The Iliad of Homer
Translated by Alexander Pope

EDITED BY STEVEN SHANKMAN

Volume 2
(Books 13-24)

WIPF & STOCK · Eugene, Oregon

Wipf and Stock Publishers
199 W 8th Ave, Suite 3
Eugene, OR 97401

The Iliad of Homer, Volume 2
Translated by Alexander Pope
By Pope, Alexandar and Shankman, Steven
Copyright © 1996 by Pope, Alexandar All rights reserved.
Softcover ISBN-13: 978-1-6667-3236-8
Hardcover ISBN-13: 978-1-6667-2599-5
eBook ISBN-13: 978-1-6667-2600-8
Publication date 7/7/2021
Previously published by Penguin Classics, 1996

This edition is a scanned facsimile of the original edition published in 1996.

THE
ILIAD
OF
HOMER

VOLUME IV

THE
THIRTEENTH BOOK
OF THE
ILIAD

The ARGUMENT

**The fourth battel continued, in which *Neptune* assists
the *Greeks*: The acts of *Idomeneus***

Neptune, *concern'd for the loss of the* Grecians, *upon seeing the fortification forc'd by* Hector, *(who had enter'd the gate near the station of the* Ajaxes) *assumes the shape of* Calchas, *and inspires those heroes to oppose him: Then in the form of one of the generals, encourages the other* Greeks *who had retir'd to their vessels. The* Ajaxes *form their troops in a close phalanx, and put a stop to* Hector *and the* Trojans. *Several deeds of valour are perform'd;* Meriones *losing his spear in the encounter, repairs to seek another at the tent of* Idomeneus. *This occasions a conversation between those two warriours, who return together to the battel.* Idomeneus *signalizes his courage above the rest; he kills* Othryoneus, Asius, *and* Alcathous. Deïphobus *and* Æneas *march against him, and at length* Idomeneus *retires.* Menelaus *wounds* Helenus, *and kills* Pisander. *The* Trojans *are repuls'd in the left wing;* Hector *still keeps his ground against the* Ajaxes, *till being gaul'd by the* Locrian *slingers and archers,* Polydamas *advises to call a council of war:* Hector *approves his advice, but goes first to rally the* Trojans; *upbraids* Paris, *rejoins* Polydamas, *meets* Ajax *again, and renews the attack.*

The eight and twentieth day still continues. The scene is between the Grecian *wall and the sea-shore.*

When now the Thund'rer, on the sea-beat coast,
Had fix'd great *Hector* and his conqu'ring host;
He left them to the fates, in bloody fray
To toil and struggle thro' the well-fought day.
5   Then turn'd to *Thracia* from the field of fight
Those eyes, that shed insufferable light,
To where the *Mysians* prove their martial force,
And hardy *Thracians* tame the savage horse;
And where the far-fam'd *Hippemolgian* strays,
10   Renown'd for justice and for length of days,
Thrice happy race! that, innocent of blood,
From milk, innoxious, seek their simple food:
Jove sees delighted, and avoids the scene
Of guilty *Troy*, of arms, and dying men:
15   No aid, he deems, to either host is giv'n,
While his high law suspends the pow'rs of heav'n.
    Mean time the *Monarch of the watry main
Observ'd the Thund'rer, not observ'd in vain.
In *Samothracia*, on a mountain's brow,
20   Whose waving woods o'erhung the deeps below,
He sate; and round him cast his azure eyes,
Where *Ida*'s misty tops confus'dly rise;
Below, fair *Ilion*'s glitt'ring spires were seen,
The crowded ships, and sable seas between.
25   There, from the crystal chambers of the main,
Emerg'd, he sate; and mourn'd his *Argives* slain.

**Neptune.*

At *Jove* incens'd, with grief and fury stung,
Prone down the rocky steep, he rush'd along;
Fierce as he past, the lofty mountains nod,
The forests shake! earth trembled as he trod,   30
And felt the footsteps of th' immortal God.
From realm to realm three ample strides he took,
And, at the fourth, the distant *Ægæ* shook.
   Far in the bay his shining palace stands,
Eternal frame! not rais'd by mortal hands: 35
This having reach'd, his brass-hoof'd steeds he reins,
Fleet as the winds, and deck'd with golden manes.
Refulgent arms his mighty limbs infold,
Immortal arms, of adamant and gold.
He mounts the car, the golden scourge applies;   40
He sits superior, and the chariot flies.
His whirling wheels the glassy surface sweep;
Th' enormous monsters, rolling o'er the deep,
Gambol around him, on the watry way;
And heavy whales in aukward measures play: 45
The sea subsiding spreads a level plain,
Exults, and owns the monarch of the main;
The parting waves before his coursers fly;
The wond'ring waters leave his axle dry.
   Deep in the liquid regions lies a cave,   50
Between where *Tenedos* the surges lave,
And rocky *Imbrus* breaks the rolling wave:
There the great ruler of the azure round
Stop'd his swift chariot, and his steeds unbound,
Fed with ambrosial herbage from his hand,   55
And link'd their fetlocks with a golden band,
Infrangible, immortal: There they stay.
The father of the floods pursues his way;
Where, like a tempest, dark'ning heav'n around,
Or fiery deluge that devours the ground,   60
Th' impatient *Trojans*, in a gloomy throng,
Embattel'd roll'd, as *Hector* rush'd along.
To the loud tumult and the barb'rous cry,
The heav'ns re-echo, and the shores reply;
They vow destruction to the *Grecian* name,   65
And, in their hopes, the Fleets already flame.

But *Neptune*, rising from the seas profound,
The God whose earthquakes rock the solid ground,
Now wears a mortal form; like *Calchas* seen,
70   Such his loud voice, and such his manly mien;
His shouts incessant ev'ry *Greek* inspire,
But most th' *Ajaces*, adding fire to fire.

'Tis yours, O warriours, all our hopes to raise;
Oh recollect your ancient worth and praise!
75   'Tis yours to save us, if you cease to fear;
Flight, more than shameful, is destructive here.
On other works tho' *Troy* with fury fall,
And pour her armies o'er our batter'd wall;
There, *Greece* has strength: but this, this part o'erthrown,
80   Her strength were vain; I dread for you alone.
Here *Hector* rages like the force of fire,
Vaunts of his Gods, and calls high *Jove* his sire.
If yet some heav'nly pow'r your breast excite,
Breathe in your hearts, and string your arms to fight,
85   *Greece* yet may live, her threat'ned fleet maintain,
And *Hector*'s force, and *Jove*'s own aid, be vain.

Then with his sceptre that the deep controuls,
He touch'd the chiefs, and steel'd their manly souls;
Strength, not their own, the touch divine imparts,
90   Prompts their light limbs, and swells their daring hearts.
Then, as a falcon from the rocky height,
Her quarry seen, impetuous at the sight,
Forth-springing instant, darts her self from high,
Shoots on the wing, and skims along the sky:
95   Such, and so swift, the pow'r of Ocean flew;
The wide horizon shut him from their view.

Th' inspiring God, *Oïleus*' active son
Perceiv'd the first, and thus to *Telamon*.
Some God, my friend, some God in human form
100   Fav'ring descends, and wills to stand the storm.
Not *Calchas* this, the venerable seer;
Short as he turn'd, I saw the pow'r appear:
I mark'd his parting, and the steps he trod;
His own bright evidence reveals a God.
105   Ev'n now some energy divine I share,
And seem to walk on wings, and tread in air!

With equal ardour (*Telamon* returns)
My soul is kindled, and my bosom burns;
New rising spirits all my force alarm,
Lift each impatient limb, and brace my arm.   110
This ready arm, unthinking, shakes the dart;
The blood pours back, and fortifies my heart;
Singly methinks, yon' tow'ring chief I meet,
And stretch the dreadful *Hector* at my feet.

   Full of the God that urg'd their burning breast,   115
The heroes thus their mutual warmth express'd.
Neptune meanwhile the routed *Greeks* inspir'd;
Who breathless, pale, with length of labours tir'd,
Pant in the ships; while *Troy* to conquest calls,
And swarms victorious o'er their yielding walls:
Trembling before th' impending storm they lie,   120
While tears of rage stand burning in their eye.
Greece sunk they thought, and this their fatal hour;
But breathe new courage as they feel the pow'r.
Teucer and *Leitus* first his words excite;   125
Then stern *Peneleus* rises to the fight;
Thoas, *Deïpyrus*, in arms renown'd,
And *Merion* next, th' impulsive fury found;
Last *Nestor*'s son the same bold ardour takes,
While thus the God the martial fire awakes.   130
   Oh lasting infamy, oh dire disgrace
To chiefs of vig'rous youth, and manly race!
I trusted in the Gods, and you, to see
Brave *Greece* victorious, and her navy free:
Ah no – the glorious combate you disclaim,   135
And one black day clouds all her former fame.
Heav'ns! what a prodigy these eyes survey,
Unseen, unthought, till this amazing day!
Fly we at length from *Troy*'s oft-conquer'd bands,
And falls our fleet by such inglorious hands?   140
A rout undisciplin'd, a straggling train,
Not born to glories of the dusty plain;
Like frighted fawns from hill to hill pursu'd,
A prey to every savage of the wood:
Shall these, so late who trembled at your name,   145
Invade your camps, involve your ships in flame?

A change so shameful, say what cause has wrought?
The soldiers baseness, or the gen'ral's fault?
Fools! will ye perish for your leader's vice?
150 The purchase infamy, and life the price!
'Tis not your cause, *Achilles'* injur'd fame:
Another's is the crime, but yours the shame.
Grant that our chief offend thro' rage or lust,
Must you be cowards, if your king's unjust?
155 Prevent this evil, and your country save:
Small thought retrieves the spirits of the brave.
Think, and subdue! on dastards dead to fame
I waste no anger, for they feel no shame:
But you, the pride, the flow'r of all our host,
160 My heart weeps blood to see your glory lost!
Nor deem this day, this battel, all you lose;
A day more black, a fate more vile, ensues.
Let each reflect, who prizes fame or breath,
On endless infamy, on instant death.
165 For lo! the fated time, th' appointed shore;
Hark! the gates burst, the brazen barriers roar!
Impetuous *Hector* thunders at the wall;
The hour, the spot, to conquer, or to fall.
　　These words the *Grecians* fainting hearts inspire,
170 And list'ning armies catch the godlike fire.
Fix'd at his post was each bold *Ajax* found,
With well-rang'd squadrons strongly circled round:
So close their order, so dispos'd their Fight,
As *Pallas'* self might view with fixt delight;
175 Or had the God of war inclin'd his eyes,
The God of war had own'd a just surprize.
A chosen Phalanx, firm, resolv'd as Fate,
Descending *Hector* and his battel wait.
An iron scene gleams dreadful o'er the fields,
180 Armour in armour lock'd, and shields in shields,
Spears lean on spears, on targets targets throng,
Helms stuck to helms, and man drove man along.
The floating plumes unnumber'd wave above,
As when an earthquake stirs the nodding grove;
185 And levell'd at the skies with pointing rays,
Their brandish'd lances at each motion blaze.

Thus breathing death, in terrible array,
The close-compacted legions urg'd their way:
Fierce they drove on, impatient to destroy;
Troy charg'd the first, and *Hector* first of *Troy.*   190
As from some mountain's craggy forehead torn,
A rock's round fragment flies, with fury born,
(Which from the stubborn stone a torrent rends)
Precipitate the pond'rous mass descends:
From steep to steep the rolling ruin bounds;   195
At ev'ry shock the crackling wood resounds;
Still gath'ring force, it smoaks; and, urg'd amain,
Whirls, leaps, and thunders down, impetuous to the
          plain:
There stops – So *Hector.* Their whole force he prov'd,
Resistless when he rag'd, and when he stop'd, unmov'd.   200
    On him the war is bent, the darts are shed,
And all their faulchions wave around his head.
Repuls'd he stands, nor from his stand retires;
But with repeated shouts his army fires.
Trojans! be firm; this arm shall make your way   205
Thro' yon' square body, and that black array:
Stand, and my spear shall rout their scatt'ring pow'r,
Strong as they seem, embattel'd like a tow'r.
For he that *Juno*'s heav'nly bosom warms,
The first of Gods, this day inspires our arms.   210
    He said, and rouz'd the soul in ev'ry breast;
Urg'd with desire of fame, beyond the rest,
Forth march'd *Deïphobus*; but marching, held
Before his wary steps, his ample shield.
Bold *Merion* aim'd a stroke (nor aim'd it wide)   215
The glitt'ring jav'lin pierc'd the tough bull-hide;
But pierc'd not thro': Unfaithful to his hand,
The point broke short, and sparkled in the sand.
The *Trojan* Warriour, touch'd with timely fear,
On the rais'd orb to distance bore the spear: 220
The *Greek* retreating mourn'd his frustrate blow,
And curs'd the treach'rous lance that spar'd a foe;
Then to the ships with surly speed he went,
To seek a surer jav'lin in his tent.

225   Meanwhile with rising rage the battel glows,
The tumult thickens, and the clamour grows.
By *Teucer*'s arm the warlike *Imbrius* bleeds,
The son of *Mentor*, rich in gen'rous steeds.
E're yet to *Troy* the sons of *Greece* were led,
230   In fair *Pedæus*' verdant pastures bred,
The youth had dwelt; remote from war's alarms,
And bless'd in bright *Medesicaste*'s arms:
(This nymph, the fruit of *Priam*'s ravish'd joy,
Ally'd the warriour to the house of *Troy*.)
235   To *Troy*, when glory call'd his arms, he came,
And match'd the bravest of her chiefs in fame:
With *Priam*'s sons, a guardian of the throne,
He liv'd, belov'd and honour'd as his own.
Him *Teucer* pierc'd between the throat and ear;
240   He groans beneath the *Telamonian* spear.
As from some far-seen mountain's airy crown,
Subdu'd by steel, a tall ash tumbles down,
And foils its verdant tresses on the ground:
So falls the youth; his arms the fall resound.
245   Then *Teucer* rushing to despoil the dead,
From *Hector*'s hand a shining jav'lin fled:
He saw, and shun'd the death; the forceful dart
Sung on, and pierc'd *Amphimachus* his heart,
Cteatus' son, of *Neptune*'s forceful line;
250   Vain was his courage, and his race divine!
Prostrate he falls; his clanging arms resound,
And his broad buckler thunders on the ground.
To seize his beamy helm the victor flies,
And just had fastned on the dazling prize,
255   When *Ajax*' manly arm a jav'lin flung;
Full on the shield's round boss the weapon rung;
He felt the shock, nor more was doom'd to feel,
Secure in mail, and sheath'd in shining steel.
Repuls'd he yields; the victor *Greeks* obtain
260   The spoils contested, and bear off the slain.
Between the leaders of th' *Athenian* line,
(*Stichius* the brave, *Menestheus* the divine,)
Deplor'd *Amphimachus*, sad object! lies;
Imbrius remains the fierce *Ajaces*' prize.

.As two grim lions bear across the lawn,   265
Snatch'd from devouring hounds, a slaughter'd fawn,
In their fell jaws high-lifting thro' the wood,
And sprinkling all the shrubs with drops of blood;
So these the chief: Great *Ajax* from the dead
Strips his bright arms, *Oïleus* lops his head: 270
Toss'd like a ball, and whirl'd in air away,
At *Hector*'s feet the goary visage lay.
  The God of Ocean, fir'd with stern disdain,
And pierc'd with sorrow for his *grandson slain,
Inspires the *Grecian* hearts, confirms their hands.   275
And breathes destruction to the *Trojan* bands.
Swift as a whirlwind rushing to the fleet,
He finds the lance-fam'd *Idomen* of *Crete*;
His pensive brow the gen'rous care exprest
With which a wounded soldier touch'd his breast,   280
Whom in the chance of war a jav'lin tore,
And his sad comrades from the battel bore;
Him to the Surgeons of the camp he sent;
That office paid, he issu'd from his tent,
Fierce for the fight: To him the God begun,   285
In *Thoas'* voice, *Andræmon*'s valiant son,
Who rul'd where *Calydon*'s white rocks arise,
And *Pleuron*'s chalky cliffs emblaze the skies.
  Where's now th' imperious vaunt, the daring boast
Of *Greece* victorious, and proud *Ilion* lost?   290
  To whom the King. On *Greece* no blame be thrown,
Arms are her trade, and war is all her own.
Her hardy heroes from the well-fought plains
Nor fear with-holds, nor shameful sloth detains.
'Tis Heav'n, alas! and *Jove*'s all-pow'rful doom,   295
That far, far distant from our native home
Wills us to fall, inglorious! Oh my friend!
Once foremost in the fight, still prone to lend
Or arms, or counsels; now perform thy best,
And what thou canst not singly, urge the rest.   300
  Thus he; and thus the God, whose force can make
The solid globe's eternal basis shake.

*Amphimachus.

Ah! never may he see his native land,
But feed the vulturs on this hateful strand,
305 Who seeks ignobly in his ships to stay,
Nor dares to combate on this signal day!
For this, behold! in horrid arms I shine,
And urge thy soul to rival acts with mine:
Together let us battel on the plain;
310 Two, not the worst; nor ev'n this succour vain.
Not vain the weakest, if their force unite;
But ours, the bravest have confess'd in fight.
    This said, he rushes where the combate burns;
Swift to his tent the *Cretan* King returns.
315 From thence, two jav'lins glitt'ring in his hand,
And clad in arms that lighten'd all the strand,
Fierce on the foe th' impetuous hero drove;
Like light'ning bursting from the arm of *Jove*,
    Which to pale man the wrath of heav'n declares,
320 Or terrifies th' offending world with wars;
In streamy sparkles, kindling all the skies,
From pole to pole the trail of glory flies.
Thus his bright armour o'er the dazled throng
Gleam'd dreadful, as the Monarch flash'd along.
325   Him, near his tent, *Meriones* attends;
Whom thus he questions: Ever best of friends!
O say, in ev'ry art of battel skill'd,
What holds thy courage from so brave a field?
On some important message art thou bound,
330 Or bleeds my friend by some unhappy wound?
Inglorious here, my soul abhors to stay,
And glows with prospects of th' approaching day.
    O Prince! (*Meriones* replies) whose care
Leads forth th' embattel'd sons of *Crete* to war;
335 *This* speaks my grief; this headless lance I wield;
The rest lies rooted in a *Trojan* shield.
    To whom the *Cretan*: Enter, and receive
The wanted weapons; those my tent can give.
Spears I have store, (and *Trojan* lances all)
340 That shed a lustre round th' illumin'd wall.
Tho' I, disdainful of the distant war,
Nor trust the dart, or aim th' uncertain spear,

Yet hand to hand I fight, and spoil the slain;
And thence these trophies and these arms I gain.
Enter, and see on heaps the helmets roll'd,   345
And high-hung spears, and shields that flame with gold.
    Nor vain (said *Merion*) are our martial toils;
We too can boast of no ignoble spoils.
But those my ship contains, whence distant far,
I fight conspicuous in the van of war.   350
What need I more? If any *Greek* there be
Who knows not *Merion*, I appeal to thee.
    To this, *Idomeneus.* The fields of fight
Have prov'd thy valour and unconquer'd might;
And were some ambush for the foes design'd,   355
Ev'n there, thy courage would not lag behind.
In that sharp service, singled from the rest,
The fear of each, or valour, stands confest.
No force, no firmness, the pale coward shows;
He shifts his place, his colour comes and goes;   360
A dropping sweat creeps cold on ev'ry part;
Against his bosom beats his quiv'ring heart;
Terrour and death in his wild eye-balls stare;
With chatt'ring teeth he stands, and stiff'ning hair,
And looks a bloodless image of despair!   365
Not so the brave – still dauntless, still the same,
Unchang'd his colour, and unmov'd his frame;
Compos'd his thought, determin'd is his eye,
And fix'd his soul, to conquer or to die:
If ought disturb the tenour of his breast,   370
'Tis but the wish to strike before the rest.
    In such assays thy blameless worth is known,
And ev'ry art of dang'rous war thy own.
By chance of fight whatever wounds you bore,
Those wounds were glorious all, and all before;   375
Such as may teach, 'twas still thy brave delight
T' oppose thy bosom where the foremost fight.
But why, like infants, cold to honour's charms,
Stand we to talk, when glory calls to arms?
Go – from my conquer'd spears, the choicest take,   380
And to their owners send them nobly back.

Swift as the word bold *Merion* snatch'd a spear,
And breathing slaughter, follow'd to the war.
So *Mars* armipotent invades the plain,
385 (The wide destroyer of the race of man)
Terrour, his best lov'd son, attends his course,
Arm'd with stern boldness, and enormous force;
The pride of haughty Warriours to confound,
And lay the strength of tyrants on the ground:
390 From *Thrace* they fly, call'd to the dire alarms
Of warring *Phlegyans*, and *Ephyrian* arms;
Invok'd by both, relentless they dispose
To these, glad conquest, murd'rous rout to those.
So march'd the leaders of the *Cretan* train,
395 And their bright arms shot horrour o'er the plain.
      Then first spake *Merion*: Shall we join the right,
Or combate in the centre of the fight?
Or to the left our wanted succour lend?
Hazard and fame all parts alike attend.
400   Not in the centre, (*Idomen* reply'd)
Our ablest chieftains the main battel guide;
Each godlike *Ajax* makes that post his care,
And gallant *Teucer* deals destruction there:
Skill'd, or with shafts to gall the distant field,
405 Or bear close battel on the sounding shield.
These can the rage of haughty *Hector* tame:
Safe in their arms, the navy fears no flame;
Till *Jove* himself descends, his bolts to shed,
And hurl the blazing Ruin at our Head.
410 Great must he be, of more than human birth,
Nor feed like mortals on the fruits of earth,
Him neither rocks can crush, nor steel can wound,
Whom *Ajax* fells not on th' ensanguin'd ground.
In standing fight he mates *Achilles'* force,
415 Excell'd alone in swiftness in the course.
Then to the left our ready arms apply,
And live with glory, or with glory die.
      He said; and *Merion* to th' appointed place,
Fierce as the God of battels, urg'd his pace.
420 Soon as the foe the shining chiefs beheld
Rush like a fiery torrent o'er the field,

Their force embody'd in a tide they pour;
The rising combate sounds along the shore.
As warring winds, in *Sirius'* sultry reign,
From diff'rent quarters sweep the sandy plain;   425
On ev'ry side the dusty whirlwinds rise,
And the dry fields are lifted to the skies:
Thus by despair, hope, rage, together driv'n,
Met the black hosts, and meeting, darken'd heav'n.
All dreadful glar'd the iron face of war,   430
Bristled with upright spears, that flash'd afar;
Dire was the gleam, of breast-plates, helms and shields,
And polish'd arms emblaz'd the flaming fields:
Tremendous scene! that gen'ral horror gave,
But touch'd with joy the bosoms of the brave.   435
   Saturn's great sons in fierce contention vy'd,
And crowds of heroes in their anger dy'd.
The sire of earth and heav'n, by *Thetis* won
To crown with glory *Peleus'* godlike son,
Will'd not destruction to the *Grecian* pow'rs,   440
But spar'd a while the destin'd *Trojan* tow'rs:
While *Neptune* rising from his azure main,
Warr'd on the King of heav'n with stern disdain,
And breath'd revenge, and fir'd the *Grecian* train,
Gods of one source, of one ethereal race,   445
Alike divine, and heav'n their native place;
But *Jove* the greater, first-born of the skies,
And more than men, or Gods, supremely wise.
For this, of *Jove's* superiour might afraid,
Neptune in human form conceal'd his aid.   450
These pow'rs infold the *Greek* and *Trojan* train
In War and Discord's adamantine chain;
Indissolubly strong, the fatal tye
Is stretch'd on both, and close-compell'd they die.
   Dreadful in arms, and grown in combats grey,   455
The bold *Idomeneus* controuls the day.
First by his hand *Othryoneus* was slain,
Swell'd with false hopes, with mad ambition vain!
Call'd by the voice of war to martial fame,
From high *Cabesus'* distant walls he came;   460

Cassandra's love he sought with boasts of pow'r,
And promis'd conquest was the proffer'd dow'r.
The King consented, by his Vaunts abus'd;
The King consented, but the fates refus'd.
465   Proud of himself, and of th' imagin'd bride,
The field he measur'd with a larger stride.
Him, as he stalk'd, the *Cretan* jav'lin found;
Vain was his breast-plate to repel the wound:
His dream of glory lost, he plung'd to hell;
470   The plains resounded as the boaster fell.

    The great *Idomeneus* bestrides the dead:
And thus (he cries) behold thy promise sped!
Such is the help thy arms to *Ilion* bring,
And such the contract of the *Phrygian* King!
475   Our offers now, illustrious Prince! receive;
For such an aid what will not *Argos* give?
To conquer *Troy*, with ours thy forces join,
And count *Atrides'* fairest daughter thine.
Meantime, on farther methods to advise,
480   Come, follow to the fleet thy new allies;
There hear what *Greece* has on her part to say.
He spoke, and dragg'd the goary corse away.

    This *Asius* view'd, unable to contain,
Before his chariot warring on the plain;
485   (His valu'd Coursers, to his squire consign'd,
Impatient panted on his neck behind)
To vengeance rising with a sudden spring,
He hop'd the conquest of the *Cretan* King.
The wary *Cretan*, as his foe drew near,
490   Full on his throat discharg'd the forceful spear:
Beneath the chin the point was seen to glide,
And glitter'd, extant at the farther side.
As when the mountain-oak, or poplar tall,
Or Pine, fit mast for some great Admiral,
495   Groans to the oft-heav'd axe, with many a wound,
Then spreads a length of ruin o'er the ground.
So sunk proud *Asius* in that dreadful day,
And stretch'd before his much-lov'd coursers lay.
He grinds the dust distain'd with streaming gore,
500   And, fierce in death, lies foaming on the shore.

Depriv'd of motion, stiff with stupid fear,
Stands all aghast his trembling charioteer,
Nor shuns the foe, nor turns the steeds away,
But falls transfix'd, an unresisting prey:
Pierc'd by *Antilochus*, he pants beneath   505
The stately car, and labours out his breath.
Thus *Asius'* steeds (their mighty master gone)
Remain the prize of *Nestor*'s youthful son.
   Stabb'd at the sight, *Deïphobus* drew nigh,
And made, with force, the vengeful weapon fly.   510
The *Cretan* saw; and stooping, caus'd to glance
From his slope shield, the disappointed lance.
Beneath the spacious targe (a blazing round,
Thick with bull-hides, and brazen orbits bound,
On his rais'd arm by two strong braces stay'd)   515
He lay collected, in defensive Shade.
O'er his safe head the jav'lin idly sung,
And on the tinkling verge more faintly rung.
Ev'n then, the spear the vig'rous arm confest,
And pierc'd, obliquely, King *Hypsenor*'s breast: 520
Warm'd in his liver, to the ground it bore
The chief, his people's guardian now no more!
   Not unattended (the proud *Trojan* cries)
Nor unreveng'd, lamented *Asius* lies:
For thee, tho' hell's black portals stand display'd,   525
This mate shall joy thy melancholy shade.
   Heart-piercing anguish, at this haughty boast,
Touch'd ev'ry *Greek*, but *Nestor*'s son the most.
Griev'd as he was, his pious arms attend,
And his broad buckler shields his slaughter'd friend;   530
Till sad *Mecistheus* and *Alastor* bore
His honour'd body to the tented shore.
   Nor yet from fight *Idomeneus* withdraws;
Resolv'd to perish in his country's cause,
Or find some foe, whom heav'n and he shall doom   535
To wail his fate in death's eternal gloom.
He sees *Alcathous* in the front aspire:
Great *Æsyetes* was the hero's sire;
His spouse *Hippodamè*, divinely fair,
Anchises' eldest hope, and darling care;   540

Who charm'd her parent's and her husband's heart,
With beauty, sense, and ev'ry work or art:
He once, of *Ilion*'s youth, the loveliest boy,
The fairest she, of all the fair of *Troy*.
545   By *Neptune* now the hapless hero dies,
Who covers with a cloud those beauteous eyes,
And fetters ev'ry limb: yet bent to meet
His fate he stands; nor shuns the lance of *Crete*.
Fixt as some column, or deep-rooted oak,
550   (While the winds sleep) his breast receiv'd the stroke.
Before the pond'rous stroke his corselet yields,
Long us'd to ward the death in fighting fields.
The riven armour sends a jarring sound:
His lab'ring heart, heaves, with so strong a bound,
555   The long lance shakes, and vibrates in the wound:
Fast-flowing from its source, as prone he lay,
Life's purple tide, impetuous, gush'd away.
      Then *Idomen*, insulting o'er the slain;
Behold, *Deïphobus!* nor vaunt in vain.
560   See! on one *Greek* three *Trojan* ghosts attend,
This, my third victim, to the shades I send.
Approaching now, thy boasted might approve,
And try the prowess of the seed of *Jove*.
From *Jove*, enamour'd on a mortal dame,
565   Great *Minos*, guardian of his country, came:
Deucalion, blameless Prince! was *Minos*' heir;
His first-born I, the third from *Jupiter*:
O'er spacious *Crete*, and her bold sons I reign,
And thence my ships transport me thro' the main;
570   Lord of a host, o'er all my host I shine,
A scourge to thee, thy father, and thy line.
      The *Trojan* heard; uncertain, or to meet
Alone, with vent'rous arms, the King of *Crete*;
Or seek auxiliar force; at length decreed
575   To call some hero to partake the deed.
Forthwith *Æneas* rises to his thought;
For him, in *Troy*'s remotest lines, he sought,
Where he, incens'd at partial *Priam*, stands,
And sees superior posts in meaner hands.

To him, ambitious of so great an aid,   580
The bold *Deïphobus* approach'd, and said.
   Now, *Trojan* Prince, employ thy pious arms,
If e'er thy bosom felt fair honour's charms.
Alcathous dies, thy brother and thy friend!
Come, and the warriour's lov'd remains defend.   585
Beneath his cares thy early youth was train'd,
One table fed you, and one roof contain'd.
This deed to fierce *Idomeneus* we owe;
Haste, and revenge it on th' insulting foe.
   Æneas heard, and for a space resign'd   590
To tender pity all his manly mind;
Then rising in his rage, he burns to fight:
The *Greek* awaits him, with collected might.
As the fell boar on some rough mountain's head,
Arm'd with wild terrours, and to slaughter bred,   595
When the loud rusticks rise, and shout from far,
Attends the tumult, and expects the war;
O'er his bent back the bristly horrours rise,
Fires stream in light'ning from his sanguin eyes,
His foaming tusks both dogs and men engage,   600
But most his hunters rouze his mighty rage.
So stood *Idomeneus*, his jav'lin shook,
And met the *Trojan* with a low'ring look.
Antilochus, *Deïpyrus* were near,
The youthful offspring of the God of war,   605
Merion, and *Aphareus*, in field renown'd:
To these the warriour sent his Voice around.
Fellows in arms! your timely aid unite;
Lo, great *Æneas* rushes to the fight:
Sprung from a God, and more than mortal bold;   610
He fresh in youth, and I in arms grown old.
Else should this hand, this hour, decide the strife,
The great dispute, of glory, or of life.
   He spoke, and all as with one soul obey'd;
Their lifted bucklers cast a dreadful shade   615
Around the chief. *Æneas* too demands
Th' assisting forces of his native bands:
Paris, *Deïphobus*, *Agenor* join;
(Co-aids and captains of the *Trojan* line.)

620   In order follow all th' embody'd train;
      Like *Ida*'s flocks proceeding o'er the plain;
      Before his fleecy care, erect and bold,
      Stalks the proud ram, the father of the fold:
      With joy the swain surveys them, as he leads
625   To the cool fountains, thro' the well-known meads.
      So joys *Æneas*, as his native band
      Moves on in rank, and stretches o'er the land.
          Round dead *Alcathous* now the battel rose;
      On ev'ry side the steely circle grows;
630   Now batter'd breast-plates and hack'd helmets ring,
      And o'er their heads unheeded jav'lins sing.
      Above the rest, two tow'ring chiefs appear,
      There great *Idomeneus*, *Æneas* here.
      Like Gods of war, dispensing fate, they stood,
635   And burn'd to drench the ground with mutual blood.
      The *Trojan* weapon whizz'd along in air;
      The *Cretan* saw, and shun'd the brazen spear:
      Sent from an arm so strong, the missive wood
      Stuck deep in earth, and quiver'd where it stood.
      But *Oenomas* receiv'd the *Cretan*'s stroke,
      The forceful spear his hollow corselet broke,
      It ripp'd his belly with a ghastly wound,
      And roll'd the smoaking entrails to the ground.
      Stretch'd on the plain, he sobs away his breath,
645   And furious, grasps the bloody dust in death.
      The victor from his breast the weapon tears;
      (His spoils he could not, for the show'r of spears.)
      Tho' now unfit an active war to wage,
      Heavy with cumb'rous arms, stiff with cold age,
650   His listless limbs unable for the course;
      In standing fight he yet maintains his force:
      Till faint with labour, and by foes repell'd,
      His tir'd, slow steps, he drags from off the field.
          Deïphobus beheld him as he past,
655   And, fir'd with hate, a parting jav'lin cast:
      The jav'lin err'd, but held its course along,
      And pierc'd *Ascalaphus*, the brave and young:
      The son of *Mars* fell gasping on the ground,
      And gnash'd the dust all bloody with his wound.

Nor knew the furious father of his fall; 660
High-thron'd amidst the great *Olympian* hall,
On golden clouds th' immortal synod sate;
Detain'd from bloody war by *Jove* and *Fate.*
 Now, where in dust the breathless hero lay,
For slain *Ascalaphus* commenc'd the fray. 665
Deïphobus to seize his helmet flies,
And from his temples rends the glitt'ring prize;
Valiant as *Mars,* *Meriones* drew near,
And on his loaded arm discharg'd his spear:
He drops the weight, disabled with the pain; 670
The hollow helmet rings against the plain.
Swift as a vultur leaping on his prey,
From his torn arm the *Grecian* rent away
The reeking jav'lin, and rejoin'd his friends.
His wounded brother good *Polites* tends; 675
Around his waste his pious arms he threw,
And from the rage of combate gently drew:
Him his swift coursers, on his splendid car
Rapt from the less'ning thunder of the war;
To *Troy* they drove him, groaning from the shore, 680
And sprinkling, as he past, the sands with gore.
 Meanwhile fresh slaughter bathes the sanguin ground,
Heaps fall on heaps, and heav'n and earth resound.
Bold *Aphareus* by great *Æneas* bled;
As tow'rd the chief he turn'd his daring head, 685
He pierc'd his throat; the bending head deprest
Beneath his helmet, nods upon his breast;
His shield revers'd o'er the fall'n warriour lies;
And everlasting slumber seals his eyes.
Antilochus, as *Thoön* turn'd him round, 690
Transpierc'd his back with a dishonest wound:
The hollow vein that to the neck extends
Along the chine, his eager jav'lin rends:
Supine he falls, and to his social Train
Spreads his imploring arms, but spreads in vain. 695
Th' exulting victor leaping where he lay,
From his broad shoulders tore the spoils away;
His time observ'd; for clos'd by foes around,
On all sides thick, the peals of arms resound.

700 His shield emboss'd the ringing storm sustains,
But he impervious and untouch'd remains.
(Great *Neptune*'s care preserv'd from hostile rage
This youth, the joy of *Nestor*'s glorious age)
In arms intrepid, with the first he fought,
705 Fac'd ev'ry foe, and ev'ry danger sought;
His winged lance, resistless as the wind,
Obeys each motion of the master's mind,
Restless it flies, impatient to be free,
And meditates the distant enemy.
710 The Son of *Asius*, *Adamas*, drew near,
And struck his target with the brazen spear,
Fierce in his front: but *Neptune* wards the blow,
And blunts the jav'lin of th' eluded foe.
In the broad buckler half the weapon stood;
715 Splinter'd on earth flew half the broken wood.
Disarm'd, he mingled in the *Trojan* crew;
But *Merion*'s spear o'ertook him as he flew,
Deep in the belly's rim an entrance found,
Where sharp the pang, and mortal is the wound.
720 Bending he fell, and doubled to the ground,
Lay panting. Thus an oxe, in fetters ty'd,
While death's strong pangs distend his lab'ring side,
His bulk enormous on the field displays;
His heaving heart beats thick, as ebbing life decays.
725 The spear, the conqu'ror from his body drew,
And death's dim shadows swam before his view.
Next brave *Deipyrus* in dust was lay'd:
King *Helenus* wav'd high the *Thracian* blade,
And smote his temples, with an arm so strong,
730 The helm fell off, and roll'd amid the throng:
There, for some luckier *Greek* it rests a prize,
For dark in death the godlike owner lies!
With raging grief great *Menelaus* burns,
And fraught with vengeance, to the victor turns;
735 That shook the pond'rous lance, in act to throw,
And this stood adverse with the bended bow:
Full on his breast the *Trojan* arrow fell,
But harmless bounded from the plated steel.

As on some ample barn's well-harden'd floor,
(The winds collected at each open door) 740
While the broad fan with force is whirl'd around,
Light leaps the golden grain, resulting from the ground:
So from the steel that guards *Atrides'* heart,
Repell'd to distance flies the bounding dart.
Atrides, watchful of th' unwary foe, 745
Pierc'd with his lance the hand that grasp'd the bow,
And nail'd it to the eugh: The wounded hand
Trail'd the long lance that mark'd with blood the sand.
But good *Agenor* gently from the wound 750
The spear sollicites, and the bandage bound;
A sling's soft wool, snatch'd from a soldier's side,
At once the tent and ligature supply'd.
  Behold! *Pisander*, urg'd by fate's decree,
Springs thro' the ranks to fall, and fall by thee, 755
Great *Menelaüs!* to enhance thy fame;
High-tow'ring in the front, the warriour came.
First the sharp lance was by *Atrides* thrown;
The lance far distant by the winds was blown.
Nor pierc'd *Pisander* thro' *Atrides'* shield;
Pisander's spear fell shiver'd on the field. 760
Not so discourag'd, to the future blind,
Vain dreams of conquest swell his haughty mind;
Dauntless he rushes where the *Spartan* lord
Like light'ning brandish'd his far-beaming sword.
His left arm high oppos'd the shining shield; 765
His right, beneath, the cover'd pole-axe held;
(An olive's cloudy grain the handle made,
Distinct with studs; and brazen was the blade)
This on the helm discharg'd a noble blow;
The plume dropp'd nodding to the plain below, 770
Shorn from the crest. *Atrides* wav'd his steel:
Deep thro' his front the weighty faulchion fell.
The crashing bones before its force gave way;
In dust and blood the groaning hero lay;
Forc'd from their ghastly orbs, and spouting gore, 775
The clotted eye-balls tumble on the shore.
The fierce *Atrides* spurn'd him as he bled,
Tore off his arms, and loud-exulting, said.

Thus, *Trojans*, thus, at length be taught to fear;

780 O race perfidious, who delight in war!
Already noble deeds ye have perform'd,
A Princess rap'd transcends a navy storm'd:
In such bold feats your impious might approve,
Without th' assistance, or the fear of *Jove*.
785 The violated rites, the ravish'd dame,
Our heroes slaughter'd, and our ships on flame;
Crimes heap'd on crimes, shall bend your glory down,
And whelm in ruins yon' flagitious town.
O thou, great Father! Lord of earth and skies,
790 Above the thought of man, supremely wise!
If from thy hand the fates of mortals flow,
From whence this favour to an impious foe?
A godless crew, abandon'd and unjust,
Still breathing rapine, violence, and lust!
795 The best of things beyond their measure, cloy;
Sleeps balmy blessing, love's endearing joy;
The feast, the dance; whate'er mankind desire,
Ev'n the sweet charms of sacred numbers tire.
But *Troy* for ever reaps a dire delight
800 In thirst of slaughter, and in lust of fight.
This said, he seiz'd (while yet the carcass heav'd)
The bloody armour, which his train receiv'd:
Then sudden mix'd among the warring crew,
And the bold son of *Pylæmenes* slew.
805 *Harpalion* had thro' *Asia* travell'd far,
Following his martial father to the war;
Thro' filial love he left his native shore,
Never, ah never, to behold it more!
His unsuccessful spear he chanc'd to fling
810 Against the target of the *Spartan* King;
Thus of his lance disarm'd, from death he flies,
And turns around his apprehensive eyes.
Him, thro' the hip transpiercing as he fled,
The shaft of *Merion* mingled with the dead.
815 Beneath the bone the glancing point descends,
And driving down, the swelling bladder rends:
Sunk in his sad companion's arms he lay,
And in short pantings sobb'd his soul away;

(Like some vile worm extended on the ground)
While life's red torrent gush'd from out the wound.   820
    Him on his car the *Paphlagonian* train
In slow procession bore from off the plain.
The pensive father, father now no more!
Attends the mournful pomp along the shore,
And unavailing tears profusely shed,   825
And unreveng'd, deplor'd his offspring dead.
    Paris from far the moving sight beheld,
With pity soften'd, and with fury swell'd:
His honour'd host, a youth of matchless grace,
And lov'd of all the *Paphlagonian* race!   830
With his full strength he bent his angry bow,
And wing'd the feather'd vengeance at the foe.
A chief there was, the brave *Euchenor* nam'd,
For riches much, and more for virtue fam'd,
Who held his seat in *Corinth*'s stately town;   835
Polydus' son, a seer of old renown.
Oft' had the father told his early doom,
By arms abroad, or slow disease at home:
He climb'd his vessel, prodigal of breath,
And chose the certain, glorious path to death.   840
Beneath his ear the pointed arrow went;
The soul came issuing at the narrow vent:
His limbs, unnerv'd, drop useless on the ground,
And everlasting darkness shades him round.
    Nor knew great *Hector* how his legions yield,   845
(Wrapt in the cloud and tumult of the field)
Wide on the left the force of *Greece* commands,
And conquest hovers o'er th' *Achaian* bands:
With such a tide superiour virtue sway'd,
And *he that shakes the solid earth, gave aid.   850
But in the centre *Hector* fix'd remain'd,
Where first the gates were forc'd, and bulwarks gain'd;
There, on the margin of the hoary deep,
(Their naval station where th' *Ajaces* keep,
And where low walls confine the beating tides   855
Whose humble barrier scarce the foes divides;

Neptune.

Where late in fight, both foot and horse engag'd,
And all the thunder of the battel rag'd)
There join'd, the whole *Bœotian* strength remains,
860 The proud *Ionians* with their sweeping trains,
Locrians and *Pthians*, and th' *Epæan* force;
But join'd, repel not *Hector*'s fiery course.
The Flow'r of *Athens*, *Stichius*, *Phidas* led,
Bias, and great *Menestheus* at their head.
865 *Meges* the strong th' *Epeian* bands controul'd,
And *Dracius* prudent, and *Amphion* bold;
The *Pthians Medon*, fam'd for martial might,
And brave *Podarces*, active in the fight.
This drew from *Phylacus* his noble line;
870 *Iphyclus*' son: and that (*Oileus*) thine:
(Young *Ajax* brother, by a stol'n embrace;
He dwelt far distant from his native place,
By his fierce stepdame from his father's reign
Expell'd and exil'd, for her brother slain.)
875 These rule the *Pthians*, and their arms employ
Mixt with *Bœotians*, on the shores of *Troy*.
   Now side by side, with like unweary'd care,
Each *Ajax* labour'd thro' the field of war.
So when two lordly bulls, with equal toil,
880 Force the bright plowshare thro' the fallow soil,
Join'd to one yoke, the stubborn earth they tear,
And trace large furrows with the shining share;
O'er their huge limbs the foam descends in snow,
And streams of sweat down their sow'r foreheads flow.
885 A train of heroes follow'd thro' the field,
Who bore by turns great *Ajax*' sev'nfold shield;
Whene'er he breath'd, remissive of his might,
Tir'd with th' incessant slaughters of the fight.
No following troops his brave associate grace,
890 In close engagement an unpractised race:
The *Locrian* squadrons nor the jav'lin wield,
Nor bear the helm, nor lift the moony shield;
But skill'd from far the flying shaft to wing,
Or whirl the sounding pebble from the sling,
895 Dext'rous with these they aim a certain wound,
Or fell the distant warriour to the ground.

Thus in the van, the *Telamonian* train
Throng'd in bright arms, a pressing fight maintain;
Far in the rear the *Locrian* archers lie,
Whose stones and arrows intercept the sky,   900
The mingled tempest on the foes they pour;
Troy's scatt'ring orders open to the show'r.
   Now had the *Greeks* eternal fame acquir'd,
And the gall'd *Ilians* to their walls retir'd;
But sage *Polydamas*, discreetly brave,   905
Address'd great *Hector*, and this counsel gave.
   Tho' great in all, thou seem'st averse to lend
Impartial audience to a faithful friend:
To Gods and men thy matchless worth is known,
And ev'ry art of glorious war thy own;   910
But in cool thought and counsel to excel,
How widely differs this from warring well?
Content with what the bounteous Gods have giv'n,
Seek not alone t' engross the gifts of heav'n.
To some the pow'rs of bloody war belong,   915
To some, sweet music, and the charm of song;
To few, and wond'rous few, has *Jove* assign'd
A wise, extensive, all–consid'ring mind;
Their guardians these, the nations round confess,
And towns and empires for their safety bless.   920
If heav'n have lodg'd this virtue in my breast,
Attend, O *Hector*, what I judge the best.
See, as thou mov'st, on dangers dangers spread,
And war's whole fury burns around thy head.
Behold! distress'd within yon' hostile wall,   925
How many *Trojans* yield, disperse, or fall?
What troops, out-number'd, scarce the war maintain?
And what brave heroes at the ships lie slain?
Here cease thy fury; and the Chiefs and Kings
Convok'd to council, weigh the sum of things.   930
Whether (the Gods succeeding our desires)
To yon' tall ships to bear the *Trojan* fires;
Or quit the fleet, and pass unhurt away,
Contented with the conquest of the day.
I fear, I fear, lest *Greece* (not yet undone)   935
Pay the large debt of last revolving sun;

Achilles, great *Achilles*, yet remains
On yonder decks, and yet o'erlooks the plains!
  The counsel pleas'd; and *Hector*, with a bound,
940 Leap'd from his chariot on the trembling ground;
Swift as he leap'd, his clanging arms resound.
To guard this post (he cry'd) thy art employ,
And here detain the scatter'd youth of *Troy*:
Where yonder heroes faint, I bend my way,
945 And hasten back to end the doubtful Day.
  This said; the tow'ring Chief prepares to go,
Shakes his white plumes that to the breezes flow,
And seems a moving mountain topt with snow.
Thro' all his host, inspiring force, he flies,
950 And bids anew the martial thunder rise.
To *Panthus'* son, at *Hector's* high command,
Haste the bold leaders of the *Trojan* band:
But round the battlements, and round the plain,
For many a chief he look'd, but look'd in vain;
955 *Deïphobus*, nor *Helenus* the seer,
Nor *Asius'* son, nor *Asius'* self appear.
For these were pierc'd with many a ghastly wound,
Some cold in death, some groaning on the ground;
Some low in dust (a mournful object) lay,
960 High on the wall some breath'd their souls away.
  Far on the left, amid the throng he found
(Cheering the troops, and dealing deaths around)
The graceful *Paris*; whom, with fury mov'd,
Opprobrious, thus, th' impatient chief reprov'd.
965 Ill-fated *Paris!* Slave to womankind,
As smooth of face as fraudulent of mind!
Where is *Deïphobus*, where *Asius* gone?
The godlike father, and th' intrepid son?
The force of *Helenus*, dispensing fate,
970 And great *Othryoneus*, so fear'd of late?
Black fate hangs o'er thee from th' avenging Gods,
Imperial *Troy* from her foundations nods;
Whelm'd in thy country's ruins shalt thou fall,
And one devouring vengeance swallow all.
975 When *Paris* thus: My brother and my friend,
Thy warm impatience makes thy tongue offend.

In other battels I deserv'd thy blame,
Tho' then not deedless, nor unknown to fame:
But since yon' rampart by thy arms lay low,
I scatter'd slaughter from my fatal bow.   980
The chiefs you seek on yonder shore lie slain;
Of all those heroes, two alone remain;
Deiphobus, and *Helenus* the seer:
Each now disabled by a hostile spear.
Go then, successful, where thy soul inspires;   985
This heart and hand shall second all thy fires:
What with this arm I can, prepare to know,
Till death for death be paid, and blow for blow.
But 'tis not ours, with forces not our own
To combate; strength is of the Gods alone.   990
　　These words the hero's angry mind asswage:
Then fierce they mingle where the thickest rage.
Around *Polydamas*, distain'd with blood,
Cebrion, *Phalces*, stern *Orthæus* stood,
Palmus, with *Polypætes* the divine,   995
And two bold brothers of *Hippotion*'s line:
(Who reach'd fair *Ilion*, from *Ascania* far,
The former day; the next, engag'd in war.)
As when from gloomy clouds a whirlwind springs,
That bears *Jove*'s thunder on its dreadful wings,   1000
Wide o'er the blasted fields the tempest sweeps,
Then gather'd, settles on the hoary deeps;
Th' afflicted deeps, tumultuous, mix and roar;
The waves behind impel the waves before,
Wide-rolling, foaming high, and tumbling to the
　　　　shore.   1005
Thus rank on rank the thick battalions throng,
Chief urg'd on chief, and man drove man along:
Far o'er the plains, in dreadful order bright,
The brazen arms reflect a beamy light.
Full in the blazing van great *Hector* shin'd,   1010
Like *Mars* commission'd to confound mankind.
Before him flaming, his enormous shield
Like the broad sun, illumin'd all the field:
His nodding helm emits a streamy ray;
His piercing eyes thro' all the battel stray,   1005

And, while beneath his targe he flash'd along,
Shot terrours round, that wither'd ev'n the strong.
  Thus stalk'd he, dreadful; death was in his Look;
Whole nations fear'd: but not an *Argive* shook.
1020 The tow'ring *Ajax*, with an ample stride,
Advanc'd the first, and thus the chief defy'd.
  Hector! come on, thy empty threats forbear:
'Tis not thy arm, 'tis thund'ring *Jove* we fear:
The skill of war to us not idly giv'n,
1025 Lo! *Greece* is humbled not by *Troy*, but heav'n.
Vain are the hopes that haughty mind imparts,
To force our fleet: The *Greeks* have hands, and hearts.
Long e'er in flames our lofty navy fall,
Your boasted city and your god-built wall
1030 Shall sink beneath us, smoaking on the ground;
And spread a long, unmeasur'd ruin round.
The time shall come, when chas'd along the plain
Ev'n thou shalt call on *Jove*, and call in vain;
Ev'n thou shalt wish, to aid thy desp'rate course,
1035 The wings of falcons for thy flying horse;
Shalt run, forgetful of a warriour's fame,
While clouds of friendly dust conceal thy shame.
  As thus he spoke, behold, in open view,
On sounding wings a dexter eagle flew.
1040 To *Jove*'s glad omen all the *Grecians* rise,
And hail, with shouts, his progress thro' the skies:
Far-echoing clamours bound from side to side;
They ceas'd; and thus the Chief of *Troy* reply'd.
  From whence this menace, this insulting strain?
1045 Enormous boaster! doom'd to vaunt in vain.
So may the Gods on *Hector* life bestow,
(Not that short life which mortals lead below,
But such as those of *Jove*'s high lineage born,
The blue-ey'd Maid, or he that gilds the morn.)
1050 As this decisive day shall end the fame
Of *Greece*, and *Argos* be no more a name.
And thou, imperious! if thy madness wait
The lance of *Hector*, thou shalt meet thy fate:
That giant-corse, extended on the shore,
1055 Shall largely feast the fowls with fat and gore.

He said, and like a lion stalk'd along:
With shouts incessant earth and ocean rung,
Sent from his foll'wing host: The *Grecian* train
With answ'ring thunders fill'd the echoing plain;
A shout that tore heav'ns concave, and above   1060
Shook the fix'd splendors of the throne of *Jove*.

OBSERVATIONS
ON THE
THIRTEENTH BOOK

The epigraph on the frontispiece of Volume IV (Books 13–16) consists of the following lines:

> *Men' moveat cimex Pantilius? aut cruciet quod*
> *Vellicat absentem Demetrius? aut quod ineptus*
> *Fannius Hermogenis lædat conviva Tigelli?*
> *Plotius, & Varius, Mæcenas, Vergiliusque,*
> *Valgius, & probet hæc Octavius optimus. –*   HOR.

[Shall that bug Pantilius disturb my composure? or shall I be tormented because Demetrius criticizes me behind my back? or because that absurd Fannius, who feasts upon the hospitality of Tigellius, tries to harm me? Let but Plotius and Varius, Mæcenas and Virgil, and Vulgius, and the unexampled Octavius approve of my writing
> (Horace, *Sermones*, I.10. 78–83)]

5. *Then turn'd to* Thracia *from the field of fight.*] One might fancy at the first reading of this passage, that *Homer* here turn'd aside from the main view of his Poem, in a vain ostentation of learning, to amuse himself with a foreign and unnecessary description of the manners and customs of these nations. But we shall find, upon better consideration, that *Jupiter*'s turning aside his eyes was necessary to the conduct of the work, as it gives Opportunity to *Neptune* to assist the *Greeks*, and thereby causes all the adventures of this book. Madam *Dacier* is too refining on this occasion; when she would have it, that *Jupiter*'s *averting his eyes* signifies his abandoning the *Trojans*; in the same manner, as the scripture represents the Almighty *turning his face* from those whom he deserts. But at this rate *Jupiter* turning his eyes from

the battel, must desert both the *Trojans* and the *Greeks*; and it is evident from the context, that *Jupiter* intended nothing less than to let the *Trojans* suffer.

9. *And where the far-fam'd* Hippemolgian *strays.*] There is much dispute among the Criticks, which are the proper names, and which the epithets, in these verses: some making ἀγαυοί the Epithet to ἱππημολγοί, others ἱππημολγοί the epithet to ἀγαυοί; and ἀβίοι, which by the common interpreters is thought only an epithet, is by *Strabo* and *Ammianus Marcellinus* made the proper name of a people. In this diversity of opinions, I have chosen that which I thought would make the best figure in poetry. It is a beautiful and moral imagination, to suppose that the long life of the *Hippemolgians* was an effect of their simple diet, and a reward of their justice: And that the Supreme Being, displeased at the continued scenes of human violence and dissension, as it were recreated his eyes in contemplating the simplicity of these people.

It is observable that the same custom of living on milk is preserv'd to this day by the *Tartars*, who inhabit the same country.

27.   *At* Jove *incens'd, with grief and fury flung,*
         Prone down the rocky steep he rush'd. –

Mons. *de la Motte* has play'd the critick upon this passage a little unadvisedly. '*Neptune*, says he, is impatient to assist the *Greeks*. *Homer* tells us that this God goes first to seek his chariot in a certain place; next he arrives at another place nearer the camp; there he takes off his horses, and then he locks them fast to secure them at his return. The detail of so many particularities no way suits the majesty of a God, or the impatience in which he is described.' Another *French* writer makes answer, that however impatient *Neptune* is represented to be, none of the Gods ever go to the war without their arms; and the arms, chariot and horses of *Neptune* were at *Ægæ*. He makes but four steps to get thither; so that what M. *de la Motte* calls being slow, is swiftness itself. The God puts on his arms, mounts his chariot, and departs: nothing is more rapid than his course; he flies over the waters: The verses of *Homer* in that place run swifter than the God himself. It is sufficient to have ears, to perceive the rapidity of *Neptune*'s chariot in the very sound of those three lines, each of which is entirely compos'd of dactyles, excepting that one spondee which must necessarily terminate the verse.

Βῆ δ᾽ ἐλάαν ἐπὶ κύματ᾽, ἄταλλε δὲ κήτε᾽ ὑπ᾽ αὐτοῦ
Γηθοσύνῃ δὲ θάλασσα διίστατο, τοὶ δὲ πέτοντο
Ῥίμφα μάλ᾽, οὐδ᾽ ὑπένερθε διαίνετο χάλκεος ἄξων.

29.   – *The lofty mountains nod,*
     The forests shake! earth trembled as he trod,
     And felt the footsteps of th' immortal God.]

Longinus confesses himself wonderfully struck with the sublimity of this passage. That Critick, after having blamed the defects with which *Homer* draws the manners of his Gods, adds, that he has much better succeeded in describing their figure and persons. He owns that he often paints a God such as he is, in all his majesty and grandeur, and without any mixture of mean and terrestrial images; of which he produces this passage as a remarkable instance, and one that had challenged the admiration of all antiquity.

The book of *Psalms* affords us a description of the like sublime manner of imagery, which is parallel to this. *O God, when thou wentest forth before thy people, when thou didst march through the wilderness, the earth shook, the heavens dropped at the presence of God, even* Sinai *itself was moved at the presence of God, the God of* Israel. Ps. 68.

32.   – *Three ample strides he took.*] This is a very grand imagination, and equals, if not transcends, what he has feign'd before of the passage of this God. We are told, that at four steps he reach'd *Ægæ*, which (supposing it meant of the town of that name in *Eubœa*, which lay the nighest to *Thrace*) is hardly less than a degree at each step. One may, from a view of the map, imagine him striding from promontory to promontory, his first step on mount *Athos*, his second on *Pallene*, his third upon *Pelion*, and his fourth in *Eubœa*. *Dacier* is not to be forgiven for omitting this miraculous circumstance, which so perfectly agrees with the marvellous air of the whole passage, and without which the sublime image of *Homer* is not compleat.

33.   – *The distant Ægæ shook.*] There were three places of this name, which were all sacred to *Neptune*; an island in the *Ægean* sea mentioned by *Nicostratus*, a town in *Peloponnesus*, and another in *Eubœa*. *Homer* is supposed in this passage to speak of the last; but the question is put, why *Neptune* who stood upon a hill in *Samothrace*, instead of going on the left to *Troy*, turns to the right, and takes a way contrary to that

which leads to the army? This difficulty is ingeniously solv'd by the old Scholiast; who says, that *Jupiter* being now on mount *Ida*, with his eyes turn'd towards *Thrace*, *Neptune* could not take the direct way from *Samo-thrace* to *Troy* without being discover'd by him, and therefore fetches this compass to conceal himself. *Eustathius* is contented to say, that the Poet made *Neptune* go so far about, for the opportunity of those fine descriptions of the palace, the chariot, and the passage of this God.

43. *Th' enormous monsters rolling o'er the deep.*] This description of *Neptune* rises upon us; his passage by water is yet more pompous than that by land. The God driving thro' the seas, the whales acknowledging him, and the waves rejoicing and making way for their monarch, are full of that *marvellous* so natural to the imagination of our author. And I cannot but think the verses of *Virgil* in the fifth *Æneid* are short of his original:

> *Cæruleo per summa levis volat æquora curru:*
> *Subsidunt undæ, tumidumque; sub axe tonanti*
> *Sternitur æquor aquis: fugiunt vasto æthere nimbi.*
> *Tum variæ comitum facies, immania cete,* &c.

> [High on the waves his azure car he guides,
> Its axles thunder, and the sea subsides;
> And the smooth ocean rowls her silent tides.
> The tempests fly before their father's face,
> Trains of inferiour Gods his triumph grace;
> And monster whales before their master play.]

I fancy *Scaliger* himself was sensible of this, by his passing in silence a passage which lay so obvious to comparison.

79.   *– This part o'erthrown,*
       Our strength were vain; I dread for you alone.]

What address, and at the same time, what strength is there in these words? *Neptune* tells the two *Ajaces*, that he is only afraid for their post, and that the *Greeks* will perish by that gate, since it is *Hector* who assaults it: at every other quarter, the *Trojans* will be repuls'd. It may therefore be properly said, that the *Ajaces* only are vanquished, and that their defeat draws destruction upon all the *Greeks.* I don't think that any thing better could be invented to animate couragious men, and make them attempt even impossibilities.   *Dacier.*

83. *If yet some heav'nly pow'r,* &c.] Here *Neptune*, considering how the *Greeks* were discouraged by the knowledge that *Jupiter* assisted *Hector*, insinuates, that notwithstanding *Hector*'s confidence in that assistance, yet the power of some other God might countervail it on their part; wherein he alludes to his own aiding them, and seems not to doubt his ability of contesting the point with *Jove* himself. 'Tis with the same confidence he afterwards speaks to *Iris*, of himself and his power, when he refuses to submit to the order of *Jupiter* in the fifteenth book. *Eustathius* remarks, what an incentive it must be to the *Ajaces*, to hear those who could stand against *Hector* equall'd, in this oblique manner, to the Gods themselves.

97. *Th' inspiring God,* Oïleus' *active son – Perceiv'd the first.*] The reason has been ask'd, why the lesser *Ajax* is the first to perceive the assistance of the God? And the ancient solution of this question was very ingenious. They said that the greater *Ajax*, being slow of apprehension, and naturally valiant, could not be sensible so soon of this accession of strength as the other, who immediately perceiv'd it as not owing so much to his natural courage.

102. *Short as he turn'd, I saw the pow'r.*] This opinion, that the majesty of the Gods was such that they could not be seen face to face by men, seems to have been generally receiv'd in most nations. *Spondanus* observes, that it might be derived from sacred truth, and founded upon what God says to *Moses* in *Exodus*, ch. 33. v. 20, 23. *Man shall not see me and live: Thou shalt see my back parts, but my face thou shalt not behold.* For the farther particulars of this notion among the Heathens, see the notes on *lib.* I. v. 268 and on the 5th, v. 971.

131. *The speech of* Neptune *to the* Greeks.] After *Neptune* in his former discourse to the *Ajaces*, who yet maintain'd a retreating fight, had encouraged them to withstand the attack of the *Trojans*; he now addresses himself to those, who having fled out of the battel, and retired to the ships, had given up all for lost. These he endeavours to bring again to the engagement, by one of the most noble and spirited speeches in the whole Iliad. He represents that their present miserable condition was not to be imputed to their want of power, but to their want of resolution to withstand the enemy, whom by experience they had often found unable to resist them. But what is particularly artful, while he is endeavouring to prevail upon them, is that he does not attribute their present dejection of mind to a cowardly spirit, but to a resentment and indignation of their general's usage of their favourite hero *Achilles*. With the same softning art, he tells them, he scorns to speak thus to cowards, but is only concern'd for their misbehaviour as they are the bravest of the army. He then exhorts them for their own sake to avoid destruction, which would certainly be inevitable, if for a moment longer they delay'd to oppose so imminent a danger.

141. *A rout undisciplin'd*, &c.] I translate this line,

$$Αὔτως ἠλάσκουσαι, ἀνάλκιδες, οὐδ' ἔπι χάρμη,$$

[Thus they wander about, in a cowardly fashion, devoid of fighting spirit,]

with allusion to the want of military discipline among the *Barbarians*, so often hinted at in *Homer*. He is always opposing to this the exact and regular disposition of his *Greeks*, and accordingly a few lines after, we are told that the *Grecian* phalanxes were such, that *Mars* or *Minerva* could not have found a defect in them.

155. *Prevent this evil*, &c.] The verse in the original,

$$'Αλλ' ἀκεώμεθα θᾶσσον, ἀκεσταί τοι φρένες ἐσθλῶν.$$

may be capable of receiving another sense to this effect. If it be your resentment of *Agamemnon*'s usage of *Achilles*, that withholds you from the battel, *that evil* (viz. the dissension of those two chiefs) *may soon be remedy'd, for the minds of good men are easily calm'd and compos'd.* I had once translated it,

> *Their future strife with speed we shall redress,*
> *For noble minds are soon compos'd to peace.*

But upon considering the whole context more attentively, the other explanation (which is that of *Didymus*) appeared to me the more natural and unforc'd, and I have accordingly follow'd it.

171. *Fix'd at his post was each bold* Ajax *found*, &c.] We must here take notice of an old story, which however groundless and idle it seems, is related by *Plutarch*, *Philostratus* and others. *Ganictor* the son of *Amphidamas* King of *Euboea*, celebrating with all solemnity the funeral of his father, proclaimed according to custom several publick games, among which was the prize for Poetry. *Homer* and *Hesiod* came

to dispute for it. After they had produced several pieces on either side, in all which the audience declar'd for *Homer*, *Panides*, the brother of the deceased, who fate as one of the judges, order'd each of the contending Poets to recite that part of his works which he esteem'd the best. *Hesiod* repeated those lines which make the beginning of his second book,

> Πληϊάδων Ἀτλαγενέων ἐπιτελλομενάων,
> Ἄρχεσθ' ἀμήτου ἀρότοιό τε δυσομενάων, &c.

[Begin your harvest when the Pleiades, sprung from Atlas, are rising; and when they set, begin your ploughing.]

Homer answer'd with the verses which follow here: But the Prince preferring the peaceful subject of *Hesiod* to the martial one of *Homer*, contrary to the expectation of all, adjudg'd the Prize to *Hesiod*. The commentators upon this occasion are very rhetorical, and universally exclaim against so crying a piece of injustice. All the hardest names which learning can furnish, are very liberally bestow'd upon poor *Panides*. *Spondanus* is mighty smart, calls him *Midas*, takes him by the ear, and asks the dead Prince as many insulting questions, as any of his author's own heroes could have done. *Dacier* with all gravity tells us, that posterity prov'd a more equitable judge than *Panides*. And if I had not told this tale in my turn, I must have incurred the censure of all the schoolmasters in the nation.

173. *So close their order*, &c.] When *Homer* retouches the same subject, he has always the art to rise in his ideas above what he said before. We shall find an instance of it in this place; if we compare this manner of commending the exact discipline of an army, with what he had made use of on the same occasion at the end of the fourth Iliad. There it is said, that the most experienc'd warriour could not have reprehended any thing, had he been led by *Pallas* thro' the battel; but here he carries it farther, in affirming that *Pallas* and the God of war themselves must have admir'd this disposition of the *Grecian* forces.   *Eustathius*.

177. *A chosen Phalanx, firm*, &c.] *Homer* in these lines has given us a description of the ancient *Phalanx*, which consisted of several ranks of men closely ranged in this order. The first line stood with their spears levell'd directly forward; the second rank being armed with spears two cubits longer, levell'd them likewise forward thro' the interstices of the first; and the third in the same manner held forth their spears yet

longer, thro' the two former ranks; so that the points of the spears of the three ranks terminated in one line. All the other ranks stood with their spears erected, in readiness to advance, and fill the vacant places of such as fell. This is the account *Eustathius* gives of the Phalanx, which he observes was only fit for a body of men acting on the defensive, but improper for the attack: And accordingly *Homer* here only describes the *Greeks* ordering their battel in this manner, when they had no other view but to stand their ground against the furious assault of the *Trojans.* The same Commentator observes from *Hermolytus*, an ancient writer of *Tacticks*, that this manner of ordering the Phalanx was afterwards introduc'd among the *Spartans* by *Lycurgus*, among the *Argives* by *Lysander*, among the *Thebans* by *Epaminondas*, and among the *Macedonians* by *Charidemus.*

191. *As from some mountain's craggy forehead torn*, &c.] This is one of the noblest similes in all *Homer*, and the most justly corresponding in its circumstances to the thing described. The furious descent of *Hector* from the wall represented by a stone that flies from the top of a rock, the hero push'd on by the superior force of *Jupiter*, as the stone driven by a torrent, the ruins of the wall falling after him, all things yielding before him, the clamour and tumult around him, all imag'd in the violent bounding and leaping of the stone, the crackling of the woods, the shock, the noise, the rapidity, the irresistibility, and the augmentation of force in its progress. All these points of likeness make but the first part of this admirable simile. Then the sudden stop of the stone when it comes to the plain, as of *Hector* at the Phalanx of the *Ajaces* (alluding also to the natural situation of the ground, *Hector* rushing down the declivity of the shore, and being stopped on the level of the sea.) And lastly, the immobility of both when so stopp'd, the enemy being as unable to move him back, as he to get forward: This last branch of the comparison is the happiest in the world, and tho' not hitherto observ'd, is what methinks makes the principal beauty and force of it. The simile is copied by *Virgil, Æn.* 12.

> *Ac veluti montis saxum de vertice præceps,*
> *Cum ruit avulsum vento, seu turbidus imber*
> *Proluit, aut annis solvit sublapsa vetustas:*
> *Fertur in abruptum magno mons improbus actu*
> *Exultatque solo; sylvas, armenta, virosque*
> *Involvens secum. Disjecta per agmina Turnus*
> *Sic urbis ruit ad muros —*

[As when a fragment, from a mountain torn
By nagging tempests, or by torrents born,
Or sapp'd by time, or loosen'd from the roots,
Prone through the void the rocky ruine shoots,
Rowling from crag to crag, from steep to steep;
Down sink, at once the shepherds and their sheep,
Involv'd alike, they rush to neather ground,
Stunn'd with the shock they fall, and stunn'd from earth
    rebound:
So *Turnus*, hasting headlong to the town,
Should'ring and shoving, bore the squadrons down.
Still pressing onward, to the walls he drew.]

And *Tasso* has again copied it from *Virgil* in his 18*th* book.

Qual gran sasso tal hor, ch' ò la vecchiezza
Solve d'un monte, o svelle ira de' venti
Ruinoso dirupa, e porta, e spezza
Le selve, e con le case anco gli armenti
Tal giù trahea de la sublime altezza
L'horribil trave e merli, e arme, e gente,
Diè la torre a quel moto uno, o duo crolli;
Tremar le mura, e rimbombaro i colli.

[As an old rock, which age or stormy wind
Tears from some craggy hill or mountain steep,
Doth break, doth bruise, and into dust doth grind
Woods, houses, hamlets, herds, and folds of sheep;
So fell the beam and down with it all kind
Of arms, of weapons, and of men did sweep,
Wherewith the towers once or twice did shake,
Trembled the walls, the hills and mountains quake.]

It is but justice to *Homer* to take notice how infinitely inferior both these similes are to their original. They have taken the image without the likeness, and lost those corresponding circumstances which raise the justness and sublimity of *Homer*'s. In *Virgil* it is only the violence of *Turnus* in which the whole application consists: And in *Tasso* it has no farther allusion than to the fall of a tower in general.

There is yet another beauty in the numbers of this part. As the verses themselves make us see, the sound of them makes us hear what they represent, in the noble roughness, rapidity, and sonorous cadence that distinguishes them.

Ῥήξας, ἀσπέτῳ ὄμβρῳ ἀναιδέος ἔχματα πέτρης, &c.

[In the aftermath of a torrential downpour, tearing away the moorings of a huge boulder.]

The translation, however short it falls of these beauties, may serve to shew the reader, that there was at least an Endeavour to imitate them.

278. *Idomen of* Crete.] *Idomeneus* appears at large in this book, whose character (if I take it right) is such as we see pretty often in common life: A person of the first rank, sufficient enough of his high birth, growing into years, conscious of his decline in strength and active qualities; and therefore endeavouring to make it up to himself in dignity, and to preserve the veneration of others. The true picture of a stiff old soldier, not willing to lose any of the reputation he has acquir'd; yet not inconsiderate in danger; but by the sense of his age, and by his experience in battel, become too cautious to engage with any great odds against him: Very careful and tender of his soldiers, whom he had commanded so long that they were become old acquaintance; (so that it was with great judgment *Homer* chose to introduce him here, in performing a kind office to one of them who was wounded.) Talkative upon subjects of war, as afraid that others might lose the memory of what he had done in better days, of which the long conversation with *Meriones*, and *Ajax*'s Reproach of him in Iliad 23. v. 478 of the original, are sufficient proofs. One may observe some strokes of lordliness and state in his character: That Respect *Agamemnon* seems careful to treat him with, and the particular distinctions shewn him at table, are mention'd in a manner that insinuates they were points upon which this Prince not a little insisted. *Il.* 4. v. 257, *&c.* The vaunting of his family in this book, together with his sarcasms and contemptuous railleries on his dead enemies, favour of the same turn of mind. And it seems there was among the ancients a tradition of *Idomeneus* which strengthens this conjecture of his pride: For we find in the *Heroicks* of *Philostratus*, that before he would come to the *Trojan* war, he demanded a share in the sovereign command with *Agamemnon* himself.

I must, upon this occasion, make an observation once for all, which will be applicable to many passages in *Homer*, and afford a solution of many difficulties. It is that our Author drew several of his characters with an eye to the histories then known of famous persons, or the traditions that past in those times. One cannot believe otherwise of a

Poet, who appears so nicely exact in observing all the customs of the age he described; nor can we imagine the infinite number of minute circumstances relating to particular persons, which we meet with every where in his poem, could possibly have been invented purely as ornaments to it. This reflection will account for a hundred seeming oddnesses not only in the *characters*, but in the *speeches* of the Iliad: For as no author is more true than *Homer* to the character of the person he introduces speaking, so no one more often suits his oratory to the character of the person spoken to. Many of these beauties must needs be lost to us, yet this supposition will give a new light to several particulars. For instance, the speech I have been mentioning of *Agamemnon* to *Idomeneus* in the 4th book, wherein he puts this hero in mind of the magnificent entertainments he had given him, becomes in this view much less odd and surprizing. Or who can tell but it had some allusion to the manners of the *Cretans* whom he commanded, whose character was so well known, as to become a proverb: *The* Cretans, *evil beasts, and slow bellies.*

283. *The surgeons of the camp.*] *Podalirius* and *Machaon* were not the only physicians in the army; it appears from some passages in this poem, that each body of troops had one peculiar to themselves. It may not be improper to advertise, that the ancient physicians were all surgeons.   *Eustathius.*

325. – Meriones *attends, Whom thus he questions* –] This conversation between *Idomeneus* and *Meriones* is generally censured as highly improper and out of place, and as such is given up even by M. *Dacier,* the most zealous of our Poet's defenders. However, if we look closely into the occasion and drift of this discourse, the accusation will, I believe, appear not so well grounded. Two persons of distinction, just when the enemy is put to a stop by the *Ajaces,* meet behind the army: Having each on important occasions retired out of the fight, the one to help a wounded soldier, the other to seek a new weapon. *Idomeneus,* who is superiour in years as well as authority, returning to the battel, is surprized to meet *Meriones* out of it, who was one of his own officers (θεράπων, as *Homer* here calls him) and being jealous of his soldier's honour, demands the cause of his quitting the fight. *Meriones* having told him it was the want of a spear, he yet seems unsatisfy'd with the excuse; adding, that he himself did not approve of that distant manner of fighting with a spear. *Meriones* being touch'd to the quick with this reproach, replies, that he of all the *Greeks* had the least reason to suspect his courage: Whereupon *Idomeneus* perceiving him highly piqued, assures him he entertains no such hard thoughts of him, since he had often known his courage prov'd on such occasions, where the danger being greater, and the number smaller, it was impossible for a coward to conceal his natural infirmity: But now recollecting that a malicious mind might give a sinister interpretation to their inactivity during this discourse, he immediately breaks it off upon that reflection. As therefore this conversation has its rise from a jealousy in the most tender point of honour, I think the Poet cannot justly be blamed for suffering a discourse so full of warm sentiments to run on for about forty verses; which after all cannot be suppos'd to take up more than two or three minutes from action.

335. *This headless Lance,* &c.] We have often seen several of *Homer's* combatants lose and break their spears, yet they do not therefore retire from the battel to seek other weapons; why therefore does *Homer* here send *Meriones* on this errand? It may be said, that in the kind of fight which the *Greeks* now maintain'd drawn up into the phalanx, *Meriones* was useless without this weapon.

339. *Spears I have store,* &c.] *Idomeneus* describes his tent as a magazine, stored with variety of arms won from the enemy, which were not only laid up as useless trophies of his victories, but kept there in order to supply his own, and his friend's occasions. And this consideration shews us one reason why these warriours contended with such eagerness to carry off the arms of a vanquish'd enemy.

This gives me an occasion to animadvert upon a false remark of *Eustathius,* which is inserted in the notes on the 11*th* book, 'that *Homer,* to shew us nothing is so unseasonable in a battel as to stay to despoil the slain, feigns that most of the warriours who do it, are kill'd, wounded, or unsuccessful.' I am astonish'd how so great a mistake should fall from any man who had read *Homer,* much more from one who had read him so thoroughly, and even superstitiously, as the old Archbishop of *Thessalonica.* There is scarce a book in *Homer* that does not abound with instances to the contrary, where the conquerors strip their enemies, and bear off their spoils in triumph. It was (as I have already said in the essay on *Homer's* battels) as honourable an exploit in those days to carry off the arms, as it is now to gain a standard. But it is a strange consequence, that because our author sometimes represents a man unsuccessful in a glorious attempt, he therefore discommends the attempt itself; and is as good an argument against encountring an enemy living, as against despoiling him dead. One ought not to confound this with plundering, between which *Homer* has so well mark'd the distinction; when he constantly speaks of the spoils as glorious, but makes *Nestor* in the *6th* book, and *Hector* in the *15th*, directly forbid the pillage, as a practice that has often prov'd fatal in the midst of a victory, and sometimes even after it.

353. *To this,* Idomeneus.] There is a great deal more dialogue in *Homer* than in *Virgil.* The *Roman* Poet's are generally set speeches, those of the *Greek* more in conversation. What *Virgil* does by two words of a narration, *Homer* brings about by a speech; he hardly raises one of his heroes out of bed without some talk concerning it. There are not only replies, but rejoinders in *Homer*, a thing scarce ever to be found in *Virgil*; the consequence whereof is, that there must be in the Iliad many continued conversations (such as this of our two heroes) a little resembling common chit-chat. This renders the poem more natural and animated, but less grave and majestic. However, that such was the way of writing generally practised in those ancient times, appears from the like manner used in most of the books of the old Testament; and it particularly agreed with our Author's warm imagination, which delighted in perpetual imagery, and in painting every circumstance of what he described.

355. *In that sharp service,* &c.] In a general battel cowardise may be the more easily conceal'd, by reason of the number of the combatants; but in an ambuscade, where the soldiers are few, each must be discovered to be what he is; this is the reason why the ancients entertain'd so great an idea of this sort of war; the bravest men were always chosen to serve upon such occasions.   *Eustathius.*

384. *So* Mars *armipotent,* &c.] *Homer* varies his similitudes with all imaginable art, sometimes deriving them from the properties of animals, sometimes from natural passions, sometimes from the occurrences of life, and sometimes (as in the simile before us) from history. The invention of *Mars*'s passage from *Thrace,* (which was feign'd to be the country of that God) to the *Phlegyans* and *Ephyrians,* is a very beautiful and poetical manner of celebrating the martial genius of that people, who lived in perpetual wars.

Methinks there is something of a fine enthusiasm, in *Homer*'s manner of fetching a compass, as it were, to draw in new images besides those in which the direct point of likeness consists. *Milton* perfectly well understood the beauty of these digressive images, as we may see from the following simile, which is in a manner made up of them.

> *Thick as autumnal leaves that strow the brooks*
> *In* Vallombrosa *(where th' Etrurian shades*
> *High-overarch'd embow'r.) Or scatter'd sedge*
> *Afloat, when with fierce winds* Orion *arm'd*
> *Hath vex'd the* Red sea-*coast, (whose wave o'erthrew*
> Busiris *and his* Memphian *chivalry,*
> *While with perfidious hatred they pursu'd*
> *The sojourners of* Goshen, *who beheld*
> *From the safe shore their floating carcasses,*
> *And broken chariot-wheels) – So thick bestrown*
> *Abject and lost lay these. –*

As for the general purport of this comparison of *Homer*, it gives us a noble and majestic idea, at once of *Idomeneus* and *Meriones*, represented by *Mars* and his son *Terrour*; in which each of these heroes is greatly elevated, yet the just distinction between them preserved. The beautiful simile of *Virgil* in his 12*th Æneid* is drawn with an eye to this of our Author.

> *Qualis apud gelidi cum flumina concitus Hebri*
> *Sanguineus Mavors clypeo increpat, atque furentes*
> *Bella movens immittit equos; illi æquore aperto*
> *Ante Notos Zephyrumque volant: gemit ultima pulsu*
> *Thraca pedum: circumque atræ Formidinis ora,*
> *Iræque, Insidiæque, Dei comitatus, aguntur.*

> [Thus on the bank of *Hebrus* freezing flood
> The God of battles in his angry mood,
> Clashing his sword against his brazen shield,
> Let loose the reins, and scours along the field:
> Before the wind his fiery coursers fly,
> Groans the sad earth, resounds the rattling sky.
> Wrath, terror, treason, tumult, and despair,
> Dire faces, and deform'd, surround the car;
> Friends of the God, and followers of the war.]

396.   *– Shall we join the right,*
     Or combat in the centre of the fight,
     Or to the left our wanted succour lend?]

The common interpreters have to this question of *Meriones* given a meaning which is highly impertinent, if not downright nonsense; explaining it thus. *Shall we fight on the right, or in the middle, or on the left, for no where else doe the* Greeks *so much want assistance?* which amounts to this: 'Shall we engage where our assistance is most wanted, or where it is not wanted?' The context, as well as the words of the original, oblige us to understand it in this obvious meaning; *Shall we bring our assistance to the right, to the left, or to the centre? Since the* Greeks *being equally press'd and engag'd on all sides, equally need our aid in all parts.*

400. *Not in the centre, &c.*] There is in this answer of *Idomeneus* a small circumstance which is overlooked by the commentators, but in which the whole spirit and reason of what is said by him consists. He says he is in no fear for the centre, since it is defended by *Teucer* and *Ajax*; *Teucer* being not only most famous for the use of the bow, but likewise excellent ἐν σταδίῃ ὑσμίνῃ, in a *close standing fight*: And as for *Ajax*, tho' not so swift of foot as *Achilles*, yet he was equal to him ἐν αὐτοσταδίῃ, in the same *stedfast* manner of fighting; hereby intimating that he was secure for the centre, because that post was defended by two persons both accomplished in that part of war, which was most necessary for the service they were then engaged in; the two expressions before mentioned peculiarly signifying a firm and steady way of fighting, most useful in maintaining a post.

452. *In war and discord's adamantine chain.*] It will be necessary, for the better understanding the conduct of *Homer* in every battel he describes, to reflect on the particular kind of fight, and the circumstances that distinguish each. In this view therefore we ought to remember thro' this whole book, that the battel describ'd in it, is a fix'd close fight, wherein the armies engage in a gross compact body, without any skirmishes or feats of activity so often mentioned in the foregoing engagements. We see at the beginning of it the *Grecians* form a *Phalanx*, v. 177. which continues unbroken at the very end, v.

1106. The chief weapon made use of is a *spear*, being most proper for this manner of combat; nor do we see any other use of a chariot, but to carry off the dead or wounded (as in the instance of *Harpalion* and *Deïphobus.*)

From hence we may observe with what judgment and propriety *Homer* introduces *Idomeneus* as the chief in action on this occasion: For this hero being declined from his prime, and somewhat stiff with years, was only fit for this kind of engagement, as *Homer* expressly says in the 512*th* verse of the present book.

> Οὐ γὰρ ἔτ᾽ ἔμπεδα γυῖα ποδῶν ἦν ὁρμηθέντι,
> Οὔτ᾽ ἄρ᾽ ἐπαῖξαι μεθ᾽ ἑὸν βέλος, οὔτ᾽ ἀλέασθαι,
> Τῷ ῥα καὶ ἐν σταδίῃ μὲν ἀμύνετο νηλεὲς ἦμαρ.

(See the translation, v. 648, &c.)

452. This short but comprehensive allegory is very proper to give us an idea of the present condition of the two contending armies, who being both powerfully sustain'd by the assistance of superiour Deities, join and mix together in a close and bloody engagement, without any remarkable advantage on either side. To image to us this state of things, the Poet represents *Jupiter* and *Neptune* holding the two armies close bound by a mighty chain, which he calls the knot of contention and war, and of which the two Gods draw the extremities, whereby the enclos'd armies are compelled together, without any possibility on either side to separate or conquer. There is not perhaps in *Homer* any image at once so exact and so bold. Madam *Dacier* acknowledges, that despairing to make this passage shine in her language, she purposely omitted it in her translation: But from what she says in her annotations, it seems that she did not rightly apprehend the propriety and beauty of it. *Hobbes* too was not very sensible of it, when he translated it so oddly.

> *And thus the Saw from brother unto brother*
> *Of cruel war was drawn alternately,*
> *And many slain on one side and the other.*

471. *The great* Idomeneus *bestrides the dead:*
   And thus (he cries) –]

It seems (says *Eustathius* on this place) that the Iliad being an heroick Poem, is of too serious a nature to admit of raillery: Yet *Homer* has found the secret of joining two things that are in a manner incompatible. For this piece of raillery is so far from raising laughter, that it becomes a hero, and is capable to enflame the courage of all who hear it. It also elevates the character of *Idomeneus*, who notwithstanding he is in the midst of imminent dangers, preserves his usual gaiety of temper, which is the greatest evidence of an uncommon courage.

I confess I am of an opinion very different from this of *Eustathius*, which is also adopted by M. *Dacier*. So severe and bloody an irony to a dying person is a fault in morals, if not in poetry itself. It should not have place at all, or if it should, is ill placed here. *Idomeneus* is represented a brave man, nay a man of a compassionate nature, in the circumstance he was introduc'd in, of assisting a wounded soldier. What provocation could such an one have, to insult so barbarously an unfortunate Prince, being neither his rival nor particular enemy? True courage is inseparable from humanity, and all generous warriours regret the very victories they gain, when they reflect what a price of blood they cost. I know it may be answer'd, that these were not the manners of *Homer*'s time, a spirit of violence and devastation then reigned, even among the chosen people of God, as may be seen from the actions of *Joshua*, *&c.* However, if one would forgive the *cruelty*, one cannot forgive the *gaiety* on such an occasion. These inhuman jests the Poet was so far from being oblig'd to make, that he was on the contrary forced to break through the general serious air of his poem to introduce them. Would it not raise a suspicion, that (whatever we see of his superiour genius in other respects) his own views of morality were not elevated above the barbarity of his age? I think indeed the thing by far the most shocking in this Author, is that spirit of cruelty which appears too manifestly in the Iliad.

Virgil was too judicious to imitate *Homer* in these licences, and is much more reserv'd in his sarcasms and insults. There are not above four or five in the whole *Æneid*. That of *Pyrrhus* to *Priam* in the second book, tho' barbarous in itself, may be accounted for as intended to raise a character of horrour, and render the action of *Pyrrhus* odious; whereas *Homer* stains his most favourite characters with these barbarities. That of *Ascanius* over *Numanus* in the ninth, was a fair opportunity where *Virgil* might have indulg'd the humour of a cruel raillery, and have been excus'd by the youth and gaiety of the speaker; yet it is no more than a very moderate answer to the insolences with which he had just been provok'd by his enemy, only retorting two of his own words upon him.

> — *I, verbis virtutem illude superbis!*
> *Bis capti Phryges hæc Rutulis responsa remittunt.*

> [Go now, vain boaster, and true valor scorn;
>   The *Phrygians* twice subdu'd, yet make this third
>   return.]

He never suffers his *Æneas* to fall into this practice, but while he is on fire with indignation after the death of his friend *Pallas*: That short one to *Mezentius* is the least that could be said to such a tyrant.

> — *Ubi nunc Mezentius acer, & illa*
> *Effera vis animi? —*

> [Now, where are now thy vaunts, the fierce disdain
>   Of proud *Mezentius*, and the lofty strain?]

The worst-natur'd one I remember (which yet is more excusable than *Homer*'s) is that of *Turnus* to *Eumedes* in the 12*th* book.

> *En, agros, & quam bello, Trojane, petisti,*
> *Hesperiam metire jacens: hæc præmia, qui me*
> *Ferro ausi tentare, ferunt: sic mœnia condunt.*

> [Possess, said he, the fruit of all thy pains,
>   And measure, at thy length, our *Latian* plains.
>   Thus are my foes rewarded by my hand,
>   Thus may they build their town, and thus enjoy the
>   land.]

474. *And such the contract of the* Phrygian *King*, &c.] It was but natural to raise a question, on occasion of these and other passages in *Homer*, how it comes to pass that the heroes of different nations are so well acquainted with the stories and circumstances of each other? *Eustathius*'s solution is no ill one, that the warriours on both sides might learn the story of their enemies from the captives they took, during the course of so long a war.

511. *The* Cretan *saw, and stooping*, &c.] Nothing could paint in a more lively manner this whole action, and every circumstance of it, than the following lines. There is the posture of *Idomeneus* upon seeing the lance flying toward him; the lifting the shield obliquely to turn it aside; the arm discover'd in that position; the form, composition, materials, and ornaments of the shield distinctly specify'd; the flight of the dart over it; the sound of it first as it flew, then as it fell; and the decay of that sound on the edge of the buckler, which being thinner than the other parts, rather tinkled than rung, especially when the first force of the stroke was spent on the orb of it. All this in the compass of so few lines, in which every word is an image, is something more beautifully particular, than I remember to have met with in any Poet.

543. *He, once of* Ilion's *youth the loveliest boy.*] Some manuscripts, after these words, ὥριστος ἐνὶ Τροίῃ εὐρείῃ, insert the three following verses,

> Πρὶν Ἀντηνορίδας τραφέμεν καὶ Πάνθοου υἷας
> Πριαμίδας θ' οἳ Τρωσὶ μετέπρεπον ἱπποδάμοισιν
> Ἕως ἔθ' ἥβην εἶχεν, ὄφελλε δὲ κούριον ἄνθος;

which I have not translated, as not thinking them genuine. Mr *Barnes* is of the same opinion.

554. *His lab'ring Heart, heaves, with so strong a bound,*
The long lance shakes, and vibrates in the wound.]

We cannot read *Homer* without observing a wonderful variety in the wounds and manner of dying. Some of these wounds are painted with very singular circumstances, and those of uncommon art and beauty. This passage is a masterpiece in that way; *Alcathous* is pierc'd into the heart, which throbs with so strong a pulse, that the motion is communicated even to the distant end of the spear, which is vibrated thereby. This circumstance might appear too bold, and the effect beyond nature, were we not inform'd by the most skilful anatomists of the wonderful force of this muscle, which some of them have computed to be equal to the weight of several thousand pounds.

Lower, de Corde. Borellus & alii.

578. *Incens'd at partial* Priam, *&c.*] *Homer* here gives the reason why *Æneas* did not fight in the foremost ranks. It was against his inclination that he serv'd *Priam*, and he was rather engag'd by honour and reputation to assist his country, than by any disposition to aid that Prince. This passage is purely historical, and the ancients have preserv'd to us a tradition which serves to explain it. They say that *Æneas* became suspected by *Priam*, on account of an oracle which prophesied he should in process of time rule over the *Trojans.* The King therefore shew'd him no great degree of esteem or consideration, with design to discredit, and render him despicable to the people. *Eustathius.* This envy of *Priam*, and this report of the oracle, are mention'd by *Achilles* to *Æneas* in the 20*th* Book.

> – ἦ σέ γε θυμὸς ἐμοὶ μαχέσασθαι ἀνώγει,
> Ἐλπόμενον Τρώεσσιν ἀνάξειν ἱπποδάμοισι,
> Τιμῆς τῆς Πριάμου; ἀτὰρ εἴ κεν ἔμ' ἐξεναρίξῃς
> Οὔ τοι τοὔνεκά γε Πρίαμος γέρας ἐν χερὶ θήσει.
> Εἰσὶν γὰρ οἱ παῖδες. –

(See v. 216, &c. of the translation.)

And *Neptune* in the same book,

> Ἤδη γὰρ Πριάμου γενεὴν ἤχθηρε Κρονίων.
> Νῦν δὲ δὴ Αἰνείαο βίη Τρώεσσιν ἀνάξει,
> Καὶ παιδῶν παῖδες, τοί κεν μετόπισθε γένωνται.

(In the translation, v. 355, &c.)

I shall conclude this note with the character of *Æneas*, as it is drawn by *Philostratus*, wherein he makes mention of the same tradition. '*Æneas* (says this Author) was inferior to *Hector* in battel only, in all else equal, and in prudence superior. He was likewise skilful in whatever related to the Gods, and conscious of what destiny had reserv'd for him after the taking of *Troy.* Incapable of fear, never discompos'd, and particularly possessing himself in the article of danger. *Hector* is reported to have been call'd the hand, and *Æneas* the head of the *Trojans*; and the latter more advantag'd their affairs by his caution, than the former by his fury. These two heroes were much of the same age, and the same stature: The air of *Æneas* had something in it less bold and forward, but at the same time more fix'd and constant.'

Philostrat. Heroic.

621. *Like* Ida's *flocks,* &c.] *Homer*, whether he treats of the customs of men or beasts, is always a faithful interpreter of nature. When sheep leave the pasture and drink freely, it is a certain sign, that they have found good pasturage, and that they are all found; 'tis therefore upon this account, that *Homer* says the shepherd rejoices. *Homer*, we find, well understood what *Aristotle* many ages after him remark'd, *viz.* that sheep grow fat by drinking. This therefore is the reason, why shepherds are accustom'd to give their flocks a certain quantity of salt every five days in the summer, that they may by this means drink the more freely.   *Eustathius.*

655. *And, fir'd with hate.*] *Homer* does not tell us the occasion of this hatred; but since his days, *Simonides* and *Ibycus* write, that *Idomeneus* and *Deïphobus* were rivals, and both in love with *Helen.* This very well agrees with the ancient tradition which *Euripides* and *Virgil* have follow'd: for after the death of *Paris*, they tell us she was espous'd to *Deïphobus.*   *Eustathius.*

720. *Bending he fell, and doubled to the ground, Lay panting.* –] The original is,

> – ὁ δ' ἑσπόμενος περὶ δουρὶ,
> ῎Ησπαιρ'. –

The versification represents the short broken pantings of the dying warriour, in the short sudden break at the second syllable of the second line. And this beauty is, as it happens, precisely copied in the *English.* It is not often that a Translator can do this justice to *Homer*, but he must be content to imitate these graces and proprieties at more distance, by endeavouring at something parallel, tho' not the same.

728. *King* Helenus.] The appellation of King was not anciently confin'd to those only who bore the sovereign dignity, but applied also to others. There was in the island of *Cyprus* a whole order of officers call'd Kings, whose business it was to receive the relations of informers, concerning all that happen'd in the island, and to regulate affairs accordingly.   *Eustathius.*

739. *As on some ample barn's well-harden'd floor.*] We ought not to be shock'd at the frequency of these similes taken from the ideas of a rural life. In early times, before politeness had rais'd the esteem of arts subservient to luxury, above those necessary to the subsistence of mankind, agriculture was the employment of persons of the greatest esteem and distinction: We see in sacred history Princes busy at sheep-shearing; and in Time of the *Roman* common-wealth, a Dictator taken from the plough. Wherefore it ought not to be wonder'd at that allusions and comparisons of this kind are frequently used by ancient heroic writers, as well to raise, as illustrate their descriptions. But since these arts are fallen from their ancient dignity, and become the drudgery of the lowest people, the images of them are likewise sunk into meanness, and without this consideration, must appear to common readers unworthy to have place in Epic poems. It was perhaps thro' too much deference to such tastes, that *Chapman* omitted this simile in his translation.

751.   *A sling's soft wool, snatch'd from a soldier's side,*
  At once the tent and ligature supply'd.]

The words of the original are these,

   Ἀυτὴν δὲ ξυνέδησεν ἐϋστρεφεῖ οἰὸς ἀώτῳ
   Σφενδόνῃ, ἣν ἄρα οἱ θεράπων ἔχε ποιμένι λαῶν.

This passage, by the Commentators ancient and modern, seems rightly understood in the sense express'd in this translation: The word σφενδόνη properly signifying a *Sling*; which (as *Eustathius* observes from an old Scholiast) was anciently made of woollen strings. *Chapman* alone dissents from the common interpretation, boldly pronouncing that slings are no where mention'd in the Iliad, without giving any reason for his opinion. He therefore translates the word σφενδόνη, a *scarf*, by no other authority but that he says, *it was a fitter thing to hang a wounded arm in, than a Sling*; and very prettily wheedles his reader into this opinion by a most gallant imagination, that *his squire might carry this scarf about him as a favour of his own or of his master's mistress.* But for the use he has found for this scarf, there is not any pretence from the original; where it is only said the wound was bound up, without any mention of hanging the arm. After all, he is hard put to it in his translation; for being resolv'd to have a *Scarf*, and oblig'd to mention *Wool*, we are left entirely at a loss to know from whence he got the latter.

A like passage recurs near the end of this book, where the Poet says the *Locrians* went to war without shield or spear, only armed,

   Τόξοισι καὶ ἐϋστρόφεῖ οἰὸς ἀώτῳ.   v. 716.

Which last expression, as all the Commentators agree, signifies a *sling*, tho' the word σφενδόνη is not used. *Chapman* here likewise, without any colour of authority, dissents from the common opinion; but very inconstant in his errours, varies his mistake, and assures us, *this expression is the true Periphrasis of a light kind of armour, call'd a* Jack, *by which all our archers used to serve in of old, and which were ever quilted with wool.*

766. *The cover'd pole-axe.*] *Homer* never ascribes this weapon to any but the *Barbarians*, for the battel-axe was not used in war by the politer nations. It was the favourite weapon of the *Amazons.*

Eustathius.

779. *The speech of* Menelaus.] This speech of *Menelaus* over his dying enemy, is very different from those with which *Homer* frequently makes his heroes insult the vanquish'd, and answers very well the character of this good-natur'd Prince. Here are no insulting taunts, no cruel sarcasms, nor any sporting with the particular misfortunes of the dead: The invectives he makes are general, arising naturally from a remembrance of his wrongs, and being almost nothing else but a recapitulation of them. These reproaches come most justly from this Prince, as being the only person among the *Greeks* who had receiv'd any personal injury from the *Trojans.* The apostrophe he makes to *Jupiter*, wherein he complains of his protecting a wicked people, has given occasion to censure *Homer* as guilty of impiety, in making his heroes tax the Gods with Injustice: But since, in the former part of this speech, it is expressly said, that *Jupiter* will certainly punish the *Trojans* by the destruction of their city for violating the laws of hospitality, the latter part ought only to be consider'd as a complaint to *Jupiter* for delaying that vengeance: This reflection being no more than what a pious suffering mind, griev'd at the flourishing condition of prosperous wickedness, might naturally fall into. Not unlike this is the complaint of the prophet *Jeremiah*, ch. 12. v. 1. *Righteous art thou, O Lord, when I plead with thee: yet let me talk with thee of thy judgments. Wherefore doth the way of the wicked prosper? Wherefore are all they happy that deal very treacherously?*

Nothing can more fully represent the cruelty and injustice of the *Trojans*, than the observation with which *Menelaus* finishes their character, by saying, that they have a more strong, constant, and insatiable appetite after bloodshed and rapine, than others have to satisfy the most agreeable pleasures and natural desires.

795. *The best of things beyond their measure cloy.*] These words comprehend a very natural sentiment, which perfectly shews the wonderful folly of men: They are soon weary'd with the most agreeable things, when they are innocent, but never with the most toilsome things in the world, when injust and criminal.   *Eustathius. Dacier.*

797. *The dance.*] In the Original it is call'd ἀμύμων, *the blameless dance*; to distinguish (says *Eustathius*) what sort of dancing it is that *Homer* commends. For there were two kinds of dancing practis'd among the ancients, the one reputable, invented by *Minerva*, or by *Castor* and *Pollux*; the other dishonest, of which *Pan*, or *Bacchus*, was the author. They were distinguish'd by the name of the tragic, and the comic or satyric dance. But those which probably our Author commends were certain military dances used by the greatest heroes. One of this sort was known to the *Macedonians* and *Persians*, practis'd by *Antiochus* the Great, and the famous *Polyperchon.* There was another which was danc'd in compleat armour, call'd the *Pyrrhick*, from *Pyrrhicus* the *Spartan* its inventor, which continu'd in fashion among the *Lacedæmonians. Scaliger* the father remarks, that this dance was too laborious to remain long in use even among the ancients; however it seems that labour could not discourage this bold Critick from reviving that laudable kind of dance in the presence of the Emperor *Maximilian* and his whole court. It is not to be doubted but the performance rais'd their admiration; nor much to be wonder'd at, if they desir'd to see more than once so extraordinary a spectacle, as we have it in his own Words. *Poëtices, lib.* 1. *cap.* 18. *Hanc saltationem* [Pyrrhicam] *nos & sæpe, & diu, coram Divo Maximiliano, jussu Bonifacii patrui*, non sine stupore totius Germaniæ, *repræsentavimus.* [Long and often have we performed this Pyrrhic dance before divine Maximilian by the command of his uncle Boniface, to the amazement of all Germany.]

819. *Like some vile worm extended on the ground.*] I cannot be of *Eustathius*'s opinion, that this simile was design'd to debase the character of *Harpalion*, and to represent him in a mean and disgraceful view, as one who had nothing noble in him. I rather think from the character he gives of this young man, whose piety carry'd him to the wars to attend his father, and from the air of this whole passage, which is tender and pathetick, that he intended this humble comparison only as a mortifying picture of human misery and mortality. As to the verses which *Eustathius* alledges for a proof of the cowardice of *Harpalion*,

> Ἂψ δ' ἑτάρων εἰς ἔθνος ἐχάζετο κῆρ' ἀλεείνων
> Πάντοσε παπταίνων. –

[Shunning death, he fell back into the band of his companions, looking cautiously about, in every direction.]

The retreat described in the first verse is common to the greatest heroes in *Homer*; the same words are applied to *Deïphobus* and *Meriones* in this book, and to *Patroclus* in the 16*th*, v. 817 of the *Greek*. The same thing in other words is said even of the great *Ajax*, *Il*. 15. v. 728. And we have *Ulysses* describ'd in the 4*th*, v. 497. with the same circumspection and fear of the darts: tho' none of those warriors have the same reason as *Harpalion* for their retreat or caution, he alone being unarm'd, which circumstance takes away all imputation of cowardice.

823. *The pensive father.*] We have seen in the 5*th* Iliad the death of *Pylæmenes* general of the *Paphlagonians*: How comes he then in this place to be introduced as following the funeral of his son? *Eustathius* informs us of a most ridiculous solution of some criticks, who thought it might be the ghost of this unhappy father, who not being yet interr'd, according to the opinion of the ancients, wander'd upon the earth. *Zenodotus* not satisfy'd with this (as indeed he had little reason to be) chang'd the name of *Pylæmenes* into *Kylæmenes*. *Didymus* thinks there were two of the same name; as there are in *Homer* two *Schedius*'s, two *Eurymedon*'s, and three *Adrastus*'s. And others correct the verse by adding a negative, μετὰ δ' οὔ σφι πατὴρ κίε; *his father did* not *follow his chariot with his face bath'd in tears*. Which last, if not of more weight than the rest, is yet more ingenious.   *Eustathius. Dacier.*

> *Nor did his valiant father (now no more)*
> *Pursue the mournful pomp along the shore,*
> *No sire surviv'd, to grace th' untimely bier,*
> *Or sprinkle the cold ashes with a tear.*

840. *And chose the certain, glorious path to death.*] Thus we see *Euchenor* is like *Achilles*, who fail'd to *Troy*, tho' he knew he should fall before it: This might somewhat have prejudic'd the character of *Achilles*, every branch of which ought to be single, and superior to all others, as he ought to be without a rival in every thing that speaks a hero: Therefore we find two essential differences between *Euchenor* and *Achilles*, which preserve the superiority of the hero of the poem. *Achilles*, if he had not fail'd to *Troy*, had enjoy'd a long life; but *Euchenor* had been soon cut off by some cruel disease. *Achilles* being independent, and as a King, could have liv'd at ease at home, without being obnoxious to any disgrace; but *Euchenor* being but a private man, must either have gone to the war, or been expos'd to an ignominious penalty.   *Eustathius. Dacier.*

845. *Nor knew great Hector,* &c.] Most part of this book being employ'd to describe the brave resistance the *Greeks* made on their left under *Idomeneus* and *Meriones*; the Poet now shifts the scene, and returns to *Hector*, whom he left in the center of the army, after he had pass'd the wall, endeavouring in vain to break the phalanx where *Ajax* commanded. And that the reader might take notice of this change of place, and carry distinctly in his mind each scene of action, *Homer* is very careful in the following lines to let us know that *Hector* still continues in the place where he had first pass'd the wall, at that part of it which was lowest, (as appears from *Sarpedon*'s having pull'd down one of its battlements on foot, *lib.* 12.) and which was nearest the station where the ships of *Ajax* were laid, because that hero was probably thought a sufficient guard for that part. As the poet is so very exact in describing each scene as in a chart or plan, the reader ought to be careful to trace each action in it; otherwise he will see nothing but confusion in things which are in themselves very regular and distinct. This observation is the more necessary, because even in this place, where the Poet intended to prevent any such mistake, *Dacier* and other interpreters have apply'd to the present action what is only a recapitulation of the time and place describ'd in the former book.

861. Pthians.] These *Pthians* are not the troops of *Achilles*, for those were call'd *Pthiotes*; but they were the troops of *Protesilaus* and *Philoctetes.*   *Eustathius.*

879. *So when two lordly bulls,* &c.] The image here given of the *Ajaces* is very lively and exact; there being no circumstance of their present condition that is not to be found in the comparison, and no particular in the comparison that does not resemble the action of the heroes. Their strength and labour, their unanimity and nearness to each other, the difficulties they struggle against, and the sweat occasion'd by the struggling, perfectly corresponding with the simile.

937.   Achilles, *great* Achilles, *yet remains*
         On yonder decks, and yet o'erlooks the plains.]

There never was a nobler encomium than this of *Achilles.* It seems enough to so wise a counsellor as *Polydamas*, to convince so intrepid a warriour as *Hector*, in how great danger the *Trojans* stood, to say, Achilles *sees us.* 'Tho' he abstains from the fight, he still casts his eye on the battel; it is true, we are a brave army, and yet keep our ground, but still *Achilles* sees us, and we are not safe.' This reflection makes him a God, a single regard of whom can turn the fate of armies, and determine the destiny of a whole people. And how nobly is this thought extended in the progress of the poem, where we shall see in the 16*th* book the *Trojans* fly at the first sight of his armour, worn by *Patroclus*; and in the 18*th* their defeat compleated by his sole appearance, unarm'd, on his ship.

939. Hector, *with a bound, Leap'd from his chariot.*] *Hector* having in the last book alighted, and caused the *Trojans* to leave their chariots behind them, when they pass'd the trench, and no mention of any chariot but that of *Asius* since occurring in the battel; we must necessarily infer, either that *Homer* has neglected to mention the advance of the chariots, (a circumstance which should not have been omitted) or else, that he is guilty here of a great mistake in making *Hector* leap from his chariot. I think it evident, that this is really a slip of the Poet's memory: For in this very book, v. 533 (of the original) we see *Polites* leads off his wounded brother to the place where his chariot remain'd behind the army. And again in the next book, *Hector* being wounded, is carried out of the battel in his soldier's arms to the place where his horses and chariot waited at a distance from the battel,

$$- \tau \grave{o} \nu \; \delta' \; \ddot{a} \rho' \; \dot{\epsilon} \tau a \hat{\imath} \rho o \iota$$
$$X \epsilon \rho \sigma \grave{\imath} \nu \; \dot{a} \epsilon \acute{\imath} \rho a \nu \tau \epsilon \varsigma \; \phi \acute{\epsilon} \rho o \nu \; \dot{\epsilon} \kappa \; \pi \acute{o} \nu o \upsilon, \; \ddot{o} \phi \rho' \; \ddot{\imath} \kappa \epsilon \theta' \; \ddot{\imath} \pi \pi o \upsilon \varsigma$$
$$\text{'}\Omega \kappa \acute{\epsilon} a \varsigma \; o \ddot{\imath} \; o \acute{\imath} \; \ddot{o} \pi \iota \sigma \theta \epsilon \; \mu \acute{a} \chi \eta \varsigma \; \mathbb{\eta} \delta \grave{\epsilon} \; \pi \tau o \lambda \acute{\epsilon} \mu o \iota o$$
$$\text{"}E \sigma \tau a \sigma a \nu. \qquad\qquad\qquad Lib.\; 14.\; v.\; 428.$$

[His companions carried him out of the battle, raising him up with their hands until they reached their swift horses, where they had .placed them, to the rear of the fighting and the battle.]

But what puts it beyond dispute, that the chariots continued all this time in the place where they first quitted them, is a passage in the beginning of the fifteenth book, where the *Trojans* being overpower'd by the *Greeks*, fly back over the wall and trench till they came to the place where their chariots stood,

$$O \acute{\imath} \; \mu \grave{\epsilon} \nu \; \delta \grave{\eta} \; \pi a \rho' \; \ddot{o} \chi \epsilon \sigma \phi \iota \nu \; \dot{\epsilon} \rho \eta \tau \acute{\upsilon} o \nu \tau o \; \mu \acute{\epsilon} \nu o \nu \tau \epsilon \varsigma. \quad Lib.\; 15.\; v.\; 3.$$

[They restrained themselves, remaining by their chariots.]

Neither *Eustathius* nor *Dacier* have taken any notice of this incongruity, which would tempt one to believe they were willing to overlook what they could not excuse. I must honestly own my opinion, that there are several other negligences of this kind in *Homer*. I cannot think otherwise of the passage in the present book concerning *Pylæmenes*, notwithstanding the excuses of the Commentators which are there given. The very using the same name in different places for different persons, confounds the reader in the story, and is what certainly would be better avoided: So that 'tis to no purpose to say, there might as well be two *Pylæmenes*'s as two *Schedius*'s, two *Eurymedons*, two *Ophelestes*'s, &c. since it is more blameable to be negligent in many instances than in one. *Virgil* is not free from this, as *Macrobius* has observ'd. *Sat. l. 5. c.* 15. But the abovemention'd names are proofs of that Critick's being greatly mistaken in affirming that *Homer* is not guilty of the same. It is one of those many errors he was led into, by his partiality to *Homer* above *Virgil*.

948. *And seems a moving mountain topt with snow.*] This simile is very short in the original, and requires to be open'd a little to discover its full beauty. I am not of Mad. *Dacier*'s opinion, that the lustre of *Hector*'s armour was that which furnish'd *Homer* with this image; it seems rather to allude to the plume upon his helmet, in the action of shaking which, this hero is so frequently painted by our Author, and from thence distinguish'd by the remarkable epithet κορυθαίολος. This is a very pleasing image, and very much what Painters call *picturesque*. I fancy it gave the hint for a very fine one in *Spenser*, where he represents the person of *Contemplation* in the figure of a venerable old man almost consum'd with study.

> *His snowy locks adown his shoulders spread,*
> *As hoary frost with spangles doth attire*
> *The mossy branches of an oak half dead.*

965. *Ill-fated* Paris.] The reproaches which *Hector* here casts on *Paris*, give us the character of this hero, who in many things resembles *Achilles*; being (like him) injust, violent, and impetuous, and making no distinction between the innocent and criminal. 'Tis he who is obstinate in attacking the entrenchments, yet asks an account of those who were slain in the attack from *Paris*; and tho' he ought to blame himself for their deaths, yet he speaks to *Paris*, as if thro' his cowardice he had suffer'd these to be slain, whom he might have preserv'd if he had fought courageously.   *Eustathius.*

1005. *Wide-rowling, foaming high, and tumbling to the shore.*] I have endeavour'd in this verse to imitate the confusion, and broken sound of the original, which images the tumult and roaring of many waters.

$$\text{Κύματα παφλάζοντα πολυφλοίσβοιο θαλάσσης}$$
$$\text{Κυρτὰ, φαληριόωντα. } -$$

1037. *Clouds of rolling dust.*] A Critick might take occasion from hence, to speak of the exact time of the year in which the actions of the Iliad are suppos'd to have happen'd. And (according to the grave manner of a learned Dissertator) begin by informing us, that he has found it must be the *summer* season, from the frequent mention made of clouds of *dust*: Tho' what he discovers might be full as well inferr'd from common sense, the summer being the natural season for a campaign. However he should quote all these passages at large; and adding to the article of *dust* as much as he can find of the *sweat* of the heroes, it might fill three pages very much to his own satisfaction. It would look well to observe farther, that the fields are describ'd flowery, *Il.* 2. v. 546. that the branches of a tamarisk tree are flourishing, *Il.* 10. v. 767. that the warriours sometimes wash themselves in the sea, *Il.* 10. v. 674. and sometimes refresh themselves by cool breezes from the sea, *Il.* 11. v. 762. that *Diomed* sleeps out of his tent on the ground, *Il.* 10. v. 170. that the flies are very busy about the dead body of *Patroclus*, *Il.* 19. v. 30. that *Apollo* covers the body of *Hector* with a cloud to prevent its being scorch'd, *Il.* 23. All this would prove the very thing which was said at first, that it was *summer*. He might next proceed to enquire, what precise critical time of summer? And here the mention of new-made Honey in *Il.* 11. v. 771. might be of great service in the investigation of this important matter: He would conjecture from hence, that it must be near the end of summer, honey being seldom taken till that time; to which having added the plague which rages in book 1. and remark'd, that infections of that kind generally proceed from the extremest heats, which heats are not till near the *autumn*; the learned enquirer might hug himself in this discovery, and conclude with triumph.

If any one think this too ridiculous to have been ever put in practice, he may see what *Bossu* has done to determine the precise season of the *Æneid, lib.* 3. *ch.* 12. The memory of that learned Critick fail'd him, when he produc'd as one of the proofs that it was autumn, a passage in the 6*th* book, where the fall of the leaf is only mention'd in a *simile.* He has also found out a beauty in *Homer,* which few even of his greatest admirers can believe he intended; which is, that to the *violence* and *fury* of the *Iliad* he artfully adapted the *heat* of *summer,* but to the *Odyssey* the *cooler and maturer* Season of *autumn,* to correspond with the *sedateness* and *prudence* of *Ulysses.*

THE
FOURTEENTH BOOK
OF THE
ILIAD

The ARGUMENT

Juno deceives *Jupiter* by the Girdle of *Venus*

Nestor *sitting at the table with* Machaon, *is alarm'd with the encreasing clamour of the war, and hastens to* Agamemnon: *On his way he meets that Prince with* Diomed *and* Ulysses, *whom he informs of the extremity of the danger.* Agamemnon *proposes to make their escape by night, which* Ulysses *withstands; to which* Diomed *adds his advice, that, wounded as they were, they should go forth and encourage the army with their presence; which advice is pursued.* Juno *seeing the partiality of* Jupiter *to the* Trojans, *forms a design to over-reach him; she sets off her charms with the utmost care, and (the more surely to enchant him) obtains the magick girdle of* Venus. *She then applies herself to the God of* Sleep, *and with some difficulty, persuades him to seal the eyes of* Jupiter; *this done, she goes to Mount* Ida, *where the God, at first sight, is ravish'd with her beauty, sinks in her embraces, and is laid asleep.* Neptune *takes advantage of his slumber, and succours the* Greeks: Hector *is struck to the ground with a prodigious stone by* Ajax, *and carry'd off from the battel: Several actions succeed; till the* Trojans *much distress'd, are obliged to give way: The lesser* Ajax *signalizes himself in a particular manner.*

But nor the genial feast, nor flowing bowl,
Could charm the cares of *Nestor*'s watchful soul;
His startled ears th' encreasing cries attend;
Then thus, impatient, to his wounded friend.

5   What new alarm, divine *Machaon*, say,
What mixt events attend this mighty day?
Hark! how the shouts divide, and how they meet,
And now come full, and thicken to the fleet!
Here, with the cordial draught dispel thy care,

10 Let *Hecamede* the strength'ning bath prepare,
Refresh thy wound, and cleanse the clotted gore;
While I th' adventures of the day explore.

He said: and seizing *Thrasimedes'* shield,
(His valiant offspring) hasten'd to the field;

15 (That day, the son his father's buckler bore)
Then snatch'd a lance, and issu'd from the door.
Soon as the prospect open'd to his view,
His wounded eyes the scene of sorrow knew;
Dire disarray! the tumult of the fight,

20 The wall in ruins, and the *Greeks* in flight.
As when old Ocean's silent surface sleeps,
The waves just heaving on the purple deeps;
While yet th' expected tempest hangs on high,
Weighs down the cloud, and blackens in the sky,

25 The mass of waters will no wind obey;
Jove sends one gust, and bids them roll away.
While wav'ring counsels thus his mind engage,
Fluctuates, in doubtful thought, the *Pylian* sage;

To join the host, or to the Gen'ral haste,
Debating long, he fixes on the last: 30
Yet, as he moves, the fight his bosom warms;
The field rings dreadful with the clang of arms;
The gleaming faulchions flash, the jav'lins fly;
Blows echo blows, and all or kill, or die.

   Him, in his march, the wounded Princes meet,   35
By tardy steps ascending from the fleet.
The King of men, *Ulysses* the divine,
And who to *Tydeus* owes his noble line.
(Their ships at distance from the battel stand,
In lines advanc'd along the shelving strand;   40
Whose bay, the fleet unable to contain
At length, beside the margin of the main,
Rank above rank, the crowded ships they moor;
Who landed first lay highest on the shore.)
Supported on their spears, they took their way,   45
Unfit to fight, but anxious for the day.
Nestor's approach alarm'd each *Grecian* breast,
Whom thus the Gen'ral of the host addrest.

   O grace and glory of th' *Achaian* name!
What drives thee, *Nestor*, from the field of fame?   50
Shall then proud *Hector* see his boast fulfill'd,
Our fleets in ashes, and our heroes kill'd?
Such was his threat, ah now too soon made good,
On many a *Grecian* bosom writ in blood.
Is ev'ry heart inflam'd with equal rage   55
Against your King, nor will one chief engage?
And have I liv'd to see with mournful eyes
In ev'ry *Greek* a new *Achilles* rise?

   Gerenian Nestor then. So Fate has will'd;
And all-confirming Time has Fate fulfill'd.   60
Not he that thunders from th' aërial bow'r,
Not *Jove* himself, upon the past has pow'r.
The wall, our late inviolable bound,
And best defence, lies smoking on the ground:
Ev'n to the ships their conqu'ring arms extend,   65
And groans of slaughter'd *Greeks* to heav'n ascend.
On speedy measures then employ your thought;
In such distress if counsel profit ought;

Arms cannot much: Tho' *Mars* our souls incite,
70   These gaping wounds withhold us from the fight.
     To him the Monarch. That our army bends,
     That *Troy* triumphant our high fleet ascends,
     And that the rampart, late our surest trust,
     And best defence, lies smoking in the dust:
75   All this from *Jove*'s afflictive hand we bear,
     Who, far from *Argos*, wills our ruin here.
     Past are the days when happier *Greece* was blest,
     And all his favour, all his aid confest;
     Now heav'n averse, our hands from battel ties,
80   And lifts the *Trojan* glory to the skies.
     Cease we at length to waste our blood in vain,
     And launch what ships lie nearest to the main;
     Leave these at anchor till the coming night:
     Then if impetuous *Troy* forbear the fight,
85   Bring all to sea, and hoist each sail for flight.
     Better from evils, well foreseen, to run,
     Than perish in the danger we may shun.
       Thus he. The sage *Ulysses* thus replies,
     While anger flash'd from his disdainful eyes.
90   What shameful words (unkingly as thou art)
     Fall from that trembling tongue, and tim'rous heart?
     Oh were thy sway the curse of meaner pow'rs,
     And thou the shame of any host but ours!
     A Host, by *Jove* endu'd with martial might,
95   And taught to conquer, or to fall in fight:
     Advent'rous combats and bold wars to wage,
     Employ'd our youth, and yet employs our age.
     And wilt thou thus desert the *Trojan* plain?
     And have whole streams of blood been spilt in vain?
100 In such base sentence if thou couch thy fear,
     Speak it in whispers, lest a *Greek* should hear.
     Lives there a man so dead to fame, who dares
     To think such meanness, or the thought declares?
     And comes it ev'n from him whose sov'reign sway
105 The banded legions of all *Greece* obey?
     Is this a Gen'ral's voice, that calls to flight,
     While war hangs doubtful, while his soldiers fight?

What more could *Troy*? What yet their fate denies
Thou giv'st the foe: all *Greece* becomes their prize.
No more the troops, (our hoisted sails in view,   110
Themselves abandon'd) shall the fight pursue,
Thy ships first flying with despair shall see,
And owe destruction to a Prince like thee.
   Thy just reproofs (*Atrides* calm replies)
Like arrows pierce me, for thy words are wise.   115
Unwilling as I am to lose the host,
I force not *Greece* to quit this hateful coast.
Glad I submit, whoe'er, or young or old,
Ought, more conducive to our weal, unfold.
   Tydides cut him short, and thus began.   120
Such counsel if you seek, behold the man
Who boldly gives it, and what he shall say,
Young tho' he be, disdain not to obey:
A youth, who from the mighty *Tydeus* springs,
May speak to councils and assembled Kings.   125
Hear then in me the great *Oenides'* son,
Whose honour'd dust (his race of glory run)
Lies whelm'd in ruins of the *Theban* wall,
Brave in his life, and glorious in his fall.
With three bold sons was gen'rous *Prothous* blest,   130
Who *Pleuron*'s walls and *Calydon* possest;
Melas and *Agrius*, but (who surpast
The rest in courage) *Oeneus* was the last.
From him, my sire. From *Calydon* expell'd,
He past to *Argos*, and in exile dwell'd;   135
The monarch's daughter there (so *Jove* ordain'd)
He won, and flourish'd where *Adrastus* reign'd;
There rich in fortune's gifts, his acres till'd,
Beheld his vines their liquid harvest yield,
And num'rous flocks that whiten'd all the field.   140
Such *Tydeus* was, the foremost once in fame!
Nor lives in *Greece* a stranger to his name.
Then, what for common good my thoughts inspire,
Attend, and in the son, respect the sire.
Tho' fore of battel, tho' with wounds opprest,   145
Let each go forth, and animate the rest,

Advance the glory which he cannot share,
Tho' not partaker, witness of the war.
But lest new wounds on wounds o'erpower us quite,
150 Beyond the missile jav'lin's sounding flight,
Safe let us stand; and from the tumult far,
Inspire the ranks, and rule the distant war.
　　He added not: The list'ning Kings obey,
Slow moving on; *Atrides* leads the way.
155 The God of ocean (to inflame their rage)
Appears a warriour furrow'd o'er with age;
Prest in his own, the Gen'ral's hand he took,
And thus the venerable hero spoke.
　　Atrides, lo! with what disdainful eye
160 *Achilles* sees his country's forces fly;
Blind impious man! whose anger is his guide,
Who glories in unutterable pride!
So may he perish, so may *Jove* disclaim
The wretch relentless, and o'erwhelm with shame!
165 But heav'n forsakes not thee: O'er yonder sands
Soon shalt thou view the scatter'd *Trojan* bands
Fly diverse; while proud Kings, and Chiefs renown'd,
Driv'n heaps on heaps, with clouds involv'd around
Of rolling dust, their winged wheels employ
170 To hide their ignominious heads in *Troy*.
　　He spoke, then rush'd amid the warriour crew;
And sent his voice before him as he flew,
Loud, as the shout encountring armies yield,
When twice ten thousand shake the lab'ring field;
175 Such was the voice, and such the thund'ring sound
Of him, whose trident rends the solid ground.
Each *Argive* bosom beats to meet the fight,
And grizly war appears a pleasing sight.
　　Meantime *Saturnia* from *Olympus'* brow,
180 High-thron'd in gold, beheld the fields below;
With joy the glorious conflict she survey'd,
Where her great brother gave the *Grecians* aid.
But plac'd aloft, on *Ida*'s shady height
She sees her *Jove*, and trembles at the sight.
185 *Jove* to deceive, what methods shall she try,
What arts, to blind his all-beholding eye?

At length she trusts her pow'r; resolv'd to prove
'The old, yet still successful, cheat of love':
Against his wisdom to oppose her charms,
And lull the Lord of Thunders in her arms.   190
    Swift to her bright apartment she repairs,
Sacred to dress, and beauty's pleasing cares:
With skill divine had *Vulcan* form'd the bow'r,
Safe from access of each intruding pow'r.
Touch'd with her secret key, the doors unfold: 195
Self-clos'd behind her shut the valves of gold.
Here first she bathes; and round her body pours
Soft oils of fragrance, and ambrosial show'rs:
The winds perfum'd, the balmy gale convey
Thro' heav'n, thro' earth, and all th' aërial way: 200
Spirit divine! whose exhalation greets
The sense of Gods with more than mortal sweets.
Thus while she breath'd of heav'n, with decent pride
Her artful hands the radiant tresses ty'd;
Part on her head in shining ringlets roll'd,   205
Part o'er her shoulders wav'd like melted gold.
Around her next a heav'nly mantle flow'd,
That rich with *Pallas'* labour'd colours glow'd;
Large clasps of gold the foldings gather'd round,
A golden zone her swelling bosom bound.   210
Far-beaming pendants tremble in her ear,
Each gemm illumin'd with a triple star.
Then o'er her head she casts a veil more white
Then new fal'n snow, and dazling as the light.
Last her fair feet celestial sandals grace.   215
Thus issuing radiant, with majestic pace,
Forth from the dome th' imperial Goddess moves,
And calls the Mother of the *Smiles* and *Loves.*
    How long (to *Venus* thus apart she cry'd)
Shall human strifes celestial minds divide?   220
Ah yet, will *Venus* aid *Saturnia's* joy,
And set aside the cause of *Greece* and *Troy?*
    Let heav'n's dread empress (*Cytheræa* said)
Speak her request, and deem her will obey'd.
Then grant me (said the Queen) those conqu'ring
        charms,   225
That pow'r, which mortals and immortals warms,

That love, which melts mankind in fierce desires,
And burns the sons of heav'n with sacred fires!
  For lo! I haste to those remote abodes,
230 Where the great parents (sacred source of Gods!)
Ocean and *Tethys* their old empire keep,
On the last limits of the land and deep.
In their kind arms my tender years were past;
What-time old *Saturn*, from *Olympus* cast,
235 Of upper heav'n to *Jove* resign'd the reign,
Whelm'd under the huge mass of earth and main.
For strife, I hear, has made the union cease,
Which held so long that ancient pair in peace.
What honour, and what love shall I obtain,
240 If I compose those fatal feuds again?
Once more their minds in mutual ties engage,
And what my youth has ow'd, repay their age.
  She said. With awe divine the Queen of Love
Obey'd the sister and the wife of *Jove*:
245 And from her fragrant breast the zone unbrac'd,
With various skill and high embroid'ry grac'd.
In this was ev'ry art, and ev'ry charm,
To win the wisest, and the coldest warm:
Fond love, the gentle vow, the gay desire,
250 The kind deceit, the still-reviving fire,
Persuasive speech, and more persuasive sighs,
Silence that spoke, and eloquence of eyes.
This on her hand the *Cyprian* Goddess laid;
Take this, and with it all thy wish, she said:
255 With smiles she took the charm; and smiling prest
The pow'rful *Cestus* to her snowy breast.
  Then *Venus* to the courts of *Jove* withdrew;
Whilst from *Olympus* pleas'd *Saturnia* flew.
O'er high *Pieria* thence her course she bore,
260 O'er fair *Emathia*'s ever pleasing shore,
O'er *Hæmus'* hills with snows eternal crown'd;
Nor once her flying foot approach'd the ground.
Then taking wing from *Athos'* lofty steep,
She speeds to *Lemnos* o'er the rowling deep,
265 And seeks the cave of Death's half-brother, *Sleep*.

Sweet pleasing Sleep! (*Saturnia* thus began)
Who spread'st thy empire o'er each God and man;
If e'er obsequious to thy *Juno*'s will,
O Pow'r of Slumbers! hear, and favour still.
Shed thy soft dews on *Jove*'s immortal eyes,   270
While sunk in love's entrancing joys he lies.
A splendid footstool, and a throne, that shine
With gold unfading, *Somnus*, shall be thine;
The work of *Vulcan*; to indulge thy ease,
When wine and feasts thy golden humours please.   275
    Imperial Dame (the balmy pow'r replies)
Great *Saturn*'s heir, and empress of the skies!
O'er other Gods I spread my easy chain;
The Sire of all, old *Ocean*, owns my reign,
And his hush'd waves lie silent on the main.   280
But how, unbidden, shall I dare to steep
Jove's awful temples in the dew of sleep?
Long since too vent'rous, at thy bold command,
On those eternal lids I laid my hand;
What-time, deserting *Ilion*'s wasted plain,   285
His conqu'ring son, *Alcides*, plow'd the main:
When lo! the deeps arise, the tempests roar,
And drive the hero to the *Coan* shore:
Great *Jove* awaking, shook the blest abodes
With rising wrath, and tumbled Gods on Gods;   290
Me chief he sought, and from the realms on high
Had hurl'd indignant to the nether sky,
But gentle *Night*, to whom I fled for aid,
(The friend of earth and heav'n) her wings display'd;
Impow'r'd the wrath of Gods and men to tame,   295
Ev'n *Jove* rever'd the venerable dame.
    Vain are thy fears (the Queen of heav'n replies,
And speaking, rolls her large, majestic eyes)
Think'st thou that *Troy* has *Jove*'s high favour won,
Like great *Alcides*, his all-conqu'ring son?   300
Hear, and obey the mistress of the skies,
Nor for the deed expect a vulgar prize;
For know, thy lov'd-one shall be ever thine,
The youngest *Grace*, *Pasithaë* the divine.

305   Swear then (he said) by those tremendous floods
That roar thro' hell, and bind th' invoking Gods:
Let the great parent Earth one hand sustain,
And stretch the other o'er the sacred main.
Call the black *Titans* that with *Chronos* dwell,
310   To hear, and witness from the depths of hell;
That she, my lov'd one, shall be ever mine,
The youngest *Grace*, *Pasithaë* the divine.

The Queen assents, and from th' infernal bow'rs
Invokes the sable subtartarean pow'rs,
315   And those who rule th' inviolable floods,
Whom mortals name the dread *Titanian* Gods.

Then swift as wind, o'er *Lemnos* smoaky isle,
They wing their way, and *Imbrus'* sea-beat soil,
Thro' air unseen involv'd in darkness glide,
320   And light on *Lectos*, on the point of *Ide*.
(Mother of savages, whose echoing hills
Are heard resounding with a hundred rills)
Fair *Ida* trembles underneath the God;
Hush'd are her mountains, and her forests nod.
325   There on a fir, whose spiry branches rise
To join its summit to the neighb'ring skies,
Dark in embow'ring shade, conceal'd from sight,
Sate *Sleep*, in likeness of the bird of night.
(*Chalcis* his name with those of heav'nly birth,
330   But call'd *Cymindis* by the race of earth.)

To *Ida*'s top successful *Juno* flies;
Great *Jove* surveys her with desiring eyes:
The God, whose light'ning sets the heav'ns on fire,
Thro' all his bosom feels the fierce desire;
335   Fierce as when first by stealth he seiz'd her charms,
Mix'd with her soul, and melted in her arms.
Fix'd on her eyes he fed his eager look,
Then press'd her hand, and thus with transport spoke.

Why comes my Goddess from th' æthereal sky,
340   And not her steeds and flaming chariot nigh?

Then she – I haste to those remote abodes,
Where the great parents of the deathless Gods,
The rev'rend *Ocean* and grey *Tethys* reign,
On the last limits of the land and main.

I visit these, to whose indulgent cares   345
I owe the nursing of my tender years.
For strife, I hear, has made that union cease,
Which held so long this ancient pair in peace.
The steeds, prepar'd my chariot to convey
O'er earth and seas, and thro' th' aërial way,   350
Wait under *Ide*: Of thy superiour pow'r
To ask consent, I leave th' *Olympian* bow'r;
Nor seek, unknown to thee, the sacred cells
Deep under seas, where hoary *Ocean* dwells.
   For that (said *Jove*) suffice another day;   355
But eager love denies the least delay.
Let softer cares the present hour employ,
And be these moments sacred all to joy.
Ne'er did my soul so strong a passion prove,
Or for an earthly, or a heav'nly love: 360
Not when I press'd *Ixion*'s matchless dame,
Whence rose *Perithous* like the Gods in fame.
Not when fair *Danaë* felt the show'r of gold
Stream into life, whence *Perseus* brave and bold.
Not thus I burn'd for either *Theban* dame,   365
(*Bacchus* from this, from that *Alcides* came).
Not *Phœnix*' daughter, beautiful and young,
Whence godlike *Rhadamanth* and *Minos* sprung.
Not thus I burn'd for fair *Latona*'s face,
Nor comelier *Ceres*' more majestick grace.   370
Not thus ev'n for thyself I felt desire,
As now my veins receive the pleasing fire.
   He spoke; the Goddess with the charming eyes
Glows with celestial red, and thus replies.
Is this a scene for love? On *Ida*'s height,   375
Expos'd to mortal, and immortal sight;
Our joys prophan'd by each familiar eye;
The sport of heav'n, and fable of the sky!
How shall I e'er review the blest abodes,
Or mix among the senate of the Gods?   380
Shall I not think, that, with disorder'd charms,
All heav'n beholds me recent from thy arms?
With skill divine has *Vulcan* form'd thy bow'r,
Sacred to love and to the genial hour;

385   If such thy will, to that recess retire,
      And secret there indulge thy soft desire.
          She ceas'd, and smiling with superiour love,
      Thus answer'd mild the cloud-compelling *Jove.*
      Nor God, nor mortal shall our joys behold,
390   Shaded with clouds, and circumfus'd in gold,
      Not ev'n the sun, who darts thro' heav'n his rays,
      And whose broad eye th' extended earth surveys.
          Gazing he spoke, and kindling at the view,
      His eager arms around the Goddess threw.
395   Glad earth perceives, and from her bosom pours
      Unbidden herbs, and voluntary flow'rs;
      Thick new-born vi'lets a soft carpet spread,
      And clust'ring *Lotos* swell'd the rising bed,
      And sudden hyacinths the turf bestrow,
400   And flamy *Crocus* made the mountain glow.
      There golden clouds conceal the heav'nly pair,
      Steep'd in soft joys, and circumfus'd with air;
      Celestial dews, descending o'er the ground,
      Perfume the mount, and breathe *Ambrosia* round.
405   At length with love and sleep's soft pow'r opprest,
      The panting Thund'rer nods, and sinks to rest.
          Now to the navy born on silent wings,
      To *Neptune*'s ear soft *Sleep* his message brings;
      Beside him sudden, unperceiv'd he stood,
410   And thus with gentle words address'd the God.
          Now, *Neptune!* now, th' important hour employ,
      To check a while the haughty hopes of *Troy*:
      While *Jove* yet rests, while yet my vapours shed
      The golden vision round his sacred head;
415   For *Juno*'s love, and *Somnus*' pleasing ties,
      Have clos'd those awful and eternal eyes.
          Thus having said, the pow'r of slumber flew,
      On human lids to drop the balmy dew.
      Neptune, with zeal encreas'd, renews his care,
420   And tow'ring in the foremost ranks of war,
      Indignant thus – Oh once of martial fame!
      O *Greeks!* if yet ye can deserve the name!
      This half-recover'd day shall *Troy* obtain?
      Shall *Hector* thunder at your ships again?

Lo still he vaunts, and threats the fleet with fires,   425
While stern *Achilles* in his wrath retires.
One hero's loss too tamely you deplore,
Be still your selves, and we shall need no more.
Oh yet, if glory any bosom warms,
Brace on your firmest helms, and stand to arms: 430
His strongest spear each valiant *Grecian* wield,
Each valiant *Grecian* seize his broadest shield;
Let, to the weak, the lighter arms belong,
The pond'rous targe be wielded by the strong.
(Thus arm'd) not *Hector* shall our presence stay;   435
My self, ye *Greeks!* my self will lead the way.
    The troops assent; their martial arms they change,
The busy chiefs their banded legions range.
The Kings, tho' wounded, and oppress'd with pain,
With helpful hands themselves assist the train.   440
The strong and cumb'rous arms the valiant wield,
The weaker warriour takes a lighter shield.
Thus sheath'd in shining brass, in bright array,
The legions march, and *Neptune* leads the way:
His brandish'd faulchion flames before their eyes,   445
Like light'ning flashing thro' the frighted skies.
Clad in his might th' earth-shaking pow'r appears;
Pale mortals tremble, and confess their fears.
    Troy's great defender stands alone unaw'd,
Arms his proud host, and dares oppose a God: 450
And lo! the God, and wond'rous man appear;
The sea's great ruler there, and *Hector* here.
The roaring main, at her great master's call,
Rose in huge ranks, and form'd a watry wall
Around the ships: Seas hanging o'er the shores,   455
Both armies join: Earth thunders, Ocean roars.
Not half so loud the bellowing deeps resound,
When stormy winds disclose the dark profound;
Less loud the winds, that from th' *Æolian* hall
Roar thro' the woods, and make whole forests fall;   460
Less loud the woods, when flames in torrents pour,
Catch the dry mountain, and its shades devour.
    With such a rage the meeting hosts are driv'n,
And such a clamour shakes the sounding heav'n.

465   The first bold jav'lin urg'd by *Hector*'s force,
       Direct at *Ajax'* bosom wing'd its course;
       But there no pass the crossing belts afford,
       (One brac'd his shield, and one sustain'd his sword.)
       Then back the disappointed *Trojan* drew,
470   And curs'd the lance that unavailing flew:
       But scap'd not *Ajax*; his tempestuous hand
       A pond'rous stone up-heaving from the sand,
       (Where heaps lay'd loose beneath the warriour's feet,
       Or serv'd to ballast, or to prop the fleet)
475   Toss'd round and round, the missive marble flings;
       On the raz'd shield the falling ruin rings:
       Full on his breast and throat with force descends;
       Nor deaden'd there its giddy fury spends,
       But whirling on, with many a fiery round,
480   Smokes in the dust, and ploughs into the ground.
       As when the bolt, red-hissing from above,
       Darts on the consecrated plant of *Jove*,
       The mountain-oak in flaming ruin lies,
       Black from the blow, and smoaks of sulphur rise;
485   Stiff with amaze the pale beholders stand,
       And own the terrours of th' almighty hand!
       So lies great *Hector* prostrate on the shore;
       His slacken'd hand deserts the lance it bore;
       His following shield the fallen chief o'erspread;
490   Beneath his helmet drop'd his fainting head;
       His load of armour, sinking to the ground,
       Clanks on the field; a dead, and hollow sound.
       Loud Shouts of triumph fill the crowded plain;
       Greece sees, in hope, *Troy*'s great defender slain:
495   All spring to seize him; storms of arrows fly;
       And thicker jav'lins intercept the sky.
       In vain an iron tempest hisses round;
       He lies protected, and without a wound.
       Polydamas, *Agenor* the divine,
       The pious warriour of *Anchises'* line,
       And each bold leader of the *Lycian* band;
       With cov'ring shields (a friendly circle) stand.
       His mournful followers, with assistant care,
       The groaning hero to his chariot bear;

His foaming coursers, swifter than the wind,   505
Speed to the town, and leave the war behind.
   When now they touch'd the mead's enamel'd side,
Where gentle *Xanthus* rolls his easy tyde,
With watry drops the chief they sprinkle round,
Plac'd on the margin of the flow'ry ground.   510
Rais'd on his knees, he now ejects the gore;
Now faints anew, low-sinking on the shore;
By fits he breathes, half views the fleeting skies,
And seals again, by fits, his swimming eyes.
   Soon as the *Greeks* the chief's retreat beheld,   515
With double fury each invades the field.
Oïlean Ajax first his jav'lin sped,
Pierc'd by whose point, the son of *Enops* bled;
(*Satnius* the brave, whom beauteous *Neis* bore
Amidst her flocks on *Satnio*'s silver shore)   520
Struck thro' the belly's rim, the warriour lies
Supine, and shades eternal veil his eyes.
An arduous battel rose around the dead;
By turns the *Greeks*, by turns the *Trojans* bled.
Fir'd with revenge, *Polydamas* drew near,   525
And at *Prothœnor* shook the trembling spear;
The driving jav'lin thro' his shoulder thrust,
He sinks to earth, and grasps the bloody dust.
Lo thus (the victor cries) we rule the field,
And thus their arms the race of *Panthus* wield: 530
From this unerring hand there flies no dart
But bathes its point within a *Grecian* heart.
Propt on that spear to which thou ow'st thy fall,
Go, guide thy darksome steps, to *Pluto*'s dreary hall!
   He said, and sorrow touch'd each *Argive* breast: 535
The soul of *Ajax* burn'd above the rest.
As by his side the groaning warriour fell,
At the fierce foe he launch'd his piercing steel;
The foe reclining, shunn'd the flying death;
But fate, *Archelochus*, demands thy breath: 540
Thy lofty birth no succour could impart,
The wings of death o'ertook thee on the dart,
Swift to perform heav'n's fatal will it fled,
Full on the juncture of the neck and head,

545 And took the joint, and cut the nerves in twain:
The dropping head first tumbled to the plain.
So just the stroke, that yet the body stood
Erect, then roll'd along the sands in blood.
     Here, proud *Polydamas*, here turn thy eyes!
550 (The tow'ring *Ajax* loud-insulting cries)
Say, is this chief extended on the plain,
A worthy vengeance for *Prothœnor* slain?
Mark well his port! his figure and his face
Nor speak him vulgar, nor of vulgar race;
555 Some lines, methinks, may make his lineage known,
Antenor's brother, or perhaps his son.
     He spake, and smil'd severe, for well he knew
The bleeding youth: *Troy* sadden'd at the view.
But furious *Acamas* aveng'd his cause;
560 As *Promachus* his slaughter'd brother draws,
He pierc'd his heart – Such fate attends you all,
Proud *Argives!* destin'd by our arms to fall.
Not *Troy* alone, but haughty *Greece* shall share
The toils, the sorrows, and the wounds of war.
565 Behold your *Promachus* depriv'd of breath,
A victim ow'd to my brave brother's death.
Not unappeas'd, he enters *Pluto*'s gate,
Who leaves a brother to revenge his fate.
     Heart-piercing anguish struck the *Grecian* host,
570 But touch'd the breast of bold *Peneleus* most:
At the proud boaster he directs his course;
The boaster flies, and shuns superior force.
But young *Ilioneus* receiv'd the spear,
Ilioneus, his father's only care:
(*Phorbas* the rich, of all the *Trojan* train
Whom *Hermes* lov'd, and taught the arts of gain)
Full in his eye the weapon chanc'd to fall,
And from the fibres scoop'd the rooted ball,
Drove thro' the neck, and hurl'd him to the plain;
580 He lifts his miserable arms in vain!
Swift his broad faulchion fierce *Peneleus* spread,
And from the spouting shoulders struck his head;
To earth at once the head and helmet fly;
The lance, yet sticking thro' the bleeding eye,

The victor seiz'd; and as aloft he shook   585
The goary visage, thus insulting spoke.
    Trojans! your great *Ilioneus* behold!
Haste, to his father let the tale be told:
Let his high roofs resound with frantic woe,
Such, as the house of *Promachus* must know;   590
Let doleful tidings greet his mother's ear,
Such, as to *Promachus'* sad spouse we bear;
When we, victorious, shall to *Greece* return,
And the pale matron in our triumphs mourn.
    Dreadful he spoke, then toss'd the head on high;   595
The *Trojans* hear, they tremble, and they fly:
Aghast they gaze around the fleet and wall,
And dread the ruin that impends on all.
    Daughters of *Jove!* that on *Olympus* shine,
Ye all-beholding, all-recording nine!   600
O say, when *Neptune* made proud *Ilion* yield,
What chief, what hero first embru'd the field?
Of all the *Grecians*, what immortal name,
And whose blest trophies, will ye raise to fame?
    Thou first, great *Ajax!* on th' ensanguin'd plain   605
Laid *Hyrtius*, leader of the *Mysian* train.
Phalces and *Mermer*, *Nestor*'s son o'erthrew.
Bold *Merion*, *Morys* and *Hippotion* slew.
Strong *Periphætes* and *Prothoön* bled,
By *Teucer*'s arrows mingled with the dead.   610
Pierc'd in the flank by *Menelaüs'* steel,
His people's pastor, *Hyperenor* fell;
Eternal darkness wrapt the warriour round,
And the fierce soul came rushing thro' the wound.
But stretch'd in heaps before *Oïleus'* son,   615
Fall mighty numbers; mighty numbers run;
Ajax the less, of all the *Grecian* race
Skill'd in pursuit, and swiftest in the chace.

OBSERVATIONS

ON THE

FOURTEENTH BOOK

The Poet, to advance the character of *Nestor*, and give us a due esteem for his conduct and circumspection, represents him as deeply sollicitous for the common good: In the very article of mirth or relaxation from the toils of war, he is all attention to learn the fate and issue of the battel: And through his long use and skill in martial events, he judges from the nature of the uproar still encreasing, that the fortune of the day is held no longer in suspense, but inclines to one side.

Eustathius.

1. *But nor the genial feast.*] At the end of the 11*th* book we left *Nestor* at the table with *Machaon.* The attack of the entrenchments, describ'd thro' the 12*th* and 13*th* books, happen'd while *Nestor* and *Machaon* sate at the table; nor is there any improbability herein, since there is nothing performed in those two books, but what might naturally happen in the space of two hours. *Homer* constantly follows the thread of his narration, and never suffers his reader to forget the train of action, or the time it employs. *Dacier.*

10. *Let* Hecamede *the bath prepare.*] The custom of women officiating to men in the bath was usual in ancient times. Examples are frequent in the *Odyssey.* And it is not at all more odd, or to be sneered at, than the custom now used in *France*, of *Valets de Chambres* dressing and undressing the ladies.

21. *As when old Ocean's silent surface sleeps.*] There are no where more finish'd pictures of nature, than those which *Homer* draws in several of his comparisons. The beauty however of some of these will be lost to many, who cannot perceive the resemblance, having never had opportu-

nity to observe the things themselves. The life of this description will be most sensible to those who have been at sea in a calm: In this Condition the water is not entirely motionless, but swells gently in smooth waves, which fluctuate backwards and forwards in a kind of balancing motion: This state continues till a rising wind gives a determination to the waves, and rolls 'em one certain way. There is scarce any thing in the whole compass of nature that can more exactly represent the state of an irresolute mind, wavering between two different designs, sometimes inclining to the one, sometimes to the other, and then moving to that point to which its resolution is at last determined. Every circumstance of this comparison is both beautiful and just; and it is the more to be admired, because it is very difficult to find sensible images proper to represent the motions of the mind; wherefore we but rarely meet with such comparisons even in the best Poets. There is one of great beauty in *Virgil*, upon a subject very like this, where he compares his hero's mind, agitated with a great variety and quick succession of thoughts, to a dancing light reflected from a vessel of water in motion.

> *Cuncta videns, magno curarum fluctuat æstu,*
> *Atque animum, nunc huc, celerem, nunc dividit illuc,*
> *In partesque; rapit varias, perque omnia versat.*
> *Sicut aquæ tremulum labris ubi lumen ahenis*
> *Sole repercussum, aut radiantis imagine lunæ,*
> *Omnia pervolitat late loca; jamque sub auras*
> *Erigitur, summique ferit laquearia tecti.*   Æn. l. 8. v. 19.

[This way and that he turns his anxious mind;
  Thinks, and rejects the counsels he design'd:
Explores himself in vain, in ev'ry part,
And gives no rest to his distracted heart.
  So when the sun by day, or moon by night,
Strike, on the polish'd brass, their trembling light,
The glitt'ring species here and there divide;
And cast their dubious beams from side to side:
Now on the walls, now on the pavement play,
And to the ceiling flash the glaring day.]

30. *He fixes on the last.*] *Nestor* appears in this place a great friend to his Prince; for upon deliberating whether he should go through the body of the *Grecian* host, or else repair to *Agamemnon*'s tent; he determines at last, and judges it the best way to go to the latter. Now because it had been ill concerted to have made a man of his age walk a great way round about in quest of his commander, *Homer* has ordered it so that he should meet *Agamemnon* in his way thither. And nothing could be better imagined than the reason, why the wounded Princes left their tents; they were impatient to behold the battel, anxious for its success, and desirous to inspirit the soldiers by their presence. The Poet was obliged to give a reason; for in *Epic* Poetry, as well as in *Dramatic*, no person ought to be introduced without some necessity, or at least some probability, for his appearance.   *Eustathius.*

39. *Their Ships at distance,* &c.] *Homer* being always careful to distinguish each scene of action, gives a very particular description of the station of the ships, shewing in what manner they lay drawn up on the land. This he had only hinted at before; but here taking occasion on the wounded heroes coming from their ships, which were at a distance from the fight (while others were engaged in the defence of those ships where the wall was broke down) he tells us, that the shore of the bay (comprehended between the *Rhætean* and *Sigæan* promontories) was not sufficient to contain the ships in one line; which they were therefore obliged to draw up in ranks, ranged in parallel lines along the shore. How many of these lines there were, the Poet does not determine. M. *Dacier*, without giving any reason for her opinion, says they were but two; one advanced near the wall, the other on the verge of the sea. But it is more than probable, that there were several intermediate lines; since the order in which the vessels lay is here described by a metaphor taken from the steps of a *scaling-ladder*; which had been no way proper to give an image only of two ranks, but very fit to represent a greater, tho' undetermined number. That there were more than two lines, may likewise be inferred from what we find in the beginning of the 11*th* book; where it is said, that the voice of *Discord*, standing on the ship of *Ulysses*, *in the middle of the fleet*, was heard as far as the stations of *Achilles* and *Ajax, whose ships were drawn up in the two extremities*: Those of *Ajax* were nearest the wall (as is expresly said in the 682d verse of the 13*th* book, *in the orig.*) and those of *Achilles* nearest the sea, as appears from many passages scatter'd thro' the Iliad.

It must be supposed that those ships were drawn highest upon land, which first approached the shore; the first line therefore consisted of those who first disembarked, which were the ships of *Ajax* and

Protesilaus; the latter of whom seems mentioned in the verse above cited of the 13*th* book, only to give occasion to observe this, for he was slain as he landed first of the *Greeks.* And accordingly we shall see in the 15*th* book, it is his ship that is first attacked by the *Trojans*, as it lay the nearest to them.

We may likewise guess how it happens, that the ships of *Achilles* were placed nearest to the sea; for in the answer of *Achilles* to *Ulysses* in the 9*th* book, v. 432. he mentions a naval expedition he had made while *Agamemnon* lay safe in the camp: So that his ships at their return did naturally lie next the sea; which, without this consideration, might appear a station not so becoming this hero's courage.

47. Nestor*'s approach alarm'd.*] That so laborious a person as *Nestor* has been described, so indefatigable, so little indulgent of his extreme age, and one that never receded from the battel, should approach to meet them; this it was that struck the Princes with amazement, when they saw he had left the field.   *Eustathius.*

81. *Cease we at length,* &c.] *Agamemnon* either does not know what course to take in this distress, or only sounds the sentiments of his nobles (as he did in the second book of the whole army.) He delivers himself first after *Nestor*'s speech, as it became a counseller to do. But knowing this advice to be dishonourable, and unsuitable to the character he assumes elsewhere, ἱδρώσει μέν τευ τελαμών [his sword-belt will sweat, *Il.* II. 388], *&c.* and considering that he should do no better than abandon his post, when before he had threaten'd the deserters with death; he reduces his counsel into the form of a proverb, disguising it as handsomly as he can under a sentence. *It is better to shun an evil,* &c. It is observable too how he has qualified the expression: He does not say, to *shun the battel,* for that had been unsoldierly; but he softens the phrase, and calls it, to shun *evil*: and this word *Evil* he applies twice together, in advising them to leave the engagement.

It is farther remarked, that this was the noblest opportunity for a General to try the temper of his officers; for he knew that in a calm of affairs, it was common with most people either out of flattery or respect to submit to their leaders: But in imminent danger, fear does not bribe them, but every one discovers his very soul, valuing all other considerations, in regard to his safety, but in the second place. He knew the men he spoke to were prudent persons, and not easy to cast themselves into a precipitate flight. He might likewise have a mind to recommend himself to his army by the means of his officers; which he was not very able to do of himself, angry as they were at him, for the affront he had offered *Achilles*, and by consequence thinking him the author of all their present calamities.   *Eustathius.*

92.   *Oh were thy sway the curse of meaner pow'rs,*
       And thou the shame of any host but ours.]

This is a noble complement to his country and to the *Grecian* army, to shew that it was an impossibility for them to follow even their General in any thing that was cowardly, or shameful; tho' the lives and safeties of 'em all were concerned in it.

104.   *And comes it ev'n from him whose sov'reign sway*
        The banded legions of all Greece *obey?*]

As who should say, that another man might indeed have utter'd the same advice, but it could not be a person of prudence; or if he had prudence, he could not be a governour, but a private man; or if a governour, yet one who had not a well-disciplin'd and obedient army; or lastly, if he had an army so condition'd, yet it could not be so large and numerous an one as that of *Agamemnon.* This is a fine climax, and of wonderful strength.   *Eustathius.*

118. *Whoe'er, or young, or old,* &c.] This nearly resembles an ancient custom at *Athens,* where in times of trouble and distress, every one, of what age or quality soever, was invited to give in his opinion with freedom by the publick cryer.   *Eustathius.*

120.] This speech of *Diomed* is naturally introduced, beginning with an answer, as if he had been call'd upon to give his advice. The counsel he proposes was that alone which could be of any real service in their present exigency: However, since he ventures to advise where *Ulysses* is at a loss, and *Nestor* himself silent, he thinks it proper to apologize for this liberty by reminding them of his birth and descent, hoping thence to add to his counsel a weight and authority which he could not from his years and experience. It can't indeed be deny'd that this historical digression seems more out of season than any of the same kind which we so frequently meet with in *Homer,* since his birth and parentage must have been sufficiently known to all at the siege, as he here tells them. This must be own'd a defect not altogether to be excus'd in the Poet, but which may receive some alleviation, if consider'd as a fault of temperament. For he had certainly a strong inclination to genealogical stories, and too frequently takes occasion to gratify this humour.

135. *He fled to* Argos.] This is a very artful colour: He calls the flight of his father for killing one of his brothers, *travelling and dwelling at* Argos, without mentioning the cause and occasion of his retreat. What immediately follows (*so* Jove *ordain'd*) does not only contain in it a disguise of his crime, but is a just motive likewise for our compassion.

Eustathius.

146. *Let each go forth and animate the rest.*] It is worth a remark, with what management and discretion the Poet has brought these four Kings, and no more, towards the engagement, since these are sufficient alone to perform all that he requires. For *Nestor* proposes to them to enquire, if there be any way or means which prudence can direct for their security. *Agamemnon* attempts to discover that method. *Ulysses* refutes him as one whose method was dishonourable, but proposes no other project. *Diomed* supplies that deficiency, and shews what must be done: that wounded as they are, they should go forth to the battel; for though they were not able to engage, yet their presence would re-establish their affairs by detaining in arms those who might otherwise quit the field. This counsel is embrac'd, and readily obey'd by the rest. *Eustathius.*

179. *The Story of* Jupiter *and* Juno.] I don't know a bolder fiction in all antiquity, than this of *Jupiter*'s being deceiv'd and laid asleep, or that has a greater air of impiety and absurdity. 'Tis an observation of Mons. *de St Evremond* upon the ancient poets, which every one will agree to: 'that it is surprizing enough to find them so scrupulous to preserve probability, in actions purely human; and so ready to violate it, in representing the actions of the Gods. Even those who have spoken more sagely than the rest, of their nature, could not forbear to speak extravagantly of their conduct. When they establish their being and their attributes, they make them immortal, infinite, almighty, perfectly wise, and perfectly good: But the moment they represent them acting, there's no weakness to which they do not make 'em stoop, and no folly or wickedness they do not make 'em commit.' The same author answers this in another place by remarking, 'that truth was not the inclination of the first ages: a foolish lye or a lucky falshood gave reputation to impostors, and pleasure to the credulous. 'Twas the whole secret of the great and the wise to govern the simple and ignorant herd. The vulgar, who pay a profound reverence to mysterious errors, would have despised plain truth, and it was thought a piece of prudence to deceive them. All the discourses of the ancients were fitted to so advantagious a design. There was nothing to be seen but fictions, allegories, and similitudes, and nothing was to appear as it was in itself.'

I must needs, upon the whole, as far as I can judge, give up the morality of this fable; but what colour of excuse for it *Homer* might have from ancient tradition, or what mystical or allegorical sense might attone for the appearing impiety, is hard to be ascertain'd at this distant period of time. That there had been before his age a tradition of *Jupiter*'s being laid asleep, appears from the story of *Hercules* at *Coos*, referr'd to by our author, v. 285. There is also a passage in *Diodorus*, *lib.* 1. *c.* 7. which gives some small light to this fiction. Among other reasons which that historian lays down to prove that *Homer* travell'd into *Egypt*, he alledges this passage of the interview of *Jupiter* and *Juno*, which he says was grounded upon an *Egyptian* festival, *whereon the nuptial ceremonies of these two deities were celebrated, at which time both their tabernacles, adorned with all sorts of flowers, are carry'd by the priests to the top of a high mountain.* Indeed as the greatest part of the ceremonies of the ancient religions consisted in some symbolical representations of certain actions of their Gods, or rather deify'd mortals, so a great part of ancient poetry consisted in the description of the actions exhibited in those ceremonies. The loves of *Venus* and *Adonis* are a remarkable instance of this kind, which, tho' under different names, were celebrated by annual representations, as well in *Egypt* as in several nations of *Greece* and *Asia*: and to the images which were carry'd in these festivals, several ancient poets were indebted for their most happy descriptions. If the truth of this observation of *Diodorus* be admitted, the present passage will appear with more dignity, being grounded on religion; and the conduct of the poet will be more justifiable, if that, which has been generally counted an indecent, wanton fiction, should prove to be the representation of a religious solemnity. Considering the great ignorance we are in of many ancient ceremonies, there may be probably in *Homer* many incidents entirely of this nature; wherefore we ought to be reserv'd in our censures, lest what we decry as wrong in the Poet, should prove only a fault in his religion. And indeed it would be a very unfair way to tax any people, or any age whatever, with grossness in general, purely from the gross or absurd ideas or practices that are to be found in their religions.

In the next place, if we have recourse to allegory, (which softens and reconciles every thing) it may be imagin'd that by the congress of *Jupiter* and *Juno*, is meant the mingling of the *æther* and the *air* (which are generally said to be signify'd by these two deities.) The ancients believ'd the *æther* to be igneous, and that by its kind influence upon the air it was the cause of all vegetation: To which nothing more exactly corresponds, than the fiction of the earth putting forth her flowers immediately upon this congress. *Virgil* has some lines in the second *Georgic*, that seem a perfect explanation of the fable into this sense. In describing the spring, he hints as if something of a vivifying influence was at that time spread from the upper heavens into the air. He calls *Jupiter* expressly *Æther*, and represents him operating upon his spouse for the production of all things.

> *Tum pater omnipotens fœcundis imbribus æther*
> *Conjugis in gremio lætæ descendit, & omnes*
> *Magnus alit, magno commixtus corpore, fœtus.*
> *Parturit omnis ager,* &c.

> [For then almighty *Jove* descends and pours
> Into his buxom bride his fruitful show'rs.
> And mixing his large limbs with hers, he feeds
> Her births with kindly juice, and fosters teeming seeds.
> Then fields the blades of bury'd corn disclose, . . .]

But, be all this as it will, it is certain, that whatever may be thought of this fable in a theological or philosophical view, it is one of the most beautiful pieces that ever was produc'd by Poetry. Neither does it want its moral: an ingenious modern writer [*Tatler* 147] (whom I am pleas'd to take any occasion of quoting) has given it us in these words.

'This passage of *Homer* may suggest abundance of instruction to a woman who has a mind to preserve or recall the affection of her husband. The care of her person and dress, with the particular blandishments woven in the *Cestus*, are so plainly recommended by this fable, and so indispensably necessary in every female who desires to please, that they need no farther explanation. The discretion likewise in covering all matrimonial quarrels from the knowledge of others, is taught in the pretended visit to *Tethys*, in the speech where *Juno* addresses herself to *Venus*; as the chaste and prudent management of a wife's charms is intimated by the same pretence for her appearing before *Jupiter*, and by the Concealment of the *Cestus* in her bosom. I shall leave this tale to the consideration of such good houswives who are never well dress'd but when they are abroad, and think it necessary to appear more agreeable to all men living than their husbands: As also to those prudent ladies, who, to avoid the appearance of being over-fond, entertain their husbands with indifference, aversion, sullen silence, or exasperating language.'

191. *Swift to her bright apartment she repairs*, &c.] This passage may be of consideration to the ladies, and, for their sakes, I take a little pains to observe upon it. *Homer* tells us that the very Goddesses, who are all over charms, never dress in sight of any one: The Queen of Heaven adorns herself in private, and the doors lock after her. In *Homer* there are no *Dieux des Ruelles*, no Gods are admitted to the toilette.

I am afraid there are some earthly Goddesses of less prudence, who have lost much of the adoration of mankind by the contrary practice. *Lucretius* (a very good judge in gallantry) prescribes as a cure to a desperate lover, the frequent sight of his mistress undress'd. *Juno* herself has suffer'd a little by the very *Muse*'s peeping into her chamber, since some nice criticks are shock'd in this place of *Homer* to find that the Goddess washes herself, which presents some idea as if she was dirty. Those who have delicacy will profit by this remark.

198. *Soft oils of fragrance.*] The practice of *Juno* in anointing her body with perfumed oils was a remarkable part of ancient *Cosmeticks*, tho' entirely disused in the modern arts of dress. It may possibly offend the niceness of modern ladies; but such of 'em as paint, ought to consider that this practice might, without much greater difficulty, be reconciled to cleanliness. This passage is a clear instance of the antiquity of this custom, and clearly determines against *Pliny*, who is of opinion that it was not so ancient as those times, where, speaking of perfum'd un-guents, he says, *Quis primus invenerit non traditur; Iliacis temporibus non erant* [Who first discovered them has not been recorded; at the time of the *Trojan* war, they did not exist], lib. 13. c. 1. Besides the custom of anointing Kings among the *Jews*, which the Christians have borrow'd, there are several allusions in the Old Testament which shew that this practice was thought ornamental among them. The *Psalmist*, speaking of the gifts of God, mentions wine and oil, the former to make glad the heart of man, and the latter to give him a chearful countenance. It seems most probable that this was an eastern invention, agreeable to the luxury of the *Asiaticks*, among whom the most proper ingredients for these unguents were produc'd; from them this custom was propagated among the *Romans*, by whom it was esteem'd a pleasure of a very refin'd nature. Whoever is curious to see instances of their expence and delicacy therein, may be satisfied in the three first chapters of the thirteenth book of *Pliny*'s natural history.

203. *Thus while she breath'd of Heav'n*, &c.] We have here a compleat picture from head to foot of the dress of the fair sex, and of the mode between two and three thousand years ago. May I have leave to observe the great simplicity of *Juno*'s dress, in comparison with the innumerable equipage of a modern toilette? The Goddess, even when she is setting herself out on the greatest occasion, has only her own locks to tie, a white veil to cast over them, a mantle to dress her whole body, her pendants, and her sandals. This the Poet expresly says was *all her dress* [πάντα κόσμον;] and one may reasonably conclude it was all that was used by the greatest princesses and finest beauties of those times. The good *Eustathius* is ravish'd to find, that here are no washes for the face, no dyes for the hair, and none of those artificial embellishments since in practice; he also rejoices not a little, that *Juno* has no looking-glass, tire-woman, or waiting maid. One may preach till doomsday on this subject, but all the commentators in the world will never prevail upon a lady to stick one pin the less in her gown, except she can be convinced, that the ancient dress will better set off her person.

As the *Asiaticks* always surpass'd the *Grecians* in whatever regarded magnificence and luxury, so we find their women far gone in the contrary extreme of dress. There is a passage in *Isaiah*, Ch. 3. that gives us a particular of their wardrobe, with the number and uselessness of their ornaments; and which I think appears very well in contrast to this of *Homer*. *The bravery of their tinkling ornaments about their feet, and their cauls, and their round tires like the moon: The chains, and the bracelets, and the mufflers, the bonnets, and the ornaments of the legs, and the headbands, and the tablets, and the ear-rings, the rings and nose-jewels, the changeable suits of apparel, and the mantles, and the wimples, and the crisping-pins, the glasses, and the fine linen, and the hoods, and the veils.*

I could be glad to ask the ladies which they should like best to imitate, the *Greeks*, or the *Asiaticks?* I would desire those that are handsome and well-made, to consider, that the dress of *Juno* (which is the same they see in *statues*) has manifestly the advantage of the present, in displaying whatever is beautiful: That the charms of the *neck* and *breast* are not less laid open, than by the modern stays; and that those of the *leg* are more gracefully discover'd, than even by the hoop-petticoat: That the fine turn of the *arms* is better observ'd; and that several natural graces of the *shape* and *body* appear much more conspicuous. It is not to be deny'd but the *Asiatic* and our present modes were better contriv'd to conceal some people's defects, but I don't speak to such people: I speak only to ladies of that beauty, who can make any fashion prevail by their being seen in it; and who put others of their sex under the wretched necessity of being like them in their habits, or not being like them at all. As for the rest, let 'em follow the mode of *Judæa*, and be content with the name of *Asiaticks*.

216. *Thus issuing radiant,* &c.] Thus the Goddess comes from her apartment against her spouse in compleat armour. The pleasures of women mostly prevail by pure cunning, and the artful management of their persons; for there is but one way for the weak to subdue the mighty, and that is by pleasure. The Poet shews at the same time, that men of understanding are not master'd without a great deal of artifice and address. There are but three ways, whereby to overcome another, by violence, by persuasion, or by craft: *Jupiter* was invincible by main force; to think of persuading was as fruitless, after he had pass'd his nod to *Achilles*; therefore *Juno* was obliged of necessity to turn her thoughts entirely upon craft; and by the force of pleasure it is, that she insnares and manages the God.   *Eustathius.*

218. *And calls the Mother of the* Smiles *and* Loves.] Notwithstanding all the Pains *Juno* has been at, to adorn herself, she is still conscious that neither the natural beauty of her person, nor the artificial one of her dress, will be sufficient to work upon a husband. She therefore has recourse to the *Cestus* of *Venus*, as a kind of love-charm, not doubting to enflame his mind by *magical enchantment*; a folly which in all ages has possest her sex. To procure this, she applies to the Goddess of Love; from whom hiding her real design under a feign'd

story, (another propriety in the character of the fair) she obtains the valuable present of this wonder-working girdle. The allegory of the *Cestus* lies very open, though the impertinences of *Eustathius* on this head are unspeakable. In it are comprized the most powerful *incentives* to love, as well as the strongest *effects* of the passion. The just admiration of this passage has been always so great and universal, that the *Cestus* of *Venus* is become proverbial. The beauty of the lines which in a few words comprehend this agreeable fiction, can scarce be equall'd. So beautiful an original has produc'd very fine imitations, wherein we may observe a few additional figures, expressing some of the improvements which the affectation, or artifice, of the fair sex have introduc'd into the art of love since *Homer*'s days. *Tasso* has finely imitated this description in the magical girdle of *Armida. Gierusalemme liberata*, Cant. 16.

> *Teneri Sdegni, e placide e tranquille*
> *Repulse, e cari vezzi, e liete paci,*
> *Sorrisi, parrolette, e dolci stille*
> *Di pianto, e sospir tronchi, e molli baci.*

> [Of mild denays, of tender scorns, of sweet
> Repulses, war, peace, hope, despair, joy, fear,
> Of smiles, jests, mirth, wo, grief, and sad regret,
> Sighs, sorrows, tears, embracements, kisses dear.]

Mons. *de la Motte*'s imitation of this fiction is likewise wonderfully beautiful.

> *Ce tissu, le simbole, & la cause à la fois,*
> *Du pouvoir d'l'amour, du charme de ses loix.*
> *Elle enflamme les yeux, de cet ardeur qui touche;*
> *D'un sourire enchanteur, elle anime la bouche;*
> *Passionne la voix, en adoucit les sons,*
> *Prête ces tours heureux, plus forts que les raisons;*
> *Inspire, pour toucher, ces tendres stratagêmes,*
> *Ces resus attirans, l'ecueil des sages mêmes.*
> *Et la nature enfin, y voulut renfermer,*
> *Tout ce qui persuade, & ce qui fait aimer.*
>   *En prenant ce tissu, que Venus lui presente,*
> *Junon n'etoit que belle, elle devient charmante.*
> *Les graces, & les ris, les plaisirs, & les jeux,*
> *Surpris cherchent Venus, doutent qui l'est des deux.*

L'amour même trompé, trouve Junon plus belle;
Et son arc à la main, déjà vole après elle.

[This garment, the symbol and, at the same time, the
      cause
of the power of love, of the spell cast by its laws.
It sets the eyes on fire with that ardour that so moves the
      soul;
with a captivating smile it animates the mouth;
it impassions the voice, it softens its sounds,
it lends to it that tone of sweet suggestiveness that is
      stronger than reason;
it inspires those tender stratagems that are so affecting,
those enticing refusals that have shipwrecked even the
      wise.
And nature has, in a word, wished to contain within it
all that is persuasive, all that inspires love.
   Upon taking up this garment that Venus had given to
      her,
Juno was not only beautiful, but she became captivating.
Gracefulness, laughter, pleasure, and playfulness –
all astonished – expect to find Venus, and wonder which
      of the two goddesses she is.
Cupid, himself deceived, finds Juno the more beautiful;
and, bow in hand, he immediately flies after her.]

Spencer, in his 4*th* book, Canto 5. describes a girdle of *Venus* of a very
different nature; for as this had the power to raise up loose desires in
others, that had a more wonderful faculty to suppress them in the
person that wore it: But it had a most dreadful quality, to burst
asunder whenever tied about any but a chaste bosom. Such a girdle,
'tis to be fear'd, would produce effects very different from the other:
Homer's *Cestus* would be a peace-maker to reconcile man and wife; but
Spencer's *Cestus* would probably destroy the good agreement of many a
happy couple.

255. *– And prest The pow'rful* Cestus *to her snowy breast.*] *Eustathius*
takes notice, that the word *Cestus* is not the name, but epithet only, of
Venus's girdle; tho' the epithet has prevail'd so far as to become the
proper name in common use. This has happen'd to others of our
Author's epithets; the word *Pygmy* is of the same nature. *Venus* wore

this girdle below her neck, and in open sight, but *Juno* hides it in her bosom, to shew the difference of the two characters: It suits well with *Venus* to make a shew of whatever is engaging in her; but *Juno*, who is a matron of prudence and gravity, ought to be more modest.

264. *She speeds to* Lemnos *o'er the rolling deep,*
And seeks the cave of Death's half-brother, Sleep.]

In this fiction *Homer* introduces a new divine personage: It does not appear whether this God of *Sleep* was a God of *Homer's* creation, or whether his pretensions to divinity were of more ancient date. The Poet indeed speaks of him as of one formerly active in some heavenly transactions. Be this as it will, succeeding Poets have always acknowledg'd his title. *Virgil* would not let his *Æneid* be without a person so proper for poetical machinery; tho' he has employ'd him with much less art than his master, since he appears in the fifth book without provocation or commission, only to destroy the *Trojan* pilot. The criticks, who cannot see all the allegories which the commentators pretend to find in *Homer's* divinities, must be obliged to acknowledge the reality and propriety of this; since every thing that is here said of this imaginary Deity is justly applicable to Sleep. He is called the *Brother of Death*; said to be protected by *Night*; and is employed very naturally to lull a husband to rest in the embraces of his wife; which effect of this *conjugal opiate* even the modest *Virgil* has remark'd in the persons of *Vulcan* and *Venus*, probably with an eye to this passage of *Homer.*

– Placidumque petivit
Conjugis infusus gremio per membra soporem.

[He snatch'd the willing Goddess to his arms;
    'Till in her lap infus'd, he lay possess'd
    Of full desire, and sunk to pleasing rest.]

264. *To* Lemnos.] The commentators are hard put to it, to give a reason why *Juno* seeks for *Sleep* in *Lemnos.* Some finding out that *Lemnos* anciently abounded with wine, inform us that it was a proper place of residence for him, wine being naturally a great provoker of sleep. Others will have it, that this God being in love with *Pasithaë*, who resided with her sister the wife of *Vulcan*, in *Lemnos*, it was very probable he might be found haunting near his mistress. Other commentators perceiving the weakness of these conjectures, will have it that *Juno* met *Sleep* here by mere accident; but this is contradictory to the whole thread of the narration. But who knows whether *Homer* might not design this fiction as a piece of raillery upon the sluggishness of the *Lemnians*; tho' this character of them does not appear? A kind of satire like that of *Ariosto*, who makes the Angel find *Discord* in a monastery? Or like that of *Boileau* in his *Lutrin*, where he places *Mollesse* in a dormitory of the Monks of St *Bernard*?

266. *Sweet-pleasing Sleep,* &c.] *Virgil* has copied some part of this conversation between *Juno* and *Sleep*, where he introduces the same Goddess making a request to *Æolus*. *Scaliger*, who is always eager to depreciate *Homer*, and zealous to praise his favourite Author, has highly censured this passage: But notwithstanding this critick's judgment, an impartial reader will find, I don't doubt, much more art and beauty in the original than the copy. In the former, *Juno* endeavours to engage *Sleep* in her design by the promise of a proper and valuable present; but having formerly run a great hazard in a like attempt, he is not prevail'd upon. Hereupon the Goddess, knowing his passion for one of the *Graces*, engages to give her to his desires: This hope brings the lover to consent, but not before he obliges *Juno* to confirm her promise by an oath in a most solemn manner, the very words and ceremony whereof he prescribes to her. These are all beautiful and poetical circumstances, most whereof are untouch'd by *Virgil*, and which *Scaliger* therefore calls low and vulgar. He only makes *Juno* demand a favour from *Æolus*, which he had no reason to refuse; and promise him a reward, which it does not appear he was fond of. The *Latin* Poet has indeed with great judgment added one circumstance concerning the promise of children,

> — *& pulchra faciat te prole parentem.*

[And make thee father of a happy line.]

And this is very conformable to the religion of the *Romans*, among whom *Juno* was suppos'd to preside over human births; but it does not appear she had any such office in the *Greek* theology.

272. *A splendid footstool.*] Notwithstanding the cavils of *Scaliger*, it may be allow'd, that an easy chair was no improper present for *Sleep*. As to the footstool, Mad. *Dacier*'s observation is a very just one; that besides its being a conveniency, it was a mark of honour, and was far from presenting any low or trivial idea. 'Tis upon that account we find it so frequently mention'd in scripture, where the earth is call'd *the footstool of the throne of God.* In *Jeremiah, Judæa* is call'd (as a mark of distinction) the footstool of the feet of God. *Lament.* 2. v. 1. *And he remember'd not the footstool of his feet, in the day of his wrath.* We see here the same image, founded no doubt upon the same customs.

Dacier.

279. *The Sire of all, old* Ocean.] '*Homer* (says *Plutarch*) calls the Sea *Father of All*, with a view to this doctrine, that all things were generated from water. *Thales* the *Milesian*, the head of the *Ionick* sect who seems to have been the first author of Philosophy, affirmed water to be the principle from whence all things spring, and into which all things are resolved; because the prolific seed of all animals is a moisture; all Plants are nourished by moisture; the very sun and stars, which are fire, are nourished by moist vapours and exhalations; and consequently he thought the world was produced from this element.' Plut. *Opin. of Philos.* lib. 1. c. 3.

281. *But how, unbidden,* &c.] This particularity is worth remarking; *Sleep* tells *Juno* that he dares not approach *Jupiter* without his own order; whereby he seems to intimate, that a spirit of a superiour kind may give itself up to a voluntary cessation of thought and action, tho' it does not want this relaxation from any weakness or necessity of its nature.

285. *What-time deserting* Ilion's *wasted plain,* &c.] One may observe from hence, that to make falsity in fables useful and subservient to our designs, it is not enough to cause the story to resemble truth, but we are to corroborate it by parallel places; which method the Poet uses elsewhere. Thus many have attempted great difficulties, and surmounted 'em. So did *Hercules*, so did *Juno*, so did *Pluto.* Here therefore the Poet feigning that *Sleep* is going to practise insidiously upon *Jove*, prevents the strangeness and incredibility of the tale, by squaring it to an ancient story; which ancient story was, that *Sleep* had once before got the mastery of *Jove* in the case of *Hercules.*

Eustathius.

296. *Ev'n* Jove *rever'd the venerable dame.*] *Jupiter* is represented as unwilling to do any thing that might be offensive or ungrateful to *Night*; the Poet (says *Eustathius*) instructs us by this, that a wise and honest man will curb his wrath before any awful and venerable persons: Such was *Night* in regard of *Jupiter*, feign'd as an ancestor, and honourable on account of her antiquity and power. For the *Greek* theology teaches that *Night* and *Chaos* were before all things. Wherefore it was held sacred to obey the *Night* in the conflicts of war, as we find by the admonitions of the heralds to *Hector* and *Ajax* in the 7*th* Iliad.

Milton has made a fine use of this ancient opinion in relation to *Chaos* and *Night*, in the latter part of his second book, where he describes the passage of *Satan* thro' their empire. He calls them,

> *– Eldest* Night
> *And* Chaos, *ancestors of nature; –*

And alludes to the same, in those noble verses,

> *– Behold the throne*
> *Of* Chaos, *and his dark pavillion spread*
> *Wide on the wasteful deep: with him enthron'd*
> *Sate sable-vested* Night, *eldest of things*
> *The consort of his reign. –*

That fine apostrophe of *Spenser* has also the same allusion, book 1.

> *O thou, most ancient grandmother of all,*
> *More old than* Jove, *whom thou at first didst breed,*
> *Or that great house of Gods cœlestial;*
> *Which was begot in* Dæmogorgon's *hall,*
> *And saw'st the secrets of the world unmade.*

307. *Let the great parent Earth one hand sustain,*
      And stretch the other o'er the sacred main, &c.]

There is something wonderfully solemn in this manner of swearing proposed by *Sleep* to *Juno*. How answerable is this idea to the dignity of the Queen of the Goddesses, where Earth, Ocean, and Hell itself, where the whole creation, all things visible and invisible, are called to be witnesses of the oath of the Deity.

311. *That she, my lov'd one,* &c.] *Sleep* is here made to repeat the words of *Juno*'s promise, than which repetition nothing, I think, can be more beautiful or better placed. The lover fired with these hopes,

insists on the promise, dwelling with pleasure on each circumstance that relates to his fair one. The throne and footstool, it seems, are quite out of his head.

323. *Fair* Ida *trembles.*] It is usually supposed at the approach or presence of any heavenly being, that upon their motion all should shake that lies beneath them. Here the Poet giving a description of the descent of these Deities upon the ground at *Lectos*, says that the loftiest of the wood trembled under their feet: Which expression is to intimate the lightness and swiftness of the motions of heavenly beings; the wood does not shake under their feet from any corporeal weight, but from a certain awful dread and horrour.   *Eustathius.*

328. *In likeness of a bird of night.*] This is a bird about the size of a hawk, entirely black; and that is the reason why *Homer* describes *Sleep* under its form. Here (says *Eustathius*) *Homer* lets us know, as well as in many other places, that he is no stranger to the language of the Gods. *Hobbes* has taken very much from the dignity of this supposition, in translating the present lines in this manner.

> *And there sate* Sleep *in likeness of a fowl,*
> *Which Gods do* Chalcis *call, but men an owl.*

We find in *Plato*'s *Cratylus* a discourse of great subtilty, grounded chiefly on this observation of *Homer*, that the Gods and men call the same thing by different names. The Philosopher supposes that in the original language every thing was express'd by a word, whose sound was naturally apt to mark the nature of the thing signified. This great work he ascribes to the Gods, since it required more knowledge both in the nature of sounds and things, than man had attained to. This resemblance, he says, was almost lost in modern languages by the unskilful alterations men had made, and the great licence they had taken in compounding of words. However, he observes there were yet among the *Greeks* some remains of this original language, of which he gives a few instances, adding, that many more were to be found in some of the barbarous languages, that had deviated less from the original, which was still preserved entire among the Gods. This appears a notion so uncommon, that I could not forbear to mention it.

345. *— To whose indulgent cares I owe the nursing,* &c.] The allegory of this is very obvious. *Juno* is constantly understood to be the *air*; and we are here told she was nourished by the vapours which rise from the *Ocean* and the *Earth.* For *Tethys* is the same with *Rhea.*

Eustathius.

359.] This Courtship of *Jupiter* to *Juno* may possibly be thought pretty singular. He endeavours to prove the ardour of his passion to her, by the instances of its warmth to other women. A great many people will look upon this as no very likely method to recommend himself to *Juno*'s favour. Yet, after all, something may be said in defence of *Jupiter*'s way of thinking, with respect to the Ladies. Perhaps a man's love to the sex in general may be no ill recommendation of him to a particular. And to be known, or thought to have been successful with a good many, is what some moderns have found no unfortunate qualification in gaining a lady, even a most virtuous one like *Juno*, especially one who (like her) has had the experience of a married state.

395. *Glad earth perceives,* &c.] It is an observation of *Aristotle* in the 25*th* chapter of his Poeticks, that when *Homer* is obliged to describe any thing of itself absurd or too improbable, he constantly contrives to blind and dazle the judgment of his readers with some shining description. This passage is a remarkable instance of that artifice, for having imagined a fiction of very great absurdity, that the Supreme Being should be laid aside in a female embrace, he immediately, as it were to divert his reader from reflecting on his boldness, pours forth a great variety of poetical ornaments; by describing the various flowers the earth shoots up to compose their couch, the golden clouds that encompassed them, and the bright heav'nly dews that were shower'd round them. *Eustathius* observes it as an instance of *Homer*'s modest conduct in so delicate an affair, that he has purposely adorn'd the bed of *Jupiter* with such a variety of beautiful flowers, that the reader's thoughts being entirely taken up with these ornaments, might have no room for loose imaginations. In the same manner an ancient scholiast has observ'd, that the golden cloud was contriv'd to lock up this action from any farther enquiry of the reader.

395.] I cannot conclude the notes on this story of *Jupiter* and *Juno*, without observing with what particular care *Milton* has imitated the several beautiful parts of this episode, introducing them upon different occasions as the subjects of his poem would admit. The circumstance of *Sleep*'s sitting in likeness of a bird on the fir-tree upon mount *Ida*, is alluded to in his *4th* book, where *Satan* sits in likeness of a cormorant on the tree of life. The creation is made to give the same tokens of joy at the performance of the nuptial rites of our first parents, as she does here at the congress of *Jupiter* and *Juno*.   *Lib*. 8.

> *— To the nuptial bow'r*
> *I led her blushing like the morn, all heav'n*
> *And happy constellations on that hour*
> *Shed their selectest influence; the earth*
> *Gave sign of gratulation, and each hill;*
> *Joyous the birds; fresh gales and gentle airs*
> *Whisper'd it to the woods, and from their wings*
> *Flung rose, flung odours from the spicy shrub.*

Those lines also in the *4th* book are manifestly from the same original.

> *— Roses and jessamine*
> *Rear'd high their flourish'd heads between, and wrought*
> *Mosaic, underfoot the violet,*
> *Crocus and hyacinth with rich inlay*
> *Broider'd the ground. —*

Where the very turn of *Homer*'s verses is observed, and the cadence, and almost the words, finely translated.

But it is with wonderful judgment and decency he has used that exceptionable passage of the dalliance, ardour, and enjoyment: That which seems in *Homer* an impious fiction, becomes a moral lesson in *Milton*; since he makes that lascivious rage of the passion the immediate effect of the sin of our first parents after the fall. *Adam* expresses it in the words of *Jupiter*.

> *For never did thy beauty since the day*
> *I saw thee first, and wedded thee, adorn'd*
> *With all perfections, so enflame my sense,*
> *With ardour to enjoy thee, fairer now*
> *Than ever; bounty of this virtuous tree!*
> *   So said he, and forbore not glance or toy*
> *Of amorous intent, well understood*
> *Of Eve, whose eye darted contagious fire.*
> *Her hand he seiz'd, and to a shady bank*
> *Thick over-head with verdant roof embow'r'd,*

> *He led her, nothing loath: flow'rs were the couch,*
> *Pansies, and violets, and asphodel,*
> *And hyacinth; earth's freshest, softest lap.*
> *There they their fill of love and love's disport*
> *Took largely, of their mutual guilt the seal;*
> *The solace of their sin, till dewy* Sleep
> *Oppress'd them, weary of their amorous play.*   Milton, *l.* 9.

417. *The pow'r of slumbers flew.*] M. *Dacier* in her translation of this passage has thought fit to dissent from the common interpretation, as well as obvious sense of the words. She restrains the general expression ἐπὶ κλυτὰ φῦλ᾽ ἀνθρώπων, *the famous nations of men*, to signify only the country of the *Lemnians*, who, she says, were much *celebrated* on account of *Vulcan.* But this strain'd interpretation cannot be admitted, especially when the obvious meaning of the words express what is very proper and natural. The God of *Sleep* having hastily delivered his message to *Neptune*, immediately leaves the hurry of the battel, (which was no proper scene for him) and retires among the tribes of mankind. The word κλυτά [famous], on which M. *Dacier* grounds her criticism, is an expletive epithet very common in *Homer*, and no way fit to point out one certain nation, especially in an author one of whose most distinguishing characters is particularity in description.

442. *The weaker warriour takes a lighter shield.*] *Plutarch* seems to allude to this passage in the beginning of the life of *Pelopidas.* '*Homer*, says he, makes the bravest and stoutest of his warriours march to battel in the best arms. The *Grecian* legislators punish'd those who cast away their shields, but not those who lost their spears or their swords, as an intimation that the care of preserving and defending our selves is preferable to the wounding our enemy, especially in those who are Generals of armies, or Governors of states.' *Eustathius* has observ'd, that the Poet here makes the best warriours take the largest shields and longest spears, that they might be ready prepar'd, with proper arms, both offensive and defensive, for a new kind of fight, in which they are soon to be engaged when the fleet is attack'd. Which indeed seems the most rational account that can be given for *Neptune*'s advice in this exigence.

Mr. *Hobbes* has committed a great oversight in this place; he makes the wounded princes (who it is plain were unfit for the battel, and do not engage in the ensuing fight) put on arms as well as the others; whereas they do no more in *Homer* than see their orders obey'd by the rest as to this change of arms.

444. *The legions march, and* Neptune *leads the way.*] The chief Advantage the *Greeks* gain by the Sleep of *Jupiter* seems to be this: *Neptune* unwilling to offend *Jupiter*, has hitherto concealed himself in disguised shapes; so that it does not appear that *Jupiter* knew of his being among the *Greeks*, since he takes no notice of it. This precaution hinders him from assisting the *Greeks* otherwise than by his advice. But upon the intelligence receiv'd of what *Juno* had done, he assumes a form that manifests his divinity, inspiring courage into the *Grecian* chiefs, appearing at the head of their army, brandishing a sword in his hand, the sight of which struck such a terrour into the *Trojans* that, as *Homer* says, none durst approach it. And therefore it is not to be wonder'd, that the *Trojans* who are no longer sustain'd by *Jupiter*, immediately give way to the enemy.

452. *And lo the God, and wondrous man appear.*] What magnificence and nobleness is there in this idea? where *Homer* opposes *Hector* to *Neptune*, and equalizes him in some degree to a God. *Eustathius.*

453. *The roaring main,* &c.] This swelling and inundation of the sea towards the *Grecian* camp, as if it had been agitated by a storm, is meant for a prodigy, intimating that the waters had the same resentments with their commander *Neptune*, and seconded him in his quarrel.   *Eustathius.*

457. *Not half so loud,* &c.] The Poet having ended the episode of *Jupiter* and *Juno*, returns to the battel, where the *Greeks* being animated and led on by *Neptune*, renew the fight with vigour. The noise and outcry of this fresh onset, he endeavours to express by these three sounding comparisons; as if he thought it necessary to awake the reader's attention, which by the preceding descriptions might be lull'd into a forgetfulness of the fight. He might likewise design to shew how soundly *Jupiter* slept, since he is not awak'd by so terrible an uproar.

This passage cannot be thought justly liable to the objections which have been made against heaping comparisons one upon another, whereby the principal object is lost amidst too great a variety of different images. In this case the principal image is more strongly impressed on the mind by a multiplication of similes, which are the natural product of an imagination labouring to express something very vast: But finding no single idea sufficient to answer its conceptions, it endeavours by redoubling the comparisons to supply this defect: The different sounds of waters, winds, and flames, being as it were united in one. We have several instances of this sort even in so castigated and reserv'd a Writer as *Virgil*, who has joined together the images of this passage in the *4th Georgic*, v. 261. and apply'd them, beautifully softened by a kind of parody, to the buzzing of a bee-hive.

> *Frigidus ut quondam sylvis immurmurat Auster,*
> *Ut mare sollicitum stridet refluentibus undis,*
> *Æstuat ut clausis rapidus fornacibus ignis.*

> [As when the woods by gentle winds are stirred;
> Such stifled noise as the close furnace hides,
> Or dying murmurs of departing tides.]

Tasso has not only imitated this particular passage of *Homer*, but likewise added to it.   *Cant.* 9. *st.* 22.

> *Rapido sì che torbida procella*
> *De cavernosi monti esce piu tarda:*
> *Fiume, ch' alberi insieme, e case svella:*
> *Folgore, che le torri abbatta, & arda:*
> *Terremoto, che 'l mondo empia d' horrore,*
> *Son picciole sembianze al suo furore.*

> [As swift as hideous *Boreas'* hasty blast,
> From hollow rocks when first his storms out burst,
> The raging floods that trees and rocks down cast,
> Thunders that towns and towers drive to dust:
>   Earthquakes, to tear the world in twain that threat,
>   Are nought, compared to his fury great.]

480. *Smokes in the dust, and ploughs into the ground.*]

> Στρόμβον δ' ὡς ἔσσευε βαλών, &c.

[Having thrown the rock, he (Ajax) sent it (or him, i.e. Hector) spinning, like a top.]

These words are translated by several as if they signify'd that *Hector* was turn'd round with the blow, like a whirlwind; which would enhance the wonderful greatness of *Ajax*'s strength. *Eustathius* rather inclines to refer the words to the stone itself, and the violence of its motion. *Chapman*, I think, is in the right to prefer the latter, but he should not have taken the interpretation to himself. He says, it is above the wit of man to give a more fiery illustration both of *Ajax*'s strength and *Hector*'s; of *Ajax*, for giving such a force to the stone, that it could not spend itself on *Hector*; but afterwards turn'd upon the earth with that violence; and of *Hector*, for standing the blow so solidly; for without that consideration, the stone could never have recoil'd so fiercely. This image, together with the noble simile following it, seem to have given *Spencer* the hint of those sublime verses.

> *As when almighty* Jove, *in wrathful mood,*
> *To wreak the guilt of mortal sins is bent,*
> *Hurls forth his thund'ring dart, with deadly food*
> *Enroll'd, of flames, and smouldring dreariment:*
> *Thro' riven clouds, and molten firmament,*
> *The fierce three-forked engine making way,*
> *Both lofty tow'rs and highest trees hath rent,*
> *And all that might his dreadful passage stay,*
> *And shooting in the earth, casts up a mound of clay.*
> *His boist'rous club so bury'd in the ground,*
> *He could not rear again,* &c. –

533. *Propt on that spear,* &c.] The occasion of this sarcasm of *Poly-damas* seems taken from the attitude of his falling enemy, who is transfixed with a spear thro' his right shoulder. This posture bearing some resemblance to that of a man leaning on a staff, might probably suggest the conceit.

The speech of *Polydamas* begins a long string of sarcastick raillery, in which *Eustathius* pretends to observe very different characters. This of *Polydamas*, he says, is *pleasant*, that of *Ajax*, *heroic*; that of *Acamas*, *plain*; and that of *Peneleus*, *pathetick.*

599. *Daughters of* Jove! &c.] Whenever we meet with these fresh invocations in the midst of action, the Poets would seem to give their readers to understand, that they are come to a point where the description being above their own strength, they have occasion for supernatural assistance; by this artifice at once exciting the reader's attention, and gracefully varying the narration. In the present case, *Homer* seems to triumph in the advantage the *Greeks* had gain'd in the flight of the *Trojans*, by invoking the *Muses* to snatch the brave actions of his heroes from oblivion, and set them in the light of eternity. This power is vindicated to them by the Poets on every occasion, and it is to this task they are so solemnly and frequently summoned by our Author. *Tasso* has, I think, introduced one of these invocations in a very noble and peculiar manner; where, on occasion of a battel by night, he calls upon the *Night* to allow him to draw forth those mighty deeds which were performed under the concealment of her shades, and to display their glories, notwithstanding that disadvantage, to all posterity.

> *Notte, che nel profondo oscuro seno*
> *Chiudesti, e ne l' oblio fatto si grande;*
> *Piacciati, ch' io nel tragga, e'n bel sereno*
> *A la future età lo spieghi, e mande.*
> *Viva la fame loro, e trà lor gloria*
> *Splenda del fosco tuo l' alta memoria.*

[Worthy of royal lists and brightest day,
Worthy a golden trump and laurel crown,
The actions were and wonders of that fray,
Which sable night did in black bosom drown:
Yet, night, consent that I their acts display,
And make their deeds to future ages known,
    And in records of long enduring story,
    Enroll their praise, their fame, their worth and glory.]

THE
FIFTEENTH BOOK
OF THE
ILIAD

The ARGUMENT

The fifth Battel, at the Ships; and the Acts of *Ajax*

Jupiter *awaking, sees the* Trojans *repuls'd from the trenches,* Hector *in a swoon, and* Neptune *at the head of the* Greeks: *He is highly incens'd at the artifice of* Juno, *who appeases him by her submissions; she is then sent to* Iris *and* Apollo. Juno *repairing to the assembly of the Gods, attempts with extraordinary address to incense them against* Jupiter; *in particular she touches* Mars *with a violent resentment: He is ready to take arms, but is prevented by* Minerva. Iris *and* Apollo *obey the orders of* Jupiter; Iris *commands* Neptune *to leave the battel, to which, after much reluctance and passion, he consents.* Apollo *re-inspires* Hector *with vigour, brings him back to the battel, marches before him with his* Ægis, *and turns the fortune of the fight. He breaks down great part of the* Grecian *wall; the* Trojans *rush in and attempt to fire the first line of the fleet, but are, as yet, repell'd by the greater* Ajax *with a prodigious slaughter.*

Now in swift flight they past the trench profound,
And many a chief lay gasping on the ground:
Then stopp'd, and panted, where the chariots lie;
Fear on their cheek, and horrour in their eye.
5 Meanwhile awaken'd from his dream of Love,
On *Ida*'s summit sate imperial *Jove*:
Round the wide fields he cast a careful view,
There saw the *Trojans* fly, the *Greeks* pursue,
These proud in arms, those scatter'd o'er the plain;
10 And, 'midst the war, the Monarch of the main.
Not far, great *Hector* on the dust he spies,
(His sad associates round with weeping eyes)
Ejecting blood, and panting yet for breath,
His senses wandring to the verge of death.
15 The God beheld him with a pitying look,
And thus, incens'd, to fraudful *Juno* spoke.
  O thou, still adverse to th' eternal will,
For ever studious in promoting ill!
Thy arts have made the god-like *Hector* yield,
20 And driv'n his conqu'ring squadrons from the field.
Can'st thou, unhappy in thy wiles! withstand
Our pow'r immense, and brave th' almighty hand?
Hast thou forgot, when bound and fix'd on high,
From the vast concave of the spangled sky,
25 I hung thee trembling, in a golden chain;
And all the raging Gods oppos'd in vain?
Headlong I hurl'd them from th' *Olympian* hall,
Stunn'd in the whirl, and breathless with the fall.

For godlike *Hercules* these deeds were done,
Nor seem'd the vengeance worthy such a son;   30
When by thy wiles induc'd, fierce *Boreas* tost
The shipwrack'd hero on the *Coan* coast:
Him thro' a thousand forms of death I bore,
And sent to *Argos*, and his native shore.
Hear this, remember, and our fury dread,   35
Nor pull th' unwilling vengeance on thy head,
Lest arts and blandishments successless prove,
Thy soft deceits, and well-dissembled love.
    The Thund'rer spoke: Imperial *Juno* mourn'd,
And trembling, these submissive words return'd.   40
    By ev'ry oath that pow'rs immortal ties,
The foodful earth, and all-infolding skies,
By thy black waves, tremendous *Styx!* that flow
Thro' the drear realms of gliding ghosts below:
By the dread honours of thy sacred head,   45
And that unbroken vow, our virgin bed!
Not by my arts the ruler of the main
Steeps *Troy* in blood, and rages round the plain;
By his own ardour, his own pity sway'd
To help his *Greeks*; he fought, and disobey'd: 50
Else had thy *Juno* better counsels giv'n,
And taught submission to the Sire of heav'n.
    Think'st thou with me? fair Empress of the skies!
(Th' immortal Father with a smile replies!)
Then soon the haughty Sea-God shall obey,   55
Nor dare to act, but when we point the way.
If truth inspires thy tongue, proclaim our will
To yon' bright synod on th' *Olympian* hill;
Our high decree let various *Iris* know,
And call the God that bears the silver bow.   60
Let her descend, and from th' embattel'd plain
Command the Sea-god to his wat'ry reign:
While *Phœbus* hastes, great *Hector* to prepare
To rise afresh, and once more wake the war,
His lab'ring bosom re-inspires with breath,   65
And calls his senses from the verge of death.
Greece chas'd by *Troy* ev'n to *Achilles'* fleet,
Shall fall by thousands at the hero's feet.

He, not untouch'd with pity, to the plain
70   Shall send *Patroclus*, but shall send in vain.
What youth he slaughters under *Ilion*'s walls?
Ev'n my lov'd son, divine *Sarpedon* falls!
Vanquish'd at last by *Hector*'s lance he lies.
Then, nor till then, shall great *Achilles* rise:
75   And lo! that instant, godlike *Hector* dies.
From that great hour the war's whole fortune turns,
Pallas assists, and lofty *Ilion* burns.
Not till that day shall *Jove* relax his rage,
Nor one of all the heav'nly host engage
80   In aid of *Greece*. The promise of a God
I gave, and seal'd it with th' almighty nod,
Achilles' glory to the stars to raise;
Such was our word, and fate the word obeys.
   The trembling Queen (th' almighty order giv'n)
85   Swift from th' *Idæan* summit shot to heav'n.
As some way-faring man, who wanders o'er
In thought, a length of lands he trod before,
Sends forth his active mind from place to place,
Joins hill to dale, and measures space with space:
90   So swift flew *Juno* to the blest abodes,
If thought of man can match the speed of Gods.
There sate the pow'rs in awful synod plac'd;
They bow'd, and made obeysance as she pass'd,
Thro' all the brazen dome: With goblets crown'd
95   They hail her Queen; the *Nectar* streams around.
Fair *Themis* first presents the golden bowl,
And anxious asks, what cares disturb her soul?
   To whom the white-arm'd Goddess thus replies:
Enough thou know'st the tyrant of the skies,
100   Severely bent his purpose to fulfill,
Unmov'd his mind, and unrestrain'd his will.
Go thou, the feasts of heav'n attend thy call;
Bid the crown'd Nectar circle round the hall;
But *Jove* shall thunder thro' th' ethereal dome,
105   Such stern decrees, such threatned woes to come,
As soon shall freeze mankind with dire surprize,
And damp th' eternal banquets of the skies.

The Goddess said, and sullen took her place;
Blank horrour sadden'd each celestial face.
To see the gath'ring grudge in ev'ry breast,   110
Smiles on her lips a spleenful joy exprest,
While on her wrinkled front, and eyebrow bent,
Sate stedfast care, and low'ring discontent.
Thus she proceeds – Attend ye pow'rs above!
But know, 'tis madness to contest with *Jove*:   115
Supreme he sits; and sees, in pride of sway,
Your vassal Godheads grudgingly obey;
Fierce in the majesty of pow'r controuls,
Shakes all the thrones of Heav'n, and bends the poles.
Submiss, immortals! all he wills, obey;   120
And thou, great *Mars*, begin and shew the way.
Behold *Ascalaphus!* behold him die,
But dare not murmur, dare not vent a sigh;
Thy own lov'd boasted offspring lies o'erthrown,
If that lov'd boasted offspring be thy own.   125
    Stern *Mars*, with anguish for his slaughter'd son,
Smote his rebelling breast, and fierce begun.
Thus then, Immortals! thus shall *Mars* obey;
Forgive me, Gods, and yield my vengeance way:
Descending first to yon' forbidden plain,   130
The God of battels dares avenge the slain;
Dares, tho' the thunder bursting o'er my head
Should hurl me blazing on those heaps of dead.
    With that, he gives command to *Fear* and *Flight*
To join his rapid coursers for the fight: 135
Then grim in arms, with hasty vengeance flies;
Arms, that reflect a radiance thro' the skies.
And now had *Jove*, by bold rebellion driv'n,
Discharg'd his wrath on half the host of heav'n;
But *Pallas* springing thro' the bright abode,   140
Starts from her azure throne to calm the God.
Struck for th' immortal race with timely fear,
From frantic *Mars* she snatch'd the shield and spear;
Then the huge helmet lifting from his head,
Thus, to th' impetuous homicide she said.   145
    By what wild passion, furious! art thou tost?
Striv'st thou with *Jove*? Thou art already lost.

Shall not the Thund'rer's dread command restrain,
And was imperial *Juno* heard in vain?
150 Back to the skies would'st thou with shame be driv'n,
And in thy guilt involve the host of heav'n?
Ilion and *Greece* no more should *Jove* engage;
The skies would yield an ampler scene of rage,
Guilty and guiltless find an equal fate,
155 And one vast ruin whelm th' *Olympian* state.
Cease then thy offspring's death unjust to call;
Heroes as great have dy'd, and yet shall fall.
Why should heav'n's law with foolish man comply,
Exempted from the race ordain'd to die?
160   This menace fix'd the warriour to his throne;
Sullen he sate, and curb'd the rising groan.
Then *Juno* call'd (*Jove*'s orders to obey)
The winged *Iris*, and the God of Day.
Go wait the Thund'rer's will (*Saturnia* cry'd)
165 On yon' tall summit of the fount-ful *Ide*:
There in the father's awful presence stand,
Receive, and execute his dread command.
   She said, and sate: the God that gilds the day,
And various *Iris* wing their airy way.
170 Swift as the wind, to *Ida*'s hills they came,
(Fair nurse of fountains and of savage game.)
There sate th' Eternal; he, whose nod controuls
The trembling world, and shakes the steady poles.
Veil'd in a mist of fragrance him they found,
175 With clouds of gold and purple circled round.
Well-pleas'd the Thund'rer saw their earnest care,
And prompt obedience to the Queen of Air;
Then (while a smile serenes his awful brow)
Commands the Goddess of the show'ry bow.
180   *Iris!* descend, and what we here ordain
Report to yon' mad tyrant of the main.
Bid him from fight to his own deeps repair,
Or breathe from slaughter in the fields of air.
If he refuse, then let him timely weigh
185 Our elder birthright, and superiour sway.
How shall his rashness stand the dire alarms,
If heav'ns omnipotence descend in arms?

Strives he with me, by whom his pow'r was giv'n,
And is there equal to the Lord of Heav'n?

 Th' Almighty spoke; the Goddess wing'd her flight 190
To sacred *Ilion* from th' *Idæan* height.
Swift as the rat'ling hail, or fleecy snows
Drive thro' the skies, when *Boreas* fiercely blows;
So from the clouds descending *Iris* falls;
And to blue *Neptune* thus the Goddess calls. 195

 Attend the mandate of the Sire above,
In me behold the messenger of *Jove*:
He bids thee from forbidden wars repair
To thy own deeps, or to the fields of air.
This if refus'd, he bids thee timely weigh 200
His elder birthright, and superiour sway.
How shall thy rashness stand the dire alarms,
If heav'ns omnipotence descend in arms?
Striv'st thou with him, by whom all pow'r is giv'n?
And art thou equal to the Lord of Heav'n? 205

 What means the haughty Sov'reign of the skies,
(The King of Ocean thus, incens'd, replies)
Rule as he will his portion'd realms on high;
No vassal God, nor of his train am I.
Three Brother Deities from *Saturn* came, 210
And ancient *Rhea*, earth's immortal dame:
Assign'd by lot, our triple rule we know;
Infernal *Pluto* sways the shades below;
O'er the wide clouds, and o'er the starry plain,
Ethereal *Jove* extends his high domain; 215
My court beneath the hoary waves I keep,
And hush the roarings of the sacred deep:
Olympus, and this earth, in common lie;
What claim has here the tyrant of the sky?
Far in the distant clouds let him controul, 220
And awe the younger brothers of the pole;
There to his children his commands be giv'n,
The trembling, servile, second race of heav'n.

 And must I then (said she) O Sire of Floods!
Bear this fierce answer to the King of Gods? 225
Correct it yet, and change thy rash intent;
A noble mind disdains not to repent.

To elder brothers guardian fiends are giv'n,
To scourge the wretch insulting them and heav'n.
230   Great is the profit (thus the God rejoin'd)
When ministers are blest with prudent mind:
Warn'd by thy words, to pow'rful *Jove* I yield,
And quit, tho' angry, the contended field.
Not but his threats with justice I disclaim,
235   The same our honours, and our birth the same.
If yet, forgetful of his promise giv'n
To *Hermes*, *Pallas*, and the Queen of heav'n;
To favour *Ilion*, that perfidious place,
He breaks his faith with half th' ethereal race;
240   Give him to know, unless the *Grecian* train
Lay yon' proud structures level with the plain,
Howe'er th' offence by other Gods be past,
The wrath of *Neptune* shall for ever last.
    Thus speaking, furious from the field he strode,
245   And plung'd into the bosom of the flood.
The Lord of Thunders from his lofty height
Beheld, and thus bespoke the Source of light.
    Behold! the God whose liquid arms are hurl'd
Around the globe, whose earthquakes rock the world;
250   Desists at length his rebel-war to wage,
Seeks his own seas, and trembles at our rage!
Else had my wrath, heav'ns thrones all shaking round,
Burn'd to the bottom of the seas profound;
And all the gods that round old *Saturn* dwell,
255   Had heard the thunders to the deeps of hell.
Well was the crime, and well the vengeance spar'd;
Ev'n pow'r immense had found such battel hard.
Go thou, my son! the trembling *Greeks* alarm,
Shake my broad *Ægis* on thy active arm,
260   Be godlike *Hector* thy peculiar care,
Swell his bold heart, and urge his strength to war:
Let *Ilion* conquer, till th' *Achaian* train
Fly to their ships and *Hellespont* again:
Then *Greece* shall breathe from toils – the Godhead said;
265   His will divine the son of *Jove* obey'd.
Not half so swift the sailing falcon flies,
That drives a turtle thro' the liquid skies;

As *Phœbus* shooting from th' *Idæan* brow,
Glides down the mountain to the plain below.
There *Hector* seated by the stream he sees,   270
His sense returning with the coming breeze;
Again his pulses beat, his spirits rise;
Again his lov'd companions meet his eyes;
Jove thinking of his pains, they past away.
To whom the God who gives the golden day.   275
    Why sits great *Hector* from the field so far,
What grief, what wound, withholds him from the war?
    The fainting hero, as the vision bright
Stood shining o'er him, half unseal'd his sight:
What blest immortal, with commanding breath,   280
Thus wakens *Hector* from the sleep of death?
Has fame not told, how, while my trusty sword
Bath'd *Greece* in slaughter, and her battel gor'd,
The mighty *Ajax* with a deadly blow
Had almost sunk me to the shades below?   285
Ev'n yet, methinks, the gliding ghosts I spy,
And hell's black horrours swim before my eye.
    To him *Apollo.* Be no more dismay'd;
See, and be strong! the Thund'rer sends thee aid,
Behold! thy *Phœbus* shall his arms employ,   290
Phœbus, propitious still to thee, and *Troy*.
Inspire thy warriours then with manly force,
And to the ships impel thy rapid horse:
Ev'n I will make thy fiery coursers way,
And drive the *Grecians* headlong to the sea.   295
    Thus to bold *Hector* spoke the son of *Jove*,
And breath'd immortal ardour from above.
As when the pamper'd steed, with reins unbound,
Breaks from his stall, and pours along the ground;
With ample strokes he rushes to the flood,   300
To bathe his sides and cool his fiery blood.
His head now freed, he tosses to the skies;
His mane dishevel'd o'er his shoulders flies;
He snuffs the females in the well known plain,
And springs, exulting, to his fields again: 305
Urg'd by the voice divine, thus *Hector* flew,
Full of the God; and all his hosts pursue.

As when the force of men and dogs combin'd
Invade the mountain goat, or branching hind;
310   Far from the hunter's rage secure they lie,
Close in the rock, (not fated yet to die)
When lo! a Lion shoots across the way:
They fly; at once the chasers and the prey.
So *Greece*, that late in conq'ring troops pursu'd,
315   And mark'd their progress thro' the ranks in blood,
Soon as they see the furious chief appear,
Forget to vanquish, and consent to fear.

   Thoas with grief observ'd his dreadful course,
Thoas, the bravest of th' *Ætolian* force:
320   Skill'd to direct the jav'lin's distant flight,
And bold to combate in the standing fight;
Nor more in councils fam'd for solid sense,
Than winning words and heav'nly eloquence.
Gods! what portent (he cry'd) these eyes invades?
325   Lo! *Hector* rises from the *Stygian* shades!
We saw him, late, by thund'ring *Ajax* kill'd:
What God restores him to the frighted field;
And not content that half of *Greece* lie slain,
Pours new destruction on her sons again?
330   He comes not, *Jove!* without thy pow'rful will;
Lo! still he lives, pursues, and conquers still!
Yet hear my counsel, and his worst withstand;
The *Greek*'s main body to the fleet command;
But let the few whom brisker spirits warm,
335   Stand the first onset, and provoke the storm:
Thus point your arms; and when such foes appear,
Fierce as he is, let *Hector* learn to fear.

   The warriour spoke, the list'ning *Greeks* obey,
Thick'ning their ranks, and form a deep array.
340   Each *Ajax*, *Teucer*, *Merion*, gave command,
The valiant leader of the *Cretan* band,
And *Mars*-like *Meges*: These the chiefs excite,
Approach the foe, and meet the coming fight.
Behind, unnumber'd multitudes attend,
345   To flank the navy, and the shores defend.
Full on the front the pressing *Trojans* bear,
And *Hector* first came tow'ring to the war.

Phœbus himself the rushing battel led;
A veil of clouds involv'd his radiant head:
High-held before him, *Jove*'s enormous shield   350
Portentous shone, and shaded all the field,
Vulcan to *Jove* th' immortal gift consign'd,
To scatter hosts, and terrify mankind.
The *Greeks* expect the shock; the clamours rise
From diff'rent parts, and mingle in the skies.   355
Dire was the hiss of darts, by heroes flung,
And arrows leaping from the bowstring sung;
These drink the life of gen'rous warriours slain;
Those guiltless fall, and thirst for blood in vain.
As long as *Phœbus* bore unmov'd the shield,   360
Sate doubtful Conquest hov'ring o'er the field;
But when aloft he shakes it in the skies,
Shouts in their ears, and lightens in their eyes,
Deep horrour seizes ev'ry *Grecian* breast,
Their force is humbled, and their fear confest.   365
So flies a herd of oxen, scatter'd wide,
No swain to guard 'em, and no day to guide,
When two fell Lions from the mountain come,
And spread the carnage thro' the shady gloom.
Impending *Phœbus* pours around 'em fear,   370
And *Troy* and *Hector* thunder in the rear.
Heaps fall on heaps: the slaughter *Hector* leads;
First great *Arcesilas*, then *Stichius* bleeds;
One to the bold *Bœotians* ever dear,
And one *Menestheus*' friend, and fam'd compeer.   375
Medon and *Iäsus*, *Æneas* sped;
This sprung from *Phelus*, and th' *Athenians* led;
But hapless *Medon* from *Oïleus* came;
Him *Ajax* honour'd with a brother's name,
Tho' born of lawless love: From home expell'd,   380
A banish'd man, in *Phylace* he dwell'd,
Press'd by the vengeance of an angry wife;
Troy ends, at last, his labours and his life.
Mecystes next, *Polydamas* o'erthrew;
And thee, brave *Clonius!* great *Agenor* slew.   385
By *Paris*, *Deiochus* inglorious dies,
Pierc'd thro' the shoulder as he basely flies.

Polites' arm laid *Echius* on the plain;
Stretch'd on one heap, the victors spoil the slain.
390   The *Greeks* dismay'd, confus'd, disperse or fall,
Some seek the trench, some skulk behind the wall,
While these fly trembling, others pant for breath,
And o'er the slaughter stalks gigantic Death.
On rush'd bold *Hector*, gloomy as the night,
395   Forbids to plunder, animates the fight,
Points to the fleet: For by the Gods, who flies,
Who dares but linger, by this hand he dies:
No weeping sister his cold eye shall close,
No friendly hand his fun'ral pyre compose.
400   Who stops to plunder, in this signal hour,
The birds shall tear him, and the dogs devour.
    Furious he said; the smarting scourge resounds;
The coursers fly; the smoaking chariot bounds:
The hosts rush on; loud clamours shake the shore;
405   The horses thunder, earth and ocean roar!
Apollo, planted at the trench's bound,
Push'd at the bank: down sunk th' enormous mound:
Roll'd in the ditch the heapy ruin lay;
A sudden road! A long and ample way.
410   O'er the dread fosse (a late-impervious space)
Now steeds, and men, and cars, tumultuous pass.
The wond'ring crowds the downward level trod;
Before them flam'd the shield, and march'd the God.
Then with his hand he shook the mighty wall;
415   And lo! the turrets nod, the bulwarks fall.
Easy, as when ashore an infant stands,
And draws imagin'd houses in the sands;
The sportive wanton, pleas'd with some new play,
Sweeps the slight works and fashion'd domes away.
420   Thus vanish'd, at thy touch, the tow'rs and walls;
The toil of thousands in a moment falls.
    The *Grecians* gaze around with wild despair,
Confus'd, and weary all the pow'rs with pray'r;
Exhort their men, with praises, threats, commands;
425   And urge the Gods, with voices, eyes, and hands.
Experienc'd *Nestor* chief obtests the skies,
And weeps his country with a father's eyes.

O *Jove!* if ever, on his native shore,
One *Greek* enrich'd thy shrine with offer'd gore;
If e'er, in hope our country to behold,   430
We paid the fattest firstlings of the fold;
If e'er thou sign'st our wishes with thy nod;
Perform the promise of a gracious God!
This day, preserve our navies from the flame,
And save the reliques of the *Grecian* name.   435
    Thus pray'd the sage: Th' Eternal gave consent,
And peals of thunder shook the firmament.
Presumptuous *Troy* mistook th' accepting sign,
And catch'd new fury at the voice divine.
As, when black tempests mix the seas and skies,   440
The roaring deeps in watry mountains rise,
Above the sides of some tall ship ascend,
Its womb they deluge, and its ribs they rend:
Thus loudly roaring, and o'erpow'ring all,
Mount the thick *Trojans* up the *Grecian* wall;   445
Legions on legions from each side arise;
Thick sound the keels; the storm of arrows flies.
Fierce on the ships above, the cars below,
These wield the mace, and those the jav'lin throw.
    While thus the thunder of the battel rag'd,   450
And lab'ring armies round the works engag'd;
Still in the tent *Patroclus* sate, to tend
The good *Eurypylus*, his wounded friend.
He sprinkles healing balmes, to anguish kind,
And adds discourse, the med'cine of the mind.   455
But when he saw, ascending up the fleet,
Victorious *Troy*: then, starting from his seat,
With bitter groans his sorrows he exprest,
He wrings his hands, he beats his manly breast.
Tho' yet thy state require redress (he cries)   460
Depart I must: What horrours strike my eyes?
Charg'd with *Achilles'* high commands I go,
A mournful witness of this scene of woe:
I haste to urge him, by his country's care,
To rise in arms, and shine again in war.   465
Perhaps some fav'ring God his soul may bend;
The voice is pow'rful of a faithful friend.

He spoke; and speaking, swifter than the wind
Sprung from the tent, and left the war behind.
470 Th' embody'd *Greeks* the fierce attack sustain,
But strive, tho' num'rous, to repulse in vain.
Nor could the *Trojans*, thro' that firm array,
Force, to the fleet and tents, th' impervious way.
As when a shipwright, with *Palladian* art,
475 Smooths the rough wood, and levels ev'ry part;
With equal hand he guides his whole design,
By the just rule, and the directing line.
The martial leaders, with like skill and care,
Preserv'd their line, and equal kept the war.
480 Brave deeds of arms thro' all the ranks were try'd,
And ev'ry ship sustain'd an equal tide.
At one proud bark, high-tow'ring o'er the fleet
Ajax the great, and God-like *Hector* meet:
For one bright prize the matchless chiefs contend;
485 Nor this the ships can fire, nor that defend;
One kept the shore, and one the vessel trod;
That fix'd as Fate, this acted by a God.
The Son of *Clytius*, in his daring hand,
The deck approaching, shakes a flaming brand;
490 But pierc'd by *Telamon*'s huge lance expires;
Thund'ring he falls, and drops th' extinguish'd fires.
Great *Hector* view'd him with a sad survey,
As stretch'd in dust before the stern he lay.
Oh! all of *Trojan*, all of *Lycian* race!
495 Stand to your arms, maintain this arduous space!
Lo! where the son of royal *Clytius* lies,
Ah save his arms, secure his obsequies!
    This said, his eager jav'lin sought the foe:
But *Ajax* shunn'd the meditated blow.
500 Not vainly yet the forceful lance was thrown;
It stretch'd in dust unhappy *Lycophron*:
An exile long, sustain'd at *Ajax*' board,
A faithful servant to a foreign lord;
In peace, in war, for ever at his side,
505 Near his lov'd master, as he liv'd, he dy'd.
From the high poop he tumbles on the sand,
And lies, a lifeless load, along the land.

With anguish *Ajax* views the piercing sight,
And thus inflames his brother to the fight.
   Teucer, behold! extended on the shore   510
Our friend, our lov'd companion! now no more!
Dear as a parent, with a parent's care,
To fight our wars, he left his native air.
This death deplor'd to *Hector*'s rage we owe;
Revenge, revenge it on the cruel foe.   515
Where are those darts on which the Fates attend?
And where the bow, which *Phœbus* taught to bend?
   Impatient *Teucer*, hastening to his aid,
Before the chief his ample bow display'd;
The well-stor'd quiver on his shoulders hung: 520
Then hiss'd his arrow, and the bowstring sung.
Clytus, *Pisenor*'s son, renown'd in fame,
(To thee, *Polydamas!* an honour'd name)
Drove thro' the thickest of th' embattel'd plains
The startling steeds, and shook his eager reins.   525
As all on glory ran his ardent mind,
The pointed death arrests him from behind:
Thro' his fair neck the thrilling arrow flies;
In youth's first bloom reluctantly he dies.
Hurl'd from the lofty seat, at distance far,   530
The headlong coursers spurn his empty car;
Till sad *Polydamas* the steeds restrain'd,
And gave, *Astynous*, to thy careful hand;
Then, fir'd to vengeance, rush'd amidst the foe;
Rage edg'd his sword, and strengthen'd ev'ry blow.   535
   Once more bold *Teucer*, in his country's cause,
At *Hector*'s breast a chosen arrow draws;
And had the weapon found the destin'd way,
Thy fall, great *Trojan!* had renown'd that day.
But *Hector* was not doom'd to perish then: 540
Th' all-wise Disposer of the fates of men,
(Imperial *Jove*) his present death withstands;
Nor was such glory due to *Teucer*'s hands.
At his full stretch, as the tough string he drew,
Struck by an arm unseen, it burst in two;   545
Down drop'd the bow: the shaft with brazen head
Fell innocent, and on the dust lay dead.

Th' astonish'd archer to great *Ajax* cries;
Some God prevents our destin'd enterprize:
550   Some God, propitious to the *Trojan* foe,
Has, from my arm unfailing, struck the bow,
And broke the nerve my hands had twin'd with art,
Strong to impel the flight of many a dart.
     Since Heav'n commands it (*Ajax* made reply)
555   Dismiss the bow, and lay thy arrows by;
Thy arms no less suffice the lance to wield,
And quit the quiver for the pond'rous shield.
In the first ranks indulge thy thirst of fame,
Thy brave example shall the rest inflame.
560   Fierce as they are, by long successes vain;
To force our fleet, or ev'n a ship to gain,
Asks toil, and sweat, and blood: Their utmost might
Shall find its match – No more: 'Tis ours to fight.
     Then *Teucer* laid his faithless bow aside;
565   The four-fold buckler o'er his shoulder ty'd;
On his brave head a crested helm he plac'd,
With nodding horse-hair formidably grac'd;
A dart, whose point with brass refulgent shines,
The warriour wields; and his great brother joins.
570   This *Hector* saw, and thus express'd his joy.
Ye troops of *Lycia*, *Dardanus*, and *Troy!*
Be mindful of yourselves, your ancient fame,
And spread your glory with the navy's flame.
Jove is with us; I saw his hand, but now,
575   From the proud archer strike his vaunted bow.
Indulgent *Jove!* how plain thy favours shine,
When happy nations bear the marks divine!
How easy then, to see the sinking state
Of realms accurs'd, deserted, reprobate!
580   Such is the fate of *Greece*, and such is ours:
Behold, ye warriors, and exert your pow'rs.
Death is the worst; a fate which all must try;
And, for our country, 'tis a bliss to die.
The gallant man, tho' slain in fight he be,
585   Yet leaves his nation safe, his children free;
Entails a debt on all the grateful state;
His own brave friends shall glory in his fate;

His wife live honour'd, all his race succeed;
And late posterity enjoy the deed!
   This rouz'd the soul in ev'ry *Trojan* breast: 590
The god-like *Ajax* next his *Greeks* addrest.
How long, ye warriours of the *Argive* race,
(To gen'rous *Argos* what a dire disgrace!)
How long, on these curs'd confines will ye lie,
Yet undetermin'd, or to live, or die!   595
What hopes remain, what methods to retire,
If once your vessels catch the *Trojan* fire?
Mark how the flames approach, how near they fall,
How *Hector* calls, and *Troy* obeys his call!
Not to the dance that dreadful voice invites,   600
It calls to death, and all the rage of fights.
'Tis now no time for wisdom or debates;
To your own hands are trusted all your fates:
And better far, in one decisive strife,
One day should end our labour, or our life;   605
Than keep this hard-got inch of barren sands,
Still press'd, and press'd by such inglorious hands.
   The list'ning *Grecians* feel their Leader's Flame,
And ev'ry kindling bosom pants for fame.
Then mutual slaughters spread on either side;   610
By *Hector* here the *Phocian Schedius* dy'd;
There pierc'd by *Ajax*, sunk *Laodamas*,
Chief of the foot, of old *Antenor*'s race.
Polydamas laid *Otus* on the sand,
The fierce commander of th' *Epeian* band.   615
His lance bold *Meges* at the victor threw;
The victor stooping, from the death withdrew:
(That valu'd life, O *Phœbus!* was thy care)
But *Cræsmus'* bosom took the flying spear:
His corps fell bleeding on the slipp'ry shore;   620
His radiant arms triumphant *Meges* bore.
Dolops, the son of *Lampus* rushes on,
Sprung from the race of old *Laomedon*,
And fam'd for prowess in a well-fought field;
He pierc'd the centre of his sounding shield: 625
But *Meges*, *Phyleus'* ample breastplate wore,
(Well known in fight on *Selles'* winding shore,

For King *Euphetes* gave the golden mail,
Compact, and firm with many a jointed scale)
630   Which oft, in cities storm'd, and battels won,
Had sav'd the father, and now saves the son.
Full at the *Trojan*'s head he urg'd his lance,
Where the high plumes above the helmet dance,
New ting'd with *Tyrian* dye: In dust below,
635   Shorn from the crest, the purple honours glow.
Meantime their fight the *Spartan* King survey'd,
And stood by *Meges*' side, a sudden aid,
Thro' *Dolops*' shoulder urg'd his forceful dart,
Which held its passage thro' the panting heart,
640   And issu'd at his breast. With thund'ring sound
The warriour falls, extended on the ground.
In rush the conqu'ring *Greeks* to spoil the slain;
But *Hector*'s voice excites his kindred train;
The hero most, from *Hicetaon* sprung,
645   Fierce *Melanippus*, gallant, brave, and young.
He (e'er to *Troy* the *Grecians* cross'd the main)
Fed his large oxen on *Percote*'s plain;
But when oppress'd, his country claim'd his care,
Return'd to *Ilion*, and excell'd in war:
650   For this, in *Priam*'s court he held his place,
Belov'd no less than *Priam*'s royal race.
Him *Hector* singled, as his troops he led,
And thus inflam'd him, pointing to the dead.
　　Lo *Melanippus!* lo where *Dolops* lies;
655   And is it thus our royal kinsman dies?
O'ermatch'd he falls; to two at once a prey,
And lo! they bear the bloody arms away!
Come on – a distant war no longer wage,
But hand to hand thy country's foes engage:
660   Till *Greece* at once, and all her glory end;
Or *Ilion* from her tow'ry height descend,
Heav'd from the lowest stone; and bury all,
In one sad sepulchre, one common fall.
　　Hector (this said) rush'd forward on the foes:
665   With equal ardour *Melanippus* glows:
Then *Ajax* thus – Oh *Greeks!* respect your fame,
Respect your selves, and learn an honest shame:

Let mutual reverence mutual warmth inspire,
And catch from breast to breast the noble fire.
On valour's side the odds of combate lie,   670
The brave live glorious, or lamented die;
The wretch that trembles in the field of fame,
Meets death, and worse than death, eternal shame.
     His gen'rous sense he not in vain imparts;
It sunk, and rooted in the *Grecian* hearts.   675
They join, they throng, they thicken at his call,
And flank the navy with a brazen wall;
Shields touching shields in order blaze above,
And stop the *Trojans*, tho' impell'd by *Jove.*
The fiery *Spartan* first, with loud applause,   680
Warms the bold son of *Nestor* in his cause.
Is there (he said) in arms a youth like you,
So strong to fight, so active to pursue?
Why stand you distant, nor attempt a deed?
Lift the bold lance, and make some *Trojan* bleed.   685
     He said, and backward to the lines retir'd;
Forth rush'd the youth, with martial fury fir'd,
Beyond the foremost ranks; his lance he threw,
And round the black battalions cast his view.
The troops of *Troy* recede with sudden fear,   690
While the swift jav'lin hiss'd along in air.
Advancing *Melanippus* met the dart
With his bold breast, and felt it in his heart:
Thund'ring he falls; his falling arms resound,
And his broad buckler rings against the ground.   695
The victor leaps upon his prostrate prize;
Thus on a roe the well-breath'd beagle flies,
And rends his side, fresh-bleeding with the dart
The distant hunter sent into his heart.
Observing *Hector* to the rescue flew;   700
Bold as he was, *Antilochus* withdrew:
So when a savage, ranging o'er the plain,
Has torn the shepherd's dog, or shepherd swain;
While conscious of the deed, he glares around,
And hears the gath'ring multitude resound,   705
Timely he flies the yet-untasted food,
And gains the friendly shelter of the wood.

So fears the youth; all *Troy* with shouts pursue,
While stones and darts in mingled tempest flew;
710 But enter'd in the *Grecian* ranks, he turns
His manly breast, and with new fury burns.

    Now on the fleet the Tydes of *Trojans* drove,
Fierce to fulfill the stern decrees of *Jove*:
The Sire of Gods, confirming *Thetis'* pray'r,
715 The *Grecian* ardour quench'd in deep despair;
But lifts to glory *Troy*'s prevailing bands,
Swells all their hearts, and strengthens all their hands.
On *Ida*'s top he waits with longing eyes,
To view the navy blazing to the skies;
720 Then, nor till then, the scale of war shall turn,
The *Trojans* fly, and conquer'd *Ilion* burn.
These fates revolv'd in his almighty mind,
He raises *Hector* to the work design'd,
Bids him with more than mortal fury glow,
725 And drives him, like a light'ning, on the foe.
So *Mars*, when human crimes for vengeance call,
Shakes his huge jav'lin, and whole armies fall.
Not with more rage a conflagration rolls,
Wraps the vast mountains, and involves the poles.
730 He foams with wrath; beneath his gloomy brow
Like fiery meteors his red eye-balls glow:
The radiant helmet on his temples burns,
Waves when he nods, and lightens as he turns:
For *Jove* his splendour round the chief had thrown,
735 And cast the blaze of both the hosts on one.
Unhappy glories! for his fate was near,
Due to stern *Pallas*, and *Pelides'* spear:
Yet *Jove* deferr'd the death he was to pay,
And gave what fate allow'd, the honours of a day!
740   Now all on fire for fame, his breast, his eyes
Burn at each foe, and single ev'ry prize;
Still at the closest ranks, the thickest fight,
He points his ardour, and exerts his might.
The *Grecian* phalanx moveless as a tow'r,
745 On all sides batter'd, yet resists his pow'r:
So some tall rock o'erhangs the hoary main,
By winds assail'd, by billows beat in vain,

Unmov'd it hears, above, the tempest blow,
And sees the watry mountains break below.
Girt in surrounding flames, he seems to fall   750
Like fire from *Jove*, and bursts upon them all:
Bursts as a wave, that from the clouds impends,
And swell'd with tempests on the ship descends;
White are the decks with foam; the winds aloud
Howl o'er the masts, and sing thro' ev'ry shroud: 755
Pale, trembling, tir'd, the sailors freeze with fears;
And instant death on ev'ry wave appears.
So pale the *Greeks* the eyes of *Hector* meet,
The chief so thunders, and so shakes the fleet.
    As when a lion, rushing from his den,   760
Amidst the plain of some wide-water'd fen,
(Where num'rous oxen, as at ease they feed,
At large expatiate o'er the ranker mead;)
Leaps on the herds before the herdsman's eyes;
The trembling herdsman far to distance flies: 765
Some lordly bull (the rest dispers'd and fled)
He singles out; arrests, and lays him dead.
Thus from the rage of *Jove*-like *Hector* flew
All *Greece* in heaps; but one he seiz'd, and slew.
Mycenian Periphes, a mighty name,   770
In wisdom great, in arms well known to fame:
The minister of stern *Euristheus'* ire
Against *Alcides*, *Copreus*, was his sire:
The son redeem'd the honours of the race,
A son as gen'rous as the sire was base;   775
O'er all his country's youth conspicuous far,
In ev'ry virtue, or of peace or war:
But doom'd to *Hector*'s stronger force to yield!
Against the margin of his ample shield
He struck his hasty foot: his heels up-sprung;   780
Supine he fell; his brazen helmet rung.
On the fall'n chief th' invading *Trojan* prest,
And plung'd the pointed jav'lin in his breast.
His circling friends, who strove to guard too late
Th' unhappy hero; fled, or shar'd his fate.   785
    Chas'd from the foremost line, the *Grecian* train
Now man the next, receding tow'rd the main:

Wedg'd in one body at the tents they stand,
Wall'd round with sterns, a gloomy, desp'rate band.
790 Now manly shame forbids th' inglorious flight;
Now fear itself confines them to the fight:
Man courage breathes in man; but *Nestor* most
(The sage preserver of the *Grecian* host)
Exhorts, adjures, to guard these utmost shores;
795 And by their parents, by themselves, implores.
     O Friends! be men: your gen'rous breasts inflame
With mutual honour, and with mutual shame!
Think of your hopes, your fortunes; all the care
Your wives, your infants, and your parents share:
800 Think of each living father's rev'rend head;
Think of each ancestor with glory dead;
Absent, by me they speak, by me they sue;
They ask their safety and their fame from you:
The Gods their fates on this one action lay,
805 And all are lost, if you desert the day.
     He spoke, and round him breath'd heroic fires;
Minerva seconds what the sage inspires.
The mist of darkness *Jove* around them threw,
She clear'd, restoring all the war to view;
810 A sudden ray shot beaming o'er the plain,
And shew'd the shores, the navy, and the main:
Hector they saw, and all who fly, or fight,
The scene wide-opening to the blaze of light.
First of the field, great *Ajax* strikes their eyes,
815 His port majestick, and his ample size:
A pond'rous mace, with studs of iron crown'd,
Full twenty cubits long, he swings around.
Nor fights like others, fix'd to certain stands,
But looks a moving tow'r above the bands;
820 High on the decks, with vast gigantic stride,
The godlike hero stalks from side to side.
So when a horseman from the watry mead
(Skill'd in the manage of the bounding steed)
Drives four fair coursers, practis'd to obey,
825 To some great city thro' the publick way;
Safe in his art, as side by side they run,
He shifts his seat, and vaults from one to one;
And now to this, and now to that he flies;

Admiring numbers follow with their eyes.
From ship to ship thus *Ajax* swiftly flew,   830
No less the wonder of the warring crew.
As furious, *Hector* thunder'd threats aloud,
And rush'd enrag'd before the *Trojan* croud:
Then swift invades the ships, whose beaky prores
Lay rank'd contiguous on the bending shores.   835
So the strong eagle from his airy height,
Who marks the swan's or crane's embody'd flight,
Stoops down impetuous, while they light for food,
And stooping, darkens with his wings the flood.
Jove leads him on with his almighty hand,   840
And breathes fierce spirits in his following band.
The warring nations meet, the battel roars,
Thick beats the combat on the sounding prores.
Thou wouldst have thought, so furious was their fire,
No force could tame them, and no toil could tire;   845
As if new vigour from new fights they won,
And the long battel was but then begun.
Greece yet unconquer'd, kept alive the war,
Secure of death, confiding in despair;
Troy in proud hopes already view'd the main   850
Bright with the blaze, and red with heroes slain!
Like strength is felt, from hope, and from despair,
And each contends, as his were all the war.
　'Twas thou, bold *Hector!* whose resistless hand
First seiz'd a ship on that contested strand;   855
The same which dead *Protesilaüs* bore,
The first that touch'd th' unhappy *Trojan* shore:
For this in arms the warring nations stood,
And bath'd their gen'rous breasts with mutual blood.
No room to poize the lance, or bend the bow;   860
But hand to hand, and man to man they grow.
Wounded, they wound; and seek each other's hearts
With faulchions, axes, swords, and shorten'd darts.
The faulchions ring, shields rattle, axes sound,
Swords flash in air, or glitter on the ground;   865
With streaming blood the slipp'ry shores are dy'd,
And slaughter'd heroes swell the dreadful tyde.
　Still raging *Hector* with his ample hand
Grasps the high stern, and gives this loud command.

870　　Haste, bring the flames! the toil of ten long years
　　　Is finish'd; and the day desir'd appears!
　　　This happy day with acclamations greet,
　　　Bright with destruction of yon' hostile fleet.
　　　The coward-counsels of a tim'rous throng
875　Of rev'rend dotards, check'd our glory long:
　　　Too long *Jove* lull'd us with lethargic charms,
　　　But now in peals of thunder calls to arms;
　　　In this great day he crowns our full desires,
　　　Wakes all our force, and seconds all our fires.
880　　He spoke – The warriours, at his fierce command,
　　　Pour a new deluge on the *Grecian* band.
　　　Ev'n *Ajax* paus'd (so thick the jav'lins fly)
　　　Step'd back, and doubted or to live, or die.
　　　Yet where the oars are plac'd, he stands to wait
885　What chief approaching dares attempt his fate;
　　　Ev'n to the last, his naval charge defends,
　　　Now shakes his spear, now lifts, and now protends,
　　　Ev'n yet, the *Greeks* with piercing shouts inspires,
　　　Amidst attacks, and deaths, and darts, and fires.
890　　O friends! O heroes! names for ever dear,
　　　Once Sons of *Mars*, and thunderbolts of war!
　　　Ah! yet be mindful of your old renown,
　　　Your great forefathers virtues, and your own.
　　　What aids expect you in this utmost strait?
895　What bulwarks rising between you and fate?
　　　No aids, no bulwarks your retreat attend,
　　　No friends to help, no city to defend.
　　　This spot is all you have, to lose or keep;
　　　There stand the *Trojans*, and here rolls the deep.
900　'Tis hostile ground you tread; your native lands
　　　Far, far from hence: your fates are in your hands.
　　　　Raging he spoke; nor farther wastes his breath,
　　　But turns his jav'lin to the work of death.
　　　Whate'er bold *Trojan* arm'd his daring hands,
905　Against the sable ships with flaming brands,
　　　So well the chief his naval weapon sped,
　　　The luckless warriour at his stern lay dead:
　　　Full twelve, the boldest, in a moment fell,
　　　Sent by great *Ajax* to the shades of hell.

OBSERVATIONS

ON THE

FIFTEENTH BOOK

Adam, in *Paradise lost*, awakes from the Embrace of *Eve*, in much the same humour with *Jupiter* in this place. Their Circumstance is very parallel; and each of them, as soon as his passion is over, full of that resentment natural to a superiour, who is imposed upon by one of less worth and Sense than himself, and imposed upon in the worst manner, by shews of tenderness and love.

23. *Hast thou forgot*, &c.] It is in the original to this effect. *Have you forgot how you swung in the air when I hung a load of two anvils at your feet, and a chain of gold on your hands?* 'Tho' it is not my design,' says M. *Dacier*, 'to give a reason for every story in the pagan theology, yet I can't prevail upon my self to pass over this in silence. The physical allegory seems very apparent to me: *Homer* mysteriously in this place explains the nature of the *Air*, which is *Juno*; the two anvils which she had at her feet are the two elements, earth and water; and the chains of gold about her Hands are the *æther*, or fire, which fills the superiour region: The two grosser elements are called anvils, to shew us, that in these two elements only, arts are exercis'd. I don't know but that a moral allegory may here be found, as well as a physical one; the Poet by these masses tied to the feet of *Juno*, and by the chain of gold with which her hands were bound, might signify, that not only domestick affairs should like Fetters detain the wife at home; but that proper and beautiful works like chains of gold ought to employ her hands.'

The physical part of this note belongs to *Heraclides Ponticus*, *Eustathius*, and the Scholiast: M. *Dacier* might have been contented with the credit of the moral one, as it seems an observation no less singular in a Lady.

23.] *Eustathius* tells us, that there were in some manuscripts of *Homer* two verses which are not to be found in any of the printed editions, (which *Hen. Stephens* places here.)

> Πρίν γ' ὅτε δὴ σ' ἀπέλυσα ποδῶν, μύδρους δ' ἐνὶ Τροίῃ
> Κάββαλον ὄφρα πέλοιτο καὶ ἐσσομένοισι πυθέσθαι.

[Before I loosed your feet from the fetters, I cast down into Troy masses of burning metal as a lesson to future generations.]

By these two verses *Homer* shews us, that what he says of the punishment of *Juno* was not an invention of his own, but founded upon an ancient tradition. There had probably been some statue of *Juno* with anvils at her feet, and chains on her hands; and nothing but chains and anvils being left by time, superstitious people rais'd this story; so that *Homer* only follow'd common report. What farther confirms it, is what *Eustathius* adds, that there were shewn near *Troy* certain ruins, which were said to be the remains of these masses.   *Dacier.*

43. *And thy black waves, tremendous* Styx!] The epithet *Homer* here gives to *Styx* is κατειβόμενον, *subterlabens* [flowing in the depths], which I take to refer to its passage thro' the infernal regions. But there is a refinement upon it, as if it signify'd *ex alto stillans*, falling drop by drop from on high. *Herodotus* in his sixth book, writes thus. 'The *Arcadians* say, that near the city *Nonacris* flows the water of *Styx*, and that it is a small rill, which distilling from an exceeding high rock, falls into a little cavity or bason, environ'd with a hedge.' *Pausanias*, who had seen the place, gives light to this passage of *Herodotus*. 'Going from *Phereus*, says he, in the country of the *Arcadians*, and drawing towards the West, we find on the left the city of *Clytorus*, and on the right that of *Nonacris*, and the fountain of *Styx*, which from the height of a shaggy precipiece falls drop by drop upon an exceeding high rock, and before it has travers'd this rock, flows into the river *Crathis*; this water is mortal both to man and beast, and therefore it is said to be an infernal fountain. *Homer* gives it a place in his Poems, and by the description which he delivers, one would think he had seen it.' This shews the wonderful exactness of *Homer* in the description of places which he mentions. The Gods swore by *Styx*, and this was the strongest oath they could take; but we likewise find that men too swore by this fatal water: for *Herodotus* tells us, that *Cleomenes* going to

Arcadia to engage the *Arcadians* to follow him in a war against *Sparta*, had a design to assemble at the city *Nonacris*, and make them swear by the water of this fountain.   *Dacier. Eustath.* in *Odyss.*

47. *Not by my arts,* &c.] This apology is well contriv'd; *Juno* could not swear that she had not deceiv'd *Jupiter*, for this had been entirely false, and *Homer* would be far from authorizing perjury by so great an example. *Juno*, we see, throws part of the fault on *Neptune*, by shewing she had not acted in concert with him.   *Eustathius.*

67. Greece *chas'd by* Troy, &c.] In this discourse of *Jupiter*, the Poet opens his design, by giving his reader a sketch of the principal events he is to expect. As this conduct of *Homer* may to many appear no way artful, and since it is a principal article of the charge brought against him by some late *French* criticks, it will not be improper here to look a little into this dispute. The case will be best stated by translating the following passage from Mr *de la Motte*'s *Reflections sur la Critique.*

'I could not forbear wishing that *Homer* had an art, which he seems to have neglected, that of preparing events without making them known beforehand, so that when they happen one might be surprized agreeably. I could not be quite satisfied to hear *Jupiter*, in the middle of the Iliad, give an exact abridgment of the remainder of the action. Mad. *Dacier* alledges as an excuse, that this past only between *Jupiter* and *Juno*; as if the reader was not let into the secret, and had not as much share in the confidence.'

She adds, 'that as we are capable of a great deal of pleasure at the representation of a tragedy which we have seen before, so the surprizes which I require are no way necessary to our entertainment. This I think a pure piece of Sophistry: One may have two sorts of pleasure at the representation of a tragedy; in the first place, that of taking part in an action of importance the first time it passes before our eyes, of being agitated by fear and hope for the persons one is most concern'd about, and in fine, of partaking their felicity or misfortune, as they happen to succeed, or be disappointed.

'This therefore is the first pleasure which the poet should design to give his auditors, to transport them by pathetick surprizes which excite terrour or pity. The second pleasure must proceed from a view of that art which the author has shewn in raising the former.

' 'Tis true, when we have seen a piece already, we have no longer that first pleasure of the surprize, at least not in all its vivacity; but there still remains the second, which could never have its turn, had not the poet labour'd successfully to excite the first, it being upon that indispensable obligation that we judge of his art.

'The art therefore consists in telling the hearer only what is necessary to be told him, and in telling him only as much as is requisite to the design of pleasing him. And although we know this already when we read it a second time, we yet taste the pleasure of that order and conduct which the art required.

'From hence it follows, that every poem ought to be contrived for the first impression it is to make. If it be otherwise, it gives us (instead of two pleasures which we expected) two sorts of disgusts; the one, that of being cool and untouch'd when we should be mov'd and transported; the other, that of perceiving the defect which caus'd that disgust.

'This, in one word, is what I have found in the Iliad. I was not interested or touch'd by the adventures, and I saw it was this cooling preparation that prevented my being so.'

It appears clearly that M. *Dacier*'s Defence no way excuses the poet's conduct; wherefore I shall add two or three considerations which may chance to set it in a better light. It must be own'd that a surprize artfully managed, which arises from unexpected revolutions of great actions, is extremely pleasing. In this consists the principal pleasure of a Romance or well writ Tragedy. But besides this, there is in the relation of great events a different kind of pleasure which arises from the artful unravelling a knot of actions, which we knew before in the gross. This is a delight peculiar to History and Epic Poetry, which is founded on History. In these kinds of writing, a preceding summary knowledge of the events described does no way damp our curiosity, but rather makes it more eager for the detail. This is evident in a good history, where generally the reader is affected with a greater delight in proportion to his preceding knowledge of the facts described: The pleasure in this case is like that of an Architect's first view of some magnificent building, who was before well acquainted with the proportions of it. In an Epic Poem the case is of a like nature; where, as if the historical Fore-knowledge were not sufficient, the most judicious poets never fail to excite their reader's curiosity by some small sketches of their design; which like the outlines of a fine picture, will necessarily raise in us a greater desire to see it in its finish'd colouring.

Had our author been inclined to follow the method of managing our passions by surprizes, he could not well have succeeded by this manner in the subject he chose to write upon, which being a story of great importance, the principal events of which were well known to the *Greeks*, it was not possible for him to alter the ground-work of his piece; and probably he was willing to mark, sometimes by anticipation, sometimes by recapitulations, how much of his story was founded on historical truths, and that what is superadded were the poetical ornaments.

There is another consideration worth remembering on this head, to justify our author's conduct. It seems to have been an opinion in those early times, deeply rooted in most countries and religions, that the actions of men were not only foreknown, but predestinated by a superior being. This sentiment is very frequent in the most ancient writers both sacred and prophane, and seems a distinguishing character of the writings of the greatest antiquity. *The word of the Lord was fulfill'd* is the principal observation in the history of the Old Testament, and Διὸς δ' ἐτελείετο βουλή [the will of Zeus was being fulfilled] is the declared and most obvious moral of the Iliad. If this great moral be fit to be represented in poetry, what means so proper to make it evident, as this introducing *Jupiter* foretelling the events which he had decreed?

86. *As some way-faring man,* &c.] The discourse of *Jupiter* to *Juno* being ended, she ascends to heaven with wonderful celerity, which the poet explains by this comparison. On other occasions he has illustrated the action of the mind by sensible images from the motion of the bodies; here he inverts the case, and shews the great velocity of *Juno*'s flight by comparing it to the quickness of thought. No other comparison could have equall'd the speed of an heavenly being. To render this more beautiful and exact, the poet describes a traveller who revolves in his mind the several places which he has seen, and in an instant passes in imagination from one distant part of the earth to another. *Milton* seems to have had it in his eye in that elevated passage,

> *— The speed of Gods*
> *Time counts not, tho' with swiftest minutes wing'd.*

As the sense in which we have explain'd this passage is exactly literal, as well as truly sublime, one cannot but wonder what should induce both *Hobbes* and *Chapman* to ramble so wide from it in their translations.

> *This said, went* Juno *to* Olympus *high.*
> *As when a man looks o'er an ample plain,*
> *To any distance quickly goes his eye:*
> *So swiftly* Juno *went with little pain.*

Chapman's is yet more foreign to the subject,

> *But as the mind of such a man, that hath a great way gone,*
> *And either knowing not his way, or then would let alone*
> *His purpos'd journey; is distract, and in his vexed mind*
> *Resolves now not to go, now goes, still many ways inclin'd –*

102. *Go thou, the feasts of heav'n attend thy call.*] This is a passage worthy our observation. *Homer* feigns, that *Themis*, that is Justice, presides over the feasts of the Gods; to let us know, that she ought much more to preside over the feasts of men.   *Eustathius.*

114. Juno'*s speech to the Gods.*] It was no sort of exaggeration what the ancients have affirm'd of *Homer*, that the examples of all kinds of oratory are to be found in his works. The present speech of *Juno* is a masterpiece in that sort, which seems to say one thing, and persuades another: For while she is only declaring to the Gods the orders of *Jupiter*, at the time that she tells them they must obey, she fills them with a reluctance to do it. By representing so strongly the superiority of his power, she makes them uneasy at it, and by particularly advising that God to submit, whose temper could least brook it, she incites him to downright rebellion. Nothing can be more sly and artfully provoking, than that stroke on the death of his darling son. *Do thou, O* Mars, *teach obedience to us all, for 'tis upon thee that* Jupiter *has put the severest trial:* Ascalaphus *thy son lies slain by his means: Bear it with so much temper and moderation, that the world may not think he was thy son.*

134. *To* Fear *and* Flight. –] *Homer* does not say, that *Mars* commanded they should join his horses to his chariot, which horses were call'd *Fear* and *Flight. Fear* and *Flight* are not the names of the horses of *Mars*, but the names of two furies in the service of this God: It appears likewise by other passages, that they were his children, book 13. v. 299. This is a very ancient mistake; *Eustathius* mentions it as an error of *Antimachus*, yet *Hobbes* and most others have fallen into it.

164. *Go wait the Thund'rer's Will.*] 'Tis remarkable, that whereas it is familiar with the Poet to repeat his errands and messages, here he introduces *Juno* with very few words, where she carries a dispatch from *Jupiter* to *Iris* and *Apollo.* She only says, '*Jove* commands you to attend him on Mount *Ida,*' and adds nothing of what had pass'd between herself and her consort before. The reason of this brevity is not only that she is highly disgusted with *Jupiter*, and so unwilling to tell her tale from the anguish of her heart; but also because *Jupiter* had given her no commission to relate fully the subject of their discourse: wherefore she is cautious of declaring what possibly he would have concealed. Neither does *Jupiter* himself in what follows reveal his decrees: For he lets *Apollo* only so far into his will, that he would have him discover and rout the *Greeks*: Their good fortune, and the success which was to ensue, he hides from him, as one who favour'd the cause of *Troy.* One may remark in this passage *Homer*'s various conduct and discretion concerning what ought to be put in practice, or left un-done; whereby his reader may be inform'd how to regulate his own affairs.   *Eustathius.*

210.   *Three brother deities, from* Saturn *came,*
        And ancient Rhea, *earth's immortal dame:*
        Assign'd by lot, our triple rule we know, &c.

Some have thought the *Platonic* Philosophers drew from hence the notion of their *Triad* (which the Christian *Platonists* since imagined to be an obscure hint of the *Sacred Trinity.*) The *Trias* of *Plato* is well known, τὸ αὐτὸ ὄν, ὁ νοῦς ὁ δημιουργός, ἡ τοῦ κόσμου ψυχή [the one itself, the intelligence and master-craftsman, the soul of the Universe]. In his *Gorgias* he tells us, τὸν Ὅμηρον (*auctorem sc. fuisse*) τῆς τῶν δημιουργικῶν Τριαδικῆς ὑποστάσεως [that *Homer* was the originator of the tripartite essence of the master-craftsman]. See *Proclus in Plat. Theol. lib.* 1. *c.* 5. *Lucian Philopatr. Aristotle de cœlo, l.* 1. *c.* 1. speaking of the *Ternarian* Number from *Pythagoras*, has these words; Τὰ τρία πάντα, καὶ τὸ τρὶς πάντη. Καὶ πρὸς τὰς ἁγιστείας τῶν θεῶν χρώμεθα τῷ ἀριθμῷ τούτῳ. Καθάπερ γάρ φασι καὶ οἱ Πυθαγόρειοι, τὸ πᾶν καὶ τὰ πάντα τοῖς τρισὶν ὥρισται. Τελευτὴ γὰρ καὶ μέσον καὶ ἀρχὴ τὸν ἀριθμὸν ἔχει τὸν τοῦ παντός· ταῦτα τὸν τῆς τριάδος [All things are three, and three is in all things. And we make use of this number in the worship of the Gods. For, as the Pythagoreans say, the 'all' and everything that makes up the all are determined by these three (dimensions). For the end, the middle, and the beginning have the number of the 'all'. And these same things have the number of the triad]. From which passage *Trapezuntius* endeavour'd very seriously to prove, that *Aristotle* had a perfect knowledge of the *Trinity*. *Duport* (who furnish'd me with this note, and who seems to be sensible of the folly of *Trapezuntius*) nevertheless in his *Gnomologia Homerica*, or comparison of our author's sentences with those of the Scripture, has placed opposite to this verse that of St *John*. *There are three who give testimony in heaven, the Father, the Son, and the Holy Ghost.* I think this the strongest instance I ever met with of the manner of thinking of such men, whose too much learning has made them mad.

Lactantius, de Fals. Relig. lib. 1. *cap.* 11. takes this fable to be a remain of ancient history, importing, that the empire of the then known world was divided among the three brothers; to *Jupiter* the oriental part, which was call'd Heaven, as the Region of light, or the sun: to *Pluto* the occidental, or darker regions: and to *Neptune* the sovereignty of the seas.

228. *To elder brothers.*] *Iris*, that she may not seem to upbraid *Neptune* with weakness of judgment, out of regard to the greatness and dignity of his person, does not say that *Jupiter* is stronger or braver; but attacking him from a motive not in the least invidious, superiority of age, she says sententiously, that the *Furies* wait upon our elders. The *Furies* are said to wait upon men in a double sense: either for evil, as they did upon *Orestes* after he had slain his mother; or else for their good, as upon elders when they are injur'd, to protect them and avenge their wrongs. This is an instance that the Pagans look'd upon birthright as a right divine.   *Eustathius.*

252. *Else had our wrath, &c.*] This representation of the terrours which must have attended the conflict of two such mighty powers as *Jupiter* and *Neptune*, whereby the elements had been mix'd in confusion, and the whole frame of nature endangered, is imaged in these few lines with a nobleness suitable to the occasion. *Milton* has a thought very like it in his fourth book, where he represents what must have happen'd if *Satan* and *Gabriel* had encounter'd.

– Not only Paradise
In this commotion, but the starry cope
Of heav'n, perhaps, and all the elements
At least had gone to wrack, disturb'd and torn

> *With violence of this conflict, had not soon*
> *Th' Almighty, to prevent such horrid fray, &c.*

274. Jove *thinking of his pains, they past away.*] *Eustathius* observes, that this is a very sublime representation of the power of *Jupiter*, to make *Hector*'s pains cease from the moment wherein *Jupiter* first turn'd his thoughts towards him. *Apollo* finds him so far recovered, as to be able to sit up, and know his friends. Thus much was the work of *Jupiter*; the God of health perfects the cure.

298. *As when the pamper'd steed.*] This comparison is repeated from the sixth book, and we are told that the ancient criticks retain'd no more than the two first verses and the four last in this place, and that they gave the verses two marks; by the one (which was the *asterism*) they intimated, that the four lines were very beautiful; but by the other (which was the *obelus*) that they were ill placed. I believe an impartial reader who considers the two places will be of the same opinion.

Tasso has improv'd the justness of this simile in his sixteenth book [xxviii], where *Rinaldo* returning from the arms of *Armida* to battel, is compared to the steed that is taken from his pastures and mares to the service of the war: The reverse of the circumstance better agreeing with the occasion.

> *Qual feroce destrier, ch'al faticoso*
> *Honor de l'arme vincitor sia tolto,*
> *E lascivo marito in vil riposo*
> *Frà gli armenti, e ne'paschi erri disciolto;*
> *Se'l desta o suon di tromba, o luminoso*
> *Acciar, colà tosto annittendo è volto;*
> *Già già brama l'arringo, e l'huom sùl dorso*
> *Portando, urtato riurtar nel corso.*

[As the fierce steed for age withdrawn from war,
  Wherein the glorious beast had always won,
  That in vile rest, from fight sequester'd far,
  Feeds with the males at rest, his service done;
  If arms he see, or hear the trumpet's jar,
  He neigheth loud, and thither fast doth run,
      And wisheth on his back the armed knight,
      Longing for jousts, for tournaments, and fight.]

311. *Far from the hunters rage.*] *Dacier* has a pretty remark on this passage, that *Homer* extended destiny (that is, the care of providence) even over the beasts of the field; an opinion that agrees perfectly with true theology. In the book of *Jonas*, the regard of the creator extending to the meanest rank of his creatures, is strongly express'd in those words of the Almighty, where he makes his compassion to the brute beasts one of the reasons against destroying *Nineveh. Shall I not spare the great city, in which there are more than sixscore thousand persons, and also much cattel?* And what is still more parallel to this passage, in St *Matth.* ch. 10. *Are not two sparrows sold for a farthing? And yet one of them shall not fall to the ground, without your father.*

362. *But when aloft he shakes.*] *Apollo* in this passage, by the mere shaking his *Ægis*, without acting offensively, annoys and puts the *Greeks* into disorder. *Eustathius* thinks that such a motion might possibly create the same confusion, as hath been reported by historians to proceed from *panic fears*: or that it might intimate some dreadful confusion in the air, and a noise issuing from thence; a notion which seems to be warranted by *Apollo*'s outcry, which presently follows in the same verse. But perhaps we need not go so far to account for this fiction of *Homer*: The sight of a hero's armour often has the like effect in an Epic Poem: The Shield of Prince *Arthur* in *Spencer* works the same wonders with this *Ægis* of *Apollo*.

386.　*By* Paris, Deiochus *inglorious dies,*
　　　　Pierc'd thro' the shoulder as he basely flies.]

Here is one that falls under the spear of *Paris*, smitten in the extremity of his shoulder, as he was flying. This gives occasion to a pretty observation in *Eustathius*, that this is the only *Greek* who falls by a wound in the back, so careful is *Homer* of the honour of his countrymen. And this remark will appear not ill grounded, if we except the death of *Eioneus* in the beginning of *lib.* 6.

396. *For by the Gods, who flies,* &c.] It sometimes happens (says *Longinus*) that a writer in speaking of some person, all on a sudden puts himself in that other's place, and acts his part; a figure which marks the impetuosity and hurry of passion. It is this which *Homer* practises in these verses; the Poet stops his narration, forgets his own person, and instantly, without any notice, puts this precipitate menace into the mouth of his furious and transported hero. How must his discourse have languish'd, had he stay'd to tell us, Hector *then said these, or the like words?* Instead of which, by this unexpected transition he prevents the reader, and the transition is made before the Poet himself seems sensible he had made it. The true and proper place for this figure is when the time presses, and when the occasion will not allow of any delay: It is elegant then to pass from one person to another, as in that of *Hecatæus. The herald, extremely discontented at the orders he had received, gave command to the* Heraclidæ *to withdraw. – It is no way in my power to help you; if therefore you would not perish entirely, and if you would not involve me too in your ruin, depart, and seek a retreat among some other people.*   Longinus, *ch.* 23.

416. *As when ashore an infant stands.*] This simile of the sand is inimitable; it is not easy to imagine any thing more exact and emphatical to describe the tumbling and confus'd heap of a wall, in a moment. . Moreover the comparison here taken from sand is the juster, as it rises from the very place and scene before us. For the wall here demolished, as it was founded on the coast, must needs border on the sand; wherefore the similitude is borrowed immediately from the subject matter under view.   *Eustathius.*

428. *Oh* Jove! *if ever,* &c.] The form of *Nestor*'s prayer in this place resembles that of *Chryses* in the first book. And it is worth remarking, that the Poet well knew what shame and confusion the reminding one of past benefits is apt to produce. From the same topick *Achilles* talks with his mother, and *Thetis* herself accosts *Jove*; and likewise *Phœnix* where he holds a parley with *Achilles.* This righteous prayer hath its wished accomplishment.   *Eustathius.*

438. *Presumptuous* Troy *mistook the sign.*] The thunder of *Jupiter* is design'd as a mark of his acceptance of *Nestor*'s prayers, and a sign of his favour to the *Greeks.* However, there being nothing in the prodigy particular to the *Greeks,* the *Trojans* expound it in their own favour, as they seem warranted by their present success. This self-partiality of men in appropriating to themselves the protection of heaven, has always been natural to them. In the same manner *Virgil* makes *Turnus* explain the transformation of the *Trojan* ships into nymphs, as an ill omen to the *Trojans.*

> *Trojanos hæc monstra petunt, his Jupiter ipse*
> *Auxilium solitum eripuit. –*

> [These monsters for the *Trojans* fate are meant,
> And are by *Jove* for black presages sent.]

History furnishes many instances of oracles, which by reason of this partial interpretation, have proved an occasion to lead men into great misfortunes: It was the case of *Crœsus* in his wars with *Cyrus*; and a like mistake engaged *Pyrrhus* to make war upon the *Romans*.

448. *On the ships above, the cars below.*] This is a new sort of battel, which *Homer* has never before mentioned; the *Greeks* on their ships, and the *Trojans* in their chariots, fight as on a plain.   *Eustathius.*

472. *Nor could the* Trojans – *Force to the fleet and tents th' impervious way.*] *Homer* always marks distinctly the place of battel; he here shews us clearly, that the *Trojans* attacked the first line of the fleet that stood next the wall, or the vessels which were drawn foremost on the land: These vessels were a strong rampart to the tents, which were pitch'd behind, and to the other line of the navy which stood nearer to the sea; to penetrate therefore to the tents, they must necessarily force the first line, and defeat the troops which defended it.   *Eustathius.*

582. *Death is the worst,* &c.]   'Tis with very great address, that to the bitterness of death, he adds the advantages that were to accrue after it. And the ancients are of opinion, that 'twou'd be as advantageous for young soldiers to read this lesson, concise as it is, as all the volumes of *Tyrtæus*, wherein he endeavours to raise the spirits of his countrymen. *Homer* makes a noble enumeration of the parts wherein the happiness of a city consists. For having told us in another place, the three great evils to which a town, when taken, is subject; the slaughter of the men, the destruction of the place by fire; the leading of their wives and children into captivity: now he reckons up the blessings that are contrary to those calamities. To the slaughter of the men indeed he makes no opposition; because it is not necessary to the well-being of a city, that every individual should be saved, and not a man slain.

Eustathius.

590. *The god-like* Ajax *next.*] The oration of *Hector* is more splendid and shining that that of *Ajax*, and also more solemn, from his sentiments concerning the favour and assistance of *Jupiter.* But that of *Ajax* is the more politick, fuller of management, and apter to persuade: For it abounds with no less than seven generous arguments to inspire resolution. He exhorts his people even to death, from the danger to which their navy was exposed, which if once consumed, they were never like to get home. And as the *Trojans* were bid to die, so he bids his men dare to die likewise: and indeed with great necessity, for the *Trojans* may recruit after the engagement, but for the *Greeks*, they had no better way than to hazard their lives; and if they should gain nothing else by it, yet at least they would have a speedy dispatch, not a lingring and dilatory destruction.   *Eustathius.*

677. *And flank the Navy with a brazen wall.*] The Poet has built the *Grecians* a new sort of Wall out of their Arms; and perhaps one might say, 'twas from this Passage *Apollo* borrow'd that Oracle which he gave to the *Athenians* about their Wall of Wood; in like manner, the *Spartans* were said to have a Wall of Bones: If so, we must allow the God not a little obliged to the Poet.   *Eustathius.*

723. *He raises* Hector, &c.] This picture of *Hector*, impuls'd by *Jupiter*, is a very finish'd piece, and excels all the drawings of this hero which *Homer* has given us in so various attitudes. He is here represented as an instrument in the hand of *Jupiter*, to bring about those designs the God had long projected: And as his fatal hour now approaches, *Jove* is willing to recompence his hasty death with this short-liv'd glory. Accordingly, this being the last scene of victory he is to appear in, the Poet introduces him with all imaginable pomp, and adorns him with all the terrour of a conqueror: His Eyes sparkle with fire, his mouth foams with fury, his figure is compared to the God of War, his rage is equall'd to a conflagration and a storm, and the destruction he causes is resembled to that which a lion makes among the herds. The Poet, by this heap of comparisons, raises the idea of the hero higher than any single description could reach.

736. *– His fate was near – Due to stern* Pallas.] It may be ask'd, what *Pallas* has to do with the *Fates*, or what power has she over them? *Homer* speaks thus, because *Minerva* has already resolv'd to succour *Achilles*, and deceive *Hector* in the combate between these two heroes, as we find in book 22. Properly speaking, *Pallas* is nothing but the knowledge and wisdom of *Jove*, and it is wisdom which presides over the councels of his providence; therefore she may be look'd upon as drawing all things to the fatal term to which they are decreed.   *Dacier.*

752. *Bursts as a Wave, &c.*] *Longinus,* observing that oftentimes the principal beauty of writing consists in the judicious assembling together of the great circumstances, and the strength with which they are marked in the proper place, chuses this passage of *Homer* as a plain instance of it. 'Where (says that noble critick) in describing the terrour of a tempest, he takes care to express whatever are the accidents of most dread and horrour in such a situation: He is not content to tell us that the mariners were in danger, but he brings them before our eyes, as in a picture, upon the Point of being every Moment overwhelmed by every wave; nay the very words and syllables of the description give us an image of their peril.' He shews, that a Poet of less judgment would amuse himself in less important circumstances, and spoil the whole effect of the image by minute, ill-chosen, or superfluous particulars. Thus *Aratus* endeavouring to refine upon that line,

> *And instant death on ev'ry wave appears!*

He turn'd it thus,

> *A slender plank preserves them from their fate.*

Which, by flourishing upon the thought, has lost the loftiness and terrour of it, and is so far from improving the image, that it lessens and vanishes in his management. By confining the danger to a single line, he has scarce left the shadow of it; and indeed the word *preserves* takes away even that. The same critick produces a fragment of an old poem on the *Arimaspians,* written in this false taste, whose Author, he doubts not, imagined he had said something wonderful in the following affected verses. I have done my best to give 'em the same turn, and I believe there are those, who will not think 'em bad ones.

> *Ye pow'rs! what madness! How, on ships so frail,*
> *(Tremendous thought!) can thoughtless mortals sail?*
> *For stormy seas they quit the pleasing plain,*
> *Plant woods in waves, and dwell amidst the main.*
> *Far o'er the deep (a trackless path) they go,*
> *And wander oceans, in pursuit of woe.*
> *No ease their hearts, no rest their eyes can find,*

On heav'n their looks, and on the waves their mind;
Sunk are their spirits, while their arms they rear;
And Gods are weary'd with their fruitless pray'r.

796. Nestor's *speech.*] This popular harangue of *Nestor* is justly extoll'd as the strongest and most persuasive piece of oratory imaginable. It contains in it every motive by which men can be affected; the preservation of their wives and children, the secure possession of their fortunes, the respect of their living parents, and the due regard for the memory of those that were departed: By these he diverts the *Grecians* from any thoughts of flight in the article of extreme peril.   *Eustathius.*

This noble exhortation is finely imitated by *Tasso, Jerusalem. l.* 20 [xx. xxv–xxvi].

> *– O valoroso, hor via con questa*
> *Faccia, a ritor la preda a noi rapita.*
> *L'imagine ad alcuno in mente desta,*
> *Glie la figura quasi, e glie l'addita*
> *De la pregante patria e de la mesta*
> *Supplice famiglivola sbigottita.*
> *Credi (dicea) che la tua patria spieghi*
> *Per la mia lingua in tui parole i preghi.*
>   *Guarda tù le mie leggi, e i sacri Tempi*
> *Fà, ch'io del sangue mio non bagni, e lavi,*
> *Assicura le virgini da gli empi,*
> *E i sepolchri, e le cinere de gli avi.*
> *A te piangendo i lor passati tempi*
> *Mostran la bianca chioma i vecchi gravi:*
> *A tè la moglie, e le mammelle, e'l petto,*
> *Le cune, e i figli, e'l marital suo letto.*

[But to the bold, 'Go, hardy knight (he says),
His prey out of this lion's paws go tear.'
To some before his thoughts the shape he lays,
And makes therein the image true appear,
How his sad country him entreats and prays,
His house, his loving wife, his children dear:
  'Suppose (quoth he) thy country doth beseech
  And pray thee thus: suppose this is her speech:
"Defend my laws, uphold my temples brave,
My blood from washing of my streets withhold;

From ravishing my virgins keep, and save
Thine ancestors' dead bones and ashes cold;
To thee thy fathers' dear and parents' grave
Show their uncover'd heads, white, hoary, old;
    To thee thy wife, her breasts with tears o'erspread,
    Thy sons their cradles show, their marriage bed." ']

814. *First of the field, great* Ajax.] In this book, *Homer*, to raise the valour of *Hector*, gives him *Neptune* for an antagonist; and to raise that of *Ajax*, he first opposed to him *Hector*, supported by *Apollo*, and now the same *Hector* impelled and seconded by *Jupiter* himself. These are strokes of a master-hand.   *Eustathius.*

824. *Drives four fair coursers*, &c.] The comparison which *Homer* here introduces, is a demonstration that the art of mounting and managing horses was brought to so great a perfection in these early times, that one man could manage four at once, and leap from one to the other even when they run full speed. But some object, that the custom of riding was not known in *Greece* at the time of the *Trojan* war: Besides, they say the comparison is not just, for the horses are said to run full speed, whereas the ships stand firm and unmoved. Had *Homer* put the comparison in the mouth of one of his heroes, the objection had been just, and he guilty of an inconsistency: but it is he himself who speaks: Saddle-horses were in use in his age, and any poet may be allowed to illustrate pieces of antiquity by images familiar to his own times. This is sufficient for the first objection; nor is the second more reasonable; for it is not absolutely necessary that comparisons should correspond in every particular; it suffices if there be a general resemblance. This is only introduced to shew the Agility of *Ajax*, who passes swiftly from one vessel to another, and is therefore entirely just.   *Eustathius.*

856. *The same that dead* Protesilaus *bore.*] *Homer* feigns that *Hector* laid hold on the ship of the dead *Protesilaus*, rather than on that of any other, that he might not disgrace any of his *Grecian* Generals.
    Eustathius.

874.   *The coward-counsels of a tim'rous throng*
     Of rev'rend dotards. —]

Homer adds this with a great deal of art and prudence, to answer beforehand all the objections which he well foresaw might be made, because *Hector* never till now attacks the *Grecians* in their camp, or endeavours to burn their navy. He was retained by the elders of *Troy*, who frozen with fear at the sight of *Achilles*, never suffered him to march from the ramparts. Our Author forgets nothing that has the resemblance of truth; but he had yet a farther reason for inserting this, as it exalts the glory of his principal hero: These elders of *Troy* thought it less difficult to defeat the *Greeks*, tho' defended with strong entrenchments, while *Achilles* was not with them; than to overcome them without entrenchments when he assisted them. And this is the reason that they prohibited *Hector* before, and permit him now, to sally upon the enemy.   *Dacier.*

877. *But now* Jove *calls to arms,* &c.] *Hector* seems to be sensible of an extraordinary impulse from heaven, signified by these words, *the most mighty hand of* Jove *pushing him on.* 'Tis no more than any other person would be ready to imagine, who should rise from a state of distress or indolence, into one of good fortune, vigour, and activity.
                                    Eustathius.

890. *The speech of* Ajax.] There is great strength, closeness, and spirit in this speech, and one might (like many criticks) employ a whole page in extolling and admiring it in general terms. But sure the perpetual rapture of such commentators, who are always giving us exclamations instead of criticisms, may be a mark of great admiration, but of little judgment. Of what use is this either to a reader who has a taste, or to one who has not? To admire a fine passage is what the former will do without us, and what the latter cannot be taught to do by us. However we ought gratefully to acknowledge the good nature of most people, who are not only pleased with this superficial applause given to fine passages, but are likewise inclined to transfer to the critick, who only points at these beauties, part of the admiration justly due to the Poet. This is a cheap and easy way to fame, which many writers ancient and modern have pursued with great success. Formerly indeed this sort of authors had modesty, and were humbly content to call their perform-ances only *Florilegia* or *Posies*: But some of late have passed such collections on the world for criticisms of great depth and learning, and seem to expect the same flowers should please us better, in these paltry nosegays of their own making up, than in the native gardens where they grew. As this practice of extolling without giving reasons is very

convenient for most writers, so it excellently suits the ignorance or laziness of most readers, who will come into any sentiment rather than take the trouble of refuting it. Thus the complement is mutual: For as such criticks do not tax their readers with any thought to understand them, so their readers in return advance nothing in opposition to such criticks. They may go roundly on, admiring and exclaiming in this manner; *What an exquisite spirit of poetry – How beautiful a circumstance – What delicacy of sentiments – With what art has the Poet – In how sublime and just a manner – How finely imagined – How wonderfully beautiful and poetical* – And so proceed, without one reason to interrupt the course of their eloquence, most comfortably and ignorantly apostrophising to the end of the chapter.

THE
SIXTEENTH BOOK
OF THE
ILIAD

The ARGUMENT

The sixth battel: The acts and death of *Patroclus*

Patroclus *(in pursuance of the request of* Nestor *in the eleventh book) entreats* Achilles *to suffer him to go to the assistance of the* Greeks *with* Achilles*'s troops and armour. He agrees to it, but at the same time charges him to content himself with rescuing the fleet, without farther pursuit of the enemy. The armour, horses, soldiers, and officers of* Achilles *are described.* Achilles *offers a libation for the success of his friend, after which* Patroclus *leads the* Myrmidons *to battel. The* Trojans *at the sight of* Patroclus *in* Achilles*'s armour, taking him for that hero, are cast into the utmost consternation: He beats them off from the vessels,* Hector *himself flies,* Sarpedon *is kill'd, tho'* Jupiter *was averse to his fate. Several other particulars of the battel are described; in the heat of which,* Patroclus, *neglecting the orders of* Achilles, *pursues the foe to the walls of* Troy; *where* Apollo *repulses and disarms him,* Euphorbus *wounds him, and* Hector *kills him, which concludes the book.*

So warr'd both armies on th' ensanguin'd shore,
While the black vessels smoak'd with human gore.
Meantime *Patroclus* to *Achilles* flies;
The streaming tears fall copious from his eyes;
5 Not faster, trickling to the plains below,
From the tall rock the sable waters flow.
Divine *Pelides*, with compassion mov'd,
Thus spoke, indulgent to his best belov'd.
　　Patroclus, say, what grief thy bosom bears,
10 That flows so fast in these unmanly tears?
No girl, no infant whom the mother keeps
From her lov'd breast, with fonder passion weeps;
Not more the mother's soul that infant warms,
Clung to her knees, and reaching at her arms,
15 Than thou hast mine! Oh tell me, to what end
Thy melting sorrows thus pursue thy friend?
　　Griev'st thou for me, or for my martial band?
Or come sad tidings from our native land?
Our fathers live, (our first, most tender care)
20 Thy good *Menœtius* breathes the vital air,
And hoary *Peleus* yet extends his days;
Pleas'd in their age to hear their children's praise.
　　Or may some meaner cause thy pity claim?
Perhaps yon' reliques of the *Grecian* name,
25 Doom'd in their ships to sink by fire and sword,
And pay the forfeit of their haughty lord?
Whate'er the cause, reveal thy secret care,
And speak those sorrows which a friend would share.

A sigh, that instant, from his bosom broke,
Another follow'd, and *Patroclus* spoke.   30
   Let *Greece* at length with pity touch thy breast,
Thy self a *Greek*; and, once, of *Greeks* the best!
Lo! ev'ry chief that might her fate prevent,
Lies pierc'd with wounds, and bleeding in his tent.
Eurypylus, Tydides, Atreus' son,   35
And wise *Ulysses*, at the navy groan
More for their country's wounds, than for their own.
Their pain, soft arts of pharmacy can ease,
Thy breast alone no lenitives appease.
   May never rage like thine my soul enslave,   40
O great in vain! unprofitably brave!
Thy country slighted in her last distress,
What friend, what man, from thee shall hope redress?
No – men unborn, and ages yet behind,
Shall curse that fierce, that unforgiving mind.   45
   O man unpitying! if of man thy race;
But sure thou spring'st not from a soft embrace,
Nor ever am'rous hero caus'd thy birth,
Nor ever tender Goddess brought thee forth.
Some rugged rock's hard entrails gave thee form,   50
And raging seas produc'd thee in a storm,
A soul well-suiting that tempestuous kind,
So rough thy manners, so untam'd thy mind.
   If some dire Oracle thy breast alarm,
If ought from *Jove*, or *Thetis*, stop thy arm,   55
Some beam of comfort yet on *Greece* may shine,
If I but lead the *Myrmidonian* line:
Clad in thy dreadful arms if I appear,
Proud *Troy* shall tremble, and desert the war:
Without thy person *Greece* shall win the day,   60
And thy mere image chase her foes away.
Press'd by fresh forces, her o'erlabour'd train
Shall quit the ships, and *Greece* respire again.
   Thus, blind to fate! with supplicating breath,
Thou beg'st his arms, and in his arms, thy death.   65
Unfortunately good! a boding sigh
Thy friend return'd; and with it, this reply.

  Patroclus! thy *Achilles* knows no fears;
  Nor words from *Jove*, nor *oracles* he hears;
70 Nor ought a mother's caution can suggest;
  The tyrant's pride lies rooted in my breast.
  My wrongs, my wrongs, my constant thought engage,
  Those, my sole oracles, inspire my rage:
  I made him tyrant; gave him pow'r to wrong
75 Ev'n me: I felt it; and shall feel it long.
  The maid, my black-ey'd maid, he forc'd away,
  Due to the toils of many a well-fought day;
  Due to my conquest of her father's reign;
  Due to the votes of all the *Grecian* train.
80 From me he forc'd her; me, the bold and brave;
  Disgrac'd, dishonour'd, like the meanest slave.
  But bear we this – the wrongs I grieve, are past;
  'Tis time our fury should relent at last:
  I fix'd its date; the day I wish'd appears:
85 Now *Hector* to my ships his battel bears,
  The flames my eyes, the shouts invade my ears.
  Go then *Patroclus!* court fair honour's charms
  In *Troy's* fam'd fields, and in *Achilles'* arms:
  Lead forth my martial *Myrmidons* to fight,
90 Go save the fleets, and conquer in my right.
  See the thin reliques of their baffled band,
  At the last edge of yon' deserted land!
  Behold all *Ilion* on their ships descends;
  How the cloud blackens, how the storm impends!
95 It was not thus, when, at my sight amaz'd,
  Troy saw and trembled, as this helmet blaz'd:
  Had not th' injurious King our friendship lost,
  Yon' ample trench had bury'd half her host.
  No camps, no bulwarks now the *Trojans* fear,
100 Those are not dreadful, no *Achilles* there:
  No longer flames the lance of *Tydeus'* son;
  No more your Gen'ral calls his heroes on;
  Hector, alone, I hear; his dreadful breath
  Commands your slaughter, or proclaims your death.
105 Yet now, *Patroclus*, issue to the plain;
  Now save the ships, the rising fires restrain,
  And give the *Greeks* to visit *Greece* again.

But heed my words, and mark a friend's command
Who trusts his fame and honours in thy hand,
And from thy deeds expects, th' *Achaian* host   110
Shall render back the beauteous maid he lost:
Rage uncontroul'd thro' all the hostile crew,
But touch not *Hector*, *Hector* is my due.
Tho' *Jove* in thunder should command the war,
Be just, consult my glory, and forbear.   115
The fleet once sav'd, desist from farther chace,
Nor lead to *Ilion*'s walls the *Grecian* race;
Some adverse God thy rashness may destroy;
Some God, like *Phœbus*, ever kind to *Troy*.
Let *Greece*, redeem'd from this destructive strait,   120
Do her own work, and leave the rest to fate.
Oh! would to all th' immortal pow'rs above,
Apollo, *Pallas*, and almighty *Jove!*
That not one *Trojan* might be left alive,
And not a *Greek* of all the race survive;   125
Might only we the vast destruction shun,
And only we destroy th' accursed town!

   Such conf'rence held the chiefs: while on the strand,
Great *Jove* with conquest crown'd the *Trojan* band.
Ajax no more the sounding storm sustain'd,   130
So thick, the darts an iron tempest rain'd:
On his tir'd arm the weighty buckler hung;
His hollow helm with falling jav'lins rung;
His breath, in quick, short pantings, comes, and goes,
And painful sweat from all his members flows.   135
Spent and o'erpow'r'd, he barely breathes at most;
Yet scarce an army stirs him from his post:
Dangers on dangers all around him grow,
And toil to toil, and woe succeeds to woe.

   Say, Muses, thron'd above the starry frame,   140
How first the navy blaz'd with *Trojan* flame?
   Stern *Hector* wav'd his sword; and standing near
Where furious *Ajax* ply'd his ashen spear,
Full on the lance a stroke so justly sped,
That the broad faulchion lopp'd its brazen head: 145
His pointless spear the warriour shakes in vain;
The brazen head falls sounding on the plain.

Great *Ajax* saw, and own'd the hand divine,
Confessing *Jove*, and trembling at the sign;
150 Warn'd, he retreats. Then swift from all sides pour
The hissing brands; thick streams the fiery show'r;
O'er the high stern the curling volumes rise,
And sheets of rolling smoke involve the skies.
      Divine *Achilles* view'd the rising flames,
155 And smote his thigh, and thus aloud exclaims.
Arm, arm, *Patroclus!* Lo, the blaze aspires!
The glowing ocean reddens with the fires.
Arm, e'er our vessels catch the spreading flame;
Arm, e'er the *Grecians* be no more a name;
160 I haste to bring the troops. – The hero said;
The friend with ardour and with joy obey'd.
      He cas'd his limbs in brass, and first around
His manly legs, with silver buckles bound
The clasping greaves; then to his breast applies
165 The flamy cuirass, of a thousand dyes;
Emblaz'd with studs of gold his faulchion shone,
In the rich belt, as in a starry zone.
Achilles' shield his ample shoulders spread,
Achilles' helmet nodded o'er his head.
170 Adorn'd in all his terrible array,
He flash'd around intolerable day.
Alone, untouch'd, *Pelides'* jav'lin stands,
Not to be pois'd but by *Pelides'* hands:
From *Pelion's* shady brow the plant entire
175 Old *Chiron* rent, and shap'd it for his sire;
Whose son's great arm alone the weapon wields,
The death of heroes, and the dread of fields.
      Then brave *Automedon* (an honour'd name,
The second to his Lord in love and fame,
180 In peace his friend, and part'ner of the war)
The winged coursers harness'd to the car.
Xanthus and *Balius*, of immortal breed,
Sprung from the wind, and like the wind in speed;
Whom the wing'd *Harpye*, swift *Podarge*, bore,
185 By *Zephyr* pregnant on the breezy shore.
Swift *Pedasus* was added to their side,
(Once great *Aëtion's*, now *Achilles'* pride)

Who, like in strength, in swiftness, and in grace,
A mortal courser match'd th' immortal race.
      Achilles speeds from tent to tent, and warms   190
His hardy *Myrmidons* to blood and arms.
All breathing death, around their chief they stand,
A grim, terrific, formidable band:
Grim as voracious wolves that seek the springs
When scalding thirst their burning bowels wrings   195
(When some tall stag, fresh-slaughter'd in the wood,
Has drench'd their wide, insatiate throats with blood)
To the black fount they rush, a hideous throng,
With paunch distended, and with lolling tongue,
Fire fills their eye, their black jaws belch the gore,   200
And gorg'd with slaughter, still they thirst for more.
Like furious rush'd the *Myrmidonian* crew,
Such their dread strength, and such their deathful view.
      High in the midst the great *Achilles* stands,
Directs their order, and the war commands.   205
He, lov'd of *Jove*, had launch'd for *Ilion*'s shores
Full fifty vessels, mann'd with fifty oars:
Five chosen leaders the fierce bands obey,
Himself supreme in valour, as in sway.
      First march'd *Menestheus*, of celestial birth,   210
Deriv'd from thee, whose waters wash the earth,
Divine *Sperchius! Jove*-descended flood!
A mortal mother mixing with a God.
Such was *Menestheus*, but miscall'd by fame
The son of *Borus*, that espous'd the dame.   215
      Eudorus next; whom *Polymele* the gay,
Fam'd in the graceful dance, produc'd to day.
Her, sly *Cyllenius* lov'd; on her would gaze,
As with swift step she form'd the running maze:
To her high chamber, from *Diana*'s quire,   220
The God pursu'd her, urg'd, and crown'd his fire.
The son confess'd his father's heav'nly race,
And heir'd his mother's swiftness in the chace.
Strong *Echeclëus*, blest in all those charms
That pleas'd a God, succeeded to her arms;   225
Not conscious of those loves, long hid from fame,
With gifts of price he sought and won the dame;

Her secret offspring to her sire she bare;
Her sire caress'd him with a parent's care.
230   *Pisander* follow'd; matchless in his art
To wing the spear, or aim the distant dart;
No hand so sure of all th' *Emathian* line,
Or if a surer, great *Patroclus!* thine.
The fourth by *Phœnix'* grave command was grac'd;
235   *Laërces'* valiant offspring led the last.
Soon as *Achilles*, with superiour care,
Had call'd the chiefs, and order'd all the war,
This stern remembrance to his troops he gave:
Ye far-fam'd *Myrmidons*, ye fierce and brave!
140   Think with what threats you dar'd the *Trojan* throng,
Think what reproach these ears endur'd so long,
'Stern Son of *Peleus* (thus ye us'd to say,
While restless, raging, in your ships you lay)
Oh nurs'd with gall, unknowing how to yield!
245   Whose rage defrauds us of so fam'd a field.
If that dire fury must for ever burn,
What make we here? Return, ye Chiefs, return!'
Such were your words – Now Warriours grieve no more.
Lo there the *Trojans!* bath your swords in gore!
250   This day shall give you all your soul demands;
Glut all your hearts! and weary all your hands!
Thus while he rowz'd the fire in ev'ry breast,
Close, and more close, the list'ning cohorts prest;
Ranks wedg'd in ranks; of arms a steely ring
255   Still grows, and spreads, and thickens round the King.
As when a circling wall the builder forms,
Of strength defensive against winds and storms,
Compacted stones the thick'ning work compose,
And round him wide the rising structure grows.
260   So helm to helm, and crest to crest they throng,
Shield urg'd on shield, and man drove man along:
Thick, undistinguish'd plumes, together join'd,
Float in one sea, and wave before the wind.
Far o'er the rest, in glitt'ring pomp appear,
265   There, bold *Automedon*; *Patroclus* here;
Brothers in arms, with equal fury fir'd;
Two friends, two bodies with one soul inspir'd.

But mindful of the Gods, *Achilles* went
To the rich coffer, in his shady tent:
There lay on heaps his various garments roll'd,   270
And costly furs, and carpets stiff with gold.
(The presents of the silver-footed dame)
From thence he took a bowl, of antique frame,
Which never man had stain'd with ruddy wine,
Nor rais'd in off'rings to the pow'rs divine,   275
But *Peleus'* son; and *Peleus'* son to none
Had rais'd in off'rings, but to *Jove* alone.
This ting'd with sulphur, sacred first to flame,
He purg'd; and wash'd it in the running stream.
Then cleans'd his hands; and fixing for a space   280
His eyes on heaven, his feet upon the place
Of sacrifice, the purple draught he pour'd
Forth in the midst; and thus the God implor'd.
   Oh thou Supreme! high-thron'd, all height above!
Oh Great! *Pelasgic, Dodonæan Jove!*   285
Who 'midst surrounding frosts, and vapours chill,
Preside on bleak *Dodona*'s vocal hill:
(Whose groves, the *Selli,* race austere! surround,
Their feet unwash'd, their slumbers on the ground;
Who hear, from rustling oaks, thy dark decrees;   290
And catch the fates, low-whisper'd in the breeze.)
Hear, as of old! Thou gav'st, at *Thetis* pray'r,
Glory to me, and to the *Greeks* despair:
Lo to the dangers of the fighting field
The best, the dearest of my friends, I yield: 295
Tho' still determin'd, to my ships confin'd,
Patroclus gone, I stay but half behind.
Oh! be his guard thy providential care,
Confirm his heart, and string his arm to war:
Press'd by his single force, let *Hector* see   300
His Fame in Arms not owing all to me.
But when the fleets are sav'd from foes and fire,
Let him with conquest and renown retire;
Preserve his arms, preserve his social train,
And safe return him to these eyes again!   305
   Great *Jove* consents to half the chief's request,
But heav'ns eternal doom denies the rest;

To free the fleet was granted to his pray'r;
His safe return, the winds dispers'd in air.
310 Back to his tent the stern *Achilles* flies,
And waits the combate with impatient eyes.
    Meanwhile the troops beneath *Patroclus'* care,
Invade the *Trojans*, and commence the war.
As wasps, provok'd by children in their play,
315 Pour from their mansions by the broad high-way,
In swarms the guiltless traveller engage,
Whet all their stings, and call forth all their rage;
All rise in arms, and with a gen'ral cry
Assert their waxen domes, and buzzing progeny.
320 Thus from the tents the fervent legion swarms,
So loud their clamours, and so keen their arms.
Their rising rage *Patroclus'* breath inspires,
Who thus inflames them with heroick fires.
    Oh warriours, part'ners of *Achilles'* praise!
325 Be mindful of your deeds in ancient days:
Your godlike master let your acts proclaim,
And add new glories to his mighty name.
Think, your *Achilles* sees you fight: Be brave,
And humble the proud monarch whom you save.
330   Joyful they heard, and kindling as he spoke,
Flew to the fleet, involv'd in fire and smoke.
From shore to shore the doubling shouts resound,
The hollow ships return a deeper sound.
The war stood still, and all around them gaz'd,
335 When great *Achilles'* shining armour blaz'd:
Troy saw, and thought the dread *Achilles* nigh,
At once they see, they tremble, and they fly.
    Then first thy spear, divine *Patroclus!* flew,
Where the war rag'd, and where the tumult grew.
340 Close to the stern of that fam'd ship, which bore
Unblest *Protesilaus* to *Ilion's* shore,
The great *Pæonian*, bold *Pyrechmes*, stood;
(Who led his bands from *Axius'* winding flood)
His shoulder-blade receives the fatal wound;
345 The groaning warriour pants upon the ground.
His troops, that see their country's glory slain,
Fly diverse, scatter'd o'er the distant plain.

Patroclus' arm forbids the spreading fires,
And from the half-burn'd ship proud *Troy* retires:
Clear'd from the smoke the joyful navy lies;   350
In heaps on heaps the foe tumultuous flies;
Triumphant *Greece* her rescu'd decks ascends,
And loud acclaim the starry region rends.
So when thick clouds inwrap the mountain's head,
O'er heav'ns expanse like one black cieling spread;   355
Sudden, the Thund'rer, with a flashing ray,
Bursts thro' the darkness, and lets down the day:
The hills shine out, the rocks in prospect rise,
And streams, and vales, and forests strike the eyes;
The smiling scene wide opens to the sight,   360
And all th' unmeasur'd *Æther* flames with light.
    But *Troy* repuls'd, and scatter'd o'er the plains,
Forc'd from the navy, yet the fight maintains.
Now ev'ry *Greek* some hostile hero slew,
But still the foremost, bold *Patroclus* flew: 365
As *Areïlycus* had turn'd him round,
Sharp in his thigh he felt the piercing wound;
The brazen-pointed spear, with vigour thrown,
The thigh transfix'd, and broke the brittle bone:
Headlong he fell. Next *Thoas* was thy chance,   370
Thy breast, unarm'd, receiv'd the *Spartan* lance.
Phylides' dart (as *Amphiclus* drew nigh)
His blow prevented, and transpierc'd his thigh,
Tore all the brawn, and rent the nerves away:
In darkness, and in death, the warriour lay.   375
    In equal arms two sons of *Nestor* stand,
And two bold brothers of the *Lycian* band:
By great *Antilochus*, *Atymnius* dies,
Pierc'd in the flank, lamented youth! he lies.
Kind *Maris*, bleeding in his brother's wound,   380
Defends the breathless carcase on the ground;
Furious he flies, his murd'rer to engage,
But godlike *Thrasimed* prevents his rage,
Between his arm and shoulder aims a blow;
His arm falls spouting on the dust below: 385
He sinks, with endless darkness cover'd o'er,
And vents his soul effus'd with gushing gore.

Slain by two brothers, thus two brothers bleed,
Sarpedon's friends, *Amisodarus'* seed;
390   *Amisodarus*, who by furies led,
The bane of men, abhorr'd *Chimæra* bred;
Skill'd in the dart in vain, his sons expire,
And pay the forfeit of their guilty Sire.
    Stopp'd in the tumult *Cleobulus* lies,
395   Beneath *Oïleus'* arm, a living prize;
A living prize not long the *Trojan* stood;
The thirsty faulchion drank his reeking blood:
Plung'd in his throat the smoaking weapon lies;
Black death, and fate unpitying, seal his eyes.
400   Amid the ranks, with mutual thirst of fame,
Lycon the brave, and fierce *Peneleus* came;
In vain their jav'lins at each other flew,
Now, met in Arms, their eager Swords they drew.
On the plum'd crest of his *Bœotian* foe,
405   The daring *Lycon* aim'd a noble blow;
The sword broke short; but his, *Peneleus* sped
Full on the juncture of the neck and head:
The head, divided by a stroke so just,
Hung by the skin: the body sunk to dust.
410   O'ertaken *Neamas* by *Merion* bleeds,
Pierc'd thro' the shoulder as he mounts his steeds;
Back from the car he tumbles to the ground:
His swimming eyes eternal shades surround.
    Next *Erymas* was doom'd his fate to feel,
415   His open'd mouth receiv'd the *Cretan* steel:
Beneath the brain the point a passage tore,
Crash'd the thin bones, and drown'd the teeth in gore:
His mouth, his eyes, his nostrils pour a flood;
He sobs his soul out in the gush of blood.
420   As when the flocks neglected by the swain
(Or kids, or lambs) lie scatter'd o'er the plain,
A troop of wolves th' unguarded charge survey,
And rend the trembling, unresisting prey.
Thus on the foe the *Greeks* impetuous came;
425   *Troy* fled, unmindful of her former fame.
    But still at *Hector* godlike *Ajax* aim'd,
Still, pointed at his breast, his jav'lin flam'd:

The *Trojan* chief, experienc'd in the field,
O'er his broad shoulders spread the massy shield,
Observ'd the storm of darts the *Grecians* pour,   430
And on his buckler caught the ringing show'r.
He sees for *Greece* the scale of conquest rise,
Yet stops, and turns, and saves his lov'd allies.
    As when the hand of *Jove* a tempest forms,
And rolls the cloud to blacken heav'n with storms,   435
Dark o'er the fields th' ascending vapour flies,
And shades the sun, and blots the golden skies:
So from the ships, along the dusky plain,
Dire *Flight* and *Terrour* drove the *Trojan* train.
Ev'n *Hector* fled; thro' heaps of disarray   440
The fiery coursers forc'd their Lord away:
While far behind, his *Trojans* fall confus'd,
Wedg'd in the trench, in one vast carnage bruis'd.
Chariots on chariots roll; the clashing spokes
Shock; while the madding steeds break short their yokes: 445
In vain they labour up the steepy mound;
Their Charioteers lie foaming on the ground.
Fierce on the rear, with Shouts, *Patroclus* flies;
Tumultuous clamour fills the fields and skies;
Thick drifts of dust involve their rapid flight,   450
Clouds rise on clouds, and heav'n is snatch'd from sight.
Th' affrighted steeds, their dying Lords cast down,
Scour o'er the fields, and stretch to reach the town.
Loud o'er the rout was heard the victor's cry,
Where the war bleeds, and where the thickest die.   455
Where horse and arms, and chariots lie o'erthrown,
And bleeding heroes under axles groan.
No stop, no check, the steeds of *Peleus* knew;
From bank to bank th' immortal coursers flew,
High-bounding o'er the fosse: the whirling car   460
Smoaks thro' the ranks, o'ertakes the flying war,
And thunders after *Hector*; *Hector* flies,
Patroclus shakes his lance; but fate denies.
Not with less noise, with less impetuous force,
The tyde of *Trojans* urge their desp'rate course,   465
Than when in Autumn *Jove* his fury pours,
And earth is loaden with incessant show'rs,

(When guilty mortals break th' eternal laws,
And judges brib'd, betray the righteous cause)
470   From their deep beds he bids the rivers rise,
And opens all the floodgates of the skies:
Th' impetuous torrents from their hills obey,
Whole fields are drown'd, and mountains swept away;
Loud roars the deluge till it meets the main;
475   And trembling man sees all his labours vain!
    And now the chief (the foremost troops repell'd)
Back to the ships his destin'd progress held,
Bore down half *Troy* in his resistless way,
And forc'd the routed ranks to stand the day.
480   Between the space where silver *Simoïs* flows,
Where lay the fleets, and where the rampires rose,
All grim in dust and blood, *Patroclus* stands,
And turns the slaughter on the conqu'ring bands.
First *Pronous* dy'd beneath his fiery dart,
485   Which pierc'd below the shield his valiant heart.
Thestor was next; who saw the chief appear,
And fell the victim of his coward fear;
Shrunk up he sate, with wild and haggard eye,
Nor stood to combate, nor had force to fly:
490   *Patroclus* mark'd him as he shunn'd the war,
And with unmanly tremblings shook the car,
And dropp'd the flowing reins. Him 'twixt the jaws
The jav'lin sticks, and from the chariot draws:
As on a rock that overhangs the main,
495   An angler, studious of the line and cane,
Some mighty fish draws panting to the shore;
Not with less ease the barbed jav'lin bore
The gaping dastard: As the spear was shook,
He fell, and life his heartless breast forsook.
500   Next on *Eryalus* he flies; a stone
Large as a rock, was by his fury thrown.
Full on his crown the pond'rous fragment flew,
And burst the helm, and cleft the head in two:
Prone to the ground the breathless warriour fell,
505   And death involv'd him with the shades of hell.
Then low in dust *Epaltes*, *Echius*, lie;
Ipheas, *Evippus*, *Polymelus*, die;

Amphoterus, and *Erymas* succeed,
And last, *Tlepolemus* and *Pyres* bleed.
Where'er he moves, the growing slaughters spread   510
In heaps on heaps; a monument of dead.

When now *Sarpedon* his brave friends beheld
Grov'ling in dust, and gasping on the field,
With this reproach his flying host he warms,
Oh stain to honour! oh disgrace to arms!   515
Forsake, inglorious, the contended plain;
This hand, unaided, shall the war sustain:
The task be mine this hero's strength to try,
Who mows whole troops, and makes an army fly.

He spake; and speaking, leaps from off the car;   520
Patroclus lights, and sternly waits the war.
As when two vulturs on the mountain's height
Stoop with resounding pinions to the fight;
They cuff, they tear, they raise a screaming cry:
The desert echoes, and the rocks reply: 525
The warriours thus oppos'd in arms, engage
With equal clamours, and with equal rage.

Jove view'd the combate, whose event foreseen,
He thus bespoke his Sister and his Queen.
The hour draws on; the destinies ordain,   530
My godlike son shall press the *Phrygian* plain:
Already on the verge of death he stands,
His life is ow'd to fierce *Patroclus'* hands.
What passions in a parent's breast debate!
Say, shall I snatch him from impending Fate,   535
And send him safe to *Lycia*, distant far
From all the dangers and the toils of war;
Or to his doom my bravest offspring yield,
And fatten, with celestial blood, the field?

Then thus the goddess with the radiant eyes: 540
What words are these, O sov'reign of the skies?
Short is the date prescrib'd to mortal man;
Shall *Jove*, for one, extend the narrow span,
Whose bounds were fix'd before his race began?
How many sons of Gods, foredoom'd to death,   545
Before proud *Ilion*, must resign their breath!

Were thine exempt, debate would rise above,
And murm'ring pow'rs condemn their partial *Jove.*
Give the bold chief a glorious fate in fight;
550   And when th' ascending soul has wing'd her flight,
Let *Sleep* and *Death* convey, by thy command,
The breathless body to his native land.
His friends and people, to his future praise,
A marble tomb and pyramid shall raise,
555   And lasting honours to his ashes give;
His fame ('tis all the dead can have!) shall live.
    She said; the cloud-compeller overcome,
Assents to Fate, and ratifies the Doom.
Then, touch'd with grief, the weeping heav'ns distill'd
560   A show'r of blood o'er all the fatal field.
The God, his eyes averting from the plain,
Laments his son, predestin'd to be slain,
Far from the *Lycian* shores, his happy native reign.
    Now met in arms, the combatants appear,
565   Each heav'd the shield, and pois'd the lifted spear:
From strong *Patroclus'* hand the jav'lin fled,
And pass'd the groin of valiant *Thrasymed,*
The nerves unbrac'd no more his bulk sustain,
He falls, and falling bites the bloody plain.
570   Two sounding darts the *Lycian* leader threw;
The first aloof with erring fury flew,
The next transpierc'd *Achilles'* mortal steed,
The gen'rous *Pedasus,* of *Theban* breed;
Fix'd in the shoulders joint, he reel'd around;
Rowl'd in the bloody dust, and paw'd the slipp'ry
575   ground.
His sudden fall th' entangled harness broke;
Each axle crackled, and the chariot shook:
When bold *Automedon,* to disengage
The starting coursers, and restrain their rage,
580   Divides the traces with his Sword, and freed
Th' incumber'd chariot from the dying steed:
The rest move on, obedient to the rein;
The car rowls slowly o'er the dusty plain.
    The tow'ring chiefs to fiercer fight advance,
585   And first *Sarpedon* whirl'd his weighty lance,

Which o'er the warriour's shoulder took its course,
And spent in empty air its dying force.
Not so *Patroclus'* never-erring dart;
Aim'd at his breast, it pierc'd the mortal part
Where the strong fibres bind the solid heart.   590
Then, as the mountain oak, or poplar tall,
Or pine (fit mast for some great admiral)
Nods to the axe, till with a groaning sound
It sinks, and spreads its honours on the ground:
Thus fell the King; and laid on earth supine,   595
Before his chariot stretch'd his form divine:
He grasp'd the dust distain'd with streaming gore,
And pale in death, lay groaning on the shore.
So lies a bull beneath the lion's paws,
While the grim savage grinds with foamy jaws   600
The trembling limbs, and sucks the smoaking blood;
Deep groans, and hollow roars, rebellow thro' the wood.
    Then to the leader of the *Lycian* band
The dying chief address'd his last command.
Glaucus, be bold; thy task be first to dare   605
The glorious dangers of destructive war,
To lead my troops, to combate at their head,
Incite the living, and supply the dead.
Tell 'em, I charg'd them with my latest breath
Not unreveng'd to bear *Sarpedon*'s death.   610
What grief, what shame must *Glaucus* undergo,
If these spoil'd arms adorn a *Grecian* foe?
Then as a friend, and as a warriour, fight;
Defend my body, conquer in my right;
That taught by great examples, all may try   615
Like thee to vanquish, or like me to die.
    He ceas'd; the fates suppress'd his lab'ring breath,
And his eyes darken'd with the shades of death.
Th' insulting victor with disdain bestrode
The prostrate prince, and on his bosom trod;   620
Then drew the weapon from his panting heart,
The reeking fibres clinging to the dart;
From the wide wound gush'd out a stream of blood,
And the soul issu'd in the purple flood.

625   His flying Steeds the *Myrmidons* detain,
        Unguided now, their mighty master slain.
        All-impotent of aid, transfix'd with grief,
        Unhappy *Glaucus* heard the dying chief.
        His painful arm, yet useless with the smart
630   Inflicted late by *Teucer*'s deadly dart,
        Supported on his better hand he stay'd;
        To *Phœbus* then ('twas all he could) he pray'd.
            All-seeing Monarch! whether *Lycia*'s coast
        Or sacred *Ilion*, thy bright presence boast,
635   Pow'rful alike to ease the wretche's smart;
        Oh hear me! God of ev'ry healing art!
        Lo! stiff with clotted blood, and pierc'd with pain,
        That thrills my arm and shoots thro' ev'ry vein,
        I stand unable to sustain the spear,
640   And sigh, at distance from the glorious war.
        Low in the dust is great *Sarpedon* laid,
        Nor *Jove* vouchsaf'd his hapless off'ring aid.
        But thou, O God of Health! thy succour lend,
        To guard the reliques of my slaughter'd friend.
645   For thou, tho' distant, can'st restore my might,
        To head my *Lycians*, and support the fight.
            Apollo heard; and suppliant as he stood,
        His heav'nly hand restrain'd the flux of blood;
        He drew the dolours from the wounded part,
650   And breath'd a spirit in his rising heart.
        Renew'd by art divine, the hero stands,
        And owns th' assistance of immortal hands.
        First to the fight his native troops he warms,
        Then loudly calls on *Troy*'s vindictive arms;
655   With ample strides he stalks from place to place,
        Now fires *Agenor*, now *Polydamas*;
        Æneas next, and *Hector* he accosts;
        Inflaming thus the rage of all their hosts.
            What thoughts, regardless chief! thy breast employ?
660   Oh too forgetful of the friends of *Troy!*
        Those gen'rous friends, who, from their country far,
        Breathe their brave souls out in another's war.
        See! where in dust the great *Sarpedon* lies,
        In action valiant, and in council wise,

Who guarded right, and kept his people free;   665
To all his *Lycians* lost, and lost to thee!
Stretch'd by *Patroclus*' arm on yonder plains,
Oh save from hostile rage his lov'd remains:
Ah let not *Greece* his conquer'd trophies boast,
Nor on his corpse revenge her heroes lost.   670
   He spoke; each leader in his grief partook,
Troy, at the loss, thro' all her legions shook.
Tranfix'd with deep regret, they view o'erthrown
At once his country's pillar, and their own;
A chief, who led to *Troy*'s beleaguer'd wall   675
A host of heroes, and outshin'd them all.
Fir'd, they rush on; First *Hector* seeks the foes,
And with superiour vengeance greatly glows.
   But o'er the dead the fierce *Patroclus* stands,
And rouzing *Ajax*, rouz'd the list'ning bands.   680
   Heroes, be men! be what you were before;
Or weigh the great occasion, and be more.
The chief who taught our lofty walls to yield,
Lies pale in death, extended on the field.
To guard his body *Troy* in numbers flies;   685
'Tis half the glory to maintain our prize.
Haste, strip his arms, the slaughter round him spread,
And send the living *Lycians* to the dead.
   The heroes kindle at his fierce command;
The martial squadrons close on either hand: 690
Here *Troy* and *Lycia* charge with loud alarms,
Thessalia there, and *Greece*, oppose their arms.
With horrid shouts they circle round the slain;
The clash of armour rings o'er all the plain.
Great *Jove*, to swell the horrors of the fight,   695
O'er the fierce armies pours pernicious night,
And round his son confounds the warring hosts,
His fate ennobling with a croud of ghosts.
   Now *Greece* gives way, and great *Epigeus* falls;
Agacleus' son, from *Budium*'s lofty walls: 700
Who chas'd for murder thence, a suppliant came
To *Peleus*, and the silver-footed dame;
Now sent to *Troy*, *Achilles*' arms to aid,
He pays due vengeance to his kinsman's shade.

705   Soon as his luckless hand had touch'd the dead,
       A rock's large fragment thunder'd on his head;
       Hurl'd by *Hectorean* force, it cleft in twain
       His shatter'd helm, and stretch'd him o'er the slain.
           Fierce to the van of fight *Patroclus* came;
710   And, like an eagle darting at his game,
       Sprung on the *Trojan* and the *Lycian* band;
       What grief thy heart, what fury urg'd thy hand,
       Oh gen'rous *Greek!* when with full vigour thrown
       At *Stenelaüs* flew the weighty stone,
715   Which sunk him to the dead: when *Troy*, too near
       That arm, drew back; and *Hector* learn'd to fear.
       Far as an able hand a lance can throw,
       Or at the lists, or at the fighting foe;
       So far the *Trojans* from their lines retir'd;
720   Till *Glaucus'* turning, all the rest inspir'd.
       Then *Bathyclæus* fell beneath his rage,
       The only hope of *Chalcon*'s trembling age:
       Wide o'er the land was stretch'd his large domain,
       With stately seats, and riches, blest in vain:
725   Him, bold with youth, and eager to pursue
       The flying *Lycians*, *Glaucus* met, and slew;
       Pierc'd thro' the bosom with a sudden wound,
       He fell, and falling, made the fields resound.
       Th' *Achaians* sorrow for their hero slain;
730   With conqu'ring shouts the *Trojans* shake the plain,
       And crowd to spoil the dead: The *Greeks* oppose;
       An iron circle round the carcase grows.
           Then brave *Laogonus* resign'd his breath,
       Dispatch'd by *Merion* to the shades of death:
735   On *Ida*'s holy hill he made abode,
       The Priest of *Jove*, and honour'd like his God.
       Between the jaw and ear the jav'lin went;
       The soul, exhaling, issu'd at the vent.
       His Spear *Æneas* at the victor threw,
740   Who stooping forward from the death withdrew;
       The lance hiss'd harmless o'er his cov'ring shield,
       And trembling strook, and rooted in the field;
       There yet scarce spent, it quivers on the plain,
       Sent by the great *Æneas'* arm in vain.

Swift as thou art (the raging hero cries)   745
And skill'd in dancing to dispute the prize,
My spear, the destin'd passage had it found,
Had fix'd thy active vigour to the ground.
  Oh valiant leader of the *Dardan* host!
(Insulted *Merion* thus retorts the boast)   750
Strong as you are, 'tis mortal force you trust,
An arm as strong may stretch thee in the dust.
And if to this my lance thy Fate be giv'n,
Vain are thy vaunts; Success is still from heav'n;
This instant sends thee down to *Pluto*'s coast,   755
Mine is the glory, his thy parting ghost.
  O friend (*Menœtius'* son this answer gave)
With words to combate, ill befits the brave:
Not empty boasts the sons of *Troy* repell,
Your swords must plunge them to the shades of hell.   760
To speak, beseems the council; but to dare
In glorious action, is the task of war.
  This said, *Patroclus* to the battel flies;
Great *Merion* follows, and new shouts arise:
Shields, helmets rattle, as the warriours close;   765
And thick and heavy sounds the storm of blows.
As thro' the shrilling vale, or mountain ground,
The labours of the woodman's axe resound;
Blows following blows are heard re-echoing wide,
While crackling forests fall on ev'ry side.   770
Thus echo'd all the fields with loud alarms,
So fell the warriours, and so rung their arms.
  Now great *Sarpedon*, on the sandy shore,
His heav'nly form defac'd with dust and gore,
And stuck with darts by warring heroes shed,   775
Lies undistinguish'd from the vulgar dead.
His long-disputed corpse the chiefs inclose,
On ev'ry side the busy combate grows;
Thick, as beneath some shepherd's thatch'd abode,
(The pails high-foaming with a milky flood,)   780
The buzzing flies, a persevering train,
Incessant swarm, and chas'd, return again.
  Jove view'd the combate with a stern survey,
And eyes that flash'd intolerable day;

785 Fix'd on the field his sight, his breast debates
The vengeance due, and meditates the fates;
Whether to urge their prompt effect, and call
The force of *Hector* to *Patroclus'* fall,
This instant see his short-liv'd trophies won,

790 And stretch him breathless on his slaughter'd son;
Or yet, with many a soul's untimely flight,
Augment the fame and horrour of the fight?
To crown *Achilles'* valiant friend with praise
At length he dooms; and that his last of days

795 Shall set in glory; bids him drive the foe;
Nor unattended, see the shades below.
Then *Hector*'s mind he fills with dire dismay;
He mounts his car, and calls his hosts away;
Sunk with *Troy*'s heavy fates, he sees decline

800 The scales of *Jove*, and pants with awe divine.
    Then, nor before, the hardy *Lycians* fled,
And left their monarch with the common dead:
Around, in heaps on heaps, a dreadful wall
Of carnage rises, as the heroes fall.

805 (So *Jove* decreed!) At length the *Greeks* obtain
The prize contested, and despoil the slain.
The radiant arms are by *Patroclus* born,
Patroclus' ships the glorious spoils adorn.
    Then thus to *Phœbus*, in the realms above,

810 Spoke from his throne the cloud-compelling *Jove.*
Descend, my *Phœbus!* on the *Phrygian* plain,
And from the fight convey *Sarpedon* slain;
Then bathe his body in the crystal flood,
With dust dishonour'd, and deform'd with blood:

815 O'er all his limbs ambrosial odours shed,
And with celestial robes adorn the dead.
Those rites discharg'd, his sacred corpse bequeath
To the soft arms of silent *Sleep* and *Death*;
They to his friends the mournful charge shall bear,

820 His friends a tomb and pyramid shall rear;
What honours mortals after death receive,
Those unavailing honours we may give!
    Apollo bows, and from mount *Ida*'s height,
Swift to the field precipitates his flight;

Thence from the war the breathless hero bore,   825
Veil'd in a cloud, to silver *Simoïs'* shore:
There bath'd his honourable wounds, and drest
His manly members in th' immortal vest;
And with perfumes of sweet ambrosial dews,
Restores his freshness, and his form renews.   830
Then *Sleep* and *Death*, two twins of winged race,
Of matchless swiftness, but of silent pace,
Receiv'd *Sarpedon*, at the God's command,
And in a moment reach'd the *Lycian* land;
The corpse amidst his weeping Friends they laid,   835
Where endless honours wait the sacred shade.
    Meanwhile *Patroclus* pours along the plains,
With foaming coursers, and with loosen'd reins.
Fierce on the *Trojan* and the *Lycian* crew,
Ah blind to fate! thy headlong fury flew: 840
Against what fate and pow'rful *Jove* ordain,
Vain was thy friend's command, thy courage vain.
For he, the God, whose counsels uncontroll'd,
Dismay the mighty, and confound the bold:
The God who gives, resumes, and orders all,   845
He urg'd thee on, and urg'd thee on to fall.
    Who first, brave hero! by that arm was slain,
Who last, beneath thy vengeance, press'd the plain;
When heav'n itself thy fatal fury led,
And call'd to fill the number of the dead?   850
Adrestus first; *Autonous* then succeeds;
Echeclus follows; next young *Megas* bleeds;
Epistor, Menalippus, bite the ground;
The slaughter, *Elasus* and *Mulius* crown'd:
Then sunk *Pylartes* to eternal night;   855
The rest dispersing, trust their fates to flight.
    Now *Troy* had stoop'd beneath his matchless pow'r,
But flaming *Phœbus* kept the sacred tow'r.
Thrice at the battlements *Patroclus* strook,
His blazing *Ægis* thrice *Apollo* shook: 860
He try'd the fourth; when, bursting from the cloud,
A more than mortal voice was heard aloud.
    Patroclus! cease: This Heav'n-defended wall
Defies thy lance; not fated yet to fall;

865   Thy friend, thy greater far, it shall withstand,
       Troy shall not stoop ev'n to *Achilles'* hand.
          So spoke the God who darts celestial fires:
       The *Greek* obeys him, and with awe retires.
       While *Hector* checking at the *Scæan* gates
870   His panting coursers, in his breast debates,
       Or in the field his forces to employ,
       Or draw the troops within the walls of *Troy.*
       Thus while he thought, beside him *Phœbus* stood,
       In *Asius'* shape, who reign'd by *Sangar's* flood;
875   (Thy brother, *Hecuba!* from *Dymas* sprung;
       A valiant warriour, haughty, bold, and young.)
       Thus he accosts him. What a shameful sight!
       Gods! is it *Hector* that forbears the fight?
       Were thine my vigour, this successful spear
880   Should soon convince thee of so false a fear.
       Turn then, ah turn thee to the field of fame,
       And in *Patroclus'* blood efface thy shame.
       Perhaps *Apollo* shall thy arms succeed,
       And heav'n ordains him by thy lance to bleed.
885   So spoke th' inspiring God; then took his flight,
       And plung'd amidst the tumult of the fight.
       He bids *Cebrion* drive the rapid car;
       The lash resounds; the coursers rush to war.
       The God the *Grecians* sinking souls deprest,
890   And pour'd swift spirits thro' each *Trojan* breast.
       Patroclus lights, impatient for the fight;
       A spear his left, a stone employs his right:
       With all his nerves he drives it at the foe;
       Pointed above, and rough and gross below:
895   The falling ruin crush'd *Cebrion's* head,
       (The lawless offspring of King *Priam's* bed,)
       His front, brows, eyes, one undistinguish'd wound,
       The bursting balls drop sightless to the ground.
       The charioteer, while yet he held the rein,
900   Struck from the car, falls headlong on the plain.
       To the dark shades the soul unwilling glides,
       While the proud victor thus his fall derides,
          Good heav'ns! what active feats yon' artist shows,
       What skilful divers are our *Phrygian* foes!

Mark with what ease they sink into the sand!   905
Pity! that all their practice is by land.
　　Then rushing sudden on his prostrate prize,
To spoil the carcase fierce *Patroclus* flies:
Swift as a lion, terrible and bold,
That sweeps the fields, depopulates the fold;   910
Pierc'd thro' the dauntless heart, then tumbles slain;
And from his fatal courage finds his bane.
At once bold *Hector* leaping from his car,
Defends the body, and provokes the war.
Thus for some slaughter'd hind, with equal rage,   915
Two lordly rulers of the wood engage;
Stung with fierce hunger, each the prey invades,
And echoing roars rebellow thro' the shades.
Stern *Hector* fastens on the warriour's head,
And by the foot *Patroclus* drags the dead.   920
While all around, confusion, rage, and fright
Mix the contending hosts in mortal fight.
So pent by hills, the wild winds roar aloud
In the deep bosom of some gloomy wood;
Leaves, arms, and trees aloft in air are blown,   925
The broad oaks crackle, and the *Sylvans* groan;
This way and that, the ratt'ling thicket bends,
And the whole forest in one crash descends.
Not with less noise, with less tumultuous rage,
In dreadful shock the mingled hosts engage.   930
Darts show'r'd on darts, now round the carcase ring;
Now flights of arrows bounding from the string:
Stones follow stones; some clatter on the fields,
Some, hard and heavy, shake the sounding shields.
But where the rising whirlwind clouds the plains,   835
Sunk in soft dust the mighty chief remains,
And stretch'd in death, forgets the guiding reins!
　　Now flaming from the *Zenith*, *Sol* had driv'n
His fervid orb thro' half the vault of heav'n;
While on each host with equal tempest fell   940
The show'ring darts, and numbers sunk to hell.
But when his ev'ning wheels o'erhung the main,
Glad conquest rested on the *Grecian* train.

Then from amidst the tumult and alarms,
945   They draw the conquer'd corpse, and radiant arms.
Then rash *Patroclus* with new fury glows,
And breathing slaughter, pours amid the foes.
Thrice on the press like *Mars* himself he flew,
And thrice three heroes at each onset slew.
950   There ends thy glory! there the fates untwine
The last, black remnant of so bright a line.
Apollo dreadful stops thy middle way;
Death calls, and heav'n allows no longer day!
    For lo! the God, in dusky clouds enshrin'd,
Approaching dealt a stagg'ring blow behind.
995   The weighty shock his neck and shoulders feel;
His eyes flash sparkles, his stunn'd senses reel
In giddy darkness: Far to distance flung,
His bounding helmet on the champain rung.
960   *Achilles'* plume is stain'd with dust and gore;
That plume, which never stoop'd to earth before,
Long us'd, untouch'd, in fighting fields to shine,
And shade the temples of the man divine.
Jove dooms it now on *Hector's* helm to nod;
965   Not long – for fate pursues him, and the God.
    His spear in shivers falls: His ample shield
Drops from his arm: His baldrick strows the field:
The corselet his astonish'd breast forsakes:
Loose is each joint; each nerve with Horrour shakes.
970   Stupid he stares, and all-assistless stands:
Such is the force of more than mortal hands!
    A *Dardan* youth there was, well-known to fame,
From *Panthus* sprung, *Euphorbus* was his name;
Fam'd for the manage of the foaming horse,
975   Skill'd in the dart, and matchless in the course:
Full twenty Knights he tumbled from the car,
While yet he learn'd his rudiments of war.
His vent'rous spear first drew the hero's gore;
He strook, he wounded, but he durst no more;
980   Nor tho' disarm'd, *Patroclus'* fury stood:
But swift withdrew the long-protended wood,
And turn'd him short, and herded in the croud.

Thus, by an arm divine, and mortal spear,
Wounded at once, *Patroclus* yields to fear,
Retires for succour to his social train,   985
And flies the fate, which heav'n decreed, in vain.
Stern *Hector*, as the bleeding chief he views,
Breaks thro' the ranks, and his retreat pursues:
The lance arrests him with a mortal wound;
He falls, earth thunders, and his arms resound.   990
With him all *Greece* was sunk; that moment all
Her yet-surviving heroes seem'd to fall.
So scorch'd with heat along the desart shore,
The roaming lion meets a bristly boar,
Fast by the spring; they both dispute the flood,   995
With flaming eyes, and jaws besmear'd with blood;
At length the sov'reign savage wins the strife,
And the torn boar resigns his thirst and life.
Patroclus thus, so many chiefs o'erthrown,
So many lives effus'd, expires his own.   1000
As dying now at *Hector*'s feet he lies,
He sternly views him, and triumphing cries.

   Lie there *Patroclus!* and with thee, the joy
Thy pride once promis'd, of subverting *Troy*;
The fancy'd scenes of *Ilion* wrapt in flames,   1005
And thy soft pleasures serv'd with captive dames!
Unthinking man! I fought, those tow'rs to free,
And guard that beauteous race from lords like thee:
But thou a prey to vulturs shalt be made!
Thy own *Achilles* cannot lend thee aid;   1010
Tho much at parting that great chief might say,
And much enjoin thee, this important day.
'Return not, my brave friend (perhaps he said)
Without the bloody arms of *Hector* dead':
He spoke, *Patroclus* march'd, and thus he sped.   1015
   Supine, and wildly gazing on the skies,
With faint, expiring breath, the chief replies.

   Vain boaster! cease, and know the pow'rs divine;
Jove's and *Apollo*'s is this deed, not thine;
To heav'n is ow'd whate'er your own you call,   1020
And heav'n itself disarm'd me e'er my fall.

Had twenty mortals, each thy match in might,
Oppos'd me fairly, they had sunk in fight:
By fate and *Phœbus* was I first o'erthrown,
1025 *Euphorbus* next; the third mean part thy own.
But thou, imperious! hear my latest breath;
The Gods inspire it, and it sounds thy death.
Insulting man! thou shalt be soon, as I;
Black fate hangs o'er thee, and thy hour draws nigh;
1030 Ev'n now on life's last verge I see thee stand,
I see thee fall, and by *Achilles'* hand.
   He faints; the soul unwilling wings her way,
(The beauteous body left a load of clay)
Flits to the lone, uncomfortable coast;
1035 A naked, wand'ring, melancholy ghost!
   Then *Hector* pausing, as his eyes he fed
On the pale carcase, thus address'd the dead.
   From whence this boding speech, the stern decree
Of death denounc'd, or why denounc'd to me?
1040 Why not as well *Achilles'* fate be giv'n
To *Hector*'s lance? Who knows the will of heav'n?
   Pensive he said; then pressing as he lay
His breathless bosom, tore the lance away;
And upwards cast the corps: The reeking spear
1045 He shakes, and charges the bold charioteer.
But swift *Automedon* with loosned reins
Rapt in the chariot o'er the distant plains,
Far from his rage th' immortal coursers drove;
Th' immortal coursers were the gift of *Jove.*

OBSERVATIONS

ON THE

SIXTEENTH BOOK

We have at the entrance of this book one of the most beautiful parts of the Iliad. The two different characters are admirably sustain'd in the dialogue of the two heroes, wherein there is not a period but strongly marks not only their natural temper, but that particular disposition of mind in either, which arises from the present state of affairs. We see *Patroclus* touch'd with the deepest compassion for the misfortune of the *Greeks*, (whom the *Trojans* had forc'd to retreat to their ships, and which ships were on the point of burning) prostrating himself before the vessel of *Achilles*, and pouring out his tears at his feet. *Achilles*, struck with the grief of his friend, demands the cause of it. *Patroclus*, pointing to the ships, where the flames already began to rise, tells him he is harder than the rocks or sea which lay in prospect before them, if he is not touch'd with so moving a spectacle, and can see in cold blood his friends perishing before his eyes. As nothing can be more natural and affecting than the speech of *Patroclus*, so nothing is more lively and picturesque than the attitude he is here describ'd in.

The *Pathetic* of *Patroclus*'s speech is finely contrasted by the *Fierté* of that of *Achilles.* While the former is melting with sorrow for his countrymen, the utmost he can hope from the latter, is but to borrow his armour and troops; to obtain his personal assistance he knows is impossible. At the very instant that *Achilles* is mov'd to ask the cause of his friend's concern, he seems to say that nothing could deserve it but the death of their fathers: and in the same breath speaks of the total destruction of the *Greeks* as of too slight a cause for tears. *Patroclus*, at the opening of this speech, dares not name *Agamemnon* even for being wounded; and after he has tried to bend him by all the arguments that could affect an human breast, concludes by supposing that some oracle or supernatural inspiration is the cause that with-holds his arms. What can match the fierceness of his answer? Which implies, that not the oracles of heaven itself should be regarded, if they stood in competition with his resentment: That if he yields, it must be thro' his own mere motive: The only reason he has ever to yield, is that nature itself cannot support anger eternally: And if he yields now, it is only because he had before determin'd to do so at a certain time, (*Il.* 9. v. 773). That time was not till the flames should approach to his own ships, till the last article of danger, and that not of danger to *Greece*, but to himself. Thus his very pity has the sternest qualifications in the world. After all, what is it he yields to? Only to suffer his friend to go in his stead, just to save them from present ruin, but he expressly forbids him to proceed any farther in their assistance, than barely to put out the fires, and secure his own and his friend's return into their country: And all this concludes with a wish, that (if it were possible) every *Greek* and every *Trojan* might perish except themselves. Such is that *Wrath* of *Achilles*, that more than wrath, as the *Greek* μῆνις implies, which *Homer* has painted in so strong a colouring.

8.   *Indulgent to his best belov'd.*] The friendship of *Achilles* and *Patroclus* is celebrated by all antiquity: And *Homer*, notwithstanding the anger of *Achilles* was his profess'd subject, has found the secret to discover, thro' that very anger, the softer parts of his character. In this view we shall find him generous in his temper, despising gain and booty, and as far as his honour is not concern'd, fond of his mistress, and easy to his friend: Not proud, but when injur'd; and not more revengeful when ill us'd, than grateful and gentle when respectfully treated. 'Patroclus (says *Philostratus*, who probably grounds his assertion on some ancient tradition) was not so much elder than *Achilles* as to pretend to direct him, but of a tender, modest, and unassuming nature; constant and diligent in his attendance, and seeming to have no affections but those of his friend.' The same author has a very pretty passage, where *Ajax* is introduced enquiring of *Achilles*, 'Which of all his warlike actions were the most difficult and dangerous to him? He answers, Those which he undertook for the sake of his friends. And which (continues *Ajax*) were the most pleasing and easy? The very same, replies *Achilles.* He then asks him, Which of all the wounds he ever bore in battel was the most painful to him? *Achilles* answers, That which he receiv'd from *Hector*. But *Hector*, says *Ajax*, never gave you a wound. Yes, replies *Achilles*, a mortal one, when he slew my friend *Patroclus.*'

It is said in the life of *Alexander the Great*, that when that Prince visited the monuments of the heroes at *Troy*, and plac'd a crown upon the tomb of *Achilles*; his Friend *Hephæstion* plac'd another on that of *Patroclus*, as an intimation of his being to *Alexander* what the other was to *Achilles*. On which occasion the saying of *Alexander* is recorded; *That* Achilles *was happy indeed, for having had such a* Friend *to love him living, and such a* Poet *to celebrate him dead.*

11. *No girl, no infant, &c.*] I know the obvious translation of this passage makes the comparison consist only in the tears of the infant, applied to those of *Patroclus*. But certainly the idea of the simile will be much finer, if we comprehend also in it the mother's fondness and concern, awaken'd by this uneasiness of the child, which no less aptly corresponds with the tenderness of *Achilles* on the sight of his friend's affliction. And there is yet a third branch of the comparison, in that pursuit, and constant application the infant makes to the mother, in the same manner as *Patroclus* follows *Achilles* with his grief, till he forces him to take notice of it. I think (all these circumstances laid together) nothing can be more affecting or exact in all its views, than this similitude; which without that regard, has perhaps seem'd but low and trivial to an unreflecting reader.

31. *Let* Greece *at length with pity touch thy breast.*] The commentators labour to prove, that the words in the Original, which begin this speech, *Μὴ νεμέσα*, *Be not angry*, are not meant to desire *Achilles* to bear no farther resentment against the *Greeks*, but only not to be displeas'd at the tears which *Patroclus* sheds for their misfortune. *Patroclus* (they say) was not so imprudent to begin his intercession in that manner, when there was need of something more insinuating. I take this to be an excess of refinement: The purpose of every period in his speech is to persuade *Achilles* to lay aside his anger; why then may he not begin by desiring it? The whole question is, whether he may speak openly in favour of the *Greeks* in the first half of the verse, or in the latter? For in the same line he represents their distress.

— τοῖον γὰρ ἄχος βεβίηκεν Ἀχαιούς.

[such distress has befallen the Achaians]

'Tis plain he treats him without much reserve, calls him implacable, inexorable, and even mischievous (for αἰναρέτη implies no less.) I don't see wherein the caution of this speech consists; it is a generous, unartful petition, whereof *Achilles*'s nature would much more approve, than of all the artifice of *Ulysses* (to which he express'd his hatred in the ninth book, v. 310.)

35.   Eurypylus, Tydides, Atreus' *son,*
       And wise Ulysses. –]

Patroclus in mentioning the wounded Princes to *Achilles*, takes care not to put *Agamemnon* first, lest that odious name striking his ear on a sudden, should shut it against the rest of his discourse: Neither does he name him last, for fear *Achilles* dwelling upon it should fall into passion: But he slides it into the middle, mixing and confounding it with the rest, that it might not be taken too much notice of, and that the names which precede and follow it may diminish the hatred it might excite. Wherefore he does not so much as accompany it with an epithet.

I think the foregoing remark of *Eustathius* is very ingenious, and I have given into it so far, as to chuse rather to make *Patroclus* call him *Atreus*' son than *Agamemnon*, which yet farther softens it, since thus it might as well be imagin'd he spoke of *Menelaus*, as of *Agamemnon*.

61. *And thy mere image chase her foes away.*] It is hard to conceive a greater complement, or one that could more touch the warlike ambition of *Achilles*, than this which *Homer* puts into the mouth of *Patroclus.* It was also an encomium which he could not suspect of flattery; since the person who made it desires to hazard his life upon the security that the enemy could not support the sight of the very armour of *Achilles*: And indeed *Achilles* himself seems to entertain no less a thought, in the answer to this speech, where he ascribes the flight of *Troy* to the blazing of his helmet: a circumstance wonderfully fine, and nobly exalting the idea of this hero's terrible character. Besides all this, *Homer* had it in his view to prepare hereby the wonderful incident that is to ensue in the eighteenth book, where the very sight of *Achilles* from his ship turns the fortune of the war.

101. *No longer flames the lance of* Tydeus' *son.*] By what *Achilles* here says, joining *Diomede* to *Agamemnon* in this taunting reflection, one may justly suspect there was some particular disagreement and emulation between these two Heroes. This we may suppose to be the more natural, because *Diomede* was of all the *Greeks* confessedly the nearest in fame and courage to *Achilles*, and therefore the most likely to move

his envy, as being the most likely to supply his place. The same
sentiments are to be observ'd in *Diomede* with regard to *Achilles*; he is
always confident in his own valour, and therefore· in their greatest
extremities he no where acknowledges the necessity of appeasing *Achil-*
les, but always in council appears most forward and resolute to carry
on the war without him. For this reason he was not thought a fit
embassador to *Achilles*; and upon return from the embassy, he breaks
into a severe reflection, not only upon *Achilles*, but even upon *Agamem-*
non who had sent this embassy to him. *I wish thou hadst not sent these*
supplications and gifts to Achilles; *his insolence was extreme before, but*
now his arrogance will be intolerable; let us not mind whether he goes or
stays, but do our duty and prepare for the battel. Eustathius observes,
that *Achilles* uses this particular expression concerning *Diomede*,

> Οὐ γὰρ Τυδεΐδεω Διομήδεος ἐν παλάμῃσι
> Μαίνεται ἐγχείη –

[No longer flames the lance of *Tydeus'* son]

because it was the same boasting expression *Diomed* had apply'd to
himself, *Il.* 8. v. 111 of the original. But this having been said only to
Nestor in the heat of fight, how can we suppose *Achilles* had notice of
it? This observation shews the great diligence, if not the judgment, of
the good archbishop.

111. *Shall render back the beauteous maid.*] But this is what the *Greeks*
had already offer'd to do, and which he has refus'd; this then is an
inequality in *Achilles*'s manners. Not at all: *Achilles* is still ambitious;
when he refused these presents, the *Greeks* were not low enough, he
would not receive them till they were reduced to the last extremity,
and till he was sufficiently reveng'd by their losses.   *Dacier.*

113. *But touch not* Hector.] This injunction of *Achilles* is highly
correspondent to his ambitious character: He is by no means willing
that the conquest of *Hector* should be atchiev'd by any hand but his
own: In that point of glory he is jealous even of his dearest friend.
This also wonderfully strengthens the idea we have of his implacability
and resentment; since at the same time that nothing can move him to
assist the *Greeks* in the battel, we see it is the utmost force upon his
nature to abstain from it, by the fear he manifests lest any other should
subdue this hero.

The verse I am speaking of,

Τοὺς ἄλλους ἐνάριζ᾽ · ἀπὸ δ᾽ Ἕκτορος ἴσχεο χεῖρας,

[Go ahead and slay the others; but don't touch *Hector*]

is cited by *Diogenes Laertius* as *Homer*'s, but not to be found in the editions before that of *Barnes.* It is certainly one of the instructions of *Achilles* to *Patroclus*, and therefore properly placed in this speech; but I believe better after

– ποτὶ δ᾽, ἀγλαὰ δῶρα πόρωσιν,

[and they will bring me shining gifts]

than where he has inserted it four lines above: For *Achilles*'s instructions not beginning till v. 83.

Πείθεο δ᾽, ὥς τοι ἐγὼ μύθου τέλος ἐν φρεσὶ θείω,

[Obey this decisive word I shall put before your mind]

it is not so proper to divide this material one from the rest. Whereas (according to the method I propose) the whole context will lie in this order. *Obey my injunctions, as you consult my interest and honour. Make as great a slaughter of the* Trojans *as you will, but abstain from* Hector. *And as soon as you have repuls'd them from the ships, be satisfy'd and return: For it may be fatal to pursue the victory to the walls of* Troy.

115. *Consult my glory, and forbear.*] *Achilles* tells *Patroclus*, that if he pursues the foe too far, whether he shall be victor or vanquish'd, it must prove either way prejudicial to his glory. For by the former, the *Greeks* having no more need of *Achilles*'s aid, will not restore him his captive, nor try any more to appease him by presents: By the latter, his arms would be left in the enemy's hands, and he himself upbraided with the death of *Patroclus*.   *Dacier.*

122. *Oh would to all, &c.*] *Achilles* from his overflowing gall vents this execration: The *Trojans* he hates as professed enemies, and he detests the *Grecians* as people who had with calmness overlooked his wrongs. Some of the ancient criticks not entring into the manners of *Achilles*, would have expunged this imprecation, as uttering an universal malevolence to mankind. This violence agrees perfectly with his implacable character. But one may observe at the same time the mighty force of friendship, if for the sake of his dear *Patroclus* he will protect and secure those *Greeks*, whose destruction he wishes. What a little qualifies this bloody wish, is that we may suppose it spoken with great unreservedness, as in secret, and between friends.

Mons. *de la Motte* has a lively remark upon the absurdity of this wish. Upon the supposition that *Jupiter* had granted it, if all the *Trojans* and *Greeks* were destroy'd, and only *Achilles* and *Patroclus* left to conquer *Troy*, he asks, what would be the victory without any enemies, and the triumph without any spectators? But the answer is very obvious; *Homer* intends to paint a man in passion; the wishes and schemes of such an one are seldom conformable to reason; and the manners are preserved the better, the less they are represented to be so.

This brings into my mind that curse in *Shakespear*, where that admirable master of nature makes *Northumberland*, in the rage of his passion, wish for an universal destruction.

> *– Now let not nature's hand*
> *Keep the wild flood confin'd! Let order die,*
> *And let the world no longer be a stage*
> *To feed contention in a lingring act:*
> *But let one spirit of the first-born* Cain
> *Reign in all bosoms, that each heart being set*
> *On bloody courses, the rude scene may end,*
> *And darkness be the burier of the dead!*

130. Ajax *no more*, &c.] This description of *Ajax* wearied out with battel, is a passage of exquisite life and beauty: Yet what I think nobler than the description itself, is what he says at the end of it, that his hero even in this excess of fatigue and languor, could scarce be moved from his post by the efforts of a whole army. *Virgil* has copied the description very exactly, *Æn.* 9.

> *Ergo nec clypeo juvenis subsistere tantum*
> *Nec dextra valet: injectis sic undique telis*
> *Obruitur. Strepit assiduo cava tempora circum*
> *Tinnitu galea, & saxis solida æra fatiscunt:*
> Discussæque jubæ capiti, nec sufficit umbo
> Ictibus: *ingeminant hastis & Troes, & ipse*
> *Fulmineus Mnestheus; tum toto corpore sudor*

Liquitur, & piceum, nec respirare potestas,
Flumen agit; fessos quatit æger anhelitus artus.

[With labour spent, no longer can he wield
The heavy faulchion, or sustain the shield:
O'erwhelm'd with darts, which from afar they fling,
The weapons round his hollow temples ring:
His golden helm gives way: with strong blows
Batter'd, and flat, and beaten to his brows.
His crest is rash'd away; his ample shield
Is falsify'd, and round with jav'lins fill'd.
　　The foe now faint, the *Trojans* overwhelm:
And *Mnesteus* lays hard load upon his helm.
Sick sweat succeeds, he drops at ev'ry pore,
With driving dust his cheeks are pasted o're.
Shorter and shorter ev'ry gasp he takes,
And vain efforts, and hurtless blows he makes.]

The circumstances which I have mark'd in a different character are improvements upon *Homer*, and the last verse excellently expresses, in the short catching up of the numbers, the quick, short panting, represented in the image. The reader may add to the comparison an imitation of the same place in *Tasso*, Canto 9. *St.* 97.

Fatto intanto hà il Soldan cio, ch'e concesso
Fare a terrena forza, hor piu non puote:
Tutto e sangue e sudore; un grave, e spesso
Anhelar gli ange il petto, e i fianche scote.
Langue sotto lo scudo il brachio oppresso,
Gira la destra il ferro in pigre rote;
Spessa, e non taglia, e divenendo ottuso
Perduto il brando omai di brando hà l'uso.

[Meanwhile the Soldan in this latest charge
Had done as much as human force was able,
All sweat and blood appear'd his members large,
His breath was short, his courage wax'd unstable,
His arm grew weak to bear his mighty targe,
His hand to rule his heavy sword unable,
　　Which bruis'd, not cut, so blunted was the blade
　　It lost the use for which a sword was made.]

148.   *Great* Ajax *saw, and own'd the hand divine,*
Confessing Jove, *and trembling at the sign.*]

In the *Greek* there is added an explication of this sign, which has no other allusion to the action but a very odd one in a single phrase, or metaphor.

$$- \ \ddot{o} \ \dot{\rho}a \ \pi \acute{a} \gamma \chi \upsilon \ \mu \acute{a} \chi \eta \varsigma \ \dot{\epsilon} \pi \grave{\iota} \ \mu \acute{\eta} \delta \epsilon a \ \kappa \epsilon \hat{\iota} \rho \epsilon \iota$$
$$Z \epsilon \grave{\upsilon} \varsigma \ \dot{\upsilon} \psi \iota \beta \rho \epsilon \mu \acute{\epsilon} \tau \eta \varsigma, \ T \rho \acute{\omega} \epsilon \sigma \sigma \iota \ \delta \grave{\epsilon} \ \beta o \acute{\upsilon} \lambda \epsilon \tau o \ \nu \acute{\iota} \kappa \eta \nu.$$

Which may be translated,

So seem'd their hopes cut off by heav'ns high Lord,
So doom'd to fall before the Trojan *sword.*

Chapman endeavours to account for the meanness of this conceit, by the gross wit of *Ajax*; who seeing the head of his lance cut off, took it into his fancy that *Jupiter* would in the same manner cut off the counsels and schemes of the *Greeks.* For to understand this far-fetch'd apprehension gravely, as the commentators have done, is indeed (to use the words of *Chapman*) most *dull and Ajantical.* I believe no man will blame me for leaving these lines out of the text.

154. Achilles *view'd the rising flames.*] This event is prepared with a great deal of art and probability. That effect which a multitude of speeches was not able to accomplish, one lamentable spectacle, the sight of the flames, at length brings to pass, and moves *Achilles* to compassion. This it was (say the ancients) that moved the tragedians to make visible representations of misery; for the spectators beholding people in unhappy circumstances, find their souls more deeply touch'd, than by all the strains of rhetorick.   *Eustathius.*

162. *He cas'd his limbs in brass,* &c.] *Homer* does not amuse himself here to describe these arms of *Achilles* at length, for besides that the time permits it not, he reserves this description for the new armour which *Thetis* shall bring that hero; a description which will be plac'd in a more quiet moment, and which will give him all the leisure of making it, without requiring any force to introduce it.   *Eustathius.*

172. *Alone untouch'd* Pelides' *jav'lin stands.*] This passage affords another instance of the stupidity of the commentators, who are here most absurdly inquisitive after the reasons why *Patroclus* does not take the spear, as well as the other arms of *Achilles?* He thought himself a very happy man, who first found out, that *Homer* had certainly given this spear to *Patroclus*, if he had not foreseen that when it should be lost in his future unfortunate engagement, *Vulcan* could not furnish *Achilles* with another; being no joiner, but only a smith. *Virgil*, it seems, was not so precisely acquainted with *Vulcan*'s disability to profess the two trades: since he has, without any scruple, employed him in making a spear, as well as the other arms for *Æneas*. Nothing is more obvious than this thought of *Homer*, who intended to raise the idea of his hero, by giving him such a spear as no other could wield: The description of it in this place is wonderfully pompous.

183. *Sprung from the wind.*] It is a beautiful invention of the poet to represent the wonderful swiftness of the horses of *Achilles*, by saying they were begotten by the western wind. This fiction is truly poetical, and very proper in the way of natural allegory. However, it is not altogether improbable our author might have designed it even in the literal sense: Nor ought the notion to be thought very extravagant in a Poet, since grave naturalists have seriously vouched the truth of this kind of generation. Some of these relate as an undoubted piece of natural history, that there was anciently a breed of this kind of horses in *Portugal*, whose damms were impregnated by a western Wind: *Varro, Collumella*, and *Pliny*, are all of this opinion. I shall only mention the words of *Pliny*, Nat. Hist. lib. 8. cap. 42. *Constat in Lusitania circa Olyssiponem oppidum, & Tagum amnem, equas Favonio flante obversas animalem concipere spiritum, idque partum fieri & gigni pernicissimum* [It is well known in Lusitania, in the area around the town of Olisipo (Lisbon) and the river Tagus, when the West Wind is blowing, that the mares who are facing it conceive a living spirit, and that in this way is born an extremely swift colt]. See also the same author, *l. 4. c. 22. l. 16. c. 25.* Possibly *Homer* had this opinion in view, which we see has authority more than sufficient to give it place in poetry. *Virgil* has given us a description of this manner of conception, *Georgic* 3.

> *Continuoque avidis ubi subdita flamma medullis,*
> *Vere magis (quia vere calor redit ossibus) illæ*
> *Ore omnes versæ in Zephyrum, stant rupibus altis,*
> *Exceptantque leves auras: & sæpe sine ullis*
> *Conjugiis, vento gravidæ (mirabile dictu)*

Saxa per & scopulos & depressas convalles
Diffugiunt. –

    [When, at the spring's approach, their marrow burns,
    (For with the spring their genial warmth returns),
    The mares to cliffs of rugged rocks repair,
    And with wide nostrils snuff the western air:
    When (wondrous to relate!) the parent wind,
    Without the stallion, propagates the kind,
    Then, fir'd with am'rous rage, they take their flight
    Through plains, and mount the hills' unequal height.]

186. *Swift* Pedasus *was added to their side.*] Here was a necessity for a spare horse (as in another place *Nestor* had occasion for the same) that if by any misfortune one of the other horses should fall, there might be a fresh one ready at hand to supply his place. This is good management in the Poet, to deprive *Achilles* not only of his charioteer and his arms, but of one of his inestimable horses.   *Eustathius.*

194. *Grim as voracious wolves,* &c.] There is scarce any picture in *Homer* so much in the savage and terrible way, as this comparison of the *Myrmidons* to wolves: It puts one in mind of the pieces of *Spagnolett*, or *Salvator Rosa*: Each circumstance is made up of images very strongly coloured, and horridly lively. The principal design is to represent the stern looks and fierce appearance of the *Myrmidons*, a gaunt and ghastly train of raw-bon'd bloody-minded Fellows. But besides this, the Poet seems to have some farther views in so many different particulars of the comparison: Their eager desire of fight is hinted at by the wolves thirsting after water: Their strength and vigour for the battel is intimated by their being filled with food: And as these beasts are said to have their thirst sharper after they are gorged with Prey; so the *Myrmidons* are strong and vigorous with ease and refreshment, and therefore more ardently desirous of the combate. This image of their *strength* is inculcated by several expressions, both in the simile and the application, and seems design'd in contraste to the other *Greeks*, who are all wasted and spent with toil.

We have a picture much of this kind given us by *Milton, lib.* 10. where *Death* is let loose into the new creation, to glut his appetite, and discharge his rage upon all nature.

> *— As when a flock*
> *Of rav'nous fowls, tho' many a league remote,*
> *Against the day of battel, to a field*
> *Where armies lie encamp'd, come flying, lur'd*
> *With scent of living carcasses, design'd*
> *For Death the following day, in bloody fight.*
> *So scented the grim feature, and upturn'd*
> *His nostril wide into the murky air,*
> *Sagacious of his quarry from afar.*

And by *Tasso*, Canto 10. *St.* 2. of the furious *Soldan* covered with blood, and thirsting for fresh slaughter.

> *Come dal chiuso ovil cacciato viene*
> *Lupo tal' hor, che fugge, e si nasconde;*
> *Che se ben del gran ventre omai ripiene*
> *Ha l' ingorde voragini profonde.*
> *Avido pur di sangue anco fuor tiene*
> *La lingua, e'l sugge da le labbra immonde;*
> *Tal' ei sen gia dopo il sanguigno stratio*
> *De la sua cupa fame anco non satio.*

> [As when a savage wolf, chas'd from the fold,
> To hide his head runs to some holt or wood,
> Who though he filled hath while it might hold
> His greedy paunch, yet hung'reth after food,
> With sanguine tongue out of his lips forth roll'd,
> About his jaws that licks up foam and blood;
> So from his bloody fray the Soldan hied,
> His rage unquench'd, his wrath unsatisfied.]

211. *Deriv'd from thee, whose waters,* &c.] *Homer* seems resolved that every thing about *Achilles* shall be miraculous. We have seen his very horses are of celestial origine; and now his commanders, tho' vulgarly reputed the sons of men, are represented as the real offspring of some Deity. The Poet thus enhances the admiration of his chief hero by every circumstance with which his imagination could furnish him.

220. *To her high chamber.*] It was the custom of those times to assign the uppermost rooms to the women, that they might be the farther removed from commerce: Wherefore *Penelope* in the *Odysseis* mounts up into a garret, and there sits to her business. So *Priam*, in the 16*th* book, v. 248. had chambers for the ladies of his court, under the roof of his palace.

   The *Lacedæmonians* call'd these high apartments ὦα, and as the word also signifies *eggs*, 'tis probable it was this that gave occasion to the fable of *Helen*'s birth, who is said to be born from an *egg*.

Eustathius.

283. *And thus the God implor'd.*] Tho' the character of *Achilles* every where shews a mind sway'd with unbounded passions, and entirely regardless of all human authority and law; yet he preserves a constant respect to the Gods, and appears as zealous in the sentiments and actions of piety as any hero of the Iliad; who indeed are all remarkable this way. The present passage is an exact description and perfect ritual of the ceremonies on these occasions. *Achilles*, tho' an urgent affair call'd for his friend's assistance, would not yet suffer him to enter the fight, till in a most solemn manner he had recommended him to the protection of *Jupiter*: And this I think a stronger proof of his tenderness and affection for *Patroclus*, than either the grief he express'd at his death, or the fury he shew'd to revenge it.

285. Dodonæan Jove.] The frequent mention of *Oracles* in *Homer* and the ancient Authors, may make it not improper to give the reader a general account of so considerable a part of the *Grecian* superstition; which I cannot do better than in the words of my friend Mr *Stanyan*, in his excellent and judicious abstract of the *Grecian* History.

   'The *Oracles* were rank'd among the noblest and most religious kinds of divination; the design of them being to settle such an immediate way of converse with their Gods, as to be able by them not only to explain things intricate and obscure, but also to anticipate the knowledge of future events; and that with far greater certainty than they could hope for from men, who out of ignorance and prejudice must sometimes either conceal or betray the truth. So that this became the only safe way of deliberating upon affairs of any consequence, either publick or private. Whether to proclaim war, or conclude a peace, to institute a new form of government, or enact new laws, all was to be done with the advice and approbation of the oracle, whose determinations were always held sacred and inviolable. As to the causes of Oracles, *Jupiter* was look'd upon as the first cause of this, and all other sorts of divination; he had the book of fate before him, and out of that reveal'd either more or less, as he pleas'd, to inferior dæmons. But to argue more rationally, this way of access to the Gods has been branded as one of the earliest and grossest pieces of priestcraft, that obtain'd in the world. For the priests, whose dependance was on the Oracles, when they found the cheat had got sufficient footing, allow'd no man to consult the gods without costly sacrifices and rich presents to themselves: And as few could bear this expence, it serv'd to raise their credit among the common people, by keeping them at an awful distance. And to heighten their esteem with the better and wealthier sort, even they were only admitted upon a few stated days: By which the thing appear'd still more mysterious, and for want of this good management, must quickly have been seen through, and fall to the ground. But whatever juggling there was as to the religious part, Oracles had certainly a good effect as to the publick; being admirably suited to the genius of a people, who would join in the most desperate expedition, and admit of any change of government, when they understood by the Oracle it was the irresistible will of the Gods. This was the method *Minos*, *Lycurgus*, and all the famous law-givers took; and indeed they found the people so entirely devoted to this part of religion, that it was generally the easiest, and sometimes the only way of winning them into a compliance. And then they took care to have them deliver'd in such ambiguous terms, as to admit of different constructions according to the exigency of the times; so that they were generally interpreted to the advantage of the state, unless sometimes there happen'd to be bribery, or flattery in the case; as when *Demosthenes* complain'd that the *Pythia* spoke as *Philip* would have her. The most numerous, and of greatest repute were the Oracles of *Apollo*, who in subordination to *Jupiter*, was appointed to preside over, and inspire all sorts of prophets and diviners. And amongst these, the *Delphian* challeng'd the first place, not so much in respect of its antiquity, as its perspicuity and certainty; insomuch that the answers of the *Tripos* came to be used proverbially for clear and infallible truths. Here we must not omit the first *Pythia* or priestess of this famous Oracle in heroic verse. They found a secret charm in numbers, which made every thing look pompous and weighty. And hence it became the general practice of legislators, and philosophers, to deliver their laws and maxims in that dress: And scarce any thing in those ages was writ of excellence or moment but in verse. This was the dawn of poetry, which soon grew into repute; and so long as it serv'd to such noble purposes as religion and government, poets were highly honour'd, and admitted into a share of the administration. But by that time it arriv'd to any perfection, they pursu'd more mean and servile ends; and as they prostituted their muse, and debased the subject, they sunk proportionably in their esteem and dignity. As to the history of Oracles, we find them mention'd in the very infancy of *Greece*; and it is as uncertain when they were finally extinct, as when they began. For they often lost their prophetick faculty for some time, and recover'd it again. I know 'tis a common opinion, that they were universally silenc'd upon our Saviour's appearance in the world: And if the Devil had been permitted for so many ages to delude mankind, it might probably have been so. But we are assur'd from history, that several of them continu'd till the reign of *Julian* the apostate, and were consulted by him: And therefore I look upon the whole business as of human contrivance; an egregious imposture founded upon superstition, and carry'd on by policy and interest, till the brighter Oracles of the holy scriptures dispell'd these mists of error and enthusiasm.'

285. Pelasgic, Dodonæan Jove.] *Achilles* invokes *Jupiter* with these particular appellations, and represents to him the services perform'd by these priests and prophets, making these honours paid in his own country, his claim for the protection of this Deity. *Jupiter* was look'd upon as the first cause of all divination and Oracles, from whence he had the appellation of πανομφαῖος [author of all omens], *Il*. 8. v. 250. The first Oracle of *Dodona* was founded by the *Pelasgi*, the most ancient of all the inhabitants of *Greece*, which is confirm'd by this verse of *Hesiod*, preserv'd by the Scholiast on *Sophocles Trachin.*

Δωδώνην, φηγόν τε Πελασγῶν ἔδρανον ἧκεν.

[He came to Dodona, the oak and abode of the Pelasgi.]

The oaks of this place were said to be endow'd with voice, and prophetic spirit; the priests who gave answers concealing themselves in these trees; a practice which the pious frauds of succeeding ages have render'd not improbable.

288. *Whose groves the* Selli, *race austere!* &c.] *Homer* seems to me to say clearly enough, that these priests lay on the ground and forbore the bath, to honour by these austerities the God they serv'd; for he says, σοὶ ναίουσ' ἀνιπτόποδες [who, to please you, keep their feet unwashed] and this σοὶ can in my opinion only signify *for you*, that is to say, *to*

please you, and *for your honour*. This example is remarkable, but I do not think it singular; and the earliest antiquity may furnish us with the like of pagans, who by an austere life try'd to please their Gods. Nevertheless I am obliged to say, that *Strabo*, who speaks very much at large of these *Selli* in his *7th* book, has not taken this austerity of life for an effect of their devotion, but for a remain of the grossness of their ancestors; who being barbarians, and straying from country to country, had no bed but the earth, and never used a bath. But it is no way unlikely that what was in the first *Pelasgians* (who founded this Oracle) only custom and use, might be continu'd by these priests thro' devotion. How many things do we at this day see, which were in their original only ancient manner, and which are continu'd thro' zeal and a spirit of religion? It is very probable that these priests by this hard living had a mind to attract the admiration and confidence of a people who lov'd luxury and delicacy so much. I was willing to search into antiquity for the original of these *Selli*, priests of *Jupiter*, but found nothing so ancient as *Homer*: *Herodotus* writes in his second book, that the Oracle of *Dodona* was the ancientest in *Greece*, and that it was a long time the only one; but what he adds, that it was founded by an *Egyptian* woman, who was the priestess of it, is contradicted by this passage of *Homer*, who shews, that in the time of the *Trojan* war this temple was serv'd by men call'd *Selli*, and not by women. *Strabo* informs us of a curious ancient tradition, importing, that this temple was at first built in *Thessaly*, that from thence it was carry'd into *Dodona*, that several women who had plac'd their devotion there follow'd it, and that in process of time the priestesses used to be chosen from among the descendents of those women. To return to these *Selli*, *Sophocles*, who of all the *Greek* poets is he who has most imitated *Homer*, speaks in like manner of these priests in one of his plays, where *Hercules* says to his son *Hillus*; 'I will declare to thee a new Oracle, which perfectly agrees with this ancient one; I my self having enter'd into the sacred wood inhabited by the austere *Selli*, who lie on the ground, writ this answer of the oak, which is consecrated to my father *Jupiter*, and which renders his oracles in all languages.'   *Dacier.*

288.] *Homer* in this verse uses a word which I think singular and remarkable, ὑποφῆται [under-prophets]. I cannot believe that it was put simply for προφῆται, but am persuaded that this term includes some particular sense, and shews some custom but little known, which I would willingly discover. In the scholia of *Didymus* there is this remark: 'They call'd those who serv'd in the temple, and who explain'd the Oracles render'd by the priests, *hypothets*, or *under-prophets.*' It is certain that there were in the temples servitors, or subaltern ministers, who for the sake of gain, undertook to explain the Oracles which were obscure. This custom seems very well establish'd in the *Ion* of *Euripides*; where that young child (after having said that the priestess is seated on the tripod, and renders the Oracles which *Apollo* dictates to her) addresses himself to those who serve in the temple, and bids them go and wash in the *Castalian* fountain, to come again into the temple and explain the Oracles to those who should demand the explication of them. *Homer* therefore means to shew, that these *Selli* were, in the temple of *Dodona*, those subaltern ministers that interpreted the Oracles. But this, after all, does not appear to agree with the present passage: For, besides that the custom was not establish'd in *Homer*'s time, and that there is no footstep of it founded in that early age; these *Selli* (of whom *Homer* speaks) are not here ministers subordinate to others, they are plainly the chief priests. The explication of this word therefore must be elsewhere sought, and I shall offer my conjecture, which I ground upon the nature of this Oracle of *Dodona*, which was very different from all the other Oracles: In all other temples the priests deliver'd the Oracles which they had receiv'd from their Gods, immediately: But in the temple of *Dodona*, *Jupiter* did not utter his oracles to his priests, but to his *Selli*; he render'd them to the oaks, and the wonderful oaks render'd them to the priests, who declared them to those who consulted them: So these priests were not properly προφῆται, prophets, since they did not receive those answers from the mouth of their God immediately; but they were ὑποφῆται, under-prophets, because they receiv'd them from the mouth of the oaks, if I may say so. The oaks, properly speaking, were the prophets, the first interpreters of *Jupiter*'s Oracles; and the *Selli* were ὑποφῆται, under-prophets, because they pronounc'd what the Oaks had said. Thus *Homer* in one single word includes a very curious piece of antiquity.   *Dacier.*

306. *Great* Jove *consents to half.*] *Virgil* has finely imitated this in his 11*th Æneid.*

> *Audiit, & voti Phœbus succedere partem*
> *Mente dedit; partem volucres dispersit in auras.*
> *Sterneret ut subita turbatam morte Camillam*
> *Annuit oranti; reducem ut patria alta videret*
> *Non dedit, inque notos vocem vertere procellæ.*

> [*Apollo* heard, and granting half his pray'r,
> Shuffled in winds the rest, and toss'd in empty air.
> He gives the death desir'd; his safe return
> By southern tempests to the seas is borne.]

314. *As wasps, provok'd,* &c.] One may observe, that tho' *Homer* sometimes takes his similitudes from the meanest and smallest things in nature, yet he orders it so as by their appearance to signalize and give lustre to his greatest heroes. Here he likens a body of *Myrmidons* to a nest of wasps, not on account of their strength and bravery, but of their heat and resentment. *Virgil* has imitated these humble comparisons, as when he compares the builders of *Carthage* to bees. *Homer* has carry'd it a little farther in another place, where he compares the soldiers to flies, for their busy industry and perseverance about a dead body; not diminishing his heroes by the size of these small animals, but raising his comparisons from certain properties inherent in them, which deserve our observation.   *Eustathius.*

This brings into my mind a pretty rural simile in *Spencer*, which is very much in the simplicity of the old father of poetry.

> *As gentle shepherd in sweet even-tide,*
> *When ruddy* Phœbus *'gins to welke in west,*
> *High on a hill, his flock to viewen wide,*
> *Marks which do bite their hasty supper best;*
> *A cloud of cumb'rous gnats do him molest,*
> *All striving to infix their feeble stings,*
> *That from their noyance he no whit can rest,*
> *But with his clownish hand their tender wings*
> *He brusheth oft, and oft doth mar their murmurings.*

354. *So when thick clouds,* &c.] All the commentators take this comparison in a sense different from that in which it is here translated. They suppose *Jupiter* is here described cleaving the air with a flash of lightning, and spreading a gleam of light over a high mountain, which a black cloud held bury'd in Darkness. The application is made to *Patroclus* falling on the *Trojans*, and giving respite to the *Greeks*, who were plung'd in obscurity. *Eustathius* gives this interpretation, but at the same time acknowledges it improper in this comparison to represent the extinction of the flames by the darting of lightning. This explanation is solely founded on the expression στεροπηγερέτα Ζεύς [Zeus the lightning-compellor], *fulgurator Jupiter*, which epithet is often applied when no such action is supposed. The most obvious signification of the words in this passage, gives a more natural and agreeable image, and admits of a juster application. The simile seems to be of *Jupiter* dispersing a black cloud which had cover'd a high mountain, whereby a beautiful prospect, which was before hid in darkness, suddenly appears. This is applicable to the present state of the *Greeks*, after *Patroclus* had extinguish'd the flames, which began to spread clouds of smoak over the fleet. It is *Homer*'s design in his comparisons to apply them to the most obvious and sensible image of the thing to be illustrated; which his commentators too frequently endeavour to hide by moral and allegorical refinements; and thus injure the Poet more, by attributing to him what does not belong to him, than by refusing him what is really his own.

It is much the same image with that of *Milton* in his second book, tho' apply'd in a very different way.

> *As when from mountain tops the dusky clouds*
> *Ascending, while the north wind sleeps, o'erspread*
> *Heav'ns chearful face; the low'ring element*
> *Scowls o'er the darkned landskip snow or show'r;*
> *If chance the radiant sun with farewell sweet*
> *Extend his evening beam, the fields revive,*
> *The birds their notes renew, the bleating herds*
> *Attest their joy, that hill and vally rings.*

390. Amisodarus, *who*, &c.] *Amisodarus* was King of *Caria*; *Bellerophon* married his daughter. The ancients guess'd from this passage that the *Chimæra* was not a fiction, since *Homer* marks the time wherein she liv'd, and the Prince with whom she liv'd; they thought it was some beast of that Prince's herds, who being grown furious and mad, had done a great deal of mischief, like the *Calydonian* boar.   *Eustathius.*

433. *Yet stops, and turns, and saves his lov'd allies.*] *Homer* represents *Hector*, as he retires, making a stand from time to time, to save his troops: And he expresses it by this single word ἀνέμιμνε; for ἀναμίμνειν does not only signify to *stay*, but likewise in retiring to stop from time to time; for this is the power of the preposition ἀνά, as in the word ἀναμάχεσθαι, which signifies to *fight by fits and starts*; ἀναπαλαίειν, to *wrestle several times*, and in many others.   *Eustathius.*

459. *From bank to bank th' immortal coursers flew*, &c.] *Homer* has made of *Hector*'s horses all that poetry could make of common and mortal horses; they stand on the bank of the ditch foaming and neighing for madness that they cannot leap it. But the immortal horses of *Achilles* find no obstacle; they leap the ditch, and fly into the plain.

Eustathius.

466.   *As when in autumn* Jove *his fury pours –*
      – When guilty mortals &c.]

The Poet in this image of an inundation, takes occasion to mention a sentiment of great piety, that such calamities were the effects of divine justice punishing the sins of mankind. This might probably refer to the tradition of an universal deluge, which was very common among the ancient heathen writers; most of them ascribing the cause of this deluge to the wrath of heaven provoked by the wickedness of men. *Diodorus Siculus, l.* 15. *c.* 5. speaking of an earthquake and inundation, which destroyed a great part of *Greece* in the 101*st Olympiad*, has these Words. *There was a great dispute concerning the cause of this calamity: The natural philosophers generally ascribed such events to necessary causes, not to any divine hand: But they who had more devout sentiments gave a more probable account hereof; asserting, that it was the divine vengeance alone that brought this destruction upon men who had offended the Gods with their impiety.* And then proceeds to give an account of those crimes which drew down this punishment upon them.

This is one, among a thousand instances, of *Homer*'s indirect and oblique manner of introducing moral sentences and instructions. These agreeably break in upon his reader even in descriptions and poetical parts, where one naturally expects only painting and amusement. We have virtue put upon us by surprize, and are pleas'd to find a thing where we should never have look'd to meet with it. I must do a noble *English* poet the justice to observe, that it is this particular art that is the very distinguishing excellence of *Cooper's-Hill*; throughout which, the descriptions of places, and images rais'd by the Poet, are still tending to some hint, or leading into some reflection, upon moral life or political institution: Much in the same manner as the real sight of such scenes and prospects is apt to give the mind a compos'd turn, and incline it to thoughts and contemplations that have a relation to the object.

480.   *Between the space where silver* Simoïs *flows,*
       Where lay the ships, and where the rampires rose.]

It looks at first sight as if *Patroclus* was very punctual in obeying the orders of *Achilles*, when he hinders the *Trojans* from ascending to their town, and holds an engagement with 'em between the ships, the river, and the wall. But he seems afterwards thro' very haste to have slipt his commands, for his orders were that he should drive 'em from the ships, and then presently return; but he proceeds farther, and his death is the consequence.   *Eustathius.*

512. *When now* Sarpedon, &c.] The Poet preparing to recount the death of *Sarpedon*, it will not be improper to give a sketch of some particulars which constitute a character the most faultless and amiable in the whole Iliad. This hero is by birth superiour to all the chiefs of either side, being the only son of *Jupiter* engaged in this war. His qualities are no way unworthy his descent, since he every where appears equal in valour, prudence, and eloquence, to the most admired heroes: Nor are these excellences blemish'd with any of those defects with which the most distinguishing characters of the Poem are stain'd. So that the nicest criticks cannot find any thing to offend their delicacy, but must be obliged to own the manners of this hero perfect. His valour is neither rash nor boisterous; his prudence neither timorous nor tricking; and his eloquence neither talkative nor boasting. He never reproaches the living, or insults the dead: but appears uniform thro' his conduct in the war, acted with the same generous sentiments that engaged him in it, having no interest in the quarrel but to succour his allies in distress. This noble life is ended with a death as glorious; for in his last moments he has no other concern, but for the honour of his friends, and the event of the day.

Homer justly represents such a character to be attended with universal esteem: As he was greatly honour'd when living, he is as much lamented when dead, as the chief prop of *Troy.* The Poet by his death, even before that of *Hector*, prepares us to expect the destruction of that town, when its two great defenders are no more: and in order to make it the more signal and remarkable, it is the only death in the Iliad attended with prodigies: Even his funeral is perform'd by divine assistance, he being the only hero whose body is carried back to be interr'd in his native country, and honour'd with monuments erected to his fame. These peculiar and distinguishing honours seem appropriated by our author to him alone, as the reward of a merit superior to all his other less perfect heroes.

522. *As when two vulturs.*] *Homer* compares *Patroclus* and *Sarpedon* to two vulturs, because they appeared to be of equal strength and abilities, when they had dismounted from their chariots. For this reason he has chosen to compare them to birds of the same kind; as on another occasion, to image the like equality of strength, he resembles both *Hector* and *Patroclus* to lions; But a little after this place, diminishing the force of *Sarpedon*, he compares him to a bull, and *Patroclus* to a lion. He has placed these vulturs upon a high rock, because it is their nature to perch there, rather than in the boughs of trees. Their crooked talons make them unfit to walk on the ground, they could not fight steadily in the air, and therefore their fittest place is the rock.   *Eustathius.*

535. *Say, shall I snatch him from impending Fate.*] It appears by this passage, that *Homer* was of opinion, that the power of God could over-rule fate or destiny. It has puzzled many to distinguish exactly the notion of the heathens as to this point. Mr *Dryden* contends that *Jupiter* was limited by the destinies, or (to use his expression) was no better than book-keeper to them. He grounds it upon a passage in the tenth book of *Virgil*, where *Jupiter* mentions this instance of *Sarpedon* as a proof of his yielding to the fates. But both that and his citation from *Ovid*, amounts to no more than that *Jupiter* gave way to destiny, not that he could not prevent it; the contrary to which is plain from his doubt and deliberation in this place. And indeed whatever may be inferr'd of other poets, *Homer*'s opinion at least, as to the dispensations of God to man, has ever seem'd to me very clear, and distinctly agreeable to truth. We shall find, if we examine his whole works with an eye to this doctrine, that he assigns three causes of all the good and evil that happens in this world, which he takes a particular care to distinguish. First the *will of God*, superiour to all.

— Διὸς δ' ἐτελείετο βουλή.   *Il.* 1.

[And the will of God was working out.]

— Θεὸς διὰ πάντα τελευτᾷ.   *Il.* 19. v. 90.

[God brings all things to pass.]

— Ζεὺς ἀγαθόν τε κακόν τε διδοῖ, — &c.

[Zeus sometimes brings good and sometimes evil.

Od. 4. 237.]

Secondly, *destiny* or *fate*, meaning the laws and order of nature affecting the constitutions of men, and disposing them to good or evil, prosperity or misfortune; which the supreme being, if it be his pleasure, may over-rule (as he is inclin'd to do in this place) but which he generally suffers to take effect. Thirdly, our own *free will*, which either by prudence overcomes those natural influences and passions, or by folly suffers us to fall under them.   *Odyss.* I. v. 32.

'Ω πόποι, οἷον δή νυ Θεοὺς βροτοὶ αἰτιόωνται.
'Εξ ἡμέων γάρ φασι κάκ' ἔμμεναι· οἱ δὲ καὶ αὐτοὶ
Σφῇσιν ἀτασθαλίῃσιν ὑπὲρ μόρον ἄλγε' ἔχουσιν.

Why charge mankind on heav'n their own offence,
And call their woes the crime of providence?
Blind! who themselves their miseries create,
And perish by their folly, not their fate.

551.   *Let Sleep and Death convey, by thy command,*
The breathless body to his native land.]

The history or fable receiv'd in *Homer*'s time imported, that *Sarpedon* was interr'd in *Lycia*, but it said nothing of his death. This gave the Poet the liberty of making him die at *Troy*, provided that after his death he was carried into *Lycia*, to preserve the fable. The Expedient proposed by *Juno* solves all; *Sarpedon* dies at *Troy*, and is interr'd at *Lycia*; and what renders this probable, is, that in those times, as at this day, Princes and persons of quality who died in foreign parts, were carried into their own country to be laid in the tombs of their fathers. The antiquity of this custom cannot be doubted, since it was practis'd in the Patriarchs times: *Jacob* dying in *Egypt*, orders his children to carry him into the land of *Canaan*, where he desired to be buried. *Gen.* 49. 29.   *Dacier.*

560. *A show'r of blood.*] As to showers of a bloody colour, many both ancient and modern naturalists agree in asserting the reality of such appearances, tho' they account for 'em differently. You may see a very odd solution of 'em in *Eustathius*, Note on v. 7 of the eleventh Iliad.

What seems the most probable, is that of *Fromondus* in his *Meteorology*, who observ'd, that a shower of this kind, which gave great cause of wonder, was nothing but a quantity of very small red insects, beat down to the earth by a heavy shower, whereby the ground was spotted in several places, as with drops of blood.

572.   – Achilles' *mortal steed,*
       The gen'rous Pedasus –.]

For the other two horses of *Achilles*, *Xanthus* and *Balius*, were immortal, as we have already seen in this book. 'Tis a merry conceit of *Eustathius*, that *Pedasus* is only said to be mortal, because of the three horses he only was a gelding. 'Tis pity poor *Pedasus* had not a better fate, to have recompensed the loss of his immortality.

605. Glaucus, *be bold*, &c.] This dying speech of *Sarpedon* deserves particular notice, being made up of noble sentiments, and fully answering the character of this brave and generous Prince, which he preserves in his last moments. Being sensible of approaching death, without any transports of rage, or desire of revenge, he calls to his friend to take care to preserve his body and arms from becoming a prey to the enemy: And this he says without any regard to himself, but out of the most tender concern for his friend's reputation, who must for ever become infamous if he fails in this point of honour and duty. If we conceive this said by the expiring hero, his dying looks fix'd on his wounded disconsolate friend, the spear remaining in his body, and the victor standing by in a kind of extasy surveying his conquest; these circumstances will form a very moving picture. *Patroclus* all this time, either out of humanity or surprize, omits to pull out the spear, which however he does not long forbear, but with it drawing forth his vitals, puts a period to this gallant life.

637.   *– pierc'd with pain*
       That thrils my arm, and shoots thro' ev'ry vein.]

There seems to be an oversight in this place. *Glaucus* in the twelfth book had been wounded with an arrow by *Teucer* at the attack of the wall; and here so long after, we find him still on the field, *in the sharpest anguish of his wound, the blood not being yet stanch'd*, &c. In the speech that next follows to *Hector*, there is also something liable to censure, when he imputes to the negligence of the *Trojans* the death of

Sarpedon, of which they knew nothing till that very speech inform'd 'em. I beg leave to pass over these things without exposing or defending them, tho' such as these may be sufficient grounds for a most inveterate war among the criticks.

696. *Great* Jove – *O'er the fierce armies pours pernicious night.*] *Homer* calls here by the name of night, the whirlwinds of thick dust which rise from beneath the feet of the combatants, and which hinders them from knowing one another. Thus poetry knows how to convert the most natural things into miracles; these two armies are buried in dust round *Sarpedon*'s body; 'tis *Jupiter* who pours upon them an obscure night, to make the battel bloodier, and to honour the funeral of his son by a greater number of victims.   *Eustathius.*

746. *And skill'd in dancing.*] This stroke of raillery upon *Meriones* is founded on the custom of his country. For the *Cretans* were peculiarly addicted to this exercise, and in particular are said to have invented the *Pyrrhic* dance, which was perform'd in complete armour. See Note on v. 797. the thirteenth book.

831. *Then Sleep and Death,* &c.] It is the Notion of *Eustathius*, that by this interment of *Sarpedon*, where *Sleep* and *Death* are concerned, *Homer* seems to intimate, that there was nothing else but an empty monument of that hero in *Lycia*, for he delivers him not to any real or solid persons, but to certain unsubstantial phantoms to conduct his body thither. He was forced (continues my author) to make use of these machines, since there were no other deities he could with any likelihood employ about this work; for the ancients (as appears from *Euripides, Hippolyto*) had a superstition that all dead bodies were offensive to the Gods, they being of a nature celestial and uncorruptible. But this last remark is impertinent, since we see in this very place *Apollo* is employ'd in adorning and embalming the body of *Sarpedon.*

What I think better accounts for the passage, is what *Philostratus in Heroicis* affirms, that this alludes to a piece of antiquity. 'The *Lycians* shew'd the body of *Sarpedon*, strew'd over with aromatical spices, in such a graceful composure, that he seem'd to be only asleep: And it was this that gave rise to the fiction of *Homer*, that his rites were perform'd by *Sleep* and *Death*.'

But after all these refin'd observations, it is probable the Poet intended only to represent the death of this favourite Son of *Jupiter*, and one of his most amiable characters, in a gentle and agreeable view, without any circumstances of dread or horrour; intimating by this fiction, that he was delivered out of all the tumults and miseries of life by two imaginary deities, *Sleep* and *Death*, who alone can give mankind ease and exemption from their misfortunes.

847. *Who, first, brave hero!* &c.] The Poet in a very moving and solemn way turns his discourse to *Patroclus.* He does not accost his muse, as it is usual with him to do, but enquires of the hero himself who was the first, and who the last, who fell by his hand? This address distinguishes and signalizes *Patroclus*, (to whom *Homer* uses it more frequently, than I remember on any other occasion) as if he was some genius or divine being, and at the same time it is very pathetical and apt to move our compassion. The same kind of apostrophe is used by *Virgil* to *Camilla.*

> *Quem telo primum, quem postremum, aspera virgo!*
> *Dejicis? Aut quot humi morientia corpora fundis?*

> [Who foremost, and who last, heroick maid,
>   On the cold earth were by thy courage laid?
>   Thy spear, of mountain ash, *Eumenius* first,
>   With fury driv'n, from side to side transpierc'd.]

904. *What skilful divers,* &c.] The original is literally thus: *'Tis pity he is not nearer the sea, he would furnish good quantities of excellent oisters, and the storms would not frighten him; see how he exercises and plunges from the top of his chariot into the plain! Who would think that there were such good divers at* Troy? This seems to be a little too long; and if this passage be really *Homer*'s, I could almost swear that he intended to let us know, that a good soldier may be an indifferent jester. But I very much doubt whether this passage be his: It is very likely these five last verses were added by some of the ancient criticks, whose caprices *Homer* has frequently undergone; or perhaps some of the rhapsodists, who in reciting his verses, made additions of their own to please their auditors. And what persuades me of its being so, is, that 'tis by no means probable that *Patroclus*, who had lately blamed *Meriones* for his little raillery against *Æneas*, and told him, 'that 'twas not by raillery or invective that they were to repel the *Trojans*, but by dint of blows; that council required words, but war deeds:' It is by no means probable, I say, that the same *Patroclus* should forget that excellent precept, and amuse himself with raillery, especially in the sight of *Hector*. I am therefore of opinion that *Patroclus* said no more than this verse, Ω πόποι, &c. *Good Gods! what an active* Trojan *it is, and how cleverly he dives,* and that the five following are strangers, tho' very ancient.   *Dacier.*

I must just take notice, that however mean or ill placed these railleries may appear, there have not been wanting such fond lovers of *Homer* as have admired and imitated them. *Milton* himself is of this number, as may be seen from those very low jests, which he has put into the mouth of *Satan* and his angels in the sixth book. What *Æneas* says to *Meriones* upon his dancing is nothing so trivial as those lines, where after the displosion of their diabolical enginry, angel rowling on archangel, they are thus derided.

> *– When we propounded terms*
> *Of composition, strait they chang'd their minds,*
> *Flew off, and into strange vagaries fell,*
> *As they would dance; yet for a dance they seem'd*
> *Somewhat extravagant and wild, perhaps*
> *For joy of offer'd peace – &c.*
> *– Terms that amus'd 'em all,*
> *And stumbled many; who receives them right*
> *Had need from head to foot well understand:*
> *Not understood, this gift they have besides,*
> *They show us when our foes walk not upright.*

952. Apollo *dreadful,* &c.] If *Homer* is resolv'd to do any thing extraordinary, or arbitrary, which his readers may not very well relish, he takes care however to prepare them by degrees for receiving such innovations. He had before given us a sketch of this trick of the Gods in the 13*th* book, where *Neptune* serves *Alcathous* much in the same manner. *Apollo* here carries it a little farther; and both these are specimens of what we are to expect from *Minerva* at the death of *Hector* in *Il.* 22.

1003. *Lie there,* Patroclus! &c.] There is much spirit in this sarcasm of *Hector* upon *Patroclus*: Nor is *Achilles* exempt from the severity of the reflection, who (as he imagines) had persuaded his dearest friend to attempt exploits that were impracticable. He touches him also, for staying at home in security himself, and encouraging *Patroclus* to undertake this perilous adventure, and to seek after spoils which he was never like to enjoy.   *Eustathius.*

1026. – *Hear my latest breath,*
          The Gods inspire it. –]

It is an opinion of great antiquity, that when the soul is on the point of being delivered from the body, and makes a nearer approach to the divine nature, at such a time its views are stronger and clearer, and the mind endow'd with a spirit of true prediction. So *Artemon* of *Miletum* says in his book of dreams, that when the soul hath collected all its powers from every limb and part of the body, and is just ready to be severed from it, at that time it becomes prophetical. *Socrates* also in his defence to the *Athenians*, 'I am now arrived at the verge of life, wherein it is familiar with people to foretell what will come to pass.'   *Eustathius.*

This opinion seems alluded to in those admirable lines of *Waller*:

> *Leaving the old, both worlds at once they view,*
> *Who stand upon the threshold of the new.*

1032. *The death of* Patroclus.] I sometimes think I am in respect to *Homer* much like *Sancho Panca* with regard to *Don Quixote*. I believe upon the whole that no mortal ever came near him for wisdom, learning, and all good qualities. But sometimes there are certain starts which I cannot tell what to make of, and am forced to own that my master is a little out of the way, if not quite beside himself. The present passage of the death of *Patroclus*, attended with so many odd circumstances to overthrow this hero (who might, for all I can see, as decently have fallen by the force of *Hector*) are what I am at a loss to excuse, and must indeed (in my own opinion) give them up to the criticks. I really think almost all those parts in *Homer* which have been objected against with most clamour and fury, are honestly defensible, and none of them (to confess my private sentiment) seem to me to be faults of any consideration, except this conduct in the death of *Patro-clus*; the length of *Nestor*'s discourse in *Lib.* 11. the speech of *Achilles*'s horse in the 19*th.* the conversation of that hero with *Æneas* in *Lib.* 20. and the manner of *Hector*'s flight round the walls of *Troy* in *Lib.* 22. I hope, after so free a confession, no reasonable modern will think me touch'd with the Ὁμηρομανία of Madam *Dacier* and others. I am sensible of the extremes which mankind run into, in extolling and depreciating authors: We are not more violent and unreasonable in attacking those who are not yet establish'd in fame, than in defending those who are, even in every minute trifle. Fame is a debt, which when we have kept from people as long as we can, we pay with a prodigious interest, which amounts to twice the value of the principal. Thus 'tis with ancient works as with ancient coins, they pass for a vast deal more than they were worth at first; and the very obscurities and deformities which time has thrown upon them, are the sacred rust, which enhances their value with all true lovers of antiquity.

But as I have own'd what seem my author's faults, and subscribed to the opinion of *Horace*, that *Homer* sometimes nods; I think I ought to add that of *Longinus* as to such negligences. I can no way so well conclude the notes to this book as with the translation of it.

'It may not be improper to discuss the question in general, which of the two is the more estimable, a faulty sublime, or a faultless mediocrity? And consequently, if of two works, one has the greater number of beauties, and the other attains directly to the sublime, which of these shall in equity carry the prize? I am really persuaded that the true sublime is incapable of that purity which we find in compositions of a lower strain, and in effect that too much accuracy sinks the spirit of an author; whereas the case is generally the same with the favourites of nature, and those of fortune, who with the best oeconomy cannot, in the great abundance they are blest with, attend to the minuter articles of their expence. Writers of a cool imagination are cautious in their management, and venture nothing, merely to gain the character of being correct; but the sublime is bold and enterprizing, notwithstanding that on every advance the danger encreaseth. Here probably some will say that men take a malicious satisfaction in exposing the blemishes of an author; that his errors are never forgot, while the most exquisite beauties leave but very imperfect traces on the memory. To obviate this objection, I will solemnly declare, that in my criticisms on *Homer* and other authors, who are universally allowed to be authentic standards of the sublime, tho' I have censur'd their failings with as much freedom as any one, yet I have not presum'd to accuse them of voluntary faults, but have gently remark'd some little defects and negligences, which the mind being intent on nobler ideas did not condescend to regard. And on these principles I will venture to lay it down for a maxim, that the sublime (purely on account of its grandeur) is preferable to all other kinds of style, however it may fall into some inequalities. The Argonauticks of *Apollonius* are faultless in their kind;

and *Theocritus* hath shewn the happiest vein imaginable for pastorals, excepting those in which he has deviated from the country: And yet if it were put to your choice, would you have your name descend to posterity with the reputation of either of those poets, rather than with that of *Homer*? Nothing can be more correct than the *Erigone* of *Eratosthenes*: but is he therefore a greater poet than *Archilochus*, in whose composures perspicuity and order are often wanting; the divine fury of his genius being too impatient for restraint, and superior to law? Again, do you prefer the odes of *Bacchilides* to *Pindar*'s, or the scenes of *Ion* of *Chios* to those of *Sophocles*? Their writings are allow'd to be correct, polite, and delicate; whereas, on the other hand, *Pindar* and *Sophocles* sometimes hurry on with the greatest impetuosity, and like a devouring flame seize and set on fire whatever comes in their way; but on a sudden the conflagration is extinguish'd, and they miserably flag when no body expects it. Yet none have so little discernment as not to prefer the single *Oedipus* of *Sophocles* to all the tragedies that *Ion* ever brought on the stage.

'In our decisions therefore on the Characters of these great men, who have illustrated what is useful and necessary with all the graces and elevation of style; we must impartially confess that, with all their errors, they have more perfections than the nature of man can almost be conceiv'd capable of attaining: For 'tis merely human to excel in other kinds of writing, but the sublime ennobleth our nature, and makes near approaches to divinity: He who commits no faults, is barely read without censure; but a genius truly great excites admiration. In short, the magnificence of a single period in one of these admirable authors is sufficient to attone for all their defects: Nay farther, if any one should collect from *Homer*, *Demosthenes*, *Plato*, and other celebrated heroes of antiquity, the little errors that have escap'd them; they would not bear the least proportion to the infinite beauties to be met with in every page of their writings. 'Tis on this account that envy, thro' so many ages, hath never been able to wrest from them the prize of eloquence which their merits have so justly acquir'd: An Acquisition which they still are, and will, in all probability continue possess'd of,

> '*As long as streams in silver mazes rove,*
> *Or spring with annual green renews the grove.*'
>
> Mr FENTON.

THE
ILIAD
OF
HOMER

VOLUME V

THE
SEVENTEENTH BOOK
OF THE
ILIAD

The ARGUMENT

The seventh Battel, for the Body of *Patroclus*: The Acts of *Menelaus*

Menelaus, *upon the death of* Patroclus, *defends his body from the enemy:* Euphorbus *who attempts it, is slain.* Hector *advancing,* Menelaus *retires, but soon returns with* Ajax, *and drives him off. This* Glaucus *objects to* Hector *as a flight, who thereupon puts on the armour he had won from* Patroclus, *and renews the battel. The* Greeks *give way, till* Ajax *rallies them:* Æneas *sustains the* Trojans. Æneas *and* Hector *attempt the chariot of* Achilles, *which is borne off by* Automedon. *The horses of* Achilles *deplore the loss of* Patroclus: *Jupiter covers his body with a thick darkness: The noble prayer of* Ajax *on that occasion.* Menelaus *sends* Antilochus *to* Achilles, *with the news of* Patroclus's *death: Then returns to the fight, where, tho' attack'd with the utmost fury, he, and* Meriones *assisted by the* Ajaxes, *bear off the body to the ships.*

The time is the evening of the eight and twentieth day. The scene lies in the fields before Troy.

On the cold earth divine *Patroclus* spread,
Lies pierc'd with wounds among the vulgar dead.
Great *Menelaüs*, touch'd with gen'rous woe,
Springs to the front, and guards him from the foe:
5 Thus round her new fal'n young, the heifer moves,
Fruit of her throes, and first-born of her loves,
And anxious, (helpless as he lies, and bare)
Turns, and re-turns her, with a mother's care.
Oppos'd to each, that near the carcase came,
10 His broad shield glimmers, and his lances flame.
　　The son of *Panthus*, skill'd the dart to send,
Eyes the dead hero and insults the friend.
This hand, *Atrides*, laid *Patroclus* low;
Warriour! desist, nor tempt an equal blow:
15 To me the spoils my prowess won, resign;
Depart with life, and leave the glory mine.
　　The *Trojan* thus: The *Spartan* monarch burn'd
With generous anguish, and in scorn return'd.
Laugh'st thou not, *Jove!* from thy superiour throne,
20 When mortals boast of prowess not their own?
Not thus the lion glories in his might,
Nor panther braves his spotted foe in fight,
Nor thus the boar (those terrours of the plain)
Man only vaunts his force, and vaunts in vain.
25 But far the vainest of the boastful kind
These sons of *Panthus* vent their haughty mind.
Yet 'twas but late, beneath my conqu'ring steel
This boaster's brother, *Hyperenor*, fell,

Against our arm which rashly he defy'd,
Vain was his vigour, and as vain his pride.   30
These eyes beheld him on the dust expire,
No more to chear his spouse, or glad his sire.
Presumptuous youth! like his shall be thy doom,
Go, wait thy brother to the *Stygian* gloom;
Or while thou may'st, avoid the threaten'd fate;   35
Fools stay to feel it, and are wise too late.

    Unmov'd, *Euphorbus* thus: That action known,
Come, for my brother's blood repay thy own.
His weeping father claims thy destin'd head,
And spouse, a widow in her bridal bed.   40
On these thy conquer'd spoils I shall bestow,
To sooth a consort's and a parent's woe.
No longer then defer the glorious strife,
Let heav'n decide our fortune, fame, and life.

    Swift as the word, the missile lance he flings,   45
The well-aim'd weapon on the buckler rings,
But blunted by the brass innoxious falls.
On *Jove* the father, great *Atrides* calls,
Nor flies the jav'lin from his arm in vain,
It pierc'd his throat, and bent him to the plain;   50
Wide thro' the neck appears the grizly wound,
Prone sinks the warriour, and his arms resound.
The shining circlets of his golden hair,
Which ev'n the Graces might be proud to wear,
Instarr'd with gems and gold, bestrow the shore,   55
With dust dishonour'd, and deform'd with gore.

    As the young olive, in some sylvan scene,
Crown'd by fresh fountains with eternal green,
Lifts the gay head, in snowy flow'rets fair,
And plays and dances to the gentle air;   60
When lo! a whirlwind from high heav'n invades
The tender plant, and withers all its shades;
It lies uprooted from its genial bed,
A lovely ruin, now defac'd and dead.
Thus young, thus beautiful, *Euphorbus* lay,   65
While the fierce *Spartan* tore his arms away.
Proud of his deed, and glorious in the prize,
Affrighted *Troy* the tow'ring victor flies,

Flies, as before some mountain lion's ire
70 The village curs, and trembling swains retire;
When o'er the slaughter'd bull they hear him roar,
And see his jaws distil with smoking gore;
All pale with fear, at distance scatter'd round,
They shout incessant, and the vales resound.
75   Meanwhile *Apollo* view'd with envious eyes,
And urg'd great *Hector* to dispute the prize,
(In *Mentes'* shape, beneath whose martial care
The rough *Ciconians* learn'd the trade of war)
Forbear, he cry'd, with fruitless speed to chace
80 *Achilles'* coursers of æthereal race;
They stoop not, these, to mortal man's command,
Or stoop to none but great *Achilles'* hand.
Too long amus'd with a pursuit so vain,
Turn, and behold the brave *Euphorbus* slain!
85 By *Sparta* slain! for ever now supprest
The fire which burn'd in that undaunted breast!
   Thus having spoke, *Apollo* wing'd his flight
And mix'd with mortals in the toils of fight:
His words infix'd unutterable care
90 Deep in great *Hector*'s soul: Thro' all the war
He darts his anxious eye; and instant, view'd
The breathless hero in his blood imbru'd,
(Forth welling from the wound, as prone he lay)
And in the victor's hands the shining prey.
95 Sheath'd in bright arms, thro' cleaving ranks he flies,
And sends his voice in thunder to the skies:
Fierce as a flood of flame by *Vulcan* sent,
It flew, and fir'd the nations as it went.
Atrides from the voice the storm divin'd,
100 And thus explor'd his own unconquer'd mind.
   Then shall I quit *Patroclus* on the plain,
Slain in my cause, and for my honour slain,
Desert the arms, the relicks of my friend?
Or singly, *Hector* and his troops attend?
105 Sure where such partial favour heav'n bestow'd,
To brave the hero were to brave the God:
Forgive me, *Greece*, if once I quit the field;
'Tis not to *Hector*, but to heav'n I yield.

Yet, nor the God, nor heav'n, shou'd give me fear,
Did but the voice of *Ajax* reach my ear: 110
Still would we turn, still battle on the plains,
And give *Achilles* all that yet remains
Of his and our *Patroclus* – This, no more,
The Time allow'd: *Troy* thicken'd on the shore,
A sable scene! The terrors *Hector* led.   115
Slow he recedes, and sighing, quits the dead.
   So from the fold th'unwilling lion parts,
Forc'd by loud clamours, and a storm of darts;
He flies indeed, but threatens as he flies,
With heart indignant and retorted eyes.   120
Now enter'd in the *Spartan* ranks, he turn'd
His manly breast, and with new fury burn'd,
O'er all the black battalions sent his view,
And thro' the cloud the god-like *Ajax* knew;
Where lab'ring on the left the warriour stood,   125
All grim in arms, and cover'd o'er with blood,
There breathing courage, where the God of day
Had sunk each heart with terrour and dismay.
To him the King. Oh *Ajax*, oh my friend!
Haste, and *Patroclus*' lov'd remains defend: 130
The body to *Achilles* to restore,
Demands our care; Alas! we can no more!
For naked now, despoil'd of arms he lies;
And *Hector* glories in the dazling prize.
He said, and touch'd his heart. The raging pair   135
Pierce the thick battel, and provoke the war.
Already had stern *Hector* seiz'd his head,
And doom'd to *Trojan* dogs th'unhappy dead;
But soon as *Ajax* rear'd his tow'rlike shield,
Sprung to his car, and measur'd back the field.   140
His train to *Troy* the radiant armour bear,
To stand a trophy of his fame in war.
   Meanwhile great *Ajax* (his broad shield display'd)
Guards the dead hero with the dreadful shade;
And now before, and now behind he stood: 145
Thus in the center of some gloomy wood,
With many a step the lioness surrounds
Her tawny young, beset by men and hounds;

Elate her heart, and rouzing all her pow'rs,
150 Dark o'er the fiery balls, each hanging eye-brow low'rs.
Fast by his side, the gen'rous *Spartan* glows
With great revenge, and feeds his inward woes.
    But *Glaucus*, leader of the *Lycian* aids,
On *Hector* frowning, thus his flight upbraids.
155 Where now in *Hector* shall we *Hector* find?
A manly form, without a manly mind.
Is this, O Chief! a hero's boasted fame?
How vain, without the merit is the name?
Since battel is renounc'd, thy thoughts employ
160 What other methods may preserve thy *Troy*?
'Tis time to try if *Ilion*'s state can stand
By thee alone, nor ask a foreign hand;
Mean, empty boast! but shall the *Lycians* stake
Their lives for you? those *Lycians* you forsake?
165 What from thy thankless arms can we expect?
Thy friend *Sarpedon* proves thy base neglect:
Say, shall our slaughter'd bodies guard your walls,
While unreveng'd the great *Sarpedon* falls?
Ev'n where he dy'd for *Troy*, you left him there,
170 A feast for dogs, and all the fowls of air.
On my command if any *Lycian* wait,
Hence let him march, and give up *Troy* to fate.
Did such a spirit as the Gods impart
Impel one *Trojan* hand, or *Trojan* heart;
175 (Such, as shou'd burn in ev'ry soul, that draws
The sword for glory, and his country's cause);
Ev'n yet our mutual arms we might employ,
And drag yon' carcass to the walls of *Troy.*
Oh! were *Patroclus* ours, we might obtain
180 *Sarpedon*'s arms and honour'd corse again!
Greece with *Achilles*' friend shou'd be repaid,
And thus due honours purchas'd to his shade.
But words are vain – Let *Ajax* once appear,
And *Hector* trembles and recedes with fear;
185 Thou dar'st not meet the Terrours of his eye;
And lo! already, thou prepar'st to fly.
    The *Trojan* chief with fixt resentment ey'd
The *Lycian* leader, and sedate reply'd.

Say, is it just (my friend) that *Hector*'s ear
From such a warriour such a speech shou'd hear?   190
I deem'd thee once the wisest of thy kind,
But ill this insult suits a prudent mind.
I shun great *Ajax*? I desert my train?
'Tis mine to prove the rash assertion vain;
I joy to mingle where the battel bleeds,   195
And hear the thunder of the sounding steeds.
But *Jove*'s high will is ever uncontroll'd,
The strong he withers, and confounds the bold,
Now crowns with fame the mighty man, and now
Strikes the fresh garland from the victor's brow!   200
Come, thro' yon' squadrons let us hew the way,
And thou be witness, if I fear to day;
If yet a *Greek* the sight of *Hector* dread,
Or yet their hero dare defend the dead.
    Then turning to the martial hosts, he cries,   205
Ye *Trojans*, *Dardans*, *Lycians*, and Allies!
Be men (my friends) in action as in name,
And yet be mindful of your ancient fame.
Hector in proud *Achilles*' arms shall shine,
Torn from his friend, by right of conquest mine.   210
    He strode along the field, as thus he said:
(The sable plumage nodded o'er his head)
Swift thro' the spacious plain he sent a look;
One instant saw, one instant overtook
The distant band, that on the sandy shore   215
The radiant spoils to sacred *Ilion* bore.
There his own mail unbrac'd, the field bestrow'd;
His train to *Troy* convey'd the massy load.
Now blazing in th'immortal arms he stands,
The work and present of celestial hands;   220
By aged *Peleus* to *Achilles* given,
As first to *Peleus* by the court of heav'n:
His father's arms not long *Achilles* wears,
Forbid by fate to reach his father's years.
    Him, proud in triumph, glitt'ring from afar,   225
The God whose thunder rends the troubled air,
Beheld with pity; as apart he sate,
And conscious, look'd thro' all the scene of fate.

He shook the sacred honours of his head;
230 *Olympus* trembled, and the Godhead said:
      Ah wretched man! unmindful of thy end!
A moment's glory! and what fates attend?
In heav'nly panoply divinely bright
Thou stand'st, and armies tremble at thy sight
235 As at *Achilles* self! Beneath thy dart
Lies slain the great *Achilles'* dearer part:
Thou from the mighty dead those arms hast torn
Which once the greatest of mankind had worn.
Yet live! I give thee one illustrious day,
240 A blaze of glory e'er thou fad'st away.
For ah! no more *Andromache* shall come,
With joyful tears to welcome *Hector* home;
No more officious, with endearing charms,
From thy tir'd limbs unbrace *Pelides'* arms!
245   Then with his sable brow he gave the nod,
That seals his word; the sanction of the God.
The stubborn arms (by *Jove*'s command dispos'd)
Conform'd spontaneous, and around him clos'd;
Fill'd with the God, enlarg'd his members grew,
250 Thro' all his veins a sudden vigour flew,
The blood in brisker tides began to roll,
And *Mars* himself came rushing on his soul.
Exhorting loud thro' all the field he strode,
And look'd, and mov'd, *Achilles*, or a God.
255 Now *Mesthles*, *Glaucus*, *Medon* he inspires,
Now *Phorcys*, *Chromius*, and *Hippothous* fires;
The great *Thersilochus* like fury found,
Asteropæus kindled at the sound,
And *Ennomus*, in augury renown'd.
260 Hear all ye hosts, and hear, unnumber'd bands
Of neighb'ring nations, or of distant lands!
'Twas not for state we summon'd you so far,
To boast our numbers, and the pomp of war;
Ye came to fight; a valiant foe to chase,
265 To save our present, and our future race.
For this, our wealth, our products you enjoy,
And glean the relicks of exhausted *Troy.*

Now then to conquer or to die prepare,
To die, or conquer, are the terms of war.
Whatever hand shall win *Patroclus* slain,   270
Whoe'er shall drag him to the *Trojan* train,
With *Hector*'s self shall equal honours claim;
With *Hector* part the spoil, and share the fame.

   Fir'd by his words, the troops dismiss their fears,
They join, they thicken, they protend their spears;   275
Full on the *Greeks* they drive in firm array,
And each from *Ajax* hopes the glorious prey:
Vain hope! what numbers shall the field o'erspread,
What victims perish round the mighty dead?

   Great *Ajax* mark'd the growing storm from far,   280
And thus bespoke his brother of the war.
Our fatal day, alas! is come (my friend)
And all our wars and glories at an end!
'Tis not this corpse alone we guard in vain,
Condemn'd to vulturs on the *Trojan* plain;   285
We too must yield: The same sad fate must fall
On thee, on me, perhaps (my friend) on all.
See what a tempest direful *Hector* spreads,
And lo! it bursts, it thunders on our heads!
Call on our *Greeks*, if any hear the call,   290
The bravest *Greeks*: This hour demands them all.

   The warriour rais'd his voice, and wide around
The field re-echo'd the distressful sound.
Oh chiefs! oh princes! to whose hand is giv'n
The rule of men; whose glory is from heav'n!   295
Whom with due honours both *Atrides* grace:
Ye guides and guardians of our *Argive* race!
All, whom this well-known voice shall reach from far,
All, whom I see not thro' this cloud of war,
Come all! let gen'rous rage your arms employ,   300
And save *Patroclus* from the dogs of *Troy*.

   Oïlean Ajax first the voice obey'd,
Swift was his pace, and ready was his aid;
Next him *Idomeneus*, more slow with age,
And *Merion*, burning with a hero's rage.   305
The long-succeeding numbers who can name?
But all were *Greeks* and eager all for fame.

Fierce to the charge great *Hector* led the throng;
Whole *Troy* embodied, rush'd with shouts along.
310 Thus, when a mountain billow foams and raves,
Where some swoln river disembogues his waves,
Full in the mouth is stopp'd the rushing tide,
The boiling ocean works from side to side,
The river trembles to his utmost shore,
315 And distant rocks rebellow to the roar.
　　Nor less resolv'd, the firm *Achaian* band
With brazen shields in horrid circle stand:
Jove, pouring darkness o'er the mingled fight,
Conceals the warriours' shining helms in night:
320 To him, the chief for whom the hosts contend,
Had liv'd not hateful, for he liv'd a friend:
Dead, he protects him with superior care,
Nor dooms his carcase to the birds of air.
　　The first attack the *Grecians* scarce sustain,
325 Repuls'd, they yield; the *Trojans* seize the slain:
Then fierce they rally, to revenge led on
By the swift rage of *Ajax Telamon.*
(*Ajax*, to *Peleus'* son the second name,
In graceful stature next, and next in fame.)
330 With headlong force the foremost ranks he tore;
So thro' the thicket bursts the mountain boar,
And rudely scatters, far to distance round,
The frighted hunter and the baying hound.
The son of *Lethus*, brave *Pelasgus'* heir,
335 *Hippothous*, dragg'd the carcase thro' the war;
The sinewy ancles bor'd, the feet he bound
With thongs, inserted thro' the double wound:
Inevitable fate o'ertakes the deed;
Doom'd by great *Ajax'* vengeful lance to bleed;
340 It cleft the helmet's brazen cheeks in twain;
The shatter'd crest, and horse-hair, strow the plain:
With nerves relax'd he tumbles to the ground:
The brain comes gushing thro' the ghastly wound;
He drops *Patroclus'* foot, and o'er him spread
345 Now lies, a sad companion of the dead:
Far from *Larissa* lies, his native air,
And ill requites his parent's tender care.

Lamented youth! in life's first bloom he fell,
Sent by great *Ajax* to the shades of hell.
   Once more at *Ajax*, *Hector*'s jav'lin flies;   350
The *Grecian* marking as it cut the Skies,
Shunn'd the descending death; which hissing on,
Stretch'd in the dust the great *Iphytus'* son,
Schedius the brave, of all the *Phocian* Kind
The boldest warriour, and the noblest mind: 355
In little *Panope* for strength renown'd,
He held his seat, and rul'd the realms around.
Plung'd in his throat, the weapon drank his blood,
And deep transpiercing, thro' the shoulder stood;
In clanging arms the hero fell, and all   360
The fields resounded with his weighty fall.
   Phorcys, as slain *Hippothous* he defends,
The *Telamonian* lance his belly rends;
The hollow armour burst before the stroke,
And thro' the wound the rushing entrails broke.   365
In strong convulsions panting on the sands
He lies, and grasps the dust with dying hands.
   Struck at the sight, recede the *Trojan* train:
The shouting *Argives* strip the heroes slain.
And now had *Troy*, by *Greece* compell'd to yield,   370
Fled to her ramparts, and resign'd the field;
Greece, in her native fortitude elate,
With *Jove* averse, had turn'd the scale of fate:
But *Phœbus* urg'd *Æneas* to the fight;
He seem'd like aged *Periphas* to sight.   375
(A herald in *Anchises'* love grown old,
Rever'd for prudence, and with prudence, bold.)
   Thus he – what methods yet, oh chief! remain,
To save your *Troy*, tho' heav'n its fall ordain?
There have been heroes, who by virtuous care,   380
By valour, numbers, and by arts of war,
Have forc'd the pow'rs to spare a sinking state,
And gain'd at length the glorious odds of fate.
But you, when fortune smiles, when *Jove* declares
His partial favour, and assists your wars,   385
Your shameful efforts 'gainst your selves employ,
And force th'unwilling God to ruin *Troy*.

Æneas thro the form assum'd descries
The pow'r conceal'd, and thus to *Hector* cries.
390 Oh lasting shame! to our own fears a prey,
We seek our ramparts, and desert the day.
A God (nor is he less) my bosom warms,
And tells me, *Jove* asserts the *Trojan* arms.
   He spoke, and foremost to the combate flew:
395 The bold example all his hosts pursue.
Then first, *Leocritus* beneath him bled,
In vain belov'd by valiant *Lycomede*;
Who view'd his fall, and grieving at the chance,
Swift to revenge it, sent his angry lance;
400 The whirling lance with vig'rous force addrest,
Descends, and pants in *Apisaon*'s breast:
From rich *Pæonias*' vales the warriour came,
Next thee, *Asteropeus!* in place and fame.
Asteropeus with grief beheld the slain,
405 And rush'd to combate, but he rush'd in vain:
Indissolubly firm, around the dead,
Rank within rank, on buckler buckler spread,
And hemm'd with bristled spears, the *Grecians* stood;
A brazen bulwark, and an iron wood.
410 Great *Ajax* eyes them with incessant care,
And in an orb, contracts the crowded war,
Close in their ranks commands to fight or fall,
And stands the center and the soul of all:
Fixt on the spot they war; and wounded, wound;
415 A sanguine torrent steeps the reeking ground;
On heaps the *Greeks*, on heaps the *Trojans* bled,
And thick'ning round 'em, rise the hills of dead.
   Greece, in close order and collected might,
Yet suffers least, and sways the wav'ring fight;
420 Fierce as conflicting fires, the combate burns,
And now it rises, now it sinks by turns.
In one thick darkness all the fight was lost;
The sun, the moon, and all th'etherial host
Seem'd as extinct: day ravish'd from their eyes,
425 And all heav'n's splendors blotted from the skies.
Such o'er *Patroclus* body hung the night,
The rest in sunshine fought, and open light:

Unclouded there, th' aerial azure spread,
No vapour rested on the mountain's head,
The golden sun pour'd forth a stronger ray,   430
And all the broad expansion flam'd with day.
Dispers'd around the plain, by fits they fight,
And here, and there, their scatter'd arrows light:
But death and darkness o'er the carcase spread,
There burn'd the war, and there the mighty bled.   435
 Meanwhile the sons of *Nestor*, in the rear,
(Their fellows routed) toss the distant spear,
And skirmish wide: So *Nestor* gave command,
When from the ships he sent the *Pylian* band.
The youthful brothers thus for fame contend,   440
Nor knew the fortune of *Achilles'* friend;
In thought they view'd him still, with martial joy,
Glorious in arms, and dealing deaths to *Troy*.
 But round the corse, the heroes pant for breath,
And thick and heavy grows the work of death: 445
O'erlabour'd now, with dust, and sweat and gore,
Their knees, their legs, their feet are cover'd o'er;
Drops follow drops, the clouds on clouds arise,
And carnage clogs their hands, and darkness fills their
  eyes.
As when a slaughter'd bull's yet reeking Hide,   450
Strain'd with full force, and tugg'd from side to side,
The brawny curriers stretch; and labour o'er
Th'extended surface, drunk with fat and gore;
So tugging round the corps both armies stood;
The mangled body bath'd in sweat and blood: 455
While *Greeks* and *Ilians* equal strength employ,
Now to the ships to force it, now to *Troy*.
Not *Pallas'* self, her breast when fury warms,
Nor he, whose anger sets the world in arms,
Could blame this scene; such rage, such horror reign'd; 460
Such, *Jove* to honour the great dead ordain'd.
 Achilles in his ships at distance lay,
Nor knew the fatal fortune of the day;
He, yet unconscious of *Patroclus'* fall,
In dust extended under *Ilion*'s wall,   465

Expects him glorious from the conquer'd plain,
And for his wish'd return prepares in vain;
Tho' well he knew, to make proud *Ilion* bend,
Was more than heav'n had destin'd to his friend,
470 Perhaps to him: This *Thetis* had reveal'd;
The rest, in pity to her son, conceal'd.
    Still rag'd the conflict round the hero dead,
And heaps on heaps by mutual wounds they bled.
Curs'd be the man (ev'n private *Greeks* would say)
475 Who dares desert this well-disputed day!
First may the cleaving earth before our eyes
Gape wide, and drink our blood for sacrifice!
First perish all, e'er haughty *Troy* shall boast
We lost *Patroclus*, and our glory lost.
480   Thus they. While with one voice the *Trojans* said,
Grant this day, *Jove!* or heap us on the dead!
    Then clash their sounding arms; the clangors rise,
And shake the brazen concave of the skies.
    Meantime, at distance from the scene of blood,
485 The pensive steeds of great *Achilles* stood;
Their godlike master slain before their eyes,
They wept, and shar'd in human miseries.
In vain *Automedon* now shakes the rein,
Now plies the lash, and sooths and threats in vain;
490 Nor to the fight, nor *Hellespont* they go;
Restive they stood, and obstinate in woe:
Still as a tomb-stone, never to be mov'd,
On some good man, or woman unreprov'd
Lays its eternal weight; or fix'd as stands
495 A marble courser by the sculptor's hands,
Plac'd on the hero's grave. Along their face,
The big round drops cours'd down with silent pace,
Conglobing on the dust. Their manes, that late
Circled their arching necks, and wav'd in state,
500 Trail'd on the dust beneath the yoke were spread,
And prone to earth was hung their languid head:
Nor *Jove* disdain'd to cast a pitying look,
While thus relenting to the steeds he spoke.
    Unhappy coursers of immortal strain!
505 Exempt from age, and deathless now in vain;

Did we your race on mortal man bestow,
Only alas! to share in mortal woe?
For ah! what is there, of inferiour birth,
That breathes or creeps upon the dust of earth;
What wretched creature of what wretched kind,   510
Than man more weak, calamitous, and blind?
A miserable race! But cease to mourn.
For not by you shall *Priam*'s son be born
High on the splendid car: one glorious prize
He rashly boasts; the rest our will denies.   515
Ourself will swiftness to your nerves impart,
Ourself with rising spirits swell your heart.
Automedon your rapid flight shall bear
Safe to the navy thro' the storm of war.
For yet 'tis giv'n to *Troy*, to ravage o'er   520
The field, and spread her slaughters to the shore;
The sun shall see her conquer, till his fall
With sacred darkness shades the face of all.

   He said; and breathing in th'immortal horse
Excessive spirit, urg'd 'em to the course;   525
From their high manes they shake the dust, and bear
The kindling chariot thro' the parted war:
So flies a vulture thro' the clam'rous train
Of geese, that scream, and scatter round the plain.
From danger now with swiftest speed they flew,   530
And now to conquest with like speed pursue;
Sole in the seat the charioteer remains,
Now plies the jav'lin, now directs the reins:
Him brave *Alcimedon* beheld distrest,
Approach'd the chariot, and the chief addrest.   535

   What God provokes thee, rashly thus to dare,
Alone, unaided, in the thickest war?
Alas! thy friend is slain, and *Hector* wields
Achilles' arms triumphant in the fields.

   In happy time (the charioteer replies)   540
The bold *Alcimedon* now greets my eyes;
No *Greek* like him, the heav'nly steeds restrains,
Or holds their fury in suspended reins:
Patroclus, while he liv'd, their rage cou'd tame,
But now *Patroclus* is an empty name!   545

To thee I yield the seat, to thee resign
The ruling charge: the task of fight be mine.
  He said. *Alcimedon*, with active heat,
Snatches the reins, and vaults into the seat.
550 His friend descends. The chief of *Troy* descry'd,
And call'd *Æneas* fighting near his side.
Lo, to my sight beyond our hope restor'd,
Achilles' car, deserted of its Lord!
The glorious steeds our ready arms invite,
555 Scarce their weak drivers guide them thro' the fight:
Can such opponents stand, when we assail?
Unite thy force, my friend, and we prevail.
  The son of *Venus* to the counsel yields;
Then o'er their backs they spread their solid shields;
560 With brass refulgent the broad surface shin'd,
And thick bull-hides the spacious concave lin'd.
Them *Chromius* follows, *Aretus* succeeds,
Each hopes the conquest of the lofty steeds:
In vain, brave youths, with glorious hopes ye burn,
565 In vain advance! not fated to return.
  Unmov'd, *Automedon* attends the fight,
Implores th'Eternal, and collects his might.
Then turning to his friend, with dauntless mind:
Oh keep the foaming coursers close behind!
570 Full on my shoulders let their nostrils blow,
For hard the fight, determin'd is the foe;
'Tis *Hector* comes; and when he seeks the prize,
War knows no mean: he wins it, or he dies.
  Then thro' the field he sends his voice aloud,
575 And calls th'*Ajaces* from the warring croud,
With great *Atrides*. Hither turn (he said)
Turn, where distress demands immediate aid;
The dead, encircled by his friends, forego,
And save the living from a fiercer foe.
580 Unhelp'd we stand, unequal to engage
The force of *Hector*, and *Æneas'* rage:
Yet mighty as they are, my force to prove,
Is only mine: th'event belongs to *Jove*.
  He spoke, and high the sounding jav'lin flung,
585 Which pass'd the shield of *Aretus* the young;

It pierc'd his belt, emboss'd with curious art;
Then in the lower belly stuck the dart.
As when the pond'rous axe descending full,
Cleaves the broad forehead of some brawny bull;
Struck 'twixt the horns, he springs with many a bound,   590
Then tumbling rolls enormous on the ground:
Thus fell the youth; the air his soul receiv'd,
And the spear trembled as his entrails heav'd.
   Now at *Automedon* the *Trojan* foe
Discharg'd his lance; the meditated blow,   595
Stooping, he shun'd; the jav'lin idly fled,
And hiss'd innoxious o'er the hero's head:
Deep rooted in the ground, the forceful spear
In long vibrations spent its fury there.
With clashing falchions now the chiefs had clos'd,   600
But each brave *Ajax* heard, and interpos'd;
Nor longer *Hector* with his *Trojans* stood,
But left their slain companion in his blood:
His arms *Automedon* divests, and cries,
Accept, *Patroclus!* this mean sacrifice.   605
Thus have I sooth'd my griefs, and thus have paid
Poor as it is, some off'ring to thy shade.
   So looks the lion o'er a mangled boar,
All grim with rage, and horrible with gore;
High on the chariot at one bound he sprung,   610
And o'er his seat the bloody trophies hung.
   And now *Minerva*, from the realms of air
Descends impetuous, and renews the war;
For, pleas'd at length the *Grecian* arms to aid,
The Lord of Thunders sent the blue-ey'd Maid.   615
As when high *Jove*, denouncing future woe,
O'er the dark clouds extends his purple bow,
(In sign of tempests from the troubled air,
Or from the rage of man, destructive war).
The drooping cattel dread th'impending skies,   620
And from his half-till'd field the lab'rer flies.
In such a form the Goddess round her drew
A livid cloud, and to the battle flew.
Assuming *Phœnix'* shape, on earth she falls
And in his well-known voice to *Sparta* calls.   625

And lies *Achilles'* friend, belov'd by all,
A prey to dogs beneath the *Trojan* wall?
What shame to *Greece* for future times to tell,
To thee the greatest, in whose cause he fell!
630 O chief, oh father! (*Atreus'* son replies)
O full of days! by long experience wise!
What more desires my soul, than here, unmov'd,
To guard the body of the man I lov'd?
Ah would *Minerva* send me strength to rear
635 This weary'd arm, and ward the storm of war!
But *Hector*, like the rage of fire, we dread,
And *Jove*'s own glories blaze around his head.

Pleas'd to be first of all the pow'rs addrest,
She breathes new vigour in her hero's breast,
640 And fills with keen revenge, with fell despight,
Desire of blood, and rage, and lust of fight.
So burns the vengeful hornet (soul all o'er)
Repuls'd in vain, and thirsty still of gore;
(Bold son of Air and Heat) on angry wings
645 Untam'd, untir'd, he turns, attacks, and stings.
Fir'd with like ardour fierce *Atrides* flew,
And sent his soul with ev'ry lance he threw.

There stood a *Trojan* not unknown to fame,
Eëtion's son, and *Podes* was his name;
650 With riches honour'd, and with courage blest,
By *Hector* lov'd, his comrade, and his guest;
Thro' his broad belt the spear a passage found,
And pond'rous as he falls, his arms resound.
Sudden at *Hector*'s side *Apollo* stood,
655 Like *Phænops*, *Asius'* son, appear'd the God;
(*Asius* the great, who held his wealthy reign
In fair *Abydos* by the rolling main.)

Oh Prince (he cry'd) oh foremost once in fame!
What *Grecian* now shall tremble at thy name?
660 Dost thou at length to *Menelaus* yield?
A chief, once thought no terrour of the field;
Yet singly, now, the long disputed prize
He bears victorious, while our army flies.
By the same arm illustrious *Podes* bled,
665 The friend of *Hector*, unreveng'd, is dead!

This heard, o'er *Hector* spreads a cloud of woe,
Rage lifts his lance, and drives him on the foe.
   But now th'Eternal shook his sable shield,
That shaded *Ide*, and all the subject field
Beneath its ample verge. A rolling cloud   670
Involv'd the mount; the thunder roar'd aloud;
Th'affrighted hills from their foundations nod,
And blaze beneath the lightnings of the God:
At one regard of his all-seeing eye,
The vanquish'd triumph, and the victors fly.   675
   Then trembled *Greece*: The flight *Peneleus* led;
For as the brave *Bœotian* turn'd his head
To face the foe, *Polydamas* drew near,
And raz'd his shoulder with a shorten'd spear:
By *Hector* wounded, *Leitus* quits the plain,   680
Pierc'd thro' the wrist; and raging with the pain
Grasps his once formidable lance in vain.
   As *Hector* follow'd, *Idomen* addrest
The flaming jav'lin to his manly breast;
The brittle point before his corselet yields;   685
Exulting *Troy* with clamour fills the fields:
High on his chariot as the *Cretan* stood,
The Son of *Priam* whirl'd the missive wood;
But erring from its aim, th'impetuous spear
Strook to the dust the squire, and charioteer   690
Of martial *Merion*: *Cœranus* his name,
Who left fair *Lyctus* for the fields of fame.
On foot bold *Merion* fought; and now laid low,
Had grac'd the triumphs of his *Trojan* foe;
But the brave squire the ready coursers brought,   695
And with his life his master's safety bought.
Between his cheek and ear the weapon went,
The teeth it shatter'd, and the tongue it rent.
Prone from the seat he tumbles to the plain;
His dying hand forgets the falling rein: 700
This *Merion* reaches, bending from the car,
And urges to desert the hopeless war;
Idomeneus consents; the lash applies;
And the swift chariot to the navy flies.

705   Nor *Ajax* less the will of heav'n descry'd,
         And Conquest shifting to the *Trojan* side,
         Turn'd by the hand of *Jove.* Then thus begun,
         To *Atreus'* seed, the godlike *Telamon.*
             Alas! who sees not *Jove's* almighty hand
710   Transfers the glory to the *Trojan* band?
         Whether the weak or strong discharge the dart,
         He guides each arrow to a *Grecian* heart:
         Not so our spears: incessant tho' they rain,
         He suffers ev'ry lance to fall in vain.
715   Deserted of the God, yet let us try
         What human strength and prudence can supply;
         If yet this honour'd corps, in triumph born,
         May glad the fleets that hope not our return,
         Who tremble yet, scarce rescu'd from their fates,
720   And still hear *Hector* thund'ring at their gates.
         Some hero too must be dispatch'd to bear
         The mournful message to *Pelides'* ear;
         For sure he knows not, distant on the shore,
         His friend, his lov'd *Patroclus*, is no more.
725   But such a chief I spy not thro' the host:
         The men, the steeds, the armies all are lost
         In gen'ral darkness – Lord of Earth and Air!
         Oh King! oh Father! hear my humble pray'r:
         Dispel this cloud, the light of heav'n restore;
730   Give me to see, and *Ajax* asks no more:
         If *Greece* must perish, we thy will obey,
         But let us perish in the face of day!
             With tears the hero spoke, and at his pray'r
         The God relenting, clear'd the clouded air;
735   Forth burst the sun with all-enlight'ning ray;
         The blaze of armour flash'd against the day.
         Now, now, *Atrides!* cast around thy sight,
         If yet *Antilochus* survives the fight,
         Let him to great *Achilles'* ear convey
740   The fatal news – *Atrides* hastes away.
             So turns the lion from the nightly fold,
         Tho high in courage, and with hunger bold,
         Long gall'd by herdsmen, and long vex'd by hounds,
         Stiff with fatigue, and fretted sore with wounds;

The darts fly round him from an hundred hands,   745
And the red terrours of the blazing brands:
Till late, reluctant, at the dawn of day
Sow'r he departs, and quits th'untasted prey.
So mov'd *Atrides* from his dang'rous place
With weary limbs, but with unwilling pace;   750
The foe, he fear'd, might yet *Patroclus* gain,
And much admonish'd, much adjur'd his train.
  Oh guard these relicks to your charge consign'd,
And bear the merits of the dead in mind;
How skill'd he was in each obliging art;   755
The mildest manners, and the gentlest heart:
He was, alas! but fate decreed his end;
In death a hero, as in life a friend!
  So parts the chief; from rank to rank he flew,
And round on all sides sent his piercing view.   760
As the bold bird, endu'd with sharpest eye
Of all that wing the mid aërial sky,
The sacred eagle, from his walks above
Looks down, and sees the distant thicket move;
Then stoops, and sowsing on the quiv'ring hare,   765
Snatches his life amid the clouds of air.
Not with less quickness, his exerted sight
Pass'd this, and that way, thro' the ranks of fight:
Till on the left the chief he sought, he found;
Chearing his men, and spreading deaths around.   770
  To him the King. Belov'd of *Jove!* draw near,
For sadder tydings never touch'd thy ear;
Thy eyes have witness'd what a fatal turn!
How *Ilion* triumphs, and th'*Achaians* mourn.
This is not all: *Patroclus* on the shore,   775
Now pale and dead, shall succour *Greece* no more.
Fly to the fleet, this instant fly, and tell
The sad *Achilles* how his lov'd one fell:
He too may haste the naked corps to gain;
The arms are *Hector*'s, who despoil'd the slain.   780
  The youthful warriour heard with silent woe,
From his fair eyes the tears began to flow;
Big with the mighty grief, he strove to say
What sorrow dictates, but no word found way.

785 To brave *Laodocus* his arms he flung,
Who near him wheeling, drove his steeds along;
Then ran, the mournful message to impart,
With tear-ful eyes, and with dejected heart.
    Swift fled the youth; nor *Menelaus* stands,
790 (Tho' sore distrest) to aid the *Pylian* bands;
But bids bold *Thrasymede* those troops sustain;
Himself returns to his *Patroclus* slain.
Gone is *Antilochus* (the hero said)
But hope not, warriors! for *Achilles'* aid:
795 Tho' fierce his rage, unbounded be his woe,
Unarm'd, he fights not with the *Trojan* foe.
'Tis in our hands alone our hopes remain,
'Tis our own vigour must the dead regain;
And save our selves, while with impetuous hate
800 *Troy* pours along, and this way rolls our fate.
    'Tis well (said *Ajax*) be it then thy care
With *Merion*'s aid, the weighty corse to rear;
Myself, and my bold brother will sustain
The shock of *Hector* and his charging train:
805 Nor fear we armies, fighting side by side;
What *Troy* can dare, we have already try'd,
Have try'd it, and have stood. The hero said.
High from the ground the warriours heave the dead;
A gen'ral clamour rises at the sight:
810 Loud shout the *Trojans*, and renew the fight.
Not fiercer rush along the gloomy wood,
With rage insatiate and with thirst of blood,
Voracious hounds, that many a length before
Their furious hunters, drive the wounded boar;
815 But if the savage turns his glaring eye,
They howl aloof, and round the forest fly.
Thus on retreating *Greece* the *Trojans* pour,
Wave their thick falchions, and their jav'lins show'r:
But *Ajax* turning, to their fears they yield,
820 All pale they tremble, and forsake the field.
    While thus aloft the hero's corse they bear,
Behind them rages all the storm of war;
Confusion, tumult, Horrour, o'er the throng
Of men, steeds, chariots, urg'd the rout along:

Less fierce the winds with rising flames conspire,   825
To whelm some city under waves of fire;
Now sink in gloomy clouds the proud abodes;
Now crack the blazing temples of the Gods;
The rumbling torrent thro' the ruin rolls,
And sheets of smoak mount heavy to the poles.   830
The heroes sweat beneath their honour'd load:
As when two mules, along the rugged road,
From the steep mountain with exerted strength
Drag some vast beam, or mast's unwieldy length;
Inly they groan, big drops of sweat distill,   835
Th'enormous timber lumbring down the hill:
So these – Behind, the bulk of *Ajax* stands,
And breaks the torrent of the rushing bands.
Thus when a river swell'd with sudden rains
Spreads his broad waters o'er the level plains,   840
Some interposing hill the stream divides,
And breaks its force, and turns the winding tides.
Still close they follow, close the rear engage;
Æneas storms, and *Hector* foams with rage:
While *Greece* a heavy, thick retreat maintains,   845
Wedg'd in one body like a flight of cranes,
That shriek incessant, while the faulcon hung
High on pois'd pinions, threats their callow young.
So from the *Trojan* chiefs the *Grecians* fly,
Such the wild Terrour, and the mingled cry.   850
Within, without the trench, and all the way,
Strow'd in bright heaps, their arms and armour lay;
Such horrour *Jove* imprest! Yet still proceeds
The work of death, and still the battel bleeds.   854

OBSERVATIONS

ON THE

SEVENTEENTH BOOK

The epigraph on the frontispiece of Volume V (Books 17–21) consists of the following lines:

– Sanctos ausus recludere fontes.   VIRG.

[Having dared to set free the sacred founts.
(Virgil, *Georgics* II. 175)]

This is the only book of the Iliad which is a continued description of a battel, without any digression or episode, that serves for an interval to refresh the reader. The heav'nly machines too are fewer than in any other. *Homer* seems to have trusted wholly to the force of his own genius, as sufficient to support him, whatsoever lengths he was carried by it. But that spirit which animates the original, is what I am sensible evaporates so much in my hands; that, tho' I can't think my author tedious, I should have made him seem so, if I had not translated this book with all possible conciseness. I hope there is nothing material omitted, tho' the version consists but of sixty five lines more than the original.

However, one may observe there are more turns of fortune, more defeats, more rallyings, more accidents, in this battel, than in any other; because it was to be the last wherein the *Greeks* and *Trojans* were upon equal terms, before the Return of *Achilles*: And besides, all this serves to introduce the chief hero with the greater pomp and dignity.

3. *Great Menelaus –*] The poet here takes occasion to clear *Menelaus* from the imputations of idle and effeminate, cast on him in some parts

of the Poem; he sets him in the front of the army, exposing himself to dangers in defending the body of *Patroclus*, and gives him the conquest of *Euphorbus* who had the first hand in his Death. He is represented as the foremost who appears in his defence, not only as one of a like disposition of mind with *Patroclus*, a kind and generous friend; but as being more immediately concern'd in honour to protect from injuries the body of a hero that fell in his cause.   *Eustathius.* See Note on v. 271. of the third book.

5. *Thus round her new fal'n young,* &c.] In this comparison, as *Eustathius* has very well observed, the Poet accommodating himself to the occasion, means only to describe the affection *Menelaus* had for *Patroclus*, and the manner in which he presented himself to defend his body: And this comparison is so much the more just and agreeable, as *Menelaus* was a Prince full of goodness and mildness. He must have little sense or knowledge in Poetry, who thinks that it ought to be suppress'd. It is true, we shou'd not use it now-a-days, by reason of the low ideas we have of the animals from which it is derived; but those not being the ideas of *Homer*'s time, they could not hinder him from making a proper use of such a comparison.   *Dacier.*

id. Thus round her new fal'n young, &c.] It seems to me remarkable, that the several comparisons to illustrate the concern for *Patroclus*, are taken from the most tender sentiments of nature. *Achilles* in the beginning of the sixteenth book, considers him as a child, and himself as his mother. The sorrow of *Menelaus* is here described as that of a heifer for her young one. Perhaps these are design'd to intimate the excellent temper and goodness of *Patroclus*, which is expressed in that fine elogy of him in this book, v. 671. Πᾶσιν γὰρ ἐπίστατο μείλιχος εἶναι. *He knew how to be good-natur'd to all men.* This gave all mankind these sentiments for him, and no doubt the same is strongly pointed at by the uncommon concern of the whole army to rescue his body.

The dissimilitude of manners between these two friends, *Achilles* and *Patroclus*, is very observable: Such friendships are not uncommon, and I have often assign'd this reason for them, that it is natural for men to seek the assistance of those qualities in others, which they want themselves. That is still better if apply'd to providence, which associates men of different and contrary qualities, in order to make a more perfect system. But, whatever is customary in nature, *Homer* had a good poetical reason for it; for it affords many incidents to illustrate the manners of them both more strongly; and is what they call a contrast in painting.

11. *The Son of Panthus.*] The conduct of *Homer* is admirable in bringing *Euphorbus* and *Menelaus* together upon this occasion; for hardly any thing but such a signal revenge for the death of his brother, could have made *Euphorbus* stand the encounter. *Menelaus* putting him in mind of the death of his brother, gives occasion (I think) to one of the finest answers in all *Homer*; in which the insolence of *Menelaus* is retorted in a way to draw pity from every reader; and I believe there is hardly one, after such a speech, that would not wish *Euphorbus* had the better of *Menelaus*: A writer of Romances would not have fail'd to have giv'n *Euphorbus* the victory. But however, it was fitter to make *Menelaus*, who had received the greatest injury, do the most revengeful actions.

55. *Instarr'd with gems and gold.*] We have here a *Trojan* who used gold and silver to adorn his hair; which made *Pliny* say, that he doubted whether the women were the first that used those ornaments. *Est quidem apud eundem* [Homerum] *virorum crinibus aurum implexum, ideo nescio an prior usus a fœminis cœperit* [Indeed, according to Homer, men braided their hair with gold; and so I do not know whether this custom originated with the women] lib. 33. chap. 1. He might likewise have strengthened his doubt by the custom of the *Athenians*, who put into their hair little grashoppers of gold.   *Dacier.*

57. *As the young olive,* &c.] This exquisite Simile finely illustrates the beauty and sudden fall of *Euphorbus*, in which the allusion to that circumstance of his comely hair is peculiarly happy. *Porphyry* and *Jamblicus* acquaint us of the particular affection *Pythagoras* had for these verses, which he set to the harp, and used to repeat as his own *Epicedion.* Perhaps it was his fondness of them, which put it into his head to say, that his soul transmigrated to him from this hero. However it was, this conceit of *Pythagoras* is famous in antiquity, and has given occasion to a dialogue in *Lucian* entitled *The Cock*, which is, I think, the finest piece of that author.

65. *Thus young, thus beautiful* Euphorbus *lay.*] This is the only *Trojan* whose death the Poet laments, that he might do the more honour to *Patroclus*, his hero's friend. The comparison here used is very proper,

for the olive always preserves its beauty. But where the Poet speaks of the *Lapithæ*, a hardy and warlike people, he compares them to *Oaks*, that stand unmoved in storms and tempests; and where *Hector* falls by *Ajax*, he likens him to an *Oak* struck down by *Jove*'s thunder. Just after this soft comparison upon the beauty of *Euphorbus*, he passes to another full of strength and terrour, that of the lion.   *Eustathius.*

110. *Did but the voice of* Ajax *reach my ear.*] How observable is *Homer*'s art of illustrating the valour and glory of his heroes? *Menelaus*, who sees *Hector* and all the *Trojans* rushing upon him, would not retire if *Apollo* did not support them; and though *Apollo* does support them, he would oppose even *Apollo*, were *Ajax* but near him. This is glorious for *Menelaus*, and yet more glorious for *Ajax*, and very suitable to his character; for *Ajax* was the bravest of the *Greeks*, next to *Achilles.*   *Dacier. Eustathius.*

117. *So from the fold th'unwilling lion.*] The Beauty of the retreat of *Menelaus* is worthy notice. *Homer* is a great observer of natural imagery, that brings the thing represented before our view. It is indeed true, that lions, tygers, and beasts of prey are the only objects that can properly represent warriours; and therefore 'tis no wonder they are so often introduced: The inanimate things, as floods, fires, and storms, are the best, and only images of battels.

137. *Already had stern* Hector, &c.] *Homer* takes care, so long before hand, to lessen in his reader's mind the horror he may conceive from the cruelty that *Achilles* will exercise upon the body of *Hector*. That cruelty will be only the punishment of this which *Hector* here exercises upon the body of *Patroclus*; he drags him, he designs to cut off his head, and to leave his body upon the ramparts, expos'd to dogs and birds of prey.   *Eustathius.*

169. *You left him there a feast to dogs.*] It was highly dishonourable in *Hector* to forsake the body of a friend and guest, and against the laws of *Jupiter Xenius*, or *hospitalis.* For *Glaucus* knew nothing of *Sarpedon*'s being honoured with burial by the Gods, and sent embalmed into *Lycia.*   *Eustathius.*

193. *I shun great Ajax?*] *Hector* takes no notice of the affronts that *Glaucus* had thrown upon him, as knowing he had in some respects a just cause to be angry, but he cannot put up what he had said of his fearing *Ajax*, to which part he only replies: This is very agreeable to his heroic character.   *Eustathius.*

209. Hector *in proud* Achilles' *arms shall shine.*] The ancients have observed that *Homer* causes the arms of *Achilles* to fall into *Hector*'s power, to equal in some sort those two heroes, in the battel wherein he is going to engage them. Otherwise it might be urged, that *Achilles* could not have kill'd *Hector* without the advantage of having his armour made by the hand of a God, whereas *Hector*'s was only of the hand of a mortal; but since both were clad in armour made by *Vulcan, Achilles*'s victory will be compleat, and in its full lustre. Besides this reason (which is for necessity and probability) there is also another, for ornament; for *Homer* here prepares to introduce that beautiful episode of the divine armour, which *Vulcan* makes for *Achilles.*   *Eustathius.*

216. *The radiant arms to sacred Ilion bore.*] A difficulty may arise here, and the question may be asked why *Hector* sent these arms to *Troy*? Why did not he take them at first? There are three answers, which I think are all plausible. The first, that *Hector* having killed *Patroclus*, and seeing the day very far advanced, had no need to take those arms for a fight almost at an end. The second, that he was impatient to shew to *Priam* and *Andromache* those glorious spoils. Thirdly, he perhaps at first intended to hang them up in some temple. *Glaucus*'s speech makes him change his resolution, he runs after those arms to fight against *Ajax*, and to win *Patroclus*'s body from him.   *Dacier.*

   Homer (says *Eustathius*) does not suffer the arms to be carried into *Troy* for these reasons. That *Hector* by wearing them might the more encourage the *Trojans*, and be the more formidable to the *Greeks*: That *Achilles* may recover them again when he kills *Hector*: And that he may conquer him, even when he is strengthened with that divine armour.

231. Jupiter's *Speech to* Hector.] The Poet prepares us for the death of *Hector*, perhaps to please the *Greek* readers, who might be troubled to see him shining in their hero's arms. Therefore *Jupiter* expresses his sorrow at the approaching fate of this unfortunate Prince, promises to repay his loss of life with glory, and nods to give a certain confirmation to his words. He says, *Achilles* is the bravest *Greek*, as *Glaucus* had just said before; the Poet thus giving him the greatest commendations, by putting his praise in the mouth of a God, and of an enemy, who were neither of them like to be prejudiced in his favour.   *Eustathius.*

How beautiful is that sentiment upon the miserable state of mankind, introduced here so artfully, and so strongly enforced, by being put into the mouth of the supreme being! And how pathetic the denunciation of *Hector*'s death, by that circumstance of *Andromache*'s disappointment, when she shall no more receive her hero glorious from the battel, in the armour of his conquered enemy!

247. *The stubborn arms* &c.] The words are,

> Ἦ, καὶ κυανέῃσιν ἐπ᾽ ὀφρύσι νεῦσε Κρονίων,
> Ἕκτορι δ᾽ ἥρμοσε τεύχε᾽ ἐπὶ χροΐ.

> [The son of Kronos spoke, and with his dark brows he
>   nodded,
> And the armour was fitted on to Hector's body.]

If we give ἥρμοσε a passive signification, it will be, the arms fitted *Hector*; but if an active (as those take it who would put a greater difference between *Hector* and *Achilles*) then it belongs to *Jupiter*; and the sense will be, *Jupiter* made the arms fit for him, which were too large before: I have chosen the last as the more poetical sense.

260. *Unnumber'd bands of neighb'ring nations.*] *Eustathius* has very well explained the artifice of this speech of *Hector*, who indirectly answers all *Glaucus*'s invectives, and humbles his vanity. *Glaucus* had just spoken as if the *Lycians* were the only allies of *Troy*; and *Hector* here speaks of the numerous troops of different nations, which he expressly designs by calling them borderers upon his kingdom, thereby in some manner to exclude the *Lycians*, who were of a country more remote; as if he did not vouchsafe to reckon them. He afterwards confutes what *Glaucus* said, 'that if the *Lycians* would take his advice they would return home'; for he gives them to understand, that being hired troops, they are obliged to perform their bargain, and to fight till the war is at an end.   *Dacier.*

290. *Call on our Greeks.*] *Eustathius* gives three reasons why *Ajax* bids *Menelaus* call the *Greeks* to their assistance; instead of calling them himself. He might be ashamed to do it, lest it should look like fear and turn to his dishonour: Or the chiefs were more likely to obey *Menelaus*:

Or he had too much business of the war upon his hands, and wanted leisure more than the other.

302. Oïlean Ajax *first.*] *Ajax Oïleus* (says *Eustathius*) is the first that comes, being brought by his love to the other *Ajax*, as it is natural for one friend to fly to the assistance of another: To which we may add, he might very probably come first, because he was the swiftest of all the heroes.

318. Jove *pouring Darkness.*] *Homer*, who in all his former descriptions of battels is so fond of mentioning the lustre of the arms, here shades them in darkness, perhaps alluding to the clouds of dust that were raised; or to the throng of combatants; or else to denote the loss of *Greece* in *Patroclus*; or lastly, that as the heav'ns had mourned *Sarpedon* in showers of blood, so they might *Patroclus* in clouds of darkness.

Eustathius.

356. Panope *renown'd.*] *Panope* was a small town twenty *stadia* from *Chæronea*, on the side of mount *Parnassus*, and it is hard to know why *Homer* gives it the epithet of *renown'd*, and makes it the residence of *Schedius*, King of the *Phocians*; when it was but nine hundred paces in circuit, and had no palace, nor gymnasium, nor theatre, nor market, nor fountain; nothing in short that ought to have been in a town which is the residence of a King. *Pausanias* (in *Phocic.*) gives the reason of it; he says, that as *Phocis* was exposed on that side to the inroads of the *Bœotians*, *Schedius* made use of *Panope* as a sort of citadel, or place of arms.

Dacier.

375. *He seem'd like aged* Periphas.] The speech of *Periphas* to *Æneas* hints at the double fate, and the necessity of means. It is much like that of St *Paul*, after he was promised that no body should perish; he says, *except these abide, ye cannot be saved.*

422. *In one thick darkness,* &c.] The darkness spread over the body of *Patroclus* is artful upon several accounts. First, a fine Image of poetry. Next, a token of *Jupiter*'s love to a righteous man: But the chief design is to protract the action; which, if the *Trojans* had seen the spot, must have been decided one way or other, in a very short time. Besides, the *Trojans* having the better in the action, must have seized the body contrary to the intention of the author. There are innumerable

instances of these little niceties and particularities of conduct in *Homer*.

436. *Meanwhile the sons of Nestor, in the rear,* &c.] It is not without reason *Homer* in this place makes particular mention of the sons of *Nestor*. It is to prepare us against he sends one of them to *Achilles*, to tell him the death of his friend.

450. *As when a slaughter'd bull's yet reeking hide.*] *Homer* gives us a most lively description of their drawing the body on all sides, and instructs us in the ancient manner of stretching hides, being first made soft and supple with oil. And tho' this comparison be one of those mean and humble ones which some have objected to, yet it has also its admirers for being so expressive, and for representing to the imagination the most strong and exact idea of the subject in hand.

Eustathius.

458. *Not* Pallas *self,* &c.] *Homer* says in the original, '*Minerva* could not have found fault, tho' she were angry.' Upon which *Eustathius* ingeniously observes, how common and natural it is for persons in anger to turn criticks, and find faults where there are none.

468.   *To make proud* Ilion *bend,*
            Was more than heav'n had promis'd to his friend,
            Perhaps to him:]

In these words the Poet artfully hints at *Achilles*'s death; he makes him not absolutely to flatter himself with the hopes of ever taking *Troy*, in his own person, however he does not say this expresly, but passes it over as an ungrateful subject.   *Eustathius.*

471. *The rest, in pity to her son conceal'd.*] Here, (says the same author) we have two rules laid down for common use. One, not to tell our friends all their mischances at once, it being often necessary to hide part of them, as *Thetis* does from *Achilles*: The other, not to push men of courage upon all that is possible for them to do. Thus *Achilles*, tho' he thought *Patroclus* able to drive the *Trojans* back to their gates, yet he does not order him to do so much, but only to save the ships, and beat them back into the field.

Homer's admonishing the reader that *Achilles*'s mother had concealed the circumstance of the death of his friend when she instructed him in his fate; and that all he knew, was only that *Troy* could not be taken at that time; this is a great instance of his care of the probability, and of his having the whole plan of the Poem at once in his head. For upon the supposition that *Achilles* was instructed in his fate, it was a natural objection, how came he to hazard his friend? If he was ignorant on the other hand of the impossibility of *Troy*'s being taken at that time, he might for all he knew, be robbed by his friend (of whose valour he had so good an opinion) of that glory, which he was unwilling to part with.

484. *At distance from the scene of blood.*] If the horses had not gone aside out of the war, *Homer* could not have introduced so well what he design'd to their honour. So he makes them weeping in secret (as their master *Achilles* used to do) and afterwards coming into the battel, where they are taken notice of and pursued by *Hector. Eustathius.*

485. *The pensive steeds of great* Achilles, &c.] It adds a great beauty to the poem when inanimate things act like animate. Thus the Heavens tremble at *Jupiter*'s nod, the sea parts it self to receive *Neptune,* the groves of *Ida* shake beneath *Juno*'s feet, *&c.* As also to find animate or brute creatures addrest to, as if rational: So *Hector* encourages his horses; and one of *Achilles*'s is endued not only with speech, but with fore-knowledge of future events. Here they weep for *Patroclus,* and stand fix'd and immoveable with grief: Thus is this hero universally mourn'd, and every thing concurs to lament his loss.   *Eustathius.*

As to the particular fiction of the horses weeping, it is countenanc'd both by naturalists and historians. *Aristotle* and *Pliny* write, that these animals often deplore their masters lost in battel, and even shed tears for them. So *Solinus* c. 47. *Ælian* relates the like of elephants, when they are carried from their native country, *De animal.* lib. 10. c. 17. *Suetonius* in the life of *Cæsar,* tells us, that several horses which at the passage of the *Rubicon* had been consecrated to *Mars,* and turn'd loose on the banks, were observed for some days after to abstain from feeding, and to weep abundantly. *Proximis diebus, equorum greges quos in trajiciendo* Rubicone *flumine Marti consecrarat, ac sine custode vagos dimiserat, comperit pabulo pertinacissime abstinere, ubertimque flere.* cap. 81.

Virgil could not forbear copying this beautiful circumstance, in those fine lines on the horse of *Pallas.*

Post bellator equus, positis insignibus, Æthon,
It lacrymans, guttisque humectat grandibus ora.

[To close the pomp, *Æthon*, the steed of state,
  Is led, the fun'rals of his lord to wait.
  Stripp'd of his trappings, with a sullen pace
  He walks, and the big tears run rolling down his face.]

494. *Or fix'd, as stands a marble courser,* &c.] *Homer* alludes to the custom in those days of placing columns upon tombs, on which columns there were frequently chariots with two or four horses. This furnish'd *Homer* with this beautiful image, as if these horses meant to remain there, to serve for an immortal monument to *Patroclus.*

Dacier.

I believe M. *Dacier* refines too much in this note. *Homer* says, – ἠὲ γυναικός [or of a lady], and seems to turn the thought only on the firmness of the column, and not on the imagery of it: Which would give it an air a little too modern, like that of *Shakespear, She sate like* Patience *on a monument, smiling at* Grief. – Be it as it will, this conjecture is ingenious; and the whole comparison is as beautiful as just. The horses standing still to mourn for their master, could not be more finely represented than by the dumb sorrow of images standing over a tomb. Perhaps the very posture in which these horses are described, their heads bowed down, and their manes falling in the dust, has an allusion to the attitude in which those statues on monuments were usually represented: There are *Bas-Reliefs* that favour this conjecture.

522. *The sun shall see* Troy *conquer.*] It is worth observing with what art and oeconomy *Homer* conducts his fable, to bring on the catastrophe. *Achilles* must hear of *Patroclus*'s death; *Hector* must fall by his hand: This cannot happen if the armies continue fighting about the body of *Patroclus* under the walls of *Troy.* Therefore, to change the face of affairs, *Jupiter* is going to raise the courage of the *Trojans,* and make them repulse and chase the *Greeks* again as far as their fleet; this obliges *Achilles* to go forth tho' without arms, and thereby every thing comes to an issue.

Dacier.

555. *Scarce their weak Drivers.*] There was but one driver, since *Alcimedon* was alone upon the chariot; and *Automedon* was got down to fight.

But in poetry, as well as in painting, there is often but one moment to be taken hold on. *Hector* sees *Alcimedon* mount the chariot, before *Automedon* was descended from it; and thereupon judging of their intention, and feeling them both as yet upon the chariot, he calls to *Æneas.* He terms them both drivers in mockery, because he saw them take the reins one after the other; as if he said, that chariot had two drivers, but never a fighter. 'Tis one single *moment* that makes this image. In reading the Poets one often falls into great perplexities, for want of rightly distinguishing the point of time in which they speak.   *Dacier.*

The art of *Homer*, in this whole passage concerning *Automedon*, is very remarkable; in finding out the only proper occasion, for so renowned a person as the charioteer of *Achilles* to signalize his valour.

564.   *In vain, brave youths, with glorious hopes ye burn,*
       In vain advance! not fated to return.]

These beautiful anticipations are frequent in the Poets, who affect to speak in the character of prophets, and men inspired with the knowledge of futurity. Thus *Virgil* to *Turnus,*

    Nescia mens hominum fati. – Turno tempus erit, &c.

    [O mortals! blind is fate, who never know. –
        The time shall come when *Turnus*. . .]

So *Tasso*, Cant. 12. when *Argante* had vowed the destruction of *Tancred.*

    O vani giuramenti! Ecco contrari
    Seguir tosto gli effetti a l' alta speme:
    E cader questi in tenzon pari estinto
    Sotto colui, ch' ei fà già preso, e vinto.

    [O promise vain! it otherwise fell out:
    Men purpose, but high Gods dispose above;
        For underneath his sword this boaster died,
        Whom thus he scorn'd and threaten'd in his pride.]

And *Milton* makes the like apostrophe to *Eve* at her leaving *Adam* before she met the serpent.

        – She to him engag'd
    To be return'd by noon amid the bower,

And all things in best order to invite
Noontide repast, or afternoon's repose.
O much deceiv'd, much failing, hapless Eve!
Thou never from that hour, in paradise,
Found'st either sweet repast, or sound repose.

642. *So burns the vengeful hornet, &c.*] It is literally in the *Greek, She inspir'd the hero with the boldness of a fly.* There is no impropriety in the comparison, this animal being of all others the most persevering in its attacks, and the most difficult to be beaten off: The occasion also of the comparison being the resolute persistance of *Menelaus* about the dead body, renders it still the more just. But our present idea of the fly is indeed very low, as taken from the littleness and insignificancy of this creature. However, since there is really no meanness in it, there ought to be none in expressing it; and I have done my best in the translation to keep up the dignity of my author.

651. *By* Hector *lov'd, his comrade and his guest.*] *Podes* the favourite and companion of *Hector*, being kill'd on this occasion, seems a parallel circumstance to the death of *Achilles*'s favourite and companion; and was probably put in here on purpose to engage *Hector* on a like occasion with *Achilles.*

721. *Some hero too must be dispatch'd, &c.*] It seems odd that they did not sooner send this message to *Achilles*; but there is some apology for it from the darkness, and the difficulty of finding a proper person. It was not every body that was proper to send but one who was a particular friend to *Achilles*, who might condole with him. Such was *Antilochus* who is sent afterwards, and who, besides, had that necessary qualification of being πόδας. ὠκύς [swift-footed].   *Eustathius.*

731. *If* Greece *must perish, we thy will obey;*
         But let us perish in the face of day!]

This thought has been look'd upon as one of the sublimest in *Homer*: *Longinus* represents it in this manner. 'The thickest darkness had on a sudden cover'd the *Grecian* army, and hindered them from fighting: When *Ajax*, not knowing what course to take, cries out, *Oh Jove! disperse this darkness which covers the Greeks, and if we must perish, let us perish in the light!* This is a sentiment truly worthy of *Ajax*, he does not pray for life; that had been unworthy a hero: But because in that darkness he could not employ his valour to any glorious purpose, and vex'd to stand idle in the field of battel, he only prays that the day may appear, as being assured of putting an end to it worthy his great heart, tho' *Jupiter* himself should happen to oppose his efforts.'

M. *l' Abbé Terasson* (in his dissertation on the Iliad) endeavours to prove that *Longinus* has misrepresented the whole context and sense of this passage of *Homer*. The fact (says he) is, that *Ajax* is in a very different situation in *Homer* from that wherein *Longinus* describes him. He has not the least intention of fighting, he thinks only of finding out some fit person to send to *Achilles*; and this darkness hindering him from seeing such an one, is the occasion of his prayer. Accordingly it appears by what follows, that as soon as *Jupiter* has dispersed the cloud, *Ajax* never falls upon the enemy, but in consequence of his former thought orders *Menelaus* to look for *Antilochus*, to dispatch him to *Achilles* with the news of the death of his friend. *Longinus* (continues this author) had certainly forgot the place from whence he took this thought; and it is not the first citation from *Homer* which the ancients have quoted wrong. Thus *Aristotle* attributes to *Calypso*, the words of *Ulysses* in the twelfth book of the *Odyssey*; and confounds together two passages, one of the second, the other of the fifteenth book of the Iliad. [*Ethic. ad Nicom.* l. 2. c. 9. and l. 3. c. 11.] And thus *Cicero* ascribed to *Agamemnon* a long discourse of *Ulysses* in the second Iliad; [*De divinatione* l. 2.] and cited as *Ajax*'s, the speech of *Hector* in the seventh. [See *Aul. Gellius* l. 15. c. 6.] One has no cause to wonder at this, since the ancients having *Homer* almost by heart, were for that very reason the more subject to mistake in citing him by memory.

To this I think one may answer, that granting it was partly the occasion of *Ajax*'s prayer to obtain light, in order to send to *Achilles* (which he afterwards does) yet the thought which *Longinus* attributes to him, is very consistent with it; and the last line expresses nothing else but an heroic desire rather to die in the light, than escape with safety in the darkness.

ʼΕν δέ φάει καὶ ὄλεσσον, ἐπεί νύ τοι εὖαδεν οὕτως.

[Destroy us in broad daylight, if it so pleases you to destroy us.]

But indeed the whole speech is only meant to paint the concern and distress of a brave general: the thought of sending a messenger is only a result from that concern and distress, and so but a small circumstance; which cannot be said to occasion the pray'r.

Mons. *Boileau* has translated this passage in two lines.

> *Grand Dieu! chasse la nuit qui nous couvre les yeux,*
> *Et combats contre nous à la clarté des cieux.*

> [Great God! drive out the night that covers our eyes,
>   And fight against us under clear skies.]

And Mr *la Motte* yet better in one.

> *Grand Dieu! rends nous le jour, & combats contre nous!*

> [Great God! Give us daylight, and fight against us!]

But both these (as *Dacier* very justly observes) are contrary to *Homer's* sense. He is far from representing *Ajax* of such a daring impiety, as to bid *Jupiter* combate against him; but only makes him ask for light, that if it be his will the *Greeks* shall perish, they may perish in open day. Καὶ ὄλεσσον – (says he) that is, abandon us, withdraw from us your assistance; for those who are deserted by *Jove* must perish infallibly. This decorum of *Homer* ought to have been preserved.

756. *The mildest manners, and the gentlest heart.*] This is a fine elogium of *Patroclus: Homer* dwells upon it on purpose, lest *Achilles's* character should be mistaken; and shews by the praises he bestows here upon goodness, that *Achilles's* character is not commendable for morality. *Achilles's* manners, entirely opposite to those of *Patroclus*, are not morally good; they are only poetically so, that is to say, they are well mark'd; and discover before-hand what resolutions that hero will take: As hath been at large explain'd upon *Aristotle's* Poeticks.   *Dacier.*

781. *The youthful warriour heard with silent woe.*] *Homer* ever represents an excess of grief by a deep horrour, silence, weeping, and not enquiring into the manner of the friend's death: Nor could *Antilochus* have express'd his sorrow in any manner so moving as silence.

                                                    Eustathius.

785. *To brave* Laodocus *his arms he flung.*] *Antilochus* leaves his armour, not only that he might make the more haste, but (as the ancients conjecture) that he might not be thought to be absent by the enemies; and that seeing his armour on some other person, they might think him still in the fight.   *Eustathius.*

794.   *But hope not, Warriours! for Achilles' aid:*
        Unarm'd –]

This is an ingenious way of making the valour of *Achilles* appear the greater; who, tho' without arms, goes forth, in the next book, contrary to the expectation of *Ajax* and *Menelaus.*   *Dacier.*

825, *&c.* The heap of images which *Homer* throws together at the end of this book, makes the same action appear with a very beautiful variety. The *Description* of the burning of a city is short but very lively. That of *Ajax* alone bringing up the rear guard, and shielding those that bore the body of *Patroclus* from the whole *Trojan* host, gives a prodigious idea of *Ajax*; and as *Homer* has often hinted, makes him just second to *Achilles.* The image of the beam paints the great stature of *Patroclus*: That of the hill dividing the stream is noble and natural.

He compares the *Ajaxes* to a boar, for their fierceness and boldness; to a long bank that keeps off the course of the waters, for their standing firm and immoveable in the battel: Those that carry the dead body, to mules dragging a vast beam thro' rugged paths, for their laboriousness: The body carried, to a beam, for being heavy and inanimate: The *Trojans* to dogs, for their boldness; and to water for their agility and moving backwards and forwards: The *Greeks* to a flight of starlings and jays, for their timorousness, and swiftness.
                    Eustathius.

THE
EIGHTEENTH BOOK
OF THE
ILIAD

The ARGUMENT

The grief of *Achilles*, and new armour
made him by *Vulcan*

The news of the death of Patroclus, *is brought to* Achilles *by* Antilochus. Thetis *hearing his lamentations, comes with all her sea-nymphs to comfort him. The speeches of the mother and son on this occasion.* Iris *appears to* Achilles *by the command of* Juno, *and orders him to shew himself at the head of the intrenchments. The sight of him turns the fortune of the day, and the body of* Patroclus *is carried off by the* Greeks. *The* Trojans *call a council, where* Hector *and* Polydamas *disagree in their opinions; but the advice of the former prevails, to remain encamped in the field: The grief of* Achilles *over the body of* Patroclus.

Thetis goes to the palace of Vulcan *to obtain new arms for her son. The description of the wonderful works of* Vulcan, *and lastly, that noble one of the shield of* Achilles.

The latter part of the nine and twentieth day, and the night ensuing, take up this book. The scene is at Achilles's *tent on the sea-shore, from whence it changes to the palace of* Vulcan.

Thus like the rage of fire the combat burns,
And now it rises, now it sinks by turns.
Meanwhile, where *Hellespont*'s broad waters flow,
Stood *Nestor*'s son, the messenger of woe:
5   There sate *Achilles*, shaded by his sails,
On hoisted yards extended to the gales;
Pensive he sate; for all that fate design'd
Rose in sad prospect to his boding mind.
Thus to his soul he said. Ah! what constrains
10   The *Greeks*, late victors, now to quit the plains?
Is this the day, which heav'n so long ago
Ordain'd, to sink me with the weight of woe?
(So *Thetis* warn'd) when by a *Trojan* hand,
The bravest of the *Myrmidonian* band
15   Should lose the light? Fulfill'd is that decree;
Fal'n is the warriour, and *Patroclus* he!
In vain I charg'd him soon to quit the plain,
And warn'd to shun *Hectorean* force in vain!
    Thus while he thinks, *Antilochus* appears,
20   And tells the melancholy tale with tears.
Sad tydings, son of *Peleus!* thou must hear;
And wretched I, th'unwilling messenger!
Dead is *Patroclus!* For his corps they fight;
His naked corps; His arms are *Hector*'s right.
25   A sudden horrour shot thro' all the chief,
And wrapt his senses in the cloud of grief;
Cast on the ground, with furious hands he spread
The scorching ashes o'er his graceful head;

His purple garments, and his golden hairs,
Those he deforms with dust, and these he tears: 30
On the hard soil his groaning breast he threw,
And roll'd and grovel'd, as to earth he grew.
The virgin captives, with disorder'd charms,
(Won by his own, or by *Patroclus'* arms)
Rush'd from the tents with cries; and gath'ring round,   35
Beat their white breasts, and fainted on the ground:
While *Nestor*'s son sustains a manlier part,
And mourns the warriour with a warriour's heart;
Hangs on his arms, amidst his frantic woe,
And oft prevents the meditated blow.   40
    Far in the deep abysses of the main,
With hoary *Nereus*, and the watry train,
The Mother Goddess from her crystal throne
Heard his loud cries, and answer'd groan for groan.
The circling *Nereids* with their mistress weep,   45
And all the sea-green sisters of the deep.
Thalia, Glauce, (ev'ry wat'ry name)
Nesæa mild, and silver *Spio* came.
Cymothoë and *Cymodoce* were nigh,
And the blue languish of soft *Alia*'s eye.   50
Their locks *Actæa* and *Limnoria* rear,
Then *Proto, Doris, Panope* appear,
Thoa, Pherusa, Doto, Melita;
Agave gentle, and *Amphithoë* gay:
Next *Callianira, Callianassa* show   55
Their sister looks; *Dexamene* the slow,
And swift *Dynamene,* now cut the tides:
Iæra now the verdant wave divides:
Nemertes with *Apseudes* lifts the head,
Bright *Galatea* quits her pearly bed;   60
These *Orythia, Clymene,* attend,
Mæra, Amphinome, the train extend,
And black *Janira,* and *Janassa* fair,
And *Amatheia* with her amber hair.
All these, and all that deep in ocean held   65
Their sacred seats, the glimm'ring grotto fill'd;
Each beat her iv'ry breast with silent woe,
Till *Thetis'* sorrows thus began to flow.

Hear me, and judge, ye sisters of the main!
70   How just a cause has *Thetis* to complain?
How wretched, were I mortal, were my fate!
How more than wretched in th'immortal state!
Sprung from my bed a god-like hero came,
The bravest far that ever bore the name;
75   Like some fair olive, by my careful hand
He grew, he flourish'd, and adorn'd the land:
To *Troy* I sent him; but the fates ordain
He never, never must return again.
So short a space the light of heav'n to view,
80   So short alas! and fill'd with anguish too?
Hear how his sorrows echo thro' the shore!
I cannot ease them, but I must deplore;
I go at least to bear a tender part,
And mourn my lov'd one with a mother's heart.
85   She said, and left the caverns of the main.
All bath'd in tears, the melancholy train
Attend her way. Wide-opening part the tides,
While the long pomp the silver wave divides.
Approaching now, they touch'd the *Trojan* land;
90   Then, two by two, ascended up the strand.
Th'immortal mother, standing close beside
Her mournful offspring, to his sighs reply'd;
Along the coast their mingled clamours ran,
And thus the silver-footed dame began.
95   Why mourns my son? thy late preferr'd request
The God has granted, and the *Greeks* distrest:
Why mourns my son? thy anguish let me share,
Reveal the cause, and trust a parent's care.
He, deeply groaning – To this cureless grief
100   Not ev'n the Thund'rer's favour brings relief.
Patroclus – Ah! – say, Goddess can I boast
A pleasure now? revenge itself is lost;
Patroclus, lov'd of all my martial train,
Beyond mankind, beyond my self, is slain!
105   Lost are those arms the Gods themselves bestow'd
On *Peleus*; *Hector* bears the glorious load.
Curs'd be that day, when all the pow'rs above
Thy charms submitted to a mortal love:

Oh had'st thou still, a sister of the main,
Pursu'd the pleasures of the wat'ry reign;   110
And happier *Peleus*, less ambitious, led
A mortal beauty to his equal bed!
E'er the sad fruit of thy unhappy womb
Had caus'd such sorrows past, and woes to come.
For soon alas! that wretched offspring slain,   115
New woes, new sorrows shall create again:
'Tis not in fate th'alternate now to give;
Patroclus dead, *Achilles* hates to live.
Let me revenge it on proud *Hector*'s heart,
Let his last spirit smoak upon my dart;   120
On these conditions will I breathe: Till then,
I blush to walk among the race of men.
    A flood of tears, at this, the Goddess shed;
Ah then, I see thee dying, see thee dead!
When *Hector* falls, thou dy'st. – Let *Hector* die,   125
And let me fall! (*Achilles* made reply)
Far lyes *Patroclus* from his native plain!
He fell, and falling, wish'd my aid in vain.
Ah then, since from this miserable day
I cast all hope of my return away,   130
Since unreveng'd, a hundred ghosts demand
The fate of *Hector* from *Achilles'* hand;
Since here, for brutal courage far renown'd,
I live an idle burden to the ground,
(Others in council fam'd for nobler skill,   135
More useful to preserve, than I to kill)
Let me – But oh! ye gracious pow'rs above!
Wrath and revenge from men and Gods remove:
Far, far too dear to ev'ry mortal breast,
Sweet to the soul, as honey to the taste;   140
Gath'ring like vapours of a noxious kind
From fiery blood, and dark'ning all the mind.
Me *Agamemnon* urg'd to deadly hate;
'Tis past – I quell it; I resign to fate.
Yes – I will meet the murd'rer of my friend,   145
Or (if the Gods ordain it) meet my end.
The stroke of fate the bravest cannot shun:
The great *Alcides*, *Jove*'s unequal'd son,

To *Juno*'s hate at length resign'd his breath,
150   And sunk the victim of all-conqu'ring Death.
So shall *Achilles* fall! stretch'd pale and dead,
No more the *Grecian* hope, or *Trojan* dread!
Let me, this instant, rush into the fields,
And reap what glory life's short harvest yields.
155   Shall I not force some widow'd dame to tear
With frantic hands her long dishevell'd hair?
Shall I not force her breast to heave with sighs,
And the soft tears to trickle from her eyes?
Yes, I shall give the Fair those mournful charms –
160   In vain you hold me – Hence! my arms, my arms!
Soon shall the sanguine torrent spread so wide,
That all shall know, *Achilles* swells the tide.
      My Son (*Cærulean Thetis* made reply,
To fate submitting with a secret sigh)
165   The host to succour, and thy friends to save,
Is worthy thee; the duty of the brave.
But can'st thou, naked, issue to the plains?
Thy radiant arms the *Trojan* foe detains.
Insulting *Hector* bears the Spoils on high,
170   But vainly glories, for his fate is nigh.
Yet, yet awhile, thy gen'rous ardour stay;
Assur'd, I meet thee at the dawn of day,
Charg'd with refulgent arms (a glorious load)
Vulcanian arms, the labour of a God.
175   Then turning to the daughters of the main,
The Goddess thus dismiss'd her azure train.
      Ye sister *Nereids!* to your deeps descend,
Haste, and our father's sacred seat attend,
I go to find the architect divine,
180   Where vast *Olympus'* starry summits shine:
So tell our hoary sire – This charge she gave:
The sea-green sisters plunge beneath the wave:
Thetis once more ascends the blest abodes,
And treads the brazen threshold of the Gods.
185   And now the *Greeks*, from furious *Hector*'s force,
Urge to broad *Hellespont* their headlong course:
Nor yet their chiefs *Patroclus'* body bore
Safe thro' the tempest to the tented shore.

The horse, the foot, with equal fury join'd,
Pour'd on the rear, and thunder'd close behind;   190
And like a flame thro' fields of ripen'd corn,
The rage of *Hector* o'er the ranks was born.
Thrice the slain hero by the foot he drew;
Thrice to the skies the *Trojan* clamours flew:
As oft' th' *Ajaces* his assault sustain;   195
But check'd, he turns; repuls'd, attacks again.
With fiercer shouts his ling'ring troops he fires,
Nor yields a step, nor from his post retires;
So watchful sheperds strive to force, in vain,
The hungry lion from a carcase slain.   200
Ev'n yet, *Patroclus* had he born away,
And all the glories of th'extended day;
Had not high *Juno*, from the realms of air,
Secret, dispatch'd her trusty messenger.
The various Goddess of the show'ry bow,   205
Shot in a whirlwind to the shore below;
To great *Achilles* at his ships she came,
And thus began the many-colour'd dame.
   Rise, Son of *Peleus!* rise divinely brave!
Assist the combate, and *Patroclus* save: 210
For him the slaughter to the fleet they spread,
And fall by mutual wounds around the dead.
To drag him back to *Troy* the foe contends;
Nor with his death the rage of *Hector* ends:
A prey to dogs he dooms the corse to lie,   215
And marks the place to fix his head on high.
Rise, and prevent (if yet thou think of fame)
Thy friend's disgrace, thy own eternal shame!
   Who sends thee, Goddess! from th'etherial skies?
Achilles thus. And *Iris* thus replies.   220
I come, *Pelides!* from the Queen of *Jove*,
Th'immortal Empress of the realms above;
Unknown to him who sits remote on high,
Unknown to all the synod of the sky.
Thou com'st in vain, he cries (with fury warm'd);   225
Arms I have none, and can I fight unarm'd?
Unwilling as I am, of force I stay,
Till *Thetis* bring me at the dawn of day

Vulcanian arms: What other can I wield?
230 Except the mighty *Telamonian* shield?
That, in my friend's defence, has *Ajax* spread,
While his strong lance around him heaps the dead:
The gallant chief defends *Menœtius'* son,
And does, what his *Achilles* should have done.

235   Thy want of arms (said *Iris*) well we know,
But tho unarm'd, yet clad in terrours, go!
Let but *Achilles* o'er yon' trench appear,
Proud *Troy* shall tremble, and consent to fear;
Greece from one glance of that tremendous eye
240 Shall take new courage, and disdain to fly.

   She spoke, and past in air. The hero rose;
Her *Ægis*, *Pallas* o'er his shoulder throws;
Around his brows a golden cloud she spread;
A stream of glory flam'd above his head.

245 As when from some beleaguer'd town arise
The smokes high-curling to the shaded skies;
(See from some island, o'er the main afar,
When men distrest hang out the sign of war)
Soon as the sun in ocean hides his rays,
250 Thick on the hills the flaming beacons blaze;
With long-projected beams the seas are bright,
And Heav'ns high arch reflects the ruddy light;
So from *Achilles'* head the splendors rise,
Reflecting blaze on blaze against the skies.

255 Forth march'd the chief, and distant from the croud,
High on the rampart rais'd his voice aloud;
With her own shout *Minerva* swells the sound;
Troy starts astonish'd, and the shores rebound.
As the loud trumpet's brazen mouth from far
260 With shrilling clangor sounds th'alarm of war;
Struck from the walls, the echoes float on high,
And the round bulwarks and thick towr's reply;
So high his brazen voice the hero rear'd:
Hosts dropp'd their arms, and trembled as they heard;
265 And back the chariots roll, and coursers bound,
And steeds and men lie mingled on the ground.
Aghast they see the living light'nings play,
And turn their eye-balls from the flashing ray.

Thrice from the trench his dreadful voice he rais'd;
And thrice they fled, confounded and amaz'd.   270
Twelve in the tumult wedg'd, untimely rush'd
On their own spears, by their own chariots crush'd:
While shielded from the darts, the *Greeks* obtain
The long-contended carcase of the slain.
      A lofty bier the breathless warriour bears;   275
Around, his sad companions melt in tears:
But chief *Achilles*, bending down his head,
Pours unavailing sorrows o'er the dead.
Whom late, triumphant with his steeds and car,
He sent refulgent to the field of war,   280
(Unhappy change!) now senseless, pale, he found,
Stretch'd forth, and gash'd with many a gaping wound.
      Meantime, unweary'd with his heavenly way,
In ocean's waves th'unwilling light of day
Quench his red orb, at *Juno*'s high command,   285
And from their labours eas'd th'*Achaian* band.
The frighted *Trojans* (panting from the war,
Their steeds unharness'd from the weary car)
A sudden council call'd: Each chief appear'd
In haste, and standing; for to sit they fear'd.   290
'Twas now no season for prolong'd debate;
They saw *Achilles*, and in him their fate.
Silent they stood: *Polydamas* at last,
Skill'd to discern the future by the past,
The son of *Panthus*, thus exprest his fears;   295
(The friend of *Hector*, and of equal years:
The self-same night to both a being gave,
One wise in council, on in action brave.)
      In free debate, my friends, your sentence speak;
For me, I move, before the morning break   300
To raise our camp: Too dang'rous here our post,
Far from *Troy* walls, and on a naked coast.
I deem'd not *Greece* so dreadful, while engag'd
In mutual feuds, her King and hero rag'd;
Then, while we hop'd our armies might prevail,   305
We boldly camp'd beside a thousand sail.
I dread *Pelides* now: his rage of mind
Not long continues to the shores confin'd,

Nor to the fields, where long in equal fray
310   Contending nations won and lost the day;
For *Troy*, for *Troy*, shall henceforth be the strife,
And the hard contest not for fame, but life.
Haste then to *Ilion*, while the fav'ring night
Detains those terrours, keeps that arm from fight;
315   If but the morrow's sun behold us here,
That arm, those terrours, we shall feel, not fear;
And hearts that now disdain, shall leap with joy,
If heav'n permits them then to enter *Troy*.
Let not my fatal prophecy be true,
320   Nor what I tremble but to think, ensue.
Whatever be our fate, yet let us try
What force of thought and reason can supply;
Let us on counsel for our guard depend;
The town, her gates and bulwarks shall defend.
325   When morning dawns, our well–appointed pow'rs
Array'd in arms, shall line the lofty tow'rs.
Let the fierce hero then, when fury calls,
Vent his mad vengeance on our rocky walls,
Or fetch a thousand circles round the plain,
330   Till his spent coursers seek the fleet again:
So may his rage be tir'd, and labour'd down;
And dogs shall tear him e'er he sack the town.
    Return? (said *Hector*, fir'd with stern disdain)
What, coop whole armies in our walls again?
335   Was't not enough, ye valiant warriours say,
Nine years imprison'd in those tow'rs ye lay?
Wide o'er the world was *Ilion* fam'd of old
For brass exhaustless, and for mines of gold:
But while inglorious in her walls we stay'd,
340   Sunk were her treasures, and her stores decay'd;
The *Phrygians* now her scatter'd spoils enjoy,
And proud *Mæonia* wasts the fruits of *Troy*.
Great *Jove* at length my arms to conquest calls,
And shuts the *Grecians* in their wooden walls:
345   Dar'st thou dispirit whom the Gods incite?
Flies any *Trojan*? I shall stop his flight.
To better counsel then attention lend;
Take due refreshment, and the watch attend.

If there be one whose riches cost him care,
Forth let him bring them, for the troops to share;   350
'Tis better gen'rously bestow'd on those,
Than left the plunder of our country's foes.
Soon as the morn the purple Orient warms
Fierce on yon' navy will we pour our arms.
If great *Achilles* rise in all his might,   355
His be the danger: I shall stand the fight.
Honor, ye Gods! or let me gain, or give;
And live he glorious, whosoe'er shall live!
Mars is our common Lord, alike to all;
And oft' the victor triumphs, but to fall.   360

    The shouting host in loud applauses join'd;
So *Pallas* robb'd the many of their mind,
To their own sense condemn'd! and left to chuse
The worst advice, the better to refuse.

    While the long night extends her sable reign,   365
Around *Patroclus* mourn'd the *Grecian* train.
Stern in superiour grief *Pelides* stood;
Those slaught'ring arms, so us'd to bathe in blood,
Now clasp his clay-cold limbs: then gushing start
The tears, and sighs burst from his swelling heart.   370
The lion thus, with dreadful anguish stung,
Roars thro' the desart, and demands his young;
When the grim savage to his rifled den
Too late returning, snuffs the track of men,
And o'er the vales, and o'er the forrest bounds;   375
His clam'rous grief the bellowing wood resounds.
So grieves *Achilles*; and impetuous, vents
To all his *Myrmidons*, his loud laments.

    In what vain promise, Gods! did I engage?
When to console *Menætius*' feeble age,   380
I vow'd his much-lov'd offspring to restore,
Charg'd with rich spoils, to fair *Opuntia*'s shore!
But mighty *Jove* cuts short, with just disdain,
The long, long views of poor, designing man!
One fate the warriour and the friend shall strike,   385
And *Troy*'s black sands must drink our blood alike:
Me too, a wretched mother shall deplore,
An aged father never see me more!

Yet, my *Patroclus!* yet a space I stay,
390 Then swift pursue thee on the darksome way.
E'er thy dear relicks in the grave are laid,
Shall *Hector*'s head be offer'd to thy shade;
That, with his arms, shall hang before thy shrine;
And twelve, the noblest of the *Trojan* line,
395 Sacred to vengeance, by this hand expire;
Their lives effus'd around thy flaming pyre.
Thus let me lie till then! thus, closely prest,
Bathe thy cold face, and sob upon thy breast!
While *Trojan* captives here thy mourners stay,
400 Weep all the night, and murmur all the day:
Spoils of my arms, and thine; when, wasting wide,
Our swords kept time, and conquer'd side by side.
    He spoke, and bid the sad attendants round
Cleanse the pale corse, and wash each honour'd wound.
405 A massy caldron of stupendous frame
They brought, and plac'd it o'er the rising flame:
Then heap the lighted wood; the flame divides
Beneath the vase, and climbs around the sides:
In its wide womb they pour the rushing stream;
410 The boiling water bubbles to the brim.
The body then they bathe with pious toil,
Embalm the wounds, anoint the limbs with oil;
High on a bed of state extended laid,
And decent cover'd with a linen shade;
415 Last o'er the dead the milk-white veil they threw;
That done, their sorrows and their sighs renew.
    Meanwhile to *Juno*, in the realms above,
(His wife and sister) spoke almighty *Jove.*
At last thy will prevails: Great *Peleus'* son
420 Rises in arms: Such grace thy *Greeks* have won.
Say (for I know not) is their race divine,
And thou the mother of that martial line?
    What words are these (th'imperial dame replies,
While anger flash'd from her majestick eyes)
425 Succour like this a mortal arm might lend,
And such success mere human wit attend:
And shall not I, the second pow'r above,
Heav'ns Queen, and consort of the thund'ring *Jove,*

Say, shall not I one nation's fate command,
Not wreak my vengeance on one guilty land?   430
    So they. Meanwhile the silver-footed dame
Reach'd the *Vulcanian* dome, eternal frame!
High-eminent amid the works divine,
Where heav'ns far-beaming, brazen mansions shine.
There the lame architect the Goddess found,   435
Obscure in smoak, his forges flaming round,
While bath'd in sweat from fire to fire he flew,
And puffing loud, the roaring bellows blew.
That day no common task his labour claim'd:
Full twenty tripods for his hall he fram'd,   440
That plac'd on living wheels of massy gold,
(Wond'rous to tell) instinct with spirit roll'd
From place to place, around the blest abodes,
Self-mov'd, obedient to the beck of Gods:
For their fair handles now, o'erwrought with flow'rs,   445
In molds prepar'd, the glowing ore he pours.
Just as responsive to his thought, the frame
Stood prompt to move, the azure Goddess came:
Charis, his spouse, a grace divinely fair,
(With purple fillets round her braided hair)   450
Observ'd her ent'ring; her soft hand she press'd,
And smiling, thus the wat'ry Queen address'd.
    What, Goddess! this unusual favour draws?
All hail, and welcome! whatsoe'er the cause:
Till now a stranger, in a happy hour   455
Approach, and taste the dainties of the bow'r.
    High on a throne, with stars of silver grac'd
And various artifice, the Queen she plac'd;
A footstool at her feet: then calling, said,
Vulcan draw near, 'tis *Thetis* asks your aid.   460
    Thetis (reply'd the God) our pow'rs may claim,
An ever dear, and ever honour'd name!
When my proud mother hurl'd me from the sky,
(My awkward form, it seems, displeas'd her eye)
She, and *Eurynome*, my griefs redrest,   465
And soft receiv'd me on their silver breast.
Ev'n then, these arts employ'd my infant thought;
Chains, bracelets, pendants, all their toys I wrought.

Nine years kept secret in the dark abode,
470   Secure I lay, conceal'd from man and God:
Deep in a cavern'd rock my days were led;
The rushing ocean murmur'd o'er my head.
Now since her presence glads our mansion, say,
For such desert what service can I pay?
475   Vouchsafe, O *Thetis!* at our board to share
The genial rites, and hospitable fare;
While I the labours of the forge forego,
And bid the roaring bellows cease to blow.
    Then from his anvil the lame artist rose;
480   Wide with distorted legs, oblique he goes,
And stills the bellows, and (in order laid)
Locks in their chests his instruments of trade.
Then with a sponge the sooty workman drest
His brawny arms imbrown'd, and hairy breast.
485   With his huge scepter grac'd, and red attire,
Came halting forth the Sov'reign of the fire:
The monarch's steps two female forms uphold,
That mov'd, and breath'd, in animated gold;
To whom was voice, and sense, and science giv'n
490   Of works divine (such wonders are in heav'n!)
On these supported, with unequal gait,
He reach'd the throne where pensive *Thetis* sate;
There plac'd beside her on the shining frame,
He thus address'd the silver-footed dame.
495   Thee, welcome Goddess! what occasion calls,
(So long a stranger) to these honour'd walls?
'Tis thine, fair *Thetis*, the command to lay,
And *Vulcan*'s joy and duty to obey.
    To whom the mournful mother thus replies,
500   (The crystal drops stood trembling in her eyes)
Oh *Vulcan!* say, was ever breast divine
So pierc'd with sorrows, so o'erwhelm'd as mine?
Of all the Goddesses, did *Jove* prepare
For *Thetis* only such a weight of care?
505   I, only I, of all the wat'ry race,
By force subjected to a man's embrace,
Who, sinking now with age, and sorrow, pays
The mighty fine impos'd on length of days.

Sprung from my bed, a god-like hero came,
The bravest sure that ever bore the name;   510
Like some fair plant beneath my careful hand
He grew, he flourish'd, and he grac'd the land:
To *Troy* I sent him! but his native shore
Never, ah never, shall receive him more;
(Ev'n while he lives, he wastes with secret woe)   515
Nor I, a Goddess, can retard the blow!
Robb'd of the prize the *Grecian* Suffrage gave,
The King of nations forc'd his royal slave:
For this he griev'd; and till the *Greeks* opprest
Requir'd his arm, he sorrow'd unredrest.   520
Large gifts they promise, and their elders send;
In vain – He arms not, but permits his friend
His arms, his steeds, his forces to employ;
He marches, combates, almost conquers *Troy*:
Then slain by *Phœbus* (*Hector* had the name)   525
At once resigns his armour, life, and fame.
But thou, in pity, by my pray'r be won:
Grace with immortal arms this short-liv'd son,
And to the field in martial pomp restore,
To shine with glory, till he shines no more!   530
    To her the Artist-god. Thy griefs resign,
Secure, what *Vulcan* can, is ever thine.
O could I hide him from the fates as well,
Or with these hands the cruel stroke repel,
As I shall forge most envy'd arms, the gaze   535
Of wond'ring ages, and the world's amaze!
    Thus having said, the father of the fires
To the black labours of his forge retires.
Soon as he bade them blow, the bellows turn'd
Their iron mouths; and where the furnace burn'd,   540
Resounding breath'd: At once the blast expires,
And twenty forges catch at once the fires;
Just as the God directs, now loud, now low,
They raise a tempest, or they gently blow.
In hissing flames huge silver bars are roll'd,   545
And stubborn brass, and tin, and solid gold:
Before, deep fix'd, th'eternal anvils stand;
The pond'rous hammer loads his better hand,

His left with tongs turns the vex'd metal round,
550 And thick, strong strokes, the doubling vaults rebound.
    Then first he form'd th'immense and solid *shield*;
Rich, various artifice emblaz'd the field;
Its utmost verge a threefold circle bound;
A silver chain suspends the massy round,
555 Five ample plates the broad expanse compose,
And god-like labours on the surface rose.
There shone the image of the master Mind:
There earth, there heav'n, there ocean he design'd;
Th'unweary'd sun, the moon compleatly round;
560 The starry lights that heav'ns high convex crown'd;
The *Pleiads*, *Hyads*, with the northern team;
And great *Orion*'s more refulgent beam;
To which, around the axle of the sky,
The *Bear* revolving, points his golden eye,
565 Still shines exalted on th'ætherial plain,
Nor bathes his blazing forehead in the main.
    Two cities radiant on the shield appear,
The image one of peace, and one of war.
Here sacred pomp, and genial feast delight,
570 And solemn dance, and *Hymenæal* rite;
Along the street the new-made brides are led,
With torches flaming, to the nuptial bed;
The youthful dancers in a circle bound
To the soft flute, and cittern's silver sound:
575 Thro' the fair streets, the matrons in a row,
Stand in their porches, and enjoy the show.
    There, in the *Forum* swarm a num'rous train;
The subject of debate, a townsman slain:
One pleads the fine discharg'd, which one deny'd,
580 And bade the publick and the laws decide:
The witness is produc'd on either hand;
For this, or that, the partial people stand:
Th'appointed heralds still the noisy bands,
And form a ring, with scepters in their hands;
585 On seats of stone, within the sacred place,
The rev'rend elders nodded o'er the case;
Alternate, each th'attesting scepter took,
And rising solemn, each his sentence spoke.

Two golden talents lay amidst, in sight,
The prize of him who best adjudg'd the right.   590
    Another part (a prospect diff'ring far)
Glow'd with refulgent arms, and horrid war.
Two mighty hosts a leaguer'd town embrace,
And one would pillage, one wou'd burn the place.
Meantime the townsmen, arm'd with silent care,   595
A secret ambush on the foe prepare:
Their wives, their children, and the watchful band,
Of trembling parents on the turrets stand.
They march; by *Pallas* and by *Mars* made bold;
Gold were the Gods, their radiant garments Gold,   600
And gold their armour: These the Squadron led,
August, divine, superiour by the head!
A place for ambush fit, they found, and stood
Cover'd with shields, beside a silver flood.
Two spies at distance lurk, and watchful seem   605
If sheep or oxen seek the winding stream.
Soon the white flocks proceeded o'er the plains,
And steers slow-moving, and two shepherd swains;
Behind them, piping on their reeds, they go,
Nor fear an ambush, nor suspect a foe.   610
In arms the glitt'ring squadron rising round
Rush sudden; hills of slaughter heap the ground,
Whole flocks and herds lie bleeding on the plains,
And, all amidst them, dead, the shepherd swains!
The bellowing oxen the besiegers hear;   615
They rise, take horse, approach, and meet the war;
They fight, they fall, beside the silver flood;
The waving silver seem'd to blush with blood.
There tumult, there contention stood confest;
One rear'd a dagger at a captive's breast,   620
One held a living foe, that freshly bled
With new-made wounds; another dragg'd a dead;
Now here, now there, the carcasses they tore:
Fate stalk'd amidst them, grim with human gore.
And the whole war came out, and met the eye;   625
And each bold figure seem'd to live, or die.
    A field deep-furrow'd, next the God design'd,
The third time labour'd by the sweating hind;

The shining shares full many plowmen guide,
630 And turn their crooked yokes on ev'ry side.
Still as at either end they wheel around,
The master meets 'em with his goblet crown'd;
The hearty draught rewards, renews their toil,
Then back the turning plow-shares cleave the soil:
635 Behind, the rising earth in ridges roll'd,
And sable look'd, tho form'd of molten gold.
  Another field rose high with waving grain;
With bended sickles stand the reaper-train:
Here stretch'd in ranks the level'd swarths are found,
640 Sheaves heap'd on sheaves, here thicken up the ground.
With sweeping stroke the mowers strow the lands;
The gath'rers follow, and collect in bands;
And last the children, in whose arms are born
(Too short to gripe them) the brown sheaves of corn.
645 The rustic monarch of the field descries
With silent glee, the heaps around him rise.
A ready banquet on the turf is laid,
Beneath an ample oak's expanded shade.
The victim-ox the sturdy youth prepare;
650 The reaper's due repast, the women's care.
  Next, ripe in yellow gold, a vineyard shines,
Bent with the pond'rous harvest of its vines;
A deaper dye the dangling clusters show,
And curl'd on silver props, in order glow:
655 A darker metal mixt, intrench'd the place;
And pales of glitt'ring tin th'enclosure grace.
To this, one pathway gently winding leads,
Where march a train with baskets on their heads,
(Fair maids, and blooming youths) that smiling bear
660 The purple product of th'autumnal year.
To these a youth awakes the warbling strings,
Whose tender lay the fate of *Linus* sings;
In measur'd dance behind him move the train,
Tune soft the voice, and answer to the strain.
665 Here, herds of oxen march, erect and bold,
Rear high their horns, and seem to lowe in gold,
And speed to meadows on whose sounding shores
A rapid torrent thro' the rushes roars:

Four golden herdsmen as their guardians stand,
And nine sour dogs compleat the rustic band.   670
Two lions rushing from the wood appear'd;
And seiz'd a bull, the master of the herd:
He roar'd: in vain the dogs, the men withstood,
They tore his flesh, and drank the sable blood.
The dogs (oft' chear'd in vain) desert the prey,   675
Dread the grim terrours, and at distance bay.
    Next this, the eye the art of *Vulcan* leads
Deep thro' fair forests, and a length of meads;
And stalls, and folds, and scatter'd cotts between;
And fleecy flocks, that whiten all the scene.   680
    A figur'd dance succeeds: Such once was seen
In lofty *Gnossus*, for the *Cretan* Queen,
Form'd by *Dædalean* art. A comely band
Of youths and maidens, bounding hand in hand:
The maids in soft cymarrs of linen drest;   685
The youths all graceful in the glossy vest;
Of those the locks with flow'ry wreaths inroll'd,
Of these the sides adorn'd with swords of gold,
That glitt'ring gay, from silver belts depend.
Now all at once they rise, at once descend,   690
With well-taught feet: Now shape, in oblique ways,
Confus'dly regular, the moving maze:
Now forth at once, too swift for sight they spring,
And undistinguish'd blend the flying ring:
So whirls a wheel, in giddy circle tost,   695
And rapid as it runs, the single spokes are lost.
The gazing multitudes admire around;
Two active tumblers in the center bound;
Now high, now low, their pliant limbs they bend,
And gen'ral songs the sprightly revel end.   700
    Thus the broad shield complete the artist crown'd
With his last hand, and pour'd the ocean round:
In living silver seem'd the waves to roll,
And beat the buckler's verge, and bound the whole.
    This done, whate'er a warriour's use requires   705
He forg'd; the cuirass that outshone the fires;
The greaves of ductile tin, the helm imprest
With various sculpture, and the golden crest.

At *Thetis*' feet the finish'd labour lay;
710   She, as a falcon cuts th'Aerial way,
Swift from *Olympus*' snowy summit flies,
And bears the blazing present through the skies.

OBSERVATIONS

ON THE

EIGHTEENTH BOOK

1. *Thus like the rage of fire*, &c.] This phrase is usual in our Author, to signify a sharp battel fought with heat and fury on both parts; such an engagement like a flame, preying upon all sides, and dying the sooner, the fiercer it burns. *Eustathius.*

6. *On hoisted yards.*] The epithet ὀρθοκραιράων in this place has a more than ordinary signification. It implies that the sail-yards were hoisted up, and *Achilles*'s ships on the point to set sail. This shews that it was purely in compliance to his friend that he permitted him to succour the *Greeks*; he meant to leave 'em as soon as *Patroclus* return'd; he still remembered what he told the embassadors in the ninth Book; v. 360. *To morrow you shall see my fleet set sail.* Accordingly this is the day appointed, and he is fixed to his resolution: This circumstance wonderfully strengthens his implacable character.

7. *Pensive he sate.*] *Homer* in this artful manner prepares *Achilles* for the fatal message, and gives him these forebodings of his misfortunes, that they might be no less than he expected.

His Expressions are suitable to his concern, and delivered confusedly. 'I bad him (says he) after he had saved the ships, and repulsed the *Trojans*, to return back, and not engage himself too far.' Here he breaks off, when he should have added; 'But he was so unfortunate as to forget my advice.' As he is reasoning with himself, *Antilochus* comes in, which makes him leave the sense imperfect. *Eustathius.*

15.   *Fulfill'd is that decree;*
    Fal'n is the warriour, and Patroclus *he!*

It may be objected, that *Achilles* seems to contradict what had been said in the foregoing book, that *Thetis* concealed from her son the death of *Patroclus* in her prediction. Whereas here he says, that she had foretold he should lose the bravest of the *Thessalians.* There is nothing in this but what is natural and common among mankind: And it is still more agreeable to the hasty and inconsiderate temper of *Achilles*, not to have made that reflection till it was too late. Prophecies are only marks of divine prescience, not warnings to prevent human misfortunes; for if they were, they must hinder their own accomplishment.

21.   *Sad tydings, Son of* Peleus!]

This speech of *Antilochus* ought to serve as a model for the brevity with which so dreadful a piece of news ought to be delivered; for in two verses it comprehends the whole Affair of the death of *Patroclus*, the person that killed him, the contest for his body, and his arms in the possession of his enemy. Besides, it shou'd be observed that grief has so crowded his words, that in these two verses he leaves the verb ἀμφιμάχονται, *they fight*, without its nominative, *the Greeks* or *Trojans.* *Homer* observes this brevity upon all the like occasions. The *Greek* tragic Poets have not always imitated this discretion. In great distresses there is nothing more ridiculous than a messenger who begins a long story with pathetic descriptions; he speaks without being heard; for the person to whom he addresses himself has no time to attend him: The first word, which discovers to him his misfortune, has made him deaf to all the rest.   *Eustathius.*

25.   *A sudden horrour*, &c.] A modern *French* writer has drawn a parallel of the conduct of *Homer* and *Virgil*, in relation to the deaths of *Patroclus* and of *Pallas.* The latter is killed by *Turnus*, as the former by *Hector*; *Turnus* triumphs in the spoils of the one, as *Hector* is clad in the arms of the other; *Æneas* revenges the death of *Pallas* by that of *Turnus*, as *Achilles* the death of *Patroclus* by that of *Hector.* The grief of *Achilles* in *Homer* on the score of *Patroclus*, is much greater than that of *Æneas* in *Virgil*, for the sake of *Pallas.* *Achilles* gives himself up to despair with a weakness which *Plato* could not pardon in him, and which can only be excused on account of the long and close friendship between 'em: That of *Æneas* is more discreet, and seems more worthy of a hero. It was not possible that *Æneas* could be so deeply interested

for any man, as *Achilles* was interested for *Patroclus*: For *Virgil* had no colour to kill *Ascanius*, who was little more than a child; besides, that his hero's interest in the war of *Italy* was great enough of itself, not to need to be animated by so touching a concern as the fear of losing his son. On the other hand, *Achilles* having but very little personal concern in the war of *Troy* (as he had told *Agamemnon* in the beginning of the Poem) and knowing, besides, that he was to perish there, required some very pressing motive to engage him to persist in it, after such disgusts and Insults as he had received. It was this which made it necessary for these two great Poets to treat a subject so much in its own nature alike, in a manner so different. But as *Virgil* found it admirable in *Homer*, he was willing to approach it, as near as the oeconomy of his work would permit.

27. *Cast on the ground,* &c.] This is a fine picture of the grief of *Achilles*: We see on the one hand, the posture in which the hero receives the news of his friend's death; he falls upon the ground, he rends his hair, he snatches the ashes and casts them on his head, according to the manner of those times; (but what much enlivens it in this place, is his sprinkling embers instead of ashes in the violence of his passion.) On the other side, the captives are running from their tents, ranging themselves about him, and answering to his groans: Beside him stands *Antilochus*, fetching deep Sighs, and hanging on the arms of the hero, for fear his despair and rage should cause some desperate attempt upon his own life: There is no painter but will be touch'd with this image.

33. *The virgin captives.*] The captive maids lamented either in pity for their Lord, or in gratitude to the memory of *Patroclus*, who was remarkable for his goodness and affability; or under these pretences mourn'd for their own misfortunes and slavery.   *Eustathius.*

75. *Like some fair olive, by my careful hand.*] This passage, where the mother compares her son to a tender plant, raised and preserved with care; has a most remarkable resemblance to that in the *Psalms, Thy children like branches of olive trees round thy table.* Psal. 127.

100, 125. *The two speeches of* Achilles *to* Thetis.] It is not possible to imagine more lively and beautiful strokes of nature and passion, than those which our author ascribes to *Achilles* throughout these admirable speeches. They contain all, that the truest friend, the most tender son, and the most generous hero, could think or express in this delicate and affecting circumstance. He shews his excess of love to his mother, by wishing he had never been born or known to the world, rather than she should have endured so many sufferings on his account: He shews no less love for his friend, in resolving to revenge his death upon *Hector*, tho' his own would immediately follow. We see him here ready to meet his fate for the sake of his friend, and in the *Odyssey* we find him wishing to live again only to maintain his father's honour against his enemies. Thus he values neither life nor death, but as they conduce to the good of his friend and parents, or the encrease of his glory.

After having calmly considered the present state of his life, he deliberately embraces his approaching fate; and comforts himself under it, by a reflection on those great men, whom neither their illustrious actions, nor their affinity to heaven, could save from the general doom. A thought very natural to him, whose business it was in peace to sing their praises, and in war to imitate their actions. *Achilles*, like a man passionate of glory, takes none but the finest models; he thinks of *Hercules*, who was the son of *Jupiter*, and who had filled the universe with the noise of his immortal actions: These are the sentiments of a real hero.   *Eustathius.*

137. *Let me – But oh ye gracious powers,* &c.] *Achilles*'s words are these; 'Now since I am never to return home, and since I lie here an useless person, losing my best friend, and exposing the *Greeks* to so many dangers by my own folly; I who am superior to them all in battel – Here he breaks off, and says – May contention perish everlastingly, *&c. Achilles* leaves the sentence thus suspended, either because in his heat he had forgot what he was speaking of, or because he did not know how to end it; for he should have said, – 'Since I have done all this, I'll perish to revenge him:' Nothing can be finer than this sudden execration against discord and revenge, which breaks from the hero in the deep sense of the miseries those passions had occasioned.

Achilles could not be ignorant that he was superior to others in battel; and it was therefore no fault in him to say so. But he is so ingenuous as to give himself no farther commendation than what he undoubtedly merited; confessing at the same time, that many exceeded him in speaking: Unless one may take this as said in contempt of oratory, not unlike that of *Virgil*,

Orabunt caussas melius – &c.

[Plead better at the bar.]

153. *Let me, this instant.*] I shall have time enough for inglorious rest when I am in the grave, but now I must act like a living hero: I shall indeed lie down in death, but at the same time rise higher in glory.

Eustathius.

162. *That all shall know,* Achilles.] There is a great stress on δηρόν [long] and ἐγώ [I]. They shall soon find that their victories have been owing to the *long absence* of a hero, and that hero *Achilles.* Upon which the ancients have observed, that since *Achilles*'s anger there past in reality but a few days: To which it may be replied, that so short a time as this might well seem long to *Achilles,* who thought all unactive hours tedious and insupportable; and if the poet himself had said that *Achilles* was long absent, he had not said it because a great many days had past, but because so great a variety of incidents had happened in that time.

Eustathius.

171. – This promise of *Thetis* to present her son with a suit of armour, was the most artful method of hindering him from putting immediately in practice his resolution of fighting, which according to his violent manners, he must have done: Therefore the interposition of *Thetis* here was absolutely necessary; it was *dignus vindice nodus* [an impediment worthy of a protector].

219. *Who sends thee Goddess,* &c.] *Achilles* is amazed, that a moment after the Goddess his mother had forbid him fighting, he should receive a contrary order from the Gods: Therefore he asks what God sent her?

Dacier.

226. *Arms I have none.*] It is here objected against *Homer,* that since *Patroclus* took *Achilles'* armour, *Achilles* could not want arms while he had those of *Patroclus*; but (besides that *Patroclus* might have given his armour to his squire *Automedon,* the better to deceive the *Trojans* by making them take *Automedon* for *Patroclus,* as they took *Patroclus* for *Achilles*) this objection may be very solidly answered by saying that *Homer* has prevented it, since he made *Achilles*'s armour fit *Patroclus*'s body not without a miracle, which the Gods wrought in his favour.

Furthermore, it does not follow that because the armour of a large man fits one that is smaller, the armour of a little man should fit one that is larger.   *Eustathius.*

230. *Except the mighty* Telamonian *shield.*] *Achilles* seems not to have been of so large a stature as *Ajax:* Yet his shield 'tis likely might be fit enough for him, because his great strength was sufficient to wield it. This passage, I think, might have been made use of by the defenders of the shield of *Achilles* against the criticks, to shew that *Homer* intended the buckler of his hero for a very large one: And one would think he put it into this place, just a little before the description of that shield, on purpose to obviate that objection.

236. *But as thou art, unarm'd.*] A hero so violent and so outragious as *Achilles*, and who had but just lost the man he loved best in the world, is not likely to refuse shewing himself to the enemy, for the single reason of having no armour. Grief and despair in a great soul are not so prudent and reserv'd; but then on the other side, he is not to throw himself into the midst of so many enemies arm'd and flush'd with victory. *Homer* gets out of this nice circumstance with great dexterity, and gives to *Achilles*'s character every thing he ought to give to it, without offending either against reason or probability. He judiciously feigns, that *Juno* sent this order to *Achilles*, for *Juno* is the Goddess of royalty, who has the care of princes and kings; and who inspires them with the sense of what they owe to their dignity and character.   *Dacier.*

237. *Let but* Achilles *o'er yon' trench appear.*] There cannot be a greater instance, how constantly *Homer* carried his whole design in his head, as well as with what admirable art he raises one great idea upon another, to the highest sublime, than this passage of *Achilles*'s appearance to the army, and the preparations by which we are led to it. In the thirteenth book, when the *Trojans* have the victory, they check their pursuit of it, in the mere thought that *Achilles sees them:* In the sixteenth, they are put into the utmost consternation at the sight of his armour and chariot: In the seventeenth, *Menelaus* and *Ajax* are in despair, on the consideration that *Achilles* cannot succour them for want of armour: In the present book, beyond all expectation he does but shew himself unarm'd, and the very sight of him gives the victory to *Greece*: How extremely noble is this gradation!

246. *The smokes high-curling.*] For fires in the day appear nothing but smoak, and in the night flames are visible because of the darkness. And thus it is said in *Exodus*, That God led his people in the day with a pillar of smoak, and in the night with a pillar of fire. *Per diem in Columna nubis, & per noctem in columna ignis.*   Dacier.

247. *Seen from some Island.*] *Homer* makes choice of a town placed in an island, because such a place being besieged has no other means of making its distress known than by signals of fire; whereas a town upon the continent has other means to make known to its neighbours the necessity it is in.   *Dacier.*

259. *As the loud trumpet's,* &c.] I have already observ'd, that when the poet speaks as from himself, he may be allowed to take his comparisons from things which were not known before his time. Here he borrows a comparison from the *Trumpet*, as he has elsewhere done from *saddle-horses*, tho' neither one nor the other were used in *Greece* at the time of the *Trojan* war. *Virgil* was less exact in this respect, for he describes the trumpet as used in the sacking of *Troy*:

> *Exoritur clamorque virum clangorque tubarum.*

> [New clamours and new clangours now arise,
> The sound of trumpets mixed with fighting-cries.]

And celebrates *Misenus* as the trumpeter of *Æneas.* But as *Virgil* wrote at a time more remote from those heroic ages, perhaps this liberty may be excused. But a Poet had better confine himself to customs and manners, like a painter; and it is equally a fault in either of them to ascribe to times and nations any thing with which they were unacquainted.

One may add an observation to this note of M. *Dacier*, that the trumpet's not being in use at that time, makes very much for *Homer*'s purpose in this place. The terrour raised by the voice of his hero, is much the more strongly imaged by a sound that was unusual, and capable of striking more from its very novelty.

315. *If but the morrow's sun,* &c.] *Polydamas* says in the original, 'If *Achilles* comes to morrow *in his armour.*' There seems to lie an objection against this passage, for *Polydamas* knew that *Achilles*'s armour was won by *Hector*, he must also know that no other man's armour would fit him; how then could he know that new arms were made for him that very night? Those who are resolved to defend *Homer*, may answer, it was by his skill in prophecy; but to me this seems to be a slip of our author's memory, and one of those little *nods* which *Horace* speaks of.

333. *The Speech of* Hector.] *Hector* in this severe answer to *Polydamas*, takes up several of his words and turns them another way.

Polydamas had said Πρῶϊ δ' ὑπηοῖοι σὺν τεύχεσι θωρηχθέντες Στησόμεθ' ἄμ πύργους, 'To morrow by break of day let us put on our arms, and defend the castles and city walls,' to which *Hector* replies, Πρῶϊ δ' ὑπηοῖοι σὺν τεύχεσι θωρηχθέντες Νηυσὶν ἔπι γλαφυρῇσιν ἐγείρομεν ὀξὺν Ἄρηα, 'To morrow by break of day let us put on our arms, not to defend our selves at home, but to fight the *Greeks* before their own ships.'

Polydamas, speaking of *Achilles*, had said τῷ δ' ἄλγιον αἴ κ' ἐθέλησιν, &c. 'if he comes after we are within the walls of our city, 'twill be the worse for him, for he may drive round the city long enough before he can hurt us.' To which, *Hector* answers; 'If *Achilles* should come Ἄλγιον, αἴ κ' ἐθέλῃσι, τῷ ἔσσεται· οὔ μιν ἐγώ γε φεύξομαι ἐκ πολέμοιο, &c. ''Twill be the worse for him, as you say, because I'll fight him: οὔ μιν ἐγώ γε φεύξομαι, says *Hector*, in reply to *Polydamas*'s saying, ὅς κε φύγῃ. But *Hector* is not so far gone in passion or pride, as to forget himself; and accordingly in the next lines he modestly puts it in doubt, which of them shall conquer.   *Eustathius.*

340. *Sunk were her treasures, and her stores decay'd.*] As well by reason of the convoys, which were necessarily to be sent for with ready money; as by reason of the great allowances which were to be given to the auxiliary troops, who came from *Phrygia* and *Mæonia. Hector*'s meaning is, that since all the riches of *Troy* are exhausted, it is no longer necessary to spare themselves, or shut themselves up within their walls.   *Dacier.*

349. *If there be one,* &c.] This noble and generous proposal is worthy of *Hector*, and at the same time very artful to ingratiate himself with the soldiers. *Eustathius* farther observes that it is said with an eye to *Polydamas*, as accusing him of being rich, and of not opening the advice he had given, for any other end than to preserve his great wealth; for riches commonly make men cowards, and the desire of saving them has often occasioned men to give advice very contrary to the publick welfare.

379. *In what vain promise.*] The lamentation of *Achilles* over the body of *Patroclus* is exquisitely touch'd: It is sorrow in the extreme, but the sorrow of *Achilles*. It is nobly usher'd in by that simile of the grief of the lion: An Idea which is fully answered in the savage and bloody conclusion of this speech. One would think by the beginning of it, that *Achilles* did not know his fate, till after his departure from *Opuntium*; and yet how does that agree with what is said of his choice of the short and active life, rather than the long and inglorious one? Or did not he flatter himself sometimes, that his fate might be changed? This may be conjectured from several other passages, and is indeed the most natural solution.

404. *Cleanse the pale corse, &c.*] This custom of washing the dead, is continued amongst the *Greeks* to this Day; and 'tis a pious duty performed by the dearest friend or relation, to see it washed and anointed with a perfume, after which they cover it with linen exactly in the manner here related.

417. Jupiter *and* Juno.] *Virgil* has copied the speech of *Juno* to *Jupiter. Ast ego quæ divum incedo regina* [But I, who walk in awful state above], &c. But it is exceeding remarkable, that *Homer* should upon every occasion make marriage and discord inseparable: 'Tis an unalterable rule with him, to introduce the husband and wife in a quarrel.

440. *Full twenty tripods.*] Tripods were vessels supported on three feet, with handles on the sides; they were of several kinds, and for several uses; some were consecrated to sacrifices, some used as tables, some as seats, others hung up as ornaments on walls of houses or temples; these of *Vulcan* have an addition of wheels, which was not usual, which intimates them to be made with clock-work. Mons. *Dacier* has commented very well on this passage. If *Vulcan* (says he) had made ordinary tripods, they had not answered the greatness, power, and skill of a God. It was therefore necessary that his work should be above that of men: To effect this, the tripods were animated, and in this *Homer* doth not deviate from the probability; for every one is fully persuaded, that a God can do things more difficult than these, and that all matter will obey him. What has not been said of the statues of *Dædalus*? *Plato* writes, that they walked alone, and if they had not taken care to tie them, they would have got loose, and run from their master. If a writer in prose can speak hyperbollically of a man, may not *Homer* do it much more of a God? Nay, this circumstance with which *Homer* has embellished his poem, would have had nothing too surprizing tho' these tripods had been made by a man; for what may not be done in clock-work by an exact management of springs? This criticism is then ill grounded, and *Homer* does not deserve the ridicule they would cast on him.

The same author applies to this passage of *Homer* that rule of *Aristotle, Poetic.* Chap. 26. which deserves to be alledged at large on this occasion.

'When a poet is accused of saying any thing that is impossible; we must examine that impossibility, either with respect to *poetry*, with respect to that which is *best*, or with respect to *common fame.* First, with regard to *poetry*, The *probable impossible* ought to be preferred to the *possible, which hath no verisimilitude*, and which would not be believed; and 'tis thus that *Zeuxis* painted his pieces. Secondly, with respect to that which is *best*, we see that a thing is more excellent and more wonderful this way, and that the originals ought always to surpass. Lastly, in respect to *fame*, It is prov'd that the poet need only follow common opinion. All that appears absurd may be also justified by one of these three ways; or else by the maxim we have already laid down, that it is probable, that a great many things may happen against probability.'

A late critick has taken notice of the conformity of this passage of *Homer* with that in the first chapter of *Ezekiel, The spirit of the living creatures was in the wheels; when those went, these went, and when those stood, these stood; and when those were lifted up, the wheels were lifted up over against them; for the spirit of the living creature was in the wheels.*

459. *A footstool at her feet.*] It is at this day the usual honour paid amongst the *Greeks*, to visiters of superior quality, to set them higher than the rest of the company, and put a footstool under their feet. See note on v. 179. Book 14. This, with innumerable other customs, are still preserved in the eastern nations.

460. Vulcan *draw near, 'tis* Thetis *asks your aid.*] The story the ancients tell of *Plato*'s application of this verse is worth observing. That great philosopher had in his youth a strong inclination to poetry, and not being satisfied to compose little pieces of gallantry and amour, he tried his forces in tragedy and epic poetry; but the success was not answerable to his hopes: He compared his performance with that of *Homer*, and was very sensible of the difference. He therefore abandoned a sort of writing wherein at best he could only be the second, and turn'd his views to an other, wherein he despaired not to become the first. His anger transported him so far, as to cast all his verses into the fire. But while he was burning them, he could not help citing a verse of the very poet who had caused his chagrin. It was the present line, which *Homer* has put into the mouth of *Charis*, when *Thetis* demands arms for *Achilles.*

Ἥφαιστε πρόμολ' ὧδε, Θέτις νύ τι σεῖο χατίζει.

Plato only inserted his own name instead of that of *Thetis.*

Vulcan *draw near, 'tis* Plato *asks your aid.*

If we credit the ancients, it was the discontentment his own poetry gave him, that raised in him all the Indignation he afterwards expressed against the art itself. In which (say they) he behaved like those lovers, who speak ill of the beauties whom they cannot prevail upon.

Fraguier, Parall. de Hom. & de Platon.

461. Thetis *(reply'd the God) our pow'rs may claim,* &c.] *Vulcan* throws by his work to perform *Thetis*'s request, who had laid former obligations upon him; the Poet in this example giving us an excellent precept, that gratitude should take place of all other concerns.

.The motives which should engage a God in a new work in the night-time upon a suit of armour for a mortal, ought to be strong; and therefore artfully enough put upon the foot of gratitude: Besides, they afford at the same time a noble occasion for *Homer* to retail his theology, which he is always very fond of.

The allegory of *Vulcan*, or fire (according to *Heraclides*) is this. His Father is *Jupiter*, or the *Æther*, his mother *Juno*, or the *Air*, from whence he fell to us, whether by lightning, or otherwise. He is said to be lame, that is, to want Support, because he cannot subsist without the continual subsistance of fuel. The ætherial fire, *Homer* calls *Sol* or *Jupiter*, the inferior *Vulcan*; the one wants nothing of perfection, the other is subject to decay, and is restored by accession of materials. *Vulcan* is said to fall from heaven, because at first, when the opportunity of obtaining fire was not so frequent, men prepared instruments of brass, by which they collected the beams of the sun; or else they gained it from accidental lightning, that set fire to some combustible matter. *Vulcan* had perished when he fell from heaven unless *Thetis* and *Eurynome* had received him; that is, unless he had been preserved by falling into some convenient receptacle, or subterranean place; and so was afterwards distributed for the common necessities of mankind. To understand these strange explications, it must be known, that *Thetis* is derived from τίθημι to *lay up*, and *Eurynome* from εὐρύς and νομή, a *wide distribution.* They are called daughters of the ocean, because the vapours and exhalations of the sea forming themselves into clouds, find nourishment for lightnings.

488.   *Two female forms,*
      That mov'd and breath'd in animated gold.]

It is very probable, that *Homer* took the idea of these from the statues of *Dædalus,* which might be extant in his time. The ancients tell us, they were made to imitate life, in rolling their eyes, and in all other motions. From whence indeed it should seem, that the excellency of *Dædalus* consisted in what we call clock-work, or the management of moving figures by springs, rather than in sculpture or imagery: And accordingly, the fable of his fitting wings to himself and his son, is formed entirely upon the foundation of the former.

517. *Robb'd of the Prize,* &c.] *Thetis* to compass her design, recounts every thing to the advantage of her son; she therefore suppresses the episode of the embassy, the prayers that had been made use of to move him, and all that the *Greeks* had suffered after the return of the ambassadors; and artfully puts together two very distant things, as if they had followed each other in the same moment. He declined, says she, to succour the *Greeks,* but he sent *Patroclus.* Now between his refusing to help the *Greeks,* and his sending *Patroclus,* terrible things had fallen out; but she suppresses them, for fear of offending *Vulcan* with the recital of *Achilles*'s inflexible obduracy, and thereby create in that God an aversion to her son.   *Eustathius.*

525. *Then slain by* Phœbus (Hector *had the name*)] It is a passage worth taking notice of, that *Brutus* is said to have consulted the *Sortes Homericæ,* and to have drawn one of these lines, wherein the death of *Patroclus* is ascribed to *Apollo*: After which, unthinkingly, he gave the name of that God for the word of battel. This is remarked as an unfortunate omen by some of the ancients, tho' I forget where I met with it.

537. *The father of the fires*, &c.] The ancients (says *Eustathius*) have largely celebrated the philosophical mysteries which they imagined to be shadowed under these descriptions, especially *Damo* (supposed the Daughter of *Pythagoras*) whose explication is as follows. *Thetis*, who receives the arms, means the apt order and disposition of all things in the creation. By the fire and the wind raised by the bellows, are meant *air* and *fire* the most active of all the elements. The emanations of the fire are those *golden maids* that waited on *Vulcan.* The circular shield is the *World*, being of a sphærical figure. The Gold, the brass, the silver, and the tin are the *elements*: Gold is fire, the firm brass is earth, the silver is air, and the soft tin, water. And thus far (say they) *Homer* speaks a little obscurely, but afterwards he names them expressly, ἐν μὲν γαῖαν ἔτευξ᾽, ἐν δ᾽ οὐρανόν, ἐν δὲ θάλασσαν, to which, for the fourth element, you must add *Vulcan*, who makes the shield. The extreme circle that runs round the shield which he calls *splendid* and *threefold*, is the Zodiack; threefold in its breadth, within which all the planets move; splendid, because the sun passes always thro' the midst of it. The silver handle by which the shield is fastened at both extremities, is the *Axis* of the world, imagined to pass thro it, and upon which it turns. The five folds are those parallel circles that divide the world, the *Polar*, the *Tropicks*, and the *Æquator*.

Heraclides Ponticus thus pursues the allegory. *Homer* (says he) makes the working of his shield, that is the world, to be begun by *night*; as indeed all matter lay undistinguished in an original and universal *night*; which is called *Chaos* by the poets.

To bring the matter of the shield to separation and form, *Vulcan* presides over the work, or as we may say, an *essential warmth: All things*, says *Heraclitus*, *being made by the operation of fire.*

And because the *architect* is at this time to give a form and ornament to the world he is making, it is not rashly that he is said to be married to one of the graces.

> *On the broad shield the* maker's *hand engraves*
> *The earth and seas beneath, the pole above,*
> *The sun unwearied, and the circled moon.*

Thus in the beginning of the world, he first lays the earth as the foundation of a building, whose vacancies are fill'd up with the flowings of the sea. Then he spreads out the sky for a kind of divine roof over it, and lights the elements, now separated from their former confusion, with the *Sun*, the *Moon*,

> *And all those stars that crown the skies with fire:*

Where, by the word *crown*, which gives the idea of roundness, he again hints at the figure of the world; and tho' he cou'd not particularly name the Stars like *Aratus* (who professed to write upon them) yet he has not omitted to mention the principal. From hence he passes to represent two *allegorical* cities, one of *peace*, the other of *war*; *Empedocles* seems to have taken from *Homer* his assertion, that all things had their original from *strife* and *friendship*.

All these refinements (not to call 'em absolute whimsies) I leave just as I found 'em, to the Reader's Judgment or Mercy. They call it *Learning* to have read 'em, but I fear it is *Folly* to quote 'em.

566. *Nor bends his blazing forehead to the main.*] The criticks make use of this passage, to prove that *Homer* was ignorant of Astronomy; since he believed, that the *Bear* was the only constellation which never bathed itself in the ocean, that is to say that did not set, and was always visible; for say they, this is common to other constellations of the artick circle, as the lesser Bear, the Dragon, the greatest part of *Cepheus*, *&c.* To salve *Homer*, *Aristotle* answers, That he calls it the only one, to shew that 'tis the only one of those constellations he had spoken of, or that he has put the *only*, for the *principal* or the *most known.* *Strabo* justifies this after another manner, in the beginning of his first book, 'Under the Name of the *Bear* and the *Chariot*, *Homer* comprehends all the artick circle; for there being several other stars in that circle which never set, he could not say, that the Bear was the only one which did not bath itself in the ocean; wherefore those are deceived, who accuse the poet of ignorance, as if he knew one Bear only when there are two; for the lesser was not distinguished in his time. The *Phœnicians* were the first who observed it and made use of it in their navigation; and the figure of that sign passed from them to the *Greeks*: The same thing happened in regard to the constellation of *Berenice*'s hair, and that of *Canopus*, which received those names very lately; and as *Aratus* says well, there are several other stars which have no names. *Crates* was then in the wrong to endeavour to correct this passage, in putting οἷος for οἴη, for he tries to avoid that which there is

no occasion to avoid. *Heraclitus* did better, who put the Bear for the artick circle as *Homer* has done. *The Bear* (says he) *is the limit of the rising and setting of the stars.* Now it is the *Artic Circle*, and not the *Bear* which is that limit. 'Tis therefore evident, that by the word *Bear*, which he calls the *Wagon*, and which he says observes *Orion*, he understands the artick circle; that by the ocean he means the horizon where the stars rise and set; and by those words, *which turns in the same place, and doth not bath itself in the ocean*, he shews that the artick circle is the most northern part of the horizon, *&c.*'

Dacier on *Arist.*

Mons. *Terasson* combates this passage with great warmth. But it will be a sufficient vindication of our author to say, that some other constellations, which are likewise perpetually above the horizon in the latitude where *Homer* writ, were not at that time discovered; and that whether *Homer* knew that the Bear's not setting was occasioned by the latitude, and that in a smaller latitude it would set, is of no consequence; for if he had known it, it was still more poetical not to take notice of it.

567. *Two cities,* &c.] In one of these cities are represented all the advantages of *peace*: And it was impossible to have chosen two better emblems of peace, than *Marriages* and *Justice*. 'Tis said this city was *Athens*, for marriages were first instituted there by *Cecrops*; and Judgment upon murder was first founded there. The ancient state of *Attica* seems represented in the neighbouring fields, where the ploughers and reapers are at work, and a king is overlooking them; for *Triptolemus* who reigned there, was the first who sowed corn: This was the imagination of *Agallias Cercyreus*, as we find him cited by *Eustathius.*

579. *The fine discharg'd.*] Murder was not always punished with death, or so much as banishment; but when some fine was paid, the criminal was suffered to remain in the city. So *Iliad* 9.

> — Καὶ μέν τίς τε κασιγνήτοιο φόνοιο
> Ποινὴν, ἢ οὗ παιδὸς ἐδέξατο τεθνηῶτος.
> Καὶ ῥ' ὁ μὲν ἐν δήμῳ μένει αὐτοῦ πόλλ' ἀποτίσας.

> — *If a brother bleed,*
> *On just atonement, we remit the deed;*
> *A sire the slaughter of his son forgives,*
> *The price of blood discharg'd, the murd'rer lives.*

590. *The prize of him who best adjudg'd the right.*] *Eustathius* informs us, that it was anciently the custom to have a reward given to that judge who pronounced the best sentence. M. *Dacier* opposes this authority, and will have it, that this reward was given to the person who upon the decision of the suit appeared to have the justest cause. The difference between these two customs, in the reason of the thing, is very great: For the one must have been an encouragement to justice, the other a provocation to dissension. It were to be wanting in a due reverence to the wisdom of the ancients, and of *Homer* in particular, not to chuse the former sense: And I have the honour to be confirmed in this opinion, by the ablest judge, as well as the best practiser, of equity, my Lord *Harcourt*, at whose seat I translated this Book.

591. *Another part (a prospect diff'rent far)* &c.] The same *Agallias*, cited above, would have this city in war to be meant of *Eleusina*, but upon very slight reasons. What is wonderful is, that all the accidents and events of *war* are set before our eyes in this short compass. The several scenes are excellently disposed to represent the whole affair. Here is in the space of thirty lines a siege, a sally, an ambush, the surprize of a convoy, and a battel; with scarce a single circumstance proper to any of these, omitted.

619. There *tumult*, &c.] This is the first place in the whole description of the buckler, where *Homer* rises in his style, and uses the allegorical ornaments of Poetry; so natural was it for his imagination, (now heated with the fighting scenes of the *Iliad*) to take fire, when the image of a battel was presented to it.

627. *A field deep-furrow'd,* &c.] Here begin the descriptions of rural life, in which *Homer* appears as great a master as in the great and terrible parts of poetry. One would think, he did this on purpose to rival his contemporary *Hesiod*, on those very subjects to which his genius was particularly bent. Upon this occasion, I must take notice of that *Greek* poem, which is commonly ascribed to *Hesiod* under the Title of Ἀσπὶς Ἡρακλέος [*The Shield of Hercules*]. Some of the ancients mention such a work as *Hesiod*'s, but that amounts to no proof that this is the same: Which indeed is not an express poem upon the shield of *Hercules*, but a fragment of the story of that hero. What regards the shield is a manifest copy from this of *Achilles*; and consequently it is not of *Hesiod*. For if he was not more ancient, he was at least contemporary with *Homer*: And neither of them could be supposed to borrow so shamelessly from the other, not only the plan of entire descriptions, (as those of the marriage, the harvest, the vineyard, the ocean round the margin, *&c.*) but also whole verses together: Those of the *Parca*, in the battel, are repeated word for word,

> – ἐν δ' ὀλοὴ Κὴρ,
> Ἄλλον ζωὸν ἔχουσα νεούτατον, ἄλλον ἄουτον
> Ἄλλον τεθνεηῶτα κατὰ μόθον ἕλκε ποδοῖιν
> Εἶμα δ' ἔχ' ἀμφ' ὤμοισι δαφοινεὸν αἵματι φωτῶν.

[And on the shield was deadly Fate holding one man just wounded, another unharmed, and another – who was dead – she dragged by his feet through the press of battle. On her shoulders she wore a garment red with men's blood.]

And indeed half the poem is but a sort of *Cento* composed out of *Homer*'s verses. The reader need only cast an eye on these two descriptions, to see the vast difference of the original and the copy; and I dare say he will readily agree with the sentiment of Monsieur *Dacier*, in applying to them that famous verse of *Sannazarius*,

> *Illum hominem dices, hunc posuisse Deum.*

[You will say that a man composed that, but a god
    composed this.]

id.] I ought not to forget the many apparent allusions to the descriptions on this shield, which are to be found in those pictures of peace and war, the city and country, in the eleventh book of *Milton*: Who was doubtless fond of any occasion to shew, how much he was charmed with the beauty of all these lively images. He makes his angel paint those objects which he shews to *Adam*, in the colours, and almost the very strokes of *Homer*. Such is that passage of the harvest field,

> *His eye he open'd, and beheld a field*
> *Part arable and tilth, whereon were sheaves*
> *New-reap'd; the other part sheep-walks and folds.*
> *In midst an altar, as the landmark, stood,*
> *Rustic, of grassy ford, &c.*

That of the marriages,

> *They light the nuptial torch, and bid invoke*

> Hymen *(then first to marriage rites invok'd)*
> *With feast and musick all the tents resound.*

But more particularly, the following lines are in a manner a translation of our author.

> *One way, a band select from forage drives*
> *A herd of beeves, fair oxen, and fair kine*
> *From a fat Meadow ground; or fleecy flock,*
> *Ewes and their bleating lambs, across the plain,*
> *Their booty: Scarce with life the shepherds fly,*
> *But call in aid, which makes a bloody fray,*
> *With cruel tournament the squadrons join*
> *Where cattel pastur'd late, now scatter'd lies*
> *With carcasses and arms th'ensanguin'd Field*
> *Deserted. – Others to a city strong*
> *Lay siege, encamp'd; by battery, scale, and mine*
> *Assaulting; others from the wall defend*
> *With dart and jav'lin, stones, and sulph'rous fire:*
> *On each hand slaughter and gigantic deeds.*
>   *In other part, the scepter'd heralds call*
> *To council in the city gates: anon*
> *Grey-headed men and grave, with warriours mixt,*
> *Assemble, and harangues are heard –*

645. *The rustic monarch of the field.*] *Dacier* takes this to be a piece of ground given to a hero in reward of his services. It was in no respect unworthy such a person, in those days, to see his harvest got in, and to overlook his reapers: It is very conformable to the manners of the ancient patriarchs, such as they are describ'd to us in the holy scriptures.

662. *The fate of* Linus.] There are two interpretations of this verse in the original: That which I have chosen is confirmed by the testimony of *Herodotus* lib. 2. and *Pausanias, Bœoticis. Linus* was the most ancient name in Poetry, the first upon record who invented verse and measure among the *Grecians*: He past for the son of *Apollo* or *Mercury*, and was præceptor to *Hercules, Thamyris,* and *Orpheus.* There was a solemn custom among the *Greeks* of bewailing annually the death of their first poet: *Pausanias* informs us, that before the yearly sacrifice to the muses on mount *Helicon,* the obsequies of *Linus* were performed, who had a statue and altar erected to him, in that place. *Homer* alludes to that custom in this passage, and was doubtless fond of paying this respect to the old father of poetry. *Virgil* has done the same in that fine celebration of him, *Eclog.* 6.

> *Tum canit errantem Permessi ad flumina Gallum,*
> *Utque viro Phœbi chorus assurrexerit omnis;*
> *Ut* Linus *hæc illi, divino carmine, pastor*
> *(Floribus atque apio crines ornatus amaro)*
> *Dixerit* – &c.

> [Then sang, how *Gallus* by a Muse's hand,
> Was led and welcom'd to the sacred strand:
> The senate rising to salute their guest;
> And *Linus* thus their gratitude express'd.]

And again in the fourth *Eclogue.*

> *Non me carminibus vincet nec* Thracius Orpheus,
> *Nec* Linus; *huic mater, quamvis atque huic pater adsit,*
> Orpheo Calliopea, Lino *formosus* Apollo.

> [Not *Thracian Orpheus* should transcend my layes,
> Nor *Linus* crown'd with never-fading bayes:
> Though each his heav'nly parent shou'd inspire;
> The muse instruct the voice, and *Phœbus* tune the lyre.]

681. *A figur'd dance.*] There were two sorts of dances, the Pyrrhick, and the common dance: *Homer* has joined both in this description. We see the Pyrrhick, or military, is performed by the youths who have swords on, the other by the virgins crowned with garlands.

Here the ancient scholiasts say, that whereas before it was the custom for men and women to dance separately, the contrary practice was afterwards brought in, by seven youths, and as many virgins, who were saved by *Theseus* from the labyrinth; and that this dance was taught them by *Dædalus*: To which *Homer* here alludes. See *Dion. Halic. Hist.* l. 7. c. 68.

It is worth observing that the *Grecian* dance is still performed in this manner in the *Oriental* nations: The youths and maids dance in a ring, beginning slowly; by degrees the musick plays a quicker time, till at last they dance with the utmost swiftness: And towards the conclusion, they sing (as it is said here) in a general chorus.

702. *And pour'd the ocean round.*] *Vulcan* was the God of fire, and passes over this part of the description negligently; for which reason *Virgil* (to take a different walk) makes half his description of *Æneas*'s buckler consist in a sea fight. For the same reason he has laboured the sea-piece among his *games*, more than any other, because *Homer* had described nothing of this kind at the funeral of *Patroclus*.

OBSERVATIONS
ON THE
SHIELD OF *ACHILLES*

The Poet intending to shew in its full lustre, his Genius for description, makes choice of this interval from action and the leisure of the night, to display that talent at large in the famous buckler of *Achilles.* His intention was no less, than to draw the picture of the whole world in the compass of this shield. We see first the universe in general; the heavens are spread, the stars are hung up, the earth is stretched forth, the seas are poured round: We next see the world in a nearer and more particular view; the cities, delightful in peace, or formidable in war; the labours of the country, and the fruit of those labours, in the harvests and the vintages; the pastoral life in its pleasures and its dangers: In a word, all the occupations, all the ambitions, and all the diversions of mankind. This noble and comprehensive design he has executed in a manner that challenged the admiration of all the ancients: And how right an idea they had of this grand design, may be judged from that verse of *Ovid, Met.* 13. where he calls it

> *Clypeus* vasti *cœlatus imagine* mundi.

> ['The shield, carved with an image of the vast universe.']

It is indeed astonishing how after this the arrogance of some moderns could unfortunately chuse the noblest part of the noblest poet for the object of their blind censures. Their criticisms, however just enough upon other parts, yet, when employed on this buckler, are to the utmost weak and impotent.

> *– postquam arma Dei ad Vulcania ventum est*
> *Mortalis mucro glacies seu futiles, icta*
> *Dissiluit –*

   [But vain against the great Vulcanian shield,
     The mortal-temper'd steel deceiv'd his hand:
     The shiver'd fragments shone amid the sand.]

I design to give the reader the sum of what has been said on this subject. First, a reply to the loose and scattered objections of the criticks, by M. *Dacier*: Then the regular plan and distribution of the shield, by Mons. *Boivin*: And lastly, I shall attempt what has not yet been done, to consider it as a work of *Painting*, and prove it in all respects conformable to the most just ideas and established rules of that art.

I

It is the fate (says M. *Dacier*) of these arms of *Achilles*, to be still the occasion of quarrels and disputes. *Julius Scaliger* was the first who appeared against this part, and was followed by a whole herd. These object in the first place, that 'tis impossible to represent the movement of the figures; and in condemning the manner, they take the liberty to condemn also the subject, which they say is trivial, and not well understood. 'Tis certain that *Homer* speaks of the figures on this buckler, as if they were alive: And some of the ancients taking his expressions to the strictness of the letter, did really believe that they had all sorts of motion. *Eustathius* shewed the absurdity of that sentiment by a passage of *Homer* himself; 'That poet, says he, to shew that his figures are not animated, as some have pretended by an excessive affection for the prodigious, took care to say that they *moved and fought*, as if *they were living men.*' The ancients certainly founded this ridiculous opinion on a rule of *Aristotle*: For they thought the poet could not make his description more *admirable* and *marvellous*, than in making his figures animated, since (as *Aristotle* says) the *original should always excel the copy.* That shield is the work of a God: 'Tis the original, of which the engraving and painting of men is but an imperfect copy; and there is nothing impossible to the Gods. But they did not perceive, that by this *Homer* would have fallen into an extravagant admirable which would not have been probable. Therefore, 'tis without any necessity *Eustathius* adds, 'That 'tis possible all those figures did not stick close to the shield, but that they were detached from it, and moved by springs, in such a manner that they appeared to have motion; as *Æschylus* has feigned something like it, in his *seven*

Captains against Thebes.' But without having recourse to that conjecture, we can shew that there is nothing more simple and natural than the description of that shield, and there is not one word which *Homer* might not have said of it, if it had been the work of a man; for there is a great deal of difference between the work itself, and the description of it.

Let us examine the particulars for which they blame *Homer*. They say he describes two towns on his shield which *speak different languages.* 'Tis the *Latin* translation, and not *Homer*, that says so; the word μερό-πων [of mortals], is a common epithet of men, and which signifies only, that they have *an articulate voice.* These towns could not speak different languages, since, as the ancients have remarked, they were *Athens* and *Eleusina*, both which spake the same language. But tho' that epithet should signify, *which spake different languages*, there would be nothing very surprizing; for *Virgil* said what *Homer* it seems must not:

> *Victæ longo ordine gentes,*
> *Quam variæ linguis.* –

> [Vast crowds of vanquish'd nations march along:
> Various in arms, in habit, and in tongue.]   *Aen.* 8.

If a painter should put into a picture one town of *France* and another of *Flanders*, might not one say they were two towns which spake different languages?

Homer (they tell us) says in another place, that *we hear the harangues of two pleaders.* This is an unfair exaggeration: He only says, *two men pleaded*, that is, were represented pleading. Was not the same said by *Pliny* of *Nicomachus*, that he had painted two *Greeks*, which spake one after another? Can we express ourselves otherwise of these two arts, which tho' they are mute, yet have a language? Or in explaining a painting of *Raphael* or *Poussin*, can we prevent animating the figures, in making them speak conformably to the design of the painter? But how could the engraver represent those young shepherds and virgins that dance first in a ring, and then in setts? Or those troops which were in ambuscade? This would be difficult indeed if the workman had not the liberty to make his persons appear in different circumstances. All the objections against the young man who sings at the same time that he plays on the harp, the bull that roars whilst he is devoured by a lion, and against the musical consorts, are childish; for we can never speak of painting if we banish those expressions. *Pliny* says of *Apelles*, that he painted *Clytus* on horseback going to battel, and demanding his helmet of his squire: Of *Aristides*, that he drew a beggar whom he could almost understand, *pene cum voce* [almost with a voice]: Of *Ctesilochus*, that he had painted *Jupiter* bringing forth *Bacchus*, and crying out like a woman, *& muliebriter ingemiscentem* [groaning like a woman]: And of *Nicearchus*, that he had drawn a piece, in which *Hercules* was seen very melancholy on reflection of his madness, *Herculem tristem, insaniae pœnitentia* [a woeful Hercules, repenting his madness]. No one sure will condemn those ways of expression which are so common. The same author has said much more of *Apelles*; he tells us, he painted those things which could not be painted, as thunder; *pinxit quæ pingi non possunt*: And of *Timanthus*, that in all his Works there was something more understood than was seen; and tho' there was all the art imaginable, yet there was still more ingenuity than art: *Atque in omnibus ejus operibus, intelligitur plus semper quam pingitur; & cum ars summa sit, ingenium tamen ultra artem est.* If we take the pains to compare these expressions with those of *Homer*, we shall find him altogether excusable in his *manner* of describing the buckler.

We come now to the *matter*. If this shield (says a modern critick) had been made in a wiser age, it would have been more correct and less charged with objects. There are two things which cause the censurers to fall into this false criticism: The first is, that they think the shield was no broader than the brims of a hat, whereas it was large enough to cover a whole man. The other is, that they did not know the design of the poet, and imagined this description was only the whimsy of an irregular wit, who did it by chance, and not following nature; for they never so much as entered into the intention of the poet, nor knew the shield was designed as a representation of the universe.

'Tis happy that *Virgil* has made a buckler for *Æneas*, as well as *Homer* for *Achilles.* The *Latin* poet, who imitated the *Greek* one, always took care to accommodate those things which time had changed, so as to render them agreeable to the palate of his readers; yet he hath not only charged his shield with a great deal more work, since he paints all the actions of the *Romans* from *Ascanius* to *Augustus*; but has not avoided any of those manners of expression which offend the criticks. We see there the wolf of *Romulus* and *Remus*, who gives them her dugs *one after another, Mulcere alternos, & corpora fingere lingua* [She licked their tender limbs, and formed them as she fed. (Dryden)]: The rape of the *Sabines* and the war which followed it, *subitoque novum consurgere bellum* [And then suddenly a new war broke out.]: *Metius* torn by four Horses, and *Tullus* who draws his entrails thro' the Forest: *Porsenna* commanding the *Romans* to receive *Tarquin*, and besieging *Rome*: The geese flying to the porches of the capitol, and giving notice by their *cries* of the attack of the *Gauls.*

> *Atque, hic auratis volitans argenteus anser,*
> *Porticibus, Gallos in limine adesse* canebat.

[The silver goose before the shining gate
There flew; and by her cackle, sav'd the state.
She told the *Gauls* approach.]

We see the *Salian* dance, hell, and the pains of the damn'd; and farther off, the place of the blessed, where *Cato* presides: We see the famous battel of *Actium*, where we may distinguish the captains: *Agrippa* with the Gods, and the winds favourable; and *Anthony* leading on all the forces of the *East*, *Egypt*, and the *Bactrians*: The fight begins, The sea is red with blood, *Cleopatra* gives the signal for a retreat, and calls her troops with a *systrum. Patrio vocat agmina systro.* The Gods, or rather the monsters of *Egypt*, fight against *Neptune*, *Venus*, *Minerva*, *Mars* and *Apollo*: We see *Anthony*'s fleet beaten, and the *Nile* sorrowfully opening his bosom to receive the conquered: *Cleopatra* looks pale and almost dead at the thought of that death she had already determined; nay we see the very wind *Iapis*, which hastens her flight: We see the three triumphs of *Augustus*; that Prince consecrates three hundred temples, the Altars are filled with ladies offering up sacrifices, *Augustus* sitting at the entrance of *Apollo*'s temple, receives presents, and hangs them on the pillars of the temple; while all the conquered Nations pass by, who *speak different languages*, and are differently equipped and armed.

> *– Incedunt victæ longo ordine gentes,*
> *Quam variæ linguis, habitu tum vestis & armis.*

[Vast crowds of vanquish'd nations march along:
Various in arms, in habit, and in tongue.]

Nothing can better justify *Homer*, or shew the wisdom and judgment of *Virgil*: He was charmed with *Achilles*'s shield, and therefore would give the same ornament to his poem. But as *Homer* had painted the universe, he was sensible that nothing remained for him to do; he had no other way to take than that of prophecy, and shew what the descendant of his hero should perform; and he was not afraid to go beyond *Homer*, because there is nothing improbable in the hands of a God. If the criticks say, that this is justifying one fault by another; I desire they would agree among themselves; for *Scaliger*, who was the first that condemned *Homer*'s shield, admires *Virgil*'s; but suppose they should agree, 'twould be foolish to endeavour to persuade us, that what *Homer* and *Virgil* have done by the approbation of all ages, is not good; and to make us think that their particular taste should prevail over that of all other men. Nothing is more ridiculous than to trouble one's self to answer men, who shew so little reason in their criticisms, that we can do them no greater favour, than to ascribe it to their ignorance.

Thus far the objections are answered by Mons. *Dacier*. Since when, some others have been started, as that the objects represented on the buckler have no reference to the poem, no Agreement with *Thetis* who procured it, *Vulcan* who made it, or *Achilles* for whom it was made.

To this it is replied, that the representation of the sea was agreeable enough to *Thetis*; that the spheres and celestial fires were so to *Vulcan*; (tho' the truth is, any piece of workmanship was equally fit to come from the hands of this God) and that the images of a town besieged, a battel, and an ambuscade, were objects sufficiently proper for *Achilles.* But after all, where was the necessity that they should be so? They had at least been as fit for one hero as for another; and *Æneas*, as *Virgil* tells us, knew not what to make of the figures on his shield.

Rerumque Ignarus, imagine gaudet.

[Unknown the names, he yet admires the grace.]

I I

But still the main objection, and that in which the vanity of the moderns has triumphed the most, is, that the shield is crowded with such a multiplicity of figures, as could not possibly be represented in the compass of it. The late dissertation of Mons. *Boivin* has put an end to this cavil, and the reader will have the pleasure to be convinced of it by ocular demonstration, in the print annexed.

This author supposes the buckler to have been perfectly round: He divides the convex surface into four concentrick circles.

The circle next the center contains the globe of the earth and the sea, in miniature; he gives this circle the dimension of three inches.

The second circle is allotted for the heavens and the stars: He allows the space of ten inches between this, and the former circle.

The third shall be eight inches distant from the second. The space between these two circles shall be divided into twelve compartments, each of which makes a picture of ten or eleven inches deep.

The fourth circle makes the margin of the buckler: And the interval between this and the former, being of three inches, is sufficient to represent the waves and currents of the ocean.

All these together make but four foot in the whole in diameter. The print of these circles and divisions will serve to prove, that the figures will neither be crowded nor confused, if disposed in the proper place and order.

As to the size and figure of the shield, it is evident from the poets, that in the time of the *Trojan* war there were shields of an extraordinary magnitude. The buckler of *Ajax* is often compared by *Homer* to a tower, and in the sixth Iliad that of *Hector* is described to cover him from the shoulders to the ankles.

> Ἀμφὶ δὲ οἱ σφυρὰ τύπτε καὶ αὐχένα δέρμα κελαινὸν
> Ἄντυξ ἣ πυμάτη θέεν ἀσπίδος ὀμφαλοέσσης.   v. 117.

[The shield's large orb behind his shoulder cast,
  His neck o'ershading, to his ancle hung;
  And as he march'd, the brazen buckler rung.

                              (Pope's trans., 143–5)]

In the second verse of the description of this buckler of *Achilles*, it is said that *Vulcan* cast round it a radiant circle.

> Περὶ δ' ἄντυγα βάλλε φαεινήν.   v. 479.

[He cast a shining rim around it.]

Which proves the figure to have been round. But if it be alledged that ἄντυξ [rim] as well signifies *oval* as *circular*, it may be answered, that the circular figure better agrees to the spheres represented in the center, and to the course of the ocean at the circumference.

We may very well allow four foot diameter to this buckler: As one may suppose a larger size would have been too unwieldy, so a less would not have been sufficient to cover the breast and arm of a man of a stature so large as *Achilles*.

In allowing four foot diameter to the whole, each of the twelve compartments may be of ten or eleven inches in depth, which will be enough to contain, without any confusion, all the objects which *Homer* mentions. Indeed in this print, each compartment being but of one inch, the principal figures only are represented; but the reader may easily imagine the advantage of nine or ten inches more. However, if the criticks are not yet satisfied there is room enough, it is but taking in the literal sense the words πάντοσε δαιδάλλων [decorating it on every side], with which *Homer* begins his description, and the buckler may be supposed engraven on both sides, which supposition will double the size of each piece: The one side may serve for the general description of heaven and earth, and the other for all the particulars.

I I I

It having been now shewn, that the shield of *Homer* is blameless as to its design and disposition, and that the subject (so extensive as it is) may be contracted within the due limits; not being one vast unproportioned heap of figures, but divided into twelve regular compartiments: What remains, is to consider this piece as a complete *idea* of *painting*, and a sketch for what one may call an *universal picture.* This is certainly the light in which it is chiefly to be admired, and in which alone the criticks have neglected to place it.

There is reason to believe that *Homer* did in this, as he has done in other arts, (even in mechanicks) that is, comprehend whatever was known of it in his time; if not (as is highly probable) from thence extend his ideas yet farther, and give a more enlarged notion of it. Accordingly it is very observable, that there is scarce a species or branch of this art which is not here to be found, whether history, battel painting, landskip, architecture, fruits, flowers, animals, &c.

I think it possible that painting was arrived to a greater degree of perfection, even at that early period, than is generally supposed by those who have written upon it. *Pliny* expressly says, that it was not known in the time of the *Trojan* war. The same author, and others, represent it in a very imperfect state in *Greece*, in, or near the days of *Homer.* They tell us of one painter, that he was the first who begun to shadow; and of another, that he filled his outlines only with a single colour, and that laid on every where alike: But we may have a higher notion of the art, from those descriptions of statues, carvings, tapestries, sculptures upon armour, and ornaments of all kinds, which every where occur in our author; as well as from what he says of their beauty, the relievo, and their emulation of life itself. If we consider how much it is his constant practice to confine himself to the custom of the times whereof he writ, it will be hard to doubt but that painting and sculpture must have been then in great practice and repute.

The shield is not only described as a piece of sculpture but of painting; the outlines may be supposed engraved, and the rest enameled, or inlaid with various-coloured metals. The variety of colours is plainly distinguished by *Homer*, where he speaks of the *blackness* of the new-open'd earth, of the *several colours* of the grapes and vines; and in other places. The different metals that *Vulcan* is feigned to cast into the furnace, were sufficient to afford all the necessary colours: But if to those which are natural to the metals, we add also those which they are capable of receiving from the operation of fire, we shall find, that *Vulcan* had as great a variety of colours to make use of as any modern painter. That enamelling, or fixing colours by fire, was practised very anciently, may be conjectured from what *Diodorus* reports of one of the walls of *Babylon*, built by *Semiramis*, that *the bricks of it were painted before they were burned, so as to represent all sorts of animals.* lib. 2. chap. 4. Now it is but natural to infer, that men had made use of ordinary colours for the representation of objects, before they learnt to represent them by such as are given by the operation of Fire; one being much more easy and obvious than the other, and that sort of painting by means of fire being but an imitation of the painting with a pencil and colours. The same inference will be farther enforced from the works of tapestry, which the women of those times interweaved with many colours; as appears from the description of that veil which *Hecuba* offers to *Minerva* in the sixth Iliad, and from a passage in the twenty second where *Andromache* is represented working flowers in a piece of this kind. They must certainly have known the use of the colours themselves for painting, before they could think of dying threads with those colours, and weaving those threads close to one another, in order only to a more laborious imitation of a thing so much more easily performed by a pencil. This observation I owe to the *Abbé Fraguier.*

It may indeed be thought, that a Genius so vast and comprehensive as that of *Homer*, might carry his views beyond the rest of mankind, and that in this buckler of *Achilles* he rather designed to give a scheme of what might be performed, than a description of what really was so: And since he made a God the artist, he might excuse himself from a strict confinement to what was known and practised in the time of the *Trojan* war. Let this be as it will, it is certain that he had, whether by learning, or by strength of genius, (tho' the latter be more glorious for *Homer*) a full and exact idea of painting in all its parts; that is to say, in the *invention*, the *composition*, the *expression*, &c.

The *invention* is shewn in finding and introducing, in every subject, the *greatest*, the most *significant*, and most *suitable* objects. Accordingly in every single picture of the shield, *Homer* constantly finds out either those objects which are naturally the principal, those which most conduce to shew the subject, or those which set it in the liveliest and most agreeable light: These he never fails to dispose in the most advantagious manners, situations, and oppositions.

Next, we find all his figures differently *characterized*, in their expressions and attitudes, according to their several natures: The Gods (for instance) are distinguished in air, habit, and proportion, from men, in the fourth picture; masters from servants, in the eighth; and so of the rest.

Nothing is more wonderful than his exact observation of the *contrast*, not only between figure and figure, but between subject and subject. The city in peace is a contrast to the city in war: Between the siege in the fourth picture, and the battel in the sixth, a piece of paisage is introduced, and rural Scenes follow after. The country too is represented in war in the fifth, as well as in peace in the seventh, eighth, and ninth. The very animals are shewn in these two different states, in the tenth and eleventh. Where the subjects appear the same, he contrastes them some other way: Thus the first picture of the town in peace having a predominant air of gaiety, in the dances and pomps of the marriage; the second has a character of earnestness and sollicitude, in the dispute and pleadings. In the pieces of rural life, that of the plowing is of a different character from the harvest, and that of the harvest from the vintage. In each of these there is a contrast of the *labour* and *mirth* of the country people: In the first, some are plowing, others taking a cup of good liquor; in the next, we see the reapers working in one part, and the banquet prepared in another; in the last, the labour of the vineyard is relieved with musick and a dance. The persons are no less varied, old and young, men and women: There being women in two pictures together, namely the eighth and ninth, it is remarkable that those in the latter are of a different character from the former; they who dress the supper being ordinary women, the others who carry baskets in the vineyard, young and beautiful virgins: And these again are of an inferior character to those in the twelfth piece, who are distinguish'd as people of condition by a more elegant dress. There are three dances in the buckler; and these too are varied: That at the wedding is in a circular figure, that of the vineyard in a row, that in the last picture, a mingled one. Lastly, there is a manifest contrast in the colours; nay, ev'n in the back-grounds of the several pieces: For example, that of the plowing is of a dark tinct, that of the harvest yellow, that of the pasture green, and the rest in like manner.

That he was not a stranger to aerial *perspective*, appears in his expresly marking the distance of object from object: He tells us, for instance, that the two spies lay a little remote from the other figures; and that the oak under which was spread the banquet of the reapers, stood apart. What he says of the valley sprinkled all over with cottages and flocks, appears to be a description of a large country in perspective. And indeed a general argument for this may be drawn from the number of figures on the shield; which could not be all expressed in their full magnitude: And this is therefore a sort of proof that the art of lessening them according to perspective was known at that time.

What the criticks call the *three unities*, ought in reason as much to be observed in a picture as in a play; each should have only *one principal action*, one *instant of time*, and one *point of view*. In this method of examination also, the shield of *Homer* will bear the test: He has been more exact than the greatest painters, who have often deviated from one or other of these rules; whereas (when we examine the detail of each compartiment) it will appear,

First, that there is but one principal action in each picture, and that no supernumerary figures or actions are introduced. This will answer all that has been said of the confusion and crowd of figures on the shield, by those who never comprehended the plan of it.

Secondly, that no action is represented in one piece, which could not happen in the same instant of time. This will overthrow the objection against so many different actions appearing in one shield; which, in this case, is much as absurd as to object against so many of *Raphael's* cartoons appearing in one gallery.

Thirdly, It will be manifest that there are no objects in any one picture which could not be seen in one point of view. Hereby the *Abbé Terasson's* whole criticism will fall to the ground, which amounts but to this, that the general objects of the heavens, stars and sea, with the particular prospects of towns, fields, *&c.* could never be seen all at once. *Homer* was incapable of so absurd a thought, nor could these heavenly bodies (had he intended them for a picture) have ever been seen together from one point; for the constellations and the full moon, for example, could never be seen at once with the sun. But the celestial bodies were placed on the boss, as the ocean at the margin of the shield: These were no parts of the painting, but the former was only an ornament to the projection in the middle, and the latter a frame round about it: In the same manner as the divisions, projections, or angles of a roof are left to be ornamented at the discretion of the painter, with foliage, architecture, grotesque, or what he pleases: However his judgment will be still more commendable, if he contrives to make even these extrinsical parts, to bear some allusion to the main design: It is this which *Homer* has done, in placing a sort of sphere in the middle, and the ocean at the border, of a work, which was so expressly intended to represent the universe.

I proceed now to the detail of the shield; in which the words of *Homer* being first translated, an attempt will be made to shew with what exact order all that he describes may enter into the composition, according to the rules of painting.

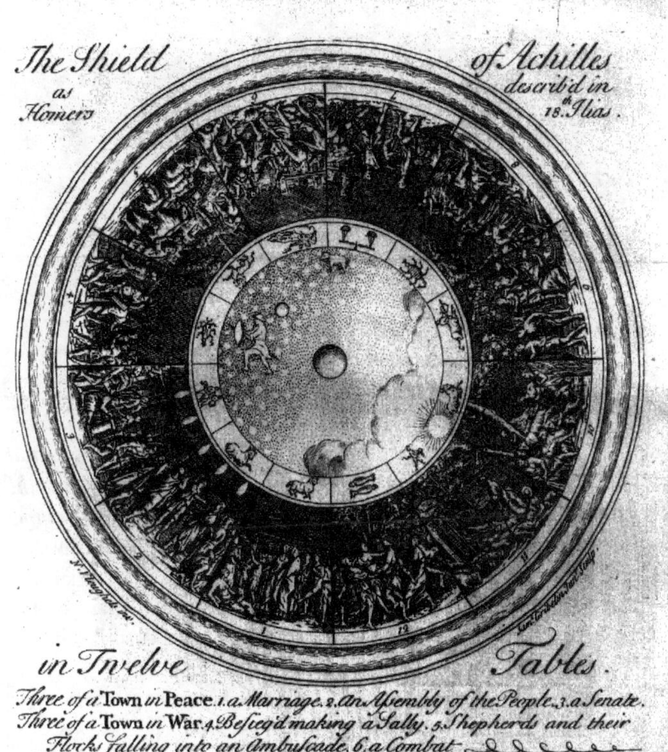

The Shield of Achilles

Engraving from the 1743 edition.
Reproduction courtesy Jack Liu

THE
SHIELD OF *ACHILLES*
Divided into its several Parts

The BOSS *of the* SHIELD

483. 'Εν μὲν γαῖαν, &c.] *Here* Vulcan *represented the earth, the heaven, the sea, the indefatigable course of the sun, the moon in her full, all the celestial signs that crown* Olympus, *the* Pleiades, *the* Hyades, *the great* Orion, *and the* Bear, *commonly call'd the* Wain, *the only constellation which never bathing itself in the ocean, turns about the pole and osberves the course of* Orion.

The sculpture of these resembled somewhat of our terrestrial and celestial globes, and took up the center of the shield: 'Tis plain by the huddle in which *Homer* expresses this, that he did not describe it as a picture for a point of sight.

The circumference is divided into twelve compartiments, each being a separate picture: as follow.

First Compartiment. *A Town in Peace*

'Εν δὲ δύω ποίησε πόλεις, &c.] *He engraved two cities; in one of them were represented nuptials and festivals. The spouses from their bridal chambers, were conducted thro' the town by the light of torches. Every mouth sung the* hymenæal *song: The youths turn'd rapidly about in a circular dance: The flute and the lyre resounded: The women, every one in the street, standing in the porches, beheld and admired.*

In this picture, the brides preceded by torch-bearers are on the foreground: The dance in circles, and musicians behind them: The street in perspective on either side, the women and spectators, in the porches, &c. dispersed thro' all the architecture.

Second Compartiment. *An Assembly of People*

Λαοὶ δ' εἰν ἀγορῇ, *&c.*] *There was seen a number of people in the market-place, and two men disputing warmly: The occasion was the payment of a fine for a murder, which one affirm'd before the people he had paid, the other denied to have received; both demanded, that the affair should be determined by the judgment of an arbiter: The acclamations of the multitude favoured sometimes the one party, sometimes the other.*

Here is a fine plan for a master-piece of *expression*; any judge of painting will see our author has chosen that *cause* which of all others, would give occasion to the greatest variety of expression: The father, the murderer, the witnesses, and the different passions of the assembly, would afford an ample field for this talent even to *Raphael* himself.

Third Compartiment. *The Senate*

Κήρυκες δ' ἄρα λαὸν. ἐρήτυον, *&c.*] *The heralds rang'd the people in order: The reverend elders were seated on seats of polish'd stone, in the sacred circle; they rose up and declared their judgment, each in his turn, with the scepter in his hand: Two talents of gold were laid in the middle of the circle, to be given to him who should pronounce the most equitable judgment.*

The judges are seated in the center of the picture; one (who is the principal figure) standing up as speaking, another in an action of rising, as in order to speak: The ground about 'em a prospect of the Forum, fill'd with auditors and spectators.

Fourth Compartiment. *A Town in War*

Τὴν δ' ἑτέρην πόλιν, *&c.*] *The other City was besieged by two glittering armies: They were not agreed, whether to sack the town, or divide all the booty of it into two equal parts, to be shared between them: Meantime the besieged secretly armed themselves for an ambuscade. Their wives, children, and old men were posted to defend the walls: The warriours marched from the town with* Pallas *and* Mars *at their head: The deities were of gold, and had golden armours, by the glory of which they were distinguished* *above the men, as well as by their superiour stature, and more elegant proportions.*

This subject may be thus disposed: The town pretty near the eye, a-cross the whole picture, with the old men on the walls: The chiefs of each army on the foreground: Their different opinions for putting the town to the sword, or sparing it on account of the booty, may be express'd by some having their hands on their swords, and looking up to the city, others stopping them, or in an action of persuading against it. Behind, in prospect, the townsmen may be seen going out from the back gates, with the two deities at their head.

Homer here gives a clear instance of what the ancients always practised; the distinguishing the Gods and Goddesses by characters of majesty or beauty somewhat superiour to nature; we constantly find this in their statues, and to this the modern masters owe the grand taste in the perfection of their figures.

Fifth Compartiment. *An Ambuscade*

Οἱ δ' ὅτε δὴ ῥ' ἵκανον, &c.] *Being arrived at the river where they designed their ambush (the place where the cattel were watered) they disposed themselves along the bank, covered with their arms: Two spies lay at a distance from them, observing when the oxen and sheep should come to drink. They came immediately, followed by two shepherds, who were playing on their pipes, without any apprehension of their danger.*

This quiet picture is a kind of *Repose* between the last, and the following, active pieces. Here is a scene of a river and trees, under which lie the soldiers, next the eye of the spectator; on the farther bank are placed the two spies on one hand, and the flocks and shepherds appear coming at a greater distance on the other.

Sixth Compartiment. *The Battle*

Οἱ μὲν τὰ προϊδόντες, &c.] *The people of the town rushed upon them, carried off the oxen and sheep, and killed the shepherds. The besiegers sitting before the town, heard the outcry, and mounting their horses, arrived at the bank of the river; where they stopped, and encountered each other with their spears. Discord, tumult, and fate raged in the midst of them. There might you see cruel Destiny dragging a dead soldier thro' the battel; two others she seized alive; one of which was mortally wounded; the other not yet hurt: The garment on her shoulders was stained with human blood: The figures appeared as if they lived, moved, and fought, you would think they really dragged off their dead.*

The sheep and two shepherds lying dead upon the fore-ground. A battle-piece fills the picture. The allegorical figure of the *Parca* or *Destiny* is the principal. This had been a noble occasion for such a painter as *Rubens*, who has with most happiness and learning, imitated the ancients in these fictitious and symbolical persons.

Seventh Compartiment. *Tillage*

’Εν δ’ ἐτίθει νειὸν μαλακήν.] *The next piece represented a large field, a deep and fruitful soil, which seemed to have been three times plowed; the labourers appeared turning their plows on every side. As soon as they came to a land's end, a man presented them a bowl of wine; cheared with this, they turned, and worked down a new furrow, desirous to hasten to the next land's end. The field was of gold, but looked black behind the plows, as if it had really been turned up; the surprizing effect of the art of* Vulcan.

The plowmen must be represented on the fore-ground, in the action of turning at the end of the furrow. The invention of *Homer* is not content with barely putting down the figures, but enlivens them prodigiously with some remarkable circumstance: The giving a cup of wine to the plowmen must occasion a fine expression in the faces.

Eighth Compartiment. *The Harvest*

’Εν δ’ ἐτιθει τέμενος, *&c.*] *Next he represented a field of corn, in which the reapers worked with sharp sickles in their hands; the corn fell thick along the furrows in equal rows: Three binders were employed in making up the sheaves: The boys attending them, gathered up the loose swarths, and carried them in their arms to be bound: The lord of the field standing in the midst of the heaps, with a scepter in his hand, rejoices in silence: His officers, at a distance, prepare a feast under the shade of an oak, and hold an ox ready to be sacrificed; while the women mix the flower of wheat for the reaper's supper.*

The reapers on the fore-ground, with their faces towards the spectators; the gatherers behind, and the children on the farther ground. The master of the field, who is the chief figure, may be set in the middle of the picture with a strong light upon him, in the action of directing and pointing with his scepter: The oak, with the Servants under it, the sacrifice, &c. on a distant ground, would altogether make a beautiful grouppe of great variety.

Ninth Compartiment. *The Vintage*

'Εν δ' ἐτίθει σταφυλῇσι, *&c.*] *He then engraved a vineyard loaden with its grapes: The vineyard was gold, but the grapes black, and the props of them silver. A trench of a dark metal, and a palisade of tin encompassed the whole vineyard. There was one path in it, by which the labourers in the vineyard passed: Young men and maids carried the fruit in woven baskets: In the middle of them a youth played on the lyre, and charmed them with his tender voice, as he sung to the strings (or as he sung the song of* Linus:) *The rest striking the ground with their feet in exact time, followed him in a dance, and accompanied his voice with their own.*

The vintage scarce needs to be painted in any colours but *Homer*'s. The youths and maids toward the eye, as coming out of the vineyard: The enclosure, pales, gate, &c. on the fore-ground. There is something inexpressibly *riant* in this piece, above all the rest.

Tenth Compartiment. *Animals*

'Εν δ' ἀγέλην ποίησε Βοῶν, *&c.*] *He graved a herd of oxen, marching with their heads erected; these oxen (inlaid with gold and tin) seemed to bellow as they quitted their stall, and run in haste to the meadows, through which a rapid river rolled with resounding streams amongst the rushes: Four herdsmen of gold attended them, followed by nine large dogs: Two terrible lions seized a bull by the throat, who roared as they dragged him along; the dogs and the herdsmen ran to his rescue, but the lions having torn the bull, devoured his entrails, and drank his blood, the herdsmen came up with their dogs and heartened them in vain; they durst not attack the lions, but standing at some distance, barked at them and shunned them.*

We have next a fine piece of animals, tame and savage: But what is remarkable, is, that these animals are not coldly brought in to be gazed upon: The herds, dogs, and lions are put into action, enough to exercise the warmth and spirit of *Rubens*, or the great taste of *Julio Romano*.

The lions may be next the eye, one holding the bull by the throat, the other tearing out his entrails: A herdsman or two heartening the dogs: All these on the fore-ground. On the second ground another grouppe of oxen, that seem to have been gone before, tossing their heads and running; other herdsmen and dogs after 'em: And beyond them, a prospect of the river.

Eleventh Compartiment. *Sheep*

'Εν δὲ νομόν, &c.] *The divine artist then engraved a large flock of white sheep, feeding along a beautiful valley. Innumerable folds, cottages, and enclosed shelters, were scattered thro' the prospect.*

This is an entire landscape without human figures, an image of nature solitary and undisturbed: The deepest repose and tranquillity is that which distinguishes it from the others.

Twelfth Compartiment. *The Dance*

'Εν δὲ χορόν, &c.] *The skilful* Vulcan *then designed the figure and various motions of a dance, like that which* Dædalus *of old contrived in* Gnossus *for the fair* Ariadne. *There the young men and maidens danced hand in hand; the maids were dressed in linen garments, the men in rich and shining stuffs: The maids had flowery crowns on their heads; the men had swords of gold hanging from their sides in belts of silver. Here they seemed to run in a ring with active feet, as swiftly as a wheel runs round when tried by the hand of the potter. There, they appeared to move in many figures, and sometimes to meet, sometimes to wind from each other. A multitude of spectators stood round, delighted with the dance. In the middle, two nimble tumblers exercised themselves in feats of activity, while the song was carried on by the whole circle.*

This picture includes the greatest number of persons: *Homer* himself has group'd them, and marked the manner of the composition. This piece would excell in the different *airs of beauty* which might be given to the young men and women, and the graceful attitudes in the various manners of dancing: On which account the subject might be fit for

Guido, or perhaps could be no where better executed than in our own country.

The BORDER *of the* SHIELD

Ἐν δ' ἐτίθει ποταμοῖο, *&c.*] *Then lastly, he represented the rapid course of the great ocean, which he made to roll its waves round the extremity of the whole circumference.*

This (as has been said before) was only the frame to the whole shield; and is therefore but slightly touched upon, without any mention of particular objects.

I ought not to end this essay, without vindicating myself from the vanity of treating of an art, which I love so much better than I understand: But I have been very careful to consult both the best performers and judges in painting. I can't neglect this occasion of saying, how happy I think myself in the favour of the most distinguish'd masters of that Art. Sir *Godfrey Kneller* in particular allows me to tell the world, that he entirely agrees with my sentiments on this subject: And I can't help wishing, that he who gives this testimony to *Homer*, would ennoble so great a design by his own execution of it. *Vulcan* never wrought for *Thetis* with more readiness and affection than Sir *Godfrey* has done for me: And so admirable a picture of the whole universe could not be a more agreeable present than he has obliged me with, in the portraits of some of those persons who are to me the dearest objects in it.

THE
NINETEENTH BOOK
OF THE
ILIAD

The ARGUMENT

The reconciliation of *Achilles* and *Agamemnon*

Thetis *brings to her son the armour made by* Vulcan. *She preserves the body of his friend from corruption, and commands him to assemble the army, to declare his resentment at an end.* Agamemnon *and* Achilles *are solemnly reconciled: The Speeches, presents, and ceremonies on that occasion.* Achilles *is with great difficulty persuaded to refrain from the battel till the troops have refreshed themselves, by the advice of* Ulysses. *The presents are conveyed to the tent of* Achilles; *where* Briseïs *laments over the body of* Patroclus. *The hero obstinately refuses all repast, and gives himself up to lamentations for his friend.* Minerva *descends to strengthen him, by the order of* Jupiter. *He arms for the fight; his appearance described. He addresses himself to his horses, and reproaches them with the death of* Patroclus. *One of them is miraculously endued with voice, and inspired to prophecy his fate; but the hero, not astonished by that prodigy, rushes with fury to the combate.*

The thirtieth day. The scene is on the sea-shore.

Soon as *Aurora* heav'd her orient head
Above the waves that blush'd with early red,
(With new-born day to gladden mortal sight,
And gild the courts of heav'n with sacred light,)
5   Th'immortal arms the Goddess-mother bears
Swift to her son: Her son she finds in tears,
Stretch'd o'er *Patroclus'* corse; while all the rest
Their Sov'reign's sorrows in their own exprest.
A ray divine her heav'nly presence shed,
10   And thus, his hand soft-touching, *Thetis* said.
     Suppress (my Son) this rage of grief, and know
It was not man, but heav'n that gave the blow;
Behold what arms by *Vulcan* are bestow'd,
Arms worthy thee, or fit to grace a god.
15   Then drops the radiant burden on the ground;
Clang the strong arms, and ring the shores around:
Back shrink the *Myrmidons* with dread surprize,
And from the broad effulgence turn their eyes.
Unmov'd, the hero kindles at the show,
20   And feels with rage divine his bosom glow:
From his fierce eye-balls living flames expire,
And flash incessant like a stream of fire:
He turns the radiant gift; and feeds his mind
On all th'immortal artist had design'd.
25   Goddess (he cry'd) these glorious arms that shine
With matchless art, confess the hand divine.
Now to the bloody battel let me bend:
But ah! the relicks of my slaughter'd friend!

In those wide wounds thro' which his spirit fled,
Shall flies, and worms obscene, pollute the dead?   30
    That unavailing care be laid aside,
(The azure Goddess to her son reply'd)
Whole years untouch'd, uninjur'd shall remain
Fresh as in life, the carcase of the slain.
But go, *Achilles*, (as affairs require)   35
Before the *Grecian* Peers renounce thine ire:
Then uncontroll'd in boundless war engage,
And heav'n with strength supply the mighty rage!
    Then in the nostrils of the slain she pour'd
Nectareous drops, and rich ambrosia showr'd   40
O'er all the corse. The flies forbid their prey,
Untouch'd it rests, and sacred from decay.
Achilles to the strand obedient went;
The Shores resounded with the voice he sent.
The heroes heard, and all the naval train   45
That tend the ships, or guide them o'er the main,
Alarm'd, transported, at the well-known sound,
Frequent and full, the great assembly crown'd;
Studious to see that terrour of the plain,
Long lost to battel, shine in arms again.   50
    Tydides and *Ulysses* first appear,
Lame with their wounds, and leaning on the spear;
These on the sacred seats of council plac'd,
The King of men, *Atrides*, came the last:
He too sore wounded by *Agenor*'s son.   55
Achilles (rising in the midst) begun.
    Oh Monarch! better far had been the fate
Of thee, of me, of all the *Grecian* state,
If, (e'er the day when by mad passion sway'd,
Rash we contended for the black-ey'd maid)   60
Preventing *Dian* had dispatch'd her dart,
And shot the shining mischief to the heart!
Then many a hero had not press'd the shore,
Nor *Troy*'s glad fields been fatten'd with our gore:
Long, long shall *Greece* the woes we caus'd, bewail,   65
And sad posterity repeat the tale.
But this, no more the subject of debate,
Is past, forgotten, and resign'd to fate:

Why should (alas) a mortal man, as I,
70   Burn with a fury that can never die?
Here then my anger ends: Let war succeed,
And ev'n as *Greece* has bled, let *Ilion* bleed.
Now call the hosts, and try, if in our sight,
Troy yet shall dare to camp a second night?
75   I deem, their mightiest, when this arm he knows,
Shall 'scape with transport, and with joy repose.
     He said: His finish'd wrath with loud acclaim
The *Greeks* accept, and shout *Pelides'* name.
When thus, not rising from his lofty throne,
80   In state unmov'd, the King of men begun.
     Hear me ye Sons of *Greece!* with silence hear!
And grant your monarch an impartial ear;
Awhile your loud, untimely joy suspend,
And let your rash, injurious clamours end:
85   Unruly murmurs, or ill-tim'd applause,
Wrong the best speaker, and the justest cause.
Nor charge on me, ye *Greeks*, the dire debate;
Know, angry *Jove*, and all-compelling *Fate*,
With fell *Erynnis*, urg'd my wrath that day
90   When from *Achilles'* arms I forc'd the prey.
What then cou'd I, against the will of heav'n?
Not by my self, but vengeful *Ate* driv'n;
She, *Jove*'s dread daughter, fated to infest
The race of mortals, enter'd in my breast.
95   Not on the ground that haughty fury treads,
But prints her lofty footsteps on the heads
Of mighty men; inflicting as she goes
Long-fest'ring wounds, inextricable woes!
Of old, she stalk'd amid the bright abodes;
100   And *Jove* himself, the Sire of Men and Gods,
The world's great ruler, felt her venom'd dart;
Deceiv'd by *Juno*'s wiles, and female art.
For when *Alcmena*'s nine long months were run,
And *Jove* expected his immortal son;
105   To Gods and Goddesses th'unruly joy
He show'd, and vaunted of his matchless boy:
From us (he said) this day an infant springs,
Fated to rule, and born a King of Kings.

Saturnia ask'd an oath, to vouch the truth,
And fix dominion on the favour'd youth.   110
The Thund'rer, unsuspicious of the fraud,
Pronounc'd those solemn words that bind a God.
The joyful Goddess, from *Olympus'* height,
Swift to *Achaian Argos* bent her flight;
Scarce sev'n moons gone, lay *Sthenelus* his wife;   115
She push'd her ling'ring infant into life:
Her charms *Alcmena*'s coming labours stay,
And stop the babe, just issuing to the day.
Then bids *Saturnius* bear his oath in mind;
'A youth (said she) of *Jove*'s immortal kind   120
Is this day born: From *Sthenelus* he springs,
And claims thy promise to be King of Kings.'
Grief seiz'd the Thund'rer, by his oath engag'd;
Stung to the soul, he sorrow'd, and he rag'd.
From his ambrosial head, where perch'd she sate,   125
He snatch'd the Fury-Goddess of Debate,
The dread, th'irrevocable oath he swore,
Th'immortal seats should ne'er behold her more;
And whirl'd her headlong down, for ever driv'n
From bright *Olympus* and the starry heav'n: 130
Thence on the nether world the fury fell;
Ordain'd with man's contentious race to dwell.
Full oft' the God his son's hard toils bemoan'd,
Curs'd the dire fury, and in secret groan'd.
Ev'n thus, like *Jove* himself, was I misled,   135
While raging *Hector* heap'd our camps with dead.
What can the errors of my rage attone?
My martial troops, my treasures, are thy own:
This instant from the navy shall be sent
Whate'er *Ulysses* promis'd at thy tent: 140
But thou! appeas'd, propitious to our pray'r,
Resume thy arms, and shine again in war.
   O King of Nations! whose superiour sway
(Returns *Achilles*) all our hosts obey!
To keep, or send the presents, be thy care;   145
To us, 'tis equal: All we ask is war.
While yet we talk, or but an instant shun
The fight, our glorious work remains undone.

Let ev'ry *Greek* who sees my spear confound
150 The *Trojan* ranks, and deal destruction round,
With emulation, what I act, survey,
And learn from thence the business of the day.
　　The Son of *Peleus* thus: And thus replies
The great in councils, *Ithacus* the wise.
155 Tho' godlike thou art by no toils opprest,
At least our armies claim repast and rest:
Long and laborious must the combate be,
When by the Gods inspir'd, and led by thee.
Strength is deriv'd from spirits and from blood,
160 And those augment by gen'rous wine and food;
What boastful son of war, without that stay,
Can last a hero thro' a single day?
Courage may prompt; but, ebbing out his strength,
Mere unsupported man must yield at length;
165 Shrunk with dry famine, and with toils declin'd,
The dropping body will desert the mind:
But built anew with strength-conferring fare,
With limbs and soul untam'd, he tires a war.
Dismiss the people then, and give command,
170 With strong repast to hearten ev'ry band;
But let the presents, to *Achilles* made,
In full assembly of all *Greece* be laid.
The King of men shall rise in publick sight,
And solemn swear (observant of the rite)
175 That spotless as she came, the maid removes,
Pure from his arms, and guiltless of his loves.
That done, a sumptuous banquet shall be made,
And the full price of injur'd honour paid.
Stretch not henceforth, O Prince! thy sov'reign might,
180 Beyond the bounds of reason and of right;
'Tis the chief praise that e'er to Kings belong'd,
To right with justice, whom with pow'r they wrong'd.
　　To him the monarch. Just is thy decree,
Thy words give joy, and wisdom breathes in thee.
185 Each due atonement gladly I prepare;
And heav'n regard me as I justly swear!
Here then awhile let *Greece* assembled stay,
Nor great *Achilles* grudge this short delay;

Till from the fleet our presents be convey'd,
And, *Jove* attesting, the firm compact made.   190
A train of noble youth the charge shall bear;
These to select, *Ulysses*, be thy care:
In order rank'd let all our gifts appear,
And the fair train of captives close the rear:
Talthybius shall the victim boar convey,   195
Sacred to *Jove*, and yon' bright orb of day.
    For this (the stern *Æacides* replies)
Some less important season may suffice,
When the stern fury of the war is o'er,
And wrath extinguish'd burns my breast no more.   200
By *Hector* slain, their faces to the sky,
All grim with gaping wounds, our heroes lie:
Those call to war! and might my voice incite,
Now, now, this instant, shou'd commence the fight.
Then, when the day's complete, let gen'rous bowls   205
And copious banquets, glad your weary souls.
Let not my palate know the taste of food,
Till my insatiate rage be cloy'd with blood:
Pale lies my friend, with wounds disfigur'd o'er,
And his cold feet are pointed to the door.   210
Revenge is all my soul! no meaner care,
Int'rest, or thought, has room to harbour there;
Destruction be my feast, and mortal wounds,
And scenes of blood, and agonizing sounds.
    O first of *Greeks* (*Ulysses* thus rejoin'd)   215
The best and bravest of the warriour-kind!
Thy praise it is in dreadful camps to shine,
But old experience and calm wisdom, mine.
Then hear my counsel, and to reason yield,
The bravest soon are satiate of the field;   220
Tho' vast the heaps that strow the crimson plain,
The bloody harvest brings but little gain:
The scale of conquest ever wav'ring lies,
Great *Jove* but turns it, and the victor dies!
The great, the bold, by thousands daily fall,   225
And endless were the grief, to weep for all.
Eternal sorrows what avails to shed?
Greece honours not with solemn fasts the dead:

Enough, when death demands the brave, to pay
230   The tribute of a melancholy day.
One chief with patience to the grave resign'd,
Our care devolves on others left behind.
Let gen'rous food supplies of strength produce,
Let rising spirits flow from sprightly juice,
235   Let their warm heads with scenes of battle glow,
And pour new furies on the feebler foe.
Yet a short interval, and none shall dare
Expect a second summons to the war;
Who waits for that, the dire effect shall find,
240   If trembling in the ships he lags behind.
Embodied, to the battel let us bend,
And all at once on haughty *Troy* descend.
    And now the delegates *Ulysses* sent,
To bear the presents from the royal tent.
245   The sons of *Nestor*, *Phyleus'* valiant heir,
Thias and *Merion*, thunderbolts of war,
With *Lycomedes* of *Creiontian* strain,
And *Melanippus*, form'd the chosen train.
Swift as the word was giv'n, the youths obey'd;
250   Twice ten bright vases in the midst they laid;
A row of six fair tripods then succeeds;
And twice the number of high-bounding steeds;
Sev'n captives next a lovely line compose;
The eighth *Briseïs*, like the blooming rose,
255   Clos'd the bright band: Great *Ithacus*, before,
First of the train, the golden talents bore;
The rest in publick view the chiefs dispose,
A splendid scene! Then *Agamemnon* rose:
The boar *Talthybius* held: The *Grecian* Lord
260   Drew the broad cutlace sheath'd beside his sword;
The stubborn bristles from the victim's brow
He crops, and off'ring meditates his vow.
His hands uplifted to th'attesting skies,
On heav'ns broad marble roof were fix'd his eyes,
265   The solemn words a deep attention draw,
And *Greece* around sate thrill'd with sacred awe.
    Witness thou first! thou greatest pow'r above!
All-good, all-wise, and all-surveying *Jove!*

And mother-earth, and heav'ns revolving light,
And ye, fell furies of the realms of night,   270
Who rule the dead, and horrid woes prepare
For perjur'd Kings, and all who falsely swear!
The black-ey'd maid inviolate removes,
Pure and unconscious of my manly loves.
If this be false, heav'n all its vengeance shed,   275
And level'd thunder strike my guilty head!
   With that, his weapon deep inflicts the wound;
The bleeding savage tumbles to the ground:
The sacred herald rolls the victim slain
(A feast for fish) into the foaming main.   280
   Then thus *Achilles.* Hear, ye *Greeks!* and know
Whate'er we feel, 'tis *Jove* inflicts the woe:
Not else *Atrides* could our rage inflame,
Nor from my arms, unwilling, force the dame.
'Twas *Jove*'s high will alone, o'eruling all,   285
That doom'd our strife, and doom'd the *Greeks* to fall.
Go then ye chiefs! indulge the genial rite;
Achilles waits ye, and expects the fight.
   The speedy council at his word adjourn'd:
To their black vessels all the *Greeks* return'd.   290
Achilles sought his tent. His train before
March'd onward, bending with the gifts they bore.
Those in the tents the squires industrious spread:
The foaming coursers to the stalls they led.
To their new seats the female captives move;   295
Briseïs, radiant as the Queen of love,
Slow as she past, beheld with sad survey
Where gash'd with cruel wounds, *Patroclus* lay.
Prone on the body fell the heav'nly fair,
Beat her sad breast, and tore her golden hair;   300
All-beautiful in grief, her humid eyes
Shining with tears, she lifts, and thus she cries.
   Ah youth! for ever dear, for ever kind,
Once tender friend of my distracted mind!
I left thee fresh in life, in beauty gay;   305
Now find thee cold, inanimated clay!
What woes my wretched race of life attend?
Sorrows on sorrows, never doom'd to end!

The first lov'd consort of my virgin bed
310 Before these eyes in fatal battel bled:
My three brave brothers in one mournful day
All trod the dark, irremeable way:
Thy friendly hand uprear'd me from the plain,
And dry'd my sorrows for a husband slain;
355 *Achilles'* care you promis'd I shou'd prove,
The first, the dearest partner of his love,
That rites divine should ratify the band,
And make me empress in his native land.
Accept these grateful tears! For thee they flow,
320 For thee, that ever felt another's woe!
    Her sister captives echo'd groan for groan,
Nor mourn'd *Patroclus'* fortunes, but their own.
The leaders press'd the chief on ev'ry side;
Unmov'd, he heard them, and with sighs deny'd.
325 If yet *Achilles* have a friend, whose care
Is bent to please him; this request forbear:
Till yonder sun descend, ah let me pay
To grief and anguish one abstemious day.
    He spoke, and from the warriours turn'd his face:
330 Yet still the Brother-Kings of *Atreus'* race,
Nestor, Idomeneus, Ulysses sage,
And *Phœnix*, strive to calm his grief and rage:
His rage they calm not, nor his grief controul;
He groans, he raves, he sorrows from his soul.
335 Thou too, *Patroclus!* (thus his heart he vents)
Once spread th'inviting banquet in our tents:
Thy sweet society, thy winning care,
Once stay'd *Achilles*, rushing to the war.
But now alas! to death's cold arms resign'd,
340 What banquet but revenge can glad my mind?
What greater sorrow could afflict my breast,
What more, if hoary *Peleus* were deceast?
(Who now, perhaps, in *Phthia* dreads to hear
His son's sad fate, and drops a tender tear.)
345 What more, should *Neoptolemus* the brave
(My only offspring) sink into the grave?
If yet that offspring lives, (I distant far,
Of all neglectful, wage a hateful war.)

I cou'd not this, this cruel stroke attend;
Fate claim'd *Achilles*, but might spare his friend.   350
I hop'd *Patroclus* might survive, to rear
My tender orphan with a parent's care,
From *Scyros* isle conduct him o'er the main,
And glad his eyes with his paternal reign,
The lofty palace, and the large domain.   355
For *Peleus* breaths no more the vital air;
Or drags a wretched life of age and care,
But till the news of my sad fate invades
His hastening soul, and sinks him to the shades.

    Sighing he said: His grief the heroes join'd,   360
Each stole a tear for what he left behind.
Their mingled grief the Sire of heav'n survey'd,
And thus, with pity, to his blue-ey'd maid.

    Is then *Achilles* now no more thy care,
And dost thou thus desert the great in war?   365
Lo, where yon' sails their canvas wings extend,
All comfortless he sits, and wails his friend:
E'er thirst and want his forces have opprest,
Haste and infuse ambrosia in his breast.

    He spoke, and sudden as the word of *Jove*   370
Shot the descending Goddess from above.
So swift thro' æther the shrill *Harpye* springs,
The wide air floating to her ample wings.
To great *Achilles* she her flight addrest,
And pour'd divine Ambrosia in his breast,   375
With nectar sweet, (refection of the Gods!)
Then, swift ascending, sought the bright abodes.

    Now issued from the ships the warriour train,
And like a deluge pour'd upon the plain.
As when the piercing blasts of *Boreas* blow,   380
And scatter o'er the fields the driving snow;
From dusky clouds the fleecy winter flies,
Whose dazling lustre whitens all the skies:
So helms succeeding helms, so shields from shields
Catch the quick beams, and brighten all the fields;   385
Broad-glitt'ring breastplates, spears with pointed rays
Mix in one stream, reflecting blaze on blaze:

Thick beats the center as the coursers bound,
With splendour flame the skies, and laugh the fields
    around.
390   Full in the midst, high tow'ring o'er the rest,
His limbs in arms divine *Achilles* drest;
Arms which the father of the fire bestow'd,
Forg'd on th'eternal anvils of the God.
Grief and revenge his furious heart inspire,
395 His glowing eye-balls roll with living fire,
He grinds his teeth, and furious with delay
O'erlooks th'embattled host, and hopes the bloody day.
    The silver cuishes first his thighs infold:
Then o'er his breast was brac'd the hollow gold:
400 The brazen sword a various baldrick ty'd,
That, starr'd with gems, hung glitt'ring at his side;
And like the moon, the broad refulgent shield
Blaz'd with long rays, and gleam'd athwart the field.
    So to night-wand'ring sailors, pale with fears,
425 Wide o'er the wat'ry waste, a light appears,
Which on the far-seen mountain blazing high,
Streams from some lonely watch-tow'r to the sky:
With mournful eyes they gaze, and gaze again;
Loud howls the storm, and drives them o'er the main.
410 Next, his high head the helmet grac'd; behind
The sweepy crest hung floating in the wind:
Like the red star, that from his flaming hair
Shakes down diseases, pestilence and war;
So stream'd the golden honours from his head,
Trembled the sparkling plumes, and the loose glories
415   shed.
    The chief beholds himself with wond'ring eyes;
His arms he poises, and his motions tries;
Buoy'd by some inward force, he seems to swim,
And feels a pinion lifting ev'ry limb.
420 And now he shakes his great paternal spear,
Pond'rous and huge! which not a *Greek* could rear.
From *Pelion*'s cloudy top an ash entire
Old *Chiron* fell'd, and shap'd it for his sire;
A spear which stern *Achilles* only wields,
425 The death of heroes, and the dread of fields.

Automedon and *Alcimus* prepare
Th' immortal coursers, and the radiant car,
(The silver traces sweeping at their side)
Their fiery mouths resplendent bridles ty'd,
The iv'ry-studded reins, return'd behind,   430
Wav'd o'er their backs, and to the chariot join'd.
The charioteer then whirl'd the lash around,
And swift ascended at one active bound.
All bright in heav'nly arms, above his squire
Achilles mounts, and sets the field on fire;   435
Not brighter, *Phœbus* in th'ethereal way,
Flames from his chariot, and restores the day.
High o'er the host, all terrible he stands,
And thunders to his steeds these dread commands.
    Xanthus and *Balius!* of *Podarges'* strain,   440
(Unless ye boast that heav'nly race in vain)
Be swift, be mindful of the load ye bear,
And learn to make your master more your care:
Thro' falling squadrons bear my slaught'ring sword,
Nor, as ye left *Patroclus*, leave your Lord.   445
    The gen'rous *Xanthus*, as the words he said,
Seem'd sensible of woe, and droop'd his head:
Trembling he stood before the golden wain,
And bow'd to dust the honours of his mane,
When, strange to tell! (So *Juno* will'd) he broke   450
Eternal silence, and portentous spoke.
    Achilles! yes! this day at least we bear
Thy rage in safety thro' the files of war:
But come it will, the fatal time must come,
Nor ours the fault, but God decrees thy doom.   455
Not thro' our crime, or slowness in the course,
Fell thy *Patroclus*, but by heav'nly force;
The bright far-shooting God who gilds the day,
(Confest we saw him) tore his arms away.
No – could our swiftness o'er the winds prevail,   460
Or beat the pinions of the western gale,
All were in vain – The fates thy death demand,
Due to a mortal and immortal hand.
    Then ceas'd for ever, by the *Furies* ty'd,
His fate-ful voice. Th' intrepid chief reply'd   465

With unabated rage – So let it be!
Portents and prodigies are lost on me.
I know my fates: To die, to see no more
My much-lov'd parents, and my native shore –
470   Enough – When heav'n ordains, I sink in night;
Now perish *Troy!* he said, and rush'd to fight.

OBSERVATIONS

ON THE

NINETEENTH BOOK

13. *Behold what arms,* &c.] 'Tis not poetry only which has had this idea, of giving divine arms to a hero; we have a very remarkable example of it in our holy books. In the second of *Maccabees*, chap. 16. *Judas* sees in a dream the prophet *Jeremiah* bringing to him a sword as from God: Tho' this was only a dream, or a vision, yet still it is the same idea. This example is likewise so much the more worthy of observation, as it is much later than the age of *Homer*; and as thereby it is seen, that the same way of thinking continued a long time amongst the oriental nations.   *Dacier.*

30. *Shall flies, and worms obscene pollute the dead?*] The care which *Achilles* takes in this place to drive away the flies from the dead body of *Patroclus*, seems to us a mean employment, and a care unworthy of a hero. But that office was regarded by *Homer*, and by all the *Greeks* of his time, as a pious duty consecrated by custom and religion; which obliged the kindred and friends of the deceased to watch his corps, and prevent any corruption before the solemn day of his funerals. It is plain this devoir was thought an indispensable one, since *Achilles* could not discharge himself of it by imposing it upon his mother. It is also clear, that in those times the preservation of a dead body was accounted a very important matter, since the Goddesses themselves, nay the most delicate of the Goddesses, made it the subject of their utmost attention. As *Thetis* preserves the body of *Patroclus*, and chases from it those insects that breed in the wounds and cause putrefaction, so *Venus* is employed day and night about that of *Hector*, in driving away the dogs to which *Achilles* had exposed it. *Apollo*, on his part, covers it with a thick cloud, and preserves its freshness amidst the greatest heats of the sun: And this care of the deities over the dead was looked upon by men as a fruit of their piety.

There is an excellent remark upon this passage in *Bossu*'s admirable treatise of the epic poem, lib. 3. c. 10. 'To speak (says this Author) of the arts and sciences as a poet ought, we should veil them under names and actions of persons fictitious and allegorical. *Homer* will not plainly say that salt has the virtue to preserve dead bodies, and prevent the flies from engendering worms in them; he will not say, that the sea presented *Achilles* a remedy to preserve *Patroclus* from putrefaction; but he will make the Sea a Goddess, and tell us, that *Thetis* to comfort *Achilles*, engaged to perfume the body with an ambrosia which should keep it a whole year from corruption: It is thus *Homer* teaches the poets to speak of arts and sciences. This example shews the nature of the things, that flies cause putrefaction, that salt preserves bodies from it; but all this is told us poetically, the whole is reduced into action, the sea is made a person who speaks and acts, and this *prosopopœia* is accompanied with passion, tenderness and affection; in a word, there is nothing which is not (according to *Aristotle*'s precept) endued with manners.'

61.   *Preventing* Dian *had dispatch'd her dart,*
   And shot the shining mischief to the heart.]

Achilles wishes *Briseïs* had died before she had occasioned so great calamities to his countreymen: I will not say, to excuse him, that his virtue here overpowers his love, but that the wish is not so very barbarous as it may seem by the phrase to a modern reader. It is not, that *Diana* had actually killed her, as by a particular stroke or judgment from heaven; it means no more than a natural death, as appears from this passage in *Odyss.* 15.

> *When age or sickness have unnerv'd the strong,*
> Apollo *comes, and* Cynthia *comes along,*
> *They bend the silver bows for sudden ill,*
> *And every shining arrow flies to kill.*

And he does not wish her death now, after she had been his mistress, but only that she had died, before he knew, or loved her.

93. *She,* Jove's *dread daughter.*] This speech of *Agamemnon,* consisting of little else than the long story of *Jupiter*'s casting *Discord* out of

heaven, seems odd enough at first sight; and does not indeed answer what I believe every reader expects, at the conference of these two Princes. Without excusing it from the justness, and proper application of the allegory in the present case, I think it a piece of artifice, very agreeable to the character of *Agamemnon*, which is a mixture of haughtiness and cunning: he cannot prevail with himself any way to lessen the dignity of the royal character, of which he every where appears jealous: Something he is obliged to say in publick, and not brooking directly to own himself in the wrong, he slurs it over with this tale. With what stateliness is it that he yields? 'I was misled (says he) but I was misled like *Jupiter*. We invest you with our powers, take our troops and our treasures: Our royal promise shall be fulfilled, but be you pacified.'

93.   *She,* Jove's *dread daughter, fated to infest*
      The race of mortals –]

It appears from hence, that the ancients owned a *Dæmon*, created by God himself, and totally taken up in doing mischief.

This fiction is very remarkable, in as much as it proves that the *Pagans* knew that a dæmon of discord and malediction was in heaven, and afterwards precipitated to earth, which perfectly agrees with holy history. St. *Justin* will have it, that *Homer* attained to the knowledge thereof in *Egypt*, and that he had even read what *Isaiah* writes, chap. 14. *How art thou fal'n from heaven, O* Lucifer, *son of the morning, how art thou cut down to the ground which didst weaken the nations?* But our poet could not have seen the prophecy of *Isaiah*, because he lived 100, or 150 years before that prophet; and this anteriority of time makes this passage the more observable. *Homer* therein bears authentick witness to the truth of the story, of an angel thrown from heaven, and gives this testimony above 100 years before one of the greatest prophets spoke of it.   *Dacier.*

145. *To keep or send the presents, be thy care.*] *Achilles* neither refuses nor demands *Agamemnon*'s presents: The first would be too contemptuous, and the other would look too selfish. It would seem as if *Achilles* fought only for pay like a mercenary, which would be utterly unbecoming a hero, and dishonourable to that character: *Homer* is wonderful as to the manners.   *Spond. Dac.*

159. *Strength is deriv'd from Spirits,* &c.] This advice of *Ulysses* that

the troops should refresh themselves with eating and drinking, was extremely necessary, after a battle of so long continuance as that of the day before: And *Achilles*'s desire that they should charge the enemy immediately, without any reflection on the necessity of that refreshment, was also highly natural to his violent character. This forces *Ulysses* to repeat that advice, and insist upon it so much: Which those criticks did not see into, who thro' a false delicacy are shock'd at his insisting so warmly upon eating and drinking. Indeed to a common reader who is more fond of heroick and romantick, than of just and natural images, this at first sight may have an air of ridicule; but I'll venture to say there is nothing ridiculous in the thing itself, nor mean and low in *Homer*'s manner of expressing it: And I believe the same of this translation, tho' I have not soften'd or abated of the Idea they are so offended with.

197. *The stern Æacides replies.*] The *Greek* verse is

> Τὸν δ' ἀπαμειβόμενος προσέφη πόδας ὠκὺς 'Αχιλλεύς.

[And then, in turn, swift-footed Achilles answered.]

Which is repeated very frequently throughout the Iliad. It is a very just remark of a *French* critick, that what makes it so much taken notice of, is the rumbling sound and length of the word ἀπαμειβόμενος: This is so true, that if in a poem or romance of the same length as the Iliad, we should repeat *The hero answer'd*, full as often, we should never be sensible of that repetition. And if we are not shocked at the like frequency of those expressions in the Æneid, *sic ore refert, talia voce refert, talia dicta dabat, vix ea fatus erat*, &c. it is only because the sound of the *Latin* words does not fill the ear like that of the *Greek* ἀπαμειβόμενος.

The discourse of the same critick upon these sort of repetitions in general, deserves to be transcribed. That useless nicety (says he) of avoiding every repetition which the delicacy of later Times has introduced, was not known to the first ages of antiquity: The books of *Moses* abound with them. Far from condemning their frequent use in the most ancient of all the poets, we should look upon them as the certain character of the age in which he liv'd: They spoke so in his time, and to have spoken otherwise had been a fault. And indeed nothing is in itself so contrary to the true sublime, as that painful and frivolous exactness, with which we avoid to make use of a proper word because it was used before. It is certain that the *Romans* were less scrupulous as to this point: You have often in a single page of *Tully*, the same word five or six times over. If it were really a fault, it is not to be conceived how an author who so little wanted variety of expressions as *Homer*, could be so very negligent herein? On the contrary, he seems to have affected to repeat the same things in the same words, on many occasions.

It was from two principles equally true, that among several people, and in several ages, two practices entirely different took their rise. *Moses*, *Homer*, and the writers of the first times, had found that repetitions of the same Words recalled the ideas of things, imprinted them much more strongly, and rendered the discourse more intelligible. Upon this principle, the custom of repeating words, phrases, and even entire speeches, insensibly established itself both in prose and poetry, especially in narrations.

The writers who succeeded them observed, even from *Homer* himself, that the greatest beauty of style consisted in variety. This they made their principle: They therefore avoided repetitions of words, and still more of whole sentences; they endeavoured to vary their transitions; and found out new turns and manners of expressing the same things.

Either of these Practices is good, but the excess of either vicious: We should neither on the one hand, thro' a love of simplicity and clearness, continually repeat the same words, phrases, or discourses; nor on the other, for the pleasure of variety, fall into a childish affectation of expressing every thing twenty different ways, tho' it be never so natural and common.

Nothing so much cools the warmth of a piece or puts out the fire of poetry, as that perpetual care to vary incessantly even in the smallest circumstances. In this, as in many other points, *Homer* has despised the ungrateful labour of too scrupulous a nicety. He has done like a great painter, who does not think himself obliged to vary all his pieces to that degree, as not one of them shall have the least resemblance to another: If the principal figures are entirely different, we easily excuse a resemblance in the landscapes, the skies, or the draperies. Suppose a gallery full of pictures, each of which represents a particular subject: In one I see *Achilles* in fury, menacing *Agamemnon*; in another the same hero with regret delivers up *Briseïs* to the heralds; in a third 'tis still *Achilles*, but *Achilles* overcome with grief, and lamenting to his mother. If the air, the gesture, the countenance, the character of

Achilles, are the same in each of these three pieces; if the ground of one of these be the same with that of the others in the composition and general design, whether it be landscape, or architecture; then indeed one should have reason to blame the painter for the uniformity of his figures and grounds. But if there be no sameness but in the folds of a few draperies, in the structure of some part of a building, or in the figure of some tree, mountain, or cloud, it is what no one would regard as a fault. The application is obvious: *Homer* repeats, but they are not the great strokes which he repeats, not those which strike and fix our attention: They are only the little parts, the transitions, the general circumstances, or familiar images, which recur naturally, and upon which the reader but casts his eye carelessly: Such as the descriptions of sacrifices, repasts, or embarquements; such in short, as are in their own nature much the same, which it is sufficient just to shew, and which are in a manner incapable of different ornaments.

209. *Pale lies my friend,* &c.] It is in the *Greek,* *lies extended in my tent with his face turned towards the door,* ἀνὰ πρόθυρον τετραμμένος, that is to say, as the scholiast has explained it, *having his feet turned towards the door.* For it was thus the *Greeks* placed their dead in the porches of their houses, as likewise in *Italy,*

> *In portam rigidos calces extendit.*   Persius.

> [He stretches his stiff heels towards the door.]

> *– Recepitque ad limina gressum*
> *Corpus ubi exanimi positum Pallantis Acetes*
> *Servabat senior –*

>   [he took his way,
> Where, new in death, lamented *Pallas* lay:
>   *Acoetes* watch'd the corps.]

Thus we are told by *Suetonius,* of the body of *Augustus* – *Equester ordo suscepit, urbique intulit, atque in vestibulo domus collocavit* [The equestrian order took it up, carried it into the city, and laid it out in a vestibule in the house].

221. *Tho' vast the heaps,* &c.] *Ulysses*'s expression in the original is very remarkable; he calls καλάμη, *straw* or *chaff,* such as are killed in the battel; and he calls ἄμητος, the *crop,* such as make their escape.

This is very conformable to the language of holy scripture, wherein those who perish are called *chaff*, and those who are saved are called *corn*.   *Dacier.*

237.   – *None shall dare*
            Expect a second summons to the war.]

This is very artful; *Ulysses*, to prevail upon *Achilles* to let the troops take repast, and yet in some sort to second his impatience, gives with the same breath orders for battel, by commanding the troops to march, and expect no farther orders. Thus tho' the troops go to take repast, it looks as if they do not lose a moment's time, but are going to put themselves in array of battel.   *Dacier.*

279–280. *Rolls the victim . . . into the main.*] For it was not lawful to eat the flesh of the victims, that were sacrificed in confirmation of oaths; such were victims of malediction.   *Eustathius.*

281. *Hear, ye* Greeks, &c.] *Achilles,* to let them see that he is entirely appeas'd, justifies *Agamemnon* himself, and enters into the reasons with which that Prince had coloured his fault. But in that justification he perfectly well preserves his character, and illustrates the advantage he has over that King who offended him.   *Dacier.*

303, *&c. The lamentation of* Briseïs *over* Patroclus.] This speech (says *Dionysius of Halicarnassus*) is not without its artifice: While *Briseïs* seems only to be deploring *Patroclus,* she represents to *Achilles* who stands by, the breach of the promises he had made her, and upbraids him with the neglect he had been guilty of in resigning her up to *Agamemnon.* He adds, that *Achilles* hereupon acknowledges the justice of her complaint, and makes answer that his promises should be performed: It was a slip in that great critick's memory, for the verse he cites is not in this part of the author, [Περὶ ἐσχηματισμένων, Part 2.]

315. Achilles' *care you promis'd,* &c.] In these days when our manners are so different from those of the ancients, and we see none of those dismal catastrophes which laid whole kingdoms waste and subjected princesses and queens to the power of the conqueror; it will perhaps seem astonishing, that a princess of *Briseïs*'s birth, the very day that

her father, brothers, and husband were killed by *Achilles*, should suffer her self to be comforted and even flattered with the hopes of becoming the spouse of the murderer. But such were the manners of those times, as ancient history testifies: And a poet represents them as they were; but if there was a necessity for justifying them, it might be said that slavery was at that time so terrible, that in truth a princess like *Briseïs* was pardonable, to chuse rather to become *Achilles*'s wife than his slave.

Dacier.

322. *Nor mourn'd* Patroclus *fortunes but their own.*] *Homer* adds this touch, to heighten the character of *Briseïs*, and to shew the difference there was between her and the other captives. *Briseïs*, as a well-born princess, really bewail'd *Patroclus* out of *gratitude*; but the others, by pretending to bewail him, wept only out of *interest.*   *Dacier.*

335. *Thou too* Patroclus, &c.] This lamentation is finely introduced: While the Generals are persuading him to take some refreshment, it naturally awakens in his mind the remembrance of *Patroclus*, who had so often brought him food every morning before they went to battel: This is very natural, and admirably well conceals the art of drawing the subject of his discourse from the things that present themselves.

Spondanus.

351. *I hop'd* Patroclus *might survive,* &c.] *Patroclus* was young, and *Achilles* who had but a short time to live, hoped that after his death his dear friend would be as a father to his son, and put him into the possession of his kingdom: *Neoptolemus* would in *Patroclus* find *Peleus* and *Achilles*; whereas when *Patroclus* was dead, he must be an orphan indeed. *Homer* is particularly admirable for the sentiments, and always follows nature.   *Dacier.*

384. *So helms succeeding helms, so shields from shields*
     Catch the quick beams, and brighten all the fields.]

It is probable the reader may think the words, *shining, splendid,* and others derived from the lustre of arms, too frequent in these books. My author is to answer for it, but it may be alledged in his excuse, that when it was the custom for every soldier to serve in armour, and when those arms were of brass before the use of iron became common, these images of lustre were less avoidable, and more necessarily frequent in descriptions of this nature.

390. *Achilles arming himself,* &c.] There is a wonderful pomp in this description of *Achilles*'s arming himself; every reader without being pointed to it, will see the extreme grandeur of all these images; but what is particular, is, in what a noble scale they rise one above another, and how the hero is set still in a stronger point of light than before; till he is at last in a manner covered over with glories: He is at first likened to the moonlight, then to the flames of a beacon, then to a comet, and lastly to the sun it self.

450. *When, strange to tell! (so* Juno *will'd) he broke*
  Eternal silence, and portentous spoke.]

It is remark'd, in excuse of this extravagant fiction of a horse speaking, that *Homer* was authorized herein by fable, tradition, and history. *Livy* makes mention of two oxen that spoke on different occasions, and recites the speech of one, which was, *Roma cave tibi* [Rome, beware!]. *Pliny* tells us, these animals were particularly gifted this way, l. 8. c. 45. *Est frequens in prodigiis priscorum, bovem locutum* [It is common, in the prodigies of the ancients, for the ox to speak]. Besides *Homer* had prepared us for expecting something miraculous from these horses of *Achilles*, by representing them to be immortal. We have seen them already sensible, and weeping at the death of *Patroclus*: And we must add to all this, that a Goddess is concerned in working this wonder: It is *Juno* that does it. *Oppian* alludes to this in a beautiful passage of his first book: Not having the original by me, I shall quote (what I believe is no less beautiful) Mr. *Fenton*'s translation of it.

> *Of all the prone creation, none display*
> *A friendlier sense of man's superiour sway:*
> *Some in the silent pomp of grief complain,*
> *For the brave chief, by doom of battel slain:*
> *And when young* Peleus *in his rapid car*
> *Rush'd on, to rouze the thunder of the war,*
> *With human voice inspir'd, his steed deplor'd*
> *The fate impending dreadful o'er his Lord.*   Cyneg. lib. 1.

Spondanus and *Dacier* fail not to bring up *Balaam*'s ass on this occasion. But methinks the commentators are at too much pains to discharge the poet from the imputation of extravagant fiction, by accounting for wonders of this kind: I am afraid, that next to the extravagance of inventing them, is that of endeavouring to reconcile such fictions to probability. Would not one general answer do better, to say once for all, that the above cited authors lived in the *age of wonders*: The taste of the world has been generally turned to the miraculous; wonders were what the people would have, and what not only the poets, but the priests, gave 'em.

464.   *Then ceas'd for ever, by the furies ty'd,*
        His fate-ful voice –]

The poet had offended against probability if he had made *Juno* take away the voice, for *Juno* (which signifies the air) is the cause of the voice. Besides, the poet was willing to intimate that the privation of the voice is a thing so dismal and melancholy, that none but the *Furies* can take upon them so cruel an employment.   *Eustathius.*

THE
TWENTIETH BOOK
OF THE
ILIAD

The ARGUMENT

The battel of the Gods, and the acts of *Achilles*

Jupiter *upon* Achilles's *returning to the battel, calls a council of the Gods, and permits them to assist either party. The terrors of the combate described, when the Deities are engaged.* Apollo *encourages* Æneas *to meet* Achilles. *After a long conversation, these two heroes encounter; but* Æneas *is preserved by the assistance of* Neptune. Achilles *falls upon the rest of the Trojans, and is upon the point of killing* Hector, *but* Apollo *conveys him away in a cloud.* Achilles *pursues the Trojans with a great slaughter.*

The same day continues. The scene is in the field before Troy.

Thus round *Pelides* breathing war and blood,
Greece sheath'd in arms, beside her vessels stood;
While near impending from a neighb'ring height,
Troy's black battalions wait the shock of fight.
5   Then *Jove* to *Themis* gives command, to call
The Gods to council in the starry hall:
Swift o'er *Olympus'* hundred hills she flies,
And summons all the senate of the skies.
These shining on, in long procession come
10   To *Jove*'s eternal adamantine dome.
Not one was absent; not a rural pow'r
That haunts the verdant gloom, or rosy bow'r,
Each fair-hair'd Dryad of the shady wood,
Each azure sister of the silver flood;
15   All but old Ocean, hoary Sire! who keeps
His ancient seat beneath the sacred deeps.
On marble thrones with lucid columns crown'd,
(The work of *Vulcan*) sate the Pow'rs around.
Ev'n *he whose trident sways the watry reign,
20   Heard the loud summons, and forsook the main,
Assum'd his throne amid the bright abodes,
And question'd thus the Sire of Men and Gods.
    What moves the God who heav'n and earth commands,
And grasps the thunder in his awful hands,
25   Thus to convene the whole ætherial state?
Is *Greece* and *Troy* the subject in debate?

*Neptune

Already met, the low'ring hosts appear,
And death stands ardent on the edge of war.
   'Tis true (the cloud-compelling pow'r replies)
This day, we call the council of the skies   30
In care of human race; ev'n *Jove*'s own eye
Sees with regret unhappy mortals die.
Far on *Olympus*' top in secret state
Ourself will sit, and see the hand of Fate
Work out our will. Celestial pow'rs! descend,   35
And as your minds direct, your succour lend
To either host. *Troy* soon must lie o'erthrown,
If uncontroll'd *Achilles* fights alone:
Their troops but lately durst not meet his eyes;
What can they now, if in his rage he rise?   40
Assist them, Gods! or *Ilion*'s sacred wall
May fall this day, tho' Fate forbids the fall.
   He said, and fir'd their heav'nly breasts with rage:
On adverse parts the warring Gods engage.
Heav'ns awful Queen; and he whose azure round   45
Girds the vast globe; the maid in arms renown'd;
Hermes, of profitable arts the sire,
And *Vulcan*, the black sov'reign of the fire:
These to the fleet repair with instant flight;
The vessels tremble as the Gods alight.   50
In aid of *Troy*, *Latona*, *Phœbus* came,
Mars fiery-helm'd, the laughter-loving Dame,
Xanthus whose streams in golden currents flow,
And the chast huntress of the silver bow.
E'er yet the Gods their various aid employ,   55
Each *Argive* bosom swell'd with manly joy,
While great *Achilles*, (terrour of the plain)
Long lost to battel, shone in arms again.
Dreadful he stood in front of all his host;
Pale *Troy* beheld, and seem'd already lost;   60
Her bravest heroes pant with inward fear,
And trembling see another God of war.
   But when the pow'rs descending swell'd the fight,
Then Tumult rose; fierce rage and pale affright
Vary'd each face; then Discord sounds alarms,   65
Earth echoes, and the nations rush to arms.

Now thro' the trembling shores *Minerva* calls.
And now she thunders from the *Grecian* walls.
Mars hov'ring o'er his *Troy*, his terrour shrouds
70 In gloomy tempests, and a night of clouds:
Now thro' each *Trojan* heart he fury pours
With voice divine from *Ilion*'s topmost tow'rs,
Now shouts to *Simoïs*, from her beauteous *hill;
The mountain shook, the rapid stream stood still.
75 Above, the Sire of Gods his thunder rolls,
And peals on peals redoubled rend the poles.
Beneath, stern *Neptune* shakes the solid ground;
The forests wave, the mountains nod around;
Thro' all their summits tremble *Ida*'s woods,
80 And from their sources boil her hundred floods.
Troy's turrets totter on the rocking plain;
And the toss'd navies beat the heaving main.
Deep in the dismal regions of the dead,
Th' infernal Monarch rear'd his horrid head,
85 Leap'd from his throne, lest *Neptune*'s arm should lay
His dark dominions open to the day,
And pour in light on *Pluto*'s drear abodes,
Abhorr'd by men, and dreadful ev'n to Gods.
    Such war th'immortals wage: Such horrors rend
90 The world's vast concave, when the Gods contend.
First silver-shafted *Phœbus* took the plain
Against blue *Neptune*, Monarch of the main:
The God of arms his giant bulk display'd,
Oppos'd to *Pallas*, war's triumphant maid.
95 Against *Latona* march'd the son of *May*;
The quiver'd *Dian*, sister of the Day,
(Her golden arrows sounding at her side)
Saturnia, Majesty of heav'n, defy'd.
With fiery *Vulcan* last in battel stands
100 The sacred flood that rolls on golden sands;
Xanthus his name with those of heavenly birth,
But call'd *Scamander* by the sons of earth.
    While thus the Gods in various league engage,
Achilles glow'd with more than mortal rage:

*Callicolone.

Hector he sought; in search of *Hector* turn'd   105
His eyes around, for *Hector* only burn'd;
And burst like light'ning thro' the ranks, and vow'd
To glut the God of Battels with his blood.
   Æneas was the first who dar'd to stay;
Apollo wedg'd him in the warriour's way,   110
But swell'd his bosom with undaunted might,
Half-forc'd, and half-persuaded to the fight.
Like young *Lycaon*, of the royal line,
In voice and aspect, seem'd the pow'r divine;
And bade the chief reflect, how late with scorn   115
In distant threats he brav'd the Goddess-born.
   Then thus the hero of *Anchises'* strain.
To meet *Pelides* you persuade in vain:
Already have I met, nor void of fear
Observ'd the fury of his flying spear;   120
From *Ida*'s woods he chas'd us to the field,
Our force he scatter'd, and our herds he kill'd;
Lyrnessus, *Pedasus* in ashes lay;
But (*Jove* assisting) I surviv'd the day.
Else had I sunk opprest in fatal fight,   125
By fierce *Achilles* and *Minerva*'s might.
Where'ere he mov'd, the Goddess shone before,
And bath'd his brazen lance in hostile gore.
What mortal man *Achilles* can sustain?
Th'immortals guard him thro' the dreadful plain,   130
And suffer not his dart to fall in vain.
Were God my aid, this arm should check his pow'r,
Tho' strong in battel as a brazen tow'r.
   To whom the Son of *Jove*, That God implore,
And be, what great *Achilles* was before.   135
From heav'nly *Venus* thou deriv'st thy strain,
And he, but from a sister of the main;
An aged Sea God, father of his line,
But *Jove* himself the sacred source of thine.
Then lift thy weapon for a noble blow,   140
Nor fear the vaunting of a mortal foe.
   This said, and spirit breath'd into his breast,
Thro' the thick troops th'embolden'd hero prest:

His vent'rous act the white-arm'd Queen survey'd,
145 And thus, assembling all the pow'rs, she said.
     Behold an action, Gods! that claims your care,
Lo great *Æneas* rushing to the war;
Against *Pelides* he directs his course,
Phœbus impels, and *Phœbus* gives him force.
150 Restrain his bold career; at least, t'attend
Our favour'd hero, let some pow'r descend.
To guard his life, and add to his renown,
We, the great armament of heav'n, came down.
Hereafter let him fall, as Fates design,
155 That spun so short his life's illustrious line:
But lest some adverse God now cross his way,
Give him to know, what pow'rs assist this day:
For how shall mortal stand the dire alarms,
When heav'ns refulgent host appear in arms?
160   Thus she, and thus the God whose force can make
The solid globe's eternal basis shake.
Against the might of man, so feeble known,
Why shou'd cœlestial pow'rs exert their own?
Suffice, from yonder mount to view the scene;
165 And leave to war the fates of mortal men.
But if th'Armipotent, or God of Light,
Obstruct *Achilles*, or commence the fight,
Thence on the Gods of *Troy* we swift descend:
Full soon, I doubt not, shall the conflict end,
170 And these, in ruin and confusion hurl'd,
Yield to our conqu'ring arms the lower world.
     Thus having said, the tyrant of the sea,
Cœrulean Neptune, rose, and led the way.
Advanc'd upon the field there stood a mound
175 Of earth congested, wall'd, and trench'd around;
In elder times to guard *Alcides* made,
(The Work of *Trojans*, with *Minerva*'s aid)
What time, a vengeful monster of the main
Swept the wide shore, and drove him to the plain.
180   Here *Neptune*, and the Gods of *Greece* repair,
With clouds encompass'd, and a veil of air:
The adverse pow'rs, around *Apollo* laid,
Crown the fair hills that silver *Simoïs* shade.

In circle close each heav'nly party sate,
Intent to form the future scheme of Fate;   185
But mix not yet in fight, tho' *Jove* on high
Gives the loud signal, and the heav'ns reply.
   Meanwhile the rushing armies hide the ground;
The trampled center yields a hollow sound:
Steeds cas'd in mail, and chiefs in armour bright,   190
The gleamy champain glows with brazen light.
Amid both hosts (a dreadful space) appear
There, great *Achilles*, bold *Æneas* here.
With tow'ring strides *Æneas* first advanc'd;
The nodding plumage on his helmet danc'd,   195
Spread o'er his breast the fencing shield he bore,
And, as he mov'd, his jav'lin flam'd before.
Not so *Pelides*; furious to engage,
He rush'd impetuous. Such the lion's rage,
Who viewing first his foes with scornful eyes,   200
Tho' all in arms the peopled city rise,
Stalks careless on, with unregarding pride;
Till at the length, by some brave youth defy'd,
To his bold spear the savage turns alone,
He murmurs fury with an hollow groan;   205
He grins, he foams, he rolls his eyes around;
Lash'd by his tail his heaving sides resound;
He calls up all his rage; he grinds his teeth,
Resolv'd on vengeance, or resolv'd on death.
So fierce *Achilles* on *Æneas* flies;   210
So stands *Æneas*, and his force defies.
E'er yet the stern encounter join'd, begun
The seed of *Thetis* thus to *Venus'* son.
   Why comes *Æneas* thro' the ranks so far?
Seeks he to meet *Achilles'* arm in war,   215
In hope the realms of *Priam* to enjoy,
And prove his merits to the throne of *Troy*?
Grant that beneath thy lance *Achilles* dies,
The partial monarch may refuse the prize;
Sons he has many; those thy pride may quell;   220
And 'tis his fault to love those sons too well.
Or, in reward of thy victorious hand,
Has *Troy* propos'd some spacious tract of land?

An ample forest, or a fair domain,
225 Of hills for vines, and arable for grain?
Ev'n this, perhaps, will hardly prove thy lot.
But can *Achilles* be so soon forgot?
Once (as I think) you saw this brandish'd spear,
And then the great *Æneas* seem'd to fear.
230 With hearty haste from *Ida*'s mount he fled,
Nor, till he reach'd *Lyrnessus*, turn'd his head.
Her lofty walls not long our progress stay'd;
Those, *Pallas*, *Jove*, and we, in ruins laid:
In *Grecian* chains her captive race were cast;
235 'Tis true, the great *Æneas* fled too fast.
Defrauded of my conquest once before,
What then I lost, the Gods this day restore.
Go; while thou may'st, avoid the threaten'd fate;
Fools stay to feel it, and are wise too late.
240   To this *Anchises*' son. Such words employ
To one that fears thee, some unwarlike boy:
Such we disdain; the best may be defy'd
With mean reproaches, and unmanly pride:
Unworthy the high race from which we came,
245 Proclaim'd so loudly by the voice of fame,
Each from illustrious fathers draws his Line;
Each Goddess-born; half human, half divine.
Thetis' this day, or *Venus'* offspring dies,
And tears shall trickle from cœlestial eyes:
250 For when two heroes, thus deriv'd, contend,
'Tis not in words the glorious strife can end.
If yet thou farther seek to learn my birth
(A tale resounded thro' the spacious earth)
Hear how the glorious origine we prove
255 From ancient *Dardanus*, the first from *Jove*:
Dardania's walls he rais'd; for *Ilion*, then,
(The city since of many-languag'd men)
Was not. The natives were content to till
The shady foot of *Ida*'s fount-ful hill.
260 From *Dardanus*, great *Erichthonius* springs,
The richest, once, of *Asia*'s wealthy kings;
Three thousand mares his spacious pastures bred,
Three thousand foals beside their mothers fed.

Boreas, enamour'd of the sprightly train,
Conceal'd his Godhead in a flowing mane, 265
With voice dissembled to his loves he neigh'd,
And cours'd the dappled beauties o'er the mead:
Hence sprung twelve others of unrival'd kind,
Swift as their mother mares, and father wind.
These lightly skimming, when they swept the plain, 270
Nor ply'd the grass, nor bent the tender grain;
And when along the level seas they flew,
Scarce on the surface curl'd the briny dew.
Such *Erichthonius* was: From him there came
The sacred *Tros*, of whom the *Trojan* name. 275
Three sons renown'd adorn'd his nuptial bed,
Ilus, *Assaracus*, and *Ganymed*:
The matchless *Ganymed*, divinely fair,
Whom heaven enamour'd snatch'd to upper air,
To bear the cup of *Jove* (ætherial guest) 280
The grace and glory of th'ambrosial feast.
The two remaining sons the line divide:
First rose *Laomedon* from *Ilus'* side;
From him *Tithonus*, now in cares grown old,
And *Priam*, (blest with *Hector*, brave and bold:) 285
Clytius and *Lampus*, ever-honour'd pair;
And *Hicetaon*, thunderbolt of war.
From great *Assaracus* sprung *Capys*, he
Begat *Anchises*, and *Anchises* me.
Such is our race: 'Tis fortune gives us birth, 290
But *Jove* alone endues the soul with worth:
He, source of pow'r and might! with boundless sway,
All human courage gives, or takes away.
Long in the field of words we may contend,
Reproach is infinite, and knows no end, 295
Arm'd or with truth or falshood, right or wrong,
So voluble a weapon is the tongue;
Wounded, we wound; and neither side can fail,
For ev'ry man has equal strength to rail:
Women alone, when in the streets they jar, 300
Perhaps excel us in this wordy war;
Like us they stand, encompass'd with the crowd,
And vent their anger, impotent and loud.

Cease then – Our business in the field of fight
305   Is not to question, but to prove our might.
To all those insults thou hast offer'd here,
Receive this answer: 'Tis my flying spear.
   He spoke. With all his force the jav'lin flung,
Fix'd deep, and loudly in the buckler rung.
310   Far on his out-stretch'd arm, *Pelides* held
(To meet the thund'ring lance) his dreadful shield,
That trembled as it stuck; nor void of fear
Saw, e'er it fell, th'immeasurable spear.
His fears were vain; impenetrable charms
315   Secur'd the temper of th'ætherial arms.
Thro' two strong plates the point its passage held,
But stopp'd, and rested, by the third repell'd;
Five plates of various metal, various mold,
Compos'd the shield; of brass each outward fold,
320   Of tin each inward, and the middle gold:
There stuck the lance. Then rising e'er he threw,
The forceful spear of great *Achilles* flew,
And pierc'd the *Dardan* shield's extremest bound,
Where the shrill brass return'd a sharper sound:
325   Thro' the thin verge the *Pelian* weapon glides.
And the slight cov'ring of expanded hides.
Æneas his contracted body bends,
And o'er him high the riven targe extends,
Sees, thro' its parting plates, the upper air,
330   And at his back perceives the quiv'ring spear:
A fate so near him, chills his soul with fright,
And swims before his eyes the many-colour'd light.
Achilles, rushing in with dreadful cries,
Draws his broad blade, and at *Æneas* flies:
335   *Æneas* rouzing as the foe came on,
(With force collected) heaves a mighty stone:
A mass enormous! which in modern days
No two of earth's degen'rate sons could raise.
But Ocean's God, whose earthquakes rock the ground,
340   Saw the distress, and mov'd the pow'rs around.
   Lo! on the brink of fate *Æneas* stands,
An instant victim to *Achilles*' hands:

By *Phœbus* urg'd; but *Phœbus* has bestow'd
His aid in vain: The man o'erpow'rs the God.
And can ye see this righteous chief attone   345
With guiltless blood, for vices not his own?
To all the Gods his constant vows were paid;
Sure, tho' he wars for *Troy*, he claims our aid.
Fate wills not this; nor thus can *Jove* resign
The future father of the *Dardan* line: 350
The first great ancestor obtain'd his grace,
And still his love descends on all the race.
For *Priam* now, and *Priam*'s faithless kind,
At length are odious to th'all-seeing mind;
On great *Æneas* shall devolve the reign,   355
And sons succeeding sons, the lasting line sustain.

    The great earth-shaker thus: To whom replies
Th'imperial Goddess with the radiant eyes.
Good as he is, to immolate or spare
The *Dardan* Prince, O *Neptune*, be thy care;   360
Pallas and I, by all that Gods can bind,
Have sworn destruction to the *Trojan* kind;
Not ev'n an instant to protract their fate,
Or save one member of the sinking state;
Till her last flame be quench'd with her last gore,   365
And ev'n her crumbling ruins are no more.

    The King of Ocean to the fight descends,
Thro' all the whistling darts his course he bends,
Swift interpos'd between the warriours flies,
And casts thick darkness o'er *Achilles*' eyes.   370
From great *Æneas*' shield the spear he drew,
And at its master's feet the weapon threw.
That done, with force divine, he snatch'd on high
The *Dardan* Prince, and bore him thro' the sky,
Smooth-gliding without step, above the heads   375
Of warring heroes, and of bounding steeds.
Till at the battel's utmost verge they light,
Where the slow *Caucons* close the rear of fight:
The Godhead there (his heav'nly form confess'd)
With words like these the panting chief address'd.   380
    What Pow'r, O Prince, with force inferior far,
Urg'd thee to meet *Achilles*' arm in war?

Henceforth beware, nor antedate thy doom,
Defrauding Fate of all thy fame to come.
385 But when the day decreed (for come it must)
Shall lay this dreadful hero in the dust,
Let then the furies of that arm be known,
Secure, no *Grecian* force transcends thy own.
  With that, he left him wond'ring as he lay,
390 Then from *Achilles* chas'd the mist away:
Sudden, returning with the stream of light,
The scene of war came rushing on his sight.
Then thus, amaz'd: What wonders strike my mind!
My spear, that parted on the wings of wind,
395 Laid here before me! and the *Dardan* Lord
That fell this instant, vanish'd from my sword!
I thought alone with mortals to contend,
But pow'rs cœlestial sure this foe defend.
Great as he is, our arm he scarce will try,
400 Content for once, with all his Gods, to fly.
Now then let others bleed – This said, aloud
He vents his fury, and inflames the crowd.
O *Greeks* (he cries, and every rank alarms)
Join battel, man to man, and arms to arms!
405 'Tis not in me, tho' favour'd by the sky,
To mow whole troops, and make whole armies fly:
No God can singly such a host engage,
Not *Mars* himself, nor great *Minerva*'s rage.
But whatsoe'er *Achilles* can inspire,
410 Whate'er of active force, or acting fire,
Whate'er this heart can prompt, or hand obey;
All, all *Achilles*, *Greeks!* is yours to-day.
Thro' yon wide host this arm shall scatter fear,
And thin the squadrons with my single spear.
415   He said: Nor less elate with martial joy,
The god-like *Hector* warm'd the troops of *Troy*.
Trojans to war! Think *Hector* leads you on;
Nor dread the vaunts of *Peleus*' haughty son.
Deeds must decide our fate. Ev'n those with words
420 Insult the brave, who tremble at their swords:
The weakest atheist-wretch all heav'n defies,
But shrinks and shudders, when the thunder flies.

Nor from yon' boaster shall your chief retire,
Not tho' his heart were steel, his hands were fire;
That fire, that steel, your *Hector* shou'd withstand,   425
And brave that vengeful heart, that dreadful hand.
   Thus (breathing rage thro' all) the hero said;
A wood of lances rises round his head,
Clamours on clamours tempest all the air,
They join, they throng, they thicken to the war.   430
But *Phœbus* warns him from high heav'n to shun
The single fight with *Thetis'* god-like son;
More safe to combate in the mingled band,
Nor tempt too near the terrours of his hand.
He hears, obedient to the God of Light,   435
And plung'd within the ranks, awaits the fight.
   Then fierce *Achilles*, shouting to the skies,
On *Troy*'s whole force with boundless fury flies.
First falls *Iphytion*, at his army's head;
Brave was the chief, and brave the host he led;   440
From great *Otrynteus* he deriv'd his blood,
His mother was a *Naïs* of the flood;
Beneath the shades of *Tmolus*, crown'd with snow,
From *Hyde*'s walls, he rul'd the lands below.
Fierce as he springs, the sword his head divides;   445
The parted visage falls on equal sides:
With loud-resounding arms he strikes the plain;
While thus *Achilles* glories o'er the slain.
   Lye there *Otryntides!* the *Trojan* earth
Receives thee dead, tho' *Gygæ* boast thy birth;   450
Those beauteous fields where *Hyllus'* waves are roll'd,
And plenteous *Hermus* swells with tides of gold,
Are thine no more – Th'insulting hero said,
And left him sleeping in eternal shade.
The rolling wheels of *Greece* the body tore,   455
And dash'd their axles with no vulgar gore.
   Demoleon next, *Antenor*'s offspring, laid
Breathless in dust, the price of rashness paid.
Th'impatient steel with full-descending sway
Forc'd thro' his brazen helm its furious way,   460
Resistless drove the batter'd skull before,
And dash'd and mingled all the brains with gore.

This sees *Hippodamas*, and seiz'd with fright,
Deserts his chariot for a swifter flight:
465 The lance arrests him: an ignoble wound
The panting *Trojan* rivets to the ground.
He groans away his soul: Not louder roars
At *Neptune*'s shrine on *Helice*'s high shores
The victim bull; the rocks rebellow round,
470 And Ocean listens to the grateful sound.
     Then fell on *Polydore* his vengeful rage,
The youngest hope of *Priam*'s stooping age:
(Whose feet for swiftness in the race surpast)
Of all his sons, the dearest, and the last.
475 To the forbidden field he takes his flight
In the first folly of a youthful knight,
To vaunt his swiftness, wheels around the plain,
But vaunts not long, with all his swiftness slain.
Struck where the crossing belts unite behind,
480 And golden rings the double back-plate join'd:
Forth thro' the navel burst the thrilling steel;
And on his knees with piercing shrieks he fell;
The rushing entrails pour'd upon the ground
His hands collect; and darkness wraps him round.
485 When *Hector* view'd, all ghastly in his gore
Thus sadly slain, th' unhappy *Polydore*;
A cloud of sorrow overcast his sight,
His soul no longer brook'd the distant fight,
Full in *Achilles'* dreadful front he came,
490 And shook his jav'lin like a waving flame.
The son of *Peleus* sees, with joy possest,
His heart high-bounding in his rising breast:
And, lo! the man, on whom black fates attend;
The man, that slew *Achilles*, in his friend!
495 No more shall *Hector*'s and *Pelides'* spear
Turn from each other in the walks of war –
Then with revengeful eyes he scan'd him o'er:
Come, and receive thy fate! He spake no more.
     Hector, undaunted, thus. Such words employ
500 To one that dreads thee, some unwarlike boy:
Such we could give, defying and defy'd,
Mean intercourse of obloquy and pride!

I know thy force to mine superiour far;
But heav'n alone confers success in war:
Mean as I am, the Gods may guide my dart,   505
And give it entrance in a braver heart.
    Then parts the lance: But *Pallas'* heav'nly breath,
Far from *Achilles* wafts the winged death:
The bidden dart again to *Hector* flies,
And at the feet of its great master lies.   510
Achilles closes with his hated foe,
His heart and eyes with flaming fury glow:
But present to his aid, *Apollo* shrouds
The favour'd hero in a veil of clouds.
Thrice struck *Pelides* with indignant heart,   515
Thrice in impassive air he plung'd the dart:
The spear a fourth time bury'd in the cloud,
He foams with fury, and exclaims aloud.
    Wretch! thou hast scap'd again. Once more thy flight
Has sav'd thee, and the partial God of Light.   520
But long thou shalt not thy just fate withstand,
If any pow'r assist *Achilles'* hand.
Fly then inglorious! But thy flight this day
Whole hecatombs of *Trojan* ghosts shall pay.
    With that, he gluts his rage on numbers slain: 525
Then *Dryops* tumbled to th'ensanguin'd plain,
Pierc'd thro' the neck: He left him panting there,
And stopp'd *Demuchus*, great *Philetor*'s heir,
Gigantick chief! Deep gash'd th'enormous blade,
And for the soul an ample passage made.   530
Laogonus and *Dardanus* expire,
The valiant sons of an unhappy sire;
Both in one instant from the chariot hurl'd,
Sunk in one instant to the nether world;
This diff'rence only their sad fates afford,   535
That one the spear destroy'd, and one the sword.
    Nor less unpity'd young *Alastor* bleeds;
In vain his youth, in vain his beauty pleads:
In vain he begs thee with a suppliant's moan,
To spare a form, an age so like thy own!   540
Unhappy boy! no pray'r, no moving art
E'er bent that fierce, inexorable heart!

While yet he trembled at his knees, and cry'd,
The ruthless falchion op'd his tender side;
545 The panting liver pours a flood of gore,
That drowns his bosom, till he pants no more.
　　Thro' *Mulius'* head then drove th'impetuous spear,
The Warriour falls, transfix'd from ear to ear.
Thy life, *Echeclus!* next the sword bereaves,
550 Deep thro' the front the pond'rous falchion cleaves;
Warm'd in the brain the smoaking weapon lies,
The purple death comes floating o'er his eyes.
Then brave *Deucalion* dy'd: The dart was flung
Where the knit nerves the pliant elbow strung;
555 He dropp'd his arm, an unassisting weight,
And stood all impotent, expecting fate:
Full on his neck the falling falchion sped,
From his broad shoulders hew'd his crested head:
Forth from the bone the spinal marrow flies,
560 And sunk in dust, the corps extended lies.
Rhigmus, whose race from fruitful *Thracia* came,
(The son of *Pireus*, an illustrious name,)
Succeeds to fate: The spear his belly rends;
Prone from his car the thund'ring chief descends:
565 The squire who saw expiring on the ground
His prostrate master, rein'd the steeds around:
His back scarce turn'd, the *Pelian* jav'lin gor'd;
And stretch'd the servant o'er his dying Lord.
As when a flame the winding valley fills,
570 And runs on crackling shrubs between the hills;
Then o'er the stubble up the mountain flies,
Fires the high woods, and blazes to the skies,
This way and that, the spreading torrent roars;
So sweeps the hero thro' the wasted shores.
575 Around him wide, immense destruction pours,
And earth is delug'd with the sanguine show'rs.
As with autumnal harvests cover'd o'er,
And thick bestrown, lies *Ceres'* sacred floor,
When round and round, with never-weary'd pain,
580 The trampling steers beat out th'unnumber'd grain.
So the fierce coursers, as the chariot rolls,
Tread down whole ranks, and crush out Heroes souls.

Dash'd from their hoofs while o'er the dead they fly,
Black, bloody drops the smoaking chariot dye:
The spiky wheels thro' heaps of carnage tore;   585
And thick the groaning axles dropp'd with gore.
High o'er the scene of death *Achilles* stood,
All grim with dust, all horrible in blood:
Yet still insatiate, still with rage on flame;
Such is the lust of never-dying Fame!   590

OBSERVATIONS

ON THE

TWENTIETH BOOK

5. *Then* Jove *to* Themis *gives command*, &c.] The poet is now to bring his hero again into action, and he introduces him with the utmost pomp and grandeur: The Gods are assembled only upon this account, and *Jupiter* permits several Deities to join with the *Trojans*, and hinder *Achilles* from over-ruling destiny itself.

The circumstance of sending *Themis* to assemble the Gods is very beautiful; she is the Goddess of justice; the *Trojans* by the rape of *Helen*, and by repeated perjuries having broken her laws, she is the properest messenger to summon a synod to bring them to punishment.

Eustathius.

Proclus has given a farther Explanation of this. *Themis* or *Justice* (says he) is made to assemble the Gods round *Jupiter*, because it is from him that all the powers of Nature take their virtue, and receive their orders; and *Jupiter* sends them to the relief of both parties, to shew that nothing falls out but by his permission, and that neither angels, nor men, nor the elements, act but according to the power which is given them.

15. *All but old Ocean.*] *Eustathius* gives two reasons why *Oceanus* was absent from this assembly: The one is because he is fabled to be the original of all the Gods, and it would have been a piece of indecency for him to see the Deities, who were all his descendents, war upon one another by joining adverse parties: The other reason he draws from the allegory of *Oceanus*, which signifies the element of water, and consequently the whole element could not ascend into the Æther; But whereas *Neptune*, the rivers, and the fountains are said to have been present, this is no way impossible, if we consider it in an allegorical sense, which implies, that the rivers, seas, and fountains supply the air with vapours, and by that means ascend into the æther.

35.   *Cælestial pow'rs! descend,*
And as your minds direct, your succour lend
To either host –]

Eustathius informs us, that the ancients were very much divided upon this passage of *Homer.* Some have criticised it, and others have answered their criticism; but he reports nothing more than the objection, without transmitting the answer to us. Those who condemned *Homer,* said *Jupiter* was for the *Trojans*; he saw the *Greeks* were the strongest, so permitted the Gods to declare themselves and go to the battel. But therein that God is deceived, and does not gain his point; for the Gods who favour the *Greeks* being stronger than those who favour the *Trojans,* the *Greeks* will still have the same advantage. I do not know what answer the partisans of *Homer* made, but for my part, I think this objection is more ingenious than solid. *Jupiter* does not pretend that the *Trojans* should be stronger than the *Greeks,* he has only a mind that the decree of destiny should be executed. Destiny had refused to *Achilles* the glory of taking *Troy,* but if *Achilles* fights singly against the *Trojans,* he is capable of forcing destiny; as *Homer* has already elsewhere said, that there had been brave men who had done so. Whereas if the Gods took part, tho' those who followed the *Grecians* were stronger than those who were for the *Trojans,* the latter would however be strong enough to support destiny, and to hinder *Achilles* from making himself master of *Troy*: This was *Jupiter*'s sole view. Thus is this passage far from being blameable, it is on the contrary very beautiful, and infinitely glorious for *Achilles.*   *Dacier.*

41.   *– Or* Ilion's *sacred wall*
May fall this day, tho' Fate forbid the fall.]

Mons. *de la Motte* criticizes on this passage, as thinking it absurd and contradictory to *Homer*'s own system, to imagine, that what Fate had ordained should not come to pass. *Jupiter* here seems to fear that *Troy* will be taken this very day in spite of destiny, ὑπὲρ μόρον. M. *Boivin* answers, that the explication hereof depends wholly upon the principles of the ancient pagan theology and their doctrine concerning Fate. It is certain, according to *Homer* and *Virgil,* that what destiny had decreed did not constantly happen in the precise time marked by destiny, the fatal moment was not to be retarded, but might be hastened: For example, that of the death of *Dido* was advanced by the blow she gave herself; her hour was not then come.

> – *Nec fato, merita nec morte peribat,*
> *Sed misera ante diem –*

> [For since she dy'd, not doom'd by heav'ns decree,
>   Or her own crime; but human casualty.]

Every violent death was accounted ὑπὲρ μόρον, that is, before the fated time, or (which is the same thing) against the natural order, *turbato mortalitatis ordine*, as the *Romans* expressed it. And the same might be said of any misfortunes which men drew upon themselves by their own ill conduct. (See the note on v. 560. *lib.* 16.) In a word, it must be allowed that it was not easy, in the pagan religion, to form the justest ideas upon a doctrine so difficult to be cleared; and upon which it is no great wonder if a poet should not always be perfectly consistent with himself, when it has puzzel'd such a number of divines and philosophers.

44.   *On adverse parts the warring Gods engage,*
      Heav'ns awful Queen, &c.]

Eustathius has a very curious remark upon this division of the Gods in *Homer*, which M. *Dacier* has entirely borrowed (as indeed no commentator ever borrowed more, or acknowledged less, than she has every where done from *Eustathius.*) This division, says he, is not made at random, but founded upon very solid reasons, drawn from the nature of those two nations. He places on the side of the *Greeks* all the Gods who preside over arts and sciences, to signify how much in that respect the *Greeks* excelled all other nations. *Juno, Pallas, Neptune, Mercury* and *Vulcan* are for the *Greeks*; *Juno*, not only as the Goddess who presides over marriage, and who is concerned to revenge an injury done to the nuptial bed, but likewise as the Goddess who represents monarchical government, which was better established in *Greece* than any where else; *Pallas*, because being the Goddess of war and wisdom, she ought to assist those who are wronged; besides the *Greeks* understood the art of war better than the *Barbarians*; *Neptune*, because he was an enemy to the *Trojans* upon account of *Laomedon*'s perfidiousness, and because most of the *Greeks* being come from islands or peninsula's they were in some sort his subjects; *Mercury*, because he is a God who presides over stratagems of war, and because *Troy* was taken by that of the wooden horse; and lastly *Vulcan*, as the declared enemy of *Mars* and of all adulterers, and as the father of arts.

52. *Mars fiery-helm'd, the laughter-loving Dame.*] The reasons why *Mars* and *Venus* engage for the *Trojans* are very obvious; the point in hand was to favour ravishers and debauchees. But the same reason, you will say, does not serve for *Apollo, Diana* and *Latona.* It is urged that *Apollo* is for the *Trojans*, because of the darts and arrows which were the principal strength of the *Barbarians*; and *Diana*, because she presided over dancing, and those *Barbarians* were great dancers; and *Latona*, as influenced by her children. *Xanthus* being a *Trojan* river is interested for his countrey.   ˙*Eustathius.*

75. *Above the Sire of Gods,* &c.] 'The images (says *Longinus*) which *Homer* gives of the combate of the Gods, have in 'em something prodigiously great and magnificent. We see in these verses, the earth opened to its very center, hell ready to disclose itself, the whole machine of the world upon the point to be destroyed and overturned: To shew that in such a conflict, heaven and hell, all things mortal and immortal, the whole creation in short was engaged in this battel, and all the extent of nature in danger.'

> *Non secus ac si qua penitus vi terra dehiscens*
> *Infernas reseret sedes & regna recludat*
> *Pallida, Diis invisa, superque immane barathrum*
> *Cernatur, trepidentque immisso lumine manes.*   Virgil.

> [So the pent vapours with a rumbling sound
> Heave from below; and rend the hollow ground:
> A sounding flaw succeeds: And from on high,
> The Gods, with hate beheld the neather sky:
> The ghosts repine at violated night.]

Madam *Dacier* rightly observes that this copy is inferior to the original on this account, that *Virgil* has made a comparison of that which *Homer* made an action. This occasions an infinite difference, which is easy to be perceived.

One may compare with this noble passage of *Homer*, the battel of the Gods and Giants in *Hesiod*'s *Theogony*, which is one of the sublimest parts of that author; and *Milton*'s battel of the *Angels* in the sixth book: The elevation, and enthusiasm of our great countryman seems owing to this original.

91. *First silver-shafted* Phœbus *took the plain,* &c.] With what art does the poet engage the Gods in this conflict! *Neptune* opposes *Apollo,* which implies that things moist and dry are in continual discord: *Pallas* fights with *Mars,* which signifies that rashness and wisdom always disagree: *Juno* is against *Diana,* that is, nothing more differs from a marriage state, than celibacy: *Vulcan* engages *Xanthus,* that is, fire and water are in perpetual variance. Thus we have a fine allegory concealed under the veil of excellent poetry, and the reader receives a double satisfaction at the same time from beautiful verses, and an instructive moral.   *Eustathius.*

119. *Already have I met,* &c.] *Eustathius* remarks that the poet lets no opportunity pass of inserting into his poem the actions that preceded the tenth year of the war, especially the actions of *Achilles* the hero of it. In this place he brings in *Æneas* extolling the bravery of his enemy and confessing himself to have formerly been vanquish'd by him: At the same time he preserves a piece of ancient history by inserting into the poem the hero's conquest of *Pedasus* and *Lyrnessus.*

121.   *From* Ida's *woods he chas'd us —*
        But Jove *assisting I surviv'd.*]

It is remarkable that *Æneas* owed his safety to his flight from *Achilles,* but it may seem strange that *Achilles* who was so fam'd for his Swiftness, should not be able to overtake him, even with *Minerva* for his guide. *Eustathius* answers, that this might proceed from the better knowledge *Æneas* might have of the ways and defiles: *Achilles* being a stranger, and *Æneas* having long kept his father's flocks in those parts.

   He farther observes, that the word φάος [light] discovers that it was in the night that *Achilles* pursued *Æneas.*

174. *Advanc'd upon the field there stood a mound,* &c.] It may not be unnecessary to explain this passage to make it understood by the reader: The poet is very short in the description, as supposing the fact already known, and hastens to the combat between *Achilles* and *Æneas.* This is very judicious in *Homer* not to dwell on a piece of history that had no relation to his action, when he has raised the reader's expecta-

tion by so pompous an introduction, and made the Gods themselves his spectators.

The story is as follows. *Laomedon* having defrauded *Neptune* of the reward he promised him for the building the walls of *Troy, Neptune* sent a monstrous whale, to which *Laomedon* exposed his daughter *Hesione*: But *Hercules* having undertaken to destroy the monster, the *Trojans* raised an intrenchment to defend *Hercules* from his pursuit: This being a remarkable piece of conduct in the *Trojans*, it gave occasion to the poet to adorn a plain narration with fiction by ascribing the work to *Pallas* the Goddess of wisdom.   *Eustathius.*

180. *Here* Neptune, *and the Gods,* &c.] I wonder why *Eustathius* and all other commentators should be silent upon this recess of the Gods: It seems strange at the first view, that so many deities, after having entered the scene of action, should perform so short a part, and immediately become themselves spectators? I conceive the reason of this conduct in the poet to be, that *Achilles* has been inactive during the greatest part of the poem; and as he is the hero of it, ought to be the chief character in it: The poet therefore withdraws the Gods from the field that *Achilles* may have the whole honour of the day, and not act in subordination to the deities: Besides, the poem now draws to a conclusion, and it is necessary for *Homer* to enlarge upon the exploits of *Achilles*, that he may leave a noble idea of his valour upon the mind of the reader.

214, &c. *The conversation of* Achilles *and* Æneas.] I shall lay before the reader the words of *Eustathius* in defence of this passage, which I confess seems to me to be faulty in the poet. The reader (says he) would naturally expect some great and terrible atchievements should ensue from *Achilles* upon his first entrance upon action. The poet seems to prepare us for it, by his magnificent introduction of him into the field: But instead of a storm, we have a calm; he follows the same method in this book as he did in the third, where when both armies were ready to engage in a general conflict, he ends the day in a single combate between two heroes: Thus he always agreeably surprizes his readers. Besides the admirers of *Homer* reap a farther advantage from this conversation of the Heroes: There is a chain of ancient history as well as a series of poetical beauties.

Madam *Dacier*'s excuse is very little better: And to shew that this is really a fault in the poet, I believe I may appeal to the taste of every reader who certainly finds himself disappointed: Our expectation is raised to see Gods and heroes engage, when suddenly it all sinks into such a combat in which neither party receives a wound; and (what is more extraordinary) the Gods are made the spectators of so small an action! What occasion was there for thunder, earthquakes, and descending deities, to introduce a matter of so little importance? Neither is it any excuse to say he has given us a piece of ancient history; we expected to read a poet, not an historian. In short, after the greatest preparation for action imaginable, he suspends the whole narration, and from the heat of a poet, cools at once into the simplicity of an historian.

258. *The natives were content to till*
      The shady foot of Ida's *fount-ful hill.*]

Κτίσσε δὲ Δαρδανίην, ἐπεὶ οὔ πω Ἴλιος ἱρὴ
Ἐν πεδίῳ πεπόλιστο πόλις μερόπων ἀνθρώπων
Ἀλλ' ἔθ' ὑπωρείας ᾤκεον πολυπίδακος Ἴδης.

[cf. trans. Pope, 256–9]

Plato and *Strabo* understand this passage as favouring the opinion that the mountainous parts of the world were first inhabited, after the universal deluge; and that mankind by degrees descended to dwell in the lower parts of the hills (which they would have the word ὑπώρεια signify) and only in greater process of time ventured into the valleys: *Virgil* however seems to have taken this word in a sense something different where he alludes to this passage.   *Æn.* 3. 109.

     – *Nondum Ilium et arces*
     Pergameæ steterant, habitabant vallibus imis.

     [E'er *Ilium* and the *Trojan* tow'rs arose,
     In humble vales they built their soft abodes:]

262. *Three thousand mares,* &c.] The number of the horses and mares of *Ericthonius* may seem incredible, were we not assured by *Herodotus* that there were in the stud of *Cyrus* at one time (besides those for the service of war) eight hundred horses and six thousand six hundred mares.   *Eustathius.*

264. *Boreas, enamour'd,* &c.] *Homer* has the happiness of making the least circumstance considerable; the subject grows under his hands,

and the plainest matter shines in his dress of poetry: Another poet would have said these horses were as swift as the wind, but *Homer* tells you that they sprung from *Boreas* the God of the wind; and thence drew their swiftness.

270. *These lightly skimming, as they swept the plain.*] The poet illustrates the swiftness of these horses by describing them as running over the standing corn, and surface of waters, without making any impression. *Virgil* has imitated these lines, and adapts what *Homer* says of these horses to the swiftness of *Camilla*.   *Æn.* 7. 809.

> *Illa vel intactæ segetis per summa volaret*
> *Gramina; nec teneras cursu læsisset aristas:*
> *Vel mare per medium, fluctu supensa tumenti*
> *Ferret iter, celeres nec tingeret æquore plantas.*

> [Flew o'er the fields, nor hurt the bearded grain:
> She swept the seas, and as she skim'd along,
> Her flying feet unbath'd on billows hung.]

The reader will easily perceive that *Virgil*'s is almost a literal translation: He has imitated the very run of the verses, which flow nimbly away in dactyls, and as swift as the wind they describe.

I cannot but observe one thing in favour of *Homer*, that there can no greater commendation be given to him, than by considering the conduct of *Virgil*: who, tho' undoubtedly the greatest poet after him, seldom ventures to vary much from his original in the passages he takes from him, as in a despair of improving, and contented if he can but equal them.

280. *To bear the cup of* Jove.] To be a cup-bearer has in all ages and nations been reckon'd an honourable employment: *Sappho* mentions it in honour of her brother *Larichus*, that he was cup-bearer to the nobles of *Mitylene*: The son of *Menelaus* executed the same office, *Hebe* and *Mercury* served the Gods in the same station.

It was the custom in the pagan worship to employ noble youths to pour the wine upon the sacrifice: In this office *Ganymede* might probably attend upon the altar of *Jupiter*, and from thence was fabled to be his cup-bearer.   *Eustath.*

339. *But Ocean's God,* &c.] The conduct of the poet in making *Æneas* owe his safety to *Neptune* in this place is remarkable: *Neptune* is an enemy to the *Trojans*, yet he dares not suffer so pious a man to fall, lest *Jupiter* should be offended: This shews, says *Eustathius*, that piety is always under the protection of God; and that favours are sometimes conferred not out of kindness, but to prevent a greater detriment; thus *Neptune* preserves *Æneas*, lest *Jupiter* should revenge his death upon the *Grecians*.

345. *And can ye see this righteous chief,* &c.] Tho' *Æneas* is represented a man of great courage, yet his piety is his most shining character: This is the reason why he is always the care of the Gods, and they favour him constantly thro' the whole poem with their immediate protection.

'Tis in this light that *Virgil* has presented him to the view of the reader: His valour bears but the second place in the *Æneis.* In the *Ilias* indeed he is drawn in miniature, and in the *Æneis* at full length; but there are the same Features in the copy, which are in the original, and he is the same *Æneas* in *Rome* as he was in *Troy*.

355. *On great Æneas shall devolve the reign,*
　　　And sons succeeding sons the lasting line sustain.]

The story of *Æneas* his founding the *Roman* empire gave *Virgil* the finest occasion imaginable of paying a complement to *Augustus*, and his countrymen, who were fond of being thought the descendants of *Troy*. He has translated these two lines literally, and put them in the nature of a prophecy; as the favourers of the opinion of *Æneas*'s sailing into *Italy*, imagine *Homer*'s to be.

　　　– Αἰνείαο βίη Τρώεσσιν ἀνάξει
　　　Καὶ παῖδες παίδων τοί κεν μετόπισθε γένωνται.

　　　[The might of Aeneas shall rule over the Trojans,
　　　　And the sons of his sons, and those who are born
　　　　　thereafter shall continue to rule over them.]

　　　Hic domus Æneæ cunctis dominabitur oris,
　　　Et nati natorum & qui nascentur ab illis.

　　　[Through the wide world th' *Æneian* house shall reign,
　　　　And children's children shall the crown sustain.]

There has been a very ancient alteration made (as *Strabo* observes) in

these two lines by substituting πάντεσσι (over all) in the room of Τρώ-
εσσι (over the Trojans). It is not improbable but *Virgil* might give
occasion for it, by his *cunctis dominabitur oris* ([the house of Aeneas]
shall rule over all lands).

Eustathius does not entirely discountenance this story: If it be
understood, says he, as a prophecy, the poet might take it from the
Sibylline oracles. He farther remarks that the poet artfully interweaves
into his poem not only the things which happened before the commence-
ment, and in the prosecution of the *Trojan* war; but other matters of
importance which happened even after that war was brought to a
conclusion. Thus for instance, we have here a piece of history not
extant in any other author, by which we are informed that the house of
Æneas succeeded to the crown of *Troas*, and to the kingdom of *Priam.*

Eustathius.

This passage is very considerable, for it ruins the famous chimæra of
the *Roman* empire, and of the family of the *Cæsars*, who both pretended
to deduce their original from *Venus* by *Æneas*, alledging that after the
taking of *Troy*, *Æneas* came into *Italy*, and this pretension is hereby
actually destroyed. This testimony of *Homer* ought to be looked upon
as an authentick act, the fidelity and verity whereof cannot be ques-
tioned. *Neptune*, as much an enemy as he is to the *Trojans*, declares
that *Æneas*, and after him his posterity, shall reign over the *Trojans.*
Wou'd *Homer* have put this prophecy in *Neptune*'s mouth, if he had not
known that *Æneas* did not leave *Troy*, but that he reigned there, and if
he had not seen in his time the descendants of that Prince reign there
likewise? That poet wrote 260 Years, or thereabouts, after the taking of
Troy, and what is very remarkable he wrote in some of the towns of
Ionia, that is to say, in the neighbourhood of *Phrygia*, so that the time
and place give such a weight to his deposition that nothing can
invalidate it. All that the historians have written concerning *Æneas*'s
voyage into *Italy*, ought to be considered as a romance, made on
purpose to destroy all historical truth, for the most ancient is posterior
to *Homer* by some ages. Before *Dionysius* of *Halicarnassus*, some
writers being sensible of the strength of this passage of *Homer*,
undertook to explain it so as to reconcile it with this fable, and they
said that *Æneas*, after having been in *Italy*, returned to *Troy*, and left
his son *Ascanius* there. *Dionysius* of *Halicarnassus*, little satisfied with
this solution, which did not seem to him to be probable, has taken
another method: He would have it that by these words, 'He shall reign
over the *Trojans*,' *Homer* meant, he shall reign over the *Trojans* whom

he shall carry with him into *Italy.* 'For is it not possible,' says he, 'that *Æneas* should reign over the *Trojans,* whom he had taken with him, though settled elsewhere?'

That historian, who wrote in *Rome* itself, and in the very reign of *Augustus,* was willing to make his court to that Prince, by explaining this passage of *Homer* so as to favour the chimæra he was possessed with. And this is a reproach that may with some justice be cast on him; for poets may by their fictions flatter Princes and welcome: 'Tis their trade. But for historians to corrupt the gravity and severity of history, to substitute fable in the place of truth, is what ought not to be pardoned. *Strabo* was much more scrupulous, for tho' he wrote his books of geography towards the beginning of *Tiberius's* reign, yet he had the courage to give a right explication to this passage of *Homer,* and to aver, that this poet said, and meant, that *Æneas* remained at *Troy,* that he reigned therein, *Priam's* whole Race being extinguished, and that he left the kingdom to his children after him. *lib.* 13. You may see this whole matter discussed in a Letter from M. *Bochart* to M. *de Segrais,* who has prefixed it to his remarks upon the translation of *Virgil.*

378. *Where the slow* Caucons *close the rear.*] The *Caucones* (says *Eustathius*) were of *Paphlagonian* extract: And this perhaps was the reason why they are not distinctly mentioned in the catalogue, they being included under the general name of *Paphlagonians:* Tho' two lines are quoted which are said to have been left out by some transcriber, and immediately followed this,

Κρῶμναν τ' αἰγιαλόν τε καὶ ὑψηλοὺς Ἐρυθίνους.

[The Cromnian shore and the Erythinian highlands.]

Which verses are these,

Καύκωνας αὖτ' ἦγε πολύκλεος υἱὸς ἀμύμιον.

[The famous, blameless son led the Caucones.]

Or as others read it, Ἄμειβος (new recruit).

Οἱ περὶ παρθένιον ποταμὸν κλυτὰ δώματ' ἔναιον.

[They dwelled in their shining homes, along the virgin
    river.]

Or according to others,

$$\text{Κατὰ δώματ' ἔναιον.}$$

[They inhabited homes.]

Yet I believe these are not *Homer*'s lines, but rather the addition of some transcriber, and 'tis evident by consulting the passage from which they are said to have been curtail'd, that they would be absurd in that place; for the second line is actually there already, and as these *Caucons* are said to live upon the banks of the *Parthenius*, so are the *Paphlagonians* in the above-mentioned passage. It is therefore more probable that the *Caucons* are included in the *Paphlagonians.*

467.   – *Not louder roars*
        At Neptune*'s shrine on* Helice*'s high shores,* &c.]

In *Helice*, a town of *Achaia*, three quarters of a league from the gulph of *Corinth*, *Neptune* had a magnificent temple where the *Ionians* offered every year to him a sacrifice of a bull; and it was with these people an auspicious sign, and a certain mark, that the sacrifice would be accepted, if the bull bellowed as he was led to the altar. After the *Ionic* migration, which happened about 140 years after the taking of *Troy*, the *Ionians* of *Asia* assembled in the fields of *Priene* to celebrate the same festival in honour of *Heliconian Neptune*; and as those of *Priene* valued themselves upon being originally of *Helice*, they chose for the King of the sacrifice a young *Prienian.* It is needless to dispute from whence the poet has taken his comparison; for as he lived 100, or 120 years after the *Ionic* migration, it cannot be doubted but he took it in the *Asian Ionia*, and at *Priene* itself; where he had probably often assisted at that sacrifice, and been witness of the ceremonies therein observed. This poet always appears strongly addicted to the customs of the *Ionians*, which makes some conjecture that he was an *Ionian* himself.   *Eustathius. Dacier.*

471. *Then fell on* Polydore *his vengeful rage.*] *Euripides* in his *Hecuba* has followed another tradition when he makes *Polydorus* the son of *Priam*, and of *Hecuba*, and slain by *Polymnestor* King of *Thrace*, after the taking of *Troy*; for according to *Homer*, he is not the son of *Hecuba*, but of *Laothoë*, as he says in the following book, and is slain by *Achilles: Virgil* too has rather chosen to follow *Euripides* than *Homer.*

489. *Full in* Achilles' *dreadful front he came.*] The great judgment of the poet in keeping the character of his hero is in this place very evident: When *Achilles* was to engage *Æneas* he holds a long conference with him, and with patience bears the reply of *Æneas*: Had he pursued the same Method with *Hector*, he had departed from his character. Anger is the prevailing passion in *Achilles*: He left the field in a rage against *Agamemnon*, and enter'd it again to be reveng'd of *Hector*: The poet therefore judiciously makes him take fire at the sight of his enemy: He describes him as impatient to kill him, he gives him a haughty challenge, and that challenge is comprehended in a single line: His impatience to be reveng'd, would not suffer him to delay it by a length of words.

513. *But present to his aid,* Apollo.] It is a common observation that a God should never be introduced into a poem but where his presence is necessary. And it may be asked why the life of *Hector* is of such importance that *Apollo* should rescue him from the hand of *Achilles* here, and yet suffer him to fall so soon after? *Eustathius* answers, that the poet had not yet sufficiently exalted the valour of *Achilles*, he takes time to enlarge upon his atchievements, and rises by degrees in his character, till he completes both his courage and resentment at one blow in the death of *Hector.* And the poet, adds he, pays a great complement to his favourite countryman, by shewing that nothing but the intervention of a God could have sav'd *Æneas* and *Hector* from the hand of *Achilles.*

541. *– No Pray'r, no moving art*
    E'er bent that fierce, inexorable heart!]

I confess it is a Satisfaction to me, to observe with what art the poet pursues his subject: The opening of the poem professes to treat of the Anger of *Achilles*; that anger draws on all the great events of the story: And *Homer* at every opportunity awakens the reader to an attention to it, by mentioning the effects of it: So that when we see in this place the hero deaf to youth, and compassion, it is what we expect: Mercy in him would offend, because it is contrary to his character. *Homer* proposes him not as a pattern for imitation; but the moral of the poem which he design'd the Reader should draw from it, is, that we should avoid anger, since it is ever pernicious in the event.

580. *The trampling steers beat out the unnumber'd grain.*] In *Greece*, instead of threshing the corn as we do, they caused it to be trod out by oxen; this was likewise practised in *Judæa*, as is seen by the law of God, who forbad the *Jews* to muzzle the ox who trod out the corn, *Non ligabis os bovis terentis in area fruges tuas* ('Thou shalt not muzzle the ox when he treadeth out the corn' [King James version]). Deuteron. 25.   *Dacier.*

The same practice is still preserved among the *Turks* and modern *Greeks.*

The similes at the end.] It is usual with our author to heap his similes very thick together at the conclusion of a book. He has done the same in the seventeenth: 'Tis the natural discharge of a vast imagination, heated in its progress, and giving itself vent in this crowd of images.

I cannot close the notes upon this book, without observing the dreadful idea of *Achilles*, which the poet leaves upon the mind of the reader. He drives his chariot over shields and mangled heaps of slain: The wheels, the axle-tree, and the horses are stain'd with blood, the hero's eyes burn with fury, and his hands are red with slaughter. A painter might form from this passage the picture of *Mars* in the fulness of his terrours, as well as *Phidias* is said to have drawn from another, that of *Jupiter* in all his majesty.

THE
TWENTY-FIRST BOOK
OF THE
ILIAD

The ARGUMENT

The battel in the river *Scamander*

The Trojans *fly before* Achilles, *some towards the town, others to the river* Scamander: *He falls upon the latter with great slaughter, takes twelve captives alive, to sacrifice to the shade of* Patroclus; *and kills* Lycaon *and* Asteropæus. Scamander *attacks him with all his waves;* Neptune *and* Pallas *assist the Hero;* Simois *joins* Scamander; *at length* Vulcan, *by the instigation of* Juno, *almost dries up the river. This combate ended, the other Gods engage each other. Meanwhile* Achilles *continues the slaughter, drives the rest into* Troy; Agenor *only makes a stand, and is conveyed away in a cloud by* Apollo; *who (to delude* Achilles) *takes upon him* Agenor's *shape, and while he pursues him in that disguise, gives the* Trojans *an opportunity of retiring into their city.*

The same day continues. The scene is on the banks, and in the stream, of Scamander.

And now to *Xanthus'* gliding stream they drove,
Xanthus, immortal progeny of *Jove*.
The river here divides the flying train.
Part to the town fly diverse o'er the plain,
5   Where late their troops triumphant bore the fight,
Now chas'd, and trembling in ignoble flight:
(These with a gather'd mist *Saturnia* shrouds,
And rolls behind the rout a heap of clouds)
Part plunge into the stream: Old *Xanthus* roars,
10   The flashing billows beat the whiten'd shores:
With cries promiscuous all the banks resound,
And here, and there, in eddies whirling round,
The flouncing steeds and shrieking warriours
        drown'd.
As the scorch'd locusts from their fields retire,
15   While fast behind them runs the blaze of fire;
Driv'n from the land before the smoky cloud,
The clust'ring legions rush into the flood:
So plung'd in *Xanthus* by *Achilles'* force,
Roars the resounding surge with men and horse.
20   His bloody lance the hero casts aside,
(Which spreading tam'risks on the margin hide)
Then, like a God, the rapid billows braves,
Arm'd with his sword, high-brandish'd o'er the waves:
Now down he plunges, now he whirls it round,
25   Deep groan'd the waters with the dying sound;
Repeated wounds the red'ning river dy'd,
And the warm purple circled on the tide.

Swift thro' the foamy flood the *Trojans* fly,
And close in rocks or winding caverns lie.
So the huge Dolphin tempesting the main,   30
In shoals before him fly the scaly train,
Confus'dly heap'd they seek their inmost caves,
Or pant and heave beneath the floating waves.
Now tir'd with slaughter, from the *Trojan* band
Twelve chosen youths he drags alive to land;   35
With their rich belts their captive arms constrains,
(Late their proud ornaments, but now their chains.)
These his attendants to the ships convey'd,
Sad Victims! destin'd to *Patroclus'* shade.
   Then, as once more he plung'd amid the flood,   40
The young *Lycaon* in his passage stood;
The son of *Priam*, whom the hero's hand
But late made captive in his father's land,
(As from a sycamore, his sounding steel
Lopp'd the green arms to spoke a chariot wheel)   45
To *Lemnos'* isle he sold the royal slave,
Where *Jason*'s son the price demanded gave;
But kind *Eëtion* touching on the shore,
The ransom'd Prince to fair *Arisbe* bore.
Ten Days were past, since in his father's reign   50
He felt the sweets of liberty again;
The next, that God whom men in vain withstand,
Gives the same youth to the same conqu'ring hand;
Now never to return! and doom'd to go
A sadder journey to the shades below.   55
His well-known face when great *Achilles* ey'd,
(The helm and visor he had cast aside
With wild affright, and dropt upon the field
His useless lance and unavailing shield.)
As trembling, panting, from the stream he fled,   60
And knock'd his fault'ring knees, the hero said.
   Ye mighty Gods! what Wonders strike my view!
Is it in vain our conqu'ring arms subdue?
Sure I shall see yon' heaps of *Trojans* kill'd
Rise from the shades, and brave me on the field: 65
As now the captive, whom so late I bound
And sold to *Lemnos*, stalks on *Trojan* ground!

Not him the sea's unmeasur'd deeps detain,
That barr such numbers from their native plain:
70   Lo! he returns! Try then, my flying spear!
Try, if the grave can hold the wanderer;
If earth at length this active Prince can seize,
Earth, whose strong grasp has held down *Hercules.*
     Thus while he spake, the *Trojan* pale with fears
75   Approach'd, and sought his knees with suppliant tears;
Loth as he was to yield his youthful breath,
And his soul shiv'ring at th' approach of death.
Achilles rais'd the spear, prepar'd to wound;
He kiss'd his feet, extended on the ground:
80   And while above the spear suspended stood,
Longing to dip its thirsty point in blood,
One hand embrac'd them close, one stopt the Dart;
While thus these melting words attempt his heart.
     Thy well-known captive, great *Achilles!* see,
85   Once more *Lycaon* trembles at thy knee.
Some pity to a suppliant's name afford,
Who shar'd the gifts of *Ceres* at thy board;
Whom late thy conqu'ring arm to *Lemnos* bore,
Far from his father, friends, and native shore;
90   A hundred oxen were his price that day,
Now sums immense thy mercy shall repay.
Scarce respited from woes I yet appear,
And scarce twelve morning suns have seen me here;
Lo! *Jove* again submits me to thy hands,
95   Again, her victim cruel fate demands!
I sprung from *Priam*, and *Laothöe* fair,
(Old *Alte*'s daughter, and *Lelegia*'s heir;
Who held in *Pedasus* his fam'd abode,
And rul'd the fields where silver *Satnio* flow'd)
100 Two sons (alas, unhappy sons) she bore;
For ah! one spear shall drink each brother's gore,
And I succeed to slaughter'd *Polydore.*
How from that arm of terrour shall I fly?
Some Dæmon urges! 'tis my doom to die!
105 If ever yet soft pity touch'd thy mind,
Ah! think not me too much of *Hector*'s kind!

Not the same mother gave thy suppliant breath,
With his, who wrought thy lov'd *Patroclus*' death.
   These words, attended with a show'r of tears,
The youth addrest to unrelenting ears: 110
Talk not of life, or ransom, (he replies)
Patroclus dead, whoever meets me, dies:
In vain a single *Trojan* sues for grace;
But least, the sons of *Priam*'s hateful race.
Die then, my friend! what boots it to deplore?   115
The great, the good *Patroclus* is no more!
He, far thy better, was foredoom'd to die,
And thou, dost thou, bewail mortality?
See'st thou not me, whom nature's gifts adorn,
Sprung from a hero, from a Goddess born;   120
The day shall come (which nothing can avert)
When by the spear, the arrow, or the dart,
By night, or day, by force or by design,
Impending death and certain fate are mine.
Die then – he said; and as the word he spoke   125
The fainting stripling sunk, before the stroke;
His hand forgot its grasp, and left the spear:
While all his trembling frame confest his fear.
Sudden, *Achilles* his broad sword display'd,
And buried in his neck the reeking blade.   130
Prone fell the youth; and panting on the land,
The gushing purple dy'd the thirsty sand:
The victor to the stream the carcass gave,
And thus insults him, floating on the wave.
   Lie there, *Lycaon!* let the fish surround   135
Thy bloated corse, and suck thy goary wound:
There no sad mother shall thy fun'rals weep,
But swift *Scamander* roll thee to the deep,
Whose ev'ry wave some wat'ry monster brings,
To feast unpunish'd on the fat of kings.   140
So perish *Troy*, and all the *Trojan* line!
Such ruin theirs, and such compassion mine.
What boots ye now *Scamander*'s worship'd stream,
His earthly honours, and immortal name;
In vain your immolated bulls are slain,   145
Your living coursers glut his gulphs in vain:

Thus he rewards you, with this bitter fate;
Thus, till the *Grecian* vengeance is compleat;
Thus is aton'd *Patroclus'* honour'd shade,
150 And the short absence of *Achilles* paid.
    These boastful words provoke the raging God;
With fury swells the violated flood.
What means divine may yet the pow'r employ,
To check *Achilles*, and to rescue *Troy*?
155 Meanwhile the hero springs in arms, to dare
The great *Asteropeus* to mortal war;
The Son of *Pelagon*, whose lofty line
Flows from the source of *Axius*, stream divine!
(Fair *Peribæa's* love the God had crown'd,
160 With all his refluent waters circled round)
On him *Achilles* rush'd: He fearless stood,
And shook two spears, advancing from the flood;
The flood impell'd him, on *Pelides'* head
T'avenge his waters choak'd with heaps of dead.
165 Near as they drew, *Achilles* thus began.
    What art thou, boldest of the race of man?
Who, or from whence? Unhappy is the sire,
Whose son encounters our resistless ire.
    O Son of *Peleus!* what avails to trace
170 (Reply'd the warriour) our illustrious race?
From rich *Pæonia's* valleys I command
Arm'd with protended spears, my native band;
Now shines the tenth bright morning since I came
In aid of *Ilion* to the fields of fame:
175 *Axius*, who swells with all the neighb'ring rills,
And wide around the floated region fills,
Begot my sire, whose spear such glory won:
Now lift thy arm, and try that hero's son!
    Threat'ning he said: The hostile chiefs advance;
180 At once *Asteropeus* discharg'd each lance,
(For both his dext'rous hands the lance cou'd wield)
One struck, but pierc'd not the *Vulcanian* shield;
One raz'd *Achilles* hand; the spouting blood
Spun forth, in earth the fasten'd weapon stood.
185 Like lightning next the *Pelian* jav'lin flies;
Its erring fury hiss'd along the skies;

Deep in the swelling bank was driv'n the spear,
Ev'n to the middle earth'd; and quiver'd there.
Then from his side the sword *Pelides* drew,
And on his foe with doubled fury flew.   190
The foe thrice tugg'd, and shook the rooted wood;
Repulsive of his might the weapon stood:
The fourth, he tries to break the spear in vain;
Bent as he stands, he tumbles to the plain;
His belly open'd with a ghastly wound,   195
The reeking entrails pour upon the ground.
Beneath the hero's feet he panting lies,
And his eye darkens, and his spirit flies:
While the proud victor thus triumphing said,
His radiant armour tearing from the dead: 200
   So ends thy glory! Such the fate they prove
Who strive presumptuous with the sons of *Jove*.
Sprung from a river didst thou boast thy line,
But great *Saturnius* is the source of mine.
How durst thou vaunt thy wat'ry progeny?   205
Of *Peleus*, *Æacus*, and *Jove*, am I;
The race of these superiour far to those,
As he that thunders to the stream that flows.
What rivers can, *Scamander* might have shown;
But *Jove* he dreads, nor wars against his son.   210
Ev'n *Achelöus* might contend in vain,
And all the roaring billows of the main.
Th'eternal Ocean, from whose fountains flow
The seas, the rivers, and the Springs below,
The thund'ring Voice of *Jove* abhors to hear,   215
And in his deep abysses shakes with fear.
   He said; then from the bank his jav'lin tore,
And left the breathless warriour in his gore.
The floating tides the bloody carcass lave,
And beat against it, wave succeeding wave;   220
Till roll'd between the banks, it lies the food
Of curling eels, and fishes of the flood.
All scatter'd round the stream (their mightiest slain)
Th'amaz'd *Pæonians* scour along the plain:
He vents his fury on the flying crew,   225
Thrasius, *Astypylus*, and *Mnesus* slew;

Mydon, *Thersilochus*, with *Ænius* fell;
And numbers more his lance had plung'd to hell;
But from the bottom of his gulphs profound,
230   *Scamander* spoke; the shores return'd the sound.
    O first of mortals! (for the Gods are thine)
In valour matchless, and in force divine!
If *Jove* have giv'n thee every *Trojan* head,
'Tis not on me thy rage should heap the dead.
235   See! my choak'd streams no more their course can keep,
Nor roll their wonted tribute to the deep.
Turn then, impetuous! from our injur'd flood;
Content, thy slaughters could amaze a God.
    In human form confess'd before his eyes
240   The river thus; and thus the Chief replies.
O sacred stream! thy word we shall obey;
But not till *Troy* the destin'd vengeance pay,
Not till within her tow'rs the perjur'd train
Shall pant, and tremble at our arms again;
245   Not till proud *Hector*, guardian of her wall,
Or stain this lance, or see *Achilles* fall.
    He said; and drove with fury on the foe.
Then to the Godhead of the silver bow
The yellow Flood began: O son of *Jove!*
250   Was not the mandate of the Sire above
Full and express? that *Phœbus* should employ
His sacred arrows in defence of *Troy*,
And make her conquer, till *Hyperion*'s fall
In awful darkness hide the face of all?
255   He spoke in vain – the chief without dismay
Ploughs thro' the boiling surge his desp'rate way.
Then rising in his rage above the shores,
From all his deep the bellowing river roars,
Huge heaps of slain disgorges on the coast,
260   And round the banks the ghastly dead are tost.
While all before, the billows rang'd on high
(A wat'ry bulwark) screen the bands who fly.
Now bursting on his head with thund'ring sound,
The falling deluge whelms the hero round:
265   His loaded shield bends to the rushing tide;
His feet, upborn, scarce the strong flood divide,

Slidd'ring, and stagg'ring. On the border stood
A spreading elm, that overhung the flood;
He seiz'd a bending bough, his steps to stay;
The plant uprooted to his weight gave way,   270
Heaving the bank, and undermining all;
Loud flash the waters to the rushing fall
Of the thick foliage. The large trunk display'd
Bridg'd the rough flood across: The hero stay'd
On this his weight, and rais'd upon his hand,   275
Leap'd from the chanel, and regain'd the land.
Then blacken'd the wild waves; the murmur rose;
The God pursues, a huger billow throws,
And bursts the bank, ambitious to destroy
The man whose fury is the fate of *Troy*.   280
He, like the warlike eagle speeds his pace,
(Swiftest and strongest of th'aërial race)
Far as a spear can fly, *Achilles* springs
At ev'ry bound; his clanging armour rings:
Now here, now there, he turns on ev'ry side,   285
And winds his course before the following tide;
The waves flow after, wheresoe'er he wheels,
And gather fast, and murmur at his heels.
So when a peasant to his garden brings
Soft rills of water from the bubbling springs,   290
And calls the floods from high, to bless his bow'rs
And feed with pregnant streams the plants and flow'rs;
Soon as he clears whate'er their passage staid,
And marks the future current with his spade,
Swift o'er the rolling pebbles, down the hills   295
Louder and louder purl the falling rills,
Before him scatt'ring, they prevent his pains,
And shine in mazy wand'rings o'er the plains.
    Still flies *Achilles*, but before his eyes
Still swift *Scamander* rolls where'er he flies: 300
Not all his speed escapes the rapid floods;
The first of men, but not a match for Gods.
Oft' as he turn'd the torrent to oppose,
And bravely try if all the pow'rs were foes;
So oft' the surge, in wat'ry mountains spread,   305
Beats on his back, or bursts upon his head.

Yet dauntless still the adverse flood he braves,
And still indignant bounds above the waves.
Tir'd by the tides, his knees relax with toil;
310   Wash'd from beneath him, slides the slimy Soil;
When thus (his eyes on heav'n's expansion thrown)
Forth bursts the hero with an angry groan.
　　Is there no God *Achilles* to befriend,
No pow'r t'avert his miserable end?
315   Prevent, oh *Jove!* this ignominious date,
And make my future life the sport of Fate.
Of all heav'ns oracles believ'd in vain,
But most of *Thetis*, must her son complain;
By *Phœbus'* darts she prophesy'd my fall,
320   In glorious arms before the *Trojan* wall.
Oh! had I dy'd in fields of battel warm,
Stretch'd like a hero, by a hero's arm!
Might *Hector*'s spear this dauntless bosom rend,
And my swift soul o'ertake my slaughter'd friend!
325   Ah no! *Achilles* meets a shameful fate,
Oh how unworthy of the brave and great!
Like some vile swain, whom on a rainy day,
Crossing a ford, the torrent sweeps away,
An unregarded carcase to the sea.
330   　　*Neptune* and *Pallas* haste to his relief,
And thus in human form address the chief:
The pow'r of Ocean first. Forbear thy fear,
O son of *Peleus!* Lo thy Gods appear!
Behold! from *Jove* descending to thy aid,
335   Propitious *Neptune*, and the blue-ey'd maid.
Stay, and the furious flood shall cease to rave:
'Tis not thy fate to glut his angry wave.
But thou, the counsel heav'n suggests, attend!
Nor breathe from combate, nor thy sword suspend,
340   Till *Troy* receive her flying sons, till all
Her routed squadrons pant behind their wall:
Hector alone shall stand his fatal chance,
And *Hector*'s blood shall smoke upon thy lance.
Thine is the glory doom'd. Thus spake the Gods;
345   Then swift ascended to the bright abodes.

Stung with new ardour, thus by heav'n impell'd,
He springs impetuous, and invades the field:
O'er all th'expanded plain the waters spread;
Heav'd on the bounding billows danc'd the dead,
Floating midst scatter'd arms; while casques of gold   350
And turn'd up bucklers glitter'd as they roll'd.
High o'er the surging tide, by leaps and bounds,
He wades, and mounts; the parted wave resounds.
Not a whole river stops the hero's course,
While *Pallas* fills him with immortal force.   355
With equal rage, indignant *Xanthus* roars,
And lifts his billows, and o'erwhelms his shores.
   Then thus to *Simoïs*: Haste, my brother flood!
And check this mortal that controuls a God:
Our bravest heroes else shall quit the fight,   360
And *Ilion* tumble from her tow'ry height.
Call then thy subject streams, and bid them roar,
From all thy fountains swell thy wat'ry store,
With broken rocks, and with a load of dead,
Charge the black surge, and pour it on his head.   365
Mark how resistless thro' the floods he goes,
And boldly bids the warring Gods be foes!
But nor that force, nor form divine to sight
Shall ought avail him, if our rage unite:
Whelm'd under our dark gulphs those arms shall lie,   370
That blaze so dreadful in each *Trojan* eye;
And deep beneath a sandy mountain hurl'd,
Immers'd remain this terrour of the world.
Such pond'rous ruin shall confound the place,
No *Greek* shall e'er his perish'd relicks grace,   375
No hand his bones shall gather, or inhume;
These his cold rites, and this his wat'ry tomb.
   He said; and on the chief descends amain,
Increas'd with gore, and swelling with the slain.
Then murm'ring from his beds, he boils, he raves,   380
And a foam whitens on the purple waves.
At ev'ry step, before *Achilles* stood
The crimson surge, and delug'd him with blood.
Fear touch'd the Queen of heav'n: She saw dismay'd,
She call'd aloud, and summon'd *Vulcan*'s aid.   385

Rise to the war! th'insulting flood requires
Thy wasteful arm: Assemble all thy fires!
While to their aid, by our command enjoin'd,
Rush the swift Eastern and the western wind:
390   These from old Ocean at my word shall blow,
Pour the red torrent on the wat'ry foe,
Corses and arms to one bright ruin turn,
And hissing rivers to their bottoms burn.
Go, mighty in thy rage! display thy pow'r,
395   Drink the whole flood, the crackling trees devour,
Scorch all the banks! and (till our voice reclaim)
Exert th'unweary'd furies of the flame!
    The Pow'r Ignipotent her word obeys:
Wide o'er the plain he pours the boundless blaze;
400   At once consumes the dead, and dries the soil;
And the shrunk waters in their chanel boil:
As when autumnal *Boreas* sweeps the sky,
And instant blows the water'd gardens dry:
So look'd the field, so whiten'd was the ground,
While *Vulcan* breath'd the fiery blast around.
Swift on the sedgy reeds the ruin preys;
Along the margin winds the running blaze:
The trees in flaming rows to ashes turn,
The flow'ry *Lotos*, and the tam'risk burn,
410   Broad elm, and cypress rising in a spire;
The wat'ry willows hiss before the fire.
Now glow the waves, the fishes pant for breath,
The eels lie twisting in the pangs of death:
Now flounce aloft, now dive the scaly fry,
415   Or gasping, turn their bellies to the sky.
At length the river rear'd his languid head,
And thus, short-panting, to the God he said.
    O *Vulcan*, oh! what pow'r resists thy might?
I faint, I sink, unequal to the fight –
420   I yield – Let *Ilion* fall; if Fate decree –
Ah – bend no more thy fiery arms on me!
    He ceas'd; wide conflagration blazing round;
The bubbling waters yield a hissing sound.
As when the flames beneath a caldron rise,
425   To melt the fat of some rich sacrifice,

Amid the fierce embrace of circling fires
The waters foam, the heavy smoak aspires:
So boils th' imprison'd flood, forbid to flow,
And choak'd with vapours, feels his bottom glow.
To *Juno* then, imperial Queen of Air,   430
The burning river sends his earnest pray'r.
    Ah why, *Saturnia*! must thy son engage
Me, only me, with all his wastfull rage?
On other Gods his dreadful arm employ,
For mightier Gods assert the cause of *Troy*.   435
Submissive I desist, if thou command,
But ah! withdraw this all-destroying hand.
Hear then my solemn oath, to yield to Fate
Unaided *Ilion*, and her destin'd state,
Till *Greece* shall gird her with destructive flame,   440
And in one ruin sink the *Trojan* name.
    His warm intreaty touch'd *Saturnia*'s ear:
She bade th' Ignipotent his rage forbear,
Recall the flame, nor in a mortal cause
Infest a God: Th'obedient flame withdraws: 445
Again, the branching streams begin to spread,
And soft re-murmur in their wonted bed.
    While these by *Juno*'s will the strife resign,
The warring Gods in fierce contention join:
Re-kindling rage each heavenly breast alarms;   450
With horrid clangor shock th' ætherial arms:
Heav'n in loud thunder bids the trumpet sound;
And wide beneath them groans the rending ground.
Jove, as his sport, the dreadful scene descries,
And views contending Gods with careless eyes.   455
The pow'r of battels lifts his brazen spear,
And first assaults the radiant Queen of War,
    What mov'd thy madness, thus to disunite
Æthereal minds, and mix all heav'n in fight?
What wonder this, when in thy frantick mood   460
Thou drov'st a mortal to insult a God;
Thy impious hand *Tydides'* jav'lin bore,
And madly bath'd it in celestial gore.
    He spoke, and smote the loud-resounding shield,
Which bears *Jove*'s thunder on its dreadful field;   465

The adamantine *Ægis* of her Sire,
That turns the glancing bolt, and forked fire.
Then heav'd the Goddess in her mighty hand
A stone, the limit of the neighb'ring land,
470   There fix'd from eldest times; black, craggy, vast:
This, at the heav'nly homicide she cast.
Thund'ring he falls; a mass of monstrous size,
And sev'n broad acres covers as he lies.
The stunning stroke his stubborn nerves unbound;
475   Loud o'er the fields his ringing arms resound:
The scornful dame her conquest views with smiles,
And glorying thus, the prostrate God reviles.
   Hast thou not yet, insatiate fury! known
How far *Minerva*'s force transcends thy own?
480   *Juno*, whom thou rebellious dar'st withstand,
Corrects thy folly thus by *Pallas'* hand;
Thus meets thy broken faith with just disgrace,
And partial aid to *Troy*'s perfidious race.
   The Goddess spoke, and turn'd her eyes away,
485   That beaming round, diffus'd celestial day.
Jove's *Cyprian* daughter, stooping on the land,
Lent to the wounded God her tender hand:
Slowly he rises, scarcely breathes with pain,
And propt on her fair arm, forsakes the plain.
490   This the bright Empress of the heav'ns survey'd,
And scoffing, thus, to War's victorious maid.
   Lo, what an aid on *Mars*'s side is seen!
The *Smiles* and *Love*'s unconquerable Queen!
Mark with what insolence, in open view,
495   She moves: Let *Pallas*, if she dares, pursue.
   Minerva smiling heard, the pair o'ertook,
And slightly on her breast the wanton strook:
She, unresisting, fell; (her spirits fled)
On earth together lay the lovers spread.
500   And like these heroes, be the fate of all
(*Minerva* cries) who guard the *Trojan* wall!
To *Grecian* Gods such let the *Phrygian* be,
So dread, so fierce, as *Venus* is to me;
Then from the lowest stone shall *Troy* be mov'd –
505   Thus she, and *Juno* with a smile approv'd.

Meantime, to mix in more than mortal fight,
The God of Ocean dares the God of Light.
What sloth has seiz'd us, when the fields around
Ring with conflicting pow'rs, and heav'n returns the
    sound?
Shall ignominious we with shame retire,   510
No deed perform'd, to our *Olympian* Sire?
Come, prove thy arm! for first the war to wage,
Suits not my greatness, or superiour age.
Rash as thou art to prop the *Trojan* throne,
(Forgetful of my wrongs, and of thy own)   515
And guard the race of proud *Laomedon!*
Hast thou forgot, how at the monarch's pray'r,
We shar'd the lengthen'd labours of a year?
Troy walls I rais'd (for such were *Jove*'s commands)
And yon' proud bulwarks grew beneath my hands: 520
Thy task it was, to feed the bellowing droves
Along fair *Ida*'s vales, and pendent groves.
But when the circling seasons in their train
Brought back the grateful day that crown'd our pain;
With menace stern the fraudful King defy'd   525
Our latent Godhead, and the prize deny'd:
Mad as he was, he threaten'd servile bands,
And doom'd us exiles far in barb'rous lands.
Incens'd, we heav'nward fled with swiftest wing,
And destin'd vengeance on the perjur'd King.   530
Dost thou, for this, afford proud *Ilion* grace,
And not like us, infest the faithless race?
Like us, their present, future sons destroy,
And from its deep foundations heave their *Troy*?
    Apollo thus: To combat for mankind   535
Ill suits the wisdom of celestial mind:
For what is man? Calamitous by birth,
They owe their life and nourishment to earth;
Like yearly leaves, that now, with beauty crown'd,
Smile on the sun; now, wither on the ground: 540
To their own hands commit the frantick scene,
Nor mix immortals in a cause so mean.
    Then turns his face, far-beaming heav'nly fires,
And from the Senior Pow'r, submiss retires;

545 Him, thus retreating, *Artemis* upbraids,
 The quiver'd huntress of the *sylvan* shades.
  And is it thus the youthful *Phœbus* flies,
 And yields to Ocean's hoary Sire, the prize?
 How vain that martial pomp, and dreadful show
550 Of pointed arrows, and the silver bow!
 Now boast no more in yon' celestial bow'r,
 Thy force can match the great Earth-shaking Pow'r.
  Silent, he heard the Queen of Woods upbraid:
 Not so *Saturnia* bore the vaunting maid;
555 But furious thus. What insolence has driv'n
 Thy pride to face the Majesty of Heav'n?
 What tho' by *Jove* the female plague design'd,
 Fierce to the feeble race of womankind,
 The wretched matron feels thy piercing dart;
560 Thy Sex's tyrant, with a tyger's heart?
 What tho' tremendous in the woodland chase,
 Thy certain arrows pierce the savage race?
 How dares thy rashness on the pow'rs divine
 Employ those arms, or match thy force with mine?
565 Learn hence, no more unequal war to wage –
 She said, and seiz'd her wrists with eager rage;
 These in her left hand lock'd, her right unty'd
 The bow, the quiver, and its plumy pride.
 About her temples flies the busy bow;
570 Now here, now there, she winds her from the blow;
 The scatt'ring arrows rattling from the case,
 Drop round, and idly mark the dusty place.
 Swift from the field the baffled huntress flies,
 And scarce restrains the torrent in her eyes:
575 So, when the falcon wings her way above,
 To the cleft cavern speeds the gentle dove,
 (Not fated yet to die) There safe retreats,
 Yet still her heart against the marble beats.
  To her, *Latona* hasts with tender care;
580 Whom *Hermes* viewing, thus declines the war.
 How shall I face the dame, who gives delight
 To him whose thunders blacken heav'n with night?
 Go matchless Goddess! triumph in the skies,
 And boast my conquest, while I yield the prize.

He spoke; and past: *Latona*, stooping low,   585
Collects the scatter'd shafts, and fallen bow,
That glitt'ring on the dust, lay here and there;
Dishonour'd relicks of *Diana*'s war.
Then swift pursu'd her to her blest abode,
Where, all confus'd, she sought the Sov'reign God;   590
Weeping she grasp'd his knees: Th' ambrosial vest
Shook with her sighs, and panted on her breast.
  The Sire, superiour smil'd; and bade her show,
What heav'nly hand had caus'd his daughter's woe?
Abash'd, she names his own imperial spouse;   595
And the pale crescent fades upon her brows.
  Thus they above: While swiftly gliding down,
Apollo enters *Ilion*'s sacred town:
The Guardian God now trembled for her wall,
And fear'd the *Greeks*, tho' Fate forbade her fall.   600
Back to *Olympus*, from the war's alarms,
Return the shining bands of Gods in arms;
Some proud in triumph, some with rage on fire;
And take their thrones around th' æthereal Sire.
  Thro' blood, thro' death, *Achilles* still proceeds,   605
O'er slaughter'd heroes, and o'er rolling steeds
As when avenging flames with fury driv'n,
On guilty towns exert the wrath of heav'n;
The pale inhabitants, some fall, some fly;
And the red vapours purple all the sky.   610
So rag'd *Achilles*: Death, and dire dismay,
And toils, and terrours, fill'd the dreadful day.
  High on a turret hoary *Priam* stands,
And marks the waste of his destructive hands;
Views, from his arm, the *Trojans* scatter'd flight,   615
And the near hero rising on his sight!
No stop, no check, no aid! With feeble pace,
And settled sorrow on his aged face,
Fast as he could, he sighing quits the walls;
And thus, descending, on the guards he calls.   620
  You to whose care our city gates belong,
Set wide your portals to the flying throng.
For lo! he comes, with unresisted sway;
He comes, and desolation marks his way!

625 But when within the walls our troops take breath,
  Lock fast the brazen bars, and shut out death.
  Thus charg'd the rev'rend monarch: Wide were flung
  The opening folds; the sounding hinges rung.
  Phœbus rush'd forth, the flying bands to meet,
630 Strook slaughter back, and cover'd the retreat.
  On heaps the *Trojans* crowd to gain the gate,
  And gladsome see their last escape from Fate:
  Thither, all parch'd with thirst, a heartless train,
  Hoary with dust, they beat the hollow plain;
635 And gasping, panting, fainting, labour on
  With heavier strides, that lengthen tow'rd the town.
  Enrag'd *Achilles* follows with his spear;
  Wild with revenge, insatiable of war.
   Then had the *Greeks* eternal praise acquir'd,
640 And *Troy* inglorious to her walls retir'd;
  But *he, the God who darts æthereal flame,
  Shot down to save her, and redeem her fame.
  To young *Agenor* force divine he gave,
  (*Antenor*'s offspring, haughty, bold and brave)
645 In aid of him, beside the beech he sate,
  And wrapt in clouds, restrain'd the hand of Fate.
  When now the gen'rous youth *Achilles* spies,
  Thick beats his heart, the troubled motions rise,
  (So, e're a storm, the waters heave and roll)
650 He stops, and questions thus his mighty soul.
   What, shall I fly this terrour of the plain?
  Like others fly, and be like others slain?
  Vain hope! to shun him by the self-same road
  Yon' line of slaughter'd *Trojans* lately trod.
655 No: with the common heap I scorn to fall –
  What if they pass'd me to the *Trojan* wall,
  While I decline to yonder path, that leads
  To *Ida*'s forests and surrounding shades?
  So may I reach, conceal'd, the cooling flood,
660 From my tir'd body wash the dirt and blood,
  As soon as night her dusky veil extends,
  Return in safety to my *Trojan* friends,

  *Apollo.

What if? – But wherefore all this vain debate?
Stand I to doubt, within the reach of Fate?
Ev'n now perhaps, e'er yet I turn the wall,   665
The fierce *Achilles* sees me, and I fall:
Such is his swiftness, 'tis in vain to fly,
And such his valour, that who stands must die.
Howe'er, 'tis better, fighting for the state,
Here, and in publick view, to meet my fate.   670
Yet sure he too is mortal; He may feel
(Like all the sons of earth) the force of steel;
One only soul informs that dreadful frame;
And *Jove*'s sole favour gives him all his fame.

   He said, and stood, collected in his might;   675
And all his beating bosom claim'd the fight.
So from some deep-grown wood a panther starts,
Rouz'd from his thicket by a storm of darts:
Untaught to fear or fly, he hears the sounds
Of shouting hunters, and of clam'rous hounds;   680
Tho' struk, tho' wounded, scarce perceives the pain,
And the barb'd jav'lin stings his breast in vain:
On their whole war, untam'd the savage flies;
And tears his hunter, or beneath him dies.
Not less resolv'd, *Antenor*'s valiant heir   685
Confronts *Achilles*, and awaits the war,
Disdainful of retreat: High-held before,
His shield (a broad circumference) he bore;
Then graceful as he stood, in act to throw
The lifted jav'lin, thus bespoke the foe.   690
   How proud *Achilles* glories in his fame!
And hopes this day to sink the *Trojan* name
Beneath her ruins! Know, that hope is vain;
A thousand woes, a thousand toils remain.
Parents and children our just arms employ,   695
And strong, and many, are the sons of *Troy*.
Great as thou art, ev'n thou may'st stain with gore
These *Phrygian* fields, and press a foreign shore.
   He said: With matchless force the jav'lin flung
Smote on his knee; the hollow cuishes rung   700
Beneath the pointed steel; but safe from harms
He stands impassive in th'æthereal arms.

Then fiercely rushing on the daring foe,
His lifted arm prepares the fatal blow.
705 But jealous of his fame, *Apollo* shrouds
The god-like *Trojan* in a veil of clouds;
Safe from pursuit, and shut from mortal view,
Dismiss'd with fame, the favour'd youth withdrew.
Meanwhile the God, to cover their escape,
710 Assumes *Agenor*'s habit, voice, and shape,
Flies from the furious chief in this disguise,
The furious chief still follows where he flies:
Now o'er the fields they stretch with lengthen'd strides,
Now urge the course where swift *Scamander* glides:
715 The God now distant scarce a stride before,
Tempts his pursuit, and wheels about the shore:
While all the flying troops their speed employ,
And pour on heaps into the walls of *Troy*.
No stop, no stay; no thought to ask, or tell,
720 Who scap'd by flight, or who by battel fell.
'Twas tumult all, and violence of flight;
And sudden joy confus'd, and mix'd affright:
Pale *Troy* against *Achilles* shuts her gate;
And nations breathe, deliver'd from their fate.

OBSERVATIONS

ON THE

TWENTY-FIRST BOOK

This book is entirely different from all the foregoing: Tho' it be a battel, it is entirely of a new and surprizing kind, diversify'd with a vast variety of imagery and description. The scene is totally chang'd, he paints the combate of his hero with the rivers, and describes a battel amidst an inundation. It is observable that tho' the whole war of the *Iliad* was upon the banks of these rivers, *Homer* has artfully left out the machinery of River-Gods in all the other battels, to aggrandize this of his hero. There is no book of the poem that has more force of imagination, or in which the great and inexhausted invention of our author is more powerfully exerted. After this description of an inundation, there follows a very beautiful contrast in that of the drought: The part of *Achilles* is admirably sustained, and the new strokes which *Homer* gives to his picture are such as are deriv'd from the very source of his character, and finish the entire draught of this Hero.

How far all that appears wonderful or extravagant in this episode, may be reconciled to probability, truth, and natural reason, will be considered in a distinct note on that head: The reader may find it on v. 447.

2. Xanthus, *immortal progeny of* Jove.] The river is here said to be the Son of *Jupiter*, on account of its being supply'd with waters that fall from *Jupiter*, that is, from heaven.   *Eustathius.*

14. *As the scorch'd locusts,* &c.] *Eustathius* observes that several countries have been much infested with armies of locusts; and that, to prevent their destroying the fruits of the earth, the countrymen by kindling large fires drove them from their fields; the locusts to avoid the intense heat were forc'd to cast themselves into the water. From

this observation the Poet draws his allusion, which is very much to the honour of *Achilles*, since it represents the *Trojans* with respect to him as no more than so many insects.

The same commentator takes notice, that because the Island of *Cyprus* in particular was used to practise this method with the locusts, some authors have conjectured that *Homer* was of that country; but if this were a sufficient reason for such a supposition, he might be said to be born in almost all the countries of the world, since he draws his observations from the customs of them all.

We may hence account for the innumerable armies of these locusts, mention'd among the Plagues of *Ægypt*, without having recourse to an immediate creation, as some good Men have imagin'd, whereas the miracle indeed consists in the wonderful manner of bringing them upon the *Ægyptians*: I have often observ'd with pleasure the similitude which many of *Homer*'s expressions bear with the holy scriptures, and that the most ancient heathen writer in the world often speaks in the idiom of *Moses*: Thus as the locusts in *Exodus* are said to be driven into *the sea*, so in *Homer* they are forc'd into a *river*.

30. *So the huge dolphin,* &c.] It is observable with what justness the author diversifies his comparisons according to the different scenes and elements he is engaged in: *Achilles* has been hitherto on the land, and compared to land animals, a lion, *&c.* Now he is in the water, the Poet derives his images from thence, and likens him to a dolphin.　　　　　　　　　　　　　　　　　*Eustathius.*

34. *Now tir'd with slaughter.*] This is admirably well suited to the character of *Achilles*, his rage bears him headlong on the enemy, he kills all that oppose him, and stops not till nature itself could not keep pace with his anger; he had determin'd to reserve twelve noble youths to sacrifice them to the *Manes* of *Patroclus*, but his resentment gives him no time to think of them, till the hurry of his passion abates, and he is tir'd with slaughter: Without this circumstance, I think an objection might naturally be raised, that in the time of a pursuit *Achilles* gave the enemy too much leisure to escape, while he busy'd himself with tying these prisoners: Tho' it is not absolutely necessary to suppose he tyed them with his own hands.

35. *Twelve chosen youths.*] This piece of cruelty in *Achilles* has appeared shocking to many, and indeed is what I think can only be

excused by considering the ferocious and vindictive spirit of this hero. 'Tis however certain that the cruelties exercised on enemies in war were authorised by the military laws of those times; nay, religion itself became a sanction to them. It is not only the fierce *Achilles*, but the pious and religious *Æneas*, whose very character is virtue and compassion, that reserves several young unfortunate captives taken in battel, to sacrifice them to the *Manes* of his favourite hero. *Æn.* 10. v. 517.

> *— Sulmone creatos*
> *Quattuor hic juvenes, totidem quos edūcat Ufens*
> *Viventes rapit; inferias quos immolet umbris,*
> *Captivoque rogi perfundat sanguine flammas.*

[Four sons of *Sulmo*, four whom *Ufens* bred,
He took in fight, and living victims led,
To please the ghost of *Pallas*; and expire
In sacrifice, before his fun'ral fire.]

And *Æn.* 11. v. 81.

> *Vinxerat & post terga manus, quos mitteret umbris,*
> *Inferias, cæso sparsuros sanguine flammam.*

[Then, pinioned with their hands behind, appear
The unhappy captives, marching in the rear,
Appointed offerings in the victor's name,
To sprinkle with their blood the funeral flame.]

And (what is very particular) the *Latin* poet expresses no disapprobation of the action, which the *Grecian* does in plain terms, speaking of this in *Iliad* 23. v. 176.

> *— Κακὰ δὲ φρεσὶ μήδετο ἔργα.*

[Evil were the deeds he pondered doing in his heart.]

41. *The young* Lycaon, &c.] *Homer* has a wonderful art and judgment in contriving such incidents as set the characteristick qualities of his heroes in the highest point of light. There is hardly any in the whole *Iliad* more proper to move pity than this circumstance of *Lycaon*, or to raise terror, than this view of *Achilles.* It is also the finest picture of them both imaginable: We see the different attitude of their persons, and the different passions which appeared in their countenances: At first *Achilles* stands erect, with surprize in his looks, at the sight of one

whom he thought it impossible to find there; while *Lycaon* is in the posture of a suppliant, with looks that plead for compassion; with one hand holding the hero's lance, and his knee with the other: Afterwards, when at his death he lets go the spear and places himself on his knees, with his arms extended, to receive the mortal wound; how lively and how strongly is this painted? I believe every one perceives the beauty of this passage, and allows that poetry (at least in *Homer*) is truly a speaking picture.

84, &c. *The speeches of* Lycaon *and* Achilles.] It is impossible for any thing to be better imagin'd than these two speeches; that of *Lycaon* is moving and compassionate, that of *Achilles* haughty and dreadful; the one pleads with the utmost tenderness, the other denies with the utmost sternness: One would think it impossible to amass so many moving arguments in so few words as those of *Lycaon*: He forgets no circumstance to soften his enemy's anger, he flatters the memory of *Patroclus*, is afraid of being thought too nearly related to *Hector*, and would willingly put himself upon him as a suppliant, and consequently as an inviolable person: But *Achilles* is immoveable, his resentment makes him deaf to entreaties, and it must be remembered that anger, not mercy, is his character.

I must confess I could have wish'd *Achilles* had spared him: There are so many circumstances that speak in his favour, that he deserved his life, had he not asked it in terms a little too abject.

There is an air of greatness in the conclusion of the speech of *Achilles*, which strikes me very much: He speaks very unconcernedly of his own death, and upbraids his enemy for asking life so earnestly, a life that was of so much less importance than his own.

121. *The day shall come —*
 When by the spear, the arrow, or the dart.

This is not spoken at random, but with an air of superiority; when *Achilles* says he shall fall by an arrow, a dart, or a spear, he insinuates that no man will have the courage to approach him in a close fight, or engage him hand to hand.   *Eustathius.*

146. *Your living coursers glut his gulphs in vain.*] It was an ancient custom to cast living horses into the sea, and into rivers, to honour, as it were, by these victims, the rapidity of their streams. This practice continued a long time, and history supplies us with examples of it: *Aurelius Victor* says of *Pompey* the younger, *Cum mari feliciter uteretur,* Neptuni *se filium confessus est, eumque bobus auratis & equo placavit* [When he wanted to use the sea with auspicious results, he confessed himself to be the son of Neptune and appeased him with golden cattle and a horse]. He offered oxen in Sacrifice, and threw a living horse into the sea, as appears from *Dion*; which is perfectly conformable to this of *Homer.*   *Eustath. Dacier.*

152. *With fury swells the violated flood.*] The poet has been preparing us for the episode of the river *Xanthus* ever since the beginning of the last book; and here he gives us an account why the river wars upon *Achilles*: It is not only because he is a river of *Troas*, but, as *Eustathius* remarks, because it is in defence of a man that was descended from a brother River-God: He was angry too with *Achilles* on another account, because he had choak'd up his current with the bodies of his countrey-men, the *Trojans.*

171. *From rich* Pæonia's – &c.] In the catalogue *Pyræchmes* is said to be commander of the *Pæonians*, where they are describ'd as bow-men; but here they are said to be arm'd with spears, and to have *Asteropæus* for their general. *Eustathius* tells us, some criticks asserted that this line in the *Cat.* v. 355.

Πηλέγονός θ' υἱὸς περιδέξιος Ἀστεροπαῖος.

[Pelegon and his son, the very dextrous Asteropaios.]

followed

Αὐτὰρ Πυραίχμης ἄγε Παίονας ἀγκυλοτόξους.

[Pyraichmes led the Paionians, who were armed with bent bows.]

but I see no reason for such an assertion. *Homer* has expressly told us in this speech that it was but ten days since he came to the aid of *Troy*; he might be made general of the *Pæonians* upon the death of *Pyræchmes*, who was kill'd in the sixteenth book. Why also might not the *Pæonians*, as well as *Teucer*, excel in the management both of the bow and the spear?

187. *Deep in the swelling bank was driv'n the spear,*
       Ev'n to the middle earth'd –]

It was impossible for the poet to give us a greater idea of the strength of *Achilles* than he has by this circumstance: His spear peirc'd so deep into the ground, that another hero of great strength could not disengage it by repeated efforts; but immediately after, *Achilles* draws it with the utmost ease: How prodigious was the force of that arm that could drive at one throw a spear half way into the earth, and then with a touch release it?

263. *Now bursting on his head,* &c.] There is a great beauty in the versification of this whole passage in *Homer*: Some of the verses run hoarse, full, and sonorous, like the torrent they describe; others by their broken cadences, and sudden stops, image the difficulty, labour, and interruption of the hero's march against it. The fall of the elm, the tearing up of the bank, the rushing of the branches in the water, are all put into such words, that almost every letter corresponds in its sound, and echoes to the sense of each particular.

274. *Bridg'd the rough flood across –*] If we had no other account of the river *Xanthus* but this, it were alone sufficient to shew that the current could not be very wide; for the poet here says that the elm stretch'd from bank to bank, and as it were made a bridge over it: The suddenness of this inundation perfectly well agrees with a narrow river.

276. *Leap'd from the chanel.*] *Eustathius* recites a criticism on this verse, in the original the word Λίμνη signifies *stagnum, palus,* a standing-water; now this is certainly contrary to the idea of a river, which always implies a *current*: To solve this, says that author, some have supposed that the tree which lay across the river stopp'd the flow of the waters, and forced them to spread as it were into a pool. Others, dissatisfy'd with this solution, think that a mistake is crept into the text, and that instead of ἐκ Λίμνης [from the standing water], should be inserted ἐκ δίνης [from the eddy]. But I do not see the necessity of having recourse to either of these solutions; for why may not the word Λίμνη signify here the *chanel* of the river, as it evidently does in the 317th verse? And nothing being more common than to substitute a part for the whole, why may not the chanel be suppos'd to imply the whole river?

289. *So when a peasant to his garden brings,* &c.] This changing of the character is very beautiful: No poet ever knew, like *Homer*, to pass from the vehement and the nervous, to the gentle and the agreeable; such transitions, when properly made, give a singular pleasure, as when in musick a master passes from the rough to the tender. *Demetrius Phalereus,* who only praises this comparison for its clearness, has not sufficiently recommended its beauty and value. *Virgil* has transfer'd it into his first book of the *Georgicks.* v. 106.

> *Deinde satis fluvium inducit, rivosque sequentes:*
> *Et cum exustus ager morientibus æstuat herbis,*
> *Ecce supercilio clivosi tramitis undam*
> *Elicit: Illa cadens raucum per levia murmur*
> *Saxa ciet, scatebrisque arentia temperat arva.*   *Dacier.*

[And calls the floods from high, to rush amain
With pregnant streams, to swell the teeming grain.
Then, when the fiery suns too fiercely play,
And shrivelled herbs on withering stems decay,
The wary ploughman, on the mountain's brow,
Undams his watery stores – huge torrents flow,
And, rattling down the rocks, large moisture yield,
Tempering the thirsty fever of the field.]

321. *Oh had I dy'd in fields of battel warm!* &c.] Nothing is more agreeable than this wish to the heroick character of *Achilles:* Glory is his prevailing passion; he grieves not that he must die, but that he should die unlike a man of honour. *Virgil* has made use of the same thought in the same circumstance, where *Æneas* is in danger of being drowned, *Æn.* 1. v. 98.

> *– O terque quaterque beati,*
> *Queis ante ora patrum* Trojæ *sub mœnibus altis*
> *Contigit oppetere! O Danaum fortissime gentis*
> *Tydide, mene Iliacis occumbere campis*
> *Non potuisse? tuaque animam hanc effundere dextra!*

[And thrice, and four times happy those, he cry'd,
That under *Ilian* walls before their parents dy'd.
Tydides, bravest of the *Grecian* train,
Why cou'd not I by that strong arm be slain.]

Lucan, in the fifth book of his *Pharsalia*, representing *Cæsar* in the same circumstance, has (I think) carry'd yet farther the character of ambition, and a boundless thirst of glory, in his hero; when, after he has repin'd in the same manner with *Achilles*, he acquiesces at last in the reflection of the glory he had already acquired,

> – *Licet ingentes abruperit actus*
> *Festinata dies fatis, sat magna peregi.*
> *Arctoas domui gentes: inimica subegi*
> *Arma manu: vidit Magnum mihi* Roma *secundum.*

> [Though fate may advance my day of departure,
> Stopping my great career, I have done enough of
>   importance and sufficient.
> I have tamed the tribes of the North; by the threat of my
>   presence,
> Nothing more, I have routed the forces gathered against
>   me;
> Rome has seen Pompey in second place, supplanted by
>   Cæsar.]

And only wishes that his obscure fate might be conceal'd, in the view that all the world might still fear and expect him.

> – *Lacerum retinete cadaver*
> *Fluctibus in mediis; desint mihi busta, rogusque,*
> *Dum metuar semper, terraque expecter ab omni.*

> [Let my mangled body, unburied,
> Unconsumed by a pyre, be borne on the waves in mid-
>   ocean:
> So will my disappearance leave all the nations uneasy,
> Every land awaiting with dread my sudden arrival.]

405. *While* Vulcan *breath'd the fiery blast around.*] It is in the original, v. 355.

> Πνοιῇ τειρόμενοι πολυμήτιος Ἡφαίστοιο.

[Worn down by the blasts of cunning Hephaistos.]

The epithet given to *Vulcan* in this verse (as well as in the 367th) Ἡφαίστοιο πολύφρονος [most wise Hephaistos], has no sort of allusion to the action describ'd: For what has his *wisdom* or *knowledge* to do with burning up the river *Xanthus?* This is usual in our author, and much exclaimed against by his modern antagonists, whom Mr. *Boileau* very well answers. 'It is not so strange in *Homer* to give these epithets to persons upon occasions which can have no reference to them; the same is frequent in modern languages, in which we call a man by the name of *Saint,* when we speak of any action of his that has not the least regard to his *sanctity*: As when we say, for example, that St. *Paul* held the garments of those who stoned St. *Stephen.*'

424. *As when the flames beneath a caldron rise.*] It is impossible to render literally such passages with any tolerable beauty. These ideas can never be made to shine in *English,* some particularities cannot be preserved; but the *Greek* language gives them lustre, the words are noble and musical.

> Ὡς δὲ λέβης ζεῖ ἔνδον ἐπειγόμενος πυρὶ πολλῷ,
> Κνίσην μελδόμενος ἀπαλοτρεφέος σιάλοιο,
> Πάντοθεν ἀμβολάδην, ὑπὸ δὲ ξύλα κάγκανα κεῖται.

> [Just so does a kitchen cauldron burn, brought to a boil by
>   a great fire,
>   Melting the fat of a plump hog –
>   It bubbles up in every direction, and dry wood lies
>   beneath it.]

All therefore that can be expected from a translator is to preserve the meaning of the simile, and embellish it with some words of affinity that carry nothing low in the sense or sound.

447. *And soft re-murmur in their wonted bed.*] Here ends the *episode* of the *river-fight*; and I must here lay before the reader my thoughts upon the whole of it: Which appears to be in part an allegory, and in part a true history. Nothing can give a better idea of *Homer*'s manner of enlivening his inanimate machines, and of making the plainest and simplest incidents noble and poetical, than to consider the whole passage in the common historical sense, which I suppose to be no more than this. There happen'd a great overflow of the river *Xanthus* during the siege, which very much incommoded the assailants: This gave occasion for the fiction of an engagement between *Achilles* and the River-God: *Xanthus* calling *Simoïs* to assist him, implies that these two neighbouring rivers joined in the inundation: *Pallas* and *Neptune* relieve *Achilles*; that is, *Pallas*, or the *wisdom* of *Achilles*, found some means to divert the waters, and turn them into the *Sea*; wherefore *Neptune*, the God of it, is feign'd to assist him. *Jupiter* and *Juno* (by which are understood the aerial regions) consent to aid *Achilles*; that may signify, that after this great flood their happened a warm, dry, windy season, which asswaged the waters, and dried the ground: And what makes this in a manner plain, is, that *Juno* (which signifies the *air*) promises to send the *north* and *west winds* to distress the river. *Xanthus* being consum'd by *Vulcan*, that is dried up with heat, prays to *Juno* to relieve him: What is this, but that the drought having drunk up his streams, he has recourse to the *air* for rains to resupply his current? Or perhaps the whole may signify no more, than that *Achilles* being on the farther side of the river, plung'd himself in to pursue the enemy; that in this adventure he run the risk of being drown'd; that to save himself he laid hold on a fallen tree, which serv'd to keep him afloat; that he was still carried down the stream to the place where was the confluence of the two rivers, which is expressed by the one calling the other to his aid, and that when he came nearer the sea (*Neptune*) he found means by his prudence (*Pallas*) to save himself from his danger.

If the reader still should think the fiction of rivers speaking and fighting is too bold, the objection will vanish by considering how much the heathen mythology authorizes the representation of rivers as persons: Nay even in old historians nothing is more common than stories of rapes committed by River-Gods: And the fiction was no way unpresidented, after one of the same nature so well known, as the engagement between *Hercules* and the river *Achelous*.

454. Jove *as his sport, the dreadful scene descries,*
       And views contending Gods with careless eyes.]

I was at a loss for the reason why *Jupiter* is said to smile at the discord of the Gods, till I found it in *Eustathius*; *Jupiter*, says he, who is the lord of nature, is well pleased with the war of the Gods, that is of earth, sea, and air, *&c.* because the harmony of all beings arises from that discord: Thus earth is opposite to water, air to earth, and water to them all; and yet from this opposition arises that discordant concord by which all nature subsists. Thus heat and cold, moist and dry, are in a continual war, yet upon this depends the fertility of the earth, and the beauty of the creation. So that *Jupiter* who according to the *Greeks* is the soul of all, may well be said to smile at this contention.

456. *The power of battels, &c.*] The combat of *Mars* and *Pallas* is plainly allegorical: Justice and Wisdom demanded that an end should be put to this terrible war: the God of war opposes this, but is worsted. *Eustathius* says that this holds forth the opposition of rage and wisdom; and no sooner has our reason subdued one temptation, but another succeeds to reinforce it, as *Venus* succours *Mars.* The poet seems farther to insinuate, that reason when it resists a temptation vigorously, easily overcomes it: So it is with the utmost facility that *Pallas* conquers both *Mars* and *Venus.* He adds, that *Pallas* retreated from *Mars* in order to conquer him; this shews us that the best way to subdue a temptation is to retreat from it.

468.   *Then heav'd the Goddess in her mighty hand*
          A Stone, &c.]

The poet has describ'd many of his heroes in former parts of his poem, as throwing stones of enormous bulk and weight; but here he rises in his image: He is describing a Goddess, and has found a way to make that action excel all human strength, and be equal to a deity.

Virgil has imitated this passage in his twelfth book, and apply'd it to *Turnus*; but I can't help thinking that the action in a mortal is somewhat extravagantly imagined: What principally renders it so, is an addition of two lines to this simile which he borrows from another part of *Homer*, only with this difference, that whereas *Homer* says no two men could raise such a stone, *Virgil* extends it to twelve.

> *– Saxum circumspicit ingens,*
> *Saxum, antiquum, ingens, campo quod forte jacebat,*
> *Limes agro positus, litem ut discerneret arvis.*

> [An antique stone he saw: the common bound
>   Of neighb'ring fields; and barrier of the ground.]

(There is a beauty in the repetition of *saxum ingens* [a huge rock], in the second line; it makes us dwell upon the image, and gives us leisure to consider the vastness of the stone:) The other two lines are as follow,

> *Vix illud, lecti bis sex cervice subirent,*
> *Qualia nunc hominum producit corpora tellus.*

> [So vast, that twelve strong men of modern days,
>   Th'enormous weight from earth cou'd hardly raise.]

May I be allowed to think too, they are not so well introduced in *Virgil*? For it is just after *Turnus* is describ'd as weaken'd and oppress'd with fears and ill omens; it exceeds probability; and *Turnus*, methinks, looks more like a knight-errant in a romance, than an hero in an epick poem.

507. *The God of Ocean dares the God of Light.*] The interview between *Neptune* and *Apollo* is very judiciously in this place enlarged upon by our author. The poem now draws to a conclusion, the *Trojans* are to be punish'd for their perjury and violence: *Homer* accordingly with a poetical justice sums up the evidence against them, and represents the very founder of *Troy* as an injurious person. There have been several references to this story since the beginning of the poem, but he forbore to give it at large till near the end of it; that it might be fresh upon the memory, and shew, the *Trojans* deserve the punishment they are going to suffer.

Eustathius gives the reason why *Apollo* assists the *Trojans*, tho' he had been equally with *Neptune* affronted by *Laomedon*: This proceeded from the honours which *Apollo* received from the posterity of *Laomedon*; *Troy* paid him no less worship than *Cilla*, or *Tenedos*; and by these means won him over to a forgiveness: But *Neptune* still was slighted, and consequently continued an enemy to the whole race.

The same author gives us various opinions why *Neptune* is said to have built the *Trojan* wall, and to have been defrauded of his wages: Some say that *Laomedon* sacrilegiously took away the treasures out of the temples of *Apollo* and *Neptune*, to carry on the fortifications: From whence it was fabled that *Neptune* and *Apollo* built the walls. Others will have it, that two of the workmen dedicated their wages to *Apollo* and *Neptune*; and that *Laomedon* detained them: So that he might in some sense be said to defraud the deities themselves, by with-holding what was dedicated to their temples.

The reason why *Apollo* is said to have kept the herds of *Laomedon* is not so clear: *Eustathius* observes that all plagues first seize upon the four-footed creation, and are suppos'd to arise from this deity: Thus *Apollo* in the first book sends the plague into the *Grecian* army: The ancients therefore made him to preside over cattel, that by preserving them from the plague, mankind might be safe from infectious diseases. Others tell us, that this employment is ascrib'd to *Apollo*, because he signifies the sun: Now the sun cloaths the pastures with grass and herbs: So that *Apollo* may be said himself to feed the cattel, by supplying them with food. Upon either of these accounts *Laomedon* may be said to be ungrateful to that deity, for raising no temple to his honour.

It is observable that *Homer* in this story ascribes the building of the wall to *Neptune* only: I should conjecture the reason might be, that *Troy* being a sea-port town, the chief strength of it depended upon its situation, so that the sea was in a manner a wall to it: Upon this account *Neptune* may not improbably be said to have built the wall.

537. *For what is man?* &c.] The poet is very happy in interspersing his poem with moral sentences; in this place he steals away his reader from war and horrour, and gives him a beautiful admonition of his own frailty. 'Shall I (says *Apollo*) contend with thee for the sake of man? Man, who is no more than a leaf of a tree, now green and flourishing, but soon wither'd away and gone?' The son of *Sirach* has an expression which very much resembles this, *Ecclus.* xiv. 18. *As the green leaves upon a thick tree some fall, and some grow, so is the generation of flesh and blood, one cometh to an end, and one is born.*

544. *And from the Senior Pow'r submiss retires.*] Two things hinder *Homer* from making *Neptune* and *Apollo* fight. First, because having already describ'd the fight between *Vulcan* and *Xanthus*, he has nothing farther to say here, for it is the same conflict between humidity and dryness. Secondly, *Apollo* being the same with destiny, and the ruin of the *Trojans* being concluded upon and decided, that God can no longer defer it.   *Dacier.*

557. *The female plague –*
Fierce to the feeble race of womankind, &c.]

The words in the original are, *Tho'* Jupiter *has made you a Lion to Women.* The meaning of this is, that *Diana* was terrible to that sex, as being the same with the moon, and bringing on the pangs of child-birth: Or else, that the ancients attributed all sudden deaths of women to the darts of *Diana*, as of men to those of *Apollo*: Which opinion is frequently alluded to in *Homer.*   *Eustathius.*

566. *She said, and seiz'd her wrists,* &c.] I must confess I am at a loss how to justify *Homer* in every point of these combats with the Gods: When *Diana* and *Juno* are to fight, *Juno* calls her an *impudent bitch,* κύον ἀδεές: When they fight, she boxes her soundly, and sends her crying and trembling to heaven: As soon as she comes thither *Jupiter* falls a laughing at her: Indeed the rest of the deities seem to be in a merry vein during all the action: *Pallas* beats *Mars*, and laughs at him, *Jupiter* sees them in the same merry mood: *Juno* when she had cuff'd *Diana* is not more serious: In short, unless there be some depths that I am not able to fathom, *Homer* never better deserv'd than in this place the censure past upon him by the ancients, that as he raised the characters of his men up to Gods, so he sunk those of Gods down to men.

Yet I think it but reasonable to conclude, from the very absurdity of all this, supposing it had no hidden meaning or allegory, that there must therefore certainly be some. Nor do I think it any inference to the contrary, that it is too obscure for us to find out: The remoteness of our times must necessarily darken yet more and more such things as were mysteries at first. Not that it is at all impossible, notwithstanding their present darkness, but they might then have been very obvious; as it is certain, allegories ought to be disguis'd, but not obscur'd: An Allegory should be like a veil over a beautiful face, so fine and transparent, as to shew the very charms it covers.

580. *Whom Hermes viewing, thus declines the war.*] It is impossible that *Mercury* should encounter *Latona*: Such a fiction would be unnatural, he being a planet, and she representing the night; for the planets owe all their lustre to the shades of the night, and then only become visible to the world.   *Eustathius.*

607.   *As when avenging Flames with Fury driv'n,*
      On guilty Towns exert the Wrath of Heaven.]

This Passage may be explain'd two ways, each very remarkable. First, by taking this Fire for a real Fire, sent from Heaven to punish a criminal City, of which we have Example in holy Writ. Hence we find that *Homer* had a Notion of this great Truth, that God sometimes exerts his Judgments on whole Cities in this signal and terrible manner. Or if we take it in the other sense, simply as a Fire thrown into a Town by the Enemies who assault it, (and only express'd thus by the Author in the same manner as *Jeremy* makes the City of *Jerusalem* say, when the *Chaldæns* burnt the Temple, *The Lord from above hath sent Fire into my Bones. Lament.* i. 13.) Yet still this much will appear understood by *Homer*, that the Fire which is cast into a City comes not properly speaking from Men, but from God who delivers it up to their Fury.   *Dacier.*

613. *High on a turret hoary* Priam, &c.] The poet still raises the idea of the courage and strength of his hero, by making *Priam* in a terrour that he should enter the Town after the routed troops: For if he had not surpassed all mortals, what could have been more desirable for an enemy, than to have let him in, and then destroy'd him?

Here again there was need of another *machine* to hinder him from entring the city; for *Achilles* being vastly speedier than those he pursued, he must necessarily overtake some of them, and the narrow gates could not let in a body of troops without his mingling with the hindmost. The story of *Agenor* is therefore admirably contriv'd, and *Apollo*, (who was to take care that the fatal decrees should be punctually executed) interposes both to save *Agenor* and *Troy*; for *Achilles* might have kill'd *Agenor*, and still entered with the troops, if *Apollo* had not diverted him by the pursuit of that phantom. *Agenor* opposed himself to *Achilles* only because he could not do better; for he sees himself reduced to a dilemma, either ingloriously to perish among the fugitives, or hide himself in the forest; both which were equally unsafe: Therefore he is purposely inspir'd with a generous resolution to try to save his countreymen, and as the reward of that service, is at last sav'd himself.

651. *What shall I fly?* &c.] This is a very beautiful soliloquy of *Agenor*, such a one as would naturally arise in the soul of a brave man, going upon a desperate enterprise: He weighs every thing in the balance of reason; he sets before himself the baseness of flight, and the courage of his enemy, till at last the thirst of glory preponderates all other considerations. From the conclusion of this speech it is evident, that the story of *Achilles* his being invulnerable except in the heel, is an invention of latter ages; for had he been so, there had been nothing wonderful in his character.   *Eustathius.*

709. *Meanwhile the God, to cover their escape,* &c.] The poet makes a double use of this fiction of *Apollo*'s deceiving *Achilles* in the Shape of *Agenor*; by these means he draws him from the pursuit, and gives the *Trojans* time to enter the city, and at the same time brings *Agenor* handsomely off from the combat. The moral of this fable is, that destiny would not yet suffer *Troy* to fall.

Eustathius fancies that the occasion of the fiction might be this: *Agenor* fled from *Achilles* to the banks of *Xanthus*, and might there conceal himself from the pursuer behind some covert that grew on the shores; this perhaps might be the whole of the story. So plain a narration would have pass'd in the mouth of an historian, but the poet dresses it in fiction, and tells us that *Apollo* (or Destiny) conceal'd him in a cloud from the sight of his enemy.

The same author farther observes, that *Achilles* by an unseasonable piece of vain-glory, in pursuing a single enemy gives time to a whole army to escape; he neither kills *Agenor*, nor overtakes the *Trojans*.

THE
ILIAD
OF
HOMER

VOLUME VI

THE
TWENTY-SECOND BOOK
OF THE
ILIAD

The ARGUMENT

The Death of *Hector*

The Trojans *being safe within the walls,* Hector *only stays to oppose* Achilles. Priam *is struck at his approach, and tries to persuade his son to re-enter the town.* Hecuba *joins her entreaties, but in vain.* Hector *consults within himself what measures to take; but at the advance of* Achilles, *his resolution fails him, and he flies;* Achilles *pursues him thrice round the walls of* Troy. *The Gods debate concerning the fate of* Hector; *at length* Minerva *descends to the aid of* Achilles. *She deludes* Hector *in the shape of* Deïphobus; *he stands the combate, and is slain.* Achilles *drags the dead body at his chariot, in the sight of* Priam *and* Hecuba. *Their lamentations, tears, and despair. Their cries reach the ears of* Andromache, *who, ignorant of this, was retired into the inner part of the palace: She mounts up to the walls, and beholds her dead husband. She swoons at the spectacle. Her excess of grief, and lamentation.*

The thirtieth day still continues. The scene lies under the walls, and on the battlements of Troy.

Thus to their bulwarks, smit with panick fear,
The herded *Ilians* rush like driven deer;
There safe, they wipe the briny drops away,
And drown in bowls the labours of the day.
5   Close to the walls advancing o'er the fields,
Beneath one roof of well-compacted shields
March, bending on, the *Greeks* embodied pow'rs,
Far-stretching in the shade of *Trojan* tow'rs.
Great *Hector* singly stay'd; chain'd down by fate,
10   There fixt he stood before the *Scæan* gate;
Still his bold arms determin'd to employ,
The guardian still of long-defended *Troy*.
    Apollo now to tir'd *Achilles* turns;
(The pow'r confest in all his glory burns)
15   And what (he cries) has *Peleus*' son in view,
With mortal speed a Godhead to pursue?
For not to thee to know the Gods is giv'n,
Unskill'd to trace the latent marks of heav'n.
What boots thee now, that *Troy* forsook the plain?
20   Vain thy past labour, and thy present vain:
Safe in their walls are now her troops bestow'd,
While here thy frantick rage attacks a God.
    The chief incens'd – Too partial God of day!
To check my conquests in the middle way:
25   How few in *Ilion* else had refuge found?
What gasping numbers now had bit the ground?
Thou robb'st me of a glory justly mine,
Pow'rful of Godhead, and of fraud divine:

Mean fame, alas! for one of heav'nly strain,
To cheat a mortal, who repines in vain.   30
   Then to the city, terrible and strong,
With high and haughty steps he tow'rd along.
So the proud courser, victor of the prize,
To the near goal with double ardour flies.
Him, as he blazing shot across the field,   35
The careful eyes of *Priam* first beheld.
Not half so dreadful rises to the sight
Thro' the thick gloom of some tempestuous night
Orion's dog (the year when autumn weighs)
And o'er the feebler stars exerts his rays;   40
Terrifick glory! for his burning breath
Taints the red air with fevers, plagues, and death.
So flam'd his fiery mail. Then wept the sage;
He strikes his rev'rend head now white with age:
He lifts his wither'd arms; obtests the skies;   45
He calls his much-lov'd son with feeble cries;
The Son, resolv'd *Achilles'* force to dare,
Full at the *Scæan* gates expects the war;
While the sad father on the rampart stands,
And thus adjures him with extended hands.   50
   Ah stay not, stay not! guardless and alone;
Hector! my lov'd, my dearest, bravest son!
Methinks already I behold thee slain,
And stretch'd beneath that fury of the plain.
Implacable *Achilles!* might'st thou be   55
To all the Gods no dearer than to me!
Thee, vultures wild should scatter round the shore,
And bloody dogs grow fiercer from thy gore.
How many valiant sons I late enjoy'd,
Valiant in vain! by thy curst árm destroy'd: 60
Or, worse than slaughter'd, sold in distant isles
To shameful bondage and unworthy toils.
Two, while I speak, my eyes in vain explore,   ⎫
Two from one mother sprung, my *Polydore*,   ⎬
And lov'd *Lycaon*; now perhaps no more!   ⎭   65
Oh if in yonder hostile camp they live,
What heaps of gold, what treasures would I give?

(Their grandsire's wealth, by right of birth their own,
Consign'd his daughter with *Lelegia*'s throne)
70 But if (which heav'n forbid) already lost,
All pale they wander on the *Stygian* coast;
What sorrows then must their sad mother know,
What anguish I? unutterable woe!
Yet less that anguish, less to her, to me,
75 Less to all *Troy*, if not depriv'd of thee,
Yet shun *Achilles!* enter yet the wall;
And spare thyself, thy father, spare us all!
Save thy dear life; or if a soul so brave
Neglect that thought, thy dearer glory save.
80 Pity, while yet I live, these silver hairs;
While yet thy father feels the woes he bears,
Yet curst with sense! a wretch, whom in his rage
(All trembling on the verge of helpless age)
Great *Jove* has plac'd, sad spectacle of pain!
85 The bitter dregs of fortune's cup to drain:
To fill with scenes of death his closing eyes,
And number all his days by miseries!
My heroes slain, my bridal bed o'erturn'd,
My daughters ravish'd, and my city burn'd,
90 My bleeding infants dash'd against the floor;
These I have yet to see, perhaps yet more!
Perhaps ev'n I, reserv'd by angry Fate
The last sad relick of my ruin'd state,
(Dire pomp of sov'reign wretchedness!) must fall,
95 And stain the pavement of my regal hall;
Where famish'd dogs, late guardians of my door,
Shall lick their mangled master's spatter'd gore.
Yet for my sons I thank ye Gods! 'twas well;
Well have they perish'd, for in fight they fell.
100 Who dies in youth, and vigour, dies the best,
Struck thro' with wounds, all honest on the breast.
But when the Fates, in fulness of their rage,
Spurn the hoar head of unresisting age,
In dust the rev'rend lineaments deform,
105 And pour to dogs the life-blood scarcely warm;
This, this is misery! the last, the worst,
That man can feel; man, fated to be curst!

He said, and acting what no words could say,
Rent from his head the silver locks away.
With him the mournful mother bears a part;   110
Yet all their sorrows turn not *Hector*'s heart:
The zone unbrac'd, her bosom she display'd;
And thus, fast-falling the salt tears, she said.
      Have mercy on me, O my son! Revere
The words of age; attend a parent's pray'r!   115
If ever thee in these fond arms I prest,
Or still'd thy infant clamours at this breast;
Ah do not thus our helpless years forego,
But by our walls secur'd, repel the foe.
Against his rage if singly thou proceed,   120
Should'st thou (but heav'n avert it!) should'st thou bleed,
Nor must thy corps lye honour'd on the bier,
Nor spouse, nor mother, grace thee with a tear;
Far from our pious rites, those dear remains
Must feast the vultures on the naked plains.   125
      So they, while down their cheeks the torrents roll;
But fix'd remains the purpose of his soul:
Resolv'd he stands, and with a fiery glance
Expects the hero's terrible advance.
So roll'd up in his den, the swelling snake   130
Beholds the traveller approach the brake;
When fed with noxious herbs his turgid veins
Have gather'd half the poisons of the plains;
He burns, he stiffens with collected ire,
And his red eye-balls glare with living fire.   135
Beneath a turret, on his shield reclin'd,
He stood, and question'd thus his mighty mind.
      Where lies my way? To enter in the wall?
Honour and shame th' ungen'rous thought recall:
Shall proud *Polydamas* before the gate   140
Proclaim, his counsels are obey'd too late,
Which timely follow'd but the former night,
What numbers had been sav'd by *Hector*'s flight?
That wise advice rejected with disdain,
I feel my folly in my people slain.   145
Methinks my suff'ring country's voice I hear,
But most, her worthless sons insult my ear,

On my rash courage charge the chance of war,
And blame those virtues which they cannot share.
150 No – If I e'er return, return I must
Glorious, my country's terrour laid in dust:
Or if I perish, let her see me fall
In field at least, and fighting for her wall.
And yet suppose these measures I forego,
155 Approach unarm'd, and parly with the foe,
The warriour-shield, the helm, and lance lay down,
And treat on terms of peace to save the town:
The wife with-held, the treasure ill detain'd,
(Cause of the war, and grievance of the land)
160 With honourable justice to restore;
And add half *Ilion*'s yet remaining store,
Which *Troy* shall, sworn, produce; that injur'd *Greece*
May share our wealth, and leave our walls in peace.
But why this thought? Unarm'd if I should go,
165 What hope of mercy from this vengeful foe,
But woman-like to fall, and fall without a blow.
We greet not here, as man conversing man,
Met at an oak, or journeying o'er a plain;
No season now for calm familiar talk,
170 Like youths and maidens in an evening walk:
War is our business, but to whom is giv'n
To die or triumph, that, determine heav'n!
  Thus pond'ring, like a God the *Greek* drew nigh;
His dreadful plumage nodded from on high;
175 The *Pelian* jav'lin, in his better hand,
Shot trembling rays that glitter'd o'er the land;
And on his breast the beamy splendors shone
Like *Jove*'s own lightning, or the rising sun.
As *Hector* sees, unusual terrours rise,
180 Struck by some God, he fears, recedes, and flies.
He leaves the gates, he leaves the walls behind;
Achilles follows like the winged wind.
Thus at the panting dove a falcon flies,
(The swiftest racer of the liquid skies)
185 Just when he holds or thinks he holds his prey,
Obliquely wheeling thro' th' aerial way;

With open beak and shrilling cries he springs,
And aims his claws, and shoots upon his wings:
No less fore-right the rapid chace they held,
One urg'd by fury, one by fear impell'd;   190
Now circling round the walls their course maintain,
Where the high watch-tow'r overlooks the plain;
Now where the fig-trees spread their umbrage broad,
(A wider compass) smoke along the road.
Next by *Scamander*'s double source they bound,   195
Where two fam'd fountains burst the parted ground;
This hot thro' scorching clefts is seen to rise,
With exhalations steaming to the skies;
That the green banks in summer's heat o'erflows,
Like crystal clear, and cold as winter-snows.   200
Each gushing fount a marble cistern fills,
Whose polish'd bed receives the falling rills;
Where *Trojan* dames, (e'er yet alarm'd by *Greece*)
Wash'd their fair garments in the days of peace.
By these they past, one chasing, one in Flight,   205
(The mighty fled, pursu'd by stronger might)
Swift was the course; no vulgar prize they play,
No vulgar victim must reward the day,
(Such as in races crown the speedy strife)
The prize contended was great *Hector*'s life.   210
As when some hero's fun'rals are decreed
In grateful honour of the mighty dead;
Where high rewards the vig'rous youth inflame,
(Some golden tripod, or some lovely dame)
The panting coursers swiftly turn the goal,   215
And with them turns the rais'd spectator's soul.
Thus three times round the *Trojan* wall they fly;
The gazing Gods lean forward from the sky:
To whom, while eager on the chace they look,
The Sire of mortals and immortals spoke.   220
   Unworthy sight! the man, belov'd of heav'n,
Behold, inglorious round yon' city driv'n!
My heart partakes the gen'rous *Hector*'s pain;
Hector, whose zeal whole hecatombs has slain,
Whose grateful fumes the Gods receiv'd with joy,   225
From *Ida*'s summits, and the tow'rs of *Troy*:

Now see him flying! to his fears resign'd,
And Fate, and fierce *Achilles*, close behind.
Consult, ye pow'rs! ('tis worthy your debate)
230   Whether to snatch him from impending fate,
Or let him bear, by stern *Pelides* slain,
(Good as he is) the lot impos'd on man?
     Then *Pallas* thus: Shall he whose vengeance forms
The forky bolt, and blackens heav'n with storms,
235   Shall he prolong one *Trojan*'s forfeit breath!
A man, a mortal, pre-ordain'd to death!
And will no murmurs fill the courts above,
No Gods indignant blame their partial *Jove*?
     Go then (return'd the Sire) without delay,
240   Exert thy will: I give the fates their way.
Swift at the mandate pleas'd *Tritonia* flies,
And stoops impetuous from the cleaving skies.
     As thro' the forest, o'er the vale and lawn,
The well-breath'd beagle drives the flying fawn;
245   In vain he tries the covert of the brakes,
Or deep beneath the trembling thicket shakes;
Sure of the vapour in the tainted dews,
The certain hound his various maze pursues.
Thus step by step, where'er the *Trojan* wheel'd,
250   There swift *Achilles* compass'd round the field.
Oft' as to reach the *Dardan* gates he bends,
And hopes th'assistance of his pitying friends,
(Whose show'ring arrows, as he cours'd below,
From the high turrets might oppress the foe.)
255   So oft' *Achilles* turns him to the plain:
He eyes the city, but he eyes in vain.
As men in slumbers seem with speedy pace,
One to pursue, and one to lead the chace,
Their sinking limbs the fancy'd course forsake,
260   Nor this can fly, nor that can overtake.
No less the lab'ring heroes pant and strain;
While that but flies, and this pursues in vain.
     What God, O Muse! assisted *Hector*'s force,
With Fate itself so long to hold the course?
265   *Phœbus* it was; who, in his latest hour,
Endu'd his knees with strength, his nerves with pow'r:

And great *Achilles*, lest some *Greek*'s advance
Should snatch the glory from his lifted lance,
Sign'd to the troops, to yield his foe the way,
And leave untouch'd the honours of the day.   270
   Jove lifts the golden balances, that show
The fates of mortal men, and things below:
Here each contending hero's lot he tries,
And weighs, with equal hand, their destinies.
Low sinks the scale surcharg'd with *Hector*'s fate;   275
Heavy with death it sinks, and hell receives the weight.
   Then *Phœbus* left him. Fierce *Minerva* flies
To stern *Pelides*, and triumphing, cries:
Oh lov'd of *Jove!* this day our labours cease,
And conquest blazes with full beams on *Greece*.   280
Great *Hector* falls; that *Hector* fam'd so far,
Drunk with renown, insatiable of war,
Falls by thy hand, and mine! nor force, nor flight
Shall more avail him, nor his God of Light.
See, where in vain he supplicates above,   285
Roll'd at the feet of unrelenting *Jove!*
Rest here: my self will lead the *Trojan* on,
And urge to meet the fate he cannot shun.
   Her voice divine the chief with joyful mind
Obey'd; and rested, on his lance reclin'd.   290
While like *Deïphobus* the martial dame
(Her face, her gesture, and her arms the same)
In show an aid, by hapless *Hector*'s side
Approach'd, and greets him thus with voice bely'd.
   Too long, O *Hector!* have I born the sight   295
Of this distress, and sorrow'd in thy flight:
It fits us now a noble stand to make,
And here, as brothers, equal fates partake.
   Then he. O Prince! ally'd in blood and fame,
Dearer than all that own a brother's name;   300
Of all that *Hecuba* to *Priam* bore,
Long try'd, long lov'd; much lov'd, but honour'd more!
Since you of all our num'rous race, alone
Defend my life, regardless of your own.
   Again the Goddess. Much my father's pray'r,   305
And much my mother's, prest me to forbear:

My friends embrac'd my knees, adjur'd my stay,
But stronger love impell'd, and I obey.
Come then, the glorious conflict let us try,
310   Let the steel sparkle, and the jav'lin fly;
Or let us stretch *Achilles* on the field,
Or to his arm our bloody trophies yield.
      Fraudful she said; then swiftly march'd before;
The *Dardan* hero shuns his foe no more.
315   Sternly they met. The Silence *Hector* broke;
His dreadful plumage nodded as he spoke.
      Enough, O son of *Peleus! Troy* has view'd
Her walls thrice circled, and her chief pursu'd.
But now some God within me bids me try
320   Thine, or my fate: I kill thee, or I die.
Yet on the verge of battel let us stay,
And for a moment's space, suspend the day;
Let heav'ns high pow'rs be call'd to arbitrate
The just conditions of this stern debate.
325   (Eternal witnesses of all below,
And faithful guardians of the treasur'd vow!)
To them I swear; if victor in the strife
Jove by these hands shall shed thy noble life;
No vile dishonour shall thy corse pursue;
330   Stript of its arms alone (the conqu'ror's due)
The rest to *Greece* uninjur'd I'll restore:
Now plight thy mutual oath, I ask no more.
      Talk not of oaths (the dreadful chief replies,
While anger flash'd from his disdainful eyes)
335   Detested as thou art, and ought to be,
Nor oath nor pact *Achilles* plights with thee:
Such pacts, as lambs and rabid wolves combine,
Such leagues, as men and furious lions join,
To such I call the Gods! One constant state
340   Of lashing rancour and eternal hate:
No thought but rage, and never-ceasing strife,
Till death extinguish rage, and thought, and life.
Rouze then thy forces this important hour;
Collect thy soul, and call forth all thy pow'r.
345   No farther subterfuge, no farther chance;
'Tis *Pallas, Pallas* gives thee to my lance.

Each *Grecian* ghost by thee depriv'd of breath,
Now hovers round, and calls thee to thy death.
  He spoke, and lanch'd his jav'lin at the foe;
But *Hector* shun'd the meditated blow: 350
He stoop'd, while o'er his head the flying spear
Sung innocent, and spent its force in air.
Minerva watch'd it falling on the land,
Then drew, and gave to great *Achilles'* hand,
Unseen of *Hector*, who, elate with joy,   355
Now shakes his lance, and braves the dread of *Troy*.
  The life you boasted to that jav'lin giv'n,
Prince! you have mist. My fate depends on heav'n.
To thee (presumptuous as thou art) unknown,
Or what must prove my fortune, or thy own.   360
Boasting is but an art, our fears to blind,
And with false terrours sink another's mind.
But know, whatever fate I am to try,
By no dishonest wound shall *Hector* die;
I shall not fall a fugitive at least,   365
My soul shall bravely issue from my breast.
But first, try thou my arm; and may this dart
End all my country's woes, deep buried in thy heart!
  The weapon flew, its course unerring held,
Unerring, but the heav'nly shield repell'd   370
The mortal dart; resulting with a bound
From off the ringing orb, it struck the ground.
Hector beheld his jav'lin fall in vain,
Nor other lance, nor other hope remain;
He calls *Deïphobus*, demands a spear,   375
In vain, for no *Deïphobus* was there.
All comfortless he stands: Then, with a sigh,
'Tis so – heav'n wills it, and my hour is nigh!
I deem'd *Deïphobus* had heard my call,
But he secure lies guarded in the wall.   380
A God deceiv'd me; *Pallas*, 'twas thy deed.
Death, and black fate approach! 'Tis I must bleed.
No refuge now, no succour from above!
Great *Jove* deserts me, and the son of *Jove*,
Propitious once, and kind! Then welcome fate!   385
'Tis true I perish, yet I perish great:

Yet in a mighty deed I shall expire,
Let future ages hear it, and admire!
   Fierce, at the word, his weighty sword he drew,
390 And, all collected, on *Achilles* flew.
So *Jove*'s bold bird, high-balanc'd in the air,
Stoops from the clouds to truss the quiv'ring hare.
Nor less *Achilles* his fierce soul prepares;
Before his breast the flaming shield he bears,
395 Refulgent orb! Above his four-fold cone
The gilded horse-hair sparkled in the sun,
Nodding at ev'ry step: (*Vulcanian* frame!)
And as he mov'd, his figure seem'd on flame.
As radiant *Hesper* shines with keener light,
400 Far-beaming o'er the silver host of night,
When all the starry train emblaze the sphere:
So shone the point of great *Achilles'* spear.
In his right hand he waves the weapon round,
Eyes the whole man, and meditates the wound;
405 But the rich mail *Patroclus* lately wore,
Securely cas'd the warriour's body o'er.
One place at length he spies, to let in fate,
Where 'twixt the neck and throat the jointed plate
Gave entrance: Thro' that penetrable part
410 Furious he drove the well-directed dart:
Nor pierc'd the windpipe yet, nor took the pow'r
Of speech, unhappy! from thy dying hour.
Prone on the field the bleeding warriour lies,
While thus triumphing, stern *Achilles* cries.
415   At last is *Hector* stretch'd upon the plain,
Who fear'd no vengeance for *Patroclus* slain:
Then Prince! you should have fear'd, what now you feel;
Achilles absent, was *Achilles* still.
Yet a short space the great avenger stay'd,
420 Then low in dust thy strength and glory lay'd.
Peaceful he sleeps, with all our rites adorn'd,
For ever honour'd, and for ever mourn'd:
While cast to all the rage of hostile pow'r,
Thee, birds shall mangle, and the dogs devour.
425   Then *Hector*, fainting at th'approach of death.
By thy own soul! by those who gave thee breath!

By all the sacred prevalence of pray'r;
Ah, leave me not for *Grecian* dogs to tear!
The common rites of sepulture bestow,
To sooth a father's and a mother's woe;   430
Let their large gifts procure an urn at least,
And *Hector*'s ashes in his country rest.

    No, wretch accurst! Relentless he replies,
(Flames, as he spoke, shot flashing from his eyes)
Not those who gave me breath shou'd bid me spare,   435
Nor all the sacred prevalence of pray'r.
Could I my self the bloody banquet join!
No – to the dogs that carcase I resign.
Shou'd *Troy*, to bribe me, bring forth all her store,
And giving thousands, offer thousands more;   440
Should *Dardan Priam*, and his weeping dame
Drain their whole realm to buy one fun'ral flame:
Their *Hector* on the pile they should not see,
Nor rob the vultures of one limb of thee.

    Then thus the chief his dying accents drew;   445
Thy rage, implacable! too well I knew:
The Furies that relentless breast have steel'd,
And curs'd thee with a heart that cannot yield.
Yet think, a day will come, when Fate's decree
And angry Gods, shall wreak this wrong on thee;   450
Phœbus and *Paris* shall avenge my fate,
And stretch thee here, before this *Scæan* gate.

    He ceas'd. The Fates supprest his lab'ring breath,
And his eyes stiffen'd at the hand of death;
To the dark realm the spirit wings its way,   455
(The manly body left a load of clay)
And plaintive glides along the dreary coast,
A naked, wand'ring, melancholy ghost!

    Achilles, musing as he roll'd his eyes
O'er the dead hero, thus (unheard) replies.   460
Die thou the first! When *Jove* and heav'n ordain,
I follow thee – He said, and stripp'd the slain.
Then forcing backward from the gaping wound
The reeking jav'lin, cast it on the ground.
The thronging *Greeks* behold with wond'ring eyes   465
His manly beauty and superiour size:

While some ignobler, the great dead deface
With wounds ungen'rous, or with taunts disgrace.
'How chang'd that *Hector!* who like *Jove* of late,
470 Sent lightning on our fleets, and scatter'd fate?'
    High o'er the slain the great *Achilles* stands,
Begirt with heroes, and surrounding bands;
And thus aloud, while all the host attends.
Princes and Leaders! Countrymen and friends!
475 Since now at length the pow'rful will of heav'n
The dire destroyer to our arm has giv'n,
Is not *Troy* fall'n already? Haste, ye pow'rs!
See, if already their deserted tow'rs
Are left unmann'd; or if they yet retain
480 The souls of heroes, their great *Hector* slain?
But what is *Troy*, or glory what to me?
Or why reflects my mind on ought but thee,
Divine *Patroclus!* Death has seal'd his eyes;
Unwept, unhonour'd, uninterr'd he lies!
485 Can his dear image from my soul depart,
Long as the vital spirit moves my heart?
If, in the melancholy shades below,
The flames of friends and lovers cease to glow,
Yet mine shall sacred last; mine, undecay'd,
490 Burn on thro' death, and animate my shade.
Meanwhile, ye sons of *Greece*, in triumph bring
The corps of *Hector*, and your *Pæans* sing.
Be this the song, slow-moving tow'rd the shore,
'*Hector* is dead, and *Ilion* is no more.'
495   Then his fell soul a thought of vengeance bred,
(Unworthy of himself, and of the dead)
The nervous ancles bor'd, his feet he bound
With thongs inserted thro' the double wound;
These fix'd up high behind the rolling wain,
500 His graceful head was trail'd along the plain.
Proud on his car th'insulting victor stood,
And bore aloft his arms, distilling blood.
He smites the steeds; the rapid chariot flies;
The sudden clouds of circling dust arise.
505 Now lost is all that formidable air;
The face divine, and long-descending hair

Purple the ground, and streak the sable sand;
Deform'd, dishonour'd, in his native land!
Giv'n to the rage of an insulting throng!
And, in his parents' sight, now dragg'd along!   510
   The mother first beheld with sad survey;
She rent her tresses, venerably grey,
And cast, far off, the regal veils away.
With piercing shrieks his bitter fate she moans,
While the sad father answers groans with groans,   515
Tears after tears his mournful cheeks o'erflow,
And the whole city wears one face of woe.
No less than if the rage of hostile fires
From her foundations curling to her spires,
O'er the proud citadel at length should rise,   520
And the last blaze send *Ilion* to the skies.
The wretched monarch of the falling state
Distracted, presses to the *Dardan* gate.
Scarce the whole people stop his desp'rate course,
While strong affliction gives the feeble force: 525
Grief tears his heart, and drives him to and fro,
In all the raging impotence of woe.
At length he roll'd in dust, and thus begun:
Imploring all, and naming one by one.
Ah! let me, let me go where sorrow calls;   530
I, only I, will issue from your walls,
(Guide or companion, friends! I ask ye none)
And bow before the murd'rer of my son.
My grief perhaps his pity may engage;
Perhaps at least he may respect my age.   535
He has a father too; a man like me,
One, not exempt from age and misery,
(Vig'rous no more, as when his young embrace
Begot this pest of me, and all my race.)
How many valiant sons, in early bloom,   540
Has that curst hand sent headlong to the tomb?
Thee, *Hector!* last: Thy loss (divinely brave)
Sinks my sad soul with sorrow to the grave.
Oh had thy gentle spirit past in peace,
The son expiring in the sire's embrace,   545

While both thy parents wept thy fatal hour,
And bending o'er thee, mix'd the tender show'r!
Some comfort that had been, some sad relief,
To melt in full satiety of grief!
550   Thus wail'd the father, grov'ling on the ground,
And all the eyes of *Ilion* stream'd around.
     Amidst her matrons *Hecuba* appears,
(A mourning Princess, and a train in tears)
Ah why has heav'n prolong'd this hated breath,
555 Patient of horrours, to behold thy death?
O *Hector*, late thy parents pride and joy,
The boast of nations! the defence of *Troy!*
To whom her safety and her fame she ow'd,
Her chief, her hero, and almost her God!
560 O fatal change! become in one sad day
A senseless corps! inanimated clay!
     But not as yet the fatal news had spread
To fair *Andromache*, of *Hector* dead;
As yet no messenger had told his fate,
565 Nor ev'n his stay without the *Scæan* gate.
Far in the close recesses of the dome,
Pensive she ply'd the melancholy loom;
A growing work employ'd her secret hours,
Confus'dly gay with intermingled flow'rs.
570 Her fair–hair'd handmaids heat the brazen urn,
The bath preparing for her Lord's return:
In vain: Alas! her Lord returns no more!
Unbath'd he lies, and bleeds along the shore!
Now from the walls the clamours reach her ear,
575 And all her members shake with sudden fear;
Forth from her iv'ry hand the shuttle falls,
As thus, astonish'd, to her maids she calls.
     Ah follow me! (she cry'd) what plaintive noise
Invades my ear? 'Tis sure my mother's voice.
580 My falt'ring knees their trembling frame desert,
A pulse unusual flutters at my heart.
Some strange disaster, some reverse of fate
(Ye Gods avert it) threats the *Trojan* state.
Far be the omen which my thoughts suggest!
585 But much I fear my *Hector*'s dauntless breast

Confronts *Achilles*; chas'd along the plain,
Shut from our walls! I fear, I fear him slain!
Safe in the crowd he ever scorn'd to wait,
And sought for glory in the jaws of fate:
Perhaps that noble heat has cost his breath,   590
Now quench'd for ever in the arms of death.
   She spoke; and furious, with distracted pace,
Fears in her heart, and anguish in her face,
Flies thro' the dome, (the maids her steps pursue)
And mounts the walls, and sends around her view.   595
Too soon her eyes the killing object found,
The god-like *Hector* dragg'd along the ground.
A sudden darkness shades her swimming eyes:
She faints, she falls; her breath, her colour flies.
Her hair's fair ornaments, the braids that bound,   600
The net that held them, and the wreath that crown'd,
The veil and diadem, flew far away;
(The gift of *Venus* on her bridal day)
Around, a train of weeping sisters stands,
To raise her sinking with assistant hands.   605
Scarce from the verge of death recall'd, again
She faints, or but recovers to complain.
   O wretched husband of a wretched wife!
Born with one fate, to one unhappy life!
For sure one star its baneful beam display'd   610
On *Priam*'s roof, and *Hippoplacia*'s shade.
From diff'rent parents, diff'rent climes we came,
At diff'rent periods, yet our fate the same!
Why was my birth to great *Aëtion* ow'd,
And why was all that tender care bestow'd?   615
Would I had never been! – O thou, the ghost
Of my dead husband! miserably lost!
Thou to the dismal realms for ever gone!
And I abandon'd, desolate, alone!
An only child, once comfort of my Pains,   620
Sad product now of hapless love, remains!
No more to smile upon his Sire! no friend
To help him now! No father to defend!
For should he 'scape the sword, the common doom!
What wrongs attend him, and what griefs to come?   625

Ev'n from his own paternal roof expell'd,
Some stranger plows his patrimonial field.
The day, that to the shades the father sends,
Robs the sad orphan of his father's friends:
630   He, wretched outcast of mankind! appears
For ever sad, for ever bath'd in tears;
Amongst the happy, unregarded he,
Hangs on the robe, or trembles at the knee,
While those his father's former bounty fed,
635   Nor reach the goblet, nor divide the bread:
The kindest but his present wants allay,
To leave him wretched the succeeding day.
Frugal compassion! Heedless they who boast
Both parents still, nor feel what he has lost,
640   Shall cry, 'Begone! Thy father feasts not here':
The wretch obeys, retiring with a tear.
Thus wretched, thus retiring all in tears,
To my sad soul *Astyanax* appears!
Forc'd by repeated insults to return,
645   And to his widow'd mother vainly mourn.
He, who with tender delicacy bred,
With princes sported, and on dainties fed,
And when still ev'ning gave him up to rest,
Sunk soft in down upon the nurse's breast,
650   Must – ah what must he not? Whom *Ilion* calls
Astyanax, from her well-guarded walls,
Is now that name no more, unhappy boy!
Since now no more the father guards his *Troy*.
But thou my *Hector* ly'st expos'd in air,
655   Far from thy parent's and thy consort's care,
Whose hand in vain, directed by her love,
The martial scarf and robe of triumph wove.
Now to devouring flames be these a prey,
Useless to thee, from this accursed day!
660   Yet let the sacrifice at least be paid,
An honour to the living, not the dead!
   So spake the mournful dame: Her Matrons hear,
Sigh back her sighs, and answer tear with tear.

OBSERVATIONS

ON THE

TWENTY-SECOND BOOK

The epigraph on the frontispiece of Volume VI (Books 22–24) consists of the following lines:

> *Qui cupit* [*sic*] *optatam cursu contingere metam,*
> *Multa tulit, fecitque puer –* HOR.

[Whoever wishes, in his race, to reach his desired goal must, as a youth, have struggled and sacrificed. (Horace, *Ars Poetica*, 412–13)]

It is impossible but the whole attention of the reader must be awaken'd in this book: The heroes of the two armies are now to encounter; all the foregoing battels have been but so many preludes and under-actions, in order to this great event: Wherein the whole fate of *Greece* and *Troy* is to be decided by the sword of *Achilles* and *Hector*.

This is the book, which of the whole *Iliad* appears to me the most charming. It assembles in it all that can be imagined of great and important on the one hand, and of tender and melancholy on the other. *Terrour* and *Pity* are here wrought up in perfection, and if the reader is not sensible of both in a high degree, either he is utterly void of all taste, or the translator of all skill, in poetry.

37. *Not half so dreadful rises*, &c.] With how much dreadful pomp is *Achilles* here introduced! How noble, and in what bold colours hath he drawn the blazing of his arms, the rapidity of his advance, the terrour of his appearance, the desolation around him; but above all, the certain death attending all his motions and his very looks; what a crowd of terrible ideas in this one simile!

But immediately after this, follows the moving image of the two aged parents, trembling, weeping, and imploring their son: That is succeeded again by the dreadful gloomy picture of *Hector*, all on fire, obstinately bent on death, and expecting *Achilles*; admirably painted in the simile of the snake roll'd up in his den and collecting his poisons: And indeed thro' the whole book this wonderful contrast and opposition of the *Moving* and of the *Terrible*, is perpetually kept up, each heightening the other: I can't find words to express how so great beauties affect me.

51. *The speech of* Priam *to* Hector.] The poet has entertain'd us all along with various scenes of slaughter and horrour: He now changes to the pathetick, and fills the mind of the reader with tender sorrows. *Eustathius* observes that *Priam* preludes to his words by actions expressive of misery: The unhappy orator introduces his speech to *Hector* with groans and tears, and rending his hoary hair. The father and the King plead with *Hector* to preserve his life and his country. He represents his own age, and the loss of many of his children; and adds, that if *Hector* falls, he should then be inconsolable, and the empire of *Troy* at an end.

It is a piece of great judgment in *Homer* to make the fall of *Troy* to depend upon the death of *Hector*: The poet does not openly tell us that *Troy* was taken by the *Greeks*, but that the reader might not be unacquainted with what happened after the period of his poem, he gives us to understand in this speech, that the city was taken, and that *Priam*, his wives, his sons and daughters, were either killed or made slaves.

76. *Enter yet the wall; and spare*, &c.] The argument that *Priam* uses (says *Eustathius*) to induce *Hector* to secure himself in *Troy* is remarkable; he draws it not from *Hector*'s fears, nor does he tell him that he is to save his own life; but he insists upon stronger motives: He tells him he may preserve his fellow-citizens, his country, and his father; and farther, persuades him not to add glory to his mortal enemy by his fall.

90. *My bleeding infants dash'd against the floor.*] Cruelties which the *Barbarians* usually exercised in the sacking of towns. Thus *Isaiah* foretels to *Babylon* that her children shall be dashed in pieces before her eyes by the *Medes. Infantes eorum allidentur in oculis eorum*, xii. 16. And *David* says to the same city, *Happy shall he be that taketh and* *dasheth thy little ones against the stones.* Psal. cxxxvii. 9. And in the prophet *Hosea*, xiii. 16. *Their infants shall be dash'd in pieces.*

Dacier.

102. *But when the Fates, &c.*] Nothing can be more moving than the image which *Homer* gives here, in comparing the different Effects produced by the view of a young man, and that of an old one, both bleeding, and extended on the dust. The old man, 'tis certain touches us most, and several reasons may be given for it; the principal is, that the young man defended himself, and his death is glorious; whereas an old man has no defence but his weakness, prayers, and tears. They must be very insensible of what is dreadful, and have no taste in poetry, who omit this passage in a translation, and substitute things of a trivial and insipid nature. *Dacier.*

114. *The speech of* Hecuba.] The speech of *Hecuba* opens with as much tenderness as that of *Priam*: The circumstance in particular of her shewing that breast to her son which had sustained his Infancy, is highly moving: It is a silent kind of oratory, and prepares the heart to listen, by prepossessing the eye in favour of the speaker.

Eustathius takes notice of the difference between the speeches of *Priam* and *Hecuba*: *Priam* dissuades him from the combat by enumerating not only the loss of his own family, but of his whole country: *Hecuba* dwells entirely upon his single death; this is a great beauty in the poet, to make *Priam* a father to his whole country; but to describe the fondness of the mother as prevailing over all other considerations, and to mention that only which chiefly affects her.

This puts me in mind of a judicious stroke in *Milton*, with regard to the several characters of *Adam* and *Eve*. When the Angel is driving them both out of Paradise, *Adam* grieves that he must leave a place where he had conversed with God and his angels; but *Eve* laments that she shall never more behold the flowers of *Eden*: Here *Adam* mourns like a man, and *Eve* like a woman.

138. *The soliloquy of* Hector.] There is much greatness in the sentiments of this whole soliloquy. *Hector* prefers death to an ignominious Life: He knows how to die with glory, but not how to live with dishonour. The reproach of *Polydamas* affects him; the scandals of the meanest people have an influence on his thoughts.

'Tis remarkable that he does not say, he fears the insults of the braver *Trojans*, but of the most worthless only. Men of merit are always the most candid; but others are ever for bringing all men to a level with themselves. They cannot bear that any one should be so bold as to excel, and are ready to pull him down to them, upon the least miscarriage. This sentiment is perfectly fine, and agreeable to the way of thinking natural to a great and sensible mind.

There is a very beautiful break in the middle of this speech. *Hector*'s mind fluctuates every way, he is calling a council in his own breast, and consulting what method to pursue: He doubts if he should not propose terms of peace to *Achilles*, and grants him very large concessions; but of a sudden he checks himself, and leaves the sentence unfinish'd. The paragraph runs thus, 'If,' says *Hector*, 'I should offer him the largest conditions, give all that *Troy* contains –' There he stops, and immediately subjoins, 'But why do I delude myself,' *&c.*

'Tis evident from this speech that the power of making peace was in *Hector*'s hands: For unless *Priam* had transferred it to him, he could not have made these propositions. So that it was *Hector* who broke the treaty in the third book; (where the very same conditions were proposed by *Agamemnon*.) 'Tis *Hector* therefore that is guilty, he is blameable in continuing the war, and involving the *Greeks* and *Trojans* in blood. This conduct in *Homer* was necessary; he observes a poetical justice, and shews us that *Hector* is a criminal, before he brings him to death.

Eustathius.

140. *Shall proud* Polydamas, &c.] *Hector* alludes to the counsel given him by *Polydamas* in the eighteenth book, which he then neglected to follow: It was, to withdraw to the city, and fortify themselves there, before *Achilles* returned to the battel.

167.   *We greet not here, as man conversing man,*
         Met at an oak, or journeying o'er a plain, &c.]

The Words literally are these, '*There is no talking with* Achilles, ἀπὸ δρυὸς οὐδ' ἀπὸ πέτρης, *from an oak, or from a rock*, (or about an oak or a rock) *as a young man and a maiden talk together.* It is thought an obscure passage, tho' I confess I am either too fond of my own explication in the above-cited verses, or they make it a very clear one. 'There is no conversing with this implacable enemy in the rage of battel; as when sauntring people talk at leisure to one another on the road, or when young men and women meet in a field.' I think the exposition of *Eustathius* more far-fetch'd, tho' it be ingenious; and therefore I must do him the justice not to suppress it. It was a common practice, says he, with the heathens, to expose such children as they either could not, or would not educate: The places where they deposited them were usually in the cavities of *rocks*, or the hollow of *oaks*: These children being frequently found and preserved by strangers, were said to be the offspring of those oaks or rocks where they were found. This gave occasion to the poets to feign that men were born of *oaks*, and there was a famous fable too of *Deucalion* and *Pyrrha*'s repairing mankind by casting *stones* behind them: It grew at last into a proverb, to signify idle tales; so that in the present passage it imports, that *Achilles will not listen to such idle tales as may pass with silly maids and fond lovers.* For fables and stories (and particularly such stories as the preservation, strange fortune, and adventures of exposed children) are the usual conversation of young men and maidens. *Eustathius* his explanation may be corroborated by a parallel place in the Odyssey; where the poet says,

$$Ο\mathring{υ}\ γὰρ\ ἀπὸ\ δρυὸς\ ἔσσι\ παλαιφάτου\ ο\mathring{υ}δ'\ ἀπὸ\ πέτρης.$$

The meaning of which passage is plainly this, *Tell me of what race you are, for undoubtedly you had a father and mother; you are not, according to the old story, descended from an* oak *or a* rock. Where the Word παλαιφάτου shews that this was become an ancient proverb even in *Homer*'s days.

180. *Struck by some God, he fears, recedes, and flies.*] I doubt not most readers are shock'd at the flight of *Hector*: It is indeed a high exaltation of *Achilles* (which was the poet's chief hero) that so brave a Man as *Hector* durst not stand him. While *Achilles* was at a distance he had fortified his heart with noble resolutions, but at his approach they all vanish, and he flies. This (as exceptionable as some may think it) may yet be allowed to be a true portrait of human nature; for distance, as it lessens all objects, so it does our fears: But where inevitable danger approaches, the stoutest hearts will feel some apprehensions at certain fate. It was the saying of one of the bravest men in this age, to one who told him he feared nothing, *Shew me but a certain danger, and I shall be as much afraid as any of you.* I don't absolutely pretend to justify this passage in every point, but only to have thus much granted me, that *Hector* was in this desperate circumstance.

First, It will not be found in the whole Iliad, that *Hector* ever thought himself a match for *Achilles. Homer* (to keep this in our minds) had just now made *Priam* tell him (as a thing known, for certainly *Priam* would not insult him at that time) that there was no comparison between his own strength, and that of his antagonist.

— ἐπεὶ ἦ πολὺ φέρτερός ἐστιν.

Secondly, We may observe with *Dacier*, the degrees by which *Homer* prepares this incident. In the 18th book the mere sight and voice of *Achilles* unarmed has terrified and put the whole *Trojan* army into disorder. In the 19th, the very sound of the cœlestial arms given him by *Vulcan*, has affrighted his own *Myrmidons* as they stand about him. In the 20th, he has been upon the point of killing *Æneas*, and *Hector* himself was not saved from him but by *Apollo*'s interposing. In that and the following book, he makes an incredible slaughter of all that oppose him; he overtakes most of those that fly from him, and *Priam* himself opens the gates of *Troy* to receive the rest.

Thirdly, *Hector* stays, not that he hopes to overcome *Achilles*, but because shame and the dread of reproach forbid him to re-enter the city; a shame (says *Eustathius*) which was a fault, that betray'd him out of his life, and ruined his Country. Nay, *Homer* adds farther, that he only stay'd by the immediate *will of heaven*, intoxicated and irresistibly bound down by *fate*.

Ἕκτορα δ' αὐτοῦ μεῖναι ὀλοὴ μοῖρ' ἐπέδησεν.

[Destructive fate bound Hector to remain.]

Fourthly, He had just been reflecting on the injustice of the war he maintained; his spirits are deprest by heaven, he expects certain death, he perceives himself abandon'd by the Gods; (as he directly says in v. 300, *&c.* of the *Greek*, and 385 of the translation) so that he might say to *Achilles* what *Turnus* does to *Æneas*,

Dii *me terrent*, *&* Jupiter *hostis.*

[Tis hostile heav'n I dread; and partial *Jove.*]

This indeed is the strongest reason that can be offered for the flight of *Hector*. He flies not from *Achilles* as a mortal hero, but from one whom he sees clad in impenetrable armour, seconded by *Minerva*, and one who had put to flight the inferior Gods themselves. This is not cowardice according to the constant principles of *Homer*, who thought it no part of a hero's character to be impious, or to fancy himself independent on the supreme being.

Indeed it had been a grievous fault, had our author suffer'd the courage of *Hector* entirely to forsake him even in this extremity: A brave man's soul is still capable of rouzing itself, and acting honourably in the last struggles. Accordingly *Hector*, tho' deliver'd over to his destiny, abandon'd by the Gods, and certain of death, yet stops and attacks *Achilles*; When he loses his spear, he draws his sword: It was impossible he should conquer, it was only in his power to fall gloriously; this he did, and it was all that man could do.

If the reader, after all, cannot bring himself to like this passage, for his own particular; yet to induce him to suspend his absolute censure, he may consider that *Virgil* had an uncommon esteem for it, as he has testify'd in transferring it almost entirely to the death of *Turnus*; where there was no necessity of making use of the like incidents: But doubtless he was touch'd with this Episode, as with one of those which interest us most of the whole Iliad, by a spectacle at once so terrible, and so deplorable. I must also add the suffrage of *Aristotle*, who was so far from looking upon this passage as ridiculous or blameable, that he esteem'd it marvellous and admirable. 'The *wonderful*,' says he, 'ought to have place in tragedy, but still more in epic poetry, which proceeds in this point even to the unreasonable: For as in epic poems one sees not the persons acting, so whatever passes the bounds of reason is proper to produce the admirable and the marvellous. For example, what *Homer* says of *Hector* pursued by *Achilles*, would appear ridiculous on the stage; for the spectators could not forbear laughing to see on one side the *Greeks* standing without any motion, and on the other *Achilles* pursuing *Hector*, and making signs to the troops not to dart at him. But all this does not appear when we read the poem: For what is wonderful is always agreeable, and as a proof of it, we find that they who relate any thing usually add something to the truth, that it may the better please those who hear it.'

The same great critick vindicates this passage in the chapter following. 'A poet, says he, is inexcusable if he introduces such things as are impossible according to the rules of poetry: but this ceases to be a fault, if by those means he attains to the End propos'd; for he has then brought about what he intended: For example, if he renders by it any part of his poem more astonishing or admirable. Such is the place in the Iliad, where *Achilles* pursues *Hector*.'

Arist. Poet. chap. 25, 26.

196. *Where two fam'd fountains.*] *Strabo* blames *Homer* for saying that one of the sources of *Scamander* was a warm fountain; whereas (says he) there is but one spring, and that cold, neither is this in the place where *Homer* fixes it, but in the mountain. It is observ'd by *Eustathius,* that tho' this was not true in *Strabo*'s days, yet it might in *Homer*'s, greater changes having happen'd in less time than that which pass'd between those two authors. *Sandys,* who was both a geographer and critick of great accuracy, as well as a traveller of great veracity, affirms as an eye witness, that there are yet some hot-water springs in that part of the country, opposite to *Tenedos.* I cannot but think that gentleman must have been particularly diligent and curious in his enquiries into the remains of a place so celebrated in poetry; as he was not only perhaps the most learned, but one of the best poets of his time: I am glad of this occasion to do his memory so much justice as to say, the *English* versification owes much of its improvement to his translations, and especially that admirable one of *Job.* What chiefly pleases me in this place, is to see the exact landskip of old *Troy,* we have a clear idea of the town itself, and of the roads and country about it; the river, the fig-trees, and every part is set before our eyes.

218. *The gazing Gods lean forward from the skies.*] We have here an instance of the great judgment of *Homer.* The death of *Hector* being the chief action of the poem; he assembles the Gods, and calls a council in heaven concerning it: It is for the same reason that he represents *Jupiter* with the greatest solemnity weighing in his scales the fates of the two heroes: I have before observ'd at large upon the last circumstance in a preceding note, so that there is no occasion to repeat it.

I wonder that none of the commentators have taken notice of this beauty; in my opinion it is a very necessary observation, and shews the art and judgment of the poet, that he has made the greatest and finishing action of the poem of such importance that it engages the Gods in debates.

226. *From* Ida's *Summits* –] It was the custom of the *Pagans* to sacrifice to the Gods upon the hills and mountains, in scripture language upon the *high places,* for they were persuaded that the Gods in a particular manner inhabited such eminences: Wherefore God order'd his people to destroy all those high places, which the nations had prophan'd by their idolatry. *You shall utterly destroy all the places wherein the nations which you shall possess served their Gods, upon the*

high mountains, and upon the hills, and under every green tree. Deut. xii.
2. 'Tis for this reason that so many kings are reproach'd in scripture
for not *taking away the high places.*   *Dacier.*

249. *Thus step by step,* &c.] There is some difficulty in this passage,
and it seems strange that *Achilles* could not overtake *Hector* whom he
excell'd so much in swiftness, especially when the poet describes him
as running in a narrower circle than *Hector*: *Eustathius* gives us many
solutions from the ancients: *Homer* has already told us that they run
for the life of *Hector*; and consequently *Hector* would exert his utmost
speed, whereas *Achilles* might only endeavour to keep him from entering
the city: Besides, *Achilles* could not directly pursue him, because he
frequently made efforts to shelter himself under the wall, and he being
oblig'd to turn him from it, he might be forced to take more steps than
Hector; but the poet, to take away all grounds of an objection, tells us
afterwards, that *Apollo* gave him a supernatural swiftness.

257. *As men in slumbers.*] This beautiful comparison has been condemn'd by some of the ancients, even so far as to judge it unworthy of
having a place in the Iliad: They say the diction is mean, and the
similitude itself absurd, because it compares the swiftness of the heroes
to men asleep, who are in a state of rest and inactivity. But there
cannot be a more groundless criticism: The poet is so far from drawing
his comparison from the repose of men asleep, that he alludes only to
their dreams: It is a race in fancy that he describes; and surely the
imagination is nimble enough to illustrate the greatest degree of
swiftness: Besides the verses themselves run with the utmost rapidity,
and imitate the swiftness they describe.   *Eustathius.*

What sufficiently proves these verses to be genuine, is, that *Virgil*
has imitated them, *Æn.* 12.

> *Ac veluti in somnis –*

[And as, when heavy sleep has clos'd the sight –]

269. *Sign'd to the troops,* &c.] The Difference which *Homer* here
makes between *Hector* and *Achilles* deserves to be taken notice of;
Hector is running away towards the walls, to the end that the *Trojans*
who are upon them may overwhelm *Achilles* with their darts; and
Achilles in turning *Hector* towards the plain, makes a sign to his
troops not to attack him. This shews the great courage of *Achilles.* Yet

this action which appears so generous has been very much condemned by the ancients; *Plutarch* in the life of *Pompey* gives us to understand, that it was look'd upon as the action of a fool too greedy of glory: Indeed this is not a single combat of *Achilles* against *Hector*, (for in that case *Achilles* would have done very ill not to hinder his troops from assaulting him) this was a rencounter in a battel, and so *Achilles* might, and ought to take all advantage to rid himself, the readiest and the surest way, of an enemy whose death would procure an entire victory to his party. Wherefore does he leave this victory to chance? Why expose himself to the hazard of losing it? Why does he prefer his private glory to the publick weal, and the safety of all the *Greeks*, which he puts to the venture by delaying to conquer, and endangering his own person? I grant it is a fault, but it must be own'd to be the fault of a hero.   *Eustathius. Dacier.*

277. *Then* Phœbus *left him –*] This is a very beautiful and poetical manner of describing a plain circumstance: The hour of *Hector*'s death was now come, and the poet expresses it by saying that *Apollo*, or *Destiny*, forsakes him: That is, the Fates no longer protect him.
                                              Eustathius.

Id. – Fierce Minerva *flies To stern* Pelides, &c.] The poet may seem to diminish the glory of *Achilles*, by ascribing the victory over *Hector* to the assistance of *Pallas*; whereas in truth he fell by the hand only of *Achilles*: But poetry loves to raise every thing into a wonder; it steps out of the common road of narration, and aims to surprize; and the poet would farther insinuate that it is a greater glory to *Achilles* to be belov'd by the Gods, than to be only excellent in valour: For many men have valour, but few the favour of heaven.   *Eustathius.*

290. *Obey'd and rested.*] The whole passage where *Pallas* deceives *Hector* is evidently an allegory: *Achilles* perceiving that he cannot overtake *Hector*, pretends to be quite spent and wearied in the pursuit; the stratagem takes effect, and recalls his enemy: This the poet expresses by saying that *Pallas*, or *Wisdom*, came to assist *Achilles*. *Hector* observing his enemy stay to rest concludes that he is quite fatigued, and immediately takes courage and advances upon him; he thinks he has him at an advantage, but at last finds himself deceiv'd: Thus making a wrong judgment he is betray'd into his death; so that his own *false judgment* is the *treacherous Pallas* that deceives him.
                                              Eustathius.

317. *The speeches of* Hector, *and of* Achilles.] There is an opposition between these speeches excellently adapted to the characters of both the heroes: That of *Hector* is full of courage, but mixt with Humanity: That of *Achilles*, of resentment and arrogance: We see the great *Hector* disposing of his own remains, and that thirst of glory which has made him live with honour, now bids him provide, as *Eustathius* observes, that what once was *Hector* may not be dishonour'd: Thus we see a sedate, calm courage, with a contempt of death, in the speeches of *Hector*. But in that of *Achilles* there is a *fierté*, and an insolent air of superiority; his magnanimity makes him scorn to steal a victory, he bids him prepare to defend himself with all his forces, and that valour and resentment which made him desirous that he might revenge himself upon *Hector* with his own hand, and forbade the *Greeks* to interpose, now directs him not to take any advantage over a brave enemy. I think both their characters are admirably sustain'd, and tho' *Achilles* be drawn with a great violence of features, yet the picture is undoubtedly like him; and it had been the utmost absurdity to have soften'd one line upon this occasion, when the soul of *Achilles* was all on fire to revenge the death of his friend *Patroclus*. I must desire the reader to carry this observation in his memory, and particularly in that place, where *Achilles* says he could eat the very flesh of *Hector*; (tho' I have a little soften'd it in the translation) v. 438.

391. *So* Jove's *bold bird*, &c.] The poet takes up some time in describing the two great heroes before they close in fight: The verses are pompous and magnificent, and he illustrates his description with two beautiful similes: He makes a double use of this conduct, which not only raises our imagination to attend to so momentous an action, but by lengthening his narration keeps the mind in a pleasing suspense, and divides it between hopes and fears for the fate of *Hector* or *Achilles*.

409. *Thro' that penetrable part Furious he drove*, &c.] It was necessary that the poet should be very particular in this point, because the arms that *Hector* wore, were the arms of *Achilles*, taken from *Patroclus*; and consequently, as they were the work of *Vulcan*, they would preserve *Hector* from the possibility of a wound: The poet therefore to give an air of probability to his story, tells us that they were *Patroclus* his arms, and as they were not made for *Hector*, they might not exactly fit his body: So that it is not improbable but there might be some place about the neck of *Hector* so open as to admit the spear of *Achilles.*   *Eustathius.*

437. *Could I my self the bloody banquet join!*] I have before hinted that there is something very fierce and violent in this passage; but I fancy that what I there observ'd will justify *Homer* in his relation, tho' not *Achilles* in his savage sentiments: Yet the poet softens the expression by making *Achilles* only wish that his heart would permit him to devour him: This is much more tolerable than a passage in the *Thebais* of *Statius*, where *Tydeus* in the very pangs of death is represented as gnawing the head of his enemy.

439. *Should* Troy, *to bribe me*, &c.] Such resolutions as *Achilles* here makes, are very natural to men in anger; he tells *Hector* that no motives shall ever prevail with him to suffer his body to be ransom'd; yet when time had cool'd his heat, and he had somewhat satisfy'd his revenge by insulting his remains, he restores them to *Priam.* This perfectly agrees with his conduct in the ninth book, where at first he gives a rough denial, and afterwards softens into an easier temper. And this is very agreeable to the nature of *Achilles*; his anger abates very slowly; it is stubborn, yet still it remits: Had the poet drawn him as never to be pacify'd, he had outrag'd nature, and not represented his hero as a man, but as a monster.   *Eustathius.*

449. *A day will come –]* *Hector* prophesies at his death that *Achilles* shall fall by the hand of *Paris.* This confirms an observation made in a former note, that the words of dying men were look'd upon as prophecies; but whether such conjectures are true or false, it appears from hence, that such opinions have prevail'd in the world above three thousand years.

467. *The great dead deface With wounds*, &c.] *Eustathius* tells us that *Homer* introduces the soldiers wounding the dead Body of *Hector*, in order to mitigate the cruelties which *Achilles* exercises upon it. For if every common soldier takes a pride in giving him a wound, what insults may we not expect from the inexorable, inflam'd *Achilles*? But I must confess myself unable to vindicate the 'poet in giving us such an idea of his countrymen. I think the former courage of their enemy should have been so far from moving them to revenge, that it should have recommended him to their esteem: What *Achilles* afterwards acts is suitable to his character, and consequently the poet is justify'd; but surely all the *Greeks* are not of his temper? *Patroclus* was not so dear to them all, as he was to *Achilles*. 'Tis true the poet represents *Achilles* (as *Eustathius* observes) enumerating the many ills they had suffer'd from *Hector*; and he seems to endeavour to infect the whole army with his resentment. Had *Hector* been living, they had been acted by a generous indignation against him: But these men seem as if they only dared approach him dead; in short, what they say over his body is a mean insult, and the stabs they give it are cowardly and barbarous.

474. *The speech of* Achilles.] We have a very fine observation of *Eustathius* on this place, that the judgment and address of *Homer* here is extremely worthy of remark: He knew, and had often said, that the gods and fate had not granted *Achilles* the glory of taking *Troy*: There was then no reason to make him march against the town after the death of *Hector*, since all his efforts must have been ineffectual. What has the poet done in this conjuncture? It was but reasonable that the first thought of *Achilles* should be to march directly to *Troy*, and to profit himself of the general consternation into which the death of *Hector* had thrown the *Trojans*. We here see he knows the duty, and does not want the ability, of a great General; but after this on a sudden he changes his design, and derives a plausible pretence from the impatience he has to pay the last devoirs to his friend. The manners of *Achilles*, and what he has already done for *Patroclus*, make this very natural. At the same time, this turning off to the tender and pathetic has a fine effect; the reader in the very fury of the hero's vengeance, perceives, that *Achilles* is still a man, and capable of softer passions.

494. 'Hector *is dead, and* Ilion *is no more*'.] I have follow'd the opinion of *Eustathius*, who thought that what *Achilles* says here was the chorus or burden of a song of triumph, in which his troops bear a part with him, as he returns from this glorious combate. *Dacier* observes that this is very correspondent to the manners of those times; and instances in that passage of the book of *Kings*, when *David* returns from the conquest of *Goliah*: The women there go out to meet him from all the cities of *Israel*, and sing a triumphal song, the chorus whereof is, Saul *has kill'd his thousands, and* David *his ten thousands*.

496. *Unworthy of himself, and of the dead.*] This inhumanity of *Achilles*

in dragging the dead body of *Hector*, has been severely (and I think indeed not without some justice) censur'd by several both ancients and moderns. *Plato* in his third book *de Republica*, speaks of it with detestation: But methinks it is a great injustice to *Homer* to reflect upon the morals of the author himself, for things which he only paints as the manners of a vicious hero.

It may justly be observ'd in general of all *Plato*'s objections against *Homer*, that they are still in a view to morality, constantly blaming him for representing ill and immoral things as the opinions or actions of his persons. To every one of these one general answer will serve, which is, that *Homer* as often describes ill things, in order to make us avoid them, as good, to induce us to follow them (which is the case with all writers whatever.) But what is extremely remarkable, and evidently shews the injustice of *Plato*'s censure is, that many of those very actions for which he blames him are expressly characterized and marked by *Homer* himself as evil and detestable, by previous expressions or cautions. Thus in the present place, before he describes this barbarity of *Achilles*, he tells us it was a most unworthy action.

— καὶ Ἕκτορα δῖον ἀεικέα μήδετο ἔργα.

[– and the treatment he was pondering for brilliant Hector
was disgraceful.]

When *Achilles* sacrifices the twelve young *Trojans* in l. 23. he repeats the same words. When *Pandarus* broke the Truce in l. 4. he told us it was a mad, unjust deed;

— τῷ δὲ φρένας ἄφρονι πεῖθεν.

[– he persuaded him, fool that he was.]

And so of the rest.

506. *The face divine, and long-descending hair.*] It is impossible to read the actions of great men without having our curiosity rais'd to know the least circumstance that relates to them: *Homer* to satisfy it, has taken care in the process of his poem to give us the shape of his heroes, and the very colour of their hair; thus he has told us that *Achilles*'s locks were yellow, and here the epithet Κυάνεαι shews us that those of *Hector* were of a darker colour: As to his person, he told us a little above that it was so handsome that all the *Greeks* were surpriz'd to see it. *Plutarch* recites a remarkable story of the beauty of *Hector*: It was reported in

Lacedæmon, that a handsome youth who very much resembled *Hector*, was arrived there; immediately the whole city run in such numbers to behold him, that he was trampled to death by the crowd. *Eustathius.*

543. *Sinks my sad soul with sorrow to the grave.*] It is in the *Greek*

Οὖ μ᾽ ἄχος ὀξὺ κατοίσεται Ἀϊδος εἴσω

[My piercing grief for him will catapult me to Hades.]

It is needless to observe to the reader with what a beautiful pathos the wretched father laments his son *Hector*: It is impossible not to join with *Priam* in his sorrows. But what I would chiefly point out to my reader, is the beauty of this line, which is particularly tender, and almost word for word the same with that of the Patriarch *Jacob*; who upon a like occasion breaks out into the same complaint, and tells his children, that if they deprive him of his son *Benjamin*, they will *bring down his grey hairs with sorrow to the grave.*

562, &c.] The grief of *Andromache*, which is painted in the following part, is far beyond all the praises that can be given it; but I must take notice of one particular which shews the great art of the poet. In order to make the wife of *Hector* appear yet more afflicted than his parents, he has taken care to encrease her affliction by *surprize*: It is finely prepared by the circumstances of her being retired to her innermost apartment, of her employment in weaving a robe for her husband (as may be conjectured from what she says afterward, v. 657.) and of her maids preparing the bath for his return: All which (as the criticks have observ'd) augment the surprize, and render this reverse of fortune much more dreadful and afflicting.

600. *Her hair's fair ornaments.*] *Eustathius* remarks, that in speaking of *Andromache* and *Hecuba*, *Homer* expatiates upon the ornaments of dress in *Andromache*, because she was a beautiful young princess; but is very concise about that of *Hecuba*, because she was old, and wore a dress rather suitable to her age and gravity, than to her state, birth, and condition. I cannot pass over a matter of such importance as a Lady's dress, without endeavouring to explain what sort of heads were worn above three thousand years ago.

It is difficult to describe particularly every ornament mentioned by the poet, but I shall lay before my female readers the Bishop's explanation. The Ἄμπυξ [head-band] was used, τὸ τὰς ἐμπροσθίας τρί-χας ἀναδεῖν, that is, to tie backwards the hair that grew on the forepart of the head: The Κεκρύφαλος was a veil of net-work that covered the hair when it was so ty'd; Ἀναδέσμη was an ornament used κύκλῳ περὶ τοὺς κροτάφους ἀναδεῖν, to tye backwards the hair that grew on the temples; and the Κρήδεμνον was a fillet, perhaps embroidered with gold, (from the expression of χρυσῆ Ἀφροδίτη [golden Aphrodite]) that bound the whole, and compleated the dress.

The Ladies cannot but be pleased to see so much learning and *Greek* upon this important subject.

Homer is in nothing more excellent than in that distinction of characters which he maintains thro' his whole poem: What *Andromache* here says, cannot be spoken properly by any but *Andromache*: There is nothing general in her sorrows, nothing that can be transferred to another character: The mother laments the son, and the wife weeps over the husband.

628. *The day that to the shades*, &c.] The following verses, which so finely describe the condition of an orphan, have been rejected by some ancient criticks: It is a proof there were always criticks of no manner of taste; it being impossible any where to meet with a more exquisite passage. I will venture to say, there are not in all *Homer* any lines more worthy of him: The beauty of this tender and compassionate image is such, that it even makes amends for the many cruel ones, with which the Iliad is too much stained. These censurers imagined this description to be of too abject and mean a nature for one of the quality of *Astyanax*; but had they considered (says *Eustathius*) that these are the words of a fond mother who feared every thing for her son, that women are by nature timorous and think all misfortunes will happen, because there is a possibility that they may; that *Andromache* is in the very height of her sorrows, in the instant she is speaking; I fancy they would have altered their opinion.

It is undoubtedly an aggravation to our misfortunes when they sink us in a moment from the highest flow of prosperity to the lowest adversity: The Poet judiciously makes use of this circumstance, the more to excite our pity, and introduces the mother with the utmost tenderness, lamenting this reverse of fortune in her son; chang'd all at once into a slave, a beggar, an orphan! Have we not examples in our own times of unhappy Princes, whose condition renders this of *Astyanax* but too probable?

647. *On dainties fed.*] It is in the *Greek*, 'Who upon his father's knees used to eat marrow and the fat of sheep.' This would seem gross if it were literally translated, but it is a figurative expression; in the style of the orientals, marrow and fatness are taken for whatever is best, tenderest, and most delicious. Thus in *Job* xxi. 24. *Viscera ejus plena sunt adipe & medullis ossa ejus irrigantur* ['His breasts are full of milk, and his bones are moistened with marrow' (King James version)]. And xxxvi. 16. *Requies autem mensæ tuæ erit plena pinguedine* ['That which should be set on thy table *should be* full of fatness' (King James version)]. In *Jer.* xxxi. 14. God says, that he will satiate the soul of the priests with fatness. *Inebriabo animam sacerdotum pinguedine.*

Dacier.

657. *The martial scarf and robe of triumph wove.*] This idea very naturally offers itself to a woman, who represents to herself the body of her husband dashed to pieces, and all his limbs dragged upon the ground uncovered; and nothing is more proper to excite pity. 'Tis well known that it was anciently the custom among princesses and great ladies to have large quantities of stuffs and moveables. This provision was more necessary in those times than now, because of the great consumption made of them on those occasions of mourning. *Dacier.*

I am of opinion that *Homer* had a farther view in expatiating thus largely upon the death of *Hector*. Every word that *Hecuba*, *Priam*, and *Andromache* speak, shews us the Importance of *Hector*: Every word adds a weight to the concluding action of the poem, and at the same time represents the sad effects of the anger of *Achilles*, which is the subject of it.

THE
TWENTY-THIRD BOOK
OF THE
ILIAD

The ARGUMENT

The Funeral of *Patroclus*

Achilles *and the* Myrmidons *do honours to the body of* Patroclus. *After the funeral feast he retires to the sea-shore, where falling asleep, the ghost of his friend appears to him, and demands the rites of burial; the next morning the soldiers are sent with mules and waggons to fetch wood for the pyre. The funeral procession, and the offering of their hair to the dead.* Achilles *sacrifices several animals, and lastly, twelve* Trojan *captives at the pile, then sets fire to it. He pays libations to the winds, which (at the instance of* Iris) *rise, and raise the flames. When the pile has burn'd all night, they gather the bones, place 'em in an urn of gold, and raise the tomb.* Achilles *institutes the funeral games: The chariot race, the fight of the* Cæstus, *the wrestling, the foot-race, the single combate, the* discus, *the shooting with arrows, the darting the javelin: The various descriptions of which, and the various success of the several antagonists, make the greatest part of the book.*

In this book ends the thirtieth day: The night following, the ghost of Patroclus *appears to* Achilles: *The one and thirtieth Day is employ'd in felling the timber for the pile; the two and thirtieth in burning it; and the three and thirtieth in the games. The scene is generally on the sea-shore.*

Thus humbled in the dust, the pensive train
Thro' the sad city mourn'd her hero slain.
The body soil'd with dust, and black with gore,
Lyes on broad *Hellespont*'s resounding shore:
5 The *Grecians* seek their ships, and clear the strand,
All, but the martial *Myrmidonian* band:
These yet assembled great *Achilles* holds,
And the stern purpose of his mind unfolds.
  Not yet (my brave companions of the war)
10 Release your smoaking coursers from the car;
But, with his chariot each in order led,
Perform due honours to *Patroclus* dead.
E'er yet from rest or food we seek relief,
Some rites remain, to glut our rage of grief.
15 The troops obey'd; and thrice in order led
(*Achilles* first) their coursers round the dead;
And thrice their sorrows and laments renew;
Tears bathe their arms, and tears the sands bedew.
For such a warriour *Thetis* aids their woe,
20 Melts their strong hearts, and bids their eyes to flow.
But chief, *Pelides*: thick succeeding sighs
Burst from his heart, and torrents from his eyes:
His slaught'ring hands, yet red with blood, he laid
On his dead friend's cold breast, and thus he said.
25 All hail, *Patroclus!* let thy honour'd ghost
Hear, and rejoice on *Pluto*'s dreary coast;
Behold! *Achilles'* promise is compleat;
The bloody *Hector* stretch'd before thy feet.

Lo! to the dogs his carcass I resign;
And twelve sad victims of the *Trojan* line   30
Sacred to vengeance, instant shall expire,
Their lives effus'd around thy fun'ral pyre.
   Gloomy he said, and (horrible to view)
Before the bier the bleeding *Hector* threw,
Prone on the dust. The *Myrmidons* around   35
Unbrac'd their armour, and the steeds unbound.
All to *Achilles'* sable ship repair,
Frequent and full, the genial feast to share.
Now from the well-fed swine black Smoakes aspire,
The bristly victims hissing o'er the fire: 40
The huge ox bellowing falls; with feebler cries
Expires the goat; the sheep in silence dies.
Around the hero's prostrate body flow'd
In one promiscuous stream, the reeking blood.
And now a band of *Argive* monarchs brings   45
The glorious victor to the king of kings.
From his dead friend the pensive warriour went,
With steps unwilling, to the regal tent.
Th'attending heralds, as by office bound,
With kindled flames the tripod-vase surround;   50
To cleanse his conqu'ring hands from hostile gore,
They urg'd in vain; the chief refus'd, and swore.
   No drop shall touch me, by almighty *Jove!*
The first and greatest of the Gods above!
Till on the pyre I place thee; till I rear   55
The grassy mound, and clip thy sacred hair.
Some ease at least those pious rites may give,
And sooth my sorrows, while I bear to live.
Howe'er, reluctant as I am, I stay,
And share your feast; but, with the dawn of day,   60
(O King of men!) it claims thy royal care,
That *Greece* the warriour's fun'ral pile prepare,
And bid the forests fall: (Such rites are paid
To heroes slumb'ring in eternal shade)
Then, when his earthly part shall mount in fire,   65
Let the leagu'd squadrons to their posts retire.
   He spoke; they hear him, and the word obey;
The rage of hunger and of thirst allay,
Then ease in sleep the labours of the day.

70 But great *Pelides*, stretch'd along the shore
Where dash'd on rocks the broken billows roar,
Lies inly groaning; while on either hand
The martial *Myrmidons* confus'dly stand:
Along the grass his languid members fall,
75 Tir'd with his chase around the *Trojan* wall;
Hush'd by the murmurs of the rolling deep,
At length he sinks in the soft arms of sleep.
When lo! the shade before his closing eyes
Of sad *Patroclus* rose, or seem'd to rise;
80 In the same robe he living wore, he came,
In stature, voice, and pleasing look, the same.
The form familiar hover'd o'er his head,
And sleeps *Achilles* (thus the phantom said)
Sleeps my *Achilles*, his *Patroclus* dead?
85 Living, I seem'd his dearest, tend'rest care,
But now forgot, I wander in the air;
Let my pale corse the rites of burial know,
And give me entrance in the realms below:
Till then, the spirit finds no resting place,
90 But here and there th' unbody'd spectres chace
The vagrant dead around the dark abode,
Forbid to cross th' irremeable flood.
Now give thy hand; for to the farther shore
When once we pass, the soul returns no more.
95 When once the last funereal flames ascend,
No more shall meet *Achilles* and his friend,
No more our thoughts to those we lov'd make known,
Or quit the dearest, to converse alone.
Me fate has sever'd from the sons of earth,
100 The fate fore-doom'd that waited from my birth:
There too it waits; before the *Trojan* wall
Ev'n great and godlike thou art doom'd to fall.
Hear then; and as in fate and love we join,
Ah suffer that my bones may rest with thine!
105 Together have we liv'd, together bred,
One house receiv'd us, and one table fed;
That golden urn thy goddess mother gave
May mix our ashes in one common grave.
      And is it thou? (he answers) to my sight
110 Once more return'st thou from the realms of night?

Oh more than brother! Think each office paid,
Whate'er can rest a discontented shade;
But grant one last embrace, unhappy boy!
Afford at least that melancholy joy.
    He said, and with his longing arms essay'd   115
In vain to grasp the visionary shade;
Like a thin smoak he sees the spirit fly,
And hears a feeble, lamentable cry.
Confus'd he wakes; amazement breaks the bands
Of golden sleep, and starting from the sands,   120
Pensive he muses with uplifted hands.
    'Tis true, 'tis certain; man, tho' dead, retains
Part of himself; th'immortal mind remains:
The form subsists, without the body's aid,
Aerial semblance, and an empty shade!   125
This night my friend, so late in battel lost,
Stood at my side, a pensive, plaintive ghost;
Ev'n now familiar, as in life, he came,
Alas! how diff'rent! yet how like the same!
    Thus while he spoke, each eye grew big with tears: 130
And now the rosy-finger'd morn appears,
Shews every mournful face with tears o'erspread,
And glares on the pale visage of the dead.
But *Agamemnon*, as the rites demand,
With mules and waggons sends a chosen band;   135
To load the timber, and the pile to rear,
A charge consign'd to *Merion*'s faithful care.
With proper instruments they take the road,
Axes to cut, and ropes to sling the load.
First march the heavy mules, securely slow,   140
O'er hills, o'er dales, o'er crags, o'er rocks they go:
Jumping high o'er the shrubs of the rough ground,
Rattle the clatt'ring cars, and the shockt axles bound.
But when arriv'd at *Ida*'s spreading woods,   145
(Fair *Ida*, water'd with descending floods)
Loud sounds the axe, redoubling strokes on strokes;
On all sides round the forest hurles her oaks
Headlong. Deep-echoing groan the thickets brown;
Then rustling, crackling, crashing, thunder down.
The wood the *Grecians* cleave, prepar'd to burn;   150
And the slow mules the same rough road return.

The sturdy woodmen equal burthens bore
(Such charge was giv'n 'em) to the sandy shore;
There on the spot which great *Achilles* show'd,
155 They eas'd their shoulders, and dispos'd the load;
Circling around the place, where times to come
Shall view *Patroclus'* and *Achilles'* tomb.
The hero bids his martial troops appear
High in their cars in all the pomp of war;
160 Each in refulgent arms his limbs attires,
All mount their chariots, combatants and squires.
The chariots first proceed, a shining train;
Then clouds of foot that smoak along the plain;
Next these a melancholy band appear,
165 Amidst, lay dead *Patroclus* on the bier:
O'er all the corse their scatter'd locks they throw;
Achilles next, opprest with mighty woe,
Supporting with his hands the hero's head,
Bends o'er th'extended body of the dead.
170 *Patroclus* decent on th'appointed ground
They place and heap the sylvan pile around.
But great *Achilles* stands apart in pray'r,
And from his head divides the yellow hair;
Those curling locks which from his youth he vow'd,
175 And sacred grew to *Sperchius'* honour'd flood:
Then sighing, to the deep his looks he cast,
And roll'd his eyes around the wat'ry waste.
   Sperchius! whose waves in mazy errours lost
Delightful roll along my native coast!
180 To whom we vainly vow'd, at our return,
These locks to fall, and hecatombs to burn:
Full fifty rams to bleed in sacrifice,
Where to the day thy silver fountains rise,
And where in shade of consecrated bow'rs
185 Thy altars stand, perfum'd with native flow'rs!
So vow'd my father, but he vow'd in vain;
No more *Achilles* sees his native plain;
In that vain hope these hairs no longer grow,
Patroclus bears them to the shades below.
190   Thus o'er *Patroclus* while the hero pray'd,
On his cold hand the sacred lock he laid.

Once more afresh the *Grecian* sorrows flow:
And now the sun had set upon their woe;
But to the King of Men thus spoke the chief.
Enough, *Atrides!* give the troops relief: 195
Permit the mourning legions to retire,
And let the chiefs alone attend the pyre;
The pious care be ours, the dead to burn –
He said: The people to their ships return:
While those deputed to inter the slain   200
Heap with a rising pyramid the plain.
A hundred foot in length, a hundred wide,
The growing structure spreads on ev'ry side;
High on the top the manly corse they lay,
And well-fed sheep, and sable oxen slay: 205
Achilles cover'd with their fat the dead,
And the pil'd victims round the body spread.
Then jars of honey, and of fragrant oil
Suspends around, low-bending o'er the pile.
Four sprightly coursers, with a deadly groan   210
Pour forth their lives, and on the pyre are thrown.
Of nine large dogs, domestick at his board,
Fall two, selected to attend their lord.
Then last of all, and horrible to tell,
Sad sacrifice! twelve *Trojan* captives fell.   215
On these the rage of fire victorious preys,
Involves and joins them in one common blaze.
Smear'd with the bloody rites, he stands on high,
And calls the spirit with a dreadful cry.

   All hail, *Patroclus!* let thy vengeful ghost   220
Hear, and exult on *Pluto*'s dreary coast.
Behold, *Achilles'* promise fully paid,
Twelve *Trojan* heroes offer'd to thy shade;
But heavier fates on *Hector*'s corse attend,
Sav'd from the flames, for hungry dogs to rend.   225
   So spake he, threat'ning: But the Gods made vain
His threat, and guard inviolate the slain:
Celestial *Venus* hover'd o'er his head,
And roseate unguents, heav'nly fragrance! shed:
She watch'd him all the night, and all the day,   230
And drove the bloodhounds from their destin'd prey.

Nor sacred *Phœbus* less employ'd his care;
He pour'd around a veil of gather'd air,
And kept the nerves undry'd, the flesh entire,
235 Against the solar beam and *Sirian* fire.
     Nor yet the pile where dead *Patroclus* lies,
Smokes, nor as yet the sullen flames arise;
But fast beside *Achilles* stood in pray'r,
Invok'd the Gods whose spirit moves the air,
240 And victims promis'd, and libations cast,
To gentle *Zephyr* and the *Boreal* blast:
He call'd th' aerial pow'rs, along the skies
To breathe, and whisper to the fires to rise.
The winged *Iris* heard the hero's call,
245 And instant hasten'd to their airy hall,
Where, in old *Zephyr*'s open courts on high,
Sate all the blustring brethren of the sky.
She shone amidst them, on her painted bow;
The rocky pavement glitter'd with the show.
250 All from the banquet rise, and each invites
The various goddess to partake the rites.
Not so, (the dame reply'd) I haste to go
To sacred Ocean, and the floods below:
Ev'n now our solemn hecatombs attend,
255 And heav'n is feasting on the world's green end,
With righteous *Æthiops* (uncorrupted train!)
Far on th' extreamest limits of the main.
But *Peleus'* son intreats, with sacrifice,
The *Western Spirit*, and the *North* to rise;
260 Let on *Patroclus'* pile your blast be driv'n,
And bear the blazing honours high to heav'n.
     Swift as the word, she vanish'd from their view;
Swift as the word, the *Winds* tumultuous flew;
Forth burst the stormy band with thund'ring roar,
265 And heaps on heaps the clouds are tost before.
To the wide main then stooping from the skies,
The heaving deeps in watry mountains rise:
Troy feels the blast along her shaking walls,
Till on the pyle the gather'd tempest falls.
270 The structure crackles in the roaring fires,
And all the night the plenteous flame aspires.

All Night *Achilles* hails *Patroclus'* soul,
With large libation from the golden bowl.
As a poor father, helpless and undone,
Mourns o'er the ashes of an only son,   275
Takes a sad pleasure the last bones to burn,
And pour in tears, e'er yet they close the urn:
So stay'd *Achilles*, circling round the shore,
So watch'd the flames, till now they flame no more.
'Twas when, emerging thro' the shades of night,   280
The morning planet told th' approach of light;
And fast behind, *Aurora*'s warmer ray
O'er the broad ocean pour'd the golden day:
Then sunk the blaze, the pyle no longer burn'd,
And to their caves the whistling winds return'd: 285
Across the *Thracian* seas their course they bore;
The ruffled seas beneath their passage roar.
Then parting from the pyle he ceas'd to weep,
And sunk to quiet in th' embrace of sleep,
Exhausted with his grief: Meanwhile the crowd   290
Of thronging *Grecians* round *Achilles* stood;
The tumult wak'd him: From his eyes he shook
Unwilling slumber, and the chiefs bespoke.
  Ye Kings and Princes of th' *Achaian* name!
First let us quench the yet remaining flame   295
With sable wine; then, (as the rites direct,)
The hero's bones with careful view select:
(Apart, and easy to be known they lie,
Amidst the heap, and obvious to the eye:
The rest around the margins will be seen,   300
Promiscuous, steeds, and immolated men)
These wrapt in double cawls of fat, prepare;
And in the golden vase dispose with care;
There let them rest, with decent honour laid,
Till I shall follow to th' infernal shade.   305
Meantime erect the tomb with pious hands,
A common structure on the humble sands;
Hereafter *Greece* some nobler work may raise,
And late posterity record our praise.
  The *Greeks* obey; where yet the embers glow   310
Wide o'er the pile the sable wine they throw,
And deep subsides the ashy heap below.

Next the white bones his sad companions place
With tears collected, in the golden vase.
315   The sacred relicks to the tent they bore;
The urn a veil of linen cover'd o'er.
That done, they bid the sepulchre aspire,
And cast the deep foundations round the pyre;
High in the midst they heap the swelling bed
320   Of rising earth, memorial of the dead.
      The swarming populace the Chief detains,
And leads amidst a wide extent of plains;
There plac'd 'em round: Then from the ships proceeds
A train of oxen, mules, and stately steeds,
325   Vases and tripods, for the fun'ral games,
Resplendent brass, and more resplendent dames.
First stood the prizes to reward the force
Of rapid racers in the dusty course.
A woman for the first, in beauty's bloom,
330   Skill'd in the needle, and the lab'ring loom;
And a large vase, where two bright handles rise,
Of twenty measures its capacious size.
The second victor claims a mare uṅbroke,
Big with a mule, unknowing of the yoke;
335   The third, a charger yet untouch'd by flame;
Four ample measures held the shining frame:
Two golden talents for the fourth were plac'd;
An ample double bowl contents the last.
These in fair order rang'd upon the plain,
340   The hero, rising, thus addrest the train.
      Behold the prizes, valiant *Greeks!* decreed
To the brave rulers of the racing steed;
Prizes which none beside our self could gain,
Should our immortal coursers take the plain;
345   (A race unrival'd, which from Ocean's God
Peleus receiv'd, and on his son bestow'd.)
But this no time our vigour to display,
Nor suit, with them, the games of this sad day:
Lost is *Patroclus* now, that wont to deck
350   Their flowing manes, and sleek their glossy neck.
Sad, as they shar'd in human grief, they stand,
And trail those graceful honours on the sand!

Let others for the noble task prepare,
Who trust the courser, and the flying car.
   Fir'd at his word, the rival racers rise;   355
But far the first, *Eumelus* hopes the prize,
Fam'd thro' *Pieria* for the fleetest breed,
And skill'd to manage the high-bounding steed.
With equal ardour bold *Tydides* swell'd
The steeds of *Tros* beneath his Yoke compell'd,   360
(Which late obey'd the *Dardan* chief's command,
When scarce a God redeem'd him from his hand)
Then *Menelaüs* his *Podargus* brings,
And the fam'd courser of the King of Kings:
Whom rich *Echepolus*, (more rich than brave)   365
To 'scape the wars, to *Agamemnon* gave,
(*Æthe* her Name) at home to end his days,
Base wealth preferring to eternal praise.
Next him *Antilochus* demands the course,
With beating heart, and chears his *Pylian* horse.   370
Experienc'd *Nestor* gives his son the reins,
Directs his judgment, and his heat restrains;
Nor idly warns the hoary sire, nor hears
The prudent son with unattending ears.
   My son! tho' youthful ardour fire thy breast,   375
The Gods have lov'd thee, and with arts have blest.
Neptune and *Jove* on thee conferr'd the skill,
Swift round the goal to turn the flying wheel.
To guide thy conduct, little precept needs;
But slow, and past their vigour, are my steeds.   380
Fear not thy rivals, tho' for swiftness known,
Compare those rivals judgment, and thy own:
It is not strength, but art, obtains the prize,
And to be swift is less than to be wise:
'Tis more by art, than force of num'rous strokes,   385
The dext'rous woodman shapes the stubborn oaks;
By Art the Pilot, thro' the boiling deep
And howling tempest, stears the fearless ship;
And 'tis the artist wins the glorious course,
Not those, who trust in chariots and in horse.   390
In vain unskilfull to the goal they strive,
And short, or wide, th' ungovern'd courser drive:

While with sure skill, tho' with inferior steeds,
The knowing racer to his end proceeds;
395   Fix'd on the goal his eye fore-runs the course,
His hand unerring steers the steady horse,
And now contracts, or now extends the rein,
Observing still the foremost on the plain.
Mark then the goal, 'tis easy to be found;
400   Yon' aged trunk, a cubit from the ground;
Of some once stately oak the last remains,
Or hardy fir, unperish'd with the rains.
Inclos'd with stones conspicuous from afar,
And round, a circle for the wheeling car.
405   (Some tomb perhaps of old, the dead to grace;
Or then, as now, the limit of a race)
Bear close to this, and warily proceed,
A little bending to the left hand steed;
But urge the right, and give him all the reins;
410   While thy strict hand his fellow's head restrains,
And turns him short; till, doubling as they roll,
The wheel's round naves appear to brush the goal.
Yet (not to break the car, or lame the horse)
Clear of the stony heap direct the course;
415   Lest thro' incaution failing, thou may'st be
A joy to others, a reproach to me.
So shalt thou pass the goal, secure of mind,
And leave unskilful swiftness far behind.
Tho' thy fierce rival drove the matchless steed
420   Which bore *Adrastus*, of celestial breed;
Or the fam'd race thro' all the regions known,
That whirl'd the car of proud *Laomedon.*
    Thus, (nought unsaid) the much-advising sage
Concludes; then sate, stiff with unwieldy age.
425   Next bold *Meriones* was seen to rise,
The last, but not least ardent for the prize.
They mount their seats; the lots their place dispose;
(Roll'd in his helmet, these *Achilles* throws.)
Young *Nestor* leads the race: *Eumelus* then;
430   And next the brother of the King of men:
Thy lot, *Meriones*, the fourth was cast;
And far the bravest, *Diomed*, was last.

They stand in order, an impatient Train;
Pelides points the barrier on the plain,
And sends before old *Phœnix* to the place,   435
To mark the racers, and to judge the race.
At once the coursers from the barrier bound;
The lifted scourges all at once resound;
Their heart, their eyes, their voice, they send before;
And up the champain thunder from the shore: 440
Thick, where they drive, the dusty clouds arise,
And the lost courser in the whirlwind flies;
Loose on their shoulders the long manes reclin'd,
Float in their speed, and dance upon the wind:
The smoaking chariots, rapid as they bound,   445
Now seem to touch the sky, and now the ground.
While hot for fame, and conquest all their care,
(Each o'er his flying courser hung in air)
Erect with ardour, pois'd upon the rein,
They pant, they stretch, they shout along the plain.   450
Now, (the last compass fetch'd around the goal)
At the near prize each gathers all his soul,
Each burns with double hope, with double pain,
Tears up the shore, and thunders tow'rd the main.
First flew *Eumelus* on *Pheretian* steeds;   455
With those of *Tros*, bold *Diomed* succeeds:
Close on *Eumelus'* back they puff the wind,
And seem just mounting on his car behind;
Full on his neck he feels the sultry breeze,
And hov'ring o'er, their stretching shadows sees.   460
Then had he lost, or left a doubtful prize;
But angry *Phœbus* to *Tydides* flies,
Strikes from his hand the scourge, and renders vain
His matchless horses labour on the plain.
Rage fills his eye with anguish, to survey   465
Snatch'd from his hope, the glories of the day.
The fraud celestial *Pallas* sees with pain,
Springs to her Knight, and gives the scourge again,
And fills his steeds with vigour. At a stroke,
She breaks his rival's chariot from the yoke;   470
No more their way the startled horses held;
The car revers'd came rat'ling on the field;

Shot headlong from his seat, beside the wheel,
Prone on the dust th' unhappy master fell;
His batter'd face and elbows strike the ground;
Nose, mouth and front, one undistinguish'd wound:
Grief stops his voice, a torrent drowns his eyes;
Before him far the glad *Tydides* flies;
Minerva's spirit drives his matchless pace,
And crowns him victor of the labour'd race.

   The next, tho' distant, *Menelaüs* succeeds;
While thus young *Nestor* animates his steeds.
Now, now, my gen'rous pair, exert your force;
Not that we hope to match *Tydides'* horse,
Since great *Minerva* wings their rapid way,
And gives their Lord the honours of the day.
But reach *Atrides!* Shall his mare out-go
Your swiftness? vanquish'd by a female foe?
Thro' your neglect, if lagging on the plain
The last ignoble gift be all we gain;
No more shall *Nestor*'s hand your food supply,
The old man's fury rises, and ye die.
Haste then; yon' narrow road before our sight
Presents th' occasion, could we use it right.

   Thus he. The coursers at their master's threat
With quicker steps the sounding champain beat.
And now *Antilochus* with nice survey,
Observes the compass of the hollow way.
'Twas where by force of wintry torrents torn,
Fast by the road a precipice was worn:
Here, where but one could pass, to shun the throng
The *Spartan* hero's chariot smoak'd along.
Close up the vent'rous youth resolves to keep,
Still edging near, and bears him tow'rd the steep.
Atrides, trembling casts his eye below,
And wonders at the rashness of his foe.
Hold, stay your steeds — What madness thus to ride
This narrow way? Take larger field (he cry'd)
Or both must fall — *Atrides* cry'd in vain;
He flies more fast, and throws up all the rein.
Far as an able arm the disk can send,
When youthful rivals their full force extend,

So far *Antilochus!* thy chariot flew
Before the King: He, cautious, backward drew
His horse compell'd; foreboding in his fears   515
The rattling ruin of the clashing cars,
The flound'ring coursers rolling on the plain,
And conquest lost thro' frantick haste to gain.
But thus upbraids his rival as he flies;
Go, furious youth! ungen'rous and unwise!   520
Go, but expect not I'll the prize resign;
Add perjury to fraud, and make it thine. –
Then to his steeds with all his force he cries;
Be swift, be vig'rous, and regain the prize!
Your rivals, destitute of youthful force,   525
With fainting knees shall labour in the course,
And yield the glory yours – The steeds obey;
Already at their heels they wing their way,
And seem already to retrieve the day.
    Meantime the *Grecians* in a ring beheld   530
The coursers bounding o'er the dusty field.
The first who mark'd them was the *Cretan* King;
High on a rising ground, above the ring,
The Monarch sate; from whence with sure survey
He well observ'd the chief who led the way,   535
And heard from far his animating cries,
And saw the foremost steed with sharpen'd eyes;
On whose broad front a blaze of shining white,
Like the full moon, stood obvious to the sight.
He saw; and rising, to the *Greeks* begun.   540
Are yonder horse discern'd by me alone?
Or can ye, all, another chief survey,
And other steeds, than lately led the way?
Those, tho' the swiftest, by some God with-held,
Lie sure disabled in the middle field: 545
For since the goal they doubled, round the plain
I search to find them, but I search in vain.
Perchance the reins forsook the driver's hand,
And, turn'd too short, he tumbled on the strand,
Shot from the chariot; while his coursers stray   550
With frantick fury from the destin'd way.

Rise then some other, and inform my sight,
(For these dim Eyes, perhaps, discern not right)
Yet sure he seems, (to judge by shape and air,)
555　The great *Ætolian* chief, renown'd in war.
　　Old man! (*Oileus* rashly thus replies)
Thy tongue too hastily confers the prize.
Of those who view the course, not sharpest ey'd,
Nor youngest, yet the readiest to decide.
560　*Eumelus'* steeds high-bounding in the chace,
Still, as at first, unrivall'd lead the race:
I well discern him, as he shakes the rein,
And hear his shouts victorious o'er the plain.
　　Thus he. *Idomeneus* incens'd rejoin'd.
565　Barb'rous of words! and arrogant of mind!
Contentious Prince! of all the *Greeks* beside
The last in merit, as the first in pride.
To vile reproach what answer can we make?
A goblet or a tripod let us stake,
570　And be the King the Judge. The most unwise
Will learn their rashness, when they pay the price.
　　He said: and *Ajax* by mad passion born,
Stern had reply'd; fierce scorn inhancing scorn
To fell extreams. But *Thetis'* god-like son
575　Awful amidst them rose; and thus begun.
　　Forbear, ye chiefs! reproachful to contend;
Much would ye blame, should others thus offend:
And lo! th'approaching steeds your contest end.
No sooner had he spoke, but thund'ring near
580　Drives, thro' a stream of dust, the charioteer;
High o'er his head the circling lash he wields;
His bounding horses scarcely touch the fields:
His car amidst the dusty whirlwind roll'd,
Bright with the mingled blaze of tin and gold;
585　Refulgent thro' the cloud: no Eye could find
The track his flying wheels had left behind:
And the fierce coursers urg'd their rapid pace
So swift, it seem'd a flight, and not a race.
Now victor at the goal *Tydides* stands,
590　Quits his bright car, and springs upon the sands;

From the hot steeds the sweaty torrents stream;
The well-ply'd whip is hung athwart the beam:
With joy brave *Sthenelus* receives the prize,
The tripod-vase, and dame with radiant eyes:
These to the ships his train triumphant leads,   595
The chief himself unyokes the panting steeds.
    Young *Nestor* follows (who by art, not force,
O'er-past *Atrides*) second in the course.
Behind, *Atrides* urg'd the race, more near
Than to the courser in his swift career   600
The following car, just touching with his heel
And brushing with his tail the whirling wheel.
Such, and so narrow now the space between
The rivals, late so distant on the green;
So soon swift *Æthe* her lost ground regain'd,   605
One length, one moment had the race obtain'd.
    Merion pursu'd, at greater distance still,
With tardier coursers, and inferior skill.
Last came, *Admetus!* thy unhappy son;
Slow dragg'd the steeds his batter'd chariot on: 610
Achilles saw, and pitying thus begun.
    Behold! the man whose matchless art surpast
The sons of *Greece!* the ablest, yet the last!
Fortune denies, but justice bids us pay
(Since great *Tydides* bears the first away)   615
To him, the second honours of the day.
    The *Greeks* consent with loud applauding cries,
And then *Eumelus* had receiv'd the prize,
But youthful *Nestor*, jealous of his fame,
Th' award opposes, and asserts his claim.   620
Think not (he cries) I tamely will resign
O *Peleus* son! the mare so justly mine.
What if the Gods, the skilful to confound,
Have thrown the horse and horseman to the ground?
Perhaps he sought not heav'n by sacrifice,   625
And vows omitted forfeited the prize.
If yet, (distinction to thy friend to show,
And please a soul desirous to bestow,)
Some gift must grace *Eumelus*; view thy store
Of beauteous handmaids, steeds, and shining ore.   630

An ample present let him thence receive,
And *Greece* shall praise thy gen'rous thirst to give.
But this, my prize, I never shall forego;
This, who but touches, warriours! is my foe.
635   Thus spake the youth, nor did his words offend;
Pleas'd with the well-turn'd flattery of a friend,
Achilles smil'd: The gift propos'd (he cry'd)
Antilochus! we shall our self provide.
With plates of brass the corselet cover'd o'er,
640   (The same renown'd *Asteropæus* wore)
Whose glitt'ring margins rais'd with silver shine;
(No vulgar gift) *Eumelus*, shall be thine.
    He said: *Automedon* at his command
The corselet brought, and gave it to his hand.
645   Distinguish'd by his friend, his bosom glows
With gen'rous joy: Then *Menelaüs* rose;
The herald plac'd the sceptre in his hands,
And still'd the clamour of the shouting bands.
Not without cause incens'd at *Nestor*'s son,
650   And inly grieving, thus the King begun:
    The praise of wisdom, in thy youth obtain'd,
An act so rash (*Antilochus*) has stain'd.
Robb'd of my glory and my just reward,
To you O *Grecians!* be my wrong declar'd:
655   So not a leader shall our conduct blame,
Or judge me envious of a rival's fame.
But shall not we, ourselves, the truth maintain?
What needs appealing in a fact so plain?
What *Greek* shall blame me, if I bid thee rise,
660   And vindicate by oath th' ill-gotten prize.
Rise if thou dar'st, before thy chariot stand,
The driving scourge high-lifted in thy hand,
And touch thy steeds, and swear, thy whole intent
Was but to conquer, not to circumvent.
665   Swear by that God whose liquid arms surround
The globe, and whose dread earthquakes heave the
      ground.
    The prudent chief with calm attention heard;
Then mildly thus: Excuse, if youth have err'd;

Superiour as thou art, forgive th' offence,
Nor I thy equal, or in years, or sense.   670
Thou know'st the errours of unripen'd age,
Weak are its counsels, headlong is its rage.
The Prize I quit, if thou thy wrath resign;
The mare, or ought thou ask'st, be freely thine,
E'er I become (from thy dear friendship torn)   675
Hateful to thee, and to the Gods forsworn.
    So spoke *Antilochus*; and at the word
The mare contested to the King restor'd.
Joy swells his soul, as when the vernal grain
Lifts the green ear above the springing plain,   680
The fields their vegetable life renew,
And laugh and glitter with the morning dew;
Such joy the *Spartan*'s shining face o'erspread,
And lifted his gay heart, while thus he said.
    Still may our souls, O gen'rous Youth! agree,   685
'Tis now *Atrides*' turn to yield to thee.
Rash heat perhaps a moment might controul,
Not break, the settled temper of thy soul.
Not but (my friend) 'tis still the wiser way
To wave contention with superiour sway;   690
For ah! how few, who should like thee offend,
Like thee, have talents to regain the friend?
To plead indulgence and thy fault attone,
Suffice thy father's merits, and thy own:
Gen'rous alike, for me, the sire and son   695
Have greatly suffer'd, and have greatly done.
I yield; that all may know, my soul can bend,
Nor is my pride preferr'd before my friend.
    He said; and pleas'd his passion to command,
Resign'd the courser to *Noëmon*'s hand,   700
Friend of the youthful chief: Himself content,
The shining charger to his vessel sent.
The golden talents *Merion* next obtain'd;
The fifth reward, the double bowl, remain'd.
Achilles this to rev'rend *Nestor* bears,   705
And thus the purpose of his gift declares.
    Accept thou this, O sacred sire! (he said)
In dear memorial of *Patroclus* dead;

Dead, and for ever lost *Patroclus* lies,
710   For ever snatch'd from our desiring eyes!
Take thou this token of a grateful heart,
Tho' 'tis not thine to hurl the distant dart,
The quoit to toss, the pond'rous mace to wield,
Or urge the race, or wrestle on the field.
715   Thy present vigour age has overthrown,
But left the glory of the past thy own.
    He said, and plac'd the goblet at his side;
With joy, the venerable King reply'd.
    Wisely and well, my son, thy words have prov'd
720   A senior honour'd, and a friend belov'd!
Too true it is, deserted of my strength,
These wither'd arms and limbs have fail'd at length.
Oh! had I now that force I felt of yore,
Known thro' *Buprasium* and the *Pylian* shore!
725   Victorious then in ev'ry solemn game
Ordain'd to *Amarynces'* mighty name;
The brave *Epeians* gave my glory way,
Ætolians, *Pylians*, all resign'd the day.
I quell'd *Clytomedes* in fights of hand,
730   And backward hurl'd *Ancæus* on the sand,
Surpast *Iphyclus* in the swift career,
Phyleus and *Polydorus*, with the spear.
The sons of *Actor* won the prize of horse,
But won by numbers, not by art or force:
735   For the fam'd twins, impatient to survey,
Prize after prize by *Nestor* born away,
Sprung to their car; and with united pains
One lash'd the coursers, while one rul'd the reins.
Such once I was! Now to these tasks succeeds
740   A younger race, that emulate our deeds:
I yield alas! (to age who must not yield?)
Tho' once the foremost hero of the field.
Go thou, my son! by gen'rous friendship led,
With martial honours decorate the dead;
745   While pleas'd I take the gift thy hands present,
(Pledge of benevolence, and kind intent)
Rejoic'd, of all the num'rous *Greeks*, to see
Not one but honours sacred age and me:

Those due distinctions thou so well can'st pay,
May the just Gods return another day.　　　　　　750
　Proud of the gift, thus spake the full of days:
Achilles heard him, prouder of the praise.
　The prizes next are order'd to the field
For the bold champions who the *Cæstus* wield.
A stately mule, as yet by toils unbroke,　　　　755
Of six years age, unconscious of the yoke,
Is to the *Circus* led, and firmly bound;
Next stands a goblet, massy, large and round.
Achilles rising, thus: Let *Greece* excite
Two heroes equal to this hardy fight;　　　　　760
Who dares his foe with lifted arms provoke,
And rush beneath the long-descending stroke?
On whom *Apollo* shall the palm bestow,
And whom the *Greeks* supreme by conquest know,
This mule his dauntless labours shall repay;　　765
The vanquish'd bear the massy bowl away.
　This dreadful combate great *Epæus* chose,
High o'er the crowd, enormous bulk! he rose,
And seiz'd the beast, and thus began to say:
Stand forth some man, to bear the bowl away!　770
(Price of his ruin:) For who dares deny
This mule my right? th'undoubted victor I.
Others, 'tis own'd, in fields of battle shine,
But the first honours of this fight are mine;
For who excells in all? Then let my foe　　　　775
Draw near, but first his certain fortune know,
Secure, this hand shall his whole frame confound,
Mash all his bones, and all his body pound:
So let his friends be nigh, a needful train
To heave the batter'd carcase off the plain.　　780
　The Giant spoke; and in a stupid gaze
The Host beheld him, silent with amaze!
'Twas thou, *Euryalus!* who durst aspire
To meet his might, and emulate thy sire,
The great *Mecistheus*; who in days of yore　　785
In *Theban* games the noblest trophy bore,
(The games ordain'd dead *Oedipus* to grace)
And singly vanquish'd the *Cadmæan* race.

Him great *Tydides* urges to contend,
790   Warm with the hopes of conquest for his friend,
Officious with the cincture girds him round;
And to his wrists the gloves of death are bound.
Amid the circle now each champion stands,
And poises high in air his iron hands;
795   With clashing gantlets now they fiercely close,
Their crackling jaws re-echoe to the blows,
And painful sweat from all their members flows.
At length *Epëus* dealt a weighty blow,
Full on the cheek of his unwary foe;
800   Beneath that pond'rous arm's resistless sway
Down dropt he, nerveless, and extended lay.
As a large fish, when winds and Waters roar,
By some huge billow dash'd against the shore,
Lies panting: Not less batter'd with his wound,
805   The bleeding hero pants upon the ground.
To rear his fallen foe, the victor lends
Scornful, his hand; and gives him to his friends;
Whose arms support him, reeling thro' the throng,
And dragging his disabled legs along;
810   Nodding, his head hangs down his shoulder o'er;
His mouth and nostrils pour the clotted gore;
Wrapt round in mists he lies, and lost to thought;
His friends receive the bowl, too dearly bought.
The third bold game *Achilles* next demands,
815   And calls the wrestlers to the level sands:
A massy tripod for the victor lies,
Of twice six oxen its reputed price;
And next, the losers spirits to restore,
A female captive, valu'd but at four.
820   Scarce did the chief the vig'rous strife propose,
When tow'r-like *Ajax* and *Ulysses* rose.
Amid the ring each nervous rival stands,
Embracing rigid with implicit hands:
Close lock'd above, their heads and arms are mixt;
825   Below, their planted feet at distance fixt:
Like two strong rafters which the builder forms
Proof to the wintry winds and howling storms,

Their tops connected, but at wider space
Fixt on the center stands their solid base.
Now to the grasp each manly body bends;   830
The humid sweat from ev'ry pore descends;
Their bones resound with blows: sides, shoulders, thighs
Swell to each gripe, and bloody tumours rise.
Nor could *Ulysses*, for his art renown'd,
O'erturn the strength of *Ajax* on the ground;   835
Nor could the strength of *Ajax* overthrow
The watchful caution of his artful foe.
While the long strife ev'n tir'd the lookers-on,
Thus to *Ulysses* spoke great *Telamon.*
Or let me lift thee, Chief, or lift thou me: 870
Prove we our force, and *Jove* the rest decree.
   He said; and straining, heav'd him off the ground
With matchless strength; that time *Ulysses* found
The strength t' evade, and where the nerves combine,
His ankle strook: The giant fell supine: 845
Ulysses following, on his bosom lies;
Shouts of applause run rattling thro the skies.
Ajax to lift, *Ulysses* next essays,
He barely stirr'd him, but he could not raise:
His knee lock'd fast, the foe's attempt deny'd;   850
And grappling close, they tumble side by side.
Defil'd with honourable dust, they roll,
Still breathing strife, and unsubdu'd of soul:
Again they rage, again to combat rise;
When great *Achilles* thus divides the prize.   855
   Your noble vigour, oh my friends, restrain;
Nor weary out your gen'rous strength in vain.
Ye both have won: Let others who excel
Now prove that prowess you have prov'd so well.
   The hero's words the willing chiefs obey,   860
From their tir'd bodies wipe the dust away,
And, cloth'd anew, the following games survey.
And now succeed the gifts, ordain'd to grace
The youths contending in the rapid race.
A silver urn that full six measures held,   865
By none in weight or workmanship excell'd:

Sidonian artists taught the frame to shine,
Elaborate, with artifice divine;
Whence *Tyrian* sailors did the prize transport,
870 And gave to *Thoas* at the *Lemnian* port:
From him descended good *Eunæus* heir'd
The glorious gift; and, for *Lycaon* spar'd,
To brave *Patroclus* gave the rich reward.
Now, the same hero's funeral rites to grace,
875 It stands the prize of swiftness in the race.
A well-fed ox was for the second plac'd;
And half a talent must content the last.
Achilles rising then bespoke the train:
Who hopes the palm of swiftness to obtain,
880 Stand forth, and bear these prizes from the plain.
     The hero said, and starting from his place,
Oïlean Ajax rises to the race;
Ulysses next; and he whose speed surpast
His youthful equals, *Nestor*'s son the last.
885 Rang'd in a line the ready racers stand;
Pelides points the barrier with his hand;
All start at once; *Oileus* led the race;
The next *Ulysses*, meas'ring pace with pace;
Behind him, diligently close, he sped,
890 As closely following as the running thread
The spindle follows, and displays the charms
Of the fair spinster's breast, and moving arms:
Graceful in motion thus, his foe he plies,
And treads each footstep e'er the dust can rise:
895 His glowing breath upon his shoulders plays;
Th' admiring *Greeks* loud acclamations raise,
To him they give their wishes, hearts, and eyes,
And send their souls before him as he flies.
Now three times turn'd in prospect of the goal,
900 The panting chief to *Pallas* lifts his soul:
Assist, O Goddess! (thus in thought he pray'd)
And present at his thought, descends the Maid.
Buoy'd by her heav'nly force, he seems to swim,
And feels a pinion lifting ev'ry limb.
905 All fierce, and ready now the prize to gain,
Unhappy *Ajax* stumbles on the plain;

(O'erturn'd by *Pallas*) where the slipp'ry shore
Was clogg'd with slimy dung, and mingled gore.
(The self-same place beside *Patroclus'* pyre,
Where late the slaughter'd victims fed the fire)   910
Besmear'd with filth, and blotted o'er with clay,
Obscene to sight, the rueful racer lay;
The well-fed bull (the second prize) he shar'd,
And left the urn *Ulysses'* rich reward.
Then, grasping by the horn the mighty beast,   915
The baffled hero thus the *Greeks* addrest.
     Accursed fate! the conquest I forego;
A Mortal I, a Goddess was my foe:
She urg'd her fav'rite on the rapid way,
And *Pallas*, not *Ulysses* won the day.   920
     Thus sow'rly wail'd he, sputt'ring dirt and gore;
A burst of laughter echo'd thro' the shore.
Antilochus, more hum'rous than the rest,
Takes the last prize, and takes it with a jest.
     Why with our wiser elders should we strive?   925
The Gods still love them, and they always thrive.
Ye see, to *Ajax* I must yield the prize:
He to *Ulysses*, still more ag'd and wise;
(A green old age unconscious of decays,
That proves the hero born in better days!)   930
Behold his vigour in this active race!
Achilles only boasts a swifter pace:
For who can match *Achilles*? He who can,
Must yet be more than hero, more than man.
     Th'effect succeeds the speech. *Pelides* cries,   935
Thy artful praise deserves a better prize.
Nor *Greece* in vain shall hear thy friend extoll'd;
Receive a talent of the purest gold.
The youth departs content. The host admire
The son of *Nestor*, worthy of his sire.   940
     Next these a buckler, spear and helm, he brings,
Cast on the plain the brazen burthen rings:
Arms, which of late divine *Sarpedon* wore,
And great *Patroclus* in short triumph bore.
Stand forth the bravest of our host! (he cries)   945
Whoever dares deserve so rich a prize!

Now grace the lists before our army's sight,
And sheath'd in steel, provoke his foe to fight.
Who first the jointed armour shall explore,
950 And stain his rival's mail with issuing gore;
The sword, *Asteropeus* possest of old,
(A *Thracian* blade, distinct with studs of gold)
Shall pay the stroke, and grace the striker's side:
These arms in common let the chief divide:
955 For each brave champion, when the combat ends,
A sumptuous banquet at our tent attends.
    Fierce at the word, uprose great *Tydeus'* son,
And the huge bulk of *Ajax Telamon.*
Clad in refulgent steel, on either hand,
960 The dreadful chiefs amid the circle stand:
Low'ring they meet, tremendous to the sight;
Each *Argive* bosom beats with fierce delight.
Oppos'd in arms not long they idly stood,
But thrice they clos'd, and thrice the charge renew'd.
965 A furious pass the spear of *Ajax* made
Thro' the broad shield, but at the corselet stay'd:
Not thus the foe: His jav'lin aim'd above
The buckler's margin, at the neck he drove.
But *Greece* now trembling for her hero's life,
970 Bade share the honours, and surcease the strife.
Yet still the victor's due *Tydides* gains,
With him the sword and studded belt remains.
    Then hurl'd the hero, thund'ring on the ground
A mass of iron, (an enormous round)
975 Whose weight and size the circling *Greeks* admire,
Rude from the furnace, and but shap'd by fire.
This mighty quoit *Aëtion* wont to rear,
And from his whirling arm dismiss in air:
The Giant by *Achilles* slain, he stow'd
980 Among his spoils this memorable load.
For this, he bids those nervous artists vie,
That teach the disk to sound along the sky.
Let him whose might can hurl this bowl, arise,
Who farthest hurls it, take it as his prize:
985 If he be one, enrich'd with large domain
Of downs for flocks, and arable for grain,

Small stock of iron needs that man provide;
His hinds and swains whole years shall be supply'd
From hence: Nor ask the neighb'ring city's aid,
For plowshares, wheels, and all the rural trade. 990
  Stern *Polyphætes* stept before the throng,
And great *Leonteus*, more than mortal strong;
Whose force with rival forces to oppose,
Uprose great *Ajax*; up *Epëus* rose.
Each stood in order: First *Epëus* threw; 995
High o'er the wond'ring crowds the whirling circle flew.
Leonteus next a little space surpast,
And third, the strength of god-like *Ajax* cast.
O'er both their marks it flew; till fiercely flung
From *Polyphætes*' arm, the *Discus* sung: 1000
Far, as a swain his whirling sheephook throws,
That distant falls among the grazing cows,
So past them all the rapid circle flies:
His friends (while loud applauses shake the skies)
With force conjoin'd heave off the weighty prize. 1005
  Those, who in skilful archery contend
He next invites the twanging bow to bend:
And twice ten axes casts amidst the round,
(Ten double-edg'd, and ten that singly wound.)
The mast, which late a first-rate galley bore, 1010
The hero fixes in the sandy shore:
To the tall top a milk-white dove they tie,
The trembling mark at which their arrows fly.
Whose weapon strikes yon' flutt'ring bird, shall bear
These two-edg'd axes, terrible in war; 1015
The single, he, whose shaft divides the cord.
He said: Experienc'd *Merion* took the word;
And skilful *Teucer*: In the helm they threw
Their lots inscrib'd, and forth the latter flew.
Swift from the string the sounding arrow flies; 1020
But flies unblest! No grateful sacrifice,
No firstling lambs, unheedful! didst thou vow,
To *Phœbus*, patron of the shaft and bow.
For this, thy well-aim'd arrow, turn'd aside,
Err'd from the dove, yet cut the cord that ty'd: 1025

A-down the main-mast fell the parted string,
And the free bird to heav'n displays her wing:
Seas, shores, and skies with loud applause resound,
And *Merion* eager meditates the wound:
1030   He takes the bow, directs the shaft above,
And following with his eye the soaring dove,
Implores the God to speed it thro' the skies,
With vows of firstling lambs, and grateful sacrifice.
The dove, in airy circles as she wheels,
1035   Amid the clouds the piercing arrow feels;
Quite thro' and thro' the point its passage found,
And at his feet fell bloody to the ground.
The wounded bird, e'er yet she breath'd her last,
With flagging wings alighted on the mast,
1040   A moment hung, and spread her pinions there,
Then sudden dropt, and left her life in air.
From the pleas'd crowd new peals of thunder rise,
And to the ships brave *Merion* bears the prize.

To close the fun'ral games, *Achilles* last
1045   A massy spear amid the circle plac'd,
And ample charger of unsullied frame,
With flow'rs high-wrought, not blacken'd yet by flame.
For these he bids the heroes prove their art,
Whose dext'rous skill directs the flying dart.
1050   Here too great *Merion* hopes the noble prize;
Nor here disdain'd the King of men to rise.
With joy *Pelides* saw the honour paid,
Rose to the Monarch and respectful said.
Thee first in virtue, as in pow'r supreme,
1055   O King of Nations! all thy *Greeks* proclaim;
In ev'ry martial game thy worth attest,
And know thee both their greatest, and their best.
Take then the prize, but let brave *Merion* bear
This beamy jav'lin in thy brother's war.
1060   Pleas'd from the hero's lips his praise to hear,
The King to *Merion* gives the brazen spear:
But, set apart for sacred use, commands
The glitt'ring charger to *Talthybius'* hands.

OBSERVATIONS
ON THE
TWENTY-THIRD BOOK

This, and the following book, which contain the description of the funeral of *Patroclus*, and other matters relating to *Hector*, are undoubtedly superadded to the grand catastrophe of the poem; for the story is compleatly finish'd with the death of that hero in the 22d Book. Many judicious criticks have been of opinion that *Homer* is blameable for protracting it. *Virgil* closes the whole scene of action with the death of *Turnus*, and leaves the rest to be imagined by the mind of the reader: He does not draw the picture at full length, but delineates it so far, that we cannot fail of imagining the whole draught. There is however one thing to be said in favour of *Homer* which may perhaps justify him in his method, that what he undertook to paint was the *anger* of Achilles: And as that anger does not die with *Hector*, but persecutes his very remains, so the poet still keeps up to his Subject; nay it seems to require that he should carry down the relation of that resentment, which is the foundation of his poem, till it is fully satisfy'd: And as this survives *Hector*, and gives the poet an opportunity of still shewing many sad effects of *Achilles*'s anger, the two following books may be thought not to be excrescencies, but essential to the poem.

Virgil had been inexcusable had he trod in *Homer*'s footsteps; for it is evident that the fall of *Turnus*, by giving *Æneas* a full power over *Italy*, answers the whole design and intention of the poem; had he gone farther he had overshot his mark: And tho' *Homer* proceeds after *Hector*'s death, yet the subject is still the anger of *Achilles*.

We are now past the war and violence of the *Ilias*, the scenes of blood are closed during the rest of the poem; we may look back with a pleasing kind of horrour upon the anger of *Achilles*, and see what dire effects it has wrought in the compass of nineteen days: *Troy* and *Greece* are both in mourning for it, heaven and earth, Gods and men, have suffer'd in the conflict. The reader seems landed upon the shore after a violent storm; and has leisure to survey the consequences of the tempest, and the wreck occasion'd by the former commotions, *Troy* weeping for *Hector*, and *Greece* for *Patroclus*. Our passions have been in an agitation since the opening of the poem; wherefore the poet, like some great master in musick, softens his notes, and melts his readers into tenderness and pity.

18. *Tears bathe their arms, and tears the sands bedew, –*
    – Thetis aids their woe –]

It is not easy to give a reason why *Thetis* should be said to excite the grief of the *Myrmidons*, and of *Achilles*; it had seem'd more natural for the mother to have compos'd the sorrows of the son, and restored his troubled mind to tranquillity.

But such a procedure would have outrag'd the character of *Achilles*, who is all along describ'd to be of such a violence of temper, that he is not easy to be pacify'd at any time, much less upon so great an incident as the death of his friend *Patroclus.* Perhaps the poet made use of this fiction in honour of *Achilles*; he makes every passion of his hero considerable, his sorrow as well as anger is important, and he cannot grieve but a Goddess attends him, and a whole Army weeps.

Some commentators fancy that *Homer* animates the very sands of the seas, and the arms of the *Myrmidons*, and makes them sensible of the loss of *Patroclus*; the preceding words seem to strengthen that opinion, because the poet introduces a Goddess to raise the sorrow of the army. But *Eustathius* seems not to give into this conjecture, and I think very judiciously; for what relation is there between the sands of the shores, and the arms of the *Myrmidons?* It would have been more poetical to have said, the sands and the rocks, than the sands and the arms; but it is very natural to say, that the soldiers wept so bitterly, that their armour and the very sands were wet with their tears. I believe this remark will appear very just by reading the verse, with a comma after τεύχεα, thus,

Δεύοντο ψάμαθοι, δεύοντο δὲ τεύχεα, φωτῶν
Δάκρυσι.

Then the Construction will be natural and easy, period will answer period in the *Greek*, and the sense in *English* will be, the sands were wet, and the arms were wet, with the tears of the mourners.

But however this be, there is a very remarkable beauty in the run of the verse in *Homer*, every word has a melancholy cadence, and the poet has not only made the sands and the arms, but even his very verse, to lament with *Achilles.*

23.   *His slaught'ring hands yet red with blood, he laid*
      On his dead friend's cold breast —]

I could not pass by this passage without observing to my reader the great beauty of this epithet, ἀνδροφόνους. An ordinary poet would have contented himself with saying, he laid his hand upon the breast of *Patroclus*, but *Homer* knows how to raise the most trivial circumstance, and by adding this one word, he laid his *deadly* hands, or his *murderous* hands, he fills our minds with great ideas, and by a single epithet recalls to our thoughts all the noble atchievements of *Achilles* thro' the Iliad.

25. *All hail,* Patroclus, *&c.*] There is in this apostrophe of *Achilles* to the ghost of *Patroclus*, a sort of savageness, and a mixture of softness and atrocity, which are highly conformable to his character.

Dacier.

51.   *To cleanse his conqu'ring hands —*
      — The chief refus'd —]

This is conformable to the custom of the orientals: *Achilles* will not be induc'd to wash, and afterwards retires to the sea-shore, and sleeps on the ground. It is just thus that *David* mourns in the scriptures; he refuses to wash, or to take any repast, but retires from company, and lies upon the earth.

78. *The Ghost of* Patroclus.] *Homer* has introduc'd into the former parts of the poem the personages of Gods and Goddesses from heav'n, and of Furies from hell: He has embellish'd it with ornaments from earth, sea, and air; and he here opens a new scene, and brings to the view a ghost, the shade of the departed friend; By these methods he diversifies his poem with new and surprizing circumstances, and awakens the attention of the reader; at the same time he very poetically adapts his language to the circumstances of this imaginary *Patroclus*, and teaches us the opinions that prevail'd in his time, concerning the state of separate souls.

92. *Forbid to cross th'irremeable flood.*] It was the common opinion of the ancients, that the souls of the departed were not admitted into the number of the happy till their bodies had receiv'd the funeral rites; they suppos'd those that wanted them wander'd an hundred years before they were wafted over the infernal river: *Virgil* perhaps had this passage of *Homer* in his view in the sixth *Æneis*, at least he coincides with his sentiments concerning the state of the departed souls.

> *Hæc omnis, quam cernis inops inhumataque turba est:*
> *Nec ripas datur horrendas, nec rauca fluenta*
> *Transportare prius, quam sedibus ossa quierunt;*
> *Centum errant annos volitantque hæc littora circum*
> *Tum demum admissi stagna exoptata revisunt.*

[The ghosts rejected, are th'unhappy crew
Depriv'd of sepulchers, and fun'ral due;
Nor dares his transport vessel cross the waves,
With such whose bones are not compos'd in graves.
A hundred years they wander on the shore,
At length, their pennance done, are wafted o're.]

It was during this interval, between death and the rites of funeral, that they supposed the only time allowed for separate spirits to appear to men; therefore *Patroclus* here tells his friend,

> *— To the farther shore*
> *When once we pass, the soul returns no more.*

For the fuller understanding of *Homer*, it is necessary to be acquainted with his notion of the state of the soul after death: He followed the philosophy of the *Ægyptians*, who supposed man to be compounded of three parts, an intelligent mind, a vehicle for that mind, and a body; the mind they call'd φρήν, or ψυχή, the vehicle εἴδωλον, *image* or *soul*, and the gross body σῶμα. The soul, in which the mind was lodg'd, was supposed exactly to resemble the body in shape, magnitude, and features; for this being in the body as the statue in its mold, so soon as it goes forth is properly the image of that body in which it was enclosed: This it was that appeared to *Achilles*, with the full resemblance of his friend *Patroclus.*   *Vid. Dacier's* life of *Pythagoras*, p. 71.

104. *Ah suffer that my bones may rest with thine!*] There is something

very pathetical in this whole speech of *Patroclus*; he begins it with kind reproaches, and blames *Achilles* with a friendly tenderness; he recounts to him the inseparable affection that had been between them in their lives, and makes it his last request, that they may not be parted even in death, but that their bones may rest in the same urn. The speech itself is of a due length; it ought not to be very short, because this apparition is an incident entirely different from any other in the whole poem, and consequently the reader would not have been satisfied with a cursory mention of it; neither ought it to be long, because this would have been contrary to the nature of such apparitions, whose stay upon earth has ever been described as very short, and consequently they cannot be supposed to use many words.

The circumstance of being buried in the same urn, is entirely conformable to the eastern custom: There are innumerable instances in the scriptures of great personages being buried with their fathers: So *Joseph* would not suffer his bones to rest in *Ægypt*, but commands his brethren to carry them into *Canaan* to the burying-place of his father *Jacob*.

124.   *The form subsists without the body's aid,*
    Aërial semblance, and an empty shade.]

The words of *Homer* are

    Ἀτὰρ φρένες οὐκ ἔνι πάμπαν.

[But there is no understanding in it.]

In which there seems to be a great difficulty; it being not easy to explain how *Achilles* can say that the ghost of his friend had no understanding, when it had but just made such a rational and moving speech: Especially when the poet introduces the apparition with the very shape, air, and voice of *Patroclus.*

But this Passage will be clearly understood, by explaining the notion which the ancients entertained of the souls of the departed, according to the fore-cited triple division of *mind, image,* and *body.* They imagined that the soul was not only separated from the body at the hour of death, but that there was a farther separation of the φρήν, or understanding, from its εἴδωλον, or vehicle; so that while the εἴδωλον, or image of the body, was in hell, the φρήν, or understanding, might be in heaven; And that this is a true explication is evident from a passage in the *Odysseis*, book 11. v. 600.

Τὸν δὲ μετ᾽, εἰσενόησα βίην, Ἡρακλείην
Εἴδωλον· αὐτὸς δὲ μετ᾽ ἀθανάτοισι θεοῖσι
Τέρπεται ἐν θαλίῃς, καὶ ἔχει καλλίσφυρον Ἥβην.

Now I the strength of Hercules *behold,*
A tow'ring spectre of gigantick mold;
A shadowy form! for high in heav'ns abodes
Himself resides, a God among the Gods:
There in the bright assemblies of the skies
He Nectar *quaffs, and* Hebe *crowns with joys.*

By this it appears that *Homer* was of opinion that *Hercules* was in heaven, while his εἴδωλον, or image, was in hell: So that when this second separation is made, the image or vehicle becomes a mere thoughtless form.

We have this whole doctrine very distinctly delivered by *Plutarch* in these words. 'Man is a compound subject; but not of two parts, as is commonly believed, because the *understanding* is generally accounted a part of the *soul*; whereas indeed it as far exceeds the soul, as the soul is diviner than the body. Now the soul, when compounded with the understanding, makes reason, and when compounded with the body, passion: Whereof the one is the source or principle of pleasure or pain, the other of vice or virtue. Man therefore properly dies two deaths; the first death makes him two of three, and the second makes him one of two.'   Plutarch *of the face in the moon.*

141.   *O'er hills, o'er dales, o'er crags, o'er rocks they go –*
       On all sides round the forest hurls her oaks
       Headlong –]

The numbers in the original of this whole passage are admirably adapted to the images the verses convey to us. Every ear must have felt the propriety of sound in this Line,

Πολλὰ δ᾽ ἄναντα, κάταντα, πάραντά τε, δόχμιά τ᾽ ἦλθον.

[They went in all directions: uphill, downhill, sideways,
    obliquely.]

That other in its kind is no less exact,

Τάμνον ἐπειγόμενοι, ταὶ δὲ μεγάλα κτυπέουσαι
Πῖπτον –

[Leaning their weight on the trees, they cut them down;
        and thundering loudly, the trees fell.]

Dionysius of *Halicarnassus* has collected many instances of these sorts of beauties in *Homer*. This description of felling the forests, so excellent as it is, is comprehended in a few lines, which has left room for a larger and more particular one in *Statius*, one of the best (I think) in that author.

> – *Cadit ardua fagus,*
> *Chaoniumque nemus, brumæque illæsa cupressus;*
> *Procumbunt piceæ, flammis alimenta supremis,*
> *Ornique, iliceæque trabes, metuendaque sulco*
> *Taxus, & infandos belli potura cruores*
> *Fraxinus, atque situ non expugnabile robur:*
> *Hinc audax abies, & odoræ vulnere pinus*
> *Scinditur, acclinant intonsa cacumina terræ*
> *Alnus amica fretis, nec inhospita vitibus ulmus,* &c.

[The lofty beech falls, and the Chaonian grove, and the cypress, unharmed by winter; the spruce-firs are laid low, food for high flames, and the ash-tree, the trunks of holm-oak and the yew (that is feared for ploughing); and the mountain-ash that will drink the unspeakable bloodshed of war, and the oak, not to be moved from its place: then the bold fir is split, the pine with its aromatic wound; the alder (friend to the sea) inclines its unshorn tip to the earth, and the non inhospitable elm to the vines.]

I the rather cite this fine passage, because I find it copied by two of the greatest poets of our own nation, *Chaucer* and *Spencer*. The first in the *Assembly of Fowls*, the second in his *Fairy Queen.* lib. 1.

> *The sailing pine, the cedar proud and tall,*
> *The vine-prop elm, the poplar never dry,*
> *The builder oak, sole king of forests all,*
> *The aspin good for staves, the cypress funeral.*
> *The laurel, meed of mighty conquerors,*
> *And poets sage: The fir that weepeth still,*
> *The willow, worn of forlorn paramours,*
> *The ewe obedient to the bender's will,*
> *The birch for shafts, the sallow for the mill,*
> *The myrrh, sweet bleeding in the bitter wound,*

> *The warlike beech, the ash for nothing ill,*
> *The fruitful olive, and the platane round,*
> *The carver holme, the maple seldom inward sound.*

160. *Each in refulgent arms, &c. –]* 'Tis not to be supposed that this was a general custom used at all funerals; but *Patroclus* being a warriour, he is buried like a soldier, with military honours.   *Eustathius.*

166. *O'er all the corse their scattered locks they throw.*] The ceremony of cutting off the hair in honour of the dead was practis'd not only among the *Greeks*, but also among other nations; thus *Statius Thebaid* VI.

> *– Tergoque & pectore fusam*
> Cæsariem *ferro minuit, sectisque jacentis*
> *Obnubit tenuia ora comis.*

[And he cut with his sword the hair that flowed over his back and breast; and he covered, with these locks, the tender face of the person who lay wounded.]

This custom is taken notice of in holy scripture: *Ezekiel* describing a great lamentation, says, *They shall make themselves utterly bald for thee,* ch. 27. v. 31. I believe it was done not only in token of sorrow, but perhaps had a concealed meaning, that as the hair was cut from the head, and was never more to be joined to it, so was the dead for ever cut off from the living, never more to return.

I must observe that this ceremony of cutting off the hair was not always in token of sorrow; *Lycophron* in his *Cassandra*, v. 976. describing a general lamentation, says

> Κρατὸς δ' ἄκουρος νῶτα καλλύνει φόβῃ.

> *A length of unshorn hair adorn'd their backs.*

And that the ancients sometimes had their hair cut off in token of *joy* is evident from *Juvenal, Sat.* 12. v. 82.

> *– Gaudent ibi vertice raso*
> *Garrula securi narrare pericula nautæ.*

[There the carefree sailors, with shaved head, Take joy in recounting their garrulous tales of danger.]

This seeming Contradiction will be solv'd by having respect to the different Practices of different Nations. If it was the general Custom of any Country to wear long Hair, then the cutting it off was a token of Sorrow; but if it was the Custom to wear short Hair, then the letting it grow long and neglecting it, shew'd that such People were Mourners.

168. *Supporting with his hands the hero's head.*] *Achilles* follows the corpse as chief mourner, and sustains the head of his friend: This last circumstance seems to be general; thus *Euripides* in the funeral of *Rhesus*, v. 886.

> Τίς ὑπὲρ κεφαλῆς θεός, ὦ Βασιλεῦ,
> Τὸν νεόδμητον ἐν χειροῖν
> φοράδην πέμπει;

What God, O king, with his hands supports the head of the deceased?

175. *And sacred grew to* Sperchius' *honour'd flood.*] It was the custom of the ancients not only to offer their own hair, but likewise to consecrate that of their children to the river-gods of their country. This is what *Pausanias* shews in his *Attics*: *Before you pass the* Cephisa (says he) *you find the tomb of* Theodorus, *who was the most excellent actor of his time for tragedy; and on the banks you see two statues, one of* Mnesimachus, *and the other of his son, who cut off his hair in honour of the rivers; for that this was in all ages the custom of the* Greeks, *may be inferred from* Homer's *poetry, where* Peleus *promises by a solemn vow to consecrate to the river* Sperchius *the hair of his son, if he returns safe from the* Trojan *war.* This custom was likewise in *Ægypt*, where *Philostratus* tells us, that *Memnon* consecrated his hair to the *Nile*. This practice of *Achilles* was imitated by *Alexander* at the funeral of *Hephæstion.*   *Spondanus.*

228. *Cœlestial* Venus, *&c.*] *Homer* has here introduced a series of allegories in the compass of a few lines: The body of *Hector* may be supposed to have continued beautiful even after he was slain; and *Venus* being the president of beauty, the poet by a natural fiction tells us it was preserv'd by that Goddess.

Apollo's covering the body with a cloud is a very natural allegory: For the sun (says *Eustathius*) has a double quality which produces contrary effects; the heat of it causes a dryness, but at the same time it exhales the vapours of the earth, from whence the clouds of heaven are formed. This allegory may be founded upon truth; there might happen to be a cool season while *Hector* lay unburied, and *Apollo*, or the sun, raising clouds which intercept the heat of his beams, by a very easy fiction in poetry may be introduced in person to preserve the body of *Hector*.

263. *The allegory of the winds.*] A poet ought to express nothing vulgarly; and sure no poet ever trespassed less against this rule than *Homer*; the fruitfulness of his invention is continually raising incidents new and surprising. Take this passage out of its poetical dress, and it will be no more than this: A strong gale of wind blew, and so increased the flame that it soon consumed the Pile. But *Homer* introduces the Gods of the winds in person: And *Iris*, or the rainbow, being (as *Eustathius* observes) a sign not only of showers, but of winds, he makes them come at her summons.

Every circumstance is well adapted: As soon as the winds see *Iris*, they rise; that is, when the rainbow appears, the wind rises: She refuses to sit, and immediately returns; that is, the rainbow is never seen long at one time, but soon appears, and soon vanishes: She returns over the ocean; that is, the bow is composed of waters, and it would have been an unnatural fiction to have described her as passing by land.

The winds are all together in the cave of *Zephyrus*, which may imply that they were there as at their general rendezvous; or that the nature of all the winds is the same; or that the western wind is in that country the most constant, and consequently it may be said that at such seasons all the winds are assembled in one corner, or rendezvous with *Zephyrus*.

Iris will not enter the cave: It is the nature of the rainbow to be stretch'd entirely upon the surface, and therefore this fiction is agreeable to reason.

When *Iris* says that the Gods are partaking hecatombs in *Æthiopia*, it is to be remembered that the Gods are represented there in the first book, before the scenes of war were opened, and now they are closed, they return thither. *Eustathius* – Thus *Homer* makes the anger of his hero so important, that it roused heaven to arms, and now when it is almost appeased, *Achilles* as it were gives peace to the Gods.

308. *Hereafter* Greece *a nobler work shall raise.*] We see how *Achilles* consults his own glory; the desire of it prevails over his tenderness for

Patroclus, and he will not permit any man, not even his beloved *Patroclus*, to share an equality of honour with himself, even in the grave.   *Eustathius.*

321. *The Games for* Patroclus.] The conduct of *Homer* in enlarging upon the games at the funeral of *Patroclus* is very judicious: There had undoubtedly been such honours paid to several heroes during this war, as appears from a passage in the ninth book, where *Agamemnon* to enhance the value of the horses which he offers *Achilles*, says, that any person would be rich that had treasures equal to the value of the prizes they had won; which races must have been run during the siege: for had they been before it, the horses would now have been too old to be of any value, this being the tenth year of the war. But the poet passes all those games over in silence, and reserves them for this season; not only in honour of *Patroclus*, but also of his hero *Achilles*; who exhibits games to a whole army; great generals are candidates for the prizes, and he himself sits the judge and arbitrator: Thus in peace as well as war the poet maintains the superiority of the character of *Achilles.*

But there is another reason why the poet deferr'd to relate any games that were exhibited at any preceding funerals: The death of *Patroclus* was the most eminent period; and consequently the most proper time for such games.

'Tis farther observable, that he chuses this peculiar time with great judgment. When the fury of the war rag'd, the army could not well have found leisure for the games, and they might have met with interruption from the enemy: But *Hector* being dead, all *Troy* is in confusion: They are in too great a consternation to make any attempts, and therefore the poet could not possibly have chosen a more happy opportunity.   *Eustathius.*

349. *Lost is* Patroclus *now,* &c.] I am not ignorant that *Homer* has frequently been blamed for such little digressions as these; in this passage he gives us the genealogy of his horses, which he has frequently told us in the preceding part of the poem. But *Eustathius* justifies his conduct, and says that it was very proper to commend the virtue of these horses upon this occasion, when horses were to contend for victory: At the same time he takes an opportunity to make an honourable mention of his friend *Patroclus*, in whose honour these games were exhibited.

It may be added as a farther justification of *Homer*, that this last circumstance is very natural: *Achilles* while he commends his horses remembers how careful *Patroclus* had been of them; His love for his friend is so great, that the minutest circumstance recalls him to his mind; and such little digressions, such avocations of thought as these, very naturally proceed from the overflows of love and sorrow.

365. *Whom rich* Echepolus, &c.] One wou'd think that *Agamemnon* might be accus'd of avarice, in dispensing a man from going to the war for the sake of a horse; but *Aristotle* very well observes, that this prince is praiseworthy for having preferr'd a horse to a person so cowardly, and so uncapable of service. It may also be conjectur'd from this passage, that even in those elder times it was the custom, that those who were willing to be excus'd from the war, should give either a horse or a man and often both. Thus *Scipio* going to *Africa* order'd the *Sicilians* either to attend him, or to give him horses or men: And *Agesilaus* being at *Ephesus* and wanting cavalry, made a proclamation, that the rich men who would not serve in the war should be dispens'd with, provided they furnish'd a man and a horse in their stead: In which, says *Plutarch*, he wisely follow'd the example of King *Agamemnon*, who excus'd a very rich coward from serving in person, for a present of a good mare.   *Eustathius. Dacier.*

371. *Experienc'd* Nestor, &c.] The poet omits no opportunity of paying honour to his old favourite *Nestor*, and I think he is no where more particularly complemented than in this book. His age had disabled him from bearing any share in the games; and yet he artfully introduces him not as a mere spectator, but as an actor in the sports. Thus he as it were wins the prize for *Antilochus*, *Antilochus* wins not by the swiftness of his horses, but by the wisdom of *Nestor*.

This fatherly tenderness is wonderfully natural: We see him in all imaginable inquietude and concern for his son; He comes to the barrier, stands beside the chariot, animates his son by his praises, and directs him by his lessons: You think the old man's soul mounts on the chariot with his *Antilochus*, to partake the same dangers, and run the same career.

Nothing can be better adapted to the character than this speech; he expatiates upon the advantages of wisdom over strength, which is a tacit complement to himself: And had there been a prize for wisdom, undoubtedly the old man would have claim'd it as his right.

Eustathius.

427. *The lots their place dispose.*] According to these lots the charioteers took their places; but to know whether they stood all in an equal Front, or one behind the other, is a difficulty: *Eustathius* says the ancients were of opinion that they did not stand in one front; because it is evident that he who had the first lot had a great advantage of the other charioteers: If he had not, why should *Achilles* cast lots? Madam *Dacier* is of opinion that they all stood a breast at the barrier, and that the first would still have a sufficient advantage, as he was nearer the bound, and stood within the rest, whereas the others must take a larger circle, and consequently were forc'd to run a greater compass of ground. *Phœnix* was plac'd as an inspector of the race, that is, says *Eustathius*, he was to make report whether they had observ'd the laws of the race in their several turnings.

Sophocles observes the same method with *Homer* in relation to the lots and inspectors, in his *Electra*.

$$- \text{Οἱ τεταγμένοι βραβεῖς}$$
$$\text{Κλήροις ἔπηλαν καὶ κατέστησαν δίφρον.}$$

The constituted judges assign'd the places according to the lots.

The ancients say that the charioteers started at the *Sigæum*, where the ships of *Achilles* lay, and ran towards the *Rhæteum*, from the ships towards the shores. But *Aristarchus* affirm'd that they run in the compass of ground of five *stadia*, which lay between the wall and the tents toward the shore. *Eustathius.*

458. *And seem just mounting on his car behind.*] A more natural image than this could not be thought of. The poet makes us spectators of the race, we see *Diomed* pressing upon *Eumelus* so closely, that his chariot seems to climb the chariot of *Eumelus.*

465. *Rage fills his eye with anguish, to survey,* &c.] We have seen *Diomed* surrounded with innumerable dangers, acting in the most perilous scenes of blood and death, yet never shed one tear: And now he weeps on a small occasion, for a mere trifle: This must be ascrib'd to the nature of mankind, who are often transported with trifles; and there are certain unguarded moments in every man's life; so that he who could meet the greatest dangers with intrepidity, may thro' Anger be betray'd into an indecency. *Eustathius.*

The reason why *Apollo* is angry at *Diomed*, according to *Eustathius*, is because he was interested for *Eumelus*, whose mares he had fed, when he serv'd *Admetus*; but I fancy he is under a mistake: This indeed is a reason why he should favour *Eumelus*, but not why he should be angry at *Diomed*. I rather think that the quarrel of *Apollo* with *Diomed* was personal; because he offer'd him a violence in the first book, and *Apollo* still resents it.

The fiction of *Minerva*'s assisting *Diomed* is grounded upon his being so wise as to take a couple of whips to prevent any mischance: So that *Wisdom*, or *Pallas*, may be said to lend him one.

Eustathius.

483. *The speech of* Antilochus *to his horses.*] I fear *Antilochus* his speech to his horses is blameable; *Eustathius* himself seems to think it a fault that he should speak so much in the very heat of the race. He commands and sooths, counsels and threatens his horses, as if they were reasonable creatures. The subsequent speech of *Menelaus* is more excusable as it is more short, but both of them are spoken in a passion, and anger we know makes us speak to every thing, and we discharge it upon the most senseless objects.

565. *The Dispute between* Idomeneus *and* Ajax.] Nothing could be more naturally imagined than this contention at a horse-race: The leaders were divided into parties, and each was interested for his friend: The poet had a two-fold design, not only to embellish and diversify his poem by such natural circumstances, but also to shew us, as *Eustathius* observes, from the conduct of *Ajax*, that passionate men betray themselves into follies, and are themselves guilty of the faults of which they accuse others.

It is with a particular decency that *Homer* makes *Achilles* the arbitrator between *Idomeneus* and *Ajax*: *Agamemnon* was his superiour in the army, but as *Achilles* exhibited the shows, he was the proper judge of any difference that should arise about them; had the contest been between *Ajax* and *Idomeneus*, considered as soldiers, the cause must have been brought before *Agamemnon*; but as they are to be considered as spectators of the games, they ought to be determined by *Achilles*.

It may not be unnecessary just to observe to the reader the judicious-ness of *Homer*'s conduct in making *Achilles* exhibit the games, and not *Agamemnon*: *Achilles* is the hero of the poem, and consequently must be the chief actor in all the great scenes of it: He had remained inactive during a great part of the poem, yet the poet makes his very inactivity contribute to the carrying on the design of his *Ilias*: And to supply his absence from many of the busy scenes of the preceding parts of it, he now in the conclusion makes him almost the sole agent: By these means he leaves a noble idea of his hero upon the mind of his Reader; as he raised our expectations when he brought him upon the stage of action, so he makes him go off with the utmost pomp and applause.

581. *High o'er his head the circling lash he wields.*] I am persuaded that the common translation of the word Κατωμαδόν, in the original of this verse, is faulty: It is rendered, *he lash'd the horses continually over the shoulders*; whereas I fancy it should be translated thus, *assidue* (equos) *agitabat scutica ab humero ducta* [He continually drove the horses with a lash whipped by his shoulder]. This naturally expresses the very action, and whirl of the whip over the driver's shoulder, in the act of lashing the horses, and agrees with the use of the same word in the 431st line of this book, where δίσκου οὖρα κατωμαδίοιο must be translated *jactus disci ab humero vibrati* [a throw of a disk hurled by his shoulder].

614. *Fortune denies, but Justice, &c.*] *Achilles* here intends to shew, that it is not just fortune should rule over virtue, but that a brave man who had performed his duty, and who did not bring upon himself his misfortune, ought to have the recompence he has deserved: And this principle is just, provided we do not reward him at the expence of another's right: *Eumelus* is a *Thessalian*, and it is probable *Achilles* has a partiality to his countryman.   *Dacier.*

633. *But this, my prize, I never shall forego* –] There is an air of bravery in this discourse of *Antilochus*: He speaks with the generosity of a gallant soldier, and prefers his honour to his interest; he tells *Achilles* if he pleases he may make *Eumelus* a richer present than his prize; he is not concern'd for the value of it, but as it was the reward of victory, he would not resign it, because that would be an acknowledgment that *Eumelus* deserved it.

The character of *Antilochus* is admirably sustained thro' this whole episode; he is a very sensible man, but transported with youthful heat, and ambitious of glory: His rashness in driving so furiously against *Menelaus* must be imputed to this; but his passions being gratify'd by the conquest in the race, his reason again returns, he owns his error, and is full of resignation to *Menelaus.*

663. *And touch thy steeds, and swear –*] 'Tis evident, says *Eustathius*, from hence, that all fraud was forbid in the chariot race; but it is not very plain what unlawful deceit *Antilochus* used against *Menelaus*: Perhaps *Antilochus* in his haste had declin'd from the race-ground, and avoided some of the uneven places of it, and consequently took an unfair advantage of his adversary; or perhaps his driving so furiously against *Menelaus* as to endanger both their chariots and their lives, might be reckon'd foul play; and therefore *Antilochus* refuses to take the oath.

679. *Joy swells his soul, as when the vernal grain, &c.*] *Eustathius* is very large in the explication of this similitude, which at the first view seems obscure: His words are these,

As the dew raises the blades of corn, that are for want of it weak and depressed, and by pervading the pores of the corn animates and makes it flourish, so did the behaviour of *Antilochus* raise the dejected mind of *Menelaus*, exalt his spirits, and restore him to a full satisfaction.

I have given the reader his interpretation, and translated it with the liberty of poetry: It is very much in the language of Scripture, and in the spirit of the Orientals.

707. *Accept thou this, O sacred sire!*] The poet in my opinion preserves a great deal of decency towards this old hero, and venerable counsellour: He gives him an honorary reward for his superior wisdom, and therefore *Achilles* calls it ἄεθλον, and not δῶρον, a prize, and not a present. The moral of *Homer* is, that princes ought no less to honour and recompense those who excel in wisdom and counsel, than those who are capable of actual service.

Achilles, perhaps, had a double view in paying him this respect, not only out of deference to his age, and wisdom, but also because he had, in a manner, won the prize by the advice he gave his son: So that *Nestor* may be said to have conquer'd in the person of *Antilochus*.   *Eustathius.*

719. Nestor's *Speech to* Achilles.] This speech is admirably well adapted to the character of *Nestor*: He aggrandizes, with an infirmity peculiar to age, his own exploits; and one would think *Horace* had him in his eye,

– Laudator temporis acti
Se puero –

[A praiser of the days when he was a boy.]

Neither is it any blemish to the Character of *Nestor* thus to be a little talkative about his own atchievements: To have described him otherwise would have been an outrage to human nature, in as much as the wisest man living is not free from the infirmities of man: and as every stage of life has some imperfection peculiar to it self.

$$-\text{'}O\ \mu\grave{\epsilon}\nu\ \check{\epsilon}\mu\pi\epsilon\delta o\nu\ \mathring{\eta}\nu\iota\acute{o}\chi\epsilon\upsilon\epsilon\nu,$$
$$-\ \text{''}E\mu\pi\epsilon\delta o\nu\ \mathring{\eta}\nu\iota\acute{o}\chi\epsilon\upsilon\text{'}.$$

[One firmly held the reins, held the reins firmly.]

The reader may observe that the old man takes abundance of pains to give reasons how his rivals came to be victors in the chariot-race: He is very solicitous to make it appear that it was not thro' any want of skill or power in himself: And in my opinion *Nestor* is never more vainglorious than in this recital of his own disappointment.

It is for the same reason he repeats the words I have cited above: He obtrudes (by that repetition) the disadvantages under which he labour'd, upon the observation of the reader, for fear he should impute the loss of the victory to his want of skill.

Nestor says that these *Moliones* overpower'd him by their *number*. The criticks, as *Eustathius* remarks, have labour'd hard to explain this difficulty; they tell us a formal story, that when *Nestor* was ready to enter the lists against these brothers, he objected against them as unfair adversaries, (for it must be remembered that they were monsters that grew together, and consequently had four hands to *Nestor*'s two) but the judges would not allow his plea, but determined, that as they grew together so they ought to be considered as one man.

Others tell us that they brought several chariots into the lists, whose charioteers combined together in favour of *Eurytus* and *Cteatus*, these brother-monsters.

Others say, that the multitude of the spectators conspir'd to disappoint *Nestor*.

I thought it necessary to give my reader these several conjectures; that he might understand why *Nestor* says he was overpower'd by $\Pi\lambda\acute{\eta}\theta\epsilon\iota$, or *numbers*; and also, because it confirms my former observation, that *Nestor* is very careful to draw his own picture in the strongest colours, and to shew it in the fairest light.

819. *A female captive valu'd but at four.*] I cannot in civility neglect a remark made upon this passage by Madam *Dacier*, who highly resents the affront put upon her sex by the ancients, who set (it seems) thrice the value upon a *tripod* as upon a beautiful female slave: Nay, she is afraid the value of women is not raised even in our days; for she says there are curious persons now living who had rather have a true antique kettle, than the finest woman alive: I confess I entirely agree with the lady, and must impute such opinions of the fair sex to want of taste in both ancients and moderns: The reader may remember that these tripods were of no use, but made entirely for show, and consequently the most satyrical critick could only say, the woman and tripod ought to have born an equal value.

826. *Like two strong rafters*, &c.] I will give the reader the words of *Eustathius* upon this similitude, which very happily represents the wrestlers in the posture of wrestling. Their heads lean'd one against the other, like the rafters that support the roof of a house; at the foot they are disjoined, and stand at a greater distance, which naturally paints the attitude of body in these two wrestlers, while they contend for victory.

849. *He barely stirr'd him, but he could not raise.*] The poet by this circumstance excellently maintains the character of *Ajax*, who has all along been described as a strong, unwieldy warriour: He is so heavy that *Ulysses* can scarce lift him. The Words that follow will bear a different meaning, either that *Ajax* lock'd his leg within that of *Ulysses*, or that *Ulysses* did it. *Eustathius* observes, that if *Ajax* gave *Ulysses* this shock, then he may be allowed to have some appearance of an equality in the contest, but if *Ulysses* gave it, then *Ajax* must be acknowledged to have been foil'd: But (continues he) it appeared to be otherwise to *Achilles*, who was the judge of the field, and therefore he gives them an equal prize, because they were equal in the contest.

Madam *Dacier* misrepresents *Eustathius* on this place, in saying he thinks it was *Ulysses* who gave the second stroke to *Ajax*, whereas it appears by the foregoing note that he rather determines otherwise in consent with the judgment given by *Achilles*.

901. *Assist, O Goddess! (thus in thought he pray'd)*] Nothing could be better adapted to the present circumstance of *Ulysses* than this prayer: It is short, and ought to be so, because the time would not allow him to make a longer; nay he prefers this petition mentally, ὃν κατὰ θυμόν [in his own heart]; all his faculties are so bent upon the race, that he does not call off his attention from it, even to speak so short a petition as seven words, which comprehend the whole of it: Such Passages as these are instances of great judgment in the poet.

924. *And takes it with a jest.*] *Antilochus* comes off very well, and wittily prevents raillery; by attributing the victory of his rivals to the protection which the Gods gave to age. By this he insinuates, that he has something to comfort himself with; (for youth is better than the prize) and that he may pretend hereafter to the same protection, since 'tis a privilege of seniority.   *Dacier.*

933. *For who can match* Achilles?] There is great art in these transient complements to *Achilles*: That hero could not possibly shew his own superiority in these games by contending for any of the prizes, because he was the exhibiter of the sports: But *Homer* has found out a way to give him the victory in two of them. In the chariot-race *Achilles* is represented as being able to conquer every opponent, and tho' he speaks it himself, the poet brings it in so happily, that he speaks it without any indecency: And in this place *Antilochus* with a very good grace tells *Achilles*, that in the foot-race no one can dispute the prize with him. Thus tho' *Diomed* and *Ulysses* conquer in the chariot and foot-race, it is only because *Achilles* is not their antagonist.

949. *Who first the jointed armour shall explore.*] Some of the ancients have been shock'd at this combat, thinking it a barbarity that men in sport should thus contend for their lives; and therefore *Aristophanes* the *Grammarian* made this alteration in the verses.

> Ὁππότερός κεν πρῶτος ἐπιγράψας χρόα καλὸν
> Φθήῃ ἐπευξάμενος διὰ τ᾽ ἔντεα, &c.

[Whichever of the two might be the first to graze his fair skin
And boast that he had stripped him of his armor.]

But it is evident that they entirely mistook the meaning and intention of *Achilles*; for he that gave the first wound was to be accounted the victor. How could *Achilles* promise to entertain them both in his tent after the combat, if he intended that one of them should fall in it? This duel therefore was only a trial of skill, and as such single combats were frequent in the wars of those ages against adversaries, so this was proposed only to shew the dexterity of the combatants in that exercise.   *Eustathius.*

971. *Yet still the victor's due* Tydides *gains.*] *Achilles* in this place acts the part of a very just arbitrator: Tho' the combat did not proceed to a full issue, yet *Diomed* had evidently the advantage, and consequently ought to be rewarded as victor, because he would have been victorious, had not the *Greeks* interpos'd.

I could have wish'd that the poet had given *Ajax* the prize in some of these contests. He undoubtedly was a very gallant soldier, and has been describ'd as repulsing a whole army; yet in all these sports he is foil'd. But perhaps the poet had a double view in this representation, not only to shew, that Strength without conduct is usually unsuccessful, but also his design might be to complement the *Greeks* his countrymen; by shewing that this *Ajax*, who had repell'd a whole army of *Trojans*, was not able to conquer any one of the *Grecian* worthies: For we find him overpower'd in three of these exercises.

985. *If he be one, enrich'd,* &c.] The poet in this place speaks in the simplicity of ancient times: The prodigious weight and size of the quoit is describ'd with a noble plainness, peculiar to the Oriental way, and agreeable to the manners of those heroick ages. He does not set down the quantity of this enormous piece of iron, neither as to its bigness nor weight, but as to the use it will be of to him who shall gain it. We see from hence, that the ancients in the prizes they propos'd, had in view not only the honourable, but the useful; a captive for work, a bull for tillage, a quoit for the provision of iron. Besides it must be remember'd, that in those times iron was very scarce; and a sure sign of this scarcity, is, that their arms were brass.

                                                                 Eustath. Dacier.

1030. *He takes the bow.*] There having been many editions of *Homer*, that of *Marseilles* represents these two rivals in archery as using two bows in the contest; and reads the verses thus,

> Σπερχόμενος δ' ἄρα Μηριόνης ἐπέθη κατ' ὀϊστὸν
> Τόξῳ, ἐν γὰρ χερσὶν ἔχε πάλαι, ὡς ἴθυνεν.

[In eager haste, Meriones placed an arrow in his bow and held it just now in his hands, as he aimed it.]

Our common editions follow the better alteration of *Antimachus*, with this only difference, that he reads it

> Ἐξείρυσε Τεύκρου τόξον.

[He drew Teucer's bow.]

And they,

> Ἐξείρυσε χειρὸς τόξον.

[He drew the bow with his hand.]

It is evident that these archers had but one bow, as they that threw the quoit had but one quoit; by these means the one had no advantage over the other, because both of them shot with the same bow. So that the common reading is undoubtedly the best, where the lines stand thus,

> Σπερχόμενος δ' ἄρα Μηριόνης ἐξείρυσε χειρὸς or Τεύκρου
> Τόξον, ἀτὰρ δὴ ὄϊστὸν ἔχε πάλαι ὡς ἴθυνεν.   *Eustath.*

[In eager haste, Meriones drew the bow with his hand (or Teucer's bow), but he had an arrow already prepared, as Teucer was taking aim.]

This *Teucer* is the most eminent man for archery of any thro' the whole Iliad, yet he is here excell'd by *Meriones*: And the poet ascribes his miscarriage to the neglect of invoking *Apollo*, the God of archery; whereas *Meriones*, who invokes him, is crown'd with success. There is an excellent moral in this passage, and the poet would teach us, that without addressing to heaven we cannot succeed: *Meriones* does not conquer because he is the better archer, but because he is the better man.

1051. *Nor here disdain'd the King of men to rise.*] There is an admirable conduct in this passage; *Agamemnon* never contended for any of the former prizes, tho' of much greater value; so that he is a candidate for this, only to honour *Patroclus* and *Achilles*. The decency which the poet uses both in the choice of the game, in which *Agamemnon* is about to contend, and the giving him the prize without a contest, is very remarkable: The game was a warlike exercise, fit for the general of an army; the giving him the prize without a contest is a decency judiciously observed, because no one ought to be suppos'd to excel the general in any military art: *Agamemnon* does justice to his own character, for whereas he had been represented by *Achilles* in the opening of the poem as a covetous person, he now puts in for the prize that is of the least value, and generously gives even that to *Talthybius.*   *Eustathius.*

As to this last particular, of *Agamemnon*'s presenting the charger to *Talthybius*, I can't but be of a different opinion. It had been an affront to *Achilles* not to have accepted of his present on this occasion, and I believe the words of *Homer*,

> Ταλθυβίῳ κήρυκι δίδου περικαλλές ἄεθλον,

[He gave the beautiful prize to Talthybius the herald;]

mean no more, than that he put it into the hands of this herald to carry it to his ships; *Talthybius* being by his office an attendant upon *Agamemnon*.

It will be expected I should here say something tending to a comparison between the games of *Homer* and those of *Virgil.* If I may own my private opinion, there is in general more variety of natural Incidents, and a more lively picture of natural passions, in the games and persons of *Homer*. On the other hand, there seems to me more art, contrivance, gradation, and a greater pomp of verse in those of *Virgil.* The *chariot-race* is that which *Homer* has most labour'd, of which *Virgil* being sensible, he judiciously avoided the imitation of what he could not improve, and substituted in its place the *naval-course*, or *ship-race.* It is in this the *Roman* poet has employ'd all his force, as if on set purpose to rival his great master; but it is extremely observable how constantly he keeps *Homer* in his eye, and is afraid to depart from his very track, even when he had vary'd the subject itself. Accordingly the accidents of the naval course have a strange resemblance with those of *Homer*'s chariot-race. He could not forbear at the very beginning to draw a part of that Description into a simile. Do not we see he has *Homer*'s chariots in his head, by these lines;

> *Non tam præcipites bijugo certamine campum*
> *Corripuere, ruuntque effusi carcere currus.*
> *Nec sic immissis aurigæ undantia lora*
> *Concussere jugis, pronique in verbera pendent.*
>
> Æn. v. v.144.

[Not fiery coursers, in a chariot race,
Invade the field with half so swift a pace.

Not the fierce driver with more fury lends
The sounding lash; and, e're the stroke descends,
Low to the wheels his pliant body bends.]

What is the encounter of *Cloanthus* and *Gyas* in the strait between the rocks, but the same with that of *Menelaus* and *Antilochus* in the hollow way? Had the galley of *Sergestus* been broken, if the chariot of *Eumelus* had not been demolish'd? Or *Mnestheus* been cast from the helm, had not the other been thrown from his seat? Does not *Mnestheus* exhort his rowers in the very Words *Antilochus* had us'd to his horses?

> *Non jam prima peto* Mnestheus, *neque vincere certo*
> *Quamquam O! sed superent quibus hoc* Neptune *dedisti;*
> *Extremos pudeat rediisse! hoc vincite, cives,*
> *Et prohibete nefas –*

[I seek not now the foremost palm to gain;
 Tho yet – But ah, that haughty wish is vain!
 Let those enjoy it whom the Gods ordain.
 But to be last, the lags of all the race,
 Redeem your selves and me from that disgrace.]

> Ἔμβητον καὶ σφῶϊ, τιταίνετον ὅττι τάχιστα.
> Ἦ τοι μὲν κείνοισιν ἐριζέμεν οὔ τι κελεύω
> Τυδείδεω ἵπποισι δαΐφρονος, οἷσιν Ἀθήνη
> Νῦν ὤρεξε τάχος –
> Ἵππους δ' Ἀτρείδαο κιχάνετε, μηδὲ λίπησθον,
> Καρπαλίμως, μὴ σφῶϊν ἐλεγχείην καταχεύῃ
> Αἴθη θῆλυς ἐοῦσα –

[cf. Pope's translation, XXIII, 483–8]

Upon the whole, the description of the Sea-Race I think has the more poetry and majesty, that of the chariots more nature, and lively incidents. There is nothing in *Virgil* so picturesque, so animated, or which so much marks the characters, as the episodes of *Antilochus* and *Menelaus*, *Ajax* and *Idomeneus*, with that beautiful interposition of old *Nestor*, (so naturally introduc'd into an affair where one so little expects him.) On the other side, in *Virgil* the description itself is nobler; it has something more ostentatiously grand, and seems a spectacle more worthy the presence of Princes and great persons.

In three other games we find the *Roman* poet contending openly with the *Grecian.* That of the *Cæstus* is in great part a verbal translation:

But it must be own'd in favour of *Virgil*, that he has vary'd from *Homer* in the event of the combate with admirable judgment and with an improvement of the moral. *Epëus* and *Dares* are described by both poets as vain boasters; but *Virgil* with more poetical justice punishes *Dares* for his arrogance, whereas the presumption and pride of *Epëus* is rewarded by *Homer*.

On the contrary, in the *foot-race*, I am of opinion that *Homer* has shewn more judgment and morality than *Virgil*. *Nisus* in the latter is unjust to his adversary in favour of his friend *Euryalus*; so that *Euryalus* wins the race by palpable fraud, and yet the poet gives him the first prize; whereas *Homer* makes *Ulysses* victorious, purely thro' the mischance of *Ajax*, and his own piety in invoking *Minerva*.

The *shooting* is also a direct copy, but with the addition of two circumstances which make a beautiful gradation. In *Homer* the first archer cuts the string that held the bird, and the other shoots him as he is mounting. In *Virgil* the first only hits the mast which the bird was fix'd upon, the second cuts the string, the third shoots him, and the fourth to vaunt the strength of his arm directs his arrow up to heaven, where it kindles into a flame, and makes a prodigy. This last is certainly superior to *Homer* in what they call the *wonderful*: but what is the intent or effect of this prodigy, or whether a reader is not at least as much surprized at it, as at the most unreasonable parts in *Homer*, I leave to those criticks who are more inclin'd to find faults than I am: Nor shall I observe upon the many literal imitations in the *Roman* poet, to object against which were to derogate from the merit of those fine passages, which *Virgil* was so very sensible of, that he was resolv'd to take them, at any rate, to himself.

There remain in *Homer* three games untouch'd by *Virgil*; the *wrestling*, the *single combate*, and the *Discus*. In *Virgil* there is only the *Lusus Trojæ* added, which is purely his own, and must be confest to be inimitable: I don't know whether I may be allow'd to say, it is worth all those three of *Homer*?

I could not forgive my self if I omitted to mention in this place the funeral games in the sixth *Thebaïd* of *Statius*; it is by much the most beautiful book of that poem. It's very remarkable, that he has follow'd *Homer* thro' the whole course of his games: There is the *chariot-race*, the *foot-race*, the *Discus*, the *Cæstus*, the *wrestling*, the *single combate* (which is put off in the same manner as in *Homer*) and the *shooting*; which last ends (as in *Virgil*) with a prodigy: Yet in the particular descriptions of each of these games this poet has not borrow'd from either of his predecessors, and his poem is so much the worse for it.

THE
TWENTY-FOURTH BOOK
OF THE
ILIAD

The ARGUMENT

The redemption of the body of *Hector*

The Gods deliberate about the redemption of Hector. Jupiter *sends* Thetis *to* Achilles *to dispose him for the restoring it, and* Iris *to* Priam, *to encourage him to go in person, and treat for it. The old King, notwithstanding the remonstrances of his Queen, makes ready for the journey, to which he is encourag'd by an omen from* Jupiter. *He sets forth in his chariot, with a waggon loaded with presents under the charge of* Idæus *the herald.* Mercury *descends in the shape of a young man, and conducts him to the pavilion of* Achilles. *Their conversation on the way.* Priam *finds* Achilles *at his table, casts himself at his feet, and begs for the body of his son;* Achilles, *mov'd with compassion, grants his request, detains him one night in his tent, and the next morning sends him home with the body: The* Trojans *run out to meet him. The lamentations of* Andromache, Hecuba, *and* Helen, *with the solemnities of the funeral.*

The time of twelve days is employ'd in this book, while the body of Hector *lies in the tent of* Achilles. *And as many more are spent in the truce allow'd for his interment. The scene is partly in* Achilles's *camp, and partly in* Troy.

Now from the finish'd games the *Grecian* band
Seek their black ships, and clear the crowded strand:
All stretch'd at ease the genial banquet share,
And pleasing slumbers quiet all their care.

5   Not so *Achilles*: He, to grief resign'd,
His friend's dear image present to his mind,
Takes his sad couch, more unobserv'd to weep,
Nor tastes the gifts of all-composing sleep.
Restless he roll'd around his weary bed,

10   And all his soul on his *Patroclus* fed:
The form so pleasing, and the heart so kind,
That youthful vigour, and that manly mind,
What toils they shar'd, what martial works they wrought,
What seas they measur'd, and what fields they fought;

15   All past before him in remembrance dear,
Thought follows thought, and tear succeeds to tear.
And now supine, now prone, the hero lay,
Now shifts his side, impatient for the day:
Then starting up, disconsolate he goes

20   Wide on the lonely beach to vent his woes.
There as the solitary mourner raves,
The ruddy morning rises o'er the waves:
Soon as it rose, his furious steeds he join'd;
The chariot flies, and *Hector* trails behind.

25   And thrice *Patroclus!* round thy monument
Was *Hector* dragg'd, then hurry'd to the tent.
There sleep at last o'ercomes the hero's eyes;
While foul in dust th' unhonour'd carcase lies,
But not deserted by the pitying skies.

For *Phœbus* watch'd it with superior care, 30
Preserv'd from gaping wounds, and tainting air;
And ignominious as it swept the field,
Spread o'er the sacred corse his golden shield.
All heav'n was mov'd, and *Hermes* will'd to go
By stealth to snatch him from th' insulting foe: 35
But *Neptune* this, and *Pallas* this denies,
And th' unrelenting Empress of the skies:
E'er since that day implacable to *Troy*,
What time young *Paris*, simple shepherd boy,
Won by destructive lust (reward obscene) 40
Their charms rejected for the *Cyprian* Queen.
But when the tenth celestial morning broke,
To heav'n assembled, thus *Apollo* spoke.

Unpitying pow'rs! how oft each holy fane
Has *Hector* ting'd with blood of victims slain? 45
And can ye still his cold remains pursue?
Still grudge his body to the *Trojans* view?
Deny to consort, mother, son, and sire,
The last sad honours of a fun'ral fire?
Is then the dire *Achilles* all your care? 50
That iron heart, inflexibly severe;
A lion, not a man, who slaughters wide
In strength of rage and impotence of pride,
Who hastes to murder with a savage joy,
Invades around, and breathes but to destroy. 55
Shame is not of his soul; nor understood,
The greatest evil and the greatest good.
Still for one loss he rages unresign'd,
Repugnant to the lot of all mankind;
To lose a friend, a brother, or a son, 60
Heav'n dooms each mortal, and its will is done:
A while they sorrow, then dismiss their care;
Fate gives the wound, and man is born to bear.
But this insatiate the commission giv'n
By fate, exceeds; and tempts the wrath of heav'n: 65
Lo how his rage dishonest drags along
Hector's dead earth insensible of wrong!
Brave tho' he be, yet by no reason aw'd,
He violates the laws of man and God.

70   If equal honours by the partial skies
Are doom'd both heroes, (*Juno* thus replies)
If *Thetis'* son must no distinction know,
Then hear, ye Gods! the Patron of the Bow.
But *Hector* only boasts a mortal claim,
75   His birth deriving from a mortal dame:
Achilles of your own ætherial race
Springs from a Goddess by a man's embrace;
(A Goddess by our self to *Peleus* giv'n,
A man divine, and chosen friend of heav'n.)
80   To grace those nuptials, from the bright abode
Your selves were present; where this Minstrel-God
(Well-pleas'd to share the feast,) amid the quire
Stood proud to hymn, and tune his youthful lyre.
    Then thus the Thund'rer checks th' imperial
        dame:
85   Let not thy wrath the court of heav'n inflame;
Their merits, nor their honours, are the same.
But mine, and ev'ry God's peculiar grace
Hector deserves, of all the *Trojan* race:
Still on our shrines his grateful off'rings lay,
90   (The only honours men to Gods can pay)
Nor ever from our smoaking altar ceast
The pure libation, and the holy feast.
Howe'er by stealth to snatch the corse away,
We will not: *Thetis* guards it night and day.
95   But haste, and summon to our courts above
The azure Queen; let her persuasion move
Her furious son from *Priam* to receive
The proffer'd ransom, and the corps to leave.
    He added not: And *Iris* from the skies,
100 Swift as a whirlwind, on the message flies,
Meteorous the face of Ocean sweeps,
Refulgent gliding o'er the sable deeps.
Between where *Samos* wide his forests spreads,
And rocky *Imbrus* lifts its pointed heads,
105 Down plung'd the maid; (the parted waves resound)
She plung'd, and instant shot the dark profound.
As bearing death in the fallacious bait
From the bent angle sinks the loaden weight;

So past the Goddess thro' the closing wave,
Where *Thetis* sorrow'd in her secret cave: 110
There plac'd amidst her melancholy train
(The blue-hair'd sisters of the sacred main)
Pensive she sate, revolving fates to come,
And wept her god-like son's approaching doom.
   Then thus the Goddess of the painted bow.   115
Arise! O *Thetis*, from thy seats below.
'Tis *Jove* that calls. And why (the Dame replies)
Calls *Jove* his *Thetis* to the hated skies?
Sad object as I am for heav'nly sight!
Ah! may my sorrows ever shun the light!   120
Howe'er be heav'ns almighty Sire obey'd –
She spake, and veil'd her head in sable shade,
Which, flowing long, her graceful person clad;
And forth she pac'd, majestically sad.
   Then thro' the world of waters, they repair   125
(The way fair *Iris* led) to upper air.
The deeps dividing, o'er the coast they rise,
And touch with momentary flight the skies.
There in the light'ning's blaze the Sire they found,
And all the Gods in shining synod round.   130
Thetis approach'd with anguish in her face,
(*Minerva* rising, gave the mourner place)
Ev'n *Juno* sought her sorrows to console,
And offer'd from her hand the nectar bowl:
She tasted, and resign'd it: Then began   135
The sacred sire of Gods and mortal man:
   Thou com'st fair *Thetis*, but with grief o'ercast,
Maternal sorrows, long, ah long to last!
Suffice, we know and we partake thy cares:
But yield to Fate, and hear what *Jove* declares.   140
Nine days are past, since all the court above
In *Hector*'s cause have mov'd the ear of *Jove*;
'Twas voted, *Hermes* from his god-like foe
By stealth should bear him, but we will'd not so:
We will, thy son himself the corse restore,   145
And to his conquest add this glory more.
Then hye thee to him, and our mandate bear;
Tell him he tempts the wrath of heav'n too far:

Nor let him more (our anger if he dread)
150 Vent his mad vengeance on the sacred dead:
But yield to ransom and the father's pray'r.
The mournful father *Iris* shall prepare,
With gifts to sue; and offer to his hands
Whate'er his honour asks, or heart demands.
155   His word the silver-footed Queen attends,
And from *Olympus'* snowy tops descends.
Arriv'd, she heard the voice of loud lament,
And echoing groans that shook the lofty tent.
His friends prepare the victim, and dispose
160 Repast unheeded, while he vents his woes.
The Goddess seats her by her pensive son,
She prest his hand, and tender thus begun.
    How long, unhappy! shall thy sorrows flow,
And thy heart waste with life-consuming woe?
165 Mindless of food, or love whose pleasing reign
Sooths weary life, and softens human pain.
O snatch the moments yet within thy Pow'r,
Nor long to live, indulge the am'rous hour!
Lo! *Jove* himself (for *Jove's* command I bear)
170 Forbids to tempt the wrath of heav'n too far,
No longer then (his fury if thou dread)
Detain the relicks of great *Hector* dead;
Nor vent on senseless earth thy vengeance vain,
But yield to ransom, and restore the slain.
175   To whom *Achilles*: Be the ransom giv'n,
And we submit, since such the will of heav'n.
    While thus they commun'd, from th' *Olympian* bow'rs
Jove orders *Iris* to the *Trojan* tow'rs.
Haste, winged Goddess! to the sacred town,
180 And urge her Monarch to redeem his son;
Alone, the *Ilian* ramparts let him leave,
And bear what stern *Achilles* may receive:
Alone, for so we will: No *Trojan* near;
Except, to place the dead with decent care,
185 Some aged herald, who with gentle hand,
May the slow mules and fun'ral car command.
Nor let him death, nor let him danger dread,
Safe thro' the foe by our protection led:

Him *Hermes* to *Achilles* shall convey,
Guard of his life, and partner of his way.   190
Fierce as he is, *Achilles'* self shall spare
His age, nor touch one venerable hair;
Some thought there must be, in a soul so brave,
Some sense of duty, some desire to save.

Then down her bow the winged *Iris* drives,   195
And swift at *Priam*'s mournful court arrives;
Where the sad sons beside their father's throne
Sate bath'd in tears, and answer'd groan with groan.
And all amidst them lay the hoary sire,
(Sad scene of woe!) His face his wrapt attire   200
Conceal'd from sight; With frantick hands he spread
A show'r of ashes o'er his neck and head.
From room to room his pensive daughters roam;
Whose shrieks and clamours fill the vaulted dome;
Mindful of those, who, late their pride and joy,   205
Lie pale and breathless round the fields of *Troy!*
Before the King *Jove*'s messenger appears,
And thus in whispers greets his trembling ears.

Fear not, oh father! no ill news I bear;
From *Jove* I come, *Jove* makes thee still his care: 210
For *Hector*'s sake these walls he bids thee leave,
And bear what stern *Achilles* may receive;
Alone, for so he wills: No *Trojan* near,
Except to place the dead with decent care,
Some aged herald, who with gentle hand   215
May the slow mules and fun'ral car command.
Nor shalt thou death, nor shalt thou danger dread;
Safe thro' the foe by his protection led;
Thee *Hermes* to *Pelides* shall convey,
Guard of thy life, and partner of thy way.   220
Fierce as he is, *Achilles'* self shall spare
Thy age, nor touch one venerable hair;
Some thought there must be, in a soul so brave,
Some sense of duty, some desire to save.

She spoke, and vanish'd. *Priam* bids prepare   225
His gentle mules, and harness to the car;
There, for the gifts, a polish'd casket lay:
His pious sons the King's command obey.

Then past the Monarch to his bridal-room,
230   Where cedar-beams the lofty roofs perfume,
And where the treasures of his empire lay;
Then call'd his Queen, and thus began to say.
     Unhappy consort of a King distrest!
Partake the troubles of thy husband's breast:
235   I saw descend the messenger of *Jove*,
Who bids me try *Achilles'* mind to move;
Forsake these ramparts, and with gifts obtain
The corps of *Hector*, at yon' navy slain.
Tell me thy thought: My heart impels to go
240   Thro' hostile camps, and bears me to the foe.
     The hoary Monarch thus. Her piercing cries
Sad *Hecuba* renews, and then replies.
Ah! whither wanders thy distemper'd mind?
And where the prudence now that aw'd mankind?
245   Thro' *Phrygia* once, and foreign regions known,
Now all confus'd, distracted, overthrown!
Singly to pass thro' hosts of foes! to face
(Oh heart of steel!) the murd'rer of thy race!
To view that deathful eye, and wander o'er
250   Those hands, yet red with *Hector*'s noble gore!
Alas! my Lord! he knows not how to spare,
And what his mercy, thy slain sons declare;
So brave! so many fall'n! To calm his rage
Vain were thy dignity, and vain thy age.
255   No – pent in this sad palace let us give
To grief the wretched days we have to live.
Still, still for *Hector* let our sorrows flow,
Born to his own, and to his parents woe!
Doom'd from the hour his luckless life begun,
260   To dogs, to vultures, and to *Peleus'* son!
Oh! in his dearest blood might I allay
My rage, and these barbarities repay!
For ah! could *Hector* merit thus? whose breath
Expir'd not meanly, in unactive death:
265   He pour'd his latest blood in manly fight,
And fell a hero in his country's right.
     Seek not to stay me, nor my soul affright
With words of omen like a bird of night;

(Reply'd unmov'd the venerable man)
'Tis heav'n commands me, and you urge in vain.   270
Had any mortal voice th'injunction laid,
Nor augur, priest, or seer had been obey'd.
A present Goddess brought the high command,
I saw, I heard her, and the word shall stand.
I go, ye Gods! obedient to your call: 275
If in yon' camp your pow'rs have doom'd my fall,
Content – By the same hand let me expire!
Add to the slaughter'd son the wretched sire!
One cold embrace at least may be allow'd,
And my last tears flow mingled with his blood!   280
    From forth his open'd stores, this said, he drew
Twelve costly carpets of refulgent hue,
As many vests, as many mantles told,
And twelve fair veils, and garments stiff with gold.
Two tripods next, and twice two chargers shine,   285
With ten pure talents from the richest mine;
And last a large well–labour'd bowl had place,
(The pledge of treaties once with friendly *Thrace*)
Seem'd all too mean the stores he could employ,
For one last look to buy him back to *Troy!*   290
    Lo! the sad father, frantick with his pain,
Around him furious drives his menial train:
In vain each slave with duteous care attends,
Each office hurts him, and each face offends.
What make ye here? Officious crowds! (he cries)   295
Hence! nor obtrude your anguish on my eyes.
Have ye no griefs at home, to fix ye there?
Am I the only object of despair?
Am I become my people's common show,
Set up by *Jove* your spectacle of woe?   300
No, you must feel him too; your selves must fall;
The same stern God to ruin gives you all:
Nor is great *Hector* lost by me alone;
Your sole defence, your guardian pow'r is gone!
I see your blood the fields of *Phrygia* drown,   305
I see the ruins of your smoking town!
Oh send me, Gods! e'er that sad day shall come,
A willing ghost to *Pluto*'s dreary dome!

He said, and feebly drives his friends away:
310   The sorrowing friends his frantick rage obey.
Next on his sons his erring fury falls,
Polites, Paris, Agathon, he calls,
His threats *Deïphobus* and *Dius* hear,
Hippothoüs, Pammon, Helenus the seer,
315   And gen'rous *Antiphon:* For yet these nine
Surviv'd, sad relicks of his num'rous line.
     Inglorious sons of an unhappy sire!
Why did not all in *Hector*'s cause expire?
Wretch that I am! my bravest offspring slain,
320   You, the disgrace of *Priam*'s house, remain!
Mestor the brave, renown'd in ranks of war,
With *Troilus,* dreadful on his rushing car,
And last great *Hector,* more than man divine,
For sure he seem'd not of terrestial line!
325   All those relentless *Mars* untimely slew,
And left me these, a soft and servile crew,
Whose days the feast and wanton dance employ,
Gluttons and flatt'rers, the contempt of *Troy!*
Why teach ye not my rapid wheels to run,
330   And speed my journey to redeem my son?
     The sons their father's wretched age revere,
Forgive his anger, and produce the car.
High on the seat the cabinet they bind:
The new-made car with solid beauty shin'd;
335   Box was the yoke, embost with costly pains,
And hung with ringlets to receive the reins;
Nine cubits long the traces swept the ground;
These to the chariot's polish'd pole they bound,
Then fix'd a ring the running reins to guide,
340   And close beneath the gather'd ends were ty'd.
Next with the gifts (the price of *Hector* slain)
The sad attendants load the groaning wain:
Last to the yoke the well-match'd mules they bring,
(The gift of *Mysia* to the *Trojan* King.)
345   But the fair horses, long his darling care,
Himself receiv'd, and harness'd to his car:
Griev'd as he was, he not this task deny'd;
The hoary herald help'd him at his side.

While careful these the gentle coursers join'd,
Sad *Hecuba* approach'd with anxious mind;   350
A golden bowl that foam'd with fragrant wine,
(Libation destin'd to the pow'r divine)
Held in her right, before the steeds she stands,
And thus consigns it to the monarch's hands.

Take this, and pour to *Jove*: that safe from harms,   355
His grace restore thee to our roof, and arms;
Since victor of thy fears, and slighting mine,
Heav'n, or thy soul, inspire this bold design:
Pray to that God, who high on *Ida*'s brow
Surveys thy desolated realms below,   360
His winged messenger to send from high,
And lead thy way with heav'nly augury:
Let the strong sov'reign of the plumy race
Tow'r on the right of yon' æthereal space.
That sign beheld, and strengthen'd from above,   365
Boldly pursue the journey mark'd by *Jove*;
But if the God his augury denies,
Suppress thy impulse, nor reject advice.

'Tis just (said *Priam*) to the sire above
To raise our hands, for who so good as *Jove*?   370
He spoke, and bad th'attendant handmaid bring
The purest water of the living spring:
(Her ready hands the ew'er and bason held)
Then took the golden cup his Queen had fill'd,
On the mid pavement pours the rosy wine,   375
Uplifts his eyes, and calls the pow'r divine.

Oh first, and greatest! heav'ns imperial Lord!
On lofty *Ida*'s holy hill ador'd!
To stern *Achilles* now direct my ways,
And teach him mercy when a father prays.   380
If such thy will, dispatch from yonder sky
Thy sacred bird, cœlestial augury!
Let the strong sov'reign of the plumy race
Tow'r on the right of yon' æthereal space:
So shall thy suppliant, strengthen'd from above,   385
Fearless pursue the journey mark'd by *Jove*.

Jove heard his pray'r, and from the throne on high
Dispatch'd his bird, cœlestial augury!

The swift-wing'd chaser of the feather'd game,
390 And known to Gods by *Percnos'* lofty name.
Wide, as appears some palace gate display'd,
So broad, his pinions stretch'd their ample shade,
As stooping dexter with resounding wings
Th'imperial bird descends in airy rings.
395 A dawn of joy in ev'ry face appears;
The mourning matron dries her tim'rous tears.
Swift on his car th'impatient monarch sprung;
The brazen portal in his passage rung.
The mules preceding draw the loaded wain,
400 Charg'd with the gifts; *Idæus* holds the rein:
The King himself his gentle steeds controuls,
And thro surrounding friends the chariot rolls.
On his slow wheels the following people wait,
Mourn at each step, and give him up to Fate;
405 With hands uplifted, eye him as he past,
And gaze upon him as they gaz'd their last.
Now forward fares the Father on his way,
Thro' the lone fields, and back to *Ilion* they.
Great *Jove* beheld him as he crost the plain,
410 And felt the woes of miserable man.
Then thus to *Hermes.* Thou whose constant cares
Still succour mortals, and attend their pray'rs;
Behold an object to thy charge consign'd,
If ever pity touch'd thee for mankind.
415 Go, guard the sire; th'observing foe prevent,
And safe conduct him to *Achilles'* tent.
    The God obeys, his golden pinions binds,
And mounts incumbent on the wings of winds,
That high thro' fields of air his flight sustain,
420 O'er the wide earth, and o'er the boundless main:
Then grasps the wand that causes sleep to fly,
Or in soft slumbers seals the wakeful eye;
Thus arm'd, swift *Hermes* steers his airy way,
And stoops on *Hellespont*'s resounding sea.
425 A beauteous youth, majestick and divine,
He seem'd; fair offspring of some princely line!
Now twilight veil'd the glaring face of day,
And clad the dusky fields in sober gray;

What time the herald and the hoary King
Their chariots stopping, at the silver spring   430
That circling *Ilus'* ancient marble flows,
Allow'd their mules and steeds a short repose.
Thro' the dim shade the herald first espies
A man's approach, and thus to *Priam* cries.
I mark some foe's advance: O King! beware;   435
This hard adventure claims thy utmost care:
For much I fear, destruction hovers nigh:
Our state asks counsel; is it best to fly?
Or, old and helpless, at his feet to fall,
(Two wretched suppliants) and for mercy call?   440
     Th' afflicted Monarch shiver'd with despair;
Pale grew his face, and upright stood his hair;
Sunk was his heart; his colour went and came;
A sudden trembling shook his aged frame:
When *Hermes* greeting, touch'd his royal hand,   445
And gentle, thus accosts with kind demand.
     Say whither, father! when each mortal sight
Is seal'd in sleep, thou wander'st thro' the night?
Why roam thy mules and steeds the plains along,
Thro' *Grecian* foes, so num'rous and so strong?   450
What couldst thou hope, should these thy treasures view,
These, who with endless hate thy race pursue?
For what defence, alas! couldst thou provide?
Thy self not young, a weak old man thy guide.
Yet suffer not thy soul to sink with dread;   455
From me no harm shall touch thy rev'rend head;
From *Greece* I'll guard thee too; for in those lines
The living image of my father shines.
     Thy words, that speak benevolence of mind
Are true, my son! (the godlike sire rejoin'd)   460
Great are my hazards; but the Gods survey
My steps, and send thee, guardian of my way.
Hail, and be blest! For scarce of mortal kind
Appear thy form, thy feature, and thy mind.
     Nor true are all thy words, nor erring wide;   465
(The sacred messenger of heav'n reply'd)
But say, convey'st thou thro' the lonely plains
What yet most precious of thy store remains,

To lodge in safety with some friendly hand?
470 Prepar'd perchance to leave thy native land.
Or fly'st thou now? What hopes can *Troy* retain?
Thy matchless son, her guard and glory, slain!
     The King, alarm'd. Say what, and whence thou art,
Who search the sorrows of a parent's heart,
475 And know so well how god-like *Hector* dy'd?
Thus *Priam* spoke, and *Hermes* thus reply'd.
     You tempt me, father, and with pity touch:
On this sad subject you enquire too much.
Oft have these eyes that godlike *Hector* view'd
480 In glorious fight with *Grecian* blood embru'd:
I saw him, when like *Jove*, his flames he tost
On thousand ships, and wither'd half a host:
I saw, but help'd not: Stern *Achilles'* ire
Forbad assistance, and enjoy'd the fire.
485 For him I serve, of *Myrmidonian* race;
One ship convey'd us from our native place;
Polyctor is my sire, an honour'd name,
Old like thy self, and not unknown to fame;
Of sev'n his sons by whom the lot was cast
490 To serve our Prince, it fell on me, the last.
To watch this quarter my adventure falls,
For with the morn the *Greeks* attack your walls;
Sleepless they sit, impatient to engage,
And scarce their rulers check their martial rage.
495   If then thou art of stern *Pelides'* train,
(The mournful Monarch thus rejoin'd again)
Ah tell me truly, where, oh where are laid
My son's dear relicks? what befalls him dead?
Have dogs dismember'd on the naked plains,
500 Or yet unmangled rest his cold remains?
     O favor'd of the skies! (Thus answer'd then
The pow'r that mediates between Gods and men)
Nor dogs nor vultures have thy *Hector* rent,
But whole he lies, neglected in the tent:
505 This the twelfth evening since he rested there,
Untouch'd by worms, untainted by the air. -
Still as *Aurora*'s ruddy beam is spread,
Round his friend's tomb *Achilles* drags the dead:

Yet undisfigur'd, or in limb or face,
All fresh he lies, with ev'ry living grace,   510
Majestical in death! No stains are found
O'er all the corse, and clos'd is ev'ry wound;
(Tho' many a wound they gave) some heav'nly care,
Some hand divine, preserves him ever fair:
Or all the host of heav'n, to whom he led   515
A life so grateful, still regard him dead.
    Thus spoke to *Priam* the cœlestial guide,
And joyful thus the royal sire reply'd.
Blest is the man who pays the Gods above
The constant tribute of respect and love!   520
Those who inhabit the *Olympian* bow'r
My son forgot not, in exalted pow'r;
And heav'n, that ev'ry virtue bears in mind,
Ev'n to the ashes of the just, is kind.
But thou, oh gen'rous youth! this goblet take,   525
A pledge of gratitude for *Hector*'s sake;
And while the fav'ring Gods our steps survey,
Safe to *Pelides*' tent conduct my way.
    To whom the latent God. O King forbear
To tempt my youth, for apt is youth to err: 530
But can I, absent from my Prince's sight,
Take gifts in secret, that must shun the light?
What from our master's int'rest thus we draw,
Is but a licens'd theft that 'scapes the law.
Respecting him, my soul abjures th' offence;   535
And as the crime, I dread the consequence.
Thee, far as *Argos*, pleas'd I could convey:
Guard of thy life, and partner of thy way.
On thee attend, thy safety to maintain,
O'er pathless forests, or the roaring main.   540
    He said, then took the chariot at a bound,
And snatch'd the reins, and whirl'd the lash around:
Before th' inspiring God that urg'd them on,
The coursers fly with spirit not their own.
And now they reach'd the naval walls, and found   545
The guards repasting, while the bowls go round;
On these the virtue of his wand he tries,
And pours deep slumber on their watchful eyes:

Then heav'd the massy gates, remov'd the bars,
550   And o'er the trenches led the rolling cars.
Unseen, thro' all the hostile camp they went,
And now approach'd *Pelides'* lofty tent.
Of fir the roof was rais'd, and cover'd o'er
With reeds collected from the marshy shore;
555   And, fenc'd with palisades, a hall of state,
(The work of soldiers) where the hero sate.
Large was the door, whose well-compacted strength
A solid pine-tree barr'd, of wond'rous length;
Scarce three strong *Greeks* could lift its mighty weight,
560   But great *Achilles* singly clos'd the gate.
This *Hermes* (such the pow'r of Gods) set wide;
Then swift alighted the cœlestial guide,
And thus, reveal'd – Hear Prince! and understand
Thou ow'st thy guidance to no mortal hand:
565   *Hermes* I am, descended from above,
The King of Arts, the messenger of *Jove*.
Farewell: To shun *Achilles'* sight I fly;
Uncommon are such favours of the sky,
Nor stand confest to frail mortality.
570   Now fearless enter, and prefer thy pray'rs;
Adjure him by his father's silver hairs,
His son, his mother! urge him to bestow
Whatever pity that stern heart can know.
   Thus having said, he vanish'd from his eyes,
575   And in a moment shot into the skies:
The King, confirm'd from heav'n, alighted there,
And left his aged herald on the car.
With solemn pace thro' various rooms he went,
And found *Achilles* in his inner tent:
580   There sate the Hero; *Alcimus* the brave,
And great *Automedon*, attendance gave:
These serv'd his person at the royal Feast;
Around, at awful distance, stood the rest.
   Unseen by these, the King his entry made;
585   And prostrate now before *Achilles* laid,
Sudden, (a venerable sight!) appears;
Embrac'd his knees, and bath'd his hands in tears;
Those direful hands his kisses press'd, embru'd

Ev'n with the best, the dearest of his blood!
    As when a wretch, (who conscious of his crime,   590
Pursu'd for murder, flies his native clime)
Just gains some frontier, breathless, pale! amaz'd!
All gaze, all wonder: Thus *Achilles* gaz'd:
Thus stood th'attendants stupid with surprize;
All mute, yet seem'd to question with their eyes: 595
Each look'd on other, none the silence broke,
Till thus at last the kingly suppliant spoke.
    Ah think, thou favour'd of the pow'rs divine!
Think of thy father's age, and pity mine!
In me, that father's rev'rend image trace,   600
Those silver hairs, that venerable face;
His trembling limbs, his helpless person, see!
In all my equal, but in misery!
Yet now, perhaps, some turn of human fate
Expels him helpless from his peaceful state;   605
Think from some pow'rful foe tho see'st him fly,
And beg protection with a feeble cry.
Yet still one comfort in his soul may rise;
He hears his son still lives to glad his eyes;
And hearing still may hope, a better day   610
May send him thee, to chase that Foe away.
No comfort to my griefs, no hopes remain,
The best, the bravest of my sons are slain!
Yet what a race; e'er *Greece* to *Ilion* came,
The pledge of many a lov'd, and loving dame: 615
Nineteen one mother bore – Dead, all are dead!
How oft, alas! has wretched *Priam* bled?
Still one was left, their loss to recompense;
His father's hope, his country's last defence.
Him too thy rage has slain! beneath thy steel   620
Unhappy in his country's cause he fell!
    For him, thro' hostile camps I bent my way,
For him thus prostrate at thy feet I lay;
Large gifts proportion'd to thy Wrath I bear;
Oh hear the wretched, and the Gods revere!   625
    Think of thy father, and this face behold!
See him in me, as helpless and as old!

Tho' not so wretched: There he yields to me,
The first of men in sov'reign misery.
630 Thus forc'd to kneel, thus grov'ling to embrace
The scourge and ruin of my realm and race;
Suppliant my children's murd'rer to implore,
And kiss those hands yet reeking with their gore!
    These words soft pity in the chief inspire,
635 Touch'd with the dear remembrance of his Sire.
Then with his hand (as prostrate still he lay)
The old man's cheek he gently turn'd away.
Now each by turns indulg'd the gush of woe;
And now the mingled tides together flow:
640 This low on earth, that gently bending o'er,
A father one, and one a son deplore:
But great *Achilles* diff'rent passions rend,
And now his Sire he mourns, and now his friend.
Th' infectious softness thro' the heroes ran;
645 One universal solemn show'r began;
They bore as heroes, but they felt as man.
    Satiate at length with unavailing woes,
From the high throne divine *Achilles* rose;
The rev'rend monarch by the hand he rais'd;
650 On his white beard and form majestick gaz'd,
Not unrelenting: Then serene began
With words to sooth the miserable man.
    Alas! what weight of anguish hast thou known?
Unhappy Prince! thus guardless and alone
655 To pass thro' foes, and thus undaunted face
The man whose fury has destroy'd thy race?
Heav'n sure has arm'd thee with a heart of steel,
A strength proportion'd to the woes you feel.
Rise then: Let reason mitigate our care:
660 To mourn, avails not: Man is born to bear.
Such is, alas! the Gods severe decree:
They, only they are blest, and only free.
Two urns by *Jove*'s high throne have ever stood,
The source of Evil one, and one of Good;
665 From thence the cup of mortal man he fills,
Blessings to these, to those distributes ills;

To most, he mingles both: The wretch decreed
To taste the bad, unmix'd, is curst indeed;
Pursu'd by wrongs, by meagre famine driv'n,
He wanders, outcast both of earth and heav'n.   670
The happiest taste not happiness sincere,
But find the cordial draught is dash'd with care.
Who more than *Peleus* shone in wealth and pow'r?
What stars concurring blest his natal hour?
A realm, a Goddess, to his wishes giv'n,   675
Grac'd by the Gods with all the gifts of heav'n!
One evil yet o'ertakes his latest day,
No race succeeding to imperial sway:
An only son! and he (alas!) ordain'd
To fall untimely in a foreign land!   680
See him, in *Troy*, the pious care decline
Of his weak age, to live the curse of thine!
Thou too, old man, hast happier days beheld;
In riches once, in children once excell'd;
Extended *Phrygia* own'd thy ample reign,   685
And all fair *Lesbos'* blissful seats contain,
And all wide *Hellespont*'s unmeasur'd main.
But since the God his hand has pleas'd to turn,
And fill thy measure from his bitter urn,
What sees the sun, but hapless heroes falls?   690
War, and the blood of men, surround thy walls!
What must be, must be. Bear thy lot, nor shed
These unavailing sorrows o'er the dead;
Thou can'st not call him from the *Stygian* shore,
But thou alas! may'st live to suffer more!   695
  To whom the King. Oh favour'd of the skies!
Here let me grow to earth! since *Hector* lies
On the bare beach, depriv'd of obsequies.
Oh give me *Hector!* to my eyes restore
His corse, and take the gifts: I ask no more.   700
Thou, as thou may'st, these boundless stores enjoy;
Safe may'st thou sail, and turn thy wrath from *Troy*;
So shall thy pity and forbearance give
A weak old man to see the light and live!
  Move me no more (*Achilles* thus replies,   705
While kindling anger sparkled in his eyes)

Nor seek by tears my steady soul to bend;
To yield thy *Hector* I my self intend:
For know, from *Jove* my Goddess-mother came,
710 (Old Ocean's daughter, silver-footed dame)
Nor com'st thou but by heav'n; nor com'st alone,
Some God impels with courage not thy own:
No human hand the weighty gates unbarr'd,
Nor could the boldest of our youth have dar'd
715 To pass our out-works, or elude the guard.
Cease; lest neglectful of high *Jove*'s command
I show thee, King! thou tread'st on hostile land;
Release my knees, thy suppliant arts give o'er,
And shake the purpose of my soul no more.
720   The Sire obey'd him, trembling and o'er-aw'd.
Achilles, like a lion, rush'd abroad:
Automedon and *Alcimus* attend,
(Whom most he honour'd, since he lost his friend;)
These to unyoke the mules and horses went,
725 And led the hoary herald to the tent;
Next heap'd on high the num'rous presents bear
(Great *Hector*'s ransome) from the polish'd car.
Two splendid mantles, and a carpet spread,
They leave; to cover, and inwrap the dead.
730 Then call the handmaids with assistant toil
To wash the body and anoint with oil;
Apart from *Priam*, lest th' unhappy sire
Provok'd to passion, once more rouze to ire
The stern *Pelides*; and nor sacred age
735 Nor *Jove*'s command, should check the rising rage.
This done, the garments o'er the corse they spread;
Achilles lifts it to the fun'ral bed:
Then, while the body on the car they laid,
He groans, and calls on lov'd *Patroclus*' shade.
740   If, in that gloom which never light must know,
The deeds of mortals touch the ghosts below:
O friend! forgive me, that I thus fulfill
(Restoring *Hector*) heav'ns unquestion'd will.
The gifts the father gave, be ever thine,
745 To grace thy *manes*, and adorn thy shrine.

He said, and entring, took his seat of state,
Where full before him rev'rend *Priam* sate:
To whom, compos'd, the God-like chief begun.
Lo! to thy pray'r restor'd, thy breathless son;
Extended on the fun'ral couch he lies;   750
And soon as morning paints the eastern skies,
The sight is granted to thy longing eyes.
But now the peaceful hours of sacred night
Demand refection, and to rest invite:
Nor thou, O father! thus consum'd with woe,   755
The common cares that nourish life, forego.
Not thus did *Niobe*, of form divine,
A parent once, whose sorrows equal'd thine:
Six youthful sons, as many blooming maids,
In one sad day beheld the *Stygian* shades;   760
These by *Apollo*'s silver bow were slain,
Those, *Cynthia*'s arrows stretch'd upon the plain.
So was her pride chastiz'd by wrath divine,
Who match'd her own with bright *Latona*'s line;
But two the Goddess, twelve the Queen enjoy'd;   765
Those boasted twelve th'avenging two destroy'd.
Steep'd in their blood, and in the dust outspread,
Nine days neglected lay expos'd the dead;
None by to weep them, to inhume them none;
(For *Jove* had turn'd the nation all to stone:)   770
The Gods themselves at length relenting, gave
Th'unhappy race the honours of a grave.
Her self a rock, (for such was heav'ns high will)
Thro' desarts wild now pours a weeping rill;
Where round the bed whence *Acheloüs* springs,   775
The wat'ry fairies dance in mazy rings,
There high on *Sipylus* his shaggy brow,
She stands her own sad monument of woe;
The rock for ever lasts, the tears for ever flow!
    Such griefs, O King! have other parents known;   780
Remember theirs, and mitigate thy own.
The care of heav'n thy *Hector* has appear'd,
Nor shall he lie unwept, and uninterr'd;
Soon may thy aged cheeks in tears be drown'd,
And all the eyes of *Ilion* stream around.   785

He said, and rising, chose the victim ewe
With silver fleece, which his attendants slew.
The limbs they sever from the reeking hide,
With skill prepare them, and in parts divide:
790   Each on the coals the sep'rate morsels lays,
And hasty, snatches from the rising blaze.
With bread the glitt'ring canisters they load,
Which round the board *Automedon* bestow'd:
The chief himself to each his portion plac'd,
795   And each indulging shar'd in sweet repast.
When now the rage of hunger was represt,
The wond'ring hero eyes his royal guest;
No less the royal guest the hero eyes;
His god-like aspect and majestick size;
800   Here, youthful grace and noble fire engage,
And there, the mild benevolence of age.
Thus gazing long, the silence neither broke,
(A solemn scene!) at length the father spoke.
    Permit me now, belov'd of *Jove!* to steep
805   My careful temples in the dew of sleep:
For since the day that numbred with the dead
My hapless son, the dust has been my bed,
Soft sleep a stranger to my weeping eyes,
My only food my sorrows and my sighs!
810   Till now, encourag'd by the grace you give,
I share thy banquet, and consent to live.
    With that, *Achilles* bad prepare the bed,
With purple soft, and shaggy carpets spread;
Forth, by the flaming lights, they bend their way,
815   And place the couches, and the cov'rings lay.
Then he: Now father sleep, but sleep not here.
Consult thy safety, and forgive my fear,
Lest any *Argive* (at this hour awake,
To ask our counsel or our orders take,)
820   Approaching sudden to our open'd tent,
Perchance behold thee, and our grace prevent.
Should such report thy honour'd person here,
The King of men the ransom might defer.
But say with speed, if ought of thy desire
825   Remains unask'd; what time the rites require

T' inter thy *Hector?* For, so long we stay
Our slaught'ring arm, and bid the hosts obey.
　　If then thy will permit (the Monarch said)
To finish all due honours to the dead,
This, of thy grace, accord: To thee are known　　　830
The fears of *Ilion*, clos'd within her town,
And at what distance from our walls aspire
The hills of *Ide*, and forests for the fire.
Nine days to vent our sorrows I request,
The tenth shall see the fun'ral and the feast;　　　835
The next, to raise his monument be giv'n;
The twelfth we war, if war be doom'd by heav'n!
　　This thy request (reply'd the chief) enjoy:
Till then, our arms suspend the fall of *Troy*.
　　Then gave his hand at parting, to prevent　　　840
The old man's fears, and turn'd within the tent;
Where fair *Briseïs* bright in blooming charms
Expects her Hero with desiring arms.
But in the porch the King and herald rest,
Sad dreams of care yet wand'ring in their breast.　　　845
Now Gods and men the gifts of sleep partake;
Industrious *Hermes* only was awake,
The King's return revolving in his mind,
To pass the ramparts, and the watch to blind.
The pow'r descending hover'd o'er his head:　　　850
And sleep'st thou, father! (thus the vision said)
Now dost thou sleep, when *Hector* is restor'd?
Nor fear the *Grecian* foes, or *Grecian* Lord?
Thy presence here shou'd stern *Atrides* see,
Thy still-surviving sons may sue for thee,　　　855
May offer all thy treasures yet contain,
To spare thy age; and offer all in vain.
　　Wak'd with the word, the trembling Sire arose,
And rais'd his friend: The God before him goes,
He joins the mules, directs them with his hand,　　　860
And moves in silence thro' the hostile land.
When now to *Xanthus*' yellow stream they drove,
(*Xanthus*, immortal progeny of *Jove*)
The winged deity forsook their view,
And in a moment to *Olympus* flew.　　　865

Now shed *Aurora* round her saffron ray,
Sprung thro' the gates of light, and gave the day:
Charg'd with their mournful load, to *Ilion* go
The Sage and King, majestically slow.
870 *Cassandra* first beholds, from *Ilion*'s spire,
The sad procession of her hoary sire,
Then, as the pensive pomp advanc'd more near,
Her breathless brother stretch'd upon the bier:
A show'r of tears o'erflows her beauteous eyes,
875 Alarming thus all *Ilion* with her cries.

　　Turn here your steps, and here your eyes employ,
Ye wretched daughters, and ye sons of *Troy!*
If e'er ye rush'd in crowds, with vast delight
To hail your hero glorious from the fight;
880 Now meet him dead, and let your sorrows flow!
Your common triumph, and your common woe.

　　In thronging crowds they issue to the plains,
Nor man, nor woman, in the walls remains.
In ev'ry face the self-same grief is shown,
885 And *Troy* sends forth one universal groan.
At *Scæa*'s gates they meet the mourning wain,
Hang on the wheels, and grovel round the slain.
The wife and mother, frantic with despair,
Kiss his pale cheek, and rend their scatter'd hair:
890 Thus wildly wailing, at the gates they lay;
And there had sigh'd and sorrow'd out the day;
But god-like *Priam* from the chariot rose:
Forbear (he cry'd) this violence of woes,
First to the palace let the car proceed,
895 Then pour your boundless sorrows o'er the dead.

　　The waves of people at his word divide,
Slow rolls the chariot thro' the following tide;
Ev'n to the palace the sad pomp they wait:
They weep, and place him on the bed of state.
900 A melancholy choir attend around,
With plaintive sighs, and musick's solemn sound:
Alternately they sing, alternate flow
Th'obedient tears, melodious in their woe.
While deeper sorrows groan from each full heart,
905 And Nature speaks at ev'ry pause of Art.

First to the corse the weeping consort flew;
Around his neck her milk-white arms she threw,
And oh my *Hector!* oh my Lord! she cries,
Snatch'd in thy bloom from these desiring eyes!
Thou to the dismal realms for ever gone!	910
And I abandon'd, desolate, alone!
An only son, once comfort of our pains,
Sad product now of hapless love, remains!
Never to manly age that son shall rise,
Or with increasing graces glad my eyes:	915
For *Ilion* now (her great defender slain)
Shall sink a smoking ruin on the plain.
Who now protects her wives with guardian care?
Who saves her infants from the rage of war?
Now hostile fleets must waft those infants o'er,	920
(Those wives must wait 'em) to a foreign shore!
Thou too my son! to barb'rous climes shalt go,
The sad companion of thy mother's woe;
Driv'n hence a slave before the victor's sword;
Condemn'd to toil for some inhuman lord.	925
Or else some *Greek* whose father prest the plain,
Or son, or brother, by great *Hector* slain;
In *Hector*'s blood his vengeance shall enjoy,
And hurl thee headlong from the tow'rs of *Troy*.
For thy stern father never spar'd a foe:	930
Thence all these tears, and all this scene of woe!
Thence, many evils his sad parents bore,
His parents many, but his consort more.
Why gav'st thou not to me thy dying hand?
And why receiv'd not I thy last command?	935
Some word thou would'st have spoke, which sadly dear,
My soul might keep, or utter with a tear;
Which never, never could be lost in air,
Fix'd in my heart, and oft repeated there!
  Thus to her weeping maids she makes her moan;	940
Her weeping handmaids echo groan for groan.
  The mournful mother next sustains her part.
Oh thou, the best, the dearest to my heart!
Of all my race thou most by heav'n approv'd,
And by th'immortals ev'n in death belov'd!	945

While all my other sons in barb'rous bands
Achilles bound, and sold to foreign lands,
This felt no chains, but went a glorious ghost
Free, and a hero, to the *Stygian* coast.
950 Sentenc'd, 'tis true, by his inhuman doom,
Thy noble corse was dragg'd around the tomb,
(The tomb of him thy warlike arm had slain)
Ungen'rous insult, impotent and vain!
Yet glow'st thou fresh with ev'ry living grace,
955 No mark of pain, or violence of face;
Rosy and fair! as *Phœbus'* silver bow
Dismiss'd thee gently to the shades below.
  Thus spoke the dame, and melted into tears.
Sad *Helen* next in pomp of grief appears:
960 Fast from the shining sluices of her eyes
Fall the round crystal drops, while thus she cries.
  Ah dearest friend! in whom the Gods had join'd
The mildest manners with the bravest mind;
Now twice ten years (unhappy years) are o'er
965 Since *Paris* brought me to the *Trojan* shore;
(Oh had I perish'd, e'er that form divine
Seduc'd this soft, this easy heart of mine!)
Yet was it ne'er my fate, from thee to find
A deed ungentle, or a word unkind:
970 When others curst the auth'ress of their woe,
Thy pity check'd my sorrows in their flow:
If some proud brother ey'd me with disdain,
Or scornful sister with her sweeping train,
Thy gentle accents soften'd all my pain.
975 For thee I mourn; and mourn my self in thee,
The wretched source of all this misery!
The fate I caus'd, for ever I bemoan;
Sad *Helen* has no friend now thou art gone!
Thro' *Troy*'s wide streets abandon'd shall I roam!
980 In *Troy* deserted, as abhorr'd at home!
  So spoke the fair, with sorrow-streaming eye:
Distressful beauty melts each stander-by;
On all around th' infectious sorrow grows;
But *Priam* check'd the torrent as it rose.

Perform, ye *Trojans!* what the rites require,   985
And fell the forests for a fun'ral pyre;
Twelve days, nor foes, nor secret ambush dread;
Achilles grants these honours to the dead.
    He spoke; and at his word, the *Trojan* train
Their mules and oxen harness to the wain,   990
Pour thro' the gates, and, fell'd from *Ida*'s crown,
Roll back the gather'd forests to the town.
These toils continue nine succeeding days,
And high in air a sylvan structure raise.
But when the tenth fair morn began to shine,   995
Forth to the pile was born the man divine,
And plac'd aloft: while all, with streaming eyes,
Beheld the flames and rolling smokes arise.
Soon as *Aurora*, daughter of the dawn,
With rosy lustre streak'd the dewy lawn;   1000
Again the mournful crowds surround the pyre,
And quench with wine the yet remaining fire.
The snowy bones his friends and brothers place
(With tears collected) in a golden vase;
The golden vase in purple palls they roll'd,   1005
Of softest texture, and inwrought with gold.
Last o'er the urn the sacred earth they spread,
And rais'd the tomb, memorial of the dead.
(Strong guards and spies, till all the rites were done,
Watch'd from the rising to the setting sun.)   1010
All *Troy* then moves to *Priam*'s court again,
A solemn, silent, melancholy train:
Assembled there, from pious toil they rest,
And sadly shar'd the last sepulchral feast.
Such honours *Ilion* to her Hero paid,   1015
And peaceful slept the mighty *Hector*'s shade.

The End of the I L I A D

OBSERVATIONS

ON THE

TWENTY-FOURTH BOOK

14. *What Seas they measur'd,* &c.] There is something very noble in these sentiments of *Achilles*: He does not recollect any soft moments, any tendernesses that had pass'd between him and *Patroclus*, but he revolves the many difficulties, the toils by land, and the dangers by sea, in which they had been companions: Thus the poet on all occasions admirably sustains the character of *Achilles*; when he play'd upon the harp in the ninth book, he sung the atchievements of Kings; and in this place there is an air of greatness in his very sorrows: *Achilles* is as much a hero when he weeps, as when he fights.

This passage in *Homer* has not escap'd the censure of *Plato*, who thought it a diminution to his character to be thus transported with grief; but the objection will vanish if we remember that all the passions of *Achilles* are in the extreme; his nature is violent, and it would have been an outrage to his general character to have represented him as mourning moderately for his friend. *Plato* spoke more like a philosopher than a critick when he blamed the behaviour of *Achilles* as unmanly: These Tears would have ill become *Plato*, but they are graceful in *Achilles.*

Besides there is something very instructive in this whole representation, it shews us the power of a sincere friendship, and softens and recommends the character of *Achilles*; the violence he used towards his enemy is alleviated by the sincerity he expresses towards his friend; he is a terrible enemy, but an amiable friend.

30. *For* Phœbus *watch'd it,* &c.] *Eustathius* says, that by this shield of *Apollo* are meant the clouds that are drawn up by the beams of the sun, which cooling and qualifying the sultriness of the air, preserved the body from decay: But perhaps the poet had something farther in his

eye when he introduc'd *Apollo* upon this occasion: *Apollo* is a physician and the God of medicaments; if therefore *Achilles* used any Arts to preserve *Hector* from decay that he might be able the longer to insult his remains, *Apollo* may properly be said to protect it with his *Ægis.*

36. *But* Neptune *this, and* Pallas *this denies.*] It is with excellent art that the poet carries on this part of his poem, he shews that he could have contriv'd another way to recover the body of *Hector*, but as a God is never to be introduc'd but when human means fail, he rejects the interposition of *Mercury*, makes use of ordinary methods, and *Priam* redeems his son: This gives an air of probability to the relation, at the same time that it advances the glory of *Achilles*; for the greatest of his enemies labours to purchase his favour, the Gods hold a consultation, and a King becomes his suppliant.   *Eustathius.*

Those seven lines, from Κλέψαι δ' ὠτρύνεσκον to Μαχλοσύνην ἀλεγεινήν, have been thought spurious by some of the ancients: They judg'd it as an indecency that the Goddess of wisdom and *Achilles* should be equally inexorable; and thought it was below the majesty of the Gods to be said to steal. Besides, say they, had *Homer* been acquainted with the judgment of *Paris*, he would undoubtedly have mention'd it before this time in his poem, and consequently that story was of a later invention: And *Aristarchus* affirms that Μαχλοσύνη [lust] is a more modern word, and never known before the time of *Hesiod*, who uses it when he speaks of the daughters of *Prætus*; and adds, that it is appropriated to signify the incontinence of women, and cannot be at all apply'd to men: Therefore others read the last verse,

Ἢ οἱ κεχαρισμένα δῶρ' ὀνόμηνε.

[Pleased with him, she gave him gifts.]

These objections are entirely gather'd from *Eustathius*; to which we may add, that *Macrobius* seems to have been one of those who rejected these verses, since he affirms that our author never mentions the judgment of *Paris*. It may be answer'd, that the silence of *Homer* in the foregoing part of the poem, as to the judgment of *Paris*, is no argument that he was ignorant of that story: Perhaps he might think it most proper to unfold the cause of the destruction of *Troy* in the conclusion of the *Ilias*; that the reader seeing the wrong done, and the punishment of that wrong immediately following, might acknowledge the justice of it.

The same reason will be an answer to the objection relating to the anger of *Pallas*: Wisdom cannot be satisfy'd without justice, and consequently *Pallas* ought not to cease from resentment, till *Troy* has suffer'd the deserts of her crimes.

I cannot think that the objection about the word $Μαχλοσύνη$ is of any weight; the date of words is utterly uncertain, and as no one has been able to determine the ages of *Homer*, and *Hesiod*, so neither can any person be assured that such words were not in use in *Homer*'s days.

52. *A Lion, not a Man, &c.*] This is a very formal condemnation of the morals of *Achilles*, which *Homer* puts into the mouth of a God. One may see from this alone that he was far from designing his hero a virtuous character, yet the poet artfully introduces *Apollo* in the midst of his reproaches, intermingling the hero's praises with his blemishes: *Brave tho' he be,* &c. Thus what is the real Merit of *Achilles* is distinguish'd from what is blameable in his character, and we see *Apollo,* or the God of wisdom, is no less impartial than just in his representation of *Achilles.*

114. *And wept her god-like son's approaching doom.*] These words are very artfully inserted by the poet. The poem could not proceed to the death of *Achilles* without breaking the Action; and therefore to satisfy the curiosity of the reader concerning the fate of this great man, he takes care to inform us that his life draws to a period, and as it were celebrates his funeral before his death.

Such circumstances as these greatly raise the character of *Achilles*; he is so truly valiant, that tho' he knows he must fall before *Troy*, yet he does not abstain from the war, but couragiously meets his death: And here I think it proper to insert an observation that ought to have been made before, which is, that *Achilles* did not know that *Hector* was to fall by his hand; if he had known it, where would have been the mighty courage in engaging him in a single combat, in which he was sure to conquer? The contrary of this is evident from the words of *Achilles* to *Hector* just before the combat,

$$- Πρὶν \ γ' \ ἢ \ ἕτερόν \ γε \ πεσόντα$$
$$Αἵματος \ ἆσαι \ ἄρηα, \ \&c. -$$

I will make no compacts with thee, says *Achilles, but one of us shall fall.*

141. *Nine days are past since all the court above,* &c.] It may be thought that so many interpositions of the Gods, such messages from heaven to earth, and down to the seas, are needless machines; and it may be imagin'd that it is an offence against probability that so many Deities should be employ'd to pacify *Achilles*: But I am of opinion that the poet conducts this whole affair with admirable judgment. The poem is now almost at the conclusion, and *Achilles* is to pass from a state of an almost inexorable resentment to a state of perfect tranquillity; such a change could not be brought about by human means; *Achilles* is too stubborn to obey any thing less than a God: This is evident from his rejecting the persuasion of the whole *Grecian* army to return to the battle: So that it appears that this machinery was necessary, and consequently a beauty to the poem.

It may be farther added, that these several incidents proceed from *Jupiter*: It is by his appointment that so many Gods are employ'd to attend *Achilles.* By these means *Jupiter* fulfills the promise mention'd in the first book, of honouring the son of *Thetis*, and *Homer* excellently sustains his character by representing the inexorable *Achilles* as not parting with the body of his mortal enemy, but by the immediate command of *Jupiter.*

If the poet had conducted these incidents merely by human means, or suppos'd *Achilles* to restore the body of *Hector* entirely out of compassion, the draught had been unnatural, because unlike *Achilles*: Such a violence of temper was not to be pacify'd by ordinary methods. Besides, he has made use of the properest personages to carry on the affair; for who could be suppos'd to have so great an influence upon *Achilles* as his own mother, who is a Goddess?

164. *And thy heart waste with life-consuming woe.*] This expression in the original is very particular. Were it to be translated literally it must be render'd, how long wilt thou eat, or prey upon thy own heart by these sorrows? And it seems that it was a common way of expressing a deep sorrow; and *Pythagoras* uses it in this sense, μὴ ἐσθίειν καρδίαν [don't consume your heart], that is, grieve not excessively, let not sorrow make too great an impression upon thy heart.   *Eustathius.*

168. *– Indulge the am'rous hour!*] The ancients (says *Eustathius*) rejected these verses because of the indecent idea they convey: The Goddess in plain terms advises *Achilles* to go to bed to his mistress, and tells him a woman will be a comfort. The good bishop is of opinion, that they ought to be rejected, but the reason he gives is as extraordinary as that of *Thetis*: Soldiers, says he, have more occasion for something to strengthen themselves with, than for women: And this is the reason, continues he, why wrestlers are forbid all commerce with that sex during the whole time of their exercise.

Dionysius of *Halicarnassus* endeavours to justify *Homer* by observing, that this advice of *Thetis* was not given him to induce him to any wantonness, but was intended to indulge a nobler passion, his desire of glory: She advises him to go to that captive who was restor'd to him in a publick manner, to satisfy his honour: To that captive, the detention of whom had been so great a punishment to the whole *Grecian* army: And therefore *Thetis* uses a very proper motive to comfort her son, by advising him to gratify at once both his love and his glory.

Plutarch has likewise labour'd in *Homer*'s justification; he observes that the poet has set the picture of *Achilles* in this place in a very fair and strong point of light: Tho' *Achilles* had so lately receiv'd his belov'd *Briseïs* from the hands of *Agamemnon*; tho' he knew that his own life drew to a sudden period, yet the hero prevails over the lover, and he does not haste to indulge his love: He does not lament *Patroclus* like a common man by neglecting the duties of life, but he abstains from all pleasures by an excess of sorrow, and the love of his mistress is lost in that of his friend.

This observation excellently justifies *Achilles*, in not indulging himself with the company of his mistress: The hero indeed prevails so much over the lover, that *Thetis* thinks her self oblig'd to recall *Briseïs* to his memory. Yet still the indecency remains. All that can be said in favour of *Thetis* is, that she was mother to *Achilles*, and consequently might take the greater freedom with her son.

Madam *Dacier* disapproves of both the former observations: She has recourse to the lawfulness of such a practice between *Achilles* and *Briseïs*; and because such commerces in those times were reputed honest, therefore she thinks the advice was decent: The married ladies are oblig'd to her for this observation, and I hope all tender mothers, when their sons are afflicted, will advise them to comfort themselves in this manner.

In short, I am of opinion that this passage outrages decency; and 'tis a sign of some weakness to have so much occasion of justification. Indeed the whole passage is capable of a serious construction, and of such a sense as a mother might express to a son with decency: And then it will run thus; 'Why art thou, my Son, thus afflicted? Why thus resign'd to sorrow? Can neither sleep nor love divert you? Short is thy date of life, spend it not all in weeping, but allow some part of it to love and pleasure!' But still the indecency lies in the manner of the expression, which must be allow'd to be almost obscene, (for such is the word μίσγεσθ' *minisceri* [engage in sexual relations]) all that can be said in defence of it is, that as we are not competent judges of what ideas words might carry in *Homer*'s time, so we ought not entirely to condemn him, because it is possible the expression might not sound so indecently in ancient as in modern ears.

189. *Him* Hermes *to* Achilles *shall convey.*] The intervention of *Mercury* was very necessary at this time, and by it the poet not only gives an air of probability to the relation, but also pays a complement to his countrymen the *Grecians*: They kept so strict a guard that nothing but a God could pass unobserv'd, and this highly recommends their military discipline; and *Priam* not being able to carry the ransom without a chariot, it would have been an offence against probability, to have suppos'd him able to have pass'd all the guards of the army in his chariot, without the assistance of some deity: *Horace* had this passage in his view, Ode the 10th of the first book.

> *Iniqua* Trojæ *castra fefellit.*

[He escaped the notice of the camp hostile to Troy.]

191.   – Achilles' *self shall spare*
   His age, nor touch one venerable hair, &c.]

It is observable that every word here is a Negative, ἄφρων, ἄσκοπος, ἀλιτήμων [without intelligence, without guidance, in a blasphemous manner]; *Achilles* is still so angry that *Jupiter* cannot say he is wise, judicious, and merciful; he only commends him negatively, and barely says he is not a madman, nor perversely wicked.

It is the observation of the ancients, says *Eustathius*, that all the causes of the sins of man are included in those three words: Man offends either out of ignorance, and then he is ἄφρων; or thro' inadvertency, then he is ἄσκοπος; or wilfully and maliciously, and then he is ἀλιτήμων. So that this description agrees very well with the present disposition of *Achilles*; he is not ἄφρων, because his resentment begins to abate; he is not ἄσκοπος, because his mother has given him instructions, nor ἀλιτήμων, because he will not offend against the injunctions of *Jupiter*.

195. *The winged* Iris *flies, &c.*] Mons. *Rapin* has been very free upon this passage, where so many machines are made use of to cause *Priam* to obtain the body of *Hector* from *Achilles.* 'This father (says he) who has so much tenderness for his son, who is so superstitious in observing the funeral ceremonies, and saving those precious remains from the dogs and vultures; ought not he to have thought of doing this himself, without being thus expressly commanded by the Gods? Was there need of a machine to make him remember that he was a father?' But this critick entirely forgets what render'd such a conduct of absolute necessity; namely, the extreme danger and (in all probability) imminent ruin both of the King and state, upon *Priam*'s putting himself into the power of his most inveterate enemy. There was no other method of recovering *Hector,* and of discharging his funeral rites (which were look'd upon by the ancients of so high importance) and therefore the message from *Jupiter* to encourage *Priam,* with the assistance of *Mercury* to conduct him, and to prepare *Achilles* to receive him with favour, was far from impertinent: It was *dignus vindice nodus* [a knot worthy of such an avenger], as *Horace* expresses it.

200. *His face his wrapt attire Conceal'd from sight.*] The poet has observ'd a great decency in this place; he was not able to express the grief of his royal mourner, and so covers what he could not represent. From this passage *Semanthes* the *Sicyonian* painter borrow'd his design in the sacrifice of *Iphigenia,* and represents his *Agamemnon,* as *Homer* does his *Priam*: *Æschylus* has likewise imitated this place, and draws his *Niobe* exactly after the manner of *Homer.*   *Eustathius.*

265.   *He pour'd his latest blood in manly fight,*
          And fell a hero —

This whole discourse of *Hecuba* is exceedingly natural, she aggravates the features of *Achilles,* and softens those of *Hector*: Her anger blinds her so much that she can see nothing great in *Achilles,* and her fondness so much, that she can discern no defects in *Hector*: Thus she draws *Achilles* in the fiercest colours, like a barbarian, and calls him ὠμηστής [savage]; But at the same time forgets that *Hector* ever fled from *Achilles,* and in the original directly tells us that he *knew not how to fear, or how to fly.*   *Eustathius.*

291. *Lo! the sad father,* &c.] This behaviour of *Priam* is very natural to a person in his circumstances: The loss of his favourite son makes so deep an Impression upon his spirits, that he is incapable of consolation; he is displeased with every body; he is angry he knows not why; the disorder and hurry of his spirits make him break out into passionate expressions, and those expressions are contain'd in short periods, very natural to men in anger, who give not themselves leisure to express their sentiments at full length: It is from the same passion that *Priam*, in the second speech, treats all his sons with the utmost indignity, calls them gluttons, dancers, and flatterers. *Eustathius* very justly remarks, that he had *Paris* particularly in his eye; but his anger makes him transfer that character to the rest of his children, not being calm enough to make a distinction between the innocent and guilty.

That passage where he runs into the praises of *Hector*, is particularly natural: His concern and fondness make him as extravagant in the commendation of him, as in the disparagement of his other sons: They are less than mortals, he more than man. *Rapin* has censur'd this anger of *Priam* as a breach of the *Manners*, and says he might have shewn himself a father, otherwise than by this usage of his children. But whoever considers his circumstances will judge after another manner. *Priam*, after having been the most wealthy, most powerful and formidable monarch of *Asia*, becomes all at once the most miserable of men; he loses in less than eight days the best of his army, and a great number of virtuous sons; he loses the bravest of them all, his glory and his defence, the gallant *Hector*. This last blow sinks him quite, and changes him so much, that he is no longer the same: He becomes impatient, frantick, unreasonable! The terrible effect of ill fortune! Whoever has the least insight into nature, must admire so fine a picture of the force of adversity on an unhappy old man.

313. *Deïphobus* and *Dius.*] It has been a dispute whether Δῖος or Ἀγανός, in v. 251. was a proper name, but *Pherecydes* (says *Eustathius*) determines it, and assures us that *Dios* was a spurious son of *Priam*.

342. *The sad attendants load the groaning wain.*] It is necessary to observe to the reader, to avoid confusion, that two cars are here prepared; the one drawn by mules, to carry the presents, and to bring back the body of *Hector*; the other drawn by horses, in which the herald and *Priam* rode.   *Eustathius.*

377. *Oh first, and greatest!* &c.] *Eustathius* observes, that there is not one instance in the whole *Ilias* of any prayer that was justly prefer'd, that fail'd of success. This proceeding of *Homer*'s is very judicious, and answers exactly to the true end of poetry, which is to please and instruct. Thus *Priam* prays that *Achilles* may cease his wrath, and compassionate his miseries; and *Jupiter* grants his request: The unfortunate king obtains compassion, and in his most inveterate enemy finds a friend.

417. *The Description of* Mercury.] A man must have no Taste for poetry that does not admire this sublime description: *Virgil* has translated it almost *verbatim* in the 4th book of the *Æneis*, v. 240.

> *– Ille patris magni parere parabat*
> *Imperio, & primum pedibus talaria nectit*
> *Aurea, quæ sublimem alis, sive æquora supra,*
> *Seu terram rapido pariter cum flamine portant.*
> *Tum virgam capit, hac animas ille evocat orco*
> *Pallentes, alias sub tristia tartara mittit;*
> *Dat somnos, adimitque, & lumina morte resignat.*

[*Hermes* obeys; with golden pinions binds
His flying feet, and mounts the western winds:
And whether o'er the seas or earth he flies,
With rapid force, they bear him down the skies.
But first he grasps within his awful hand,
The mark of sov'reign pow'r, his magick wand:
With this, he draws the ghosts from hollow graves,
With this he drives them down the *Stygian* waves;
With this he seals in sleep, the wakeful sight;
And eyes, though clos'd in death restores to light.]

It is hard to determine which is more excellent, the copy, or the original: *Merucry* appears in both pictures with equal majesty; and the *Roman* dress becomes him, as well as the *Grecian.* *Virgil* has added the latter part of the fifth, and the whole sixth line to *Homer*, which makes it still more full and majestical.

Give me leave to produce a passage out of *Milton*, of near affinity with the lines above, which is not inferior to *Homer* or *Virgil*: It is the description of the descent of an angel,

> *– Down thither, prone in flight*
> *He speeds, and thro' the vast æthereal sky*
> *Sails between worlds and worlds; with steady wing*
> *Now on the polar winds: Then with quick force*
> *Winnows the buxom air –*
> *Of beaming sunny rays a golden Tiar*
> *Circled his head; nor less his locks behind*
> *Illustrious, on his shoulders fledg'd with wings,*
> *Lay waving round. – &c.*

427. *Now twilight veil'd the glaring face of day.*] The poet by such intimations as these recalls to our minds the exact time which *Priam* takes up in this journey to *Achilles*: He set out in the evening; and by the time that he reach'd the tomb of *Ilus*, it was grown somewhat dark, which shews that this tomb stood at some distance from the city: Here *Mercury* meets him, and when it was quite dark, guides him into the presence of *Achilles.* By these methods we may discover how exactly the poet preserves the unities of time and place, that he allots space sufficient for the actions which he describes, and yet does not crowd more incidents into any interval of time than may be executed in as much as he allows: Thus it being improbable that so stubborn a man as *Achilles* should relent in a few moments, the poet allows a whole night for this affair, so that *Priam* has leisure enough to go and return, and time enough remaining to persuade *Achilles.*

447, *&c. The speech of* Mercury *to* Priam.] I shall not trouble the reader with the dreams of *Eustathius*, who tells us that this fiction of *Mercury* is partly true, and partly false: 'Tis true that his father is old; for *Jupiter* is King of the whole universe, was from eternity, and created both men and Gods: In like manner, when *Mercury* says he is the seventh child of his father, *Eustathius* affirms that he meant that there were six planets besides *Mercury.* Sure it requires great pains and thought to be so learnedly absurd: The supposition which he makes afterwards is far more natural; *Priam*, says he, might by chance meet with one of the *Myrmidons*, who might conduct him unobserv'd thro' the camp into the presence of *Achilles*, and as the execution of any wise design is ascrib'd to *Pallas*, so may this clandestine enterprize be said to be manag'd by the guidance of *Mercury.*

But perhaps this whole passage may be better explain'd by having recourse to the pagan theology: It was an opinion that obtain'd in those early days, that *Jupiter* frequently sent some friendly messengers to protect the innocent, so that *Homer* might intend to give his readers a lecture of morality, by telling us that this unhappy king was under the protection of the Gods.

Madam *Dacier* carries it farther. *Homer* (says she) instructed by tradition, knew that God sends his angels to the succour of the afflicted. The scripture is full of examples of this truth. The story of *Tobit* has a wonderful relation with this of *Homer*: *Tobit* sent his son to *Rages*, a city of *Media*, to receive a considerable sum; *Tobias* did not know the way; he found at his door a young man cloath'd with a majestick glory, which attracted admiration: It was an angel under the form of a man. This angel being ask'd who he was, answer'd (as *Mercury* does here) by a fiction: He said that he was of the children of *Israel*, that his name was *Azarias*, and that he was son of *Ananias*. This angel conducted *Tobias* in safety; he gave him instructions; and when he was to receive the recompence which the father and son offer'd him, he declar'd that he was the angel of the Lord; took his flight towards heaven, and disappear'd. Here is a great conformity in the ideas and in the style; and the example of our author so long before *Tobit*, proves, that this opinion of God's sending his angels to the aid of man was very common, and much spread amongst the pagans in those former times.   *Dacier.*

519. *Blest is the man,* &c.] *Homer* now begins after a beautiful and long fable, to give the moral of it, and display his poetical justice in rewards and punishments: Thus *Hector* fought in a bad cause, and therefore suffers in the defence of it; but because he was a good man, and obedient to the Gods in other respects, his very remains become the care of heaven.

I think it necessary to take notice to the reader, that nothing is more admirable than the conduct of *Homer* throughout his whole poem, in respect to morality. He justifies the character of *Horace*,

> *– Quid pulchrum, quid turpe, quid utile, quid non,*
> *Plenius & melius Chrysippo & Crantore dicit.*

[Homer states – more fully and better than (the philosophers) Chrysippus and Crantor – what is beautiful, what is base, what is useful and what is not.]

If the Reader does not observe the morality of the *Ilias*, he loses half, and the nobler part of its beauty: He reads it as a common romance, and mistakes the chief aim of it, which is to instruct.

531. *But can I, absent, &c.*] In the original of this place (which I have paraphras'd a little) the word Συλεύειν [to rob] is remarkable. *Priam* offers *Mercury* (whom he looks upon as a soldier of *Achilles*) a present, which he refuses, because his prince is ignorant of it: This present he calls a direct *theft* or *robbery*; which may shew us how strict the notions of justice were in the days of *Homer*, when if a prince's servant receiv'd any present without the knowledge of his master, he was esteem'd a thief and a robber.   *Eustathius.*

553. *Of fir the roof was rais'd.*] I have in the course of these observations describ'd the method of encamping used by the *Grecians*: The reader has here a full and exact description of the tent of *Achilles*: This royal pavilion was built with long palisadoes made of fir; the top of it cover'd with reeds, and the inside was divided into several apartments: Thus *Achilles* had his αὐλὴ μεγάλη, or large hall, and behind it were lodging rooms. So in the ninth book *Phœnix* has a bed prepared for him in one apartment, *Patroclus* has another for himself and his captive *Iphis*, and *Achilles* has a third for himself and his mistress *Diomeda.*

But we must not imagine that the other *Myrmidons* had tents of the like dimensions: they were, as *Eustathius* observes, inferior to this royal one of *Achilles*: Which indeed is no better than an hovel, yet agrees very well with the duties of a soldier, and the simplicity of those early times.

I am of opinion that such fixed tents were not used by the *Grecians* in their common marches, but only during the time of sieges, when their long stay in one place made it necessary to build such tents as are here describ'd; at other times they lay like *Diomed* in the tenth book, in the open air, their spears standing upright, to be ready upon any alarm; and with the hides of beasts spread on the ground instead of a bed.

It is worthy observation that *Homer* even upon so trivial an occasion as the describing the tent of *Achilles*, takes an opportunity to shew the superior strength of his hero; and tells us that three men could scarce open the door of his pavilion, but *Achilles* could open it alone.

569. *Nor stand confest to frail mortality.*] *Eustathius* thinks it was from this maxim, that the Princes of the east assum'd that air of majesty which separates them from the sight of their subjects; but I should rather believe that *Homer* copied this after the originals from some Kings of his time: it not being unlikely that this policy is very ancient.

Dacier.

571. *Adjure him by his father,* &c.] *Eustathius* observes that *Priam* does not entirely follow the instructions of *Mercury*, but only calls to his remembrance his aged father *Peleus*: And this was judiciously done by *Priam*: For what motive to compassion could arise from the mention of *Thetis*, who was a Goddess, and incapable of misfortune? Or how could *Neoptolemus* be any inducement to make *Achilles* pity *Priam*, when at the same time he flourish'd in the greatest prosperity? Therefore *Priam* only mentions his father *Peleus*, who like him, stood upon the very brink of the grave, and was liable to the same misfortunes he suffer'd. These are the remarks of *Eustathius*, but how then shall we justify *Mercury*, who gave him such improper instructions with relation to *Thetis*? All that can be said in defence of the poet is, that *Thetis*, tho' a Goddess, has thro' the whole course of the *Ilias* been describ'd as a partner in all the afflictions of *Achilles*, and consequently might be made use of as an inducement to raise the compassion of *Achilles*. *Priam* might have said, I conjure thee by the love thou bearest to thy mother, take pity on me! For if she who is a Goddess would grieve for the loss of her beloved son, how greatly must the loss of *Hector* afflict the unfortunate *Hecuba* and *Priam*?

586. *Sudden, (a venerable sight!) appears.*] I fancy this interview between *Priam* and *Achilles* would furnish an admirable subject for a painter, in the surprize of *Achilles*, and the other spectators, the attitude of *Priam*, and the sorrows in the countenance of this unfortunate King.

That circumstance of *Priam*'s kissing the hands of *Achilles* is inimitably fine; he kiss'd, says *Homer*, the hands of *Achilles*, those terrible, murderous hands that had robb'd him of so many sons: By these two words the poet recalls to our mind all the noble actions perform'd by *Achilles* in the whole *Ilias*; and at the same time strikes us with the utmost compassion for this unhappy King, who is reduc'd so low as to be oblig'd to kiss those hands that had slain his subjects, and ruin'd his kingdom and family.

598. *The Speech of* Priam *to* Achilles.] The curiosity of the reader must needs be awaken'd to know how *Achilles* would behave to this unfortunate King; it requires all the art of the poet to sustain the violent character of *Achilles*, and yet at the same time to soften him into compassion. To this end the poet uses no preamble, but breaks directly into that circumstance which is most likely to mollify him, and the two first words he utters are, μνῆσαι Πατρὸς, *see thy father, O* Achilles, *in me!* Nothing could be more happily imagin'd than this entrance into his speech; *Achilles* has every where been describ'd as bearing a great affection to his father, and by two words the poet recalls all the tenderness that love and duty can suggest to an affectionate son.

Priam tells *Achilles* that *Hector* fell in the defence of his country: I am far from thinking that this was inserted accidentally; it could not fail of having a very good effect upon *Achilles*, not only as one brave man naturally loves another, but as it implies that *Hector* had no particular enmity against *Achilles*, but that tho' he fought against him it was in defence of his country.

The reader will observe that *Priam* repeats the beginning of his speech, and recalls his father to his memory in the conclusion of it. This is done with great judgment; the poet takes care to enforce his petition with the strongest motive, and leaves it fresh upon his memory; and possibly *Priam* might perceive that the mention of his father had made a deeper impression upon *Achilles* than any other part of his petition, therefore while the mind of *Achilles* dwells upon it, he again sets him before his imagination by this repetition, and softens him into compassion.

634. *These words soft pity,* &c.] We are now come almost to the end of the poem, and consequently to the end of the anger of *Achilles*: And *Homer* has describ'd the abatement of it with excellent judgment. We may here observe how necessary the conduct of *Homer* was, in sending *Thetis* to prepare her son to use *Priam* with civility: It would have ill suited with the violent temper of *Achilles* to have used *Priam* with tenderness without such pre-admonition; nay, the unexpected sight of his enemy might probably have carried him into violence and rage: But *Homer* has avoided these absurdities; for *Achilles* being already prepared for a reconciliation, the misery of this venerable prince naturally melts him into compassion.

653. Achilles's *speech to* Priam.] There is not a more beautiful passage in the whole *Ilias* than this before us: *Homer* to shew that *Achilles* was not a mere soldier, here draws him as a person of excellent sense and sound reason: *Plato* himself (who condemns this passage) could not speak more like a true philosopher: And it was a piece of great judgment thus to describe him; for the reader would have retain'd but a very indifferent opinion of the hero of a poem, that had no qualification but mere strength: It also shews the art of the poet thus to defer this part of his character till the very conclusion of the poem: By these means he fixes an idea of his greatness upon our minds, and makes his hero go off the stage with applause.

Neither does he here ascribe more wisdom to *Achilles* than he might really be master of; for as *Eustathius* observes, he had *Chiron* and *Phœnix* for his tutors, and a Goddess for his mother.

663. *Two urns by* Jove's *high throne*, &c.] This is an admirable allegory, and very beautifully imagin'd by the poet. *Plato* has accus'd it as an impiety to say that God gives evil: But it seems borrow'd from the eastern way of speaking, and bears a great resemblance to several expressions in scripture: This in the *Psalms*, *In the hand of the Lord there is a cup, and he poureth out of the same; as for the dregs thereof, all the ungodly of the earth shall drink them.*

It was the custom of the *Jews* to give condemn'd persons just before execution, οἶνον ἐσμυρνισμένον, wine mix'd with Myrrh to make them less sensible of pain: Thus *Proverbs* xxxi. 6. *Give strong drink to him that is ready to perish.* This custom was so frequent among the *Jews*, that the cup which was given before execution, came to denote death itself, as in that passage, *Father let this cup pass from me.*

Some have suppos'd that there were three urns, one of good, and two of evil; thus *Pindar*,

Ἐν γὰρ ἐσθλὸν, πήματα σύνδυο
Δαίονται βροτοῖς ἀθάνατοι.

[For the immortals distribute two evils for every good to mortals.]

But, as *Eustathius* observes, the word ἕτερος [the one (of two)] shews that there were but two, for that word is never used when more than two are intended.

685. *Extended* Phrygia, *&c.*] *Homer* here gives us a piece of geography, and shews the full extent of *Priam*'s kingdom. *Lesbos* bounded it on the south, *Phrygia* on the east, and the *Hellespont* on the north. This kingdom, according to *Strabo* in the 13th book, was divided into nine dynasties, who all depended upon *Priam* as their king: So that what *Homer* here relates of *Priam*'s power is literally true, and confirmed by History.   *Eustathius.*

706. *While kindling anger sparkled in his eyes.*] I believe every reader must be surpriz'd, as I confess I was, to see *Achilles* fly out into so sudden a passion, without any apparent reason for it. It can scarce be imagin'd that the name of *Hector* (as *Eustathius* thinks) could throw him into so much violence, when he had heard it mention'd with patience and calmness by *Priam* in this very conference: especially if we remember that *Achilles* had actually determin'd to restore the body of *Hector* to *Priam.* I was therefore very well pleas'd to find that the words in the original would bear another interpretation, and such a one as naturally solves the difficulty. The meaning of the passage I fancy may be this: *Priam* perceiving that his address had mollify'd the heart of *Achilles*, takes this opportunity to persuade him to give over the war, and return home; especially since his anger was sufficiently satisfy'd by the fall of *Hector.* Immediately *Achilles* takes fire at this proposal, and answers, 'Is it not enough that I have determin'd to restore thy son? ask no more, lest I retract that resolution.' In this view we see a natural reason for the sudden passion of *Achilles.*

What may perhaps strengthen this conjecture is the word πρῶτον [first]; and then the sense will run thus; since I have found so much favour in thy sight, as first to permit me to live, O wouldst thou still enlarge my happiness, and return home to thy own country! *&c.*

This opinion may be farther establish'd from what follows in the latter end of this interview, where *Achilles* asks *Priam* how many days he would request for the interment of *Hector*? *Achilles* had refus'd to give over the war, but yet consents to intermit it a few days; and then the sense will be this, 'I will not consent to return home, but ask a time for a cessation, and it shall be granted.' And what most strongly speaks for this interpretation is the answer of *Priam*; I ask, says he, eleven days to bury my son, and then let the war commence again, since *it must be so*, εἴπερ ἀνάγκη; since you necessitate me to it; or since you will not be persuaded to leave these shores.

706. *While kindling anger sparkled in his eyes.*] The reader may be

pleas'd to observe that this is the last sally of the resentment of *Achilles*; and the poet judiciously describes him moderating it by his own reflection: So that his reason now prevails over his anger, and the design of the poem is fully executed.

709. *For know, from* Jove *my Goddess-mother came.*] The injustice of *La Motte*'s criticism, (who blames *Homer* for representing *Achilles* so mercenary, as to enquire into the price offer'd for *Hector*'s body before he would restore it) will appear plainly from this passage, where he makes *Achilles* expressly say, it is not for any other reason that he delivers the body, but that heaven had directly commanded it. The words are very full.

> — Διόθεν δέ μοι ἄγγελος ἦλθε
> Μήτηρ ἥ μ' ἔτεκεν, θυγάτηρ ἁλίοιο γέροντος,
> Καὶ δέ σε γινώσκω Πρίαμε φρεσίν, οὐδέ με λήθεις,
> Ὅττι Θεῶν τις ἦγε θοὰς ἐπὶ νῆας Ἀχαιῶν.

[cf. Pope's translation, ll. 709–15.]

757. *Not thus did* Niobe, &c.] *Achilles*, to comfort *Priam*, tells him a known history; which was very proper to work this effect. *Niobe* had lost all her children, *Priam* had some remaining. *Niobe*'s had been nine days extended on the earth, drown'd in their blood, in the sight of their people, without any one presenting himself to interr them: *Hector* has likewise been twelve days, but in the midst of his enemies; therefore 'tis no wonder that no one has paid him the last duties. The Gods at last interr'd *Niobe*'s children, and the Gods likewise are concern'd to procure honourable funerals for *Hector*.   *Eustathius.*

798. *The royal Guest the Hero eyes,* &c.] The poet omits no opportunity of praising his hero *Achilles*, and it is observable that he now commends him for his more amiable qualities: He softens the terrible idea we have conceiv'd of him, as a warriour, with several virtues of humanity; and the angry, vindictive soldier is become calm and compassionate. In this place he makes his very enemy admire his personage, and be astonish'd at his manly beauty. So that tho' courage be his most distinguishing character, yet *Achilles* is admirable both for the endowments of mind and body.

Ἐπικερτομέων. The sense of this word differs in this place from that it usually bears: It does not imply τραχύτητα ὑβριστικήν, any reproachful asperity of language, but εἰσήγησιν ψευδοῦς φόβου, the raising of a false fear in the old man, that he might not be concern'd at his being lodg'd in the outermost part of the tent; and by this method he gives *Priam* an opportunity of going away in the morning without observation.

Eustathius.

819. *To ask our counsel, or our orders take.*] The poet here shews the importance of *Achilles* in the army; tho' *Agamemnon* be the general, yet all the chief commanders apply to him for advice; and thus he promises *Priam* a cessation of arms for several days, purely by his own authority. The method that *Achilles* took to confirm the truth of the cessation, agrees with the custom which we use at this day, he gave him his hand upon it.

> — χεῖρα γέροντος
> Ἔλλαβε δεξιτερὴν —   *Eustathius.*

[He grabbed hold of the old man's right hand.]

900. *A melancholy choir, &c.*] This was a custom generally receiv'd, and which passed from the *Hebrews* to the *Greeks, Romans,* and *Asiaticks.* There were weepers by profession, of both sexes, who sung doleful tunes round the dead. *Ecclesiasticus* cap. 12. v. 5. *When a man shall go into the house of his eternity, there shall encompass him weepers.* It appears from St. *Matthew* xi. 17. that children were likewise employed in this office.   *Dacier.*

906, &c. *The lamentations over* Hector.] The poet judiciously makes *Priam* to be silent in this general lamentation; he has already born a sufficient share in these sorrows, in the tent of *Achilles,* and said what grief can dictate to a father and a King upon such a melancholy subject. But he introduces three women as chief mourners, and speaks only in general of the lamentation of the men of *Troy,* an excess of sorrow being unmanly: Whereas these women might with decency indulge themselves in all the lamentation that fondness and grief could suggest. The wife, the mother of *Hector,* and *Helen,* are the three persons introduced; and tho' they all mourn upon the same occasion, yet their lamentations are so different, that not a sentence that is spoken by the one, could be made use of by the other: *Andromache* speaks like a tender wife, *Hecuba* like a fond mother, and *Helen* mourns with a sorrow rising from self-accusation: *Andromache* commends-his bravery, *Hecuba* his manly beauty, and *Helen* his gentleness and humanity.

Homer is very concise in describing the funeral of *Hector*, which was but a necessary piece of conduct, after he had been so full in that of *Patroclus.*

934. *Why gav'st thou not to me thy dying hand,*
  And why receiv'd not I thy last command?]

I have taken these two lines from Mr. *Congreve*, whose translation of this part was one of his first essays in poetry. He has very justly render'd the sense of Πυκινὸν ἔπος, *dictum prudens* [prudent advice], which is meant of the words of a dying man, or one in some dangerous exigence; at which times what is spoken is usually something of the utmost importance, and deliver'd with the utmost care: Which is the true signification of the epithet Πυκινὸν [solid or prudent] in this place.

We have now past thro' the *Iliad*, and seen the Anger of *Achilles*, and the terrible effects of it, at an end: As that only was the subject of the poem, and the nature of epic poetry would not permit our author to proceed to the event of the war, it may perhaps be acceptable to the common reader to give a short Account of what happen'd to *Troy* and the chief actors in this poem, after the conclusion of it.

I need not mention that *Troy* was taken soon after the death of *Hector*, by the stratagem of the wooden horse, the particulars of which are described by *Virgil* in the second book of the *Æneis.*

Achilles fell before *Troy*, by the hand of *Paris*, by the shot of an arrow in his heel, as *Hector* had prophesied at his death, *lib.* 22.

The unfortunate *Priam* was kill'd by *Pyrrhus* the son of *Achilles.*

Ajax, after the death of *Achilles*, had a contest with *Ulysses* for the armour of *Vulcan*, but being defeated in his aim, he slew himself thro' indignation.

Helen, after the death of *Paris*, married *Deïphobus* his brother, and at the taking of *Troy* betray'd him, in order to reconcile herself to *Menelaus* her first husband, who receiv'd her again into favour.

Agamemnon at his return was barbarously murther'd by *Ægysthus* at the instigation of *Clytæmnestra* his wife, who in his absence had dishonour'd his bed with *Ægysthus.*

Diomed after the fall of *Troy* was expell'd his own country, and scarce escap'd with life from his adulterous wife *Ægiale*; but at last was receiv'd by *Daunus* in *Apulia*, and shar'd his kingdom: 'Tis uncertain how he died.

Nestor liv'd in peace, with his Children, in *Pylos* his native country.

Ulysses also after innumerable troubles by sea and land, at last return'd in safety to *Ithaca*, which is the subject of *Homer*'s *Odysses*.

I must end these notes by discharging my duty to two of my friends, which is the more an indispensable piece of justice, as the one of them is since dead: The merit of their kindness to me will appear infinitely the greater, as the task they undertook was in its own nature of much more labour, than either pleasure or reputation. The larger part of the extracts from *Eustathius*, together with several excellent observations were sent me by Mr. *Broome*: And the whole essay upon *Homer* was written upon such memoirs as I had collected, by the late Dr. *Parnell*, Archdeacon of *Clogher* in *Ireland*: How very much that gentleman's friendship prevail'd over his genius, in detaining a writer of his spirit in the drudgery of removing the rubbish of past pedants, will soon appear to the world, when they shall see those beautiful pieces of poetry the publication of which he left to my charge, almost with his dying breath.

For what remains, I beg to be excused from the ceremonies of taking leave at the end of my work; and from embarassing myself, or others, with any defences or apologies about it. But instead of endeavouring to raise a vain monument to my self, of the merits or difficulties of it (which must be left to the world, to truth, and to posterity) let me leave behind me a memorial of my friendship, with one of the most valuable men as well as finest writers, of my age and country: One who has try'd, and knows by his own experience, how hard an undertaking it is to do justice to *Homer*: And one, who (I am sure) sincerely rejoices with me at the period of my labours. To him therefore, having brought this long work to a conclusion, I desire to *dedicate* it; and to have the honour and satisfaction of placing together, in this manner, the names of Mr. *C O N G R E V E,* and of

March 25.   *A. P O P E.*
1720.

Τῶν θεῶν δὲ εὐποΐα, τὸ μὴ ἐπὶ πλέον με προκόψαι ἐν Ποιητικοῖς ἐπιτηδεύμασι, ἐν οἷς ἴσως ἂν κατεσχέθην, εἰ ἠσθόμην ἐμαυτὸν εὐόδως προϊόντα. M. AUREL. ANTON. *de seipso*, L. 1. § 17.

[It was through the beneficence of the gods that I made no more progress in my poetic pursuits, in which I would perhaps have been detained had I perceived that my efforts were successful.]

FINIS

AN INDEX OF PERSONS AND THINGS

	Book	Verse
Mestles	2	1054
MINERVA *goes to* Pandarus		
to induce him to break		
the truce	4	119
strengthens Diomed	5	109
forces Mars *from the battel*	5	45
derides Venus	5	509
prepares her self for the war	5	883
		908
asks leave of Jupiter *to go*		
to the war	5	942
speaks to Diomed	5	998
encourages Diomed *to*		
assault Mars	5	1020
her speech to Jupiter	8	39
restrains Mars *his anger*	15	140
knocks down Mars *with a*		
mighty stone	21	469
vanquishes Venus *and her*		
lover	21	498
in the shape of Deïphobus		
persuades Hector *to*		
meet Achilles	22	291
Mycenians	2	686
Myrmidons	2	834
go to the fight	16	312

·N

	Book	Verse
Nastes	2	1060
Neptune *his and* Jupiter's		
discourse concerning		
the Grecian *Wall*	7	530
his discourse with		
Idomeneus	13	289
brings help to the Greeks	12	17
encourages the two Ajax's	13	73
and the Greeks	13	131
is angry with Jupiter	15	206
advises about the		
preservation of Æneas	20	341
preserves Æneas *from*		
Achilles's *fury*	20	367
comforts Ulysses	21	333
urges Apollo *to fight*	21	450
Nereïds, *the catalogue and*		

	Book	Verse
names of them	18	42
		&c.
NESTOR *endeavours to*		
reconcile Achilles *and*		
Agamemnon	1	330
Nestor *praised by* Agamemnon	2	440
his speech to the soldiers	2	402
NESTOR	2	716
his speech to Agamemnon	4	370
exhorts the soldiers	6	84
his speech for burying the		
dead, and building a wall	7	392
blames the Greeks *for not*		
daring to encounter		
Hector	7	145
is in great danger	8	102
flies with Diomed	8	190
his advice for guards and		
refreshment	9	86
for pacifying Achilles	9	141
approves Diomed's *speech*		
to Agamemnon	9	73
goes by night to Ulysses	10	157
encourages Diomed	10	180
advises to send spies into		
the enemy's camp	10	241
recites what he did in his		
youth	11	817
goes on an uproar to know		
the cause	14	1
prays to Jupiter	15	428
exhorts the Greeks *to*		
oppose the enemy	15	796
advises his son concerning		
the race	23	369
Niobe, *her fable*	24	757
Nireus *the most handsome*		
Greek	2	817

O

	Book	Verse
Orcus *his helmet*	5	1037
Odius	2	1043

A POETICAL INDEX
TO HOMER'S *ILIAD*

The first number marks the book, the second the verse.

F·ABLE

The great *Moral* of the Iliad, that *Concord, among Governours, is the preservation of States, and Discord the ruin of them*: pursued thro' the whole *Fable*.

The Anger of Achilles breaks this union in the opening of the poem, *l.* 1. He withdraws from the body of the *Greeks*, which first interrupts the success of the common cause, *ibid.* The Army mutiny, *l.* 2. The *Trojans* break the Truce, *l.* 4. A great number of the *Greeks* slain, 7. 392. Forc'd to build Fortifications to guard their Fleet, *ibid.* In great distress from the enemy, whose victory is only stopt by the night, 8. Ready to quit their design, and return with infamy, 9. Send to *Achilles* to persuade him to a re-union, in vain, *ibid.* The distress continues; the General and all the best warriours are wounded, 11. The fortification overthrown, and the fleet set on fire, 15. *Achilles* himself shares in the misfortunes he brought upon the allies, by the loss of his friend *Patroclus*, 16. Hereupon the hero is reconciled to the General, the victory over *Troy* is compleat, and *Hector* slain by *Achilles*, 19, 20, 21, 22, *&c.*

EPISODES *or* FABLES *which are interwoven into the Poem, but foreign to its design*

The Fable of the conspiracy of the Gods against *Jupiter*, 1. 516. Of *Vulcan*'s fall from heav'n on the Island of *Lemnos*, 1. 761. The imprisonment of *Mars* by *Otus* and *Ephialtes*, 5. 475. The story of *Thamyris*, 2. 721. The embassy of *Tydeus* to *Thebes*, 4. 430. The tale of *Bellerophon*, 6. 195. Of *Lycurgus* and the *Bacchanals*, 6. 161. The war of the *Pylians* and *Arcadians*, 6. 165. The story of *Phoenix*, 9. 572. Of *Meleager* and the Wars of the *Curetes* and *Ætolians*, 9. 653. The wars of *Pyle* and *Elis*, 11. 818. The birth of *Hercules* and labour of *Alcmena*, 19. 103. The expulsion of *Ate* from heaven, 19. 93. *Vulcan*'s abode with *Thetis*, and his employment there, 18. 463. The family and history of *Troy*, 20. 255. The transformation of *Niobe*, 24. 757. Building of the walls of *Troy* by *Neptune*, 21. 518.

ALLEGORICAL FABLES

Moral.] *Prudence* restraining *Passion*, represented in the machine of *Min-*

erva descending to calm *Achilles*, 1. 261. Love alluring, and extinguishing *Honour*, in *Venus* bringing *Paris* from the combate to the arms of *Helen*, 3. 460, *&c.* True *Courage* overcoming *Passion* in *Diomed*'s conquest of *Mars* and *Venus*, by the assistance of *Pallas*, 5. 407, &c. *through that whole book.* Prayers the daughters of *Jupiter*, following *Injustice* and persecuting her at the throne of heaven, 9. 625. The *Cestus*, or girdle of *Venus*, 14. 247. The allegory of *Sleep*, 14. 265. The allegory of *Discord* cast out of heaven, to earth, 19. 93. The allegory of the two *Urns* of *Pleasure* and *Pain*, 24. 663.

Physical or Philosophical.] The combate of the *elements* till the *water* subsided, in the fable of the wars of *Juno* or the *Air*, and *Neptune* or the *Sea*, with *Jupiter* or the *Æther*, till *Thetis* put an end to 'em, 1. 516. *Fire* deriv'd from heaven to earth, imag'd by the fall of *Vulcan* on *Lemnos*, 1. 761. The gravitation of the *Planets* upon the *Sun*, in the Allegory of the *golden chain* of *Jupiter*, 8. 25. The influence of the *Æther* upon the *Air*, in the allegory of the congress of *Jupiter* and *Juno*, 14. 395. The *Air* supply'd by the vapours of the *Ocean* and *Earth*, in the story of *Juno* nourish'd by *Oceanus* and *Tethys*, 14. 231. The allegory of the *Winds*, 23. 242. The quality of *Salt* preserving dead bodies from corruption, in *Thetis* or the *Sea* preserving the body of *Patroclus*, 19. 40.

For the rest of the Allegories, *see the* System of the Gods *as acting in their allegorical characters, under the article* CHARACTERS.

ALLEGORICAL *or* FICTITIOUS PERSONS *in* HOMER

The *lying dream* sent to *Agamemnon* by *Jupiter*, 2. 7. *Fame* the messenger of *Jove*, 2. 121. *Furies*, punishers of the wicked, 3. 351. *Hebe*, or *Youth*, attending the banquets of the Gods, 4. 3. *Flight* and *Terror* attendants upon *Mars*, 4. 500. *Discord* describ'd, 4. 502. *Bellona* Goddess of war, 5. 726. The *Hours*, keepers of the gates of heaven, 5. 929. Nymphs of the mountains, 6. 532. *Night*, a Goddess, 6. 342. *Iris*, or the *Rainbow*, 8. 486. *Prayers* the daughters of *Jupiter*, 9. 625. *Eris*, or *Discord*, 11. 5. *Ilythiæ*, Goddesses presiding in women's labour, 11. 349. *Terror* the son of *Mars*, 13. 386. *Sleep*, 14. 265. *Night*, 14. 293. *Death* and *Sleep*, two twins, 16. 831. *Nereids*, or nymphs of the sea, a catalogue of them, 18. 45. *Ate*, or the Goddess of *Discord*, 19. 93. *Scamander* the River-God, 21. 231. *Fire* and *Water* made Persons in the battel of *Scamander* and *Vulcan*, 21. 387. The *East* and *West-Winds*, ibid. *Iris*, or the *Rainbow*, and the *Winds*, 23. 242.

The MARVELLOUS, *or* supernatural FICTIONS *in* HOMER

Omen of the birds and serpent representing the event of the *Trojan* war, 2. 370. The miraculous rivers *Titaresius* and *Styx*, 2. 910. The giant *Typhon* under the burning mountain *Typhœus*, 2. 952. Battel of the cranes and pygmies, 3. 6. Prodigy of a comet, 4. 101. *Diomed*'s helmet ejecting fire, 5. 6. Horses of cœlestial breed, 5. 327. Vast stone heav'd by *Diomed*, 5. 370. And *Hector*, 12. 537. And *Minerva*, 20. 470. The miraculous chariot and arms of *Pallas*, 5. 885, 907, *&c.* The *Gorgon*; helmet, and *Ægis* of *Jupiter*, *ibid.* The gates of heaven, *ibid.* The leap of immortal horses, 5. 960. Shout of *Stentor*, 5. 978. Roaring of *Mars*, 5. 1054. Helmet of *Oreus*, which render'd the wearer invisible, 5. 1036. The *blood* of the Gods, 5. 422. The immediate healing of their wounds, 5. 1116. The *chimæra*, 6. 220. Destruction by *Neptune* of the *Grecian* rampart, 12. 15. Wall push'd down by *Apollo*, 15. 415. The golden chain of *Jupiter*, 8. 25. Horses and chariot of *Jupiter*, 8. 50. His balances, weighing the fates of men, 8. 88. 22. 271. *Jupiter*'s assisting the *Trojans* by thunders and lightnings, and visible declarations of his favour, 8. 93, 165, *&c.* 17. 670. Prodigy of an eagle and fawn, 8. 297. Horses of the Gods, stables and chariots, pompously describ'd, 8. 535, *&c. Hector*'s lance of ten cubits, 8. 615. Omen of an heron, 10. 320. The descent of *Eris*, 11. 5. A shower of blood, 11. 70 – 16. 560. Omen of an eagle and serpent, 12. 230. The progress of *Neptune* thro' the seas, 13. 42. The *War* and *Discord* stretch'd over the armies, 13. 451. The loud voice of *Neptune*, 14. 173. Solemn oath of the Gods, 14. 307 – 15. 41. *Minerva* spreads a light over the army, 15. 808. *Jupiter* involves the combatants in thick darkness, 16. 695, 422. Horses begot by the wind on a harpye, 16. 183. A shower of blood, 16. 560. Miraculous transportation and interment of *Sarpedon* by *Apollo*, *Sleep* and

Death, 16. 810, *&c.* Prophecy at the hour of death, 16. 1026 – 22. 450. *Achilles* unarmed puts the whole *Trojan* army to flight on his appearance, 18. 240, *&c.* Moving tripods and living statues of *Vulcan*, 18. 440, 488. The horse of *Achilles* speaks by a prodigy, 19. 450. The battel of the Gods, 20. 63, *&c.* Horses of a miraculous extraction, the transformation of *Boreas*, 20. 264. The wonderful battel of the *Xanthus*, 21. 230, *&c. Hector*'s body preserv'd by *Apollo* and *Venus*, 23. 226. The ghost of *Patroclus*, 23. 77. The two urns of *Jupiter*, 24. 663. The vast quoit of *Aëtion*, 23. 975. The transformation of *Niobe* and her people into stones, 24. 757.

Under this head of the Marvellous *may also be included all the immediate* machines *and* appearances of the Gods *in the Poem, and their* transformations; *the* miraculous birth *of* heroes; *the* passions in human and visible forms, *and the* rest.

CHARACTERS, OR MANNERS

Characters of the GODS *of* HOMER, *as acting in the* PHYSICAL *or* MORAL *capacities of those deities*

JUPITER

Acting and governing all, as the supreme Being.] See the article *Theology* in the next *Index.*

JUNO

As the element of Air.] Her congress with *Jupiter*, or the *Æther*, and production of vegetables, 14. 390, *&c.* Her loud shout, the air being the cause of sound, 5. 978. Nourish'd by *Oceanus* and *Tethys*, 14. 231.

As Goddess of Empire and Honour.] Stops the *Greeks* from flying ignominiously, 2. 191. *and in many other places.* Incites and commands *Achilles* to revenge the death of his friend, 18. 203, *&c.* Inspires into *Helen* a contempt of *Paris*, and sends *Iris* to call her to behold the combate with *Menelaus*, 3. 185.

APOLLO

As the Sun.] Causes the plague in the heat of summer, 1. 61. Raises a phantom of clouds and vapours, 5. 545. Discovers in the morning the slaughter made the night before, 10. 606. Recovers *Hector* from fainting, and opens his eyes, 15. 280. Dazzles the eyes of the *Greeks*, and shakes his *Ægis* in their faces, 15. 362. Restores vigour to *Glaucus*, 16. 647. Preserves the body of *Sarpedon* from corruption, 16. 830. And that of *Hector*, 23. 230. Raises a cloud to conceal *Æneas*, 20. 515.

As Destiny.] Saves *Æneas* from death, 5. 441. And *Hector*, 20. 513. Saves *Agenor*, 21. 706. Deserts *Hector* when his hour is come, 22. 277.

As Wisdom.] He and *Minerva* inspire *Helenus* to keep off the general engagement by a single combate, 7.

25. Advises *Hector* to shun encountering *Achilles*, 20. 431.

MARS

As mere martial courage without conduct.] Goes to the fight against the orders of *Jupiter*, 5. 726. Again provoked to rebel against *Jupiter* by his passion, 15. 126. Is vanquish'd by *Minerva*, or *Conduct*, 21. 480.

MINERVA

As martial courage with Wisdom.] Joins with *Juno* in restraining the *Greeks* from flight, and inspires *Ulysses* to do it, 2. 210. Animates the army, 2. 525. Describ'd as leading a hero safe thro' a battel, 4. 632. Assists *Diomed* to overcome *Mars* and *Venus*, 5. 407, 1042. Overcomes them her self, 21. 480. Restrains *Mars* from rebellion against *Jupiter*, 5. 45 − 15. 140. Submits to *Jupiter*, 8. 40. Advises *Ulysses* to retire in time from the night expedition, 10. 593. Assists him throughout that expedition, 10. 350, *&c.* Discovers the ambush laid against the *Pylians* by night, and causes them to sally, 11. 851. Assists *Achilles* to conquer *Hector*, 22. 277, *&c.*

As Wisdom separately consider'd.] Suppresses *Achilles*'s passion, 1. 261. Suppresses her own anger against *Jupiter*, 4. 31. Brings to pass *Jupiter*'s Will in contriving the breach of the truce, 4. 95. Teaches *Diomed* to discern Gods from men, and to conquer *Venus*, 5. 155, *&c.* Call'd the best belov'd of *Jupiter*, 8. 48. Obtains leave of *Jupiter*, that while the other Gods do not assist the *Greeks*, she may direct 'em with her counsels, 8. 45. Is again check'd by the command of *Jupiter* and submits, 8. 506, 580. Is said to assist, or save any hero, in general thro' the Poem, when any act of prudence preserves him.

VENUS

As the passion of love.] Brings *Paris* from the fight to the embraces of *Helen*, and inflames the lovers, 3. 460, 530, &c. Is overcome by *Minerva*, or Wisdom, 5. 407. And again, 21. 500. Her *Cestos* or girdle, and the effects of it, 14. 247.

NEPTUNE

As the sea.] Overturns the *Grecian* wall with his waves, 12. 15. Assists the *Greeks* at their fleet, which was drawn up at the sea-side, 13. 67, &c. Retreats at the order of *Jupiter*, 15. 245. Shakes the whole field of battel and sea-shore with earthquakes, 20. 77.

VULCAN

Or the Element of Fire.] Falls from heaven to earth, 1. 761. Receiv'd in *Lemnos*, a place of subterraneous fires, *ibid.* His operations of various kinds, 18. 440, 468, 540. Dries up the river *Xanthus*, 21. 460. Assisted by the winds, 21. 390.

Characters of the HEROES

N.B. *The* Speeches *which depend upon, and flow from these several characters, are distinguished by an* S.

ACHILLES

Furious, passionate, disdainful, and reproachful, *lib.* 1. 155. S. 195. S. 295. S − 9. 405. S. 746. S − 24. 705.
Revengeful and implacable in the highest degree, 9. 765. 755. − 16. 68. S. 121. S. − 19. 211. S − 22. 333. S. 437. S. 18. 120. 125. S. −
Cruel, 16. 122 − 19. 395 − 21. 112 − 22. 437. S. 495. S − 23. 30 − 24. 51 −
Superiour to all men in valour, 20. 60. 437, &c. − *l.* 21. 22. throughout.
Constant and violent in friendship, 9. 730. 18. 30 − 371 − 23. 54. 272 − 24. 5 − 16. 9. S. 208. S. 18. 100. S. 380. S − 19. 335. S − 22. 482. S. −
Achilles scarce ever speaks without mention of his friend *Patroclus.*

ÆNEAS

Pious to the Gods, 5. 226. S − 20. 132. 290. 345 −
Sensible, and moral, 20. 242. 293, &c. S.
Valiant, not rash, 20. 130. 240 − S.
Tender to his friend, 13. 590.

See this character in the notes on l. 5. v. 212. *and on* l. 13. v. 578.

AGAMEMNON

Imperious and passionate, 1. 34. 729 S –
Sometimes cruel, 6. 80 – 2. 140 S –
Artful and designing, 2. 68. 95 –
Valiant and an excellent General, 4. 256.
   265, *&c.* 11. *throughout.*
Eminent for brotherly affection, 4. 183,
   &c. S. 7. 120 –

See his character in the notes on l. 11.
v. 1.

AJAX

Of superiour strength and size, and fearless on that account, 13. 410 – 7.
   227. S. 274. S – 15. 666.
Indefatigable and patient, 11. 683, *&c.*
   13. 877 – 15. *throughout* – 14. 535 –
   short in his speeches, 7. 227 – 9. 742
   – 15. 666, *&c.*

See his character in the notes on l. 7. v.
226.

DIOMED

Daring and intrepid, 5. *throughout,* and
   8. 163. 180 S – 9. 65. 820 – 10. 260 –
Proud and boasting, 6. 152 – 11. 500.
Vain of his birth, 14. 125.
Generous, 6. 265 –
Is guided by *Pallas* or Wisdom, and
   chuses *Ulysses* to direct him, 5.
   throughout. 10. 287. 335.

See his character in the notes on l. 5. v. 1.

HECTOR

A true lover of his country, 8. 621. S –
12. 284 – 15. 582. S.

Valiant in the highest degree, 3. 89 – 7.
   80. 12. 270. S – 18. 333. S – *&c.*
Excellent in conduct, 8. 610. S. – 11.
   663 –
Pious, 6. 140. 335. 605 –
Tender to his parents, 6. 315.
   – to his wife, 6. 456.
   – to his child, 6. 606.
   – to his friends, 20. 485 – 24. 962 –

See his character in the notes on l. 3. v. 53.

IDOMENEUS

An old soldier, 13. 455. 648 –
A lover of his soldiers, 13. 280 –
Talkative upon subjects of war, 13. 340
   – 355, *&c.* 4. 305. S –
Vain of his family, 13. 565, *&c.*
Stately and insulting, 13. 472 – *&c.*

See his character in the notes on l. 13.
v. 279.

MENELAUS

Valiant, 3. 35 – 13. 733 – 17.
   throughout.
Tender of the people, 10. 32 –
Gentle in his nature, 10. 138 – 23. 685 –
But fir'd by a sense of his wrongs, 2.
   711 – 3. 45 – 7. 109. S – 13. 780. S
   – 17. 640.

See his character in the notes on l. 3. v.
278.

NESTOR

Wise and experienced in council, 1. 331.
   340 – 2. 441 –
Skilful in the art of war, 2. 432. 670 – 4.
   338, *&c.* S. 7. 392. S –
Brave, 7. 165 – 11. 817 – 15. 796. S.

Eloquent, 1. 332. *&c.*
Vigilant, 10. 88. 186. 624 –
Pious, 15. 427.
Talkative thro' old age, 4. 370 – 7. 145
   – 11. 800 – 23. 373. 718 – and in
   general thro' the book.

   See his character in the notes on l. 1. v.
339. *on* 2. 402, *&c.*

PARIS

Effeminate in dress and person, 3. 27.
   55. 80. 409.
Amorous, 3. 550.
Ingenious in arts, musick, 3. 80. Build-
   ing, 6. 390.
Patient of reproof, 3. 86.
Naturally valiant, 6. 669 – 13. 985.

   See his characters in the notes on l. 3.
v. 26. 37. 86.

PATROCLUS

Compassionate of the sufferings of his
   countrymen, 11. 947 – 16. 5. 31. S.
Rash, but valiant, 16. 709.
Of a gentle nature, 19. 320 – 17. 755 –

PRIAM

A tender father to *Hector*, 22. 51. S –
   24. 275 – to *Paris*, 3. 381 – to *Helen*,
   3. 212. S.
An easy Prince, of too yielding a temper,
   7. 443.
Gentle and compassionate, 3. 211. 382.
Pious, 4. 70 – 24. 520. S.

   See his character in the notes on l. 3. v.
211.

SARPEDON

Valiant, out of principle and honour, 5.
   575. S – 12. 371. S.
Eloquent, *ibid.*
Careful only of the common cause in his
   death, 16. 605. S.

   See his character in the notes on l. 16.
v. 512.

ULYSSES

Prudent, 3. 261 – 10. 287 – 19. 218 –
Eloquent, 3. 283 – 9. 295. S. *&c.*
Valiant in the field with caution, 4. 566
   – 11. 515, *&c.*
Bold in the council with prudence, 14.
   90 –

   See his character in the notes on l. 2. v.
402. *& sparsim.*

Characters of other
HEROES

Agenor, valiant and considerate, 21. 648.
Antenor, a prudent Counsellor, 7. 418.
Ajax Oïleus, famous for swiftness, 2.
   631 – 14. 618.
Antilochus, bold-spirited, but reason-
   able; and artful, 4. 522 – 23. 505.
   618. 666. S – 23. 910, 930.
Euphorbus, beautiful and valiant, 16. 973
   – 17. 11. 57 –
Glaucus, pious to his Friend, 16. 660 –
   17. 165. 180.
Helenus, a Prophet and Hero, 6. 92.
Meriones, dauntless and faithful, 13. 325,
   &c.
Machaon, an excellent physician, 2. 890
   – 11. 630.

For other less distinguished characters, see the article, Descriptions of the Passions.

SPEECHES, OR ORATIONS

A table of the most considerable in the
ILIAD

In the exhortatory or deliberative Kind

In the vituperative kind

In the narrative

In the pathetic

In the irony, or sarcasm

DESCRIPTIONS
OR IMAGES

*A collection of the
most remarkable
throughout the Poem*

Descriptions of PLACES

Descriptions of PERSONS

Descriptions of THINGS

SIMILES

From BEASTS

Paris issuing from his apartment, 6. 652. A hound following a lion, to *Hector* following the *Grecians*, 8. 407. Dogs watching the folds, to the guards by night, 10. 211. Hounds chasing a hare thro' thick woods, to *Diomed* and *Ulysses* pursuing an enemy by night, 10. 427. A hind flying from a lion, to the *Trojans* flying from *Agamemnon*, 11. 153. Beasts flying from a lion to the same, 10. 227. Hounds chear'd by the hunter, to troops encourag'd by the General, 11. 378. A hunted boar to *Ajax*, 11. 526. A wounded deer encompass'd with wolves, to *Ulysses* surrounded by enemies, 11. 595. An ass surrounded by boys to *Ajax*, 11. 683. A fawn carry'd off by two lions, to the body of *Imbrius* carry'd by the *Ajaxes*, 13. 265. A boar enrag'd, to *Idomeneus* meeting his enemy, 13. 595. An ox rolling in the pangs of death, to a dying warriour, 13. 721. Beasts retreating from hunters, to the *Greeks* retiring, 15. 303. Oxen flying from lions, to the *Greeks* flying from *Apollo* and *Hector*, 15. 366. A hound fastening on a roe, to a hero flying on an enemy, 15. 697. A wild beast wounded and retiring from a multitude, to *Antilochus* his retreat, 15. 702. A hideous assembly of wolves, to the fierce figure of the Myrmidons, 16. 194. Wolves invading the flocks, to the *Greeks*, 16. 420. A bull torn by a lion, to *Sarpedon* kill'd by *Patroclus*, 16. 600. A bull sacrificed, to *Aretus*, 17. 588. Hounds following a boar, to the *Trojans* following *Ajax*, 17. 811. Mules dragging a beam, to heroes carrying a dead body, 17. 832. A panther hunted, to *Agenor*, 21. 978. A hound pursuing a fawn, to *Achilles* pursuing *Hector*, 22. 243.

From LIONS

A Lion rouzing at his prey, to *Menelaus* at sight of *Paris*, 3. 37. A lion falling on the flocks, and wounded by a shepherd, to *Diomed* wounded, 5. 174. A lion among heifers, to the same, 5. 206. Two young lions kill'd by hunters, to two young warriours, 5. 681. A lion destroying the sheep in their folds, to *Ulysses* slaughtering the *Thracians* asleep, 10. 564. The sowr retreat of a lion, to that of *Ajax*, 11. 675. Lion, or boar hunted, to a hero distress'd, 12. 47. A Lion rushing on the flocks, to *Sarpedon*'s march, 12. 357. A lion killing a bull, to *Hector* killing *Periphas*, 15. 760. A lion slain, after he has made a great slaughter, apply'd to *Patroclus*, 16. 909. Two lions fighting, to *Hector* and *Patroclus*, 16. 915. A lion and boar at a spring, to the same, 16. 993. A lion putting a whole village to flight, to *Menelaus*, 17. 70. Retreat of a lion, to that of *Menelaus*, 17. 117. A lioness defending her young, to his defence of *Patroclus*, 17. 145. Another retreat of a lion, to that of *Menelaus*, 17. 741. The rage and grief of a lion for his young, to that of *Achilles* for *Patroclus*, 18. 371. A lion rushing on his foe, to *Achilles*, 20. 200.

From BIRDS

A Flight of cranes or swans, to a numerous army, 2. 540. The noise of cranes, to the shouts of an army, 3. 5. An eagle preserving and fighting for her young, to *Achilles* protecting the *Grecians*, 9. 424. A falcon flying at the quarry, to *Neptune*'s flight, 13. 91. An eagle stooping at a swan, to *Hector*'s attacking a ship, 15. 836. Two vultures fighting, to *Sarpedon* and *Patroclus*, 16. 522. A vulture driving geese, to *Automedon* scattering the *Trojans*, 17. 527. An eagle casting his eyes on the quarry, to *Menelaus* looking thro' the ranks for *Antilochus*, 17. 761. Cranes afraid of falcons, to the *Greeks* afraid of *Hector* and *Æneas*, 17. 845. A dove afraid of a falcon, to *Diana* afraid of *Juno*, 21. 576. A falcon following a dove, to *Achilles* pursuing *Hector*, 22. 183. An eagle at an hare, to *Achilles* at *Hector*, 22. 391. The broad wings of an eagle extended, to palace-gates set open, 24. 391.

From SERPENTS

A traveller retreating from a serpent, to *Paris* afraid of *Menelaus*, 3. 47. A snake roll'd up in his den, and collecting his anger, to *Hector* expecting *Achilles*, 22. 130.

From INSECTS

Bees swarming, to a numerous army issuing out, 2. 111. Swarms of flies, to the same, 2. 552. Grasshoppers chirping in the sun, to old men talking, 3. 201. Wasps defending their nest, to the multitude and violence of soldiers defending a battlement, 12. 190. Wasps provok'd by children flying at the traveller, to troops violent in an attack, 16. 314. A hornet angry, to *Menelaus* incens'd, 17. 642. Locusts driv'n into a river, to the *Trojans* in *Scamander*, 21. 14.

From FIRES

A forest in flames, to the lustre of armour, 2. 534. The spreading of a conflagration, to the march of an army, 2. 948. Trees sinking in a conflagration, to squadrons falling in battel, 11. 201. The noise of fire in a wood, to that of an army in confusion, 14. 461. A conflagration, to *Hector*, 15. 728. The rumbling and rage of a fire, to the confusion and roar of a routed army, 17. 825. Fires on the hills, and beacons to give signals of distress, to the blaze of *Achilles*'s helmet, 18. 245. A fire running over fields and woods, to the progress and devastations made by *Achilles*, 20. 569. Fire boiling the waters, to *Vulcan* operating on *Scamander*, 21. 425. A fire raging in a town, to *Achilles* in the battel, 21. 608. A town on fire, 22. 518.

From ARTS

The staining of ivory, to the blood running down the thigh of *Menelaus*, 4. 170. An architect observing the rule and line, to leaders preserving the line of battel, 4. 474. An artist managing four horses, and leaping from one to another, compar'd to *Ajax* striding from ship to ship, 15. 822. A builder cementing a wall, to a leader embodying his men, 16. 256. Curriers straining to hide, to soldiers tugging for a dead body, 17. 450. Bringing a current to water a garden, to the pursuit of *Scamander* after *Achilles*, 21. 290. The placing of rafters in a building, to the posture of two wrestlers, 23. 825. The motions of a spinster, the spindle and thread, to the swiftness of a racer, 23. 889. The sinking of a plummet, to the passage of *Iris* thro' the sea, 24. 107.

From TREES

The Fall of a poplar, to that of *Simoisius*, 4. 552. Of a beautiful olive, to that of *Euphorbus*, 17. 57. Two tall oakes on the mountains, to two heroes, 12. 145. The fall of an ash, to that of *Imbrius*, 13. 241. Of a pine or oak stretch'd on the ground, to *Asius* dead, 13. 493. An oak overturn'd by a thunderbolt, to *Hector* fell'd by a stone, 14. 408. An oak, pine or poplar falling, to *Sarpedon*, 16. 591.

From the SEA

Rolling billows, to an army in motion, 2. 175. The murmurs of waves, to the noise of a multitude, 2. 249. Succession of waves, to the moving of troops, 4. 478. A fresh gale to weary mariners, like the coming of *Hector* to his troops, 7. 5. The seas settling themselves, to thick troops compos'd in order and silence, 7. 71. The sea agitated by different winds, to the army in doubt and confusion, 9. 5. The waves rolling neither way, till one wind sways 'em, to *Nestor*'s doubt and sudden resolution, 14. 21. A rock breaking the billows, to the body of *Greeks* resisting the *Trojans*, 15. 746. The sea roaring at its reception of a river into it, to the meeting of armies at a charge, 17. 310. A beacon to mariners at sea, to the light of *Achilles*'s shield, 19. 405. A dolphin pursuing

the lesser fish, to *Achilles* in *Scamander*, 21. 30.

From the SUN, MOON, STARS

The moon and stars in glory, to the brightness and number of the *Trojan* fires, 8. 687. A star sometimes shewing and sometimes hiding itself in clouds, to *Hector* seen by fits thro' the battalions, 11. 83. The sun in glory, to *Achilles*, 19. 436. The evening star, to the point of his spear, 22. 399. The dog-star rising, to *Diomed*'s dreadful appearance, 5. 8. – to *Achilles*, 22. 37. The red rays of the dog star, to *Achilles*'s helmet, 19. 412. The morning star, its beauty, to young *Astyanax*, 6. 499.

From TORRENTS, STORMS, WINDS

Torrents rushing to the vallies, to armies meeting in an engagement, 4. 516. Torrents drowning the field, to the rage of a hero, 5. 116. A Torrent stopping a shepherd, to *Hector* stopping *Diomed*, 5. 734. The violence of a torrent, to *Ajax*, 11. 615. A storm overwhelming a ship at sea, to the *Trojans* mounting a breach, 15. 440. An autumnal storm and a deluge, to the ruin of a routed army, 16. 467. A storm roaring in a wood, to armies shouting, 16. 923. The wind tossing the clouds, to *Hector* driving the *Greeks*, 11. 396. Different winds driving the dust, to different passions urging the combatants, 13. 425. A whirlwind on the waters, to a hurry of an army in motion, 13. 1000. Winds roaring thro' woods, or on the seas, to the noise of an army,

14. 457. A tempest and shipwreck, compar'd to the rage of *Hector* and terrors of the *Greeks*, 15. 752. The north wind drying a garden, to *Vulcan* drying the field after an inundation, 21. 403.

From heavenly appearances, THUNDER *and* LIGHTNING, COMETS, CLOUDS, *&c.*

A mountain shaken by thunder, to the trampling of an army, 2. 950. The blaze of a comet, to the descent of *Pallas*, 4. 101. The darkness of troops, to the gathering of clouds, 4. 314. The regular appearance of clouds on the mountain tops, to a line of battel, 5. 641. Pestilential vapors ascending, to *Mars* flying to heaven, 5. 1058. The quick flashes of lightning, to the thick sighs of *Agamemnon*, 10. 5. Thick flakes of snow, to showers of arrows, 12. 175. Snow covering the earth, to heaps of stones hiding the fields, 12. 331. The blaze of lightning, to the arms of *Idomeneus*, 13. 318. Clouds dispers'd and the prospect appearing, to the smokes being clear'd from the ships, and the navy appearing, 16. 354. A cloud shading the fields as it rises, to the rout of *Trojans* flying over the plain, 16. 434. The figure of a rainbow, to the appearance of *Pallas*, 17. 616. The lustre of snow, to that of armour, 19. 380.

From RURAL AFFAIRS

Waving of corn in the field, to the motion of plumes and spears, 2. 179.

A shepherd gathering his flocks, to a general ranging his army, 2. 562. A thick mist on the mountains, to the dust rais'd by an army, 3. 15. The bleating of flocks, to the noise of men, 4. 492. Chaff flying from the barn-floor, to the dust, 5. 611. Corn falling in ranks, to men slain in battle, 10. 90. The joy of a shepherd seeing his flock, to the joy of a General surveying his army, 13. 620. The corn bounding from the threshing-floor, to an arrow bounding from armour, 13. 739. Two bulls plowing, to two heroes labouring in a battel side by side, 13. 879. Felling of timber, to the fall of heroes in battel, 16. 767. Oxen trampling out the corn, to horses trampling on the slain, 20. 580. The morning dew reviving the corn, to the exaltation of joy in a man's mind, 23. 678.

From LOW LIFE

A Mother defending her child from a wasp, to *Minerva*'s sheltering *Menelaus* from an arrow, 4. 162. A heifer standing over her young one, to *Menelaus* guarding the body of *Patroclus*, 17. 5. Two countrymen disputing about the limits of their land, to two armies disputing a post, 12. 511. A poor woman weighing wool, the scales hanging uncertain, to the doubtful fates of two armies, 12. 521. Boys building and destroying houses of sand, to *Apollo*'s overturning the *Grecian* wall, 15. 416. A child weeping to his mother, to *Patroclus*'s supplications to *Achilles*, 16. 11.

SIMILES *exalting the characters of men by comparing them to* GODS

Agamemnon compar'd to *Jupiter*, *Mars*, and *Neptune*, 2. 564. *Ajax* to *Mars*, 7. 252. *Meriones*, to *Mars* rushing to the battel, 13. 384. *Hector*, to *Mars* destroying armies, 15. 726.

SIMILES *disadvantagious to the* CHARACTERS

Paris running from *Menelaus*, to a traveller frighted by a snake, 3. 47. A gawdy, foppish soldier, to a woman dress'd out, 2. 1063. *Teucer* skulking behind *Ajax*'s shield, to a child, 8. 325. *Thestor* pull'd from his chariot, to a fish drawn by an angler, 16. 495. *Ajax* to an ass, patient and stubborn, 11. 683. *Patroclus* weeping, to an infant, 16. 11. *Cebriones* tumbling, to a diver, 16. 904.

MISCELLANEOUS SIMILES

Soft piercing words, to snow, 3. 285. The closing of a wound, to milk turning to curd, 5. 1114. The fall of a hero, to a tower, 4. 528. Indefatigable courage, to an axe, 3. 90. *Agamemnon* weeping, to a fountain, 9. 19. *Juno* flying, to the mind passing over distant places, 15. 86. Dancers, to a wheel turning round, 18. 695. A warriour breaking the squadrons, to a mound dividing the course of a river, 17. 839. Men seeming to run in a dream, to the course of *Hector* and *Achilles*, 22. 257. A father

mourning at the funeral of his son, to *Achilles* for *Patroclus*, 23. 272. A fragment of a rock falling, to the furious descent of *Hector*, 13. 191. A poppy bending the head, to *Gorgythion* dying, 8. 371. The swift motion of the Gods, to the eye passing over a prospect, 5. 960. The smoothness of their motion, to the flight of doves, 5. 971.

VERSIFICATION

Expressing in the sound the thing describ'd

Made *abrupt* (and without conjunctions) in expressing haste, 7. 282. 15. 402.

Short, in earnest and vehement entreaties, 21. 420 – 23. 506.

Full of breaks, where disappointment is imag'd. 18. 101, 144 – 22. 378.

— where rage and fury is express'd, 18. 137.

— where grief is scarce able to go on, 18. 101. 22. 616, 650.

Broken and disorder'd in describing a stormy sea, 13. 1005.

Straining, imag'd in the sound, 15. 544.

Trembling, imag'd in the sound, 10. 446.

Panting, 13. 721.

Relaxation of all the limbs in death, 7. 18, 22.

A confused noise, 12. 410.

A hard-fought spot of ground, 12. 513, *&c.*

Tumbling of a wall, 7. 552.

Bounding of a stone from a rock, 13. 198.

A sudden stop, 13. 199.

Stiffness and slowness of old age, 13. 649, 653 – 23. 423.

A sudden fall, 23. 146.

The rustling and crashing of trees falling, 23. 147.

INDEX OF
ARTS AND SCIENCES

The first number marks the book, the second the verse.

ART MILITARY

AGRICULTURE *and* RURAL ARTS

ARCHITECTURE

ASTRONOMY

DIVINATION

GYMNASTICKS

HISTORY

MUSICK

MECHANICKS

Archery, Making a bow, and all its parts described, 4. 136, *&c.*

Chariot-making, A chariot described in all its parts, 5. 889, *&c.* 24. 335.

Poplar proper for wheels, 4. 554.

Sycamore fit for wheels, 21. 44.

Clockwork, 18. 441.

Enamelling, 18. 635.

Shipbuilding, 5. 80 – 15. 475.

Pine, a proper wood for the mast of a ship, 16. 592.

Smithery, iron-work, &c. The forge describ'd, 18. 435, 540. Bellows, 435, 482, 540. Hammer, tongs, anvil, 547.

Mixing of metals, *ibid.*

Spinning, 23. 890.

Weaving, 3. 580. 6. 580.

Embroidery, 6. 361.

Armory, and instruments of war.]

A compleat suit, that of *Paris*, 3. 410, *&c.* of *Agamemnon*, 11. 22 – *&c.*

Scale-armour, 15. 629.

Helmets, with four plumes, 5. 919 –

— without any crests, 10. 303 –

— lin'd with wool, and ornamented with boars teeth, of a particular make, 10. 311.

— lin'd with furr, 10. 397.

Bows, how made, 4. 137.

Battel-Ax, describ'd, 13. 766.

Belts, crossing each other, to hang the sword and the shield, 14. 468.

Corselets, ornamented with sculpture, 11. 33.

— how lin'd, 4. 165.

Mace, or club, 7. 170 – 15. 816.

Shields, so large as to cover from the neck to the ankles, 6. 145 – How made and cover'd, 7. 267. describ'd in every particular, 11. 43, *&c.*

Slings, 13. 899.

Spears, with brass points, 8. 617.

Ash fit to make them, 16. 143 – 19. 422.

How the wood was join'd to the point, 18. 618.

Swords, how ornamented, with ivory, gems, 19. 400.

ORATORY

See the Article Speeches *in the poetical index.*

POLICY

Kings.] Derive their honour from God, 2. 233 – 1. 315. Their names to be honour'd, 2. 313. One sole monarch, 2. 243. Hereditary right of kings represented by the sceptre of *Agamemnon* given by *Jove*, 2. 129. Kings not to be disobey'd on the one hand, nor to stretch too far their prerogative on the other, 1. 365, *&c.* Kings not absolute in council, 9. 133. Kings made so, only for their excelling others in virtue and valour, 12. 377. Vigilance continually necessary in princes, 2. 27 – 10. 102. Against monarchs delighting in war, 9. 82, *&c.* – 24. 55. The true valour, that which preserves, not destroys mankind, 6. 196. Kings may do wrong, and are oblig'd to reparation, 9. 144. Character of a great prince in war and peace, 3. 236.

Councils.] The danger of a subject's too bold advice, 1. 103. The advantage of wise counsels seconded by a wise prince, 9. 101. The use of advice, 9. 137. The singular blessing to a nation and prince, in a good and wise counsellor, 13. 918. The deliberations of the council to be free, the prince only to give a sanction to the best, 9. 133.

Laws.] deriv'd from God, and legislators his delegates, 1. 315. Committed to the care of kings, as guardians of the laws of God, 9. 129.

Tribute paid to princes from towns, 9. 206.

Taxes upon subjects to assist foreign allies, 17. 266.

Ambassadors, a sacred character, 1. 435 – 9. 261.

Voluntiers, listed into service, 11. 904.

See the Article Art Military.

PHYSICK

The praise of a physician, 11. 637.

Chiron learn'd it from *Æsculapius*, 4. 251.

Machaon and *Podalarius* professors of it, 2. 890.

   Botany.] Profess'd by skilful women, *Agamede* famous for it, 11. 877.

   Anatomy.] Of the *head*, 16. 415, *&c.*

The *eye*, 14. 577.

Under the *ear*, a wound there mortal, 13. 841.

The Juncture of the *head*, and its *nerves*, 14. 544.

The juncture of the *neck* and *chest*, the *collar-bone* and its insertion, the disjointing of which renders the arm useless, 8. 393, *&c.*

The *spinal marrow* exprest by the vein that runs along the chine, a wound there mortal, 13. 692 – 20. 559.

The *elbow*, its tendons and ligaments, 20. 554.

Blood, a great effusion of it, by cutting off the arm, the cause of immediate death, 5. 105.

The *heart* and its fibres, 16, 590.

The force of the muscle of the heart, 13. 554.

A wound in the *bladder* by piercing the *Ischiatic* joint, mortal, 13. 813.

The insertion of the thigh-bone, and its ligaments describ'd, 5. 375.

The wounds of the *Abdomen* mortal, and excessively painful, 13. 718.

The tendons of the *ankle*, 4. 597.

   Chirurgery.] extraction of darts, 4. 228.

Sucking the blood from the wound, 4. 250.

Infusion of balms into wounds, 4. 250. 5. 1111.

Washing the wound with warm water, and the use of lenitives, 11. 965.

Stanching the blood by the bitter root, 11. 983.

Ligatures of wool, 13. 752.

Use of baths for wounded men, 14. 10.

Sprinkling water to recover from fainting, 14. 509.

   Pharmacy and *Diæticks.*

The use of wine forbidden, 6. 330.

Cordial potion of *Nestor*, 11. 782, *&c.*

Infection, seizing first on animals, then men, 1. 70. Nine days the crisis of diseases, 1. 71. Fevers and plagues from the dog-star, 5. 1058 – 19. 412 – 22. 41.

PAINTING, SCULPTURE, *&c.*

See the whole shield of Achilles, *and the notes on* lib. 18.

The CHARACTERS. *Homer* distinguishes the character in the figures of Gods superior to those of men, 18. 602.

Characters of majesty.] The majesty of *Jupiter*, from whence *Phidias* copied his statue, 1. 683. Of *Mars* and *Neptune*, 2. 569.

The Majesty of a prince, in the figure of *Agamemnon*, 2. 564, *&c.* Of a wise man, in *Ulysses*'s aspect, 3. 280. Of an old man, in *Nestor* and *Priam*, 1. 330 – 24. 600. Of a young hero, in *Achilles*, 19. 390, *&c.* All variously characterized by *Homer*.

Characters of Beauty.] *Alluring* beauty in the Goddess *Venus*, 14. 250. *Majestic* beauty in *Juno*, 14. 216. Beauty of a *woman* in *Helen*, 3. 205. Beauty of a *young man*, in *Paris*, 3. 26. *Euphorbus* 17. 53, *&c.* Beauty of a *fine infant*, in *Astyanax*, 6. 497.

Beauties of the parts of the body.] Largeness and majesty of the eyes, in *Juno*'s. Blackness, in those of *Cryseïs.* Blue, in *Minerva*'s, *&c.* Eye-brows, black, graceful, 1. 683. The beauty of the cheeks, and the fairness of hair, in the epithets of *Helen.* Whiteness of the arms in those of *Juno.* Fingers rather red than pale, in the epithet of *Rosie-finger'd* to *Aurora.* Whiteness of the feet in that of *Silver-footed* to *Thetis*, &c. Colour of the skin to be painted differently according to the condition of the personages, applied to the whiteness of the thigh of *Menelaus*, 4. 175.

Character of deformity, the opposites to beauty in the several parts, consider'd in the figure of *Thersites*, 2. 263, *&c.*

For pictures of particular things, see the article Images *in the* POETICAL INDEX.

History, landscape-painting, animals, &c. In the buckler of *Achilles*, 18. at large.

The design of a goblet in *sculpture*, 11. 775.

Sculpture of a corslet, 11. 33, *&c.* Of a bowl, 23. Horses carv'd on monuments, 17. 495.

Enameling, and *in-laying*, in the buckler of *Achilles*, 18. 635. 655, and breast-plate of *Agamemnon*, 11. 35.

Tapestry, or weaving histories, flowers, *&c.* 3. 171 – 6. 580 – 22. 569.

Embroidery of garments, 6. 360.

POETRY

See the entire INDEX.

THEOLOGY

A view of HOMER's
THEOLOGY

JUPITER, *or the* **SUPREME BEING**

Superiour to all powers of heaven, 7. 244. 8. 10, *&c.* Enjoying himself in the contemplation of his glory and power, 11. 107. Self-sufficient, and above all second causes, or inferior deities, 1. 647. The other deities resort to him as their sovereign appeal, 5. 1065 – 21. 590. His will his fate, 8. 10. His sole will the cause of all humane events, 1. 8. His will takes certain and instant effect, 1. 685. His will immutable and always just, 1. 730. All-seeing, 8. 65 – 2. 4 – Supreme above all, and sole sufficient, 11. 107. The sole governor and fate of all things, 2. 147 – 16. 845. Disposer of all the glories and success of men, 17. 198. Forseeing all things, 71. 228. The giver of victory, 7. 118. Disposer of all human affairs, 9. 32. His least regard, or thought restores mankind, 15. 274. or turns the fate of armies, 17. 675. Dispenser of all the good and evil that befalls mankind, 24. 663. His favour superiour to all human means, 9. 152. His counsels unsearchable, 1. 705. *Themis* or *Justice* is his messenger, 20. 5. God prospers those who worship him, 1. 290. Constantly punishes the wicked, tho' late, 4. 194. The avenger of injustice, 4. 202. Nothing so terrible as his wrath, 5. 227. His divine justice sometimes punishes whole nations by general calamities, 16. 468. Children punished for the sins of their parents, 11. 166 and 16. 393.

The inferiour DEITIES

Have different offices under God: Some preside over elements, 18. 46 – 23. 240.

Some over cities and countries, 4. 75.

Some over words, springs, &c. 20. 12.

They have subordinate power over one another. Inferiour Deities or Angels subject to pain, imprisonment, 5. 475. 1090. Threatened by *Jupiter* to be cast into *Tartarus*, 8. 15. Are supposed to converse in a language different from that of mortals, 2. 985 – Subsist not by material food, 5. 425. Compassionate mankind, 8. 42 – 24. 412. Able to assist mortals at any distance, 16. 633. Regard and take care of those who serve them, even to their remains after death, 24. 520. No resisting heavenly powers, 5. 495. The meanness and vileness of all earthly creatures in comparison of the divine natures, 5. 535.

Prayer recommended on all enterprizes, *throughout the poem.*

Prayers intercede at the throne of heaven, 9. 624.

Opinions of the ancients concerning *hell*, the place of punishment for the wicked after death, 8. 15 – 19. 271.

Opinions of the ancients concerning the state of separate *spirits*, 23. 89, &c. 120, &c.

Variant Readings in the Poetic Text

After the first edition (quarto and folio) of 1715–20, later editions of
Pope's *Iliad* published during Pope's lifetime are the following:

1720a 6 vols., duodecimo. By Bowyer for Bernard Lintot.

1720b 6 vols., duodecimo. 'The Second Edition'. 1720–21, Vols.
I–III; 1721, Vols. I–VI. Some of the six volumes printed
by Bettenham.

1732 6 vols., duodecimo. 'The Third Edition'. Vol. III is dated
1731.

1736 6 vols., duodecimo. 'The Fourth Edition'. Woodfall for
Lintot.

1743 6 vols., duodecimo. For Henry Lintot.

NOTE: I am indebted to the Twickenham text for recording a large
number of these variant readings. Where I have not followed the
readings of the 1743 edition, I have listed these readings here; the
Twickenham text did not list all of the variant readings from the 1743
edition. The editors of the Twickenham text did not distinguish, in
their apparatus, between the folio and quarto versions of 1715–20;
references to the first edition in this list of variant readings refer to the
folio, which was the more polished of the two first editions. While I
have depended upon the Twickenham text for identifying most of the
alternative readings, I have in each instance consulted the editions
listed above in order to check the veracity of the variant readings
recorded by the editors of the Twickenham text.

In general, when I have departed from the 1743 duodecimo edition,
it has been in deference to the readings of the first-edition folio which,
as discussed in the introduction, is the last edition that Pope carefully
and systematically proofread.

The variants listed here refer to substantive alternative readings
rather than to accidentals.

I have generally not listed as variant readings those readings that
were corrected in the *errata* sheet included in the final volume of the
first edition in 1720.

Book I

1 Achilles' . . . Greece] The Wrath of *Peleus'* Son *1715–32*
The manuscript of the opening lines of Pope's translation read as follows:

wrath
The stern Pelides Rage, O Goddess! sing,
Of all the Grecian Woes the fatal Spring,
Heroes
That strowd with Warriors dead the Phrygian Plain,
Whose limbs unburyd on the hostile Shore
Devouring Dogs and greedy Vultures tore.

(Add. MSS. 4807)

2 Of . . . heav'nly] Of all the *Grecian* Woes, O *1715–32*.

72 *Pyres*] Fires *1715*. Is Pope perhaps responding to Thomas Tickell's 'Fun'ral Piles' in his rival version? Pope's MS. reading is 'The fun'ral flames reflect a dreadful blase'.

102 truths, . . . Great,] Truths . . . Great *1715*.

117 man] Priest *1715*.

267 sees] saw *1715*.

268 sparkle] sparkled *1715*.

274 forsake] forsook *1715*.

296 *Atrides*] the Monarch *1715*.

331 Experienc'd] Th'experienc'd *1715*.

343 ye] you *1715, 1732*.

360 me wise] we wise *1743* (an obvious misprint).

362 *Atrides*, seize not] *Atrides* seize not *1743*.

452–3]   Supported by the Chiefs on either Hand,
          In Silence past along the winding Strand. *1715*.

541 trickle] trickled *1715*.

557 feasts] Feasts *1743*.

607 off'ring] Victims *1715*.

608 flames] flame *1732, 1743.*

644 the] a *1715.*

667 fear?] fear; *1743.*

Book 2

50 numbers] Mountains *1715.*

110 by thousands] in Millions *1715.*

157 tens] ten *1736, 1743.*

490 hast] has *1720a–43.*

563 thousands] Millions *1715.*

587 *Peneleus*] *Peneleius 1743.*

646 *Carystos*] *Caristos 1743.*

947 sweep] swept *1715–32.*

1008 fates] Fate *1715–20b.*

Book 3

39–40]   In vain the Youths oppose, the Mastives bay,
The Lordly Savage rends the panting Prey. *1715–36.*

251 martial] manly *1715.*

253 warriour-train] martial Train *1715.*

294 a] an *1715.*

340 draws] drew *1715.*

361 ev'ry] age to *1732.*

405 weighty] mighty *1732.*

412 with silver] and silver *1715.*

416 Sustained . . . glittered] Sustains . . . glitters *1715.*

476 borrow'd] *Groea*'s *1715.*

477 She seem'd an ancient] *Groea*, her Fav'rite *1715.*

Book 4

4 goblet] Goblets *1715.*

161 from its] from the *1715.*

297 warriours] Warrior's *1715.*

349 nor] or *1715.*

487 the] their *1715–32.*

579 Pond'rous he falls;] Down sinks the Chief: *1715.*

Book 5

40 bathe . . . shake] bath'st . . . shak'st *1716.*

110 diff'ring] diff'rent *1716–32.*

201 father] father's *1743* (most probably a misprint).

229 entreat] intreat *1743.*

278 Now haste, ascend my Seat, and from the Car *1716.*

279 fight] War *1716.*

291 hear the rein] bear the rein *1743* (probably a misprint).

314–15]   I loath in lazy Fights to press the Car,
          At distance wound, or wage a flying War; *1716.*

316 strong] strung *1716.*

390 match] match'd *1716.*

851 with] in *1716.*

930 they] to *1716.*

982 the] their *1716.*

1076 reveres] revere *1715.*

Book 6

10 And] That *1716.*

71 not sex] nor Sex *1732–43.*

97 aid's] Aid's *1716–43.* (I am speculating that 'aids'' was the intended meaning, although spelt as if it was the singular possessive.)

249 consum'd] oppress'd *1716.*

Book 7

67 like] of *1743.*

176 aught] ought *1716.*

189 he] I *1716.*

248 it] 'em *1716.*

305 their jav'lins] the Javelins *1716.*

336 And first] When thus *1716.*

376 man] Chief *1716.*

416 Order] Union *1716.*

Book 8

97 hosts] Host *1716.*

276 your] our *1716.*

277 Your] Our *1716.*

318 pass'd] pass *1716.*

384 All pale and] And ey'd him *1716.*

393 note This note is missing in the edition of *1743.*

395 bowstring] Tendon *1716–20b.*

398 a] the *1716.*

464 her] the *1716.*

519 dare to combate] dare combate *1743* (an obvious misprint).

523 King] Sire *1716.*

589 Those] These *1716.*

617 brass] Steel *1716.*

638 or] and *1716.*

646 our] the *1716.*

Book 9

232 take] took *1717.*

261 you] ye *1717.*

274 porket] Porker *1717.*

561 accent] Accents *1717.*

640 fierce, and] fierce and *1743.*

781 *Diomedè*] Diomede *1720a, 1743.*

Book 10

53 pray'r] Vows *1717.*

206 th'entrenchments] the entrenchments *1743.*

241 said he] he said *1717.*

Book 11

8 fleet] Fleets *1717.*

45 brims] brim *1743.*

64 rush] rush'd *1717–20b.*

216 death] Deaths *1717.*

270 Springs] Vaults *1717.*

333 sanguine] smoaking *1717.*

534 Falls . . . earth] Supinely falls *1717.*

588 host] Hosts *1717–32.*

589 loss not] loss, not *1720a, 1743.*

701 Marks] Drinks *1717* (corrected to Prints in *Errata*).

838 at] in *1717.*

Book 12

41 and] with *1717–32.*

69 bold] brave *1717, 1720b.*

103 glorious] glories *1717–20b.*

288 t' escape] to 'scape *1717, 1720a.*

303 his] their *1736, 1743.*

309 rampart] Ramparts *1717–32.*

497 hope] Hopes *1717.*

Book 13

109 my force] the Man *1718.*

117 meanwhile] mean while *1743.*

152 yours] your's *1743.*

249 forceful] boasted *1718–1720b.*

267 high-lifting] high-lifted *1718.*

268 drops of] dropping *1718.*

409 blazing] brazen *1736, 1743.*

451 infold] inclose *1718–36.*

454 close-compell'd] Heaps on Heaps *1718–36.*

485 valu'd coursers] crowded coursers *1743.*

497 dreadful] deathful *1718–20b.*

514 and] with *1718–20b.*

889–90　　His Brave Associate had no following Band,
His Troops unpractis'd in the Fights of Stand:
1718–36.

891 For not the Spear the *Locrian* Squadrons wield, *1718–36.*

930 whose] thick *1718, 1720a.*

946 prepares] prepar'd *1718.*

985 inspires;] inspires: *1743.*

Book 14

135 past] fled *1718.*

156 warriour] Hero *1718.*

158 hero] Warrior *1718.*

162 unutterable] inutterable *1718.*

171 warriour] warring *1718–32.*

309 Titans . . . *Chronos*] Gods that round *Saturnus 1718–36.*

418 dew] drew *1743* (obvious misprint).

Book 15

44 drear] dear *1720a–43.*

48 rages] ranges *1720a–43.*

253 the] his *1718–32.*

310–11   They gain th'impervious Rock and safe retreat
          (For *Fate* preserves them) from the Hunter's
              Threat. *1718.*

420 vanish'd] vanish *1718.*

775 the] his *1718.*

Book 16

200 eye] Eyes *1718.*

226 those loves] her Love *1718.*

290 thy] their *1718.*

383 godlike] godly *1736, 1743.*

614 body,] Corpse, and *1718.*

673 view] view'd *1718.*

859 battlements] Battlement *1718.*

1010 Thy own] The fierce [*Errata 1720*]; The great *1718.*

Book 17

8 re-turns] returns *1720.*

34 Go,] To *1720.*

35 Or while] While yet *1720.*

343 thro'] from *1720.*

499 arching] arched *1732–43.*

745 an] a *1720.*

750 weary] weary'd *1720–20b.*

Book 18

205 show'ry] painted *1720.*

229 can] should *1720.*

242 shoulder] Shoulders *1720–32.*

353 purple Orient] rosie *Welkin* *1720* (*Errata 1720* corrects *Welkin* with Orient)

364 worst] worse *1720.*

395 Sacred . . . hand] Slain by this Hand, sad Sacrifice! *1720.*

477 the labours] my Labours *1720.*

482 chests] Chest *1720–32.*

566 bathes . . . in] bends . . . to *1720.*

635 Behind, the rising earth in] The new-ear'd Earth in blacker *1720.*

636 And sable] Sable it *1720.*

Book 19

336 Once] Hast *1720–32.*

338 Once] Oft' *1720–32.*

Book 20

18 Pow'rs] Gods *1720.*

540 an] and *1720–32.*

550 the front] his Front *1720.*

Book 21

3 flying] scatt'ring (*Errata 1720*).

25 groan'd] groan *1720.*

44 from a sycamore] on a Fig-tree Top *1720.*

85 trembles] trembling *1720.*

258 deep] Deeps *1720.*

294 the] their *1720.*

403 gardens] Garden *1720.*

589 her blest] the blest *1720.*

660 dirt] Dust *1720.*

Book 22

34 double] doubled *1720–20b.*

56 the Gods no dearer than] th'Immortals hateful as *1720.*

394 the flaming] his flaming *1720.*

441 his] the *1720.*

487 melancholy shades] silent Shades of Hell *1720.*

534 grief] Griefs *1720.*

Book 23

18 bathe their arms, ... the sands] drop the Sands, ... their Arms *1720.*

80 he living] the Living *1720.*

146 redoubling] rebounding *1720.*

164 a] the *1736, 1743.*

170 *Patroclus*] The Body *1720.*

174 Those] The *1720.*

279 flame] flam'd *1720–36.*

371 his son] the Son *1720.*

827 winds] Wind *1736, 1743.*

934 hero, more] Hero, or *1720–32.*

939 host] Hosts *1720–32.*

Book 24

2 Seek . . . clear] Sought . . . clear'd *1720.*

49 a fun'ral] the fun'ral *1720.*

392 stretch'd] stretch *1720.*

397 his] the *1743.*

464 Appear] Appears *1720.*

482 a host] an Host *1720.*

494 their martial] the martial *1720–32.*

679 An only] One only *1720.*

853 or *Grecian*] nor *Grecian* *1720.*

Glossary

The following definitions are cued to the specific contexts in which the words that are here defined appear in Pope's *Iliad*. These definitions are not always the primary or most obvious meanings, even in Pope's time, but they are rather meant to elucidate the meaning of words when they are used in ways that may not be familiar to the modern reader. Examples of the listed definitions are recorded, by book and line number, in parentheses; these are not intended to be exhaustive.

SJ refers to Samuel Johnson's *Dictionary of the English Language* (London, 1755); **OED** to the *Oxford English Dictionary*, Second Edition (Oxford, 1989).

ABLUTION 'The act of cleansing, or washing clean.' SJ

ACCORD *v.* 'To assent or consent to. *Obs.*' OED

ADJURE 'To impose an oath upon another, prescribing the form in which he shall swear.' SJ

ADVENTURE *n.* 'An accident, a chance' (24:491) and 'a hazard' (24:436). SJ

AEGIS The shield of Jove (Zeus).

ALARMS A call to arms.

AMAZE *n.* 'Astonishment; confusion, either of fear or wonder.' SJ

AMBIENT 'Surrounding; encompassing.' SJ

APPALL 'To depress; to discourage.' SJ

APPLY 'To have recourse to, as a solicitor or petitioner; with *to*' (9:234). SJ

APPROVE 'To prove; to show; to justify.' SJ

ARMIPOTENT 'Powerful in arms; mighty in war.' SJ

ARREARS 'That which remains behind unpaid, though due.' SJ

ART 'A science, a trade; cunning.' SJ

ARTFUL 'Cunning, skilful, dexterous.' SJ

ARTIST Artisan.

ASPERSE 'To bespatter with censure or calumny.' SJ

ASPIRE 'To rise higher' (1:608, 2:508). SJ

ATTAINT Taint.

ATTEND 'To await' SJ; 'to regard; to fix the mind upon' (13:922). SJ

ATTEST 'To bear witness of; to witness; to call to witness.' SJ

AWFUL 'That which strikes with awe; invested with dignity; that which fills with reverence.' SJ

BALDRICK An ornamented belt worn to support a sword.

BAND *v.* 'To unite together into one body or troop.' SJ

BEEVES 'Oxen.' SJ

BOARD 'Table.' SJ

BOREAS The north wind.

BOSSY Embossed, studded.

BRAKE *n.* 'A thicket of brambles, or of thorns.' SJ

BRAND 'To mark or stamp with infamy; stigmatize.' OED

BRAVE 'Courageous'; 'gallant; lofty; graceful.' SJ

BRINDLED 'Streaked; tabby.' SJ

BRUISE 'To crush; to beat into coarse powder' (11:982). SJ

BUCKLER Shield.

BUNCH 'A protuberance; a hump on the back.' OED

CAESTUS 'A contrivance consisting of thongs of bullhide, loaded with strips of iron and lead, and wound round the hands. Used by Roman boxers as a protection and to give greater weight to the blows.' OED

CANISTER Bread basket.

CARE *n.* 'The object of care, or caution, or of love.' SJ

CASQUE Helmet.

CATARACT Waterfall (12:27).

CAWL Caul, 'the omentum; the integument in which the guts are inclosed.' SJ

CENTINEL Sentinel.

CESTUS 'The girdle of Venus.' SJ

CHAMPAIN 'The field of military operations.' OED

CHANNEL BONE Neck or throat.

CHARGE *n.* 'Care; trust; custody; office.' SJ

CHARGER 'A large dish.' SJ

CHINE 'The part of the back in which the spine is found.' SJ

CINCTURE 'Something worn round the body' SJ. More specifically, a belt worn around the waist.

CIRCUS 'An open space or area for sports, with seats round for the spectators.' SJ

CISTERN 'A receptacle of water for domestick uses' (22:201). SJ

CLIFT Cliff.

CLOSE *adj.* 'Secret; private; hidden; not revealed' (1:677). SJ

COERULEAN 'Blue; sky coloured.' SJ

COFFER 'A box or chest, *esp.* a strong box in which money or valuables are kept.' OED

COMMUTUAL 'Reciprocal.' SJ

COMPACTED Joined tightly together.

COMPOSE 'To calm; to quiet' (7:81, 123, 440; 14:240). SJ

CONCLUSIVE 'Decisive.' SJ

CONDUCT *n.* 'The act of convoying or guarding'; 'behaviour' (23:379). SJ

CONE 'The conical top of a helmet.' OED

CONFESS 'To declare or acknowledge.' SJ

CONFEST 'Open; known; acknowledged; not concealed.' SJ

CONFIRM To make firm, strengthen, encourage (2:228, 16:299), as in the Latin *confirmo.*

CONFOUND To destroy.

CONGLOBE 'To gather into a round mass.' SJ

CONSISTORY 'Any solemn assembly' (10:232). SJ

CONSPIRE 'To agree together.' SJ; but used in the more common sense of 'to plot' in 6:408.

CORPS = CORSE = CORPSE

CORSLET 'A light armour for the forepart of the body.' SJ

COUCH *v.* 'To lie down on a place of repose.' SJ

COUNSEL *n.* 'Deliberation; scheme; purpose; design.' SJ

COURSER 'A swift horse; a war horse: a word not used in prose.' SJ

COVERT *n.* 'A shelter; a thicket or hiding place.' SJ

CUIRASS Breast-plate.

CUISH 'The armour that covers the thighs.' SJ

CYMARR 'A slight covering; a scarf.' SJ

DARDAN Trojan.

DASTARD *n.* and *adj.* Coward(ly).

DECENT 'Becoming, fit, suitable.' SJ

DEGEN'RATE *adj.* 'Fallen from the virtue and merit of his ancestors.' SJ

DENOUNCE 'To threaten by proclamation.' SJ

DEPEND 'To hang from'; 'to rely on' (18:323). SJ

DEPLORE To grieve over.

DEPRECATE 'To implore mercy of' (9:236). SJ

DEPUTE 'To send with a special commission; to empower one to transact instead of another.' SJ

DEVIOUS 'Out of the common track' (10:540). SJ

DEVOLVE 'To fall in succession into new hands.' SJ

DEVOTED Cursed, doomed to destruction.

DEXTER 'The right [which, for oracles, is auspicious; 13:1039, 24:393]; not the left.' SJ

DISCOV'RY 'Exploration, investigation, reconnoitring, reconaissance. *Obs.*' OED

DISDAIN *v. intrans.* 'To be moved with indignation, be indignant, take offence. *Obs.*' (18:317). OED

DISEMBOGUE 'To pour out at the mouth of a river; to vent' (17:311). SJ, who cites Skinner's derivation from the Old French *disem' oucher.*

DISHONEST 'Disgraceful; ignominious. These two senses are scarcely English, being borrowed from the Latin.' SJ; cf. *Windsor-Forest* 326, *Dunciad* (1743) 3:198.

DISTAIN To discolour or to dye.

DISTASTE *v. trans.* 'To excite the dislike or aversion of; to be distasteful to; to displease, offend.' OED

DISTEMPER *v. trans.* 'To disease; to disorder.' SJ

DISTRACT 'To pull different ways at once; to separate, divide; to fill the mind with contrary considerations; to make mad.' SJ

DOME House, home.

DOOM *n.* Judgement; *v.* to judge.

DOUBTFUL 'Uncertain; to be feared.' OED

DUCTILE 'Easy to be drawn out into length, or expanded.' SJ

EMBATTL'D Furnished with battlements; a battlement is 'an indented parapet [i.e. barrier] at the top of a wall.' OED

EMBODY'D United into a single body.

EMBRUE = IMBRUE 'To steep, to soak.' SJ

ENAMEL *v.* 'Variegate with colours.' SJ

ENCHASE Engrave.

ENGINE 'A military machine; any instrument.' SJ

ENGROSS *v. trans.* 'To gain or keep exclusive possession of.' OED

ENSANGUINE 'To smear with gore, suffuse with blood.' SJ

ENSIGN 'Badge or symbol of office or dignity.' SJ

ENVY 'Rivalry; competition; malice; malignity.' SJ
EUGH Yew tree.
EVENT Outcome.
EXPLORE To search for.
EXTANT 'Standing out to view.' SJ

FAINT 'To grow feeble; to sink into dejection' (12:323). SJ
FAN 'An instrument for winnowing grain. A basket of special form . . . used for separating the corn from the chaff by throwing it into the air. *Obs.*' OED
FANCY *n.* 'Imagination; the power by which the mind forms to itself images and representations of things, persons, or scenes of being.' SJ
FANE 'A temple; a place consecrated to religion. A poetical word.' SJ
FATAL 'Deadly' and 'proceeding by destiny, appointed by destiny.' SJ
FAULCHION Sword.
FETLOCK 'A tuft of hair as big as the hair of the mane that grows behind the pastern-joint of many horses: horses of a low size have scarce any such tuft' (13:55). SJ, quoting from *Farrier's Dictionary.*
FILE *n.* 'A line of soldiers ranged one behind another.' SJ
FLAGGY 'Weak; lax; limber; not stiff; not tense.' SJ
FLAGITIOUS 'Wicked; villainous; atrocious.' SJ
FLOUNCE 'To move with violence in the water or mire; to struggle or dash in the water.' SJ
FLOURET 'A small imperfect flower.' SJ
FOND 'Foolish; silly; indiscreet; imprudent; injudicious'; but also 'pleased in too great a degree; foolishly delighted' (1:156). SJ
FOOT 'Infantry.' SJ
FORBID *adj.* Forbidden, prohibited from (19:41).
FORE-RIGHT 'Directly forward, in or towards the front, straight ahead.' OED
FOSSE 'A ditch; a moat.' SJ
FULGID 'Shining; glittering; dazzling.' SJ

GANTLET Boxing glove. Cf. CAESTUS
GENIAL Festive.
GEN'ROUS 'Not of mean birth; noble of mind; liberal; strong; vigorous.' SJ
GENTLE 'Well born; well descended.' SJ

GLAD 'Wearing a gay appearance; fertile; bright, showy.' SJ

GLORIOUS 'Boastful; proud; haughty'; 'Noble, illustrious.' SJ

GLOW 'To burn with vehement heat' (11:986). SJ

GORGET 'The piece of armour that defends the throat.' SJ

GRATEFUL 'Pleasing; acceptable'; also 'having a due sense of benefits' (23:711). SJ

GREAVES Metal plates protecting the shin-bone.

GRIPE v. To grip. 'To hold with the fingers closed; to grasp.' SJ

GRIZLY Ghastly, horrific.

HANGER 'A short broad sword' (11:42).

HAST Haste.

HAUNCH 'The thigh; the hind hip.' SJ

HEADSTALL 'Part of the bridle [or halter] that covers the head.' SJ

HECATOMB A sacrifice of a hundred oxen, or any large and costly sacrifice.

HEIR v. 'To inherit.' SJ

HINDE or HIND A 'female of red deer' (16:915); a 'peasant' (18:628). SJ

HOLLOW adj. 'Noisy, like sound reverberated from a cavity'; 'having a void space within' (2:401).

HOMICIDE 'A murderer; a manslayer.' SJ

HONEST Honourable.

HONOUR 'Ornament; decoration'; 'Honours of the Head' (17:229) means 'hair'.

HUMOURS 'The different kind of moisture in man's body, reckoned by the old physicians to be phlegm, blood, choler, and melancholy, which, as they predominated, were supposed to determine the temper of mind; general turn or temper of mind.' SJ

HYMENAEAL 'Pertaining to marriage.' SJ

IGNIPOTENT 'Presiding over fire.' SJ

IMPEND 'To hang over.' SJ

IMPETUOUS 'Violent; fierce; vehement.' SJ

IMPLICIT 'Entangled; infolded; complicated.' SJ

IMPOTENT 'Without power of restraint'; 'weak, feeble' (20:556). SJ

INDULGENT 'Kind; gentle.' SJ

INFRANGIBLE 'Not to be broken.' SJ

INNOCENT adj. 'Pure from mischief; unhurtful; harmless in effects.' SJ

INNOXIOUS 'Free from mischievous effects'; 'pure from crimes.' SJ

INSULT *v. trans.* 'To treat with insolence or contempt. It is sometimes used with *over*' (13:558). SJ

INVEST 'To dress; to clothe; to adorn; to grace.' SJ

INVOLVE 'To inwrap, to cover with any thing circumfluent.' SJ

IRREMEABLE 'Admitting no return.' SJ

KIND *n.* 'Race; generical class.' SJ

LATENT 'Hidden; concealed; secret.' SJ

LAY *v.* 'To impose; enjoin' (11:740). SJ

LEAGUER'D Besieged.

LEAVE 'Grant of liberty; permission; allowance.' SJ

LEGAT = LEGATE 'A deputy; an ambassador.' SJ

LEV'RET 'A young hare.' SJ

LIBATION 'The act of pouring wine on the ground in honour of some god; the wine so poured.' SJ

LIGATURE Bandage.

LIST *v.* 'To enclose for combat.' SJ

LIST *n.* 'Inclosed ground in which tilts [military games at which the combatants run against each other with lances on horseback] are run and combats fought.' SJ

LIVID 'Discoloured, as with a blow; black and blue.' SJ

LOWER *v.* (rhymes with 'scour') 'To frown; to pout; to look sullen.' SJ

LOW'RING See LOWER

LUCID 'Shining; bright; glittering.' SJ

LUMBER 'Any thing useless or cumbersome.' SJ

LUSTRATION 'Purification by water.' SJ

MAGAZINE 'A storehouse, commonly an arsenal or armoury, or repository of provisions.' SJ

MAISTIFF (*maistives*, plural) 'A dog of the largest size; dogs kept to watch the house.' SJ

MANES (disyllabic) 'Ghost; shade.' SJ

MART 'A place of public traffick.' SJ

MATE *v. trans.* 'To be equal to' (13:414). SJ

MEAN *adj.* 'Wanting dignity; low-minded; base.' SJ

MISSILE *adj.* 'Thrown by the hand; striking at distance.' SJ

MISSIVE *adj.* 'Such as may be sent; used at distance.' SJ

MITRE Used by Pope (and Chapman before him) to translate the Homeric μίτρη, a belt or girdle.

MOLE Structure serving as a breakwater.

MOULDER 'To turn to dust; to crumble.' SJ

NARRATIVE *adj.* Garrulous or talkative.

NAVE 'The middle part of the wheel in which the axle moves.' SJ

NERVOUS 'Well strung; strong; vigorous.' SJ

NICE 'Accurate in judgement to minute exactness.' SJ

NOTUS The south wind.

OBLOQUY 'Censorious speech; blame; slander; reproach.' SJ

OBSCENE 'Immodest; offensive; inauspicious; ill-omened.' SJ

OBSEQUIES 'Funeral rites; funeral solemnities.' SJ

OBTEST 'To beseech, to supplicate.' SJ

OFFICIOUS 'Kind; doing good offices; importunely forward.' SJ

ORIENT *adj.* 'Rising as the sun; eastern.' SJ

ORTHIAN See Pope's note on 11:14.

PAEAN 'A song of triumph.' SJ

PALISADE 'Pales [a pale is a 'narow piece of wood joined above and below to a rail, to inclose grounds'] set by way of inclosure or defence.' SJ

PALL 'A cloak or mantle of state; the covering thrown over the dead.' SJ

PAP Nipple.

PENSIVE 'Sorrowfully thoughtful; sorrowful; melancholy.' SJ

PERIOD 'The end or conclusion' (4:206; 11:955); also 'a stated number of years; a round of time' (11:95, 12:9). SJ

PHALANX 'A troop of men closely embodied.' SJ

PINNACE 'A boat belonging to a ship of war. It seems formerly to have signified rather a small sloop [a small vessel furnished with a mast] or bark attending a larger ship.' SJ

PLIGHT *v.* To pledge, promise.

PLY *v.* 'To go in haste' (10:623); 'to solicit importunately' (11:82); 'to employ with diligence; to keep busy; to set on work; to practise diligently.' SJ

POMP 'A procession of splendour and ostentation'; 'splendour' (23:159). SJ

POMPOUS 'Splendid; magnificent; grand.' SJ

PORKET Pig.

PREFER *v.* To put forward.

PRESS *n.* 'Crowd, tumult, throng' SJ; 'a throng or crush in battle; the thick of the fight.' OED

PREVENT 'To hinder; to obviate; to obstruct'; 'to go before.' SJ

PROFFER *n.* Offer, proposal.

PROFOUND *n.* 'The deep; the main; the sea.' SJ

PROMISCUOUS 'Mingled; confused; undistinguished.' SJ

PRORE Prow of a ship.

PROTEND 'To hold out; to stretch forth.' SJ

PROVE 'To experience; make trial.' SJ

QUOIT Discus. 'The discus of the ancients is sometimes called in English quoit, but improperly; the game of quoits is a game of skill; the discus was only a trial of strength, as among us to throw the hammer.' SJ

RAMPIRES 'Ramparts.' SJ

RANGE *v. trans.* 'To place in order; to put in ranks.' SJ

RANK *v.* To arrange or draw up soldiers into rank.

REBATE *v.* 'To blunt; to beat to obtuseness; to deprive of keenness' (11:304). SJ

RECREANT 'Cowardly.' SJ

RED STAR Mars.

REFECTION 'Refreshment after hunger or fatigue.' SJ

REFLUENT *adj.* 'Running back; flowing back.' SJ

REFULGENT Shining.

REIGN *n.* 'Kingdom; dominions.' SJ

REMAIN *v. trans.* 'To await.' SJ

REMEMBRANCE 'Reminder.' SJ

REMISSIVE *adj.* 'Producing or allowing decrease *of* something.' SJ

REMIT *v. trans.* Forgive (9:744).

REMOVE *v.* Depart.

REPAIR *v.* 'To go to; to betake himself.' SJ

RESOLVE *v.* 'To melt; to be dissolved' (7:113); also 'to decree within oneself' (13:534). SJ

RESTIVE *adj.* 'Unwilling to stir; resolute against going forward; obstinate; stubborn.' SJ

RESULT *v. intrans.* 'To rebound; to spring up' OED; 'to fly back.' SJ

RESUME *v.* To take back to oneself something previously given or granted.

RETORTED *adj.* 'Thrown or cast back; returned.' OED

SACRED 'Inviolable' (cf. 19:42; 22:489); 'holy'; 'consecrated.' SJ

SALUBRIOUS 'Wholesome; healthful; promoting health.' SJ

SANCTION 'Binding force given to an oath; something which makes an oath or engagement binding; a solemn oath.' OED

SANGUINE Bloody.

SCIENCE 'Knowledge.' SJ

SCUD v. 'To run away with precipitation' (11:597). SJ

SEPULTURE n. Burial.

SERENE n. 'A calm damp evening.' SJ

SERENE v. 'To calm; to quiet; to brighten' (15:178).

SHELVING adj. 'Sloping; inclining; having declivity.' SJ

SHOCKING Assailing with a sudden and fierce attack; charging (with troops).

SIMPLE 'A single ingredient in a medicine; a drug.' SJ

SINISTER 'Left; not right; not dexter; inauspicious.' SJ

SLIDDER 'To slide with interruption.' SJ

SLOATH = SLOTH

SLOPE adj. 'Oblique; not perpendicular' (13:512). SJ

SMOAK 'To move with such swiftness as to kindle; to move very fast so as to raise dust like smoke.' SJ

SNUFF v. 'To scent.'

SOCIAL 'Easy to mix in friendly gaiety; companionable' (11:911). SJ

SOW'R = SOUR adj. 'Harsh of temper; severe.' SJ

SOWSE = SOUSE 'To fall as a bird on its prey.' SJ

SPOIL Booty. Can also mean 'the cast or stripped-off skin of any animal'. OED

STAND v. trans. 'To endure; to resist without flying or yielding.' SJ

STILL adv. 'Ever, always.' SJ

STOOP Swoop down (24:393).

STRICT 'Close; tight.' SJ

STRING v. trans. 'To make tense.' SJ

STROW 'To spread by being scattered; to besprinkle; to scatter.' SJ

STUDIOUS Zealous (19:49); 'intent on a purpose.' OED

STYGIAN 'Hellish; infernal; pertaining to Styx, one of the poetical rivers of hell.' SJ

STYLE (or STILE) v. 'To name.' SJ

STYPTICK 'Having the power to staunch [i.e. stop the flow of] blood; astringent.' SJ

SUBMISS adj. Submissive.

SUBTARTAREAN 'Being or living under Tartarus [the infernal region].' OED

SUCCEED 'To follow' SJ; also to confer success upon, to further.

SUE 'To petition.' SJ

SUPPLE *v. trans.* 'To make pliant; to make soft; to make flexible' (10:676). SJ

SUSTAIN 'To bear without yielding; to suffer; to bear as afflicted.' SJ

SWARTH = SWATH 'A line of grass cut down by the mower.' SJ

SWAY *n.* 'Power; rule; dominion; anything moving with bulk and power.' SJ

SWOLN = SWOLLEN.

SYLVAN 'One who (or something that) inhabits the woods.' OED

SYNOD 'An assembly called for consultation'; 'a conjunction of the heavenly bodies.' SJ

TALENT 'So much weight, or a sum of money, the value differing according to the different ages and countries.' SJ, citing Arbuthnot.

TAMARISK See Pope's note on 10:677.

TAPER *adj.* 'Regularly narrowed from the bottom to the top; pyramidical; conical' (10:350). SJ

TARGE 'A kind of buckler or shield borne on the left arm.' SJ

TERRIFIC 'Dreadful; causing terror.' SJ

THRILLING Piercing.

TRACE 'Harness for beasts of draught' SJ; rope connecting collar of a horse to the reins.

TRAIN *n.* 'A retinue; a number of followers or attendants.' SJ

TRIPLE DOG Cerberus, the three-headed dog guarding the entrance to Hades.

TROPHY 'Something taken from an enemy, and shewn or treasured up in proof of victory.' OED

TRUSS *v.* 'Of a bird of prey: to seize or clutch (the prey) in its talons.' OED

UNCONSCIOUS 'Having no mental perception' SJ; unknowing.

UNGRATEFUL 'Unpleasing; unacceptable' (8:253, 681). SJ

UNNERV'D 'Weak, feeble.' SJ

UNREPROV'D *adj.* 'Not censured; not liable to censure.' SJ

URGE *v.* 'To labour vehemently'; 'to incite; to push' (2:185).

VAGRANT *adj.* 'Wandering; unsettled.' SJ
VAN = VANGUARD The front of an army.
VARIOUS 'Variegated; diversified' SJ; of many colours (2:956).
VERGE Margin or border.
VEST *n.* 'A robe or gown.' OED
VIZOR Part of a helmet that covers the face.
VOLUME 'Something rolled or convolved [rolled together].' SJ
VULGAR Ordinary, common.

WAIN 'A carriage' SJ; in the *Iliad*, 'a chariot'.
WAIT *v. trans.* To escort or attend (17:34).
WARD *v. trans.* To parry or fend off (now always used with 'off').
WINDE = WIND *v.* 'To nose; to follow by scent' (10:427). SJ
WITHOUT *adv.* 'Not on the inside.' SJ

YARDS 'The supports of the sails.' SJ

ZONE 'A girdle' SJ; but also 'area', as in play on this word at 16:167.